For Tracy,
Thank you so much for all the help.
You're one hell of an editor and my favorite sister as well.
You have been a fabulous collaborator for the past five years.
I don't know if I would have made it this far without you!

Acknowledgments

I'm incredibly indebted to a number of people who have helped see this novel to fruition. First, I want to send my sister a huge thank you. Tracy was there every step of the way, as an editor, as someone to bounce ideas off of, and most importantly a cheerleader when I needed to encouragement to crank out one more chapter. I deeply appreciate all of her help. Thanks to Mom, Dad, and Ross for being test readers. Their input with the rough draft helped hone quite a bit of some unpolished sections of the novel. They also cheered me on as I wrote, edited, and sought a publisher. Their support was instrumental in seeing this book through to the end. I want to thank the crew at Interliant. They put up with me when I straggled into work tired and cranky the morning after a long writing session and supported my efforts as a fledgling writer. Even though most of us have left the company, I have some fabulous memories and great friends from my time there. When I needed a front cover for the novel, I knew exactly who to turn to, and Jenni and Jeremiah did not disappoint. They put together an incredible image that I think captures the essence of the book. Tad Williams was a great source of inspiration as I struggled halfway through the writing of the novel. Despite working on his masterful Otherland series, he still found time to send advice when I was at a troubling juncture. Lastly, I want to thank Lauren. I met her after I had already completed the novel, but she has been a rock of support as I've sought agents and publishers. I have been lucky to have her support as I took the final step on the journey to see The Ghost Hunters in print.

And thank you for purchasing this novel! With enough support, I will get my foot firmly in the door of the publishing world, and you'll see Two Princes in Avalon in the near future. Keep tuned. There will be another book out soon!

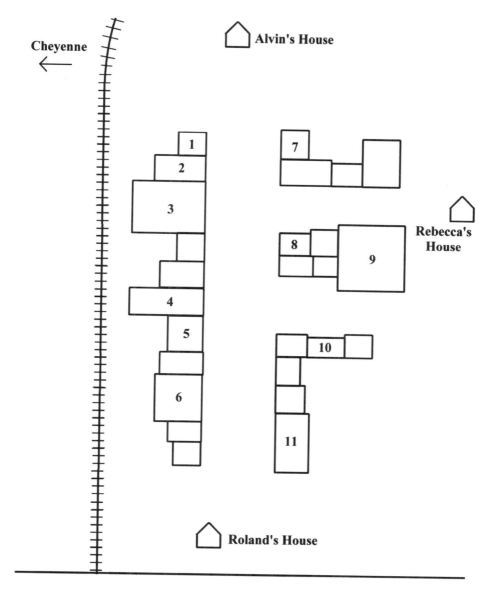

Cheyenne

Alvin's House

1

2

3

4

5

6

7

Rebecca's House

8

9

10

11

Roland's House

Legend of New Haven

1) Will's Tavern
2) Sherry's Bordello
3) Railroad Station
4) Dennis's Smithy
5) Doc Sullivan's Office
6) Sam's Supply Store

7) Church
8) New Haven Gazette Office
9) The Station House
10) The Last Frontier
11) The Rattlesnake

Book One:
The Haunting
June 20 - July 1

Chapter One

Sheriff Roland Black awakened with the rising sun on June 20, 1892, as he had every other morning for as long as he could remember. His father had been a farmer, and Roland had grown up in a farming community. Every morning, the crow would rouse him from his slumber so he could begin his day's chores. By 1892, waking early had become second nature, and the tiniest bit of light creeping through the curtains on his window would send him scurrying out of bed. Besides, it was too hot to sleep any later. The summer of 1892 was brutal in Colorado. It notched record highs that year as the heat scorched grass and livestock alike. Crops had started to wilt, and unless rain came soon, Colorado was looking at a possible food shortage. Hot weather also ushered in hot tempers, and keeping those tempers in line was Roland's job.

Roland was the Sheriff of New Haven, Colorado, a young town thriving on the railroad industry that connected America's two coasts. It was a new town, like so many that had passed before it. The railroad had connected the East and the West, and it had also left a trail of booming cities in its wake. One after another, they had arisen along the great railroads, flaring into prominence before fading into obscurity when the next town grew famous. Roland had seen many of those towns come and go during his years of gunslinging, and New Haven seemed so similar to the cities Roland had visited in his youth. That was the main reason he had come to New Haven.

Western America in the 1870's and 1880's had provided an ideal setting for men of opportunity to make their mark. As towns grew, so did their need for gambling, and that need sparked the popularity of faro and poker houses. In time, gambling became as common as drinking. Many men earned their entire keep by playing cards, while others played to pass the time or supplement their income from another job. Liquored-up men with recently earned cash provided the perfect target for prostitutes, and bordellos arose on the tail of gambling houses.

Gambling dominated Western America, and it had its own share of unwritten rules. Disputes were frequently settled by the law of the draw. Town locals or newspapers might have protested a killing, but the law rarely arrested perpetrators if they had adhered to the gambling code. Cheating was mandatory to excel at gambling and was expected, but getting caught in the act was an entirely different matter. Stacking the deck or hiding a card up the sleeve was an invitation for a duel, as were numerous other infractions. If the victim was a prominent member of society, the law would go through the motions of arresting the killer. That only notified the gambler that he should move to the next town. This was a common cycle for gamblers of the Wild West. They would gamble, then duel, move to another town, and begin the process all over again. Frequently the gambler would return to the scene of an earlier crime after all the public outcry had diminished and would calmly resume playing cards without a worry.

It was in this tumultuous setting that the gunslingers rose to fame. Billy the Kid, Wyatt Earp, and Doc Holliday were a few of the time's legends. They came from various backgrounds. Some were from wealthy families and yearned for something different than their quiet upbringing, while others had grown up in poverty and wished to live the good life. Like the gamblers, gunslingers enjoyed some leniency from the law. In fact, many of the legendary gunslingers were gamblers primarily and drew their notoriety from the disputes that arose over gambling. Doc Holliday earned his keep from playing cards, but the numerous gunfights that resulted from his gambling endeavors had earned him a different kind of reputation than that of a mere gambler.

The law did distinguish between gambler and gunslinger. Law enforcers were willing to let a man go if a duel erupted over crooked card playing, but they weren't quite so willing to turn a blind eye to unprovoked murder. Too often, though, the law simply chased the villain out of town then abandoned pursuit. Occasionally a gunslinger's crimes grew too great. Then the law would assemble a posse to track him down, or somebody would offer a substantial reward to encourage that pursuit. Wyatt Earp particularly stood out as a lawman, bounty hunter, and gunslinger. Unlike the gambler, the gunslinger usually couldn't return to the scene of his crime. Gambling had its own unwritten rules and people would forgive and forget, but unprovoked duels or shooting could last in the memory for quite some time. And so the gunslingers became drifters, riding from town to town, settling briefly here or briefly there before an inevitable gunfight or other crime forced them to move on for good.

By the late 1880's, times had changed. The railroad had indeed connected America's two coasts, and that cast the final curtain over the Wild West. Too many people had settled in the West for the gunslingers to exist any longer. In its heyday, the West had been a sparsely populated area of America, but by the late 1880's, thriving communities stretched from coast to coast. Society necessitated order, and order always started with rules and laws. At first, only known murderers and duelists were arrested, but soon even gamblers met a similar fate. Doc Holliday narrowly beat a murder charge that resulted over a cheating card opponent, but many others weren't so lucky.

Under stringent laws, the gunslingers began to disappear one by one. Billy the Kid was shot in the back, and most of the other gunslingers of the time found a similar fate. Perhaps it was poetic justice for the men who had dealt death so many times from their own guns to find death at the receiving end of a bullet. Like the gunslingers, gambling also began to wane with the stricter enforcement of laws. The gambling code had been a large part of gambling's allure. Men enjoyed the danger inherent in the game, and with the halt of duels and fights, the sport soon became a tired one. State by state and town by town, the gunslingers and gamblers were forced to stand and fight one last time or conform to the new way of life in the West. Men such as Doc Holliday and Wyatt Earp found themselves in a changing world that no longer played by their rules. At least Doc finally succumbed to tuberculosis, finding the ultimate respite from a changing time in which society no longer appreciated the gunslinger.

Sheriff Black felt the same pain that Doc and Wyatt had experienced. In fact, he had even ridden with Doc on a bounty hunt before his Tombstone days. The West had provided much joy over the years, but that crusade with Doc Holliday had been one of the highlights. All those years, Roland had ridden with abandon throughout the entire West on countless adventures, and it had nearly killed him when his culture had begun to dissipate. He understood at that point what the Indians had felt as their way of life was stripped away one piece at a time. It had seemed as if the only two choices left to him were to find a new way of life like Wyatt Earp or seek his grave like Doc Holliday, but Lady Luck had smiled upon Roland and given him a third option.

Swinging his long legs out of bed, Roland slowly rubbed the last vestiges of sleep from his eyes. His knees stiffened on him a bit, as they were prone to do in the heat of summer and the frost of winter. The Sheriff had lived through many adventures in his past and bore a number of aches and pains to prove it. Every year those aches grew worse, but they weren't enough to make him retire. He might have slowed down a bit as he aged, but he still had a sharp mind and could draw a pistol faster than anyone in town, with the possible exception of Carlos the Quick.

Stumbling over to the water basin, Sheriff Black splashed water on his face, shocking himself into some semblance of alertness. He lathered his face before carefully shaving away a day-old beard, leaving the drooping mustache that was so popular throughout the West. The Sheriff had pitch black hair that hung to just below the nape of his neck, although time had salted it with quite a bit of grey. His mustache was mostly white, but his scalp still retained a fair share of its youthful darkness. Roland had worried when his hair first began to grey, but by 1892, he felt it gave him an older, more authoritative appearance.

He was a tall man, standing just a shade over six feet. Like his last name, the Sheriff's clothes were pitch black. He wore a white shirt, but his boots, hat, vest, coat, and slacks all were the charcoal black to which the citizens of New Haven had grown accustomed. Roland had first donned black after his family died during the capture of Vicksburg, Mississippi in the Civil War, but in time it had become his trademark. During his gunslinging days, people had noticed when the blue-eyed stranger dressed in black entered their town. The citizens of New Haven loved their notorious Sheriff and would have been heartbroken if he ever changed his legendary appearance. Besides, by 1892, he didn't know what else to wear.

Fully dressed, Sheriff Black grabbed his badge of office and carefully buckled on his holster belt. He carried two Colt .45's in case one of them jammed on him. Roland always wanted to be ready to draw and fire at a moment's notice. Over the years he had seen too many men fall because they weren't. Roland's pistol had jammed on him once in his youth, and he still counted himself lucky that he only carried a scar on his left shoulder from the incident. He had lived to see another day, but afterwards he always made sure he had a backup. With two fully-loaded pistols in his holsters, Roland went outside to protect the citizens of New Haven once again.

Damn, he thought as he stepped out the door. That Thursday morning, the sun beat down on New Haven like a blazing hammer as it had for the past two weeks. Roland had lived all over the West, including Texas, California, and Arizona, but he couldn't remember the weather ever being hotter. He just hoped the temperature would drop soon and rain would come. Roland could take a week of the brutal sun but not a full three months. Tempers had already started to flare under the hot conditions, and somebody was likely to cross the line unless the weather became more favorable.

New Haven had sprung up along the train route leading to Denver. It was nearly eighty miles south of the larger city, nestled in the Colorado Rockies. The city had risen in a crude F-shaped form. One street ran north through the center of town, while two other streets shot off perpendicular to the east. A fair number of New Haven's 1,500 citizens lived inside the city, but most lived a short distance away. They rode into town to buy or sell at the market or ship goods on one of the trains coming through the town. Roland's house was on the southern side, a short walking distance from the town's main buildings. He had considered assembling his home further from the bustle of the city, but he wanted to be nearby in case trouble arose.

The streets of New Haven were empty that close to sunrise, and that's the way Roland liked them. He drew satisfaction from interacting with the other citizens of New Haven, but Sheriff Black enjoyed those quiet times even more. Mornings were always peaceful in New Haven. The troublemakers of the city stayed out late carousing and didn't awaken until far later in the day. Dennis Stanton, the blacksmith, was up as usual, but other than him, only a few farmers had risen from their beds to tend their land.

Every morning the Sheriff passed Dennis's shop during his walk to the station house, and every morning Dennis sat on his shop steps and carefully whittled a piece of wood or sketched on a piece of paper. Like most men of his profession, Dennis's arms bulged with hard muscles earned from long hours of pounding metal at the smithy. It fascinated Sheriff Black that such a large man could have the delicate hands to sculpt or paint something beautiful, but

14

the Sheriff had seen enough of Dennis's finished products to know that the blacksmith was as accomplished at the arts as he was with metals.

"Morning, Dennis. How's business?" Roland greeted as he took his customary seat next to the blacksmith. The Sheriff enjoyed visiting with him. Although Dennis was a tremendously strong man, he had a quiet, amicable personality that belied his size.

"Morning, Sheriff." Dennis was whittling that morning and carefully set down his block of wood and carving knife before answering Roland. "Business is good. It's kept me busy and all three apprentices as well. I've been thinking about bringing on another one with all the work we've had."

"Any prospects?"

"I could probably get most of the boys in town to learn the trade if I wanted." Dennis laughed. "You know boys. Show them a fire, and they'll flock to it. Half the boys in town come by to watch us in the smithy, but I was thinking about David McCarthy. He's got a good head on his shoulders and working on that farm has given him some strong arms."

"David's a good boy. You could do a lot worse. Do you think he's interested?"

"I won't know until I ask him, but I can always hope. He's come around here before to watch us, but if he's not interested, there are always plenty of others."

"That's true, Dennis." Roland laughed. Dennis's shop was one of the most popular places in town for young boys. He could remember when he was young and how hypnotic the lure of fire had been. "So what are you working on today?" He peered over at the block of wood that the blacksmith had set down.

A faint blush crept up Dennis's cheeks, and he looked bashful as he picked up his current work. Despite his large hands, he held the block delicately as if it was the most fragile thing in the world. "Betty's birthday is next week, so I'm carving this." He held it out for Roland to view.

The Sheriff whistled in amazement. The blacksmith had carved a sculpture of a rose in full bloom. There were still a few rough edges that Dennis hadn't completed, but other than that, the piece looked exquisite. "It's beautiful, Dennis. Betty'll love it."

Dennis beamed at the compliment and carefully set the sculpture back down. "I hope so. I still have some work on it, but I should have it finished by her birthday. Say, Sheriff. What was all that noise last night? It woke us in the middle of the night. I could've sworn it was a gunshot."

Roland spat on the ground in disgust. "It was Curly again. I swear one of these days I'm going to kill that son of a bitch. He and a few Riders got themselves all liquored up last night. They were over at The Snake, and nobody else was over there. I thought it would be a quiet night, but everyone knows how Curly gets when he's been drinking."

The blacksmith nodded as Roland continued his story. He had listened to many of the Sheriff's stories about the Dark Riders. Too frequently it seemed Curly or one of his other brethren inspired the Sheriff's wrath.

"Stephen Brady was playing poker with him and was winning too much. Curly got pissed at losing all his money and started talking about dueling out in the street. He and a few Riders threw Stephen into the street, and Curly tried to spook him into drawing a gun. Luckily Stephen has a brain in that thick head of his and didn't oblige him. At some point, Curly fired a shot into the air, but nobody was hurt.

"By the time I got there, Alvin had calmed everyone down. I hate that damn snake," Roland said harshly, the calm look disappearing from his face and replaced with a stern mask. Roland hated Alvin more than anyone else he could think of. "He's so polite, but I know he's working for the Riders. He might keep them in line, but I don't trust him. I have to admit, though, if he hadn't been there last night, this town would have seen some dead bodies today," Roland uttered the last statement grudgingly. He hated paying Alvin any type of compliment.

"You didn't arrest anyone?" Dennis raised an eyebrow inquisitively, not paying any attention to the Sheriff's fierce expression. He always looked that way when talking about the Mayor or the Dark Riders.

"You know me better than that, Dennis," Roland chided. The look of anger faded away, and one corner of his mouth drifted upwards in a lopsided grin that was as much of a trademark as his black clothing. "There was no need to. Alvin calmed everyone down. Curly fired his gun, but he wasn't going to hurt anyone. Arresting him would just upset the Dark Riders. This town doesn't need the Riders going after Stephen for being lucky at poker." The Sheriff shrugged his shoulders. "Besides, Curly has a quick temper, but he forgets just as fast."

"That's true. I guess that's why you're the Sheriff," Dennis agreed, and the two chatted about more pleasant matters. The main reason Roland enjoyed the blacksmith's company was for the respite it gave him from the rest of the town's problems. It was pleasant to talk about smithery, weather, the railroad, or whatever else they chose. He just didn't want to think about the Riders, Alvin, or the other issues that would surely come up later in the day. After fifteen minutes of talking with the blacksmith, Roland had to return to his job and regretfully rose to his feet.

Roland left the blacksmith behind as he walked towards the station house. When he assumed the role of Sheriff, Roland had tried to establish a presence in New Haven. Before he got there, the station house was used as the town's only courtroom and occasional jailhouse, but Roland had wanted to make it a place where one of his deputies could be found at any time. Roland had nine deputies under his command, but most of them worked during the day and early evening. Phillip Kearny worked the later shift when Roland and the other deputies sought out their beds. Even though there wasn't much need for law enforcement at that time of night, Roland wanted to be sure that if anybody was in need of assistance, they knew exactly where to find it. Robert Douglas watched it during the late afternoon and early evening, and Roland and another deputy usually stepped in for a few hours between their shifts.

Phillip was a large burly man with a big gut and a dark bushy beard who usually wore jeans and a white shirt. He had been a gunslinger in his youth and enjoyed the chance to use his skills even though time had eroded them. When Roland had asked for a volunteer for the graveyard shift, Phillip had stepped forward immediately. He was a quiet man who had never married, making him ideal for the solitary job. The remaining deputies preferred the company of other people, but Phillip didn't mind the solitude since it gave him plenty of time to read, which he enjoyed more than any person Roland knew. Years of reading had given him a squint, and the deputy had finally started wearing glasses. "Morning, Sheriff," Phillip said, looking up from the book he was reading as Roland entered the station house. He quickly laid it face-down to keep his place.

"Morning, Phillip. Anything happen last night after Curly skipped town?" His voice became rougher than when he had spoken with Dennis. Roland pulled up a chair and sat down across the desk from his deputy. The jail and station house were in one half of the building, while the courthouse stood on the other side. A thick concrete wall separated the two, and despite the fact that they shared the same roof, they might as well have been two buildings. The half in which Roland spent most of his time housed a desk and a few chairs. Two cells with iron bars lay behind a large iron door, but they were rarely occupied.

"No. It was quiet last night. Curly got everyone riled up then they all went home and slept."

"That's good. We don't need any more trouble with this damn weather."

"That's the truth," Phillip laughed. "Do you think that Curly will cause trouble tonight?"

"He shouldn't. Alvin probably told him to back off for a little while. That son of a bitch doesn't want any Riders to hurt his popularity." His lip curled into a sneer at the mention of Alvin's name. *You Goddamn snake,* he thought in contempt.

"But at least he keeps them in line. Could you imagine what would have happened last night if he hadn't shown up?"

"I don't want to talk about it," the Sheriff stated flatly in a tone that brooked no argument. The mayor was a touchy subject for Roland, and all of his deputies knew to shy away from talk of Alvin when the Sheriff was in a bad mood.

"Whatever you say," Phillip agreed in a placating tone. Sheriff Black had a storied past, and only a select few in New Haven really knew what was true and what was fiction. Consequently, most of the town's citizens and a fair share of his deputies treaded lightly around him. The Sheriff wanted to laugh when people got that fearful look in their eyes and backed away from him, but their fear had come in handy. He liked it when people obeyed him instantly whether it was from fear or respect. It made his job much easier.

After Phillip gathered his book and left, Roland leaned back behind the desk and smiled his lopsided grin in amusement as he considered the stories that had circulated about him since he had become Sheriff. According to the rumors in the saloons, Roland had been the deadliest gunslinger in the West, and the number of men killed by his guns ranged from fifty to over three hundred. He had also served in the Civil War under the direct command of General Lee, and he had supposedly gunned down hundreds of Union soldiers. Like most rumors, they touched upon the truth but managed to skew the facts.

In 1845, Roland was born the oldest child to a pair of farmers just outside of Vicksburg, Mississippi. Roland's parents never had much money, and he grew up in a meager but homey atmosphere. They owned a farm on a small plot of land that had been enough to keep the Black family fed, but little else. They had never possessed enough money to buy slaves. Not that it bothered Roland much. He had always disagreed with the institution of slavery, even though it was present everywhere around him.

With his brother and two sisters, Roland had helped his parents tend their land, harvesting enough food to get by from year to year. Despite their limited means, the Blacks were a close-knit family. Roland enjoyed hunting with his father and scuffling with his younger brother. He even liked his sisters, although they could be annoying with their giggling and horseplay. Until he turned fifteen, Roland never even gave thought to leaving home, but then serious talk of secession and a war of rebellion began to circulate.

The War didn't come as a surprise to the Blacks. For years, their neighbors had complained of Northern intervention into Southern culture. By March 1861, nobody blinked an eye when Mississippi joined a growing list of seceding states. During the first year of the war, more and more of the Blacks' neighbors enlisted in the Confederate army, but the Blacks continued to tend their land. In the summer of 1862, the harsh reality of war hit home for the Blacks as Roland ventured off to take part in the War. Roland didn't believe in all of the causes that had started the rebellion, but he was a Southerner. He fought for his homeland and all of her customs, however repugnant he might find some of them.

Roland saw little action during his first two months of enlistment. His troop had the assignment of guarding supply trains as they were delivered to Richmond, Virginia. When he arrived in the Confederate capitol in early August, General Robert E. Lee incorporated Roland's troop into his army as they prepared to march towards Manassas. The Battle of Bull Run had demonstrated the South's determination to defend their homeland, and once again, the South moved to defend the infamous site. General Pope's Union soldiers controlled the area, but General Lee quickly marched to attack him before more Northern troops could supplement the existing force already there.

The Second Battle of Bull Run marked the beginning of Roland's infamy with a gun. During the short battle, Roland amazed his fellow soldiers as he calmly stood under fire and shot down one Union soldier after another. Many of his troop didn't survive the fighting, but those who did praised Roland's accuracy with a rifle. Soldiers had pressed him for details of the battle, but they eventually quit due to his disappointing recounts. Roland didn't mean to let them down, but the whole battle was a blur. He remembered emptying his rifle, reloading it, then gunning down more troops, but that was the only image that he could recall. The soldiers around him, though, bragged that the "Black Hand of Death" could shoot an acorn at a hundred yards.

The praise baffled Roland, for he had always been a dead shot and had taken it for granted over the years. Back home, he had hunted deer with his father numerous times. When he was ten, his father had started taking him along when he went hunting, although he didn't let Roland fire the rifle at first. His father wanted to teach him the skill of hunting, not let him spoil the hunt. Several months later, Roland was finally allowed to take his first shot at a deer. After waiting for hours in the woods, the young boy had spotted a deer off in the distance behind a tree. His father turned to point out the target to his son when Roland fired at it. About to chastise his son for not being patient enough to wait for a better shot, he paused when he saw the deer was lying on the ground. Roland didn't understand what all the fuss was about. He had simply concentrated on the target, and the shot had flown true. From that day on, Roland's father always let him carry the gun.

In the army, Roland's reputation with a gun grew. General Lee had praised him and several other soldiers as heroes after the battle at Manassas. From there, Roland took place in several small raids against Northern troops. With his skill, Roland could be counted on to kill a target from a distance and escape safely. Armed with a new Spencer repeating rifle, Roland went on raid after raid and basked in the admiration of his fellow soldiers.

Roland's happiness was short-lived, though. A little over a year after joining the Confederate Army, rumors began to circulate that Vicksburg had been captured. Not bothering to ask permission to leave, Roland began a long trek home. After dodging Union troops for over a month, he arrived at his family farm to find it burned to the ground. He picked though the ashes, but whatever remains had existed were long since swept away.

The deaths of his family invoked a profound grief in the young man. He recounted all the years of laughing and working with his parents and siblings. The thought of living without them tore at his soul. In the back of his mind, Roland had always counted on coming home from the War and resuming work on his family's land with the people he loved. With that no longer an option, Roland wondered for the first time in his life what he would do with himself. The War had brought the destruction of his family, and he had no desire to take any further role in it. Roland knew he needed to leave the vicinity of Vicksburg, for there were still Union troops in the area. The War showed no signs of leaving Southern soil for years, and he'd never consider moving to the Yankees' part of the country, which left him only one choice. Donning black in remembrance of his family, Roland headed West with a hardened resolve to seek whatever fortune he could find.

Over the following twenty-five years, Roland roamed over the entire Western half of America. He never settled in any one town for too long, preferring to test the waters in another city when one grew old. Sometimes he served as a Sheriff or even armed protection. Every now and then, he would team up with a few other gunslingers and ride on bounty hunts. He had ridden with Doc Holliday once in the pursuit of a band of outlaws. Always surrounded by the exploits of famous men, Roland was delighted to find himself teamed with a legend, even though it was a short expedition. They tracked a band of four men for several days before catching them and, when the quartet refused to surrender, calmly gunned them down. Doc went off on his own after that, joining Wyatt Earp and his brothers as they moved towards Tombstone, where chaos lay in waiting.

Roland enjoyed his adventurous lifestyle and freedom to do as he wished, but that began to change in the late 1880's. By then, the West had been inundated with a surge of people moving Westward, and unfortunately, they brought their culture with them. There was plenty of bounty work as more and more states tried to exterminate the gunslingers who had preyed in the West for so long. The work kept Roland busy, but he saw the West dying one day at a time. He even knew that by hunting down outlaws he was helping that process. There was still a need for him to be Sheriff, but Roland found the work boring. The gambling houses were disappearing, and duels hardly ever occurred. Even the bordellos were shutting down as more conservative newcomers disapproved of them. The excitement of the West had died, and Roland began to wonder where he would go, as he had wondered when he returned to Vicksburg in 1863.

The answer caught him completely by surprise in the spring of 1891. Roland had just returned to Denver, Colorado to collect on a bounty when he

20

was approached by a deputy named Morgan Shields from a young railroad town called New Haven. He had met Morgan before and considered the grizzled Civil War veteran a wily and crafty gunslinger. The town's mayor had specifically wanted Roland to be the Sheriff of his town and had sent Morgan to persuade him to visit the town. Roland remembered Alvin all too well from his travels and didn't think very fondly of him, but Morgan was persistent. He rambled about what a wonderful town it was and how much Roland would love it. Eventually Roland agreed to visit the city and make up his mind, and so the pair hopped aboard the train and arrived several hours later. It only took Roland five minutes of observing New Haven before he accepted, despite his reservations over the mayor summoning him.

What Roland found in New Haven was a remnant of the culture in which he had thrived for over two decades. It was a tamed version, but there was a sense of rowdiness and free spirit that Roland thought had died along with the rest of the West. He had been amazed to count two gambling houses when he came to town the first time. Disputes over faro or poker games were settled by fisticuffs rather than guns, but that was a far cry better than most cities where faro was no longer even played. Madame Sherry ran her bordello even back then, although she had hired many new girls in the following twelve months. It seemed that no matter where he turned his eye, Roland was reminded of some part of the culture he thought had died but had resurrected itself within the city limits of New Haven, Colorado. He knew that dealing with Alvin would be a constant hassle, but the mayor paled in comparison to the thriving culture that he had discovered.

By the summer of 1892, New Haven had blossomed into a major city along the railroad connection, and Roland was proud of the thriving young town. The Last Frontier was the biggest saloon in town and boasted the most faro dealers, but there were three other places of gambling in addition to the pickup games played at private residences. There were frequent fights over cheating, and because of his past, Roland was all too happy to turn a blind eye to them. As long as nobody was seriously hurt, a bit of bloodshed helped keep the game lively and filled with enough excitement to draw newcomers. Occasionally a gun was drawn in the heat of an argument, but every man in town knew that he needed a valid excuse for shooting someone or there would be hell to pay with Sheriff Black. Even the Dark Riders left the local population alone for the most part. New Haven was probably the only place in America where they could exist, and they didn't want her citizens rising against them. Overall, Roland enjoyed his job. The people were polite, the atmosphere was nostalgic, and the work was mostly easy with the exception of the Dark Riders. Luckily they didn't cause Sheriff Black too much worry. They occasionally raised some concern or trouble, but most of the time they stayed in the background and didn't bother the people of New Haven.

Sheriff Black chuckled as he reflected on his past. The citizens of New Haven would be surprised if they knew his true story. Roland had lived through some impressive adventures, but he hadn't won hundreds of duels or nearly defeated the Union army single-handedly. He was just an old gunslinger who had come to a place that reminded him of the glory years of his youth. Others had come to New Haven for the exact same reason. Most had come for the economic opportunity that the railroads provided, but Roland had spotted a glint in the eyes or a bounce in the step of those who viewed New Haven as a paradise that captured the magic of their youth. The time passed quickly as he sat alone in the station house and looked over the empty streets, thinking back to a time when he was younger and the entire West had been as free as New Haven.

Wade Hampton arrived at the station house nearly two hours later. The young deputy barely looked a day over seventeen, although Roland knew for a fact that he was only a few months away from twenty-two. It had to be the eyes, Roland always thought. Wade had sandy blond hair and the bluest eyes Roland had ever seen. "Baby blues," Roland had often heard them called, and many of New Haven's citizens assumed that the man behind such a boyish face was innocent and sweet. They couldn't have been further from the truth. Despite his young appearance, Wade was one of the quickest gunslingers Roland had ever met, and he had met many. He carried two Colt .45's like Roland, but he wore them backwards in a pair of holsters worn high on his leg. The Sheriff preferred the ease with which he could draw his guns, but Wade enjoyed the dramatic effect of reaching across his body to draw both pistols.

Like many other youths, including Roland himself, Wade had grown up practicing with a gun. By the time he was eighteen, he was ready to head out on the road and try living in the Wild West. But before he could get there, the West had died on him. Nobody tolerated gunfights or needed deputies with steady nerves who were quick on the draw. Nobody, that was, except the citizens of New Haven. Wade perfectly embodied what Roland wanted to accomplish with New Haven's outdated ways. Without New Haven, men like Wade and Roland would be cast adrift in a society that no longer wanted them.

"Morning, Wade," Roland called out as the deputy stepped through the door.

"Morning, Sheriff. Looks like it's gonna be another hot one today."

"I think you just might be right," Roland replied drolly. "That's why we're going to keep an eye on The Snake tonight. Curly already went off last night, and I don't want any of the other Riders doing the same. When Robert shows up, I want you to go over there with Morgan and Ben. Jack's riding patrol today, and I'll be over at The Frontier with William. There will be plenty of men around tonight, and you make sure you call for help if there's even the slightest hint of trouble. With this damn weather, somebody's going to lose their temper and do something stupid. If we're lucky and we show our faces all over town, we might just discourage them."

"I don't think there'll be any trouble if there are three of us at The Snake. Curly likes to play tough, but he's spineless if you show some force. The rest of the men there won't do anything with us around either. They only get rowdy when one of the Riders riles them up and we're not there to break it up. Unless Carlos pays us a visit tonight, we should be fine."

"Sounds good. You just be sure to be careful and not brave. I mean it. You send for help if the Riders decide to cause any trouble tonight," Roland advised. He trusted Morgan to keep the younger deputy in tow. Morgan had notched his gunbelt many times, while Wade kept hoping to place one on his. Then the Sheriff walked out of the station house and across the street to The Last Frontier.

The Last Frontier was the most popular saloon in New Haven. It wasn't as rowdy as The Snake or as cheap as Will's Tavern, but it had gained such popularity because it offered the best services of all the saloons in town. It boasted three faro dealers in addition to plenty of pickup poker games. A fair number of Madam Sherry's upscale prostitutes patronized it for customers who didn't want to make the jaunt over to her brothel. The main reason so many people visited the establishment, however, was for safety. Roland usually stationed himself in The Last Frontier during his shift, and the amount of trouble caused in the saloon had decreased ever since he started doing so. George Wright owned The Frontier, and he was all too happy to have the Sheriff or one of the deputies inside to keep trouble away. His profits had soared since Roland had become Sheriff, and he also wanted to be sure he never caught a bullet meant for someone else.

Sheriff Black did want to cut down on the crime committed in the saloon, but his motives for stationing himself in The Frontier were also personal. The saloon reminded him of his years of gunslinging more than any other part of New Haven. From the card-playing to the prostitutes wandering the tavern floor, the entire establishment was a throwback to the West that Roland was accustomed to. By 1892, there weren't many saloons like The Last Frontier around anymore, and Roland wanted to enjoy its atmosphere while he could.

The saloon was empty that early in the day. The first train came through town shortly after noon, and most of the town was busy preparing to receive goods or to ship them away. During that time, the rest of the town ground to a virtual halt, but things would pick up quickly after the train had departed. Roland took a seat and waited for the inevitable tide to arrive. The staff was there as usual, but there wasn't much for them to do. They were rarely needed that early, but George liked to keep them on hand in case things got busy. Edmund stood behind the bar, pouring a drink for one of the three customers in the saloon, while one of the bargirls served the other two patrons at one of the

23

back tables. None of Sherry's girls had arrived, but they usually didn't start walking the floor until closer to dusk.

George, however, always kept busy. He constantly bustled about the bar, fastidiously cleaning, mixing, pouring, or doing whatever else was needed to help out. When Roland entered the saloon, George was meticulously cleaning the bar, although the Sheriff thought it already looked spotless. At the sight of Roland, George dropped his cloth and scurried over to him. "Howdy, Sheriff. Mighty hot day we're having," George stated the obvious as he rubbed his ample stomach.

Roland shook his head as he wondered how many times he would have to hear that comment. "Hell, George, it's been a hot month if you ask me."

"That's true, Sheriff. Say, what happened last night over at The Rattlesnake? We never heard back from you last night. Gossip's been floating around, but I thought I'd get the real story from you."

Again, Roland thought in frustration and proceeded to tell the story of Curly and his compatriots again as the morning passed by. He had to stop and restart his story as several of the staff and customers drifted over to hear the tale. Roland had grown tired of the story after telling it to Dennis that morning, and he was sick of it after the third time he had to restart from the beginning. It was with relief that Roland spotted Simon heading towards the saloon. Simon was extremely slow and not a great conversationalist, but Roland was grateful for any reason to stop telling the story of Curly's escapade the night before. "Excuse me." Roland smiled and left his crowd of avid listeners. "Morning Simon. How are you?" He greeted the deputy as he took a seat at his table. Roland spent so much time at the saloon that one of the tables by a window had been set aside for him, and nobody ever dared to take one of his seats.

"Good morning, Sheriff. I'm doing fine," Simon answered with a simple smile.

"And how's Sarah?" Roland asked.

Simon blinked then his smile grew wide. "She's doing fine. She's getting close to having the baby," he announced proudly.

"That's good," Roland answered and resisted the urge to chuckle. Simon had been telling him that every day for over a month. He'd be glad when Sarah finally gave birth so Simon would have something else to talk about.

The rest of the day flew by quietly. Roland passed the time visiting with his deputy or talking to the customers. People began to hustle up and down the streets when the afternoon train came through, but after the goods and passengers had been loaded off and on, the train continued west once again, sending many to their homes. The rest trickled into the saloon to relax early. A decent crowd had filled The Frontier by mid-afternoon, but Roland knew that most of the clientele wouldn't arrive until after the sun went down.

William Farragut showed up just before sunset, replacing Simon as Roland's assistant deputy that evening. Normally Simon would have stayed on all night, but he had been nervous lately, and Roland expected that to continue until Sarah finally gave birth. Until then, the Sheriff gave his deputy some time off to spend with his wife. Sheriff Black wanted a full crew on duty at all times, but he couldn't begrudge Simon some family time, especially considering that even Roland had been taking some personal time off lately.

The crowds began to pour into The Last Frontier as night descended upon New Haven. Faro dealers had their hands full with plenty of gamblers, and liquor ran freely as customers sauntered into the saloon. Roland noticed some of Sherry's strumpets walking the floor of the saloon. They would also patronize some of the town's other saloons, but The Last Frontier drew the largest crowds and thus most of Sherry's attention.

Roland's stomach growled with hunger as the Sheriff eyed the saloon one last time. Everything appeared to be fine so far that evening. Trouble usually didn't start that early. It always took time for the alcohol to take effect before the patrons became truly rowdy. He checked his timepiece one last time, noting it was nearing seven o'clock, and decided it was time he took his break. Sheriff Black hated to leave The Last Frontier, but he had personal matters to attend to. Besides, it would be hours before any trouble brewed in New Haven. In the meantime, William could handle matters by himself.

William stood close to Heather, one of Sherry's girls. The sandy-haired deputy had a rather notorious appetite and was known to frequent Madam Sherry's bordello. In fact, his main reason for becoming a deputy had been to attract more women, whom Roland had noticed over the years were drawn to the danger and excitement that came from carrying a gun. Roland couldn't care less about William's excursions as long as he performed his job properly, and so far, William had never let him down.

"Sheriff," Heather greeted then cast her eyes down demurely.

Roland shook his head in amusement at her coy behavior. "So shy tonight, Heather? I hate to do this to you, but could you excuse William here for just a moment?"

"All right," the dark-haired prostitute answered with a pout then turned back to William. Running a fingernail over his cheek, she breathed slowly, "I'll see you when you're finished."

Roland waited as William's eyes watched Heather strut across the saloon before darting back to the Sheriff. "She's a pretty one, William, but just wait a little while longer. I need to have dinner with Rebecca tonight. I'd appreciate it if you'd watch over The Frontier for a few hours."

"Sure, Sheriff, it's no problem." William smiled good-naturedly. As often as William had found someone to cover for him so he could make a quick trip over to Madam Sherry's, it was only right for him to return the favor every now and then. "Tell Miss White I send my regards."

"I'll do that, William. If you need any help, Wade, Morgan, and Ben are over at The Snake, and Robert's over at the station house. Jack is patrolling the streets and can be here quickly if you need him." Roland gave his last instructions, then left his deputies alone for a little while. He didn't like leaving the town, but he knew that he had a fine crew of deputies who could handle the routine problems that might occur while he was gone.

Rebecca White lived about a mile north of New Haven, just past the flour mill. It was a short enough distance to walk, but Roland wanted to spend as much time as possible with Rebecca that evening and not waste time walking. Procuring one of the six horses allocated to him and his deputies, Roland set off at a brisk pace. She could always visit him at The Last Frontier, but Rebecca hated crowds. They'd also be under the scrutiny of all its clientele. Gossip spread quickly in New Haven, and several people had already asked him about his relationship with Rebecca. Sheriff Black knew that people were naturally inquisitive, but he felt that he and Rebecca should be allowed to conduct their relationship in private without having to explain or justify it to anyone. Unfortunately that was impossible, considering her status as a widow and the events that led to her husband's death.

The Dark Riders only counted twenty-two men as official members of their gang, but they also employed the help of several other New Haven citizens. The mayor stood out as the most notable example, but Bryant White was another whom Roland believed had helped the Dark Riders from time to time. Bryant had worked for the railroad station and had access to arrival and departure times for trains all over the nation. Sheriff Black could never be certain, but his gut told him that Bryant had sold the Dark Riders information on several of those routes. The train robbery outside Denver could have been anyone's work, but Roland was quite sure that it had been the Dark Riders. Nobody could prove it had been them, and all of Roland's speculations would never hold weight in court. He had been tempted to alert the federal marshals to their possible involvement, but then he would have had the government intruding on his job. Roland liked New Haven just the way it was and didn't want to spoil it by calling in help when it wasn't needed. Besides, marshals never could have prosecuted the Dark Riders for any of their crimes. There just wasn't enough evidence to convict them.

That had been the most blatant of Bryant's possible connections to the Dark Riders, although there were numerous others that hadn't gained as much attention. Several other loads had turned up missing from trains that had passed through New Haven, and once again, Roland felt that the Dark Riders were responsible. The Dark Riders would have needed inside information to know when valuable cargo was being transported, and Bryant would have been the only one to provide that information. Around the time that Sheriff Black had noticed a flurry of railroad crimes, Bryant had begun to live beyond his means. The railroads didn't pay that much in salary so Bryant had to be receiving additional income from another source. It didn't take Sheriff Black much speculation to lay that blame at the door of the Dark Riders.

All of Roland's speculation ceased at the beginning of the year. On a cold January morning, a furious pounding on his door awakened Sheriff Black from a fitful sleep. He had arrived in the streets of New Haven to see a growing crowd around the dead body of Bryant White. Blood drenched Bryant's clothes from a vicious cut across his neck, and a nasty bludgeon wound adorned his left temple. It looked as if he had been struck with a stick or pistol-whipped, but the town doctor couldn't be sure exactly what weapon had been used. Despite all the blood on Bryant's body and clothes, there was little to be found on the snow surrounding the corpse, convincing Sheriff Black that Bryant had been killed somewhere else and deposited in the street after the crime.

Roland still hadn't found Bryant's killer. He was quite certain that none of the travelers or strangers in New Haven had committed the crime, and he was even more confident that none of New Haven's citizens would commit such a violent act. That left only the Dark Riders, but Sheriff Black couldn't determine why they would kill somebody on their payroll who could still provide valuable information. Even though the Dark Riders were the ones most likely to have killed Bryant, Roland also couldn't conclude which of them had slit his throat. And so Sheriff Black was left with a dead body, no motive, and no specific suspect for the crime.

The murder had rocked New Haven for quite some time. *The New Haven Gazette* had run articles on the slaying for over a month, speculating wildly on who could have committed the crime. Only one publication pointed a finger at the Dark Riders, but after that lone article, *The Gazette* had left the Dark Riders alone. Roland suspected that had to do with a payoff from Alvin or a threat from the Dark Riders. Even if *The Gazette* refused to cast blame towards Carlos and his gang, the citizens of New Haven directed their suspicions towards them. It was always done quietly or in private, though. Nobody was foolish enough to accuse the Dark Riders in public for fear that the same might happen to them.

Bryant's death had provided Sheriff Black a great deal of stress. It had been the only murder during his tenure, but it allowed Roland to meet Bryant's widow. She and Bryant had met and married in Philadelphia before heading West for greater economic opportunity. Their marriage had been one of convenience for her family. Rebecca had come from a poor background, and her parents were all too happy to marry one of their children off so they would have more income at their disposal. Bryant had simply been the lucky man who snared himself a young, beautiful wife.

27

Their marriage wasn't unpleasant, although it was far from happy. In the few months before his death, Bryant had begun to spend increasing amounts of time in the saloons of New Haven, leaving his young bride alone in their house. Rebecca's isolation had begun to wear upon her by the time of Bryant's murder. When Roland had knocked on Rebecca's door to give her the grim news, he was the first person other than her husband whom she had seen in several months. Grateful for company, she invited Roland into the house so he wouldn't leave. Roland had stayed for several hours and enjoyed conversing with the beautiful widow.

Roland stopped by the house frequently over the next month to keep Rebecca abreast of his investigation and to keep her company. He had sensed her need for any type of companionship when he first visited her and didn't want to abandon her to isolation so soon after her husband's death. After a few trips to her house, though, he found himself attracted to the young widow. Roland had traveled extensively in his day and had seen plenty of beautiful women. He had taken on several lovers during his years of gunslinging, but Roland had never let himself become emotionally attached to anyone. His family's death had taught him what emptiness and sorrow were, and he wanted to make sure that he never experienced such pain again. Yet Rebecca was quite different than any other woman he had ever known.

Rebecca was the most beautiful woman in New Haven. She had long, dark hair that curled down around her shoulders and emerald green eyes that threw Roland off balance whenever she looked at him. It wasn't just her beauty that attracted him. Numerous other beautiful women had thrown themselves at Roland. Even Sherry had made it perfectly clear that he was welcome in her bed whenever he wished. Yet all of those women viewed the Sheriff as an icon, somebody of status who would be prestigious to take on as a lover. Rebecca wasn't trying to use him or woo him because of his position. She simply enjoyed his company, and Roland discovered that he was growing quite attached to her. Never having fallen in love before, it was a strange feeling for Roland. At times, his attachment to Rebecca frightened Roland, but he had lived his own life of isolation since his family's death and welcomed the change.

Glimpsing her house in the distance, Sheriff Black spurred his horse into a gallop for the rest of the way. After tying the horse securely to a tether post, Roland straightened his coat one last time before knocking on Rebecca's door. He stood on her porch impatiently for several moments before it slowly opened to reveal the stunningly beautiful woman.

Rebecca smiled brightly, her eyes sparkling with merriment. Whenever she smiled, her whole face lit up with happiness. "Good evening, Roland. You got here right on time. I just finished making supper."

"Glad I could make it, Rebecca," Roland answered quietly. Normally Roland had a gruff voice and an abrupt personality, but when he spoke to Rebecca, his tone was softer and a great deal more polite.

"It wasn't a problem taking time off?" Rebecca eyebrows furrowed in genuine concern. She had told him how much she appreciated his company, but Rebecca didn't want him shirking his duties as Sheriff.

"Not at all, not at all. William's on duty, and he can take care of any problems that might come up. The real troublemakers won't hit the town until later."

Rebecca smiled in response, then rolled her eyes in amusement. "I'm sorry, Roland. I didn't mean to keep you standing outside. Please come in." Rebecca stepped aside so Roland could enter then escorted him into the dining room.

True to her word, Rebecca had already placed dinner on the table. Roland waited for her to take a seat then pushed her chair up to the table before he sat down himself. The months of isolation had given Rebecca the time to learn the art of cooking, and as much as he enjoyed her company, Roland would have kept returning to her house just to dine on her wonderful meals. That Thursday evening, she had prepared chicken stew, seasoned with homegrown vegetables and herbs. Eating a spoonful, Roland once again marveled over her wonderful cooking. "It's delicious, Rebecca." Roland knew how much she loved to hear praise, especially since Bryant had never been too keen on paying compliments.

Rebecca rewarded him with another smile. "Thank you, Roland. I'm glad you like it." She had served him the same stew several times before and had noted his appreciation for it. Armed with that knowledge, she had spent a large part of the day preparing the meal. Confident that he would continue visiting her house for her company, Rebecca felt that serving a good meal would only give him more reason to return. Besides, Roland made her happy with his visits, and if taking the time to cook a good meal could return the favor, she was all too willing to do so. "So how has your day been?"

"It's been a quiet one, thank God. After last night, I could use some peace and quiet for a change," Roland answered then proceeded to explain the previous night's adventures yet again as Rebecca listened attentively to every word. Rebecca had heard about Curly many times and wasn't too surprised that he had caused trouble again. Nonetheless, she was grateful that no harm had befallen Roland. Roland had told her that he suspected the Dark Riders of her husband's murder, and since then, she continually fretted that one of their gang would harm the Sheriff as well.

"Luckily Alvin was there to cool everyone down," Roland continued his tale. "I thought for a moment there, we were going to have a gunfight in the middle of town. That's all New Haven needs right now. Everybody's been in a foul mood with all this weather. It's only going to take one event to ignite a lot of tempers in this town."

"At least you're all right, Roland. You just be careful," Rebecca chastised him.

Reaching across the table, Roland placed his hand over Rebecca's and stared at her. He held his gaze steady as he lost himself in her emerald eyes. *I don't deserve her,* Roland told himself. He cursed the fact that he had to return to town. Roland wanted nothing more than to stay with Rebecca forever and forget about Curly, Alvin, and all the Dark Riders. "Don't you worry, Rebecca. I've got good deputies working for me, and nobody in New Haven wants to take on all of us. Alvin will keep the Riders in line, and everything will settle down. It'll just take a little time. That's all. Besides, I've managed to keep myself alive through a lot worse than the Dark Riders. I'm not ready to go quite yet."

"I know. I just worry about you. They already killed Bryant, and I don't want to lose you as well."

"You're not going to lose me. You've given me something else to think about for the first time since the War. A year ago, I might have done something stupid, but now I have you to visit. I don't want to lose that, and I'm not going to take any chances if I don't have to. I promise you, I'll be eating your meals for a long, long time," Roland soothed the widow. He was telling her the truth, though. Before he had met her, Roland would have rushed into a gunfight without a moment's hesitation, but not anymore.

Usually Rebecca grew self-conscious when they talked of their feelings for one another, which Roland understood perfectly. He too had lost family members, and it had taken him over three decades to let himself care this deeply for somebody else again. This time, however, Rebecca continued to meet his gaze and flashed her dazzling smile once again. "Thank you, Roland. You don't know how much I enjoy visiting with you. Everything was so cold and distant with Bryant. Now that I've found you, I'm just afraid of losing you too," she answered him softly, then gave a merry little laugh. "I'm sorry. I'm just rambling on tonight. Please don't mind me."

"It's no bother at all." Roland answered her smile with his own lopsided grin. *I don't deserve her,* he thought to himself again. He was about to make a joke about her being so shy, but he heard a loud knock from the study. "What was that?" Roland asked as he removed his hand from hers and lowered it to his holster. He stared at the room, but nothing seemed amiss.

Rebecca darted her eyes nervously towards the study. "I don't know. I've been hearing strange noises the past few nights—a few knocks like that and a creaking coming from the bedroom—but I thought it was my ears playing tricks on me."

"I don't think it's your ears. I heard it this time." Roland was relieved to see the study empty. "It doesn't look like we have company. I wonder what it could—" Roland halted as another loud knock sounded. Drawing one of his guns, Roland stood up and peered at the study. "I'm going to take a look, Rebecca. I want you to stay behind me."

"But Roland, it's just a noise. Do you really need a gun?" Rebecca despised guns. In her opinion, they were nothing but tools of violence. She knew Roland had to carry one to protect himself in the line of duty, but she had no desire to see one brandished in her own house.

"Just being careful," Roland answered while keeping his eyes on the study. "I don't know what's causing that noise. Let's go take a look."

After Rebecca joined him, Roland inched towards the study, his gun pointed in the direction of the noisy room while Rebecca hovered close behind him with a worried frown. They had only taken a few steps out of the dining room when the knocking began again. This time it was a deep thud as if someone was hitting a bass drum. *What the hell?* Roland thought in bewilderment.

Rebecca grabbed the back of his shirt, stopping him from going any closer to the source of the mysterious noise. "I'm scared, Roland."

Roland turned his head and forced a nonchalant smile. "Don't worry. Nothing will happen to you while I'm here," he tried to calm her then focused on the room once more. Before he could take another step, the thudding resumed. This time it wasn't a single outburst but a rhythmic pounding that chilled Roland's blood. "Rebecca, I think we should both leave the house right now." Roland didn't know what was causing the ruckus, but he had no desire to find out alone at night.

Rebecca smiled in relief as the thudding continued to blare. "That's fine with me. Let's get out of here. *Now!*" She emphasized the last word and rushed towards the front door. The thudding began to pound erratically, alternating between soft and loud noises. Before it had been a steady pattern, but now it beat in a furious tempo.

Roland backed towards the door, watching the study cautiously. He didn't know what was making that noise, but he certainly didn't want to turn his back on it. They were nearly to the front door when he heard a loud bang coming from the doorway. Looking in the direction of the new noise, Roland's jaw dropped wide open as he saw the front door opening by itself then slamming shut. "What the hell?" He whispered as Rebecca jumped back into him and screamed in pure terror.

From the kitchen, Roland heard several dishes break as the erratic thudding and door slamming continued. His eyes nearly popped out of their sockets as he saw two drinking glasses float into the air then dash themselves to pieces against the dining room wall. Books leapt into the air and began flying around the house like bats, flapping their covers like wings. *Blazes,* he thought numbly. For thirty years Roland had drawn his pistols with a steady hand, but that night his gun wavered as his hand shook with uncertainty and fear.

"How do we leave?" Rebecca screamed as she clung to his back protectively.

Roland would have suggested the front door, but it continued to bang open and shut under its own power. He frantically scanned the house and jumped back into Rebecca as the dining room table began to shake, spilling food onto the floor. The surrounding chairs also shook then launched themselves into the air. They turned lazy pirouettes, speeding up and slowing down to the erratic beat of the loud knocks booming from the study. Amidst the sudden bedlam, Roland's eyes fixed upon one of the windows. "The window," he called to Rebecca and smoothly fired two shots at it, shattering the glass. "Hurry."

The two rushed towards their new exit as noise swirled around them. Roland helped Rebecca step through the vacant window, careful of the jagged glass lining the frame's edges. Once she was safely through, Roland hiked one of his legs over the window sill and was about to step through when the fireplace flared to life. The sudden ignition of fire momentarily blinded Roland, and he paused halfway through his makeshift exit. "*Mine!*" A scratchy voice that sounded like nails being dragged over iron echoed through the house. "*Mine!*"

As frightened as he was, that voice pushed Roland over the edge. Even though spots of light clouded his vision, he stumbled out of the house, not taking any care to avoid the jagged glass along the edge of the window in his haste to escape. He hissed in pain as he cut himself in several places including a deep gash along his ribcage. Roland shrugged it aside, however, as adrenaline surged into his bloodstream and numbed the stinging wounds. Taking Rebecca's arm, Roland guided the frightened young woman towards his horse. After helping her mount, Roland awkwardly swung up behind her and spurred his horse into a canter, grunting as the bumpy gait jostled his recent wounds.

Once they had gone several hundred feet, Roland reined the horse in and took one last look at the house. If it weren't for the stinging cuts inflicted by the window, Roland would have sworn he was dreaming. The events in the house defied any explanation that he could conceive, and he could only watch in silence as he and Rebecca witnessed the phenomena from a distance. The door continued to open and shut with a great deal of noise, and an eerie blue light flickered behind several of the windows. Even that far from the house, the loud knocking echoed faintly, disturbing the perfect silence of the summer night.

"What's happening, Roland?" Rebecca sobbed as she leaned back into his comforting embrace.

Roland couldn't blame her for crying. Whatever was happening inside her house had scared him more than he had ever been in his life.

He had fearlessly faced gunslingers countless times. At least he knew that a bullet would stop them, but he had no idea how to kill a noise or flying kitchenware. "I don't know, Rebecca. I don't know." He wrapped his arms around her tightly as they watched the spectacles continue inside her house. Then he clucked the horse into a canter towards the safety of New Haven.

Chapter Two

The moon had waned to a thin crescent in the summer sky as Roland and Rebecca fled under its scant lighting from the terrifying phenomena in her house. Fortunately the sweltering heat that had plagued Colorado for the past month lessened considerably in the evening. Sweat already drenched Roland's shirt and coat, and he didn't need scorching weather to make him perspire any more profusely. His clothes stuck to his body from that sweat and the blood from wounds he had received while scrambling through the window. Numerous cuts decorated his chest, arms, and legs, and a deep wound ran along his ribcage where he had pressed against the broken pane. In his hectic scramble through the window, Roland had shrugged aside the pain, but once things settled down, his wounds began to throb agonizingly. He couldn't tell how deep the wound in his side was, but he thought it just might reach the bone. Despite constant pressure, blood still trickled slowly from the wound, and he knew that he needed to see Doc Sullivan to have it cleaned and dressed. But he wanted to take care of Rebecca first.

When they started their flight to New Haven, Rebecca huddled back into his embrace and whimpered in tears. She continued crying until they had traveled halfway to town, then abruptly lapsed into silence. Despite his repeated attempts to console her, Rebecca didn't utter a sound for the remainder of their journey. The ordeal which had wounded and frightened Roland left Rebecca in a state of shock which he could not penetrate. Roland was certain that he too would be similarly incapacitated if he hadn't lived through so many harrowing escapades in his life. He could no longer count the number of times he had narrowly escaped death during his years of gunslinging in the West, but his nerves had hardened with each event. Even those hardened nerves hadn't spared him a great deal of terror, but they had at least left him able to function after they had escaped the house.

Roland yearned to push the horse into a gallop so he could return to town faster and try to shake Rebecca out of her catatonic state, but with two of them on the horse, he was forced to continue at a slow pace. With one hand pressed firmly against his painful side, Roland wrapped his other arm protectively around the shaking widow. Although she was still silent, Rebecca gripped that arm and pressed against his damp chest as if drawing solace from him.

The slow ride gave Roland time to consider the night's events. The Sheriff wasn't one to believe in magic, but he couldn't easily dismiss the extraordinary display that he had witnessed. His first thought was to consult Chief Running Brook. Most people in New Haven didn't believe in magic, but Roland knew for a fact that the Cheyenne did. Indian magic could explain the flying furniture and flickering lights that Roland had beheld, but that explanation didn't feel right. The Cheyenne had never caused Roland any trouble before, and it didn't make sense for them to start doing so by attacking Rebecca's house with magic. The only other culprit Roland could blame was a ghost, and he considered that possibility even less likely. The only ghost that would have haunted Rebecca's house would have been her dead husband, but Bryant had been in the grave for over six months. If he had chosen to return from the dead as a ghost, surely he would have do so long before the summer. Discounting those two possibilities, Roland tried to think of a third during the trip back to New Haven, but despite stretching his imagination to the limit, he couldn't think of anything else. The events at Rebecca's house simply defied explanation.

A cool breeze swept past them, providing a brief respite from his stinging wounds as the town finally came into view. *About Goddamn time,* Roland thought in relief. Grateful for the refreshing wind, Roland guided his horse towards the lighted streets of New Haven. Not bothering to return the horse to the station house, Roland proceeded directly to The Last Frontier and dismounted awkwardly as his chest wound tightened painfully. Pressing one hand to the cut along his ribcage, he slowly tied the horse to a tether post at the front of the saloon. He rested for a moment before returning his attention to Rebecca, who still sat atop the horse.

Her eyes pointed towards the saloon, but they appeared cloudy, as if she wasn't looking at anything. Roland had always thought that Rebecca's eyes were her most beautiful feature, and it tore at his heart to see them so lifeless. "Rebecca," he called softly, hoping to break her out of her withdrawn state, but she remained silent as she stared at The Last Frontier's entrance. Placing a hand upon her leg, Roland repeated himself, "Rebecca. Come on. You need to get inside."

The touch of Roland's hand penetrated her shell, and she slowly turned her head towards him. Under the lights of New Haven, Roland noticed for the first time how pale her pallor had become. Her skin appeared to have been coated with flour, while her eyes continued to stare ahead blankly. "Roland?" She called out falteringly.

"Yes, Rebecca. It's me, Roland." Her lifelessness troubled him. He had to strain his ears to catch her soft reply, and her vacant gaze stared right past him as if he wasn't standing in front of her. Patting her leg reassuringly, Roland continued to look into her blank emerald eyes, hoping to see some signs of life in them. "Come on, Rebecca. Why don't you get off the horse, and we can go inside. I'll have George get you a room with a comfortable bed. How does that sound?" He forced his voice to sound chipper.

Her head shook back and forth several times in mute denial. "But what if it happens again?" She answered in the same barely audible tone. As terrifying as the events at her house had been, seeing Rebecca in such a state of shock frightened Roland even more. He had observed people in shock after a particularly violent gunfight, but he had never seen anybody as withdrawn as Rebecca was that night. Of course, he had never experienced anything more harrowing than the phenomena in her house.

"It won't happen again. I promise. The Last Frontier is the safest place in town. I don't know what happened at your house, but I guarantee you'll be safe here. Please come down, and let's go inside. You need to get some sleep, and everything will be better in the morning." Grabbing her hand, Roland squeezed it reassuringly. He desperately wanted Rebecca to get some rest, and he knew that's where he was headed as soon as Doc Sullivan looked at his wounds. They had begun to tighten, and it took most of his strength to stand beside Rebecca and try to calm her.

Taking a deep breath, she closed her eyes, her body beginning to shake again as she cried softly. Rebecca squeezed his hand in return then nodded weakly. She slowly slid off the horse into Roland's waiting arms. Wincing in pain, Roland's knees nearly buckled as he momentarily bore her full weight. Despite the wracking pain in his side, Roland embraced Rebecca as she threw her arms around him and cried deep choking sobs. Roland comfortingly stroked her hair as she continued to cry into his shoulder. He whispered soothingly into her ear, "Shh. It's all right, Rebecca. It's all over now. Shh."

Roland continued to console her until her tears stopped. Raising her head, Rebecca stared up into Roland's eyes, and he was relieved to see them focus upon him. She sniffed once and cast her eyes downward. "I'm sorry, Roland. I'm just not myself tonight."

Roland barked out a laugh. "Hell, Rebecca. After all we went through, I'm surprised I can still function. Don't apologize. Most *men* I know would have run out of that house crying like a little girl." He looked down at her and waited until she met his gaze before smiling his lopsided grin.

"Thank you, Roland," she answered and forced a trembling smile of her own in reply. It wasn't the dazzling smile that could knock Roland off his feet, but it was a smile nonetheless.

Thank God, he thought. Roland's spirits soared as Rebecca came out of her state of shock, and he instinctively bobbed his head and placed a kiss on her lips. Her arms locked around him as she tilted her head to accommodate him. They stood in front of The Last Frontier, dirty, bleeding, and kissing like a couple of lovestruck children, momentarily forgetting everything else but the other. Pulling his head away slightly, Roland stared at the beautiful woman who had become so important to him. It wasn't the first time they had kissed, but it seemed to have banished Rebecca's remaining fears. Her eyes once again stared back at him with some of their customary sparkle. She still didn't have her usual merry aura, but after the night's events, Roland would have been stunned if she had. "Feeling better?" He bantered lightly.

"Yes, Roland. I am."

36

Her voice had regained some of its strength, and Roland rejoiced to hear it. "Good. Why don't we head inside? I'll get you a room, and then I think you should get a good night's sleep." Roland draped a tired arm around her shoulders and leaned on her as his side tightened on him painfully once again. Pressing the other hand firmly against his ribs, Roland limped into the saloon with Rebecca's support.

Stepping inside The Last Frontier, Roland noted the quietness for the first time. The Last Frontier was the busiest saloon in town and always had a noisy crowd that could be heard in the street, but when they entered the saloon, the place was nearly empty. Besides the staff, only a handful of gamblers and a few men in the throes of the bottle remained. "What's going on?" Roland muttered to himself as the tavern's few patrons and the staff turned their heads in his direction. Every eye focused upon him expectantly, and he saw George Wright scurry his way with a worried expression on his face.

"Roland, thank God you're back!" George shouted as he approached the couple. The pudgy owner's eyes were wide with fear as his stout legs hurried across the floor.

"Where's everyone, George?" Roland asked warily as his legs trembled. He couldn't wait to have Doc Sullivan examine the wounds. None were too serious except the one along his ribs, but they all burned like wasp stings. His strength was dwindling, and he needed to get his injuries looked at before he went to sleep. The wound along his ribs would need stitching to heal properly, Roland surmised unpleasantly. As soon as Rebecca was set up in her room, he planned on visiting Sullivan then getting some sleep himself. There was nothing else for him to do that night. Roland just wanted to lay in bed and forget all about her house and the terrible phenomena that had occurred inside.

Ignoring Sheriff Black's question, George stared at them with wide eyes. He appeared to have completely forgotten what had caused him to rush to their side. "What happened to you two?"

Roland glanced at Rebecca and looked over his own clothes, noting how they must appear to the saloon owner. Rebecca had ceased her crying, but her cheeks were still puffy from her earlier bouts. Her hair was a tangled mess, and her dress was torn in several places from her climb through the window. Roland looked even worse. His clothes were ripped, and blood had soaked through them since his desperate scramble out of the house. Sweat drenched both of their clothes, and Roland thought they both looked like a pair of fighters who had just emerged from a brawl. Shaking his head, Roland rolled his eyes at their sorry state. "Nevermind. Just tell me what's going on tonight. Where's everybody?"

George continued to stare at them then shook his head as if to banish a few questions he wanted to ask. Suddenly remembering why he had rushed to meet the Sheriff, George began to babble hurriedly. "Roland, you need to get over to The Snake immediately. Wade came over here about ten minutes ago and said about a dozen Riders had come to town." The innkeeper stopped and grabbed Roland's elbow. "Roland, he said Carlos was with them. He and William lit out of here like a couple of children about ready to get a switchin', and we heard a couple of gunshots about five minutes ago. Everyone went over to see what was happening. After last night, I imagine half the people in town are over there. William said you should get over there as soon as you got back."

"Damn it to Hell," Roland swore and clenched a fist. He should have counted on the Dark Riders to make an appearance that night. It had already gone poorly, and he had only wanted to get his wounds tended to and sleep off the pain of his injuries. Sleep, however, wasn't in his immediate future. *Goddamn it,* he fumed. Roland just hoped that he could resolve the conflict quickly. In such a large group, the Dark Riders usually caused quite a bit of trouble, and if Carlos was with them, they would be even more emboldened. Roland prayed a gunfight could be avoided. He was always prepared to put his life on the line for his job, but Roland wouldn't be effective when he had already sustained wounds. His side throbbed, and his arms were slowly growing numb.

"Roland?" Rebecca called softly and gently ran a hand through his hair. "Are you all right?"

Sheriff Black laughed coarsely as she tried to soothe him. Only moments before, it had been he who had to comfort her. "I'm all right. I want you to stay here. I need to go see what's happening at The Snake. George, Rebecca's going to need a room upstairs, and give me the one next to hers. Make sure she gets anything she needs. We can settle up when I get back," Roland ordered the saloon owner then pulled Rebecca aside. George nodded wordlessly and backed away from the couple.

"You're not going over there, are you?" Rebecca asked in a worried tone. George stopped and stared back at them, but Roland shot him a stern gaze. The saloon owner darted his eyes away and quickly scurried back to the bar.

Once George was out of hearing range, Roland bent over painfully and placed his mouth next to Rebecca's ear. "Rebecca, I have to go. I don't want to, but I have to."

"Do you have to go? You're already hurt. Can't Jack handle everything?" She asked insistently.

"I'd stay if I could, but Jack can't handle the Riders by himself. I'm probably the only one they fear. Hell, none of this would have happened if I had been around," Roland cursed bitterly. He hated to leave Rebecca alone for even a short time after the events at her house, but the Dark Riders had taken precedence over his personal concerns.

38

"I'm sorry. I didn't mean to take you away from your job," Rebecca said quietly and looked down at the floor.

"It's not your fault, Rebecca," Roland told her immediately. "I wanted to join you for dinner. If I can't let the deputies look after the town for an hour, then it's not a safe town. Now, listen. I don't want you telling anybody what happened tonight. Tell them the horse bucked us if anyone asks. We don't need rumors floating around before we find out what happened."

"All right, Roland. I'll do that. You just be careful. Don't be foolish. You're already hurt, and you're in no condition for any fights." Her lips pursed in a worried grimace.

"I promise. I'll be back as soon as I can." Roland gave her a quick kiss then limped out of the saloon to join his deputies. He untied his horse, then laboriously mounted it, grunting as pain coursed through his side. The Rattlesnake was only a short distance away, but Roland didn't know if he could walk that far. Spurring the horse into a trot, Roland rode towards The Snake, cursing each agonizing jolt of the horse's gait. He clung to the horse's neck for dear life and tried to keep from falling out of the saddle as his strength continued to dwindle. As he turned the corner, Roland considered trying to draw one of his pistols, but he knew the effort would be futile. He wanted to resolve the situation peacefully and riding up with a gun in hand wouldn't be the way to accomplish that goal. Roland just prayed that Alvin had already shown up to calm the outlaws and keep them from causing even more trouble.

A large crowd had gathered outside of the saloon to witness the confrontation. The Rattlesnake was second only to The Last Frontier in terms of popularity, but it attracted a seedier brand of customers. The Dark Riders patronized The Snake when they came to town. Before Roland had become Sheriff, the Riders had frequented The Last Frontier, but once he established his presence there, Carlos and his men had sought a rowdier atmosphere and found it at The Snake. The Sheriff had often been tempted to place more of his deputies there, but he knew that the Dark Riders would have simply moved on to a different saloon. The Snake's owner had even asked Sheriff Black to stay out of his establishment for fear that he would drive away all of the customers. Roland didn't have enough deputies to watch every saloon in town, so he usually left The Snake and its patrons alone. He had most of the troublemakers in the city isolated in one spot, and Roland preferred them in one location rather than spread over the entire city.

The crowd outside The Rattlesnake that night was composed mainly of spectators, although Roland noticed its usual patrons bunched by the door and watching the activities taking place on the street. Sheriff Black counted five of his deputies outside The Snake and nearly a dozen of the Dark Riders. Four of his men stood defiantly between the Dark Riders and the crowd that had gathered. Morgan Shields stood most prominently among the deputies, his long white hair blowing under the gentle summer wind. Besides Jack, Morgan was Roland's favorite deputy, and he was glad the old gunslinger was there that night. Wade had a feral grin on his face in anticipation of a possible confrontation, while William and Ben looked slightly edgy, although ready to put their lives on the line. The Sheriff had taken his time when selecting his deputies, and he was glad that patience had paid off. He didn't want men who would bolt at the first sign of a gunfight, nor eager men whose itchy trigger fingers could ignite one. Roland was confident in the ability of those four deputies, and while he wasn't looking for a fight, he felt a lot more secure with those men on his side.

The Dark Riders lounged in front of The Rattlesnake, trying to bait his deputies. Curly was there and drunk as usual. He had long blond hair and a short beard. His overcoat was thrown wide open, revealing the pair of Colt .45's that he was ready to use. Wild Carl and Mad Dog were also present. They were another pair of Dark Riders who frequently came to town and became intoxicated. Mad Dog had tangled brown hair and dirty clothes, while Wild Carl had thinning blond hair and a lazy eye that made people uncomfortable when he stared at them. Marshall Drake was Carlos's second in command. He didn't try to bait Roland's deputies as the other Dark Riders but stood back calmly with his hand near his holster. Five of the Banditos had also ridden to town. Carlos had fled Mexico years ago bringing along a few of his men. Carlos had picked up English over the years, but the Banditos barely spoke a word of it. Roland had few dealings with them since they only came to town when Carlos made one of his rare excursions.

Just as George had reported, Carlos stood in the street, wearing his customary sneer. The expression on his face announced clearly what he thought of the deputies confronting him and his men. Carlos was the leader of the Dark Riders, although he usually kept out of sight. According to the rumor mill, Carlos had killed over a hundred men in Mexico before fleeing to America to avoid the authorities. Sheriff Black didn't hold much stock in rumors, but he was glad that Carlos stayed out of town most of the time. Somebody with that much reputation could usually back it up with some degree of skill. So far, he had only been belligerent when entering town, but Sheriff Black feared it was just a matter of time before Carlos finally decided to push his luck too far. He was a tall man, towering over even Roland, and had a bushy mustache and brown eyes. He wore a wide-brimmed hat and a tan overcoat, and he held a shotgun in his hands. Roland knew that he also had a Colt .45 strapped to his thigh.

Luckily Alvin Buckner stood next to Carlos, calmly talking with Jack Logan, Roland's most trusted deputy. Alvin had achieved a small bit of notoriety for being a gunslinger in his youth, but he had settled down years ago after being shot in the leg. He didn't like to speak of that particular shooting and still bore a limp and cane from the incident. The first time Roland had met him, Alvin was flushed and excited from just winning a duel, even though his opponent had managed to graze his right shoulder. When Roland came to New Haven, he was amazed to see the cultured, eloquent man that Alvin had become. His white hair was perfectly combed, and he wore a polished, urbane smile as well as a fancy suit. The citizens of New Haven had liked Alvin so much, they had elected him mayor of their town. They thought he was a polite gentleman who always kept the Dark Riders from causing any real harm, but Roland knew better.

He knew that Alvin was working with the Dark Riders and that the gentleman act was a façade. Carlos was the power behind the Dark Riders, but Alvin was the brains behind their operation. Alvin had grown too old to be an effective gunslinger any longer, so he instead used his intelligence to guide the Dark Riders in their illegal activities. New Haven provided Alvin the ideal setting to be the gang's contact man. He could buy information about train schedules and stagecoach departures as well as scout out public sentiment towards the Dark Riders. Using the prestige of his elected office, Alvin could effectively stand up for the Dark Riders when necessary. As much as he hated the mayor, Roland was grateful to see him that night. Alvin knew that if the Dark Riders pitched a shoot-out in the middle of town, some of Roland's men would be killed as well as several citizens. That would ensure the entire town's wrath, and it would only be a matter of time before the Dark Riders were tracked down and killed.

Slowly sliding one of his legs off the horse, Sheriff Black grunted as pain coursed through his side. He prayed that Alvin could keep Carlos and the rest of the Dark Riders in line. Roland didn't think he could remain on his feet much longer, let alone survive a shoot-out. Placing a hand along the wound in his side, Roland limped towards the crowd. "Let me through," Roland called out as he pushed through. A startled buzz rippled through the people as they noted the arrival of their Sheriff. The participants of the confrontation also noticed his arrival. All of his deputies broke into smiles as he arrived on the scene, and most of the Dark Riders scowled at his intrusion.

Spotting the Sheriff wading through the crowd of onlookers, Carlos started to point the shotgun towards him, but Alvin quickly reached out and grabbed his arm, shaking his head at the gunslinger. "Jack," Roland greeted cheerfully as he joined the three. Despite the pain shooting through his body, he forced his face into a flippant grin. "Alvin, Carlos," he greeted the Dark Rider and mayor in the same upbeat tone, nodding his head to each. "Why don't you tell me what's going on here tonight."

Carlos looked over Roland, noting the blood that stained his clothes and the way Sheriff Black pressed a hand against his side. Carlos straightened his back and looked down at Roland. His face twisted into another sneer, and he spat upon the ground. "What's the matter, Sheriff? Did you get your ass whipped by one of the barmaids at The Frontier?" He taunted Roland in his thick accent then coarsely chuckled at his own humor.

I should shoot you right now, you son of a bitch, Roland thought but held his tongue. He ignored the Dark Rider and shifted his eyes to the mayor. "Alvin, you tell me what's going on." Roland knew he could count on Alvin to be amicable and try to smooth things over peacefully. Left to his own devices, Carlos would gleefully start a gunfight, but Alvin had no desire for that. His power came from keeping the Dark Riders in check. Besides, a large portion of New Haven was watching them, and the one thing that Alvin guarded more preciously than the Dark Riders' safety was his reputation. It would certainly take a beating if anyone died that night.

"Roland, it's nothing to get upset over. I was just telling Jack we should all go home and forget it ever happened," Alvin explained in a saccharine tone. He assumed his innocent expression that he always showed Roland in public, even though both he and Roland knew it was a sham.

You Goddamn snake, Roland snarled to himself but held his tongue once more. He knew that Alvin was lying and trying to upset him in front of everyone else, but the safety of his men and the rest of the town was more important. "That's fine, Alvin," Roland told the mayor, and his tone had a harder edge to it. "But I want to know what's going on. It looks like Carlos and his men are about to start a gunfight."

Alvin spread his hands wide and smiled, but his eyes narrowed spitefully towards Roland. "As I was telling Jack, it wasn't Carlos's fault. Your deputies were hassling them, and a few tempers got riled. Nothing would have happened. I think it would be best for everyone if Carlos and the rest of the Riders went home. Don't you?" His face stretched into a smug look of satisfaction. He knew that he was upsetting Roland, but the Sheriff couldn't do anything in front of the whole town. There were too many eyes looking on, and Roland would be the one blamed if anything bad happened.

Roland growled at the back of his throat. He wanted to throw the whole damn lot in jail for the night, but as much as hated it, Alvin was right. The Dark Riders leaving town was in everyone's best interests, but he'd be damned if he let them get away without any punishment. His business dealings with Alvin had deteriorated into a chess match during his tenure as Sheriff. They'd banter back and forth until they finally came to an agreement. Roland hated the games of words he played with Alvin, but they were the only way to deal with the Dark Riders barring violence, so he endured them with a huge amount of salt. "Fine," he said curtly. "I want all of them gone in the next five minutes, but I don't want any of them back in town for a week." Sheriff Black issued his demands and waited for Alvin's counter proposal.

The old gunslinger rubbed his chin thoughtfully as he considered the Sheriff's words. "A whole week out of the city? That seems rather excessive, Roland. How about we make it tonight and tomorrow night? That will give everyone time to cool down, and it doesn't punish Carlos and his men unfairly." Alvin watched Sheriff Black with a feral expression. He knew that Roland wanted the situation defused peacefully as soon as possible, and that knowledge allowed him to press the Sheriff's orders.

Unfairly? Roland wanted to laugh at Alvin's offer. He was positive that the Dark Rider had instigated the whole affair that evening, although he'd have to wait until the Riders left town before he could talk to Jack. Roland just wanted Alvin to shut his mouth and accept his orders, but that was unlikely to happen. The Sheriff couldn't remember a time that he had passed judgment upon the Dark Riders and Alvin hadn't pestered him relentlessly until he had lessened the sentence.

Normally Roland would have backed down and been more flexible when dealing with Alvin, but that night's events had already put him in a foul mood. The phenomena in Rebecca's house had confounded and injured him, but he could at least strike back at Alvin. For too long, Carlos and Alvin had forced him into compliance with the threat of violence. *But not tonight,* he thought grimly. He slid a hand onto the butt of his right pistol and calmly stroked its hammer with the ball of his finger. "Two days?" He rasped harshly. "I'm telling you this one more time, Alvin. They're gone for a Goddamn week. Do you understand?"

Carlos didn't look frightened by Roland's gesture and gripped his shotgun even tighter. He planted his feet firmly in the earth. "Are you threatening me, Sheriff? You look a little tired for a gunfight. The Riders go where they want to go, and if you get in our way, we'll put you down." Carlos told Roland, his sneer deepening.

"Don't be a fool," Alvin cursed at the Dark Rider. He stepped in front of Carlos and turned his back to the Sheriff. "You just get over with the rest of your men and leave town when I say to leave. Is that clear?"

Carlos looked at Roland with contempt then turned his attention to Alvin. "We can take him and his men. If he tries to make us leave, we'll put him and all of his deputies down."

"You just shut up and let me handle this. I swear if you shoot one more bullet tonight, I'll kill you myself. Now get over there with the rest of your men, and let us talk." Alvin placed a hand upon his hip and watched Carlos with stern eyes. The Dark Rider looked on the verge of retorting, but he chose to hold his silence. He threw Sheriff Black a hostile glance and spat on the ground derisively before ambling over to where the other Dark Riders were standing. "Let's talk, Roland. In private," Alvin told Roland. His eyebrows lowered maliciously, but Roland knew that he was one of the few people in town who saw past his polished smile.

"Jack, why don't you join Morgan? I want to talk to Alvin alone here for a moment." The deputy nodded and wordlessly followed the Sheriff's order. Once they were alone, Sheriff Black turned his attention solely on Alvin. "A week, Alvin. I'm not backing down this time. Just accept it and get them out of town. I know you don't want a shoot-out."

"You're bluffing. You wouldn't risk a gunfight. Just accept two days, and we can all go home."

Roland was about to reply when pain lanced through his side. He hissed as a spasm ripped along his ribs and left him short of breath. His anger at Alvin hadn't abated, but Roland knew that he couldn't delay medical help any longer. His strength was nearly gone, and he was beginning to feel lightheaded. He held up a hand in supplication. "Let's decide on somewhere between two and seven days then. Just get them to leave town and come by The Frontier when you get finished. We can discuss it then."

"Are you all right?" The mayor looked at him with more curiosity than concern.

"I'm fine. Just get them out of here now. I need to get off my feet, and I think we both want the Riders gone while I'm still able to stand."

Alvin studied Roland carefully and paused before nodding his head. "All right, Roland. I'll get them to leave, but you'd better not go back on your word. Somewhere between two and seven. If you're lying, I'll have Carlos bring every Rider into town every night for the next month. Am I clear?"

"Perfectly. Now get them out of here, and don't hurry to The Frontier. Give me an hour."

Alvin tapped his chin and studied Roland carefully. The polished smile never left his lips, but his eyes narrowed. Finally the mayor nodded. "Fine, Roland. I'll see you in one hour."

Sheriff Black limped over to his men as Alvin rounded up the Dark Riders. Carlos had a few heated words with him, but eventually he followed Alvin's orders and mounted his horse. A path opened in the crowd as the Dark Riders slowly rode down the street in a single line. Alvin turned around with his polished grin. The mayor began to greet his constituents as a smattering of applause broke out, but most of the onlookers went back to their normal lives now that the ordeal was over. A great many were obviously disappointed that it hadn't ended with some excitement, but Roland was pleased with the result.

As Alvin shook hands and soothed the fears of New Haven's voters, Roland leaned against The Snake and addressed his men. "Morgan, I want you to take William and Wade and make sure the Riders leave town. I don't want someone pounding on my door tonight telling me they're starting more trouble. Come to The Frontier when they're gone. Ben, you go fetch Doc Sullivan and tell him to bring his medical bag with him. Jack, you tell me what the hell happened tonight."

"Are you all right, Sheriff?" Ben piped up immediately. "You've got blood all over you. Did you get in a fight? You don't look good. Were you shot? Or were—" he broke off as Roland interrupted him.

"I fell off my horse, Ben," Roland cut him off roughly. It was the only way to get through to Ben. "It's nothing serious. Now everyone get moving. I'm fine." His words seemed to calm everyone. Even Morgan looked concerned over his appearance, but they all nodded when he gave them their orders.

"Yes, sir," William quipped as he and the other two deputies followed the Dark Riders' trail. Ben climbed onto his horse and galloped down the street towards Doc Sullivan's house. Roland hoped Ben was quick about it. He was getting more and more tired by the minute.

Jack watched Ben disappear down the street then cast a dubious glance towards Roland. "You don't expect us to believe that happened from falling off a horse, do you?" Jack Logan was the only one of Roland's deputies who would question him when he was in a bad mood. Roland had met Jack nearly two decades before, and when the old gunslinger had passed through New Haven eight months ago, Roland had quickly convinced him to stay. Time had turned his hair and mustache iron grey, but he was still quick with a gun. More importantly, he had a level head and would speak his mind. Sometimes the other deputies grew afraid of Roland's wrath, but Jack had known Roland when he was a gunslinger and knew that the rumors circulating about the Sheriff were blown out of proportion.

The Sheriff barked out a laugh and nearly choked as pain tore through his side. "No, I don't expect to you to believe it, but I expect you to shut up about it," he answered then gave Jack a stern gaze to say that he meant every word. It wasn't to scare Jack, just to let him know that Roland was serious.

Waving a hand in dismissal, Jack acquiesced to Roland's request. "It's none of my business, Roland."

Good, Roland thought. He was too tired to argue with Jack. "I'm going to sit down until Sullivan shows up. I want you to tell me what happened." Roland breathed a sigh of relief as he finally took a sat down on the ground and let his weary muscles rest.

"Well, from what I gathered from Wade, the Riders showed up about an hour ago and headed over to The Snake. Ben and Morgan sent Wade to round up everyone in case of trouble while they kept an eye on the place. Robert's still at the station house, but everyone else showed up. Right after they left, Curly started making a scene again. I guess he's still upset from last night. He was arguing over a poker hand and had started to push people around when Ben and Morgan intervened.

"At that point, Carlos and every Rider in the place started talking about a duel in the streets. By the time we came back with Wade, they had dragged Ben and Morgan into the street. The Riders were pretty brave when they're facing two men, but I guess five men gave them pause. I managed to keep Carlos in line until Alvin showed up, then Alvin kept them in line until you got here."

"What about the gunshots? George said he heard two gunshots."

"That was Carlos. He was just blowing off some steam. He fired two shots at Wade's feet to let us know he was serious."

"That's about what I expected. 'Unfair punishment.' It figures Alvin would say you were 'hassling' them. I should throw every damn Rider out of town for a month and see how he likes that." Roland laughed bitterly then took a deep, calming breath as a tremor ran along his ribcage.

"How was Alvin?"

"The same as always. He plays nice around voters, but as soon as they turn their backs, he's a Goddamn snake." Sheriff Black coughed out a chuckle, and Jack joined him in laughter. As they waited for Ben to return with Doc Sullivan, Roland and his deputy mocked their mayor as Alvin chatted away with the citizens of New Haven.

Just as the crowd had dissipated, Ben rode down the street with the stuffy town doctor behind him. Doc Sullivan had been the doctor of New Haven since before Roland had even come to the town. Prior to being the lone doctor of New Haven, Doctor Richard Sullivan had practiced medicine in Boston, Massachusetts, fighting for business with all of the other doctors in town. Tired of the relentless competition for patients, he had moved west to a place where he would be the sole authority on medical matters. Roland had to admit that Doc Sullivan was perhaps the best doctor he had ever seen, but he still couldn't stand the man. The doctor's skill and absence of competitors had swelled his head with arrogance, and he usually performed his practice with an overinflated ego that grated at Roland's nerves.

"Sheriff, Ben told me that you'd been injured," the stout doctor announced in his nasal voice. Ben escorted Doc Sullivan all the way to Roland's side then helped the little teapot off his horse. The doctor was a short, pudgy man who often reminded Roland of his teapot at home, and the Sheriff had a hard time blocking that mental image when dealing with him.

"Yeah, I fell off a horse about an hour ago."

"Is that so?" The doctor asked rhetorically as he knelt beside the wounded Sheriff. "Well, let me take a look." Roland grimaced in pain as Doc Sullivan opened his shirt and probed at the cut along his side. He suddenly looked up at Roland accusingly. "This is from a knife or some sort of blade. Why'd you tell me it was from a fall?"

Roland closed his eyes in frustration and exhaustion. *I don't have time for this.* He just wanted the cut stitched up so he could return to The Frontier and get some sleep. "Does it really matter how it got there?"

The doctor straightened his posture then nudged his glasses up with a knuckle. "No, it doesn't, but I would like to—"

"Just stitch it up, Doc," Roland broke him off. "I have an appointment I need to keep. It's been a long night, and I don't have to explain myself to you," Sheriff Black rasped harshly. He had been through enough events that night, and if the doctor didn't start bandaging him up soon, Roland swore he would shoot him dead right there on the street.

"Well, all right, but I'd still like to know what happened." Doc Sullivan rambled on and on. The entire time he stitched Roland's side, the doctor shot pestering question after question about the wound's source. Roland would have barked at the doctor to be silent, but he was busy grinding his teeth as the doctor cleaned his wound then slowly sewed it closed.

After tending to the large cut, Doc Sullivan methodically dressed the other minor injuries that Roland had sustained. "You should avoid any heavy physical activity for the next week," the doctor explained as he tied the last bandage around Roland's upper arm.

"One week? I have to work tomorrow," Roland stated flatly.

"Impossible, Sheriff. If you push yourself too hard, the wound in your side will break open again. Maybe a week is a bit much. Could you rest for the next three days?"

"I can't be away from the town that long. I can sit around the saloon and not do anything strenuous. Is that good enough?"

The doctor considered Roland's offer for a moment. He idly stroked his neatly trimmed beard and looked to the sky as if it held the answers to Roland's question. "All right. Go back to work. I don't think I can stop you, but you be careful and don't go running around. If you overdo it, you'll reinjure yourself and have to rest more than a few days. I mean it. That cut in your side was nearly to the bone, and if you start riding around tomorrow, it will break open again."

"That sounds fine. Drop by the station house tomorrow, and one of my men will pay you for your services," Roland dismissed the little man. Doc Sullivan puffed up with self-importance then strutted to his horse with a jaunt of arrogance in his step. "I swear one of these days, I'm going to knock his head right out of the clouds," the Sheriff joked as the doctor left earshot, and then he slowly came to his feet. His wounds still ached dully, but they weren't the throbbing fury that had pained his body before.

Now sleep, Roland thought wearily. It had been a long night, and he couldn't wait to return to The Frontier and collect on some much-deserved rest. The Sheriff limped to his horse and draped his weary arms over the saddle. "Jack, can you give me a hand here?"

The deputy broke off his conversation with Ben and trotted over to the Sheriff. He knelt by the horse and cradled his hands together for Roland to use as a step. Roland placed a foot in the deputy's palms, and Jack shoveled him awkwardly onto his mount as Roland tried to keep from stretching his tender side. Roland squirmed around for a moment before slowly assuming a seated position. Black spots swirled in front of his eyes as he felt the world suddenly lurch. Wrapping his arms around the neck of his horse, Roland waited for his sense of balance to return.

"You all right?" Jack looked up at the Sheriff with a concerned expression.

Roland blinked several times, attempting to make the black spots floating through his vision disappear. "Can you ride to The Frontier with me? I don't want to pass out and wake up in the middle of the street."

"Sure, Roland. Give me a second to fetch my horse." The Sheriff waited for Jack to mount his own horse, and then the two slowly rode towards The Last Frontier in silence.

Sheriff Black didn't mind the silence. Ever since dinner at Rebecca's house, events had swirled about him and not allowed him to catch his breath. He was exhausted and sore and simply wanted to sleep fitfully and forget about his problems for a little while. In all the excitement of the Dark Riders, Roland hadn't thought any further of the extraordinary events at Rebecca's house, and he intended to keep it that way now that things had settled down. There was nothing more he could do about it that night, and he would put off speculation on the subject until the following day after a good night's sleep. His conversation with Alvin still loomed before he could go to bed, but Roland could deal with the mayor even though he was exhausted. It wasn't the first time the two had negotiated a punishment for the Dark Riders, and Roland was an old hand at it after a year as Sheriff.

Jack rode along quietly as well, although his face showed that he was thinking about something. Finally the deputy spoke up and asked Roland what had been perplexing him. "Roland, what really happened to you tonight?"

"I already told you. I don't want to talk about it."

Jack decided to press the issue. "We've known each other a long time, Roland. You know I'd do anything to keep this town safe, and I know you'd do the same. For God's sake, don't go running after whoever took a knife to you. This town needs you as Sheriff. New Haven can't afford to have you run off on a vendetta."

Roland tipped back his head and laughed. He still didn't want to discuss Rebecca's house, but he had never thought that Jack would have speculated about his wounds and struck so far from the truth. "Jack, it's not a knife wound.

I wasn't attacked by anybody, and I'm not doing anything stupid. So let's just drop the subject."

"But if it's not a knife wound, what is it? That cut sure isn't from falling off a horse."

Normally Sheriff Black admired Jack's tenacity. Most of the deputies kept their mouths shut when Roland was in a bad mood, but not Jack. The events of that evening, however, were a very touchy issue, and Roland didn't wish to discuss them. "Jack, I'm going to say this one last time. I don't want to talk about it. As soon as I know what the hell happened tonight, I promise you'll be the first to know, but until then, I want you to drop the subject. I'm not asking, Jack. I'm telling you."

Jack had been around Roland long enough to know when to push and when to keep quiet, and he wisely switched the topic. "That's fine, Roland. So how long do you think the Riders will stay out of town?"

Roland spat on the ground in disgust. "It's up to Alvin. Sullivan told me I need to rest for at least three days, so I won't be riding around town during that time. I should be able to convince Alvin to keep them away until I'm able to move around. He doesn't want them running roughshod over New Haven anymore than I do, and if they know I can't get up and fight, they'll raise hell every night until I'm better."

"Do you think Alvin will see it that way? He's always looked out for their interests before."

"Alvin might be a Goddamn snake, but he's not a stupid one. If they start making trouble every night, even he won't be able to cover for them. Alvin needs for them to cause some trouble, but he doesn't want them shooting people in the streets. If I'm off my feet, they'll swarm over the town, whether he likes it or not. No offense to you, Jack, but I'm the only one the Dark Riders fear. Probably because I'm the only one with a reputation hanging over my head."

Jack waved a hand in the air, dismissing Roland's statement. "No offense taken, Roland. We all know you're the Sheriff in New Haven, and we wouldn't want it any other way." His face suddenly broke into a mischievous grin. "Personally, I don't mind if the Dark Riders don't consider me a threat. I don't want them gunning after me if they ever get too nervous."

"Thanks for your support," Sheriff Black replied dryly.

By the time they reached The Frontier, Roland's entire body yearned to find a bed. His muscles protested every time he moved, and his eyelids had grown heavy and required Roland's constant attention to keep from closing. *Not much longer*, the Sheriff kept telling himself. Soon Alvin would pay his visit, then he could sleep the night away in complete bliss. He just hoped he could stay awake that long. The mayor didn't take kindly to being slighted, and the last thing Roland needed was trouble from the Dark Riders.

After tying his horse to a post, Jack helped Roland out of his saddle. Pain once again flared in his injured side, and Roland thought he would pass out for a moment. He slumped in Jack's grip as the pain slowly receded. "Roland?" Jack asked worriedly.

"I'm fine, Jack. Just give me a moment." Roland kept his eyes closed as he felt the pain deaden into a dull ache once more. Flexing his legs, he unsteadily came to his feet. "Jack, do you mind making sure I get inside?"

"No problem, Roland. Take your time. Don't push yourself too hard." Jack dipped his shoulder as Roland swung an arm around it, then the deputy guided the limping Sheriff into the saloon.

The patrons had returned to The Last Frontier with the Dark Riders safely out of town. The bargirls scrambled between the bar and the thirsty clientele, while the card dealers had their hands full with plenty of gamblers. Nearly every one of them paused to stare as Roland limped into the establishment with Jack's help. Roland made an effort to keep his face locked in a flat, hostile expression and fought the urge to smile as his storied past once again came to his aid. One by one, the patrons resumed their drinking or card games as he cast his furious gaze around the saloon.

George hustled over to the pair as the environment turned festive once again. "Sheriff, are you all right?"

"I'm fine. Where's Rebecca?"

"She's already upstairs. I put her in the quietest room in the house. She looked pretty worried, Sheriff. She said you two had fallen from your horse." George stated the last sentence as if he didn't believe it.

Roland had no intention of bandying words with the saloon owner. His priorities were talking with Alvin and going to sleep. "That's exactly what happened, George. It was the damnedest thing. We were just riding along, and the damn horse bucked us. We'll both be fine," Roland responded in a tone that warranted no argument. "I'll be taking the room next to Rebecca's."

"But, Sheriff, I've already rented that room out tonight. I thought you would want Rebecca in a quiet room, so I put her in the back room upstairs. There were already people sleeping in the room next to hers, and I couldn't kick them out as this time of night."

"Move them," Roland stated flatly.

"I can't do that. It's bad for business. I have another room available just down the hall. Won't that do?"

"I said to move them."

"All right, all right, you can have the room. Are you happy?"

Roland rewarded the saloon owner with his lopsided grin. "Perfectly happy, George. Think of it as payment for all the protection you've received from me and my deputies."

"Fine, Sheriff," George responded in a pouty voice. Kicking customers out of their rooms in the middle of the night wouldn't help his reputation any, but the couple staying in the room were travelers and wouldn't ever pay him any money again after they left. "Is there anything else you need?"

"Yes. If Alvin shows up, send him up to my room."

"I'll do that. Let me go move the people out of your room, then you can lie down." George scurried upstairs and headed down the hall towards the set of rooms where Roland and Rebecca would be staying. He appeared again soon after, escorting an angry-looking pair of travelers to their new room.

"They don't look too happy about swapping rooms," Jack commented drolly.

"No, they don't. It's not our problem, though. They're George's customers."

Jack laughed at Roland's reply as George marched down the stairs. The saloon owner didn't look too thrilled with their moving either, and he presented Roland with the key to his room with a huff and great deal of displeasure. "Those people weren't pleased with being woken up and moved to a different room. I hope you appreciate this."

"I do, George. Now if you'll excuse us, I really have to go lie down." Roland dismissed the saloon owner and slowly climbed up the stairs with Jack's help. They had to stop once as Roland's side flared painfully, and he gripped the banister to maintain his balance. It quickly subsided, though, and the two resumed their ascent.

Once they reached the top, Roland leaned against a wall and caught his breath. "Damn, I need to get some sleep. Thanks for your help, Jack."

"You're welcome, Roland. Do you need anything else?"

"No, I should be fine. I want you to stay at The Frontier until I'm feeling stronger. William can use some help. I'll be staying here, but I won't be good for anything if trouble breaks out. And make sure that the Dark Riders left town. If you don't hear from Wade, wake me up."

"Sure, it's not a problem. If you're fine, I'll just head on down to the floor and keep an eye on things tonight. People have their blood boiling over the Dark Riders, and somebody might do something stupid."

"Good luck."

"Thanks. Sleep well, Roland. We can use you back as soon as possible."

"I'll do that," Roland replied then limped down the hall, keeping one arm steadied against the wall to help his balance. George had put him and Rebecca in the back of the saloon near his own room. The noise coming from the customers was impossible to block completely, but the rooms were far enough away where the loud reverie below was sufficiently muted.

Holding the key in his hand, Roland paused at the doorway to his room. He needed to lie down and rest his weary body, but he wanted to make sure Rebecca had settled in her room all right. The night had worn on him, but he could only imagine what Rebecca must be feeling. At least Roland still had a house he could return to when he was feeling better. He wouldn't let Rebecca return to hers until he found out what had happened that evening.

He knocked softly on her door several times. "Rebecca, are you still up?" He called softly in case she was sleeping. When she didn't answer the door, he knocked again and waited impatiently outside her door. He was just about to leave when the door opened a crack.

"Roland? Is that you?" Rebecca stood behind the barely opened door, peering out with bleary eyes.

"Yes, it's me. Did I wake you?"

"Hmm," she murmured affirmatively. "It was a light sleep, though. My nerves are a bit high-strung tonight for some reason." She gave him a sleepy smile.

"I'm sorry. I just wanted to be sure you were all right and to let you know I made it back safely."

"Thanks. I would've woken up tomorrow scared to death. I'm glad you're back safe. Did the Riders cause much trouble?"

"Nothing too bad. Just their normal routine. They got a lot of people excited then they left when Alvin told them to."

"Good. I'm glad Alvin can keep them in line. I'd hate for you to have to fight them someday."

"Don't worry. I'll be fine. I've survived far worse than the Dark Riders, and I'm not about to get myself shot on account of them."

Rebecca smiled in response. "How's your side?"

"Doc Sullivan stitched it up and told me to rest for the next week, but I talked him down to one night and taking it easy for a while."

Placing her hands on her hips, Rebecca tried to give him a stern look that failed miserably in her tired state. "Do you plan on following his orders, or are you going to run around and play Sheriff until it gets worse?"

Reaching out his hand, Roland gently stroked her hair. "You can relax. I plan on obeying the doctor's orders. I'm staying in the next room tonight, then I'll be relaxing in the saloon for at least the next few days. Jack'll be here, and he can take care of any problems."

"Then why don't you stay at home and rest in bed while Jack watches after this place?"

"I might not be able to fight, but I still need to be here. People expect to see me here. If I'm gone, they might get a little braver. With this weather we don't need people running around thinking they can do whatever they want because the Sheriff is at home resting."

"All right, but what about me? I can't go back to the house, Roland. Not ever."

"Don't worry. I'm not letting you go back to that house until I know what happened tonight. You can stay at my house until we know yours is safe."

Cupping his hand in hers, Rebecca lightly kissed his fingertips. "Thank you, Roland. I was so afraid about what I would do tomorrow."

"You're welcome." Her kiss sent shivers down his spine, and goosebumps broke out on his weary arms.

Rebecca looked down at the floor nervously. "I don't know what I'd do without you, Roland."

Roland grinned foolishly as she spoke to him. Rebecca was very self-conscious when it came to expressing her feelings for him, which made the few times that she did special. Steeling himself against the pain in his side, Roland drew Rebecca into his embrace and gently kissed her. Her hands reached up and entwined themselves in his hair as she enthusiastically returned the kiss. Roland felt his blood begin to heat and broke off the kiss while he still could. "Rebecca, I need to go now." He told her and tried to slow his breathing.

Rebecca shuffled her feet nervously on the floor, and her hands played with the sides of her shift. "Do you have to go?" She asked wistfully.

Reaching out and cupping her chin gently, Roland waited for her to meet his gaze. "I still have to talk with Alvin tonight, and I'm about ready to pass out from these wounds. Besides, we don't want gossip spreading all over town about us. What would people say about that? The Sheriff and the widow sleeping in the same room." Roland chuckled and flashed his lopsided grin.

"I don't care what everyone else says. I just care what you think, Roland," she told him seriously. He was surprised that her eyes stayed focused upon his face. Usually she stared at the floor or anywhere else except him when she expressed her personal feelings.

Roland dropped his smile and gazed at Rebecca with a somber expression. He knew how difficult it was for Rebecca to open up and show her feelings, let alone to ask him to stay with her that night. The entire time he had known her, Rebecca had lived in a shell of self-protection. Her invitation was the most forward he had ever seen her be, and he wanted her to know how badly he wished to take her up on that offer. "I understand, and I wish I could. But my side is killing me, and the opinion of the town does matter. I'm still the Sheriff in New Haven, and it doesn't do any good for me to tarnish my reputation. It wouldn't matter to most people if I joined you tonight, but it would to some. And you never know when I might need their help or support. Besides tomorrow night we'll be together at my house, and we'll be alone."

His words calmed Rebecca, and her mouth turned into a wistful grin. "I just don't want to sleep alone tonight."

"Neither do I, but it's only tonight, and I'll be in the next room."

"Okay. Thanks again for everything, Roland."

"It's my pleasure." Roland smiled and kissed her once again, although more chastely. He was sorely tempted to join her, and he knew that if they shared another passionate kiss, he wouldn't hesitate. Pulling his head up, Roland ran a finger softly over her cheek. "Good night, Rebecca."

"Good night, Roland." Rebecca squeezed his hand one last time then closed the door.

Roland stood in the hallway outside her door, tempted to knock again and take her up on the invitation to share her bed. He quickly unlocked his door and entered his own room before that temptation grew too great. There was still his conversation with Alvin, and more than that, he wasn't ready to progress that far. He had been with numerous women during his years of gunslinging, but he wanted it to be special with Rebecca. After living as a bachelor for nearly fifty years, he was actually considering settling down with one woman for the rest of his life. He wanted the first time with her to be something they would both remember fondly, not an occasion when he was so exhausted. There would be plenty of time to pursue that pleasure when he was healed.

His clothes were tattered and torn after his night's ordeals. Blood, sweat, and dust had settled in and stiffened them, while gaping holes marked where Roland hadn't been so lucky when scrambling through Rebecca's window. As he peeled off the ruined remains of his clothing, Roland contemplated what he would do about her. Their relationship had progressed faster than he anticipated and had grown into something that confused him. He had never thought about marrying before he had met Rebecca, but now it seemed only proper to make her his wife.

Roland stopped undressing as he thought of marriage and carefully considered the idea. He had never wanted to marry before he met Rebecca, but she filled the emptiness that had existed for so long in his life. Roland decided right then that he would wed Rebecca, and the first bed they shared would be their marriage bed. The thought invigorated Roland, and he found himself in a wonderful mood for the first time since he had savored Rebecca's delicious cooking earlier that evening. He would need to ask Reverend Thatcher to perform the ceremony and procure nice clothes for him and Rebecca. If he could arrange those two things, they could even be married the following day. The more he considered the notion, the more excited Roland became. He would just have to see how he felt in the morning, but if he could get around the following afternoon, he intended to make Rebecca White his wife the following night.

Stripped to his smallclothes, Roland eased himself onto the bed. His own bed was more comfortable, but Roland had slept in far worse. This one would be enough for him to relax his tired body. Lying down, Roland thought about his future with Rebecca and tried to keep his mind alert so he could remain awake for Alvin's visit. He was in far too good a mood to allow Alvin's petulance to cause him worry. And so he kept his mind occupied with the excitement of his decision to marry, staving off the slumber that called to him.

He fought off exhaustion for nearly half an hour, but eventually when Alvin still hadn't arrived, it caught up with him. His eyes slowly drifted shut, and his body sank into the feather mattress as his mind wandered towards the threshold of sleep. A knock on his door abruptly yanked Roland into alertness, and he rubbed a hand over his eyes, wiping away the sleep that had nearly claimed him. "Who is it?"

"It's Alvin, Roland. Let me in," the mayor's muted voice sounded from the hallway.

"Just a second." Roland's body protested loudly when he rose from the bed and came to his feet. He pressed a hand against the cut on his side as it twinged painfully. Lurching to the door, he clumsily unlocked it and swung it open.

Contrary to Roland's battered appearance, Alvin was sharply dressed as always. The mayor made it a habit to wear a pressed suit every day, and his long grey hair looked as if Alvin carried a comb with him at all times. Roland supposed that it all fit in with the debonair image that Alvin had cultivated. The mayor raised an eyebrow as he looked at Roland's bruised and bandaged body. "Blazes, Roland. What the hell happened to you? You looked bad at The Snake, but I didn't realize it was this bad."

"Let's just say I fell off a horse, Alvin, and leave it at that. If you don't mind, I'm going to lie down. It's been a tiring day," Roland announced and eased himself back onto the mattress, propping his back against the headboard. His pleasant mood darkened as he dealt with Alvin. Roland couldn't wait for the mayor to leave so he could go back to thinking about his upcoming marriage to Rebecca.

Alvin looked at Roland with amused eyes. "A horse accident?" He shook his head mockingly. "Whatever you say, Roland. Now why don't we get to the business at hand? I believe I suggested two days."

"I'm too tired to argue with you tonight, Alvin. Let's just make it five days. Sullivan told me to rest my side for a week, but I talked him down to three days. Even then, I'll still be weak and in no condition to fight. Neither one of us wants the Riders in town when I can't stop them from causing trouble. We both know without me on duty, they feel a hell of a lot braver."

The mayor took a deep breath and considered Roland's offer for a moment. "Sullivan will give me the same diagnosis if I ask him?" The Sheriff nodded once. "Fine, five days it is, but mend fast, Roland. They'll be back on the sixth day no matter how strong you are. Carlos will want to show the entire city he's not afraid of you."

Alvin's smug answer irritated Roland. He was simply trying to keep the citizens of New Haven safe, and the mayor had to make unsubtle threats. "You just tell Carlos to lay off. My patience is growing awfully thin, Alvin. He pulls another stunt like tonight, and I swear I'll start locking them up. You want to push me, I'll push back." He stared at the mayor with a dangerous glint in his eyes.

"You say that now, Roland, but will you really back up that talk? If you declare war on Carlos, a lot of people will die. Some of your men, maybe a few women or children. It would only be a matter of time before the government intervened. Where will your precious culture be then? We both came to this town because we missed our past. I know you won't jeopardize that with a foolish show of stubbornness." He smirked at the Sheriff.

"Don't try me, Alvin. I've had a really bad day, and I don't need any trouble right now. If you think I'll let you bully me into doing whatever you want, you're wrong. You might have Carlos wrapped around your finger, but I'm still Sheriff, damn it. Tell him to back off, or I'll make him back off."

"Roland, you can barely stand, and you're making threats?" Alvin quipped sardonically.

"Don't underestimate me, Alvin, and don't think you can keep pushing me around. One of these days Carlos is going to get out of hand, and you won't be able to stop him. I'm not going to let that happen. If there's even one more incident like tonight, I'm kicking them all out of town."

"Would you risk all of your deputies in a gunfight for that?" Alvin asked rhetorically. "I don't think so. You care too much for all the good people of this town. The Dark Riders will continue to come to town, and if you want to avoid serious trouble with them, you'll have to deal with me. I'm sure after a good night's rest, you'll see things my way in the morning. There's always been a truce between us, and I trust you won't break it. Get better, Roland, and try not to fall off another horse." Alvin laughed then left the room, closing the door behind him.

Chapter Three

Sheriff Black awakened four or five hours after sunrise the following day. He squinted as sunlight poured in through the curtains of his window and was surprised he had slept so late. Roland couldn't remember the last time he had slept more than an hour past dawn, but he was glad for the extra rest. Although his muscles were still sore from the previous night's activities, they had clearly benefited from a good night's sleep.

His first thought upon waking was of his plan to marry Rebecca, yet his thoughts soon turned to the phenomena that had occurred at her house. He didn't know what had caused the terrifying events, and he knew of only one man who might have a clue. Whatever had transpired the previous night had been magical or even spiritual, and Chief Running Brook was the foremost expert on that realm of studies in Colorado. Running Brook was the Chief of a tribe of Cheyenne Indians who hadn't been swept out of the state in America's western movement. America's government had made many hollow promises to the tribes over the years but had actually managed to keep only a select few of them. Luckily for Running Brook and his people, their tribe had been granted a small reservation and allowed to stay there as well.

They lived about ten miles west of New Haven, and Roland had encountered few problems concerning them. Some of the citizens occasionally muttered about ousting the Injuns, but the majority of the local population possessed an indifference to their neighbors. In return, the Cheyenne kept to themselves and never gave New Haven anything to worry about. Roland had even met with Running Brook several times and considered the Chief to be a very intelligent man. Running Brook knew that the White Man had killed most of his people and wouldn't hesitate to do the same to the Cheyenne, so his tribe strived for harmony with the young town and avoided contact. Convinced that they wanted nothing more than peace, Sheriff Black had dismissed them as a cause for worry.

Only once had Roland encountered a major problem over their presence, and luckily it was stopped before anyone got hurt. The previous winter, Curly had gotten himself liquored up at The Snake with a few other Riders. He had started to rant and rave about ridding the area of its "Injun problem" and talked a few of the Riders and locals into riding with him. Roland heard about it and immediately rounded up his deputies. By the time they caught up with Curly, the Dark Riders had crept into the woods directly behind the Cheyenne camp. Roland and his deputies stopped them before they could harm anyone, and that was one of the few times the Sheriff did lock up Curly in one of his cells.

Running Brook had laughed about the incident afterwards. He knew that most of the people in New Haven didn't consider him a threat and that Curly's failed attack had been an isolated occasion. He also knew that Roland was on his side and could persuade New Haven to leave his people alone. The incident did rouse some furor for a few weeks in town, though. *The Gazette* had run several articles calling for driving the Cheyenne out, but Roland went to work soothing tempers and worries. After a week, the story grew stale, and most people shifted back to their neutral disposition towards the Cheyenne.

Roland didn't want to upset the balance by visiting Running Brook. The citizens of New Haven were mostly good people at heart, but they spread gossip without a care in the world. Sheriff Black considered how, in the eyes of people, his adventures as a gunslinger had transformed him into a ruthless, killing machine that had preyed on the West. He knew that in two days' time, there would be crazy rumors flying that there was trouble with the Cheyenne that he had to oversee, and some people would probably even blame his injuries on the Indians. He didn't want to cause anyone concern, especially in the brutal heat. Roland was still convinced that somebody would lose his temper in the hot temperatures and do something stupid. With Rebecca's house, the Riders, and the heat to worry about, the one thing the Sheriff didn't need was for a mob to form, demanding the removal of the Cheyenne.

He decided to wait before consulting Running Brook. Roland wanted to revisit the house in daylight and see if another phenomenon occurred before seeking out the Cheyenne Chief. The previous night, he had been so terrified that he didn't even consider returning to the house, but after a night of rest, he had calmed down and thought he could escape safely if strange things began to occur. He had been wounded the last time he exited the house, but he blamed that on himself; it had been his own fault that he scrambled wildly through the window. The furniture had floated in the air and the loud knocking had echoed through the house, but none of those things had even threatened him or Rebecca. The scratchy voice that had called before he fled the house had frightened him quite a bit, and it still put a chill in his blood. He didn't know what the voice had been or why it had called "mine," but he pushed those thoughts aside. It didn't matter what the voice had meant by that single word. All Roland had to do was stay calm when he returned to the house. If strange things happened, he would calmly and carefully leave the house without injury, then he would go to the Cheyenne camp and consult Running Brook.

Shaking his head, Roland banished all thoughts of Rebecca's house from his mind. He might plan on returning to the house, but that would have to wait until his side had healed. Despite his confidence that he could emerge from the house safely, Roland wasn't about to return until he was at full strength, which would be at least three days. In the meantime, he intended to relax and enjoy his recovery time. Shifting his thoughts back to Rebecca, Roland again considered his idea of marrying her. It seemed like a hare-brained scheme after sleeping on the decision. Yet it felt like the right decision. He loved Rebecca, and it was only right to marry her. "Damn straight," Roland muttered to himself and solidified his intention of marrying Rebecca that night.

Proposing to Rebecca, however, meant getting out of bed, and that was the last thing Roland wanted to do. His body had recovered much of its strength during his long slumber, but his muscles had also stiffened on him while he lay in bed. Sleep called for him to close his eyes and return, and Roland quickly sat up before he gave in and slept the day away. His muscles screamed in protest as he got up, and the wound in his side tingled a bit. Roland tentatively put a hand to the bandage covering the cut in his side and was relieved to see that although it was tender, the wound was no longer painful to the touch. Propelling himself into a standing position, Roland grunted as his muscles once again protested his physical exertion, but he ignored their cries and slowly began to stretch his arms and legs. He was careful to favor his tender left side so the wound wouldn't break open. It didn't hurt so far that morning, but Roland didn't want to risk it. If he reinjured himself he could forget any idea of getting married that night. In a few minutes, the blood began to flow to his aching muscles, and Roland deemed that he was ready to go downstairs and face the world.

Roland's clothes were still tattered and torn and had begun to smell overnight, but they were all he had to wear. After putting on his ragged outfit, Roland splashed some water on his face and stepped into the hallway. He heard chatter coming from downstairs and wondered how many of the staff had already made their way to The Last Frontier. Jack should have arrived at The Frontier by that late hour, and Roland felt his deputy could handle everything by himself. Pushing all concern for the saloon out of his mind, Roland walked down the hallway and knocked on Rebecca's door.

Several moments later, he heard a muffled groan followed by shuffling footsteps. There was a long pause as the footsteps reached the door, then it opened a crack as Rebecca peered from behind it with eyes puffy from lack of sleep. "Good Morning, Roland," she greeted then covered her mouth as she yawned.

"Good morning, Rebecca." Roland smiled at her as she opened the door for him to enter. Stepping inside, he shut the door behind him then wrapped an arm around Rebecca and kissed her. Rebecca tipped her head back and responded warmly. He was surprised when he felt her hand slide tentatively up his back. He held the kiss for another moment before he ended it. There would be plenty of time to kiss her after they were married, and he was anxious to propose to Rebecca. He planned to do so as soon as he had rustled up better clothing. He figured that love was in the heart but he didn't want to look bloody and battered when he asked her. "So how did you sleep last night?"

Rebecca huddled against his chest and shivered. "I had nightmares all night. I kept tossing and turning and waking up. I'm scared, Roland. What happened last night at my house?"

"I don't know, Rebecca, but you're safe now. You don't have to return to your house until we know it's safe. You've got a place to stay until then. There's nothing to be afraid of," Roland comforted her in a soft voice.

"But, Roland, all of my things are there. I have nothing to wear except the dress from yesterday, and it's torn."

"Don't worry, Jack's downstairs. I'll ask him if you can borrow a few of Dotty's dresses. As soon as this side heals, I'm going back to the house, and I'll gather all of yours."

Pushing back from his chest, Rebecca looked up at him with worried eyes. "You can't go back, Roland," she pleaded with him. "What if something happens to you? I can't lose you."

"Rebecca, nothing will happen to me," he told her and took her hands in his own. "I'm going back during the day when I can see everything fine. If you remember what happened last night, nothing there could have hurt us. The only reason I'm injured is because we panicked and climbed through the window. I'll be ready this time, and I won't get hurt." Roland forced some confident bravado into his voice so that Rebecca wouldn't know that he still had a few slight doubts about returning to the house.

"Do you have to go, Roland? Can't you send Jack or someone else?"

"No, Rebecca. It has to be me. I don't want anyone else knowing about your house. If anyone heard of this, they'd blame the Cheyenne and Indian magic, and that's the last thing I need right now. I'm definitely too weak to stop an angry mob from grabbing their guns and attacking the Cheyenne."

Rebecca took a deep breath then looked at Roland with a resigned expression. "All right. Just tell me before you go?"

Pulling her to him, Roland gently stroked her hair and looked into her emerald eyes. "I'll let you know before I go, but please don't worry. I promise everything will be better really soon."

"Promise?" Rebecca asked wistfully.

"Yes, I promise," Roland answered confidently and bent his head to kiss her once again. It only lasted for a moment, but it was enough to enliven Roland's spirits. He would need all the energy he could muster to ride out to his house and back. His body felt better than it had the previous night, but he was still weak. Roland pulled away from her embrace as his side began to twinge and leaned against one of the bedroom walls.

"Are you all right, Roland?"

"Yeah, I'm fine. I'm still a little sore from last night, but I'll be okay. Trust me."

"Don't you push yourself, Roland. You follow Sullivan's advice."

"I will. I just have to ride back to my house, and after that I'll be good and sit downstairs the rest of the day. I promise."

"What? I thought you said you were going to rest. You're going to hurt yourself if you go riding all over town playing Sheriff."

"I'm not playing Sheriff. I need to go back to my house and get some decent clothes, then I've got a surprise for you."

"A surprise?"

"A surprise," Roland answered in a light bantering tone.

"What kind of surprise?"

"Well, it wouldn't be a surprise if I told you, so you'll just have to wait and see."

"Oh really?"

"Yes, really. Now hurry up and get dressed. I'm starved. We'll get George to throw us some food together." Roland smiled at her and gently pushed her away so she could get ready to go downstairs. He was anxious to get started that day. It wasn't that long of a ride to his house, but Roland wanted to complete it as soon as possible. He couldn't wait until he returned to the saloon and proposed to Rebecca. Every time he thought about it, his heart beat faster in excitement. Forcing himself to take a deep, relaxing breath, Roland watched as Rebecca thrust her arms into the tattered dress from the previous night. Roland laughed as she shrugged her shoulders, for they both looked wretched. He wasn't looking forward to the questions that were bound to be asked and reconsidered the thought of them both going downstairs for breakfast. "Rebecca, why don't you wait for me up here?"

She paused in the midst of raking her fingers through her hair. "Why? Don't you want me to go with you?"

Roland smiled ruefully at her. "We both look terrible. Can you imagine the kinds of questions everyone will ask if they see us both looking the way we do? I tell you what. I'll have George send some food up here, and I'll ride back to the house real quick for some clean clothes. I can talk to Jack when I go downstairs and have him borrow some of those dresses from Dotty right now. That way we can both have clean clothes on and not look like a couple of beggars. Then I'll give you your surprise, and we can spend the rest of the day together."

"Do you have to go? I just woke up, and you're already leaving."

"I really need to get some better clothes. I promise you won't even miss me, and I think you'll be glad when I get back."

She gave him a mocking grin. "All right, but you'd better get back here quickly."

Roland scurried to the door and paused before opening it. "I don't think this is what Doc Sullivan had in mind when he told me to rest," he quipped then winked at Rebecca before dashing out of the room. His heart raced in excitement as he left her room. Soon he would be back wearing his best suit and would ask Rebecca to marry him. Despite the tenderness in his side, Roland wanted to skip down the hallway.

Jack was sitting at the bar with George as Roland came down the staircase. The rest of the staff hadn't arrived at the saloon yet, and Roland guessed it was just George's loud voice he had heard in the hallway upstairs. Jack nodded politely when he saw the Sheriff, and George's eyes widened again as Roland's clothing attested to the wounds he had sustained.

"Jack. George." Roland nodded to both men as he pulled up a barstool beside them.

"How you feeling this morning, Roland?" Jack asked.

"Fine, Jack. Thanks for asking. George, do you suppose you could rustle up some breakfast for me and Rebecca?"

"No problem, Sheriff. How's Miss White doing this morning?"

"She's doing much better. She's a little bit tired, but she'll be fine. That was a rough fall we both took last night," Roland commented drolly and shot his deputy a stare so Jack wouldn't ask again where the wounds had come from. The Sheriff was in far too good a mood to argue with Jack.

"It must have been. You look like hell if you don't mind me saying. If you two will excuse me, I'll go get some food for you and Miss White."

"Thanks, George. Jack, I have a favor to ask you as well," Roland told his deputy as George headed behind the bar towards the kitchen.

Jack raised an eyebrow. "What's that, Roland?"

"I'd appreciate it if Rebecca could borrow one of Dotty's Sunday dresses. I could return it tomorrow."

"What does she need a dress for, especially a good one? Why can't she go home and get one?"

"It's a long story, Jack, but—"

"I've got plenty of time to listen." Jack broke in and stared at Roland for a long moment. "What in Sam Hill's going on? You and Rebecca both get injured and claim it came from a horse fall when you and I both know that's a lie. Then you ask to borrow a good Sunday dress when I'm sure Rebecca has a dresser full of them. Are you in some type of trouble, Roland?"

The Sheriff shook his head ruefully. He was in trouble all right, but it wasn't the type of trouble that Jack thought. Roland would have loved to tell Jack about Rebecca's house, but he didn't trust anybody with that secret. He would either look like a fool in front of the entire town, or they would believe him and blame it on the Cheyenne. Neither was a choice that Roland particularly liked. "I'm not in any trouble. It's a surprise. I'll tell you all about it when I get back."

"You're not lying to me?" The deputy looked at Roland skeptically.

"No, I'm not lying. Now can she borrow a dress or not? It's important, damn it."

Jack spread his hands in supplication. "Sure, Roland. I'll go fetch one from Dotty as soon as William gets here. He dropped by last night after you went upstairs and said he'd come in to town early today. No offense, Roland. I'd leave you here alone, but not with you being so weak."

"That's fine. I need to leave for a little bit anyway."

"What are you talking about? Where are you going?"

"I need to go home and get some clothes." He glanced down over his clothes, and his face turned into a look of disgust. "These things have seen their final day and need to be buried. Don't worry, it's a short trip. I'll take it at a slow walk all the way to the house and back. I don't think my side will break open if I travel a half-mile on horseback."

"Roland, Sullivan told you to take it easy, not to run around town," Jack chided, giving him an amused glance. He had known Roland a long time and had been certain that Roland wouldn't follow Sullivan's instructions.

"Blazes, Jack. You sound like an old woman. Don't nag at me. It won't kill me. My side feels much better today, and I'm only riding a short distance. I'll be back before William gets here."

Jack once again spread his hands in supplication. He was just giving Roland a hard time, for Jack knew that once Roland had made up his mind to do something there was nothing that he could do to stop the Sheriff. "Do whatever you want, but be careful. We don't want you down any longer than you have to be."

"Trust me. I'll be back to normal in a few days. I've never had an injury that could hold me back, and I don't intend to let this one either," Roland assured his deputy, then his eyes lit up as George walked towards them with a pair of plates. "That was quick, George," the Sheriff commented, and his stomach growled. The haunting at Rebecca's house had interrupted dinner the night before, and he hadn't eaten in quite some time.

"We had some of last night's food still warm, Sheriff," George answered as he set the plates on the bar. "Shall I go get Miss White?"

Roland had hastily shoved a few scraps of food into his mouth as George talked and took a moment to swallow the morsels. "Can you take it up to her, Jack? I'll be back in about an hour," the Sheriff replied and grabbed a piece of chicken off the plate. He took a bite off the drumstick and stood up. His muscles were a bit stiff, but at least his side no longer hurt. He probably shouldn't ride back to his house, but he couldn't wait to propose to Rebecca and wouldn't do so until he had decent clothing. "Take care of everything for me, Jack. I'll be back soon." He tipped his hat to the pair and headed out the door.

Jack had moved their horses while he had slept, so Roland made the short jaunt over to the station house, walking slowly to protect his tender side.

He spotted his horse and laboriously mounted, hurrying as much as he could so Robert wouldn't see him. Roland wanted to return to his house then back to the saloon as quickly as possible, and he wouldn't do that if he had to answer his deputy's questions about the previous night. He awkwardly squirmed his way into the saddle as he tried to avoid stretching his left side. It twinged once, but it ceased its protesting as soon as he had settled himself on the horse. Clucking the horse into a walk, Roland began the trip home.

As it had done for every day the past week, the sun blazed in the summer sky that Friday morning. Roland felt a light sweat break on his forehead as he slowly rode back to his house. Even though he normally walked between the saloon and his home on foot, the trip seemed to drag forever. Roland was in a hurry to get back to the saloon. He couldn't wait to propose to Rebecca and see the surprise and joy on her face. Tempted to push the horse harder, Roland curbed his impatience and continued the slow gait. His side was only a bit tender that morning, and he intended to keep it that way.

Eventually he caught sight of his house. The horse's pace appeared to slow as he approached his destination, but he finally reached it. Roland gingerly dismounted and grimaced as his side twinged once again. Placing a hand over his side, Roland straightened out his back and rolled his head from back and forth. The trip had only been a short one, but his muscles had tightened slightly during the ride. His brief stretching seemed to get the blood circulating back to his muscles, and he headed inside feeling much better.

Once he had stepped through the door, Roland gratefully took off his tattered clothing. Down to his smallclothes, he walked over to the water basin and splashed some water on his stubbly face. After spreading lather over his chin and cheeks, Roland carefully swiped away his day-old beard. He smoothed down the tips of his mustache, and after a careful inspection in the mirror, Roland retrieved his best set of clothes from the dresser. If there was ever an occasion that warranted his good suit, surely it was his wedding. As was normal for Roland, the coat, slacks, vest, and boots he selected were pitch black. Even the hat he chose to replace the battered one from the night before was dark. Checking his appearance one last time in the mirror, Roland walked back to his horse.

As Roland slowly climbed into the saddle again, he felt a wild exhilaration. He was finally going to get married. After all these years and at his old age, he was going to marry the sweetest and most beautiful woman in New Haven, and his heart was ready to burst. Roland's side tightened for a moment, but he dismissed the pain and placed his hand over the wound. All he could focus on was returning to town and proposing to Rebecca, and he wasn't going to let an injury lessen his happiness. A tiny voice at the back of his mind questioned if she would say yes, but Roland shut it out.

Tapping the horse with his foot, Roland began a slow walk back towards The Frontier. He felt on top of the world, and as the horse moved away from his house, Roland suddenly had an idea and pulled in the reins. Roland yearned to return to the saloon and propose to Rebecca, but he hated to see her get married in another woman's dress. She would be much more comfortable in one of her own dresses. He himself wore his best clothes, and she should be allowed the same luxury. Her house still frightened Roland, and he had intended to return only when he was at full strength. The journey to his house had tired him more than he thought it would, but he thought he was strong enough to keep riding for a while. As long as he stayed calm, Roland was confident he could enter the house safely and, if anything bizarre happened, leave safely as well.

Rebecca's house wasn't far from Roland's, or he wouldn't have even considered the idea. It wasn't on his way back to town, but the trip didn't go too far astray. Angling his horse towards his new destination, Roland began his slow journey. As the trip to his own house did, the ride to Rebecca's seemed to drag forever at his slow pace. About to burst with impatience, Roland once again stopped himself from pressing the horse into a faster gait. Getting himself injured would not bode well for his wedding day. Although it seemed to take hours, Roland reached her house fairly quickly.

Looking at it, Roland could scarcely believe that the bizarre phenomena had transpired the previous night. When Roland had first visited Rebecca, he thought the house was a very cozy one. Bryant had purchased the house with his money from the Dark Riders, and his additional income allowed him to have a house far, far larger than Roland's. The size was deceptive, though, for Rebecca had taken a fair amount of time decorating it while Bryant spent his time in town. Her touch had given it a warm, homey feel that belied its great size. Every room had been personally decorated by Rebecca, and each of them had the aura of her touch upon them. Roland knew he was probably biased because of his feelings for Rebecca, but he still felt the house was a far warmer house than his efficient yet bleak home. That's what made the previous night's occurrence so mind-boggling. He would have expected a ghost in an abandoned mansion, not in Rebecca's tidy home.

He considered drawing a gun as his horse crept closer to the house but decided against it. If there were any more phenomena inside, a gun wouldn't help him. A bullet wouldn't have much luck stopping a floating dish or moving door. It could even hurt him by accident, so he left his guns in their holster and approached the house. As details of the house became visible, Roland was glad to see the door standing ajar. It had unnerved him to see it opening and closing on its own the night before, and if it had been doing so as he rode up, Roland wouldn't have hesitated to turn around immediately. Riding to the tether post at the front of the house, Roland carefully dismounted and clutched his side as it once again tightened. Luckily the pain receded once he had his feet on the ground. Roland set his jaw determinately and approached the house.

He paused at the entrance for a moment and stared at the door. For all he knew it would start opening and closing again with him halfway through, but he took a deep breath and stepped into the house. He exhaled with relief as he entered safely then whistled as he beheld the disaster inside. *Blazes,* he thought in amazement. Rebecca had always taken great care to keep her house immaculate, but the phenomena from the night before had undone her hard work. All the furniture had been moved into a big pile in the center of the living room, and books had been strewn all over the study. Glass fragments from broken dishes littered the kitchen floor, and some of them had been swept all the way into the living room. If Rebecca ever decided to stay at the house again, she would have one hell of a cleaning project on her hands.

"Hello?" Roland called out tentatively. He didn't think anyone would answer and fervently hoped that nobody would. "Hello?" Roland called out once more, and when no answer was forthcoming, he walked into the living room. His boots crushed tiny fragments of glass, giving a crunching echo to his footsteps as he approached the massive pile of furniture.

The kitchen table, all of its chairs, and the living room furniture had been thrown together into a crude pyramid in the middle of the floor. Roland hesitantly touched one of the chairs and jerked his hand back as he expected it to once again return to life. Yet the furniture remained dormant as Roland stood before it. Emboldened by its lack of movement, Roland gritted his teeth and pulled the chair several feet away from the pyramid. The strain caused his side to twitch tenderly, and he placed his hand over it as he watched the chair. He half-expected it to slide back to the pyramid, but it remained lifeless before him.

"I'll be damned," Roland laughed as he took a seat in the chair to catch his breath. He had pushed himself by riding to Rebecca's house as well as his own, and his side still twinged from pulling the chair. In spite of his exhaustion, Roland was filled with relief that everything was all right at the house. Clearly whatever had happened in the house the night before was an isolated incident, and Roland had to laugh at his own caution. There was one hell of a mess to clean up, but Roland was sure that the house was safe once again. That only served to brighten his already sunny mood.

Chuckling, Roland pushed himself out of the chair and only felt a brief pang of pain from his side. He wasn't looking forward to the ride back to New Haven. Sullivan had been right in telling him to take it easy, and Roland was beginning to pay the price for not following the doctor's advice. Hopefully he could make it back to the saloon and have a chance to recuperate before he married Rebecca that evening. Roland shook his head as he thought of his original purpose for coming to the house and gingerly approached Rebecca's bedroom.

Opening the door, Roland expected to see more of the disaster that had swept through Rebecca's house, but this room was meticulously clean. Whatever had wrecked the rest of her house had spared the bedroom. The bed was neatly made, and like the house had been before the previous night, not a single item lay on the floor. Roland couldn't help but smile. At least her clothes would be fine. He had worried that he would return to the house to find all her clothes destroyed, and it buoyed his spirits to see something left untouched.

Roland rummaged through her dresser in an attempt to find a suitable wedding dress. He nearly picked the yellow dress Rebecca wore to church occasionally, but he hesitated as he caught sight of the green dress under it. Rebecca had worn that dress the first time he had met her. Even though it had been a somber moment as he informed her of Bryant's death, Roland remembered the way the dress had matched the color of her eyes. She had worn the dress several times since then, and it always left him speechless. Gathering the dress, Roland swung it over his shoulder and turned to leave the house. He stopped before he left the room and returned to the dresser. Rebecca would need more than one gown to wear, and he didn't think she would want to return to the house so soon after the previous night. Plucking several more from the dresser as well as a few shifts, Roland left the house with his load of clothes.

Awkwardly untying his horse while holding the bundle of clothes, Roland carefully placed the green dress between several others so it wouldn't gather any dust or dirt during his trip back to town. Clutching the bundle in the crook of his arm, Roland laboriously climbed into the saddle of his horse, struggling to keep the dresses from becoming wrinkled or dirty. A sharp burst of pain shot through the wound in his side, and Roland closed his eyes and sucked in his breath as he waited for it to pass. The wound throbbed for a moment or two, but it faded quickly. Roland waited to make sure it wasn't going to flare up again, and once he was satisfied that it wouldn't, he clucked the horse into a walk.

The day's efforts continued to wear upon Roland. Mainly it was his muscles that troubled Roland. They felt rubbery after riding the horse to Rebecca's house, and he yearned to sit down and rest his weary body. Roland still had a long day ahead of him, and he knew he needed to regain some of his strength or he would never make it. Other than his weakening strength and a few bumps that caused his side to grumble, Roland's return trip passed uneventfully. Soon New Haven was in sight, and as he rode into town, Roland spotted Ben. Roland ducked his head in hopes of avoiding his deputy, but he was a hard target to miss when he was carrying an armful of dresses.

"Sheriff!" Ben cried out from across the street, a smile lighting his face. Even if his body hadn't ached painfully and he wanted to hurry back to Rebecca, Roland would have tried to avoid Ben. Benjamin Wallace was the most boyish of all Roland's deputies, even though he wasn't the youngest. He was just over thirty years old and had sandy blond hair and a boyish smile that always made him look younger. Roland often thought he and Wade could be brothers, but their similarities stopped with their appearance. Wade was a deputy because he had a thirst for adventure that could only be satisfied in New Haven. Ben was a deputy because he cared for the people of New Haven and wanted to keep them safe. The most notable difference was Ben's talkativeness. The deputy could ask more questions than Roland would have ever believed possible.

That Friday morning Roland was in even less of a mood to deal with Ben, and he grimaced when the deputy hailed him. "Ben," Roland greeted as the deputy crossed the street to talk to him.

"Sheriff," Ben nodded. "It sure is hot. Can you ever remember it being this hot?" Ben stopped to squint at the bundle Roland was carrying and looked up at him curiously. "Why are you carrying those dresses? Are they for Miss White? How is she? You both looked bad—" he broke off as Roland interrupted him.

"They're for Rebecca," he told Ben curtly. The only way to shut him up was to cut him off. Luckily Ben was used to it and never seemed to get upset by people cutting him off. "Have you seen Thatcher anywhere today?" The only other way to make him stop asking questions was to ask one in return.

"No, Sheriff. I haven't, but he should be over at the church. That's where he usually is. What do you need Reverend Thatcher for? Do you—"

"Nothing important, Ben. I just needed to ask a favor of him," Roland cut off Ben again. "How's everything here in town?"

"Quiet. After last night, everybody should calm down. The Dark Riders are gone for at least a few more days, so there shouldn't be any trouble." Ben told him confidently. "Do you think Carlos will cause much trouble when he gets back? He looked really mad last night. I was telling Morgan he looked—" Ben broke off again as Roland quickly butted in.

"They'll either quiet down or be excited enough to do something stupid. You just be ready for any trouble. I'm not going to be available tonight, so let's make sure that nothing happens."

"That's what we're doing, Sheriff, although I think we're overdoing it a bit. I'm riding patrol today, and we have people stationed all over town. Jack's watching The Frontier, and Wade is keeping an eye on The Snake. Morgan's been riding around as well. Don't worry, we have enough men on duty to discourage people from getting into trouble."

"So you're just riding on patrol this afternoon?"

"Yes, sir. Morgan told me —"

"Good, then you can take this bundle for me," Roland broke in once more.

"Sure, Sheriff." Ben smiled and carefully folded the bundle over one of his arms.

Roland exhaled in relief as the load was lifted from his grasp. The dresses weren't too heavy, but holding them had begun to wear on his sore body. "Thanks, Ben. Take those over to The Frontier and make sure that Rebecca gets them. I have one more errand to run, then I'll be right over there. Sound good?"

"What type of errand?" Ben asked as he shifted the clothes around to settle comfortably on his shoulder. "Do you—"

"Nothing important, Ben. You just take those clothes to Rebecca, and I'll see you over there," Roland snapped then tapped his horse with his foot before the deputy could ask any more questions. He truly liked Ben, but sometimes the deputy was quite a handful. Jack had once speculated that the only way to keep Ben quiet would be to nail a board over his mouth, and that would only work for a little while. Luckily Ben followed Roland's instructions, and he was able to ride to the church without the inquisitive deputy in tow. He just hoped the Reverend was there. His body was tired and sore, and Roland didn't think he had the strength to track him down all over town.

The church was directly across the street from Madam Sherry's bordello, which had always amused Roland. Reverend Thatcher had a more tolerant view than most other preachers, but he still didn't approve of prostitution. That location, however, had been one of the few inside the city that were available for the new church. Roland hadn't been in New Haven at the time, but from what he heard, it had actually been Sherry who had disapproved of Reverend Thatcher and not the other way around. By the time Roland had become Sheriff, the two had settled into an amicable relationship. Thatcher was a man of God, but he had tempered his religious beliefs with a worldly attitude. He might not approve of Sherry's establishment or the activities that went on inside, but he never preached about it. That might have had more to do with the fact that a good number of his congregation stumbled from Sherry's bordello over to the church on Sunday mornings.

The church was a medium-sized two story building that could accommodate the sixty to seventy people who attended the Sunday services. Thatcher lived on the second floor by himself. He had been married, but his wife died of pneumonia several years ago. After her death, he had moved west to spread the word of God in a region that he felt had been lacking a church presence. Most days Thatcher could be found puttering around the church, writing his sermons or cleaning the sanctuary. Occasionally he went out to visit members of his congregation, but whenever Roland had needed Thatcher, he had been able to find him inside the church.

Just as Roland expected, the Reverend was busy dusting when Roland limped into the church. He was a short, bald man who was almost as stuffy as George Wright. Roland had always liked the man. Unlike many preachers Roland had met over the years, Thatcher cared for the well-being of his congregation whatever their sins might be. Even some of Sherry's girls attended his services, and while Thatcher might not care for their occupation, he welcomed them into his church with open arms. He paused in the midst of his cleaning when Roland entered and beamed a smile at the Sheriff. "Roland. It's good to see you. What brings you here today?"

"Reverend, I wanted to ask you a favor." Roland limped up to the short man and shook his hand.

"Sure, Roland. Anything I can help with, I'd be glad to."

"I was wondering if you could spare the time to perform a wedding tonight."

"I'd love to. Who's getting married?" Thatcher asked as he rubbed his hands in satisfaction. He loved performing marriages. Those and baptisms were probably the two things he enjoyed most about his line of work.

"Well, I'm getting married," Roland said a bit awkwardly. It still felt strange to think that he was actually going to marry Rebecca.

Thatcher stopped rubbing his hands and looked at Roland dumbfoundedly. "You? You're getting married? To Miss White, I presume?" Like the rest of the town and even Roland himself, the Reverend had thought the Sheriff would stay a bachelor forever, despite the rumors floating around town about his relationship with Bryant's widow.

"Yes, I'm marrying Rebecca, and I'd really appreciate it if you could perform the ceremony tonight."

"My, my, Roland. I never thought I'd see the day when you settled down, but yes. I'd be happy to perform the ceremony, but can't it wait a few more days? Sunday is only two days away."

"No, it can't. It's a long story, but I'd like for you to marry us tonight."

Thatcher thought about it for a moment then nodded. "Okay, tonight it is. Someday you'll have to tell me what the rush is all about. Did you have a particular time for this urgent wedding of yours?"

"Um, how about eight? Does that sound all right to you?" Roland waited for the Reverend to nod again. "Good. Rebecca and I will meet you here at eight o'clock. Is there anything you need for us to do beforehand?"

"Not really. Normally couples plan out the wedding several weeks in advance, but as long as you don't mind a simple ceremony, there's nothing I need from you two except your attendance."

"Great, I'll see you then." Roland beamed and shook Thatcher's hand one more time. Limping back to his horse, Roland barely noticed the soreness in his muscles as his sunny mood soared to even greater heights. He had retrieved good clothes for both himself and Rebecca and arranged for the wedding to be performed Now all he had to do was propose to Rebecca. His stomach fluttered for a moment with nervousness. He thought she would accept his offer, but he wasn't absolutely positive. Roland hoped she would after all the trouble he had gone to. He would be quite embarrassed if Thatcher was all set to perform the wedding and the bride declined to show up. *She'll say yes,* Roland kept telling himself hopefully.

Despite his giddiness, Roland felt the effects of his activities that morning as he climbed onto his horse, and it only grew worse as he clucked his mount towards The Last Frontier. As he rode up to the saloon, Roland breathed a sigh of relief. His journey that day had been a short one, but it had left him exhausted. The wound in his side throbbed, and Roland cupped a hand over it to make sure it didn't start bleeding again. The muscles in his arms and legs had grown numb, and it took most of Roland's attention to guide the horse back to the saloon. If he was to be married that night, Roland knew he needed a good nap first. He would have a long night ahead of him and would need all of the stamina he could muster.

Gritting his teeth, Roland swung out of the saddle and nearly collapsed as his side screamed in agony. He held onto the horse and closed his eyes as pain ripped through his body. The pain subsided into a dull ache, but as Roland opened his eyes, tiny specks of light floated lazily through his vision. The world seemed to lurch then settled into an unsettling spinning motion that made Roland nauseous. Luckily the sensation faded quickly as it had the night before. Once he felt safe to let go of his mount, Roland tied it to the tether post and limped into the saloon.

It was still early afternoon, and the saloon was virtually empty. The afternoon train arrived at 1:30 that day, and most of the town was busy preparing what they wanted to ship on it. There would be a large crowd later, but for the meantime, it was just the staff, Jack, and a few customers.

"Roland." The Sheriff turned his head to see Jack sitting at the bar and waving him over. "Glad you made it back. I was beginning to wonder if you had collapsed along the way before Ben came in."

"Where is he?" Roland asked as he sat down beside his deputy with relief. His strength was nearly gone, but his muscles stopped much of their complaining after he took a seat.

"He just went upstairs with all those dresses. Did you have to bring back her entire wardrobe?"

"Yeah, I did. She's going to need some clothes. Hers were ruined last night in the fall." Roland didn't care whether Jack believed him or not. Unlike Ben, Jack would keep his silence now that Roland had told him he didn't wish to discuss what had transpired the previous night. Grimacing as his side once again tightened on him, Roland turned his attention to the bartender. "Hey, Edmund. Get me a shot of whiskey."

"Sure thing, Sheriff," he replied, grabbing a shot glass and a bottle. Edmund deftly poured a full glass for Roland and slid it across the bar.

Roland picked up the glass and swallowed it all without hesitation. Everything seemed to lurch about him momentarily, but the pain in his side and his sore muscles stopped their protesting as the whiskey hit his system with a warm, numbing sensation. "Thanks, Edmund. I needed that." The bartender nodded then drifted to the other side of the bar to chat with a customer. Roland returned his attention to Jack, who was watching him with an amused grin. "Sorry, Jack. My side was hurting, and a shot of whiskey is always a good painkiller."

"I told you not to ride around town, but you wouldn't listen. It didn't break open again, did it?" He asked Roland with a resigned look on his face.

"No, it's just sore. That's it. Have you had a chance to get that dress from Dotty yet?"

"No. I was just about to leave and let Ben watch the place while I was gone. I take it you don't need them anymore. It looks like she has enough dresses to last her a while."

"Yeah, don't worry about it. I figured Rebecca's house wasn't too far from mine, so I went and got a few of hers while I was out." Looking around, Roland made sure nobody was listening to him or Jack. Satisfied that nobody was eavesdropping, Roland continued his conversation with the deputy. "Jack, I have another favor to ask."

Jack arched his eyebrows and gave Roland an exasperated look. "What is it this time? Please tell me you don't want to borrow some of my clothes."

"No, nothing like that. Listen, keep this quiet. I'm going to ask Rebecca to marry me tonight, and I was wondering if you would be my best man."

"Good God, I don't believe it. Roland Black is going to get married. I've heard everything now," Jack joked, his face breaking into a mischievous grin. He shook his head ruefully, then held out a hand to Roland. "I'd be glad to. Congratulations, Roland."

"Thanks, Jack. I appreciate it." Roland shook Jack's hand and smiled. "I just talked to Thatcher, and he said he could perform the ceremony at eight tonight. I guess I should go upstairs and ask her if she'll take me now."

"You talked to Thatcher, and you haven't asked her yet?" Jack asked him incredulously.

"I wanted it to be a surprise. I just hope she'll accept."

"Of course she will, Roland. She loves you. Anybody can see that despite the way you try to hide it."

"Thanks for the boost of confidence. I'll be down in a little while," Roland replied then headed for the staircase. His face broke into a wide grin as he finally limped up the stairs to propose to Rebecca. *Rebecca Black,* he thought to himself over and over. He kept one hand on the banister just in case his body broke out in pain again, but he made it to the top of the staircase without a problem.

Ben appeared as Roland started walking down the hallway. The deputy's face broke into one of his customary smiles, and he stopped to talk to the Sheriff. "Hey, Sheriff. I just gave Rebecca those dresses, and she seemed awfully surprised I did. She asked me where I got them, and when I told her you gave them to me, she got all worried. Kept asking me if you were all right. I told her you were still injured, but other than that you were fine. Why was she so worried, Sheriff? Did she—"

"It's a long story, Ben, but I'm really busy right now. I'll tell you all about it later," Roland answered abruptly before Ben could drag him into a drawn-out conversation. Ben nodded pleasantly as if Roland hadn't cut him off, but the Sheriff didn't even notice. His attention was focused solely on Rebecca.

As he limped towards Rebecca's room, butterflies began to flutter in Roland's stomach. Despite his confidence that Rebecca would accept his offer, Roland was still nervous over the whole idea of marriage. A year ago he had thought he would die a bachelor, and even after meeting Rebecca, Roland still hadn't thought he would ever get married. But he had gone too far in setting up the marriage to turn back at that point because of cold feet. Taking a deep breath, Roland tried to settle his nerves and knocked on her door.

"Who is it?" Rebecca's voice came through the door.

He had to clear his throat before he could answer. "It's Roland."

A sudden flurry of footsteps rushed towards the door, and it was abruptly yanked open. Rebecca had donned the blue dress he had brought back. After just putting on the dress, her hair needed to be combed, but Roland thought she looked beautiful. Her eyes glowed with relief, and she threw her arms around him. "I'm so glad you're back," she muttered into his chest.

"Careful," Roland cautioned as his side twinged painfully. Her arms loosened their grip, and he breathed a sigh of relief as the pain faded. Returning her soft embrace, Roland spoke softly into her ear, "I told you I wouldn't be gone too long."

"I know, but why did you go back to the house? You could have been killed." She looked up at him with teary eyes. "I can't lose you, Roland. It was bad when Bryant died, but if you died, I don't know what I would do."

"I'm not going to die, Rebecca. You've made me realize how much I need someone else in my life, and I'm not about to leave you." Roland told her somberly and looked deep into her eyes.

"Then why did you go back to the house? You're still hurt from last night."

"I was careful. The house looked safe, so I went inside. Don't worry, I was ready to run at a moment's notice if anything strange happened. You have a pretty big mess to clean up, but other than that, it's safe to go back. Please, don't cry. I wasn't in any danger."

"But anything could have happened, Roland, and you promised you would tell me before you went back," she accused him.

"I know I did, but I also told you I had a surprise for you. I had to go back to your house before I could give it to you."

Rebecca looked at him with a baffled expression. "The dresses are my surprise?" She was glad to have clean clothes, but she thought he had something else in mind when he had mentioned a surprise that afternoon.

"That's just part of it."

"Well, where's the rest?" Rebecca let her worry and irritation at Roland fade once she realized he wasn't injured and was beginning to wonder about the surprise that Roland kept hinting at. He was being cryptic with his answers, and she had no idea what he intended to give her.

Roland smiled at her and assumed an innocent expression. "Oh, did you want the rest of it? I couldn't tell."

Rebecca shook her head in amusement. "Yes, Roland. I would love to see the rest of this surprise of yours."

"In that case, why don't we go inside your room, and I'll tell you all about it."

"Okay, but you had better stop giving all these hints. I want to know what it is," she replied as she unwrapped her arms from around him.

"Trust me." Roland gave her his lopsided grin and ushered her out of the hallway. Shutting the door behind him, Roland turned back to Rebecca who watched him with a curious gaze. The butterflies in his stomach fluttered wildly now that he was about to propose, and Roland took a deep calming breath to steady his nerves.

"Well, Roland?" She crossed her arms under her breasts and tapped her foot impatiently.

"Why did you pick the blue dress?"

Rebecca shot him an odd glance. "Why? Is there something wrong with this one?"

"No. I just think you should put the green one on instead. It seems a little more appropriate."

"I know you like it, Roland, but that's one of my best dresses. I didn't want to wear it in a saloon. Besides, we still have to ride back to your house, and I didn't want to get it dirty."

"Well, that may be, but I still think you should put it on," Roland told her seriously as his stomach churned in nervousness.

"Why? You're being awfully strange, Roland."

74

"Tonight's a special occasion, so I thought you should wear your best dress."

"What's happening tonight, besides getting out of this saloon and going to your house?"

Taking a deep breath, Roland grabbed her hand and sank to one knee. His body complained loudly as he knelt on the floor, but Roland ignored it and focused all of his attention on her face. He had always thought that Rebecca was the most beautiful person he had ever met, but at that moment, her beauty was so radiant, it outshone the sun. "Rebecca White, I love you, and I want to spend the rest of my life with you. Will you marry me?"

Rebecca's face broke into a huge smile as she knelt down with him. As tears joyfully rolled down her cheeks, she grabbed his face and kissed him with all her heart, and even though she didn't answer with words, Roland was perfectly happy with her reply.

Chapter Four

Roland and Rebecca lost track of everything else as they knelt on the floor kissing. It was as if the world had stopped moving, and the only thing that mattered was each other. All of Roland's injuries and all their worries about Rebecca's house faded into the background, and they simply reveled in their moment of happiness. Eventually Roland drew back and stared into Rebecca's teary eyes. "I told you I had a surprise."

Pausing to wipe her eyes, Rebecca gave him a trembling smile in return. "Oh, Roland. I can't believe you asked. I thought you'd never want to get married."

"Neither did I, but I guess you captured my heart." He brushed a tear off her cheek with a callused finger, then smiled a mischievous grin. "So I take it you accept," he bantered.

Rebecca rolled her eyes. "Of course I accept," she replied then leaned forward to kiss Roland once more. It was a brief kiss although it sent Roland's blood racing while it lasted. Pulling back, Rebecca gave him a mock serious expression. "And it took you long enough too."

"Well, I guess it just took me a while to figure out what I wanted. Are you sure you're okay with getting married like this? I know you would have liked to plan out the wedding, but I can't wait another day, Rebecca."

"Roland, you'll be there, and that's all I need. What else could I ask for?" She smiled at him, then kissed his nose. "Now where's the dress?"

"Dress?" Roland asked confusedly. "What dress are you talking about?"

"My wedding dress. Come on, where'd you put it?"

Roland looked at Rebecca strangely. "I thought you'd be happy wearing the green dress."

Rebecca grabbed Roland's shirt, and her eyes grew wide. "Roland, are you telling me you didn't bring my wedding gown?"

"What wedding gown? I thought you'd want to wear the green dress. You look beautiful in it."

"No, it's not that I don't like it. I already have a wedding gown. It's the same one I married Bryant in, and my mother married my father in it. It's been passed down three generations, and I can't get married without it."

Roland closed his eyes and snorted in disgust. "I can't believe it, Rebecca. Where do you keep it? I looked all over your room, and I didn't see a wedding gown."

"I keep it in the bottom drawer of my dresser, right next to the green dress. I don't know how you could have missed it."

"Are you sure, Rebecca? I looked in there, and I didn't see a wedding gown. I even pulled out several dresses next to the green one, and there wasn't any wedding gown near it."

"Yes, I'm sure. I've always kept it in same drawer." Rebecca looked at the ground as she thought for a moment. "Maybe it got moved somehow. After last night, maybe the dress moved itself."

Roland shook his head in frustration. "No, that doesn't make sense. The bedroom is the only room in the house where nothing happened. The rest of the house is a mess, but your room wasn't even touched. The bed's even made. Maybe I just missed it somehow."

"How could you have missed it?"

"I don't know. Maybe I was in a hurry, or maybe I just wasn't paying attention. All I know is that I didn't see it."

"I know it's in there, Roland." Rebecca paused and pursed her lips. "Are you sure the house is safe?"

"Well, I was in it, and nothing happened this time. I even moved some of the furniture. There were no sounds from the study or floating dishes or moving furniture. I'm pretty sure it's safe again. Why?"

"If it's safe, we can go back and get the dress."

Roland was flabbergasted. "You want to go back to the house? I thought you were terrified of it."

"I am, Roland. It scares me to death, but you went back and didn't get hurt. I love you and want to marry you tonight, and I need the dress if we want to do it. It's *important* to me."

Damn it, Roland swore to himself. When he had first thought of getting married that night, he had known it was a foolhardy idea, and now he had proof that it was. Roland wasn't scared to go back to the house. He just didn't know if his body could take any more riding that day. But it was for Rebecca, and he would at least make the effort. Roland would have walked through fire if it would make Rebecca happy. "All right. We'll go get the dress at five. It's almost noon, and five hours of sleep will do me some good. I need to rest before I get back on a horse. If we leave by five, that gives us plenty of time to fetch the dress and get back in time for Thatcher."

Rebecca rewarded him with one of her dazzling smiles, and her eyes began to fill with tears again. "Oh, thank you, Roland, thank you." She threw her arms around him and kissed him warmly.

Roland enjoyed her display of gratitude, but he regretfully broke the kiss off. "Well, I'm glad to see my efforts are appreciated." Roland winked at her playfully. "I'd love to stay in here and kiss you, but I have to get some rest if we actually want to go through with this tonight." His mouth drooped into its trademark lopsided grin. "Besides, we'll have all night for that, and if you want me to be awake for it, I need to sleep now."

A blush spread up Rebecca's cheeks, and she cast her eyes aside bashfully. "Roland," she chastised.

Chuckling, Roland cupped her chin in his palm. "You weren't so shy last night," he joked, but then his face turned serious. "God, I love you, Rebecca, and I can't wait to marry you. But I really need to lay down for a while. I'm exhausted."

"Okay, Roland, but what should I do now?" Rebecca asked nervously. Months of isolation had left her uncomfortable around strangers, and she had not enjoyed spending time by herself in the saloon. She liked George, Jack, Morgan, and the rest of the deputies, but she wasn't comfortable sitting in a saloon and chatting with them.

"You could take a nap too. Tonight's probably going to be a late night, but if you're not tired, I've got some books behind the bar. George can give you one of them if you ask," Roland replied as he came to his feet. He grimaced as his side tightened.

"Are you okay, Roland?" Rebecca asked and put a supporting arm around him.

Roland bent over and waited for his side to stop its complaining then slowly straightened his back. "I'll be fine. I just need to lay down for a little bit." He leaned over and kissed Rebecca chastely on the forehead. "I love you, Rebecca White."

Rebecca looked up at him and had to struggle not to burst out laughing with joy. "I love you too, Roland Black." Then she placed her hands on her hips and tried to give him a stern look, but she failed as her mouth refused to bend into anything but a smile. "Now, go take your nap. You're marrying me tonight whether you're tired or not."

"Yes, ma'am," Roland replied, tipping his hat towards her, then he limped out of her room. He paused halfway through the door. "Just remember to wake me at five. It's not too long of a ride to your house, but I just want to make sure we have plenty of time."

Roland's heart beat wildly as he stepped into the hallway and closed the door behind him. *Yes!* He exulted. He had been so nervous before proposing to her that he didn't think he would be able to utter the words, but hearing her accept had put a smile on his face that wouldn't go away. Despite the pain and exhaustion plaguing his body, Roland felt like running down to the floor of the saloon and shouting out that he and Rebecca were getting married. He couldn't wait until that evening. Already the hours that remained before Reverend Thatcher performed the ceremony seemed to stretch into months, although Roland knew they would pass quickly. When he awakened from his nap, he and Rebecca would be rushed up until the time they stood before the preacher to speak their vows.

After taking off his coat and boots, Roland carefully folded his coat over a chair. It probably wouldn't have wrinkled if he had thrown the coat on the floor, and normally Roland wouldn't have cared if it did. Yet he was getting married that night and wanted to look his best. Roland slid into bed with relief. Once again it wasn't the most comfortable bed he had slept in, but the feather mattress was all Roland needed. His muscles stopped their constant nagging, and a soothing lethargy seeped into him. Even his side felt better. The wound still tingled to remind him it was there, but it no longer caused him any pain.

He hadn't thought he would be able to go to sleep after Rebecca had accepted his offer. Roland had been ready to run ten miles at that point, but once he relaxed on the bed, he was more worried that she wouldn't be able to wake him up in five hours. Roland was upset with himself for not spotting Rebecca's wedding gown. He could have sworn he had looked through all her dresses carefully, but he must have passed it over somehow. Those extra hours of sleep would have done his body wonders, but he would just have to rest the following day. It wasn't every day he got married, and it was with visions of his upcoming wedding floating through his head that he fell asleep.

A loud knocking awakened Roland, and he peered at the door with blurry eyes. He tried to call out and ask who was there, but his body didn't respond to his commands. Roland didn't know how long he had slept, but he knew he wanted to close his eyes and rest some more. His body fought against him, demanding that he go back to sleep, and Roland wearily closed his eyes.

The knocking was persistent, though. No sooner than Roland had closed his eyes, it resumed again, and the tired Sheriff squirmed from under the sheets in resignation. "Just a minute," he mumbled to the door and placed a hand over his tender side as he slowly sat up. His body was tired, and it fought Roland's efforts vigorously. He nearly gave up and closed his eyes, but he forced himself to stand up and try to get the blood circulating to his weary muscles. Once he had propelled himself into motion, much of his body's protesting dissipated. He needed more sleep, but Roland was just thankful that the pain he had felt earlier had disappeared. He could deal with exhaustion, but he wasn't sure if he could ride to Rebecca's house and get married if his side continued to protest.

Rubbing his eyes, Roland shuffled to the door. "Who is it?"

"It's Rebecca. You told me to wake you," her muffled voice came through the door in reply.

Opening the door, Roland squinted at Rebecca. "Is it five already?"

Rebecca's eyes squinted, and she looked at the floor guiltily. "Actually, it's about half past," she admitted.

"What?" Roland asked in alarm

"Calm down, Roland. We have plenty of time, and if we don't make it exactly on time, I don't think Thatcher's going to turn us away." Rebecca reached out and patted his cheek. "Now hurry up, sleepyhead. Time to get dressed."

"You're right," Roland admitted and forced himself to take a deep breath. "Give me a minute here. I'm still half-asleep," Roland mumbled then stepped back from the door so she could enter. She still wore the blue dress he had brought back from her house, and her hair looked as if it had been recently brushed. Roland thought she was as beautiful as the most colorful sunrise. "So what did you do while I slept?"

"I've been downstairs talking to Jack, George, and William. I was just going to borrow a book, but Jack asked me if you had proposed. So I sat down and started chatting with him, and the next thing I knew it was past five."

"Good, I'm glad you didn't hole up in your room. It's good to see you visiting with people."

"It was fun. It's just taking me a while to get used to being out in public again. I've been so used to spending all my time in the house and not talking to anyone. You're really the only person I've talked with since I moved here."

Roland stopped in the process of putting on his coat and walked over to Rebecca. Placing his hands on her upper arms, Roland bent down and placed a kiss upon her forehead. "Just be yourself, Rebecca. I've always thought you were a wonderful person, and if you act the same way around everyone else, they'll think the same."

A faint blush crept up Rebecca's cheeks, and she looked at the floor self-consciously. "Thank you, Roland. It's just taking some time."

"Take all the time you need. Just don't stop talking to me. Okay?"

Rebecca smiled warmly at him. "Okay. I think I can do that much."

"Good. Let me put my coat on, and we can go get that dress of yours," Roland remarked as he slung his weary arm into his coat sleeves, then the two left the room. He grabbed the lantern from his room on the way out as well. It was nearing dusk, and he had no intention of entering Rebecca's house without any light. Roland's body felt better once they had stepped into the hallway, although he had a slight limp to his step. He placed a hand against his tender side and made sure he favored his other leg. So far, it wasn't causing him any pain, but he wanted to make sure it stayed that way.

Jack caught sight of the two as Rebecca led the limping Sheriff down the stairs, and the deputy rose from his barstool and approached them. "Rebecca. Roland," he greeted and tipped his hat.

"Jack. How have things been around town today?"

"They've been fine. No problems so far. Listen, Roland, I know you don't like people telling you what to do, but let me go to her house instead of you. You're going to wind up hurting yourself."

Roland shook his head. "Rebecca and I need to do this by ourselves. Don't worry about me. Just keep this town safe for a few more hours, and I promise I'll be back."

"At least let me send Wade or Morgan with you."

"No, Jack. You need them here. If the Riders come back early, I want as many men in town as possible."

Jack rolled his eyes in frustration. "Okay. Do what you want, but just try to take care of yourself. This town can't afford to have you get hurt again."

"All right, we'll be careful. We'll meet you back here in a few hours, then we can all go to the church."

"Sounds good. See you later. Rebecca." Jack tipped his hat once more and ambled back to his barstool.

"Shall we head on then?" Roland turned to Rebecca, smiled, and offered his other arm to his fiancée. Smiling back, she took his arm, and the two left the saloon. The weather was still blazing hot. Sweat already lined his brow, and he knew it wouldn't be a pleasant ride in the summer heat. At least it was nearly dark. The temperatures would fall significantly once the sun set for the evening.

Technically the horses were intended for deputies only, but Roland felt he could bend that rule, considering the special circumstances. Picking two of the more gentle colts, Roland untied them from the tether post and handed a pair of reins to Rebecca. She had a little difficulty climbing into the saddle, but she managed to seat herself atop her mount. Roland had a few problems as a burst of pain flared in his side, and he took a few deep breaths once he had seated himself in his own saddle. The pain again faded quickly, but Roland was starting to worry about the injury. Perhaps Sullivan had been right, and he should continue to rest. But he pushed those thoughts aside. He was getting married that night and could rest all he wanted after they had been through the ceremony.

His side occasionally twinged, but other than those few instances, Roland felt fine during the brief ride. That morning, the slow pace had seemed to drag for hours, but he had Rebecca to keep him company on his second trip that evening. They passed the time by talking, and Roland was surprised when her house suddenly came into sight. The sun had nearly disappeared by that time, and only a tiny violet piece was still visible. Roland was just glad that he had thought to bring a lantern. He guided his horse to the tether post in front of the house under the waning light and awkwardly dismounted. He placed a hand against his side and grunted as pain flared briefly.

"Is it bothering you again?" Rebecca looked at him with a concerned expression.

"Just a little. It's nothing to worry about. I'll be fine," Roland replied then tied their horses to the tether post in front of the house. With the horses secured, Roland held out his hand and waited for Rebecca to take it. Then holding her hand, he escorted her towards the house. Roland turned on the lantern and paused before opening the door. He turned back to Rebecca. "Just remember. It's all over. The house is a mess, but nothing will happen to us."

"I know, Roland. Let's get this over with," she told him in a trembling voice.

"All right," Roland answered and slowly swung the door open.

Rebecca gasped as she observed the wreckage under the scant lighting of Roland's lantern. The chair Roland had moved still sat apart from the pyramid of furniture in the middle of the room. He was relieved to see it hadn't moved. If the chair had been even a foot from where he had left it, Roland would have yanked Rebecca out of the house and been back in New Haven as quickly as possible.

"Oh my God," Rebecca uttered as she stared at the disaster in shock. She had always worked so hard to maintain the house, and it upset her greatly to see it in shambles. "This could take weeks to clean."

Roland wrapped an arm around her. "We'll worry about that later. We've got a wedding to get to, and you've got a place to stay in the meantime. There will be time to clean this up after things slow down."

Rebecca shook her head and tried to shift her focus away from the disaster. "You're right. I just can't believe how bad it is. You told me it was a mess, but not this bad."

"It's the sort of thing you need to see to believe. Now, let's go get that dress and get back to town." Roland was in a hurry to leave the house. He had felt much more comfortable that afternoon when the sun was up, but the house's dark interior sent shivers down Roland's spine. The lantern provided enough light to see, but not enough to make Roland completely at ease.

"All right," Rebecca agreed then followed Roland as he detoured around the furniture lumped in the middle of the floor. He could feel her squeeze his hand tightly as she stared at the pile of furniture. He admired her bravery for coming back to the house and couldn't wait to marry her.

Roland paused as they neared her bedroom. He could sense Rebecca's uneasiness and wanted to allay her fears. "See, there's nothing to worry about. Everything's quiet now."

"You're right. I just want to get out of here. It reminds of me of last night."

"Well hurry up and get your dress, and we can leave." Roland smiled and opened the bedroom door.

Rebecca breathed a sigh of relief as she beheld her bedroom. It was just as Roland had testified. The bed was made, and the dresser had been left alone as well. Walking over to the dresser, Rebecca opened the bottom drawer and ruffled through the dresses inside. "See, I told you," she chastised Roland as she pulled out a white gown.

Roland scratched his head in perplexity. "I don't know how the hell I missed it. I thought. Oh well, you have it now. Let's get back to town."

"Okay, but let me get my necklace while we're here. It'll just take a second." Rebecca opened the jewelry box on top of her dresser. She removed a few items and set them down beside the box before pulling out a beautiful pearl necklace. Roland remembered seeing the necklace before. Bryant had purchased it shortly after the train robbery in Denver, giving Roland another reason to think both he and the Dark Riders had been responsible for the crime. After he had told Rebecca of his suspicions, she hadn't worn the necklace since, but she could put her feelings aside for that one day. They were getting married, and Rebecca wanted to look as good as possible, even if that meant wearing jewelry that was purchased with dirty money. "I've got it." Rebecca held up the necklace for Roland to observe, then she put it on. "Let's go."

"Sounds good to me." Roland took the dress from her and slung it over one shoulder carefully. Holding out his other arm for her to take, Roland escorted her towards the bedroom door. He couldn't help but smile as they crossed the bedroom. They finally had everything they needed for the wedding to proceed, and Roland thought his heart would burst. Rebecca looked so beautiful walking beside him, and he leaned over to tell her just that when the bedroom door slammed shut.

"Oh my God," Rebecca cried out then covered her mouth with her hands. "Oh God. Oh God."

"Take the dress, Rebecca," Roland told the shaken woman, but she continued to stare at the door with frightened eyes. "Rebecca," he raised his voice, but she still looked straight ahead as if she hadn't heard him. Grabbing her shoulder, he squeezed firmly. "Rebecca, look at me."

She jerked her head around to face him, her hair swinging wildly about her neck. Her eyes were wide with terror, and the blood had drained from her face, making her look pale as milk. "Oh my God, Roland, it's happening again."

"Rebecca, take the dress." Roland insisted firmly. He wanted them to get out of the house as quickly as possible, but he wanted to keep his hands free so he could deal with anything that threatened them. Roland thought they would emerge safely if they kept calm, although his heart raced in his chest as he felt terror begin to well within him.

"What?" Rebecca whimpered and edged closer to Roland. She looked about the room wildly to see if any objects were moving or floating through the air. Rebecca had been afraid to return to the house, but she had felt safe doing so with Roland after he had proclaimed it safe. Now the house had justified her fears, and she was terrified that they wouldn't escape with their lives.

"Damn it, Rebecca. Look at me," Roland barked and waited for Rebecca to return her attention to him. She turned her head towards him, but her eyes kept darting about, looking for any objects that might hurt them. "Rebecca, take the dress. We're getting out of here, but I need my hands free," Roland told her tensely. He wanted to get out before events escalated, but Rebecca kept peering about and not hearing his words. "Rebecca, would you—" Roland broke off as he heard a loud knock come from the other side of the door.

Rebecca wrapped her arms around him, and he threw the dress on the bed and held her back awkwardly as he gripped the lantern in an iron fist. They stood in front of the door quietly and stared at it. Roland didn't know what to expect. They had left the house when events had escalated the night before, and he was afraid what might happen this time. He could hear his heart beating wildly in his chest, and he felt the blood pour through Rebecca's veins as her pulse quickened in fright.

They both jumped as they heard another loud knock come from the den. It was exactly the same noise they had heard the night before, and Roland decided to leave the house immediately. The previous night, it had taken a little time for the events to grow strong enough to actually hurt someone, and Roland intended to be gone long before that happened again.

"Rebecca," Roland shouted loud enough to break through her withdrawn state. Rebecca turned her frightened gaze upon him, and Roland winced at the terror that was painted on her face. "Rebecca, grab the dress. We're leaving now."

She shook her head fiercely in denial. "We can't leave. Oh God. We'll be killed," She babbled wildly.

"Stop that, Rebecca. Calm down. We got out last night, and we'll leave tonight. Grab the dress, we're going now!" Roland barked in a tone that brooked no argument. He looked at the bedroom window for a few moments then decided against using it as an exit. That's how he had been injured the night before. He moved towards the bedroom door as Rebecca scurried over the bed to pick up the dress.

He jumped back as the door swung open on its own. Roland was surprised to see the den undisturbed. He had expected furniture to be floating in the air and dishes smashing themselves to pieces, but everything was perfectly still. The only noises he could hear were Rebecca's frightened breathing and his heart racing in his chest. Cautiously stepping out of the bedroom, Roland turned back to Rebecca. She had huddled against the bed in terror, staring at him with vacant eyes. Forcing the muscles in his face into a strained smile, Roland held a hand out to her. "See? I told you it would be safe. Now let's go."

Rebecca continued to huddle protectively against the bed for a moment, then came to her feet in an unsteady motion. She jerked her head about and peered around the room, afraid something would leap out at her.

"Come on, Rebecca," Roland called urgently and was about to walk into the room to get her when he heard another loud knock directly behind him. He jumped forward and quickly turned around, but there was nothing there. The only thing he could see was the giant pyramid of furniture in the middle of the room.

He swung his head over his shoulder to see if Rebecca had left the room, but she had retreated back to the bed. Her face was pale as milk, and her eyes stared vacantly at the door. "Oh God. Oh God," she kept chanting to herself as fear paralyzed her. Rebecca continued to back up until she bumped against the bedroom wall, then she slowly sat down. Drawing her knees up to her chest, Rebecca wrapped her arms around them and curled into a protective ball.

"Damn it," Roland swore as he watched Rebecca retreat further into the room instead of fleeing with him. He stalked towards her so he could make her leave but only went two steps before the bedroom door slammed shut. Roland's jaw dropped, and he stared at the door for a moment before shaking off his surprise. Taking a deep breath, Roland marched towards it again and turned the doorknob.

It moved freely in his hand, but the door refused to open. He shot the door a perplexed look, then tried turning the doorknob again. This time, he pushed his shoulder into it, but the door remained securely shut. He attempted to open it one last time and threw himself at the door with all of his strength. His side erupted in pain, but he might as well have been hurling himself against a mountainside.

"Rebecca?" Roland pressed his face up the door and shouted. He waited for a reply, but no sound emerged from the other side. Raising his hand to pound on the door, he jumped in startlement as another loud knock boomed directly above him. Wildly looking around, Roland still couldn't see the source of the noise. The knocking was beginning to worry Roland. He had no idea what was causing the phenomena in her house, and he really didn't care. Roland just wanted to get Rebecca safely out of the house before she was hurt.

Turning back to the door, Roland pounded on it with a balled fist. "Rebecca?" He called worriedly. "Rebecca? Damn it, if you're okay, answer me," he barked, growing more scared by the second. Roland put the lantern on the floor so he could put his shoulder into bursting the door down.

The doorknob began to twist back and forth, and Roland took a step back in fear. He stared at it as the knob shook violently. "Roland, it won't open," Rebecca's muffled voice cried from the bedroom.

Roland rushed back to the door and pressed himself against it. "Rebecca? Are you okay?" He panted. Fear ate at him as he futilely struggled to open the door. *Open, Goddamn you,* Roland swore to himself.

"The door won't open, Roland," Rebecca babbled from the other side worriedly.

He twisted the doorknob forcefully and pushed on the door. "Damn it to hell," Roland swore when it still refused to yield. "Rebecca, step back from the door. I'm going to break it down," he shouted through the door, but he didn't hear any reply. "Rebecca, did you hear me? Stand back. I don't want you to get hurt."

"I'm away from the door, Roland. Break it down!" Rebecca screamed from the bedroom.

Roland backed up to the pyramid of furniture and gathered his dwindling strength. He paused for a moment when another knock boomed behind him. Not bothering to look for its source, Roland took a deep breath and hurled himself into motion. He hit the door with a loud thud, but instead of breaking it down, Roland was hurled backwards from the impact. Pain erupted in his side as he hit the floor, and he closed his eyes and bit his lip as it coursed through him.

"Roland? It's still not open!" Rebecca shrieked in terror, although Roland barely heard her through the door.

Taking a deep breath, he forced himself into a seated position and nearly passed out as his side throbbed agonizingly. Pressing a hand against the wound and then bringing it before his eyes, Roland was relieved not to see any blood. "Just a second!" He shouted out and put his hands on the floor. Steeling himself against the inevitable pain, Roland pushed against the floor and made himself stand up. His side screamed as it was stretched once again, and Roland had to bend over to keep from passing out.

Black spots danced through his vision, and he knew that they had to leave the house soon while he still had some strength. He tried to straighten his back, but Roland's side spasmed wildly and the room seemed to spin. Bending over and closing his eyes, Roland was relieved when his side stopped complaining and his sense of balance returned. Holding one of his arms out, Roland lurched blindly towards the bedroom door and stopped as his hand pressed against it. A loud knock sounded within the bedroom, and it was followed by a shrill, metallic shrieking. Roland heard Rebecca whimpering fearfully inside as he leaned against the door wearily. "Rebecca, get away from the door. Do you understand?" He shouted as loud as he could.

"Yes, Roland. Hurry," her strained voice came through the door.

Drawing a pistol from one of his holsters, Roland cocked it and took aim at the doorknob. *Without the latch, it has to open,* Roland told himself and fired. His first shot tore through the door and launched splinters into the air. Roland squinted and tried to brush away the wood dust that was floating in the air. Pushing on the door, Roland cursed as it still refused to open. Taking a step back, Roland took aim carefully and set his stance as he prepared to empty his gun into the door.

A loud knock boomed behind him, and Roland took his eyes off the door to look around. His heart raced even faster as he saw the chair he had moved earlier begin to shake under its own power. Instinctively he pointed his pistol at the chair and smoothly fired a shot at it. It tore a hole through the back, but the chair continued to shake, oblivious of the bullet that had just struck it. "Goddamn it," Roland swore and turned his back to the chair. *It can't hurt me*, Roland repeated to himself. *Just shoot the latch out, get Rebecca, and leave.*

His next shot tore another hole in the door, but before he took another one, a softer set of knocks began approaching him from behind. Roland turned his head to see what was happening this time, and his gun slipped from his fingers as his jaw dropped open in surprise. The chair had ceased to shake in one spot. It continued to dance about, its legs striking the floor with faint, wooden knocks, but it had begun to move in his direction. "What the hell?" Roland wondered out loud as he stared at the chair making its way towards him.

Picking his gun back up, Roland hurriedly fired three more shots into the door. His finger kept pulling the trigger even after that, and Roland forced himself to calm down as he realized he was out of bullets. Taking a deep breath, Roland gathered his remaining strength and prepared to hurl himself at the door, but he was struck in the back and knocked to the floor, his gun slipping from his hand again and sliding across the room.

Roland lay breathless on the floor as his side screamed furiously at him. He attempted to sit up but quickly abandoned the idea as his body erupted in pain. Something kicked his shin, and Roland looked up to see the chair floating in the air. He stared at it in wonder but was quickly shaken out of his reverie as the chair launched itself at his head. Throwing his arms up protectively, Roland was able to protect his head, but the chair smashed itself against his arms. Roland bit his lip to keep from crying out in pain. "Rebecca, run!" He shouted weakly. Roland wasn't sure he would survive the ordeal, but he meant to see Rebecca through it safely.

The chair had floated back into the air after it struck Roland and hovered there as he shouted to Rebecca. He kept a nervous eye on it as he lay painfully on the ground and tried to catch his breath. Roland knew he had to gather his strength quickly or he wouldn't make it out of the house. Despite the furious pain in his side, Roland forced himself to sit and was knocked back to the floor as the chair swooped down and struck his face. His head hit the floor loudly, and blood dripped from his nose. "Son of a bitch," Roland swore at the chair as it began to turn lazily in the air above him. It seemed oblivious of him, but when he tried to sit up again, it flew down and crashed into his chest.

Roland lay down on the ground and closed his eyes in defeat as even greater pain flared in his side. Even his bullet wound twenty years ago hadn't caused as much pain as he was feeling at the moment. A minute ago he could have walked out of the house under his own power, but not after the blow he had taken to his ribs. He felt blood trickle from the wound in his side as it broke open. "Get out, Rebecca," he muttered weakly as he felt unconsciousness steal over him.

"*Mine!*" The same ominous voice echoed through the house, and Roland heard a loud scream come from the bedroom. "*Mine!*" The voice repeated itself. Roland opened his eyes and looked about the room slowly, but the only activity was the chair spinning above him. "Bryant?" He called out. "Bryant, is that you? For the love of God, leave us alone." Roland closed his eyes and waited for the voice to reply. Without warning the chair stopped spinning and dropped to the floor, narrowly missing Roland's head.

He lay on the floor and waited for the chair to launch itself at him again, but it remained still where it had fallen over. His entire body was a nest of pain, and he had to grit his teeth to keep from crying out. *Rebecca,* he thought grimly and forced himself to crawl towards the room despite the pain in his side. He tried to sit once he had reached the door, but his body protested loudly. Roland collapsed back to the ground and looked up at the doorknob. He was so close, but his strength had finally deserted him.

"Rebecca?" Roland called out faintly. He hadn't heard a sound from the bedroom since she had screamed, and he desperately hoped she wasn't injured like he was. With his bleeding side shrieking painfully every time he tried to sit, Roland knew he would need her help if he wanted to leave the house. If she needed assistance to leave the house as well, they wouldn't stand a chance of getting out. "Damn it," Roland swore when no answer came from the bedroom, and he hit the door in frustration. He watched in amazement as it slowly swung open, and the door knob and surrounding wood fell to the floor with a loud clank.

Pushing the door all the way open, Roland stared in horror at Rebecca. Under the dim lighting of his lantern, he could see that she lay on the bed, jerking her arms and legs about and gurgling a horrifying noise. "Rebecca," Roland called to her, but she continued to thrash about on the bed, oblivious of him. Frantically Roland pushed himself into a sitting position, despite the horrible agony it caused him. He leaned against the doorframe and took a deep breath before flexing his legs and standing up.

The world tottered on its foundation as black spots once again floated before Roland's eyes. He hunched over and pressed a hand to his bleeding side as dizziness overwhelmed him. Lurching forward, Roland grasped at a bedpost to help him regain his sense of balance. He closed his eyes for a moment as the room began to spin faster. When he reopened them, the room still spun but not as quickly as before. Breathing a sigh of relief, Roland turned his attention back to Rebecca.

Rebecca's thrashing hadn't abated as he unsteadily made his way to the bed, and he watched in horror as she jerked about. Her eyes had rolled back in their sockets, and only the whites of them showed. A deep gurgling came from within her throat, and spittle leaked from the sides of her mouth as she violently tossed her head from one side to the other. "Rebecca?" Roland whispered. "Oh my God, Rebecca. Can you hear me?" He called to her as she continued to writhe in some horrible dance upon her bed.

Roland let go of the bedpost and made his way to her side. The wound along his ribs cried with every step he took, but Roland shook off the pain as his worry for Rebecca took over. He grabbed at her hand, but Rebecca shook it out of his grasp and continued to flail her limbs about wildly. "Rebecca, we have to go," Roland cried out in frustration as her arm once again passed through his grip. "Bryant, is that you? Let her go, damn it. You're dead."

Rebecca's thrashing grew stronger as Roland spoke, and he felt the air cool around him. Goosebumps broke out along his arms, and he shivered in the sudden cold. Each breath billowed out like a cloud of smoke as it condensed in the frosty temperatures. Roland wrapped his arms about himself to keep warm and shouted at Rebecca, "Rebecca, damn it! We have to go!" Yet she remained oblivious of his presence and continued to flail her limbs. If he had been healthy, Roland could have dragged her out of the house, but in his weakened condition, he could barely leave under his own power, much less assist someone else. "Rebecca, for the love of—" Roland broke off as he heard another loud knock coming from the den.

Another knock followed soon after, and Roland looked into the den with frightened eyes as noises began to boom in a slow, rhythmic pattern. The chair that had attacked Roland twitched on its side then suddenly launched into the air. It spun around slowly, dancing to the steady accompaniment of the knocking and sending a chill down Roland's spine. He didn't think it would do any good, but Roland drew his remaining pistol and aimed it at the floating chair in case it decided to launch itself at him again. Yet it ignored Roland and turned pirouettes in the air as if it was enraptured by the booming knocks that echoed throughout the house.

Roland lurched backwards a few steps involuntarily as the pyramid of furniture shook. It teetered one way then the other and paused off balance for a moment before slowly tipping over. It hit the floor with a great deal of noise, drowning out the loud knocking as furniture slid across the floor and crashed into the wall. As they came to rest, the pieces of furniture began to shake like the dancing chair and soon afterwards launched themselves into the air. The chairs all turned energetic pirouettes, but the couch spun about sluggishly as if its large size prevented it from flitting about like its smaller counterparts.

The knocking picked up its tempo, alternating between soft and loud noises. As it reached an erratic, frenzied state, the chairs began to gyrate in chaotic loops. Roland stared at the moving furniture, his gun still pointed in their direction, but a choking gurgle from Rebecca called his attention back to her. Like the furniture, Rebecca's thrashing had grown more chaotic with the frenzied beat of the knocking. Her head jerked back and forth, slamming into the pillow then touching her chin to her chest, and her hips began to buck off

89

the bed violently. Spittle covered her face, and the disturbing gurgle turned into a choking gasp that frightened Roland. Despite the pain plaguing his body, Roland grabbed her arm and tried to yank her out of the bed. Pain broke out along his side, but Roland knew he had to get Rebecca out of the house immediately. The bizarre phenomena was growing stronger by the second.

He managed to drag her shoulder off the bed in spite of the pain that threatened to overwhelm him, and Roland thought that they might just make it out of the house alive after all. Slowly she began to slide off the bed, and Roland's face broke into a tight grin until he felt his feet leave the floor. *What the hell?* Roland's body froze in fear as he floated into the air, and Rebecca's arm slipped right through his grasp. He hovered several feet in the air for a moment then began to turn a lazy cartwheel to the same beat as the couch. *Oh my God,* he thought in terror. Roland pressed a hand against his side and tried to fight off the tide of exhaustion that was depleting his body of strength. It had already been difficult to maintain his sense of balance, but as soon as he began to spin, Roland felt the world rock violently on its foundation. Despite the horrible dizziness, he tried to focus his careening vision upon Rebecca.

She had nearly slid off the bed, but as soon as Roland's grasp of her arm slipped, Rebecca moved back to the center of the mattress, continuing to shake and gyrate violently. She breathed in wheezing gasps, and each one sounded as if she might not have the strength to take another. Roland watched helplessly as she flailed about and struggled to get air into her lungs. "Damn it. You're killing her!" Roland shouted as he continued to turn about slowly. "Let us—" He broke off as a wave of energy crashed against him and sent his body hurling into the wall.

Roland fell to the floor, and pain exploded throughout his body. He closed his eyes and blanked out the rest of the house as he fought to remain conscious. Pain coursed through him, and Roland was tempted to give in to the deep sleep that sweetly beckoned him. Roland teetered on that brink, but a choking gurgle from Rebecca yanked him back from the precipice. Roland slowly opened his eyes and felt his stomach lurch as the room spun about wildly. He tried to clench the muscles in his stomach, but the wound along his ribs flared agonizingly, forcing him to relax. As soon as his muscles relaxed Roland gagged and vomited on the floor. Tears welled in his eyes as he continued to dry heave after his stomach had been emptied. *"Mine!"* The scratchy voice echoed through the house, and Roland weakly turned to the bed.

Rebecca had floated into the air as well, and she flailed her limbs as if she was swimming above the bed. Her head continued to rock back and forth and the rest of her body bucked violently as she hung in the air. The sheet beneath her floated upwards, stopping just below her. They rippled slowly like the surface of a lake which had just been struck by a rock, then slowly began to rise again. Roland watched in horror as they wrapped around Rebecca enveloping her entire body, but he was forced to lay there helplessly as his body continued to convulse in pain and nausea.

She kept thrashing violently after the sheets had wrapped around her completely, covering her like a mummy. Roland held out a hand to her hopelessly as she slowly began to spin in the air. "Rebecca," Roland croaked between retches and tried to push his way across the floor with his legs. The quilt that had laid folded at the foot of the bed floated into the air as Roland moved towards Rebecca. It hovered in the air, methodically unfolding until it spread out fully over the bed. "Leave her alone," Roland gasped weakly as the quilt began to ripple. He didn't know if Rebecca could still breathe under the sheets, but he knew that if the quilt wrapped around her as well, she would be smothered.

"Mine!" The voice repeated, and the quilt ceased its rippling and flew towards Roland. It hovered directly above him and paused there, gently rippling as he watched in resignation. Roland knew that he would probably die if he was smothered by the quilt, but he lacked even the strength to sit up, let alone run from the house. He tried to push his way out from underneath the quilt with his legs, but his body floated into the air again. Roland's stomach turned violently, and his stomach convulsed with dry heaves again as he drifted into the quilt's waiting embrace.

Roland felt his back brush against the rippling quilt and watched in horror as it draped around him. Roland gasped a deep breath as the quilt suddenly jerked into motion and enveloped his body. It pressed tightly from his head to his toes, and Roland struggled to hold his last breath. His supply of oxygen, however, was depleted as his stomach convulsed once again, causing him to retch. Inhaling with all his strength, Roland was relieved to find he could still take in a small amount of air. The quilt began to spin with Roland inside as he struggled to feed his burning lungs the air they needed.

With Roland fighting inside it, the quilt floated across the room, and he couldn't determine which direction they were going as dizziness continued to sweep over him. His head bumped against the wall painfully, then a second later his feet did the same. Roland was bent in half as the quilt dragged him through the doorway. Roland flailed his arms in a vain attempt to free himself from the quilt's grasp. "Rebecca," he gasped, but the quilt muffled his cry. Grabbing onto the doorframe, Roland tried to keep the quilt from dragging him from the room. He didn't want to leave Rebecca alone. Roland was fairly certain that they would both die, but he wanted to be with the woman he loved if he was going to be killed. The quilt stopped halfway out of the bedroom as Roland desperately clung to the frame, but it jerked forward one last time, causing the frame to slip from his grasp. "Rebecca!" Roland called out once more as he floated away from the bedroom and heard the door slam shut with a loud crash.

The knocking grew louder, deafening Roland even through the quilt. He stopped fighting to escape and simply struggled to breathe as he was dragged through the air. Sleep still called out invitingly to him as he fought to breathe under the quilt's smothering embrace. Something bumped against his legs, and Roland jerked them away defensively. Then he felt it jab into his back, and he realized that he was floating past the dancing furniture. "Please. Please let us go," Roland panted through the quilt as another piece of furniture brushed up against him.

"Mine!" The voice boomed again, and the quilt began to twist in the air, causing Roland's stomach to heave yet again. Roland struggled to call out to the strange voice, but he couldn't force the words out as he had to fight for every thin breath between retching. He weakly flailed his arms in a desperate attempt to loosen the quilt, but it remained fastened tightly around him despite his weak effort to gain more air space in its smothering confines.

Pain shot through his back as a chair launched itself at him while he lay helpless inside the quilt. Roland gasped in pain, then tried to suck in another breath to replace the air he had just coughed up. The furniture began to slam against him, striking him all over his body. Welts arose over his back, chest, and legs as the furniture kept a steady assault on the prone Sheriff. He could no longer continue his struggle for air, and Roland felt himself passing out from lack of oxygen as he was buffeted from all sides. One of the chairs smashed against his head, and Roland slumped in defeat as exhaustion washed over him. His lungs began to burn, but Roland was too tired to fight for air anymore. The furniture continued to strike him, but Roland no longer felt any pain as he slowly sank into unconsciousness.

He was jolted back awake as a giant wave of pain swept through his body. Instinctively he gasped for air and was amazed when it came easily. It took Roland a moment to realize he was laying on the floor as he took deep wheezing breaths to replenish his starving lungs. He pushed at the quilt with his right hand and was surprised again as it yielded to him. The loud knocking continued to beat erratically as he shrugged off the quilt, so he knew that Bryant—or whatever was causing the haunting—was still present. Roland couldn't figure out why the quilt had ceased its assault on him, but he concentrated on burrowing his way out of its confines as quickly as possible.

The furniture continued to dance in the air above the den floor, and books flapped their covers wildly as they flew about the study like bats. Roland tried to ignore them as he fought to rise on his hands and knees in their midst. He was able to rise from the floor through sheer adrenaline, and he took ragged breaths as he fought to maintain the position with his body crying out in pain. Raising his head slowly, Roland fought off dizziness and focused on the bedroom door. He could see it was closed, but no sounds emerged from the room. Roland wasn't sure if Rebecca was unconscious, dead, or vainly calling for help as the loud knocking drowned out all other sounds. "Rebecca," the Sheriff breathed in exhaustion and laboriously forced his arms and legs to crawl towards the bedroom. Freedom lay beyond the door behind him, but Roland was determined to bring Rebecca out safely or at least do the best he could. He loved her and wouldn't abandon her in the house while he still breathed.

Each time he had to lift a hand or knee, pain lanced through his side, but Roland was beyond feeling pain at that point. His body had been battered beyond any threshold he had ever encountered, but his mind focused on the sole task of rescuing Rebecca as he slowly made his way across the den floor. He passed under the floating furniture, but he concentrated on the bedroom door. Fortunately they continued to turn their pirouettes obliviously above him and let Roland go by without attacking him again.

It took Roland some time to cross the floor at his slow rate, but he eventually reached the bedroom door. He raised a hand off the floor and had to fight to maintain his balance as he teetered on only three points of support. Pressing his hand against the door, Roland was able to restore his balance, but the door refused to swing inward again. He had to close his eyes as dizziness swept over him, but it faded quickly. Roland opened his eyes cautiously, expecting the world to spin, but it stayed level. A darkness seemed to lurk at the edge of his vision, however, and Roland struggled to keep himself from passing out. Putting his palm flat upon the surface of the door, Roland pushed against it with what was left of his dwindling strength.

A jolt of electricity shocked Roland's palm as the door refused to budge. Tentatively he reached out and pressed his hand against the door, wincing as he expected another shock. When none came, he pushed it inward and threw all of his strength into the effort, but it still wouldn't budge. "Rebecca," Roland called weakly and pushed against the door in one last effort. Another spark jumped off the door, shocking his hand, and Roland was thrown backwards nearly ten feet. He landed painfully and closed his eyes as his muscles refused to obey any of his orders to move.

The loud knocking continued to beat around him, and the sound of breaking dishes could be heard from the kitchen as he lay helplessly. He made one more attempt to sit up, but he was suddenly yanked towards the front door. Roland curled up into a tight ball and stopped fighting against whatever was haunting Rebecca's house as he was dragged inexorably out of the house. He opened his eyes to see what was pulling him, but Roland didn't spot anything else other than the furniture moving in the room. Roland was pulled all the way to the front door, and he watched with detachment as it swung open under its own power. The invisible force kept dragging him until he lay on the wooden porch, then stopped as the front door slammed shut.

Even with the door shut, Roland could still hear the loud knocking booming through the house. His body was completely battered, and it ignored every impulse he had to go back inside. Roland desperately wanted to rescue Rebecca, but the numerous wounds he had taken in the previous two days had depleted all of his strength. He closed his eyes and lay on the porch for a few minutes as he felt a tiny amount of strength slowly creep back into his exhausted limbs. Unconsciousness beckoned him to give up and sleep, and Roland knew he had to try to move again or he would pass out and abandon Rebecca to whatever fate the house intended for her.

He tried to force himself into a crawling position, but his muscles were too weak to support him. Roland looked at the front door and cursed mentally. It was so close, but he didn't know how he was going to make it back inside, let alone rescue Rebecca from the bedroom. He stared at the door for a few more moments as bizarre sounds continued to emanate from inside. Then he had an idea. Taking a deep breath, Roland forced his body to roll towards the door. Pain flared in his side, but Roland gritted his teeth and kept rolling until he bumped into the front door.

Lying on his back, Roland stared up at the doorknob above him and stretched out an arm to grab it. He had to strain to reach the brass handle, but he was able to grip the knob. Roland took a deep breath then twisted the knob and pushed against the door with his shoulder. He had barely turned it when a huge jolt of electricity surged through the door and shocked Roland's hand, making him cry out in pain. Balling up protectively, Roland took short, ragged breaths as he shook and shivered in agony.

"*Mine!*" The voice shrieked again, and Roland was hurled off the porch as an invisible force slammed against him. Roland flew nearly twenty feet off the porch and landed painfully on the ground. He rolled to a stop and took one last look at the house as his body shut down. Eerie blue lights danced behind the windows, and the pounding knocks could still be heard even that far from the house. "*Mine!*" The voice called out one more time as blackness stole over Roland and he slipped into unconsciousness.

Chapter Five

When Roland awakened, his body was a nest of aches and pain. It seemed as if his entire body had been bruised during his expulsion from the house. He had no idea what time it was, but the pale crescent moon was still bright in the night sky, casting faint illumination upon the house. The mysterious blue lights that had flickered before he had passed out were gone, and the loud thumping had ceased its erratic beat. Roland found the quiet tranquility disturbing. They made the house seem innocent and safe although he knew that something sinister dwelled within.

Fear for Rebecca paralyzed his mind as he grimly contemplated her imprisonment inside the treacherous house, and that fear prompted him to sit up. The wound at his side tightened and screamed as he stretched it. Groaning, he put a hand against it and was relieved when he didn't feel blood. He probed at the wound gently and hissed as his fingertips grazed one of his ribs, igniting an inferno of pain. *Damn,* he swore to himself as he realized it was broken. Doc Sullivan would have to tend to his injuries at some point. He had been struck with a great deal of force as he was pulled through the air, and now that adrenaline had stopped flowing through his body, he was feeling the effects of that cruel beating.

Despite the pain, Roland continued to sit with gritted teeth and wait for his wounded side to cease its furious aching. His body called for him to lie back down and let sleep soothe the pain, but he tenaciously focused on rescuing Rebecca from the house. There would be time for him to rest his exhausted body later. He loved Rebecca, and his first priority was to help her. He wouldn't let anything harm her if it was within his power to stop it. Whether it was a ghost or all twenty-two Dark Riders, Roland was determined to overcome any obstacle that came between him and Rebecca.

A tree stump jutted from the dying grass, and Roland took a deep breath of resignation as he looked at it. Wrapping one arm protectively around his wounded ribs, Roland slowly crawled forward on three limbs. As he crawled, sharp pains rippled through his side, but he kept his eyes focused on his goal and resolutely continued. It took him an agonizingly long time to cross the short distance, and he breathed a sigh of relief when his hand slapped against the stump's wooden surface. He held it there for a moment as he gathered his strength. Then, clenching his jaw, Roland pushed downward on the stump and painfully rose to his feet. He hunched over, his arm curled around his sore ribs, and tottered for a moment as he struggled to balance himself on his exhausted legs. Roland wasn't sure at first if he could remain on his feet, but his tired muscles steadied themselves as he put pressure on them.

Roland peered forlornly at the front door. *Rebecca,* he thought hopelessly. It was so close but seemed an impossible distance to walk in his tired state. He just prayed that whatever had haunted the house was gone. Roland considered himself lucky to have survived before and didn't hold much stock in doing so again if the haunting resumed. He knew it was a foolhardy idea to reenter the house, but Roland wouldn't leave until he had done everything in his power to rescue Rebecca. After taking a deep breath, Roland determinedly put one foot forth. Exhaustion instantly pulled at every part of his body, and Roland suddenly doubted that he would have the strength to go on. Each step, however, became a little easier as he limped towards the house. He sighed with relief when he grabbed the porch banister, one hand clutching it for support as he slowly made his way up the steps.

Roland paused as he stepped up to the door and pressed an ear against it. He strained to listen, but the only sounds he could hear were the crickets' chirping through the summer air. Hesitantly Roland stretched out a hand and grasped the brass doorknob, but before he could turn it, a spark of electricity leapt from the handle, shocking his hand. Roland hissed in pain and balled his numbed hand into a weak fist. *"Mine!"* The voice shrieked again, and Roland limped off the porch as quickly as his tired muscles would allow, biting his lip to shut out the pain. His pace wasn't very fast, and Roland cringed fearfully, expecting to be struck from behind. He had already incurred enough injuries and didn't know if he could take any more. Fortunately he made it onto the dry grass safely, but he kept on putting distance between himself and the house until he had limped to the tether post.

His horse turned its head curiously in Roland's direction as he leaned against the post and watched the house cautiously. Worry for Rebecca gnawed at him, and he yearned to try one more time to enter the house. But he knew that there was no more he could do on his own. Whatever had imprisoned Rebecca and thrown him out of the house was still laying in wait, and Roland was quite sure he would receive even more injuries or die if he tried to walk through the front door again.

He was tempted to ride back to town and gather his deputies, but he didn't know if ten men would be enough to break past whatever resided in Rebecca's house. He had briefly considered seeking out Chief Running Brook that morning but decided against consulting the Cheyenne Chief for fear of alarming the citizens of New Haven. Yet after witnessing and being injured by the second terrifying manifestation, he barely gave that risk a thought. Running Brook had a reputed knowledge of ghosts and spirits, and he seemed the ideal choice for help. The journey was a considerable distance, but he would ride ten times further just to help her.

Roland curled his lip in disgust as he looked at his horse. The wound in his side had receded to a dull ache, but Roland knew that climbing onto the saddle would rekindle the pain. Walking a bit unsteadily, Roland guided the horse to the tree stump and leaned against it for support. He glanced at the house and sighed in resignation. The Cheyenne tribe lived nearly ten miles away, and he wasn't sure if his body could make that long of a trip. But Running Brook was the only person who Roland thought had a chance to help Rebecca, and that decided the matter. Stepping onto the tree stump, Roland set his jaw and awkwardly scrambled his way into the saddle, nearly passing out as pain erupted in his side. Closing his eyes, he fell forward onto his horse's neck and wrapped his arms about it. The horse neighed in frustration, but Roland kept his eyes shut and waited for the fury in his side to diminish. It receded after a few labored breaths, but Roland felt something trickle down his side. Placing a tentative hand to his wounded side, he cursed as he realized his stitches had broken open.

He continued to lean against his horse's neck as he opened his eyes and clutched it desperately as the world spun dizzyingly. It settled into some stability as Roland focused on the ground below him. Exhaustion still plagued his body, and Roland knew that he needed to get the horse into motion before he gave into sleep's tempting lure. Clucking at his horse, Roland pulled the reins and guided it towards New Haven. Each step his horse took sent stabbing pains through his side, and Roland had to clench his teeth to keep from crying out. The first twenty steps nearly killed him, and he wondered how he would ever manage to travel ten miles on horseback. Yet he continued to push his mount towards the Cheyenne camp that seemed so far away.

He gazed longingly at the lights of New Haven, but he tiredly rode north of town and across the railroad tracks before beginning the long trek through the forest. As he rode under the tall oak trees that dominated the forest, the sharp pains in his side dulled into a deep throbbing, and Roland felt a numbing lassitude sweep over his body. It killed the pain, but it also relaxed his muscles and pushed him dangerously close to the brink of unconsciousness. Roland bit down on his lip and drew blood in an effort to stave off the sleep which called to him. With each step the horse took, Roland felt his eyes grow heavier and heavier. *Find Running Brook and save Rebecca,* Roland kept thinking to himself and repeated that mantra several times in an attempt to hold his tenuous grasp on consciousness, but he knew he had undertaken a fool's quest. He might hold off sleep for a little while, but it was only a matter of time before it caught up with him. Then he would pass out and abandon Rebecca to whatever fate her house decided. He should have ridden back to town and sought out Jack's help, but it was too late to change his course of action.

Roland continued his slow westward progression for nearly another hour through gritted teeth and sheer determination. Blood had soaked through his shirt by that point, and his muscles had turned into rubber. He had fallen forward and draped his arms about his horse's neck, clinging to it for support, but even then he could barely manage to stay in the saddle. Each step threatened to knock him from his precarious perch as he struggled to remain awake. His eyes had grown too heavy to keep open, and he blindly rode onward, trusting his horse to hold a steady western course although he wouldn't have noticed if the horse had turned around and headed due east.

As his horse passed by a giant oak tree, Roland's hands slipped, and he tumbled off the horse, landing painfully on the ground. He cried out as his ribs screamed in agony, and he momentarily forgot about everything else as pain coursed through his body. Something nuzzled at his chest, and Roland forced his heavy eyelids open to see his horse standing over him. It looked curiously at Roland as if wondering why he had chosen such a strange place and method to dismount. Roland held out an exhausted hand to it, and tried to rise to his feet. *Rebecca,* he thought forlornly. He desperately wanted to climb back into the saddle and get help for her, but his tired muscles were beyond his control. He made a few more efforts to force his body into motion, then his weary arm fell to his side as he gave up. Blackness descended upon him as he closed his eyes in resignation, and his last thoughts were of Rebecca before he finally passed out.

He was awakened by a gentle shaking, and when he opened his heavy eyelids, Roland was surprised to see the hazy outline of a Cheyenne brave standing over him. The brave's features were blurred by Roland's tired eyes and the faint moonlight, but Roland thought he could make out both red and light blue paint upon the brave's face. He turned his back to Roland and called out something to the forest. Roland was dimly aware of answering voices as the brave once again turned towards him. "Sleep, Sheriff. We will care for your wounds," the Cheyenne assured Roland and knelt beside him to take a closer look at his injuries. Roland was too tired to push away the hands that gently probed at his tender ribs. "You have been badly hurt. Someday you must tell me how a great man like you became so wounded."

Roland struggled to keep his eyes open and tried to focus his gaze as the brave knelt beside him. The features were still blurry, but Roland thought he recognized the Cheyenne's voice. "Falling Thunder? Is that you?" Roland asked weakly as his eyelids slowly drifted shut.

"Yes, Sheriff. I am Falling Thunder. I am here as my father commanded." Roland was glad the brave was somebody he knew and, more importantly, somebody who could take him to Running Brook. He had met Falling Thunder on several of his previous trips to the Cheyenne camp and had liked the young brave. Falling Thunder was Running Brook's son and would probably succeed his father as Chief of their tribe. Like his father, he was one of the few Indians Roland had ever met who could speak the English language with any degree of success. Since Roland couldn't speak more than several words of the Cheyenne dialect, it made dealing with their tribe much easier. Falling Thunder was also their best hunter and frequently led hunting parties into the surrounding forest. A skilled hunter like Falling Thunder knew how to avoid the White Man when he entered the forest, and Roland was mildly surprised to encounter him.

Roland struggled to sit, but his body had lost all of its strength. He yawned once as he abandoned his efforts to rise and concentrated on ensuring that he was taken to the Cheyenne village. "Take me to Running Brook," he muttered in a weak voice.

"That is why we are here, Sheriff," Falling Thunder answered, but Roland had already passed out again and didn't hear his soft reply.

As Roland slept, he dreamed that he was walking through the forest on a cold winter night. A biting wind chilled him to the bone as the full moon shone in a cloudy sky. Under its dim lighting, he followed two sets of footprints in the light snowfall. He knew that one belonged to Rebecca, and the other came from whatever had haunted her house. The second set seemed to exude a darkness, and although he was terrified to discover what had made those ominous footprints, he trudged on, determined to rescue Rebecca.

Somewhere ahead, he heard a loud caw followed by the rustling of bushes, and Roland picked up the pace of his pursuit. The winter air grew quiet around him, and he frantically rushed ahead, scared he would lose Rebecca in the chase. He wondered if he was still on the right track in the forest's quietness, but another caw pierced the chill winter air. Staring in the direction of the telltale noise, Roland was rewarded when he saw a flickering of movement behind a set of bushes. Dashing towards them, Roland peered ahead, desperately trying to catch a glimpse of Rebecca. Dodging between barren trees, Roland once again began to fear that he had lost Rebecca, but he pressed on, desperate to find her.

He burst into a tiny clearing and stopped in his tracks, crying out in triumph as he spotted Rebecca standing by a tall oak tree. "Rebecca," Roland laughed and held out his arms to her, but the smile faded from his face as he came close enough to see her clearly. She stood with her back rigidly pressed against the tree. Her chin jutted forward, and her eyes remained steadfastly closed as if she was completely oblivious to his presence. A raven sat upon her shoulder, its head pointed away from Roland. The whole scene disturbed Roland, and he approached her warily. "Rebecca!" He shouted in an attempt to make her open her eyes.

The raven whipped its head about when he called to Rebecca and cast its black eyes upon him. It cawed once, it shrill cry echoing in the frosty air. Then with a loud rustle, it flapped its wings and flew at Roland's head. He threw his hands up protectively and ducked as it flew above him and into the winter sky. Rebecca's eyes shot open in response, and she jerked her head towards him erratically. The veins in her neck stood out as if she had to fight with all her strength just to turn her head. She reached out a hand to him imploringly, and he moved to grab it when he felt the air push him backwards. He tried to move forward with all of his strength, but it was as if an invisible wall had been erected between him and Rebecca. "Help me," Rebecca called forlornly as a cloud of smoke suddenly formed around her, shielding her from Roland's frightened eyes.

"Rebecca!" Roland screamed in horror and pushed forward in desperation. He cried out in surprise as the invisible barrier disappeared, and he fell forward, crashing to the ground. Surging back to his feet, Roland rushed to the cloud of smoke. He pushed an arm into the smoke, but he encountered no resistance. *What the hell?* He thought in confusion, then a brief gust of wind blew through the small clearing, tearing apart the cloud into tattered white tendrils. Yet when the cloud had disappeared, Rebecca was nowhere to be found. The ground was undisturbed by even a set of footprints, and although he could still feel her presence, there was no evidence showing where she had gone. "Rebecca!" Roland screamed once again, and his cry echoed through the cold forest. He was answered by a caw, and when Roland looked up, he spotted the same raven that had perched on Rebecca's shoulder, now sitting comfortably on a tree branch. Its black eyes seemed to stare malevolently at him, and he unconsciously took a step backwards. Once more the raven cawed to him, and Roland was yanked from his dream.

He awakened to a strange, rhythmic chanting, and he opened his heavy eyes to see what was causing the noise. Gasping in surprise, Roland looked up at the face of Running Brook, who peered into his eyes from no more than six inches away. They were inside a teepee, and the only light came from the opening at the top and the thin entrance. The Chief continued to scrutinize him from that close distance as Roland recovered from his momentary shock. Red paint had been smeared in three sets of matching lines, running diagonally across each of Running Brook's cheeks, and a light blue arc had been set beneath each eye. His long white hair was held back from his forehead with a simple leather band, and his dark eyes ran over Roland carefully. "Running Brook?" Sheriff Black called out tentatively. He didn't know why the Chief was looking at his face with such concentration, but Roland found it slightly unnerving.

Running Brook ignored Roland's greeting and took one last look at Roland's face before nodding his head in satisfaction. Leaning back, Running Brook crossed his legs and raised a hand in greeting. "Sheriff. You will live."

"What?" He asked drowsily.

"Your wounds. They are serious, but they were not enough to kill you. Falling Thunder found you just in time. If he had been later, you would be dead."

Once the Chief mentioned it, Roland noticed that his body's pain had disappeared. The deep bruises that had covered his body seemed to have vanished, and he couldn't even feel the wound in his side. Putting a hand inside his shirt and pressing it to his ribcage, Roland was amazed when it encountered unbroken skin. Even the stitches had been removed. The vicious cut he had taken two nights ago seemed to have disappeared completely. It was slightly tender, but the pressure he was applying would have made him pass out earlier. *Could I have slept long enough for the wounds to heal naturally?* He thought, worrying about Rebecca being left in her house during that time.

Although the pain was gone, a heavy exhaustion had fallen over Roland, and he found himself weaker than he had been when he started his expedition to find Running Brook. His jaw dropped open in wonder as he continued to probe at his side, half-expecting the pain to return, but it appeared as if his wounds had mysteriously vanished. "Oh my God. What did you do?" Doc Sullivan was the best doctor Roland had encountered during his travels in the West, but whatever Running Brook had done far exceeded Sullivan's skills.

The Chief's face stretched into a huge, satisfied grin, and he laughed in response. "Your wounds have been healed, Sheriff. I—how do you say? Persuaded your wounds to go away."

"Persuaded? Blazes, Running Brook. I had broken ribs and a nasty cut in my side. You didn't just make the pain go away. You healed me. How the hell did you do that?" He didn't know what the Chief meant by persuading his wounds to go away, but he did know that the injuries he had sustained had been serious and could have killed him. Running Brook hadn't simply patched him up or tended his wounds; he had completely healed Roland.

"I sang to your wounds and told them you would die if they did not go away. They were very bad, and it took a long time to make them all go. It took much singing to convince them, but the strength came from you. Do you not feel tired?"

It was an effort for Roland just to stay awake, and he nodded wearily as he continued to run his hand over his healed ribcage in disbelief. "I'm exhausted. I'm more tired than I was before. Why?"

"Your body had to heal, Sheriff, or you would have died. There are songs the Cheyenne know to help the body begin healing, but the power to do so must come from the one who is hurt. That is what I did to you. I sang to your body and told it to absorb all the pain of your wounds and give you strength. Your body listened, but it drew that strength from within you. For a while I feared that you would not be strong enough to overcome your injuries, but you proved me wrong. You have little strength remaining and will need several days of rest to regain it. In the meantime, you will be as weak as a newborn babe."

Roland looked at the Cheyenne Chief with skeptical eyes. It was difficult to believe that he had been healed by mere singing, but he found it hard to dispute such obvious evidence. Other than bone-deep exhaustion, all of his injuries had completely disappeared. He never would have dreamed that he could be healed so miraculously, and he began to think that Rebecca would be rescued safely after all. He had turned to the Cheyenne Chief in desperation, not certain whether Running Brook would have the ability to help. After having his wounds healed, Roland didn't have a doubt in the world that Running Brook could handle whatever was haunting Rebecca's house. "Thank you, Running Brook, but there's a reason I came here. I need your help. There's a woman in a lot of danger right now, and I need you to come with me and try to rescue her."

Running Brook looked up at the ceiling of his teepee for a moment, his face becoming very serious, then he focused his eyes upon Roland again. "I know, Sheriff. I dreamed of you last night. Would you like me to tell you about my dream?"

Roland didn't know how the Chief could have dreamed that Rebecca would need his help, but he had talked with the Cheyenne Chief before and knew that Running Brook could spin a tale for hours if given the chance. Normally Roland wouldn't be rude to his host, especially after he had administered such a miraculous healing. But Rebecca was Roland's first priority, and he didn't have time to listen to Running Brook tell one of his long tales. "Can you tell me about it later? Rebecca's in a lot of trouble, and I think you might be the only one who can help her. We really need to go to her house *right now*," Roland panted in desperation. He didn't know how long he had been unconscious, but Rebecca could already be dead or in need of medical attention. Roland didn't want to waste another minute.

"This relates to your Rebecca. I heard you speak her name in your sleep, so I also sang to the spirits of my ancestors. The Sun Father is very strong in the summer, and I asked him—"

"Spirits of your ancestors?" Roland broke in and shook his head in skepticism. He was still amazed that he had been healed, but he wasn't quite willing to stretch his belief that far. Running Brook had spoken about some of the Cheyenne lore in the past, and Roland didn't really feel the need to have the Chief explain their religion again. Rebecca was still trapped in her house, and each second could mean the difference between her living or dying. "Running Brook, I'd love to listen to your story, but I really need you to help Rebecca. She could be dying." He futilely tried to push himself off the ground, but his body had been drained of energy.

"Please, do not stir. Your body is very weak. We will go to this house in time. Be assured, your Rebecca is not dead. Evil lies in wait over her but will not harm her any more. We have until the sun sets to return."

"Evil? What are you talking about? We need to go now, Goddamn it! Rebecca needs me. Help me up!" Roland felt like he was talking to a tree stump. He hated to shout, but Running Brook appeared content to sit and tell stories. Roland remembered all too well the sight of Rebecca gurgling and floating above her bed and had no intention of waiting another moment to return.

"Be silent and listen," Running Brook told Roland and folded his arms across his chest.

Be silent? Roland thought in amazement. He had thought that Running Brook would help him, not give him a lecture. "No, you listen to me. Help me up! I need to help Rebecca. If you won't help, I'm leaving," Roland spat out in frustration.

"Fine, Sheriff. Then leave," the Cheyenne Chief replied and watched Roland patiently. Roland took his advice and tried to rise to his feet to no avail. His body simply had no strength remaining. It was a monumental effort just to keep his eyes open. Running Brook watched it all and saw when Roland finally gave up. "Now will you listen?"

"I don't have any choice," Roland answered petulantly and fumed silently. Rebecca's life might well hang in the balance, but Running Brook was intent on wasting precious time. He had thought the Chief would help.

"Good. Know your Rebecca is safe. She was attacked by a spirit from the Land of Shadows. They are strong during the night but have no power during the day. We will return to her house and rescue her, but she will not be harmed while the sun is still up."

The sun? Roland thought and looked at the entrance to the teepee. He had seen the light before, but the fact that it was sunlight hadn't sunk in. He knew that he had slept for a while but had no idea it had been so long. Roland was even further baffled by Running Brook's words. *Land of Shadows? Spirits?* Roland thought in confusion. He was interested in hearing about that later, but first he wanted to get Rebecca out of her house.

"We will go to this house later, Sheriff, but I must tell you of my dream first."

"Dream?" Roland asked out loud, and Running Brook looked at him sternly. He forced his voice to sound polite even though he was desperate to return to Rebecca's side. "Can you please tell me about this later? I know you think she's safe, but I want to see her."

"She *is* safe, Sheriff. Listen to my words first," he told Roland, and the Sheriff nodded in weary resignation. He had no other choice in his weakened condition. He certainly couldn't do anything to help Rebecca without the help of the Cheyenne, and unfortunately that meant listening to Running Brook even if it jeopardized Rebecca's safety.

"I must help you and your Rebecca. I will tell you of my dream, so you will understand. Whatever evil threatens you also threatens the Cheyenne, and the lives of my people are in danger. I must help you defeat this evil if I want my people to live. You see the red paint I wear upon my face? Falling Thunder wears it as well. All men in this camp wear red paint upon their faces.

It marks us ready for fighting. The Cheyenne are at war with an evil that threatens us, and we will defeat it. That I promise." Running Brook's face had become rigid while he spoke, and his eyes seemed to bore into Roland.

"Okay. Please tell your story," Roland replied softly. He had never seen Running Brook look so intense. Roland didn't have a clue why Rebecca's house being haunted would threaten the Cheyenne, but he wasn't about to dispute anything Running Brook said at that moment. The Chief looked like he might just hurt him if Roland dared to open his mouth in protest again. He didn't have much choice either. Until Running Brook decided to help him off the ground, Roland was too weak to do anything but lay there and wait. *Rebecca, I'm trying.*

Running Brook relaxed his face and looked up at the top of his teepee. He rubbed his hands together slowly and began his tale. "The Cheyenne put much faith in dreams. Dreams are powerful things. They can tell us about the past, the present, and even the future. All men dream, Sheriff, but few know how to use that knowledge to learn about the world around us. I am one of those few. Ever since my ninth summer, I have been able to read the true meaning of my dreams and use that meaning to help my people.

"I had a dream last night, Sheriff. In my dream, I was an Eagle, soaring high above the clouds. As you know, every Cheyenne has a token animal. It is chosen in our rite of passage to adulthood, and that animal plays an important role during the remainder of our lives. I chose the Eagle when I was younger, and I always take his form when I dream. I have come to know the Eagle well. The Eagle is a noble bird that lives in clouds and flies majestically through the heavens. His enemy is the Raven, which is an evil bird that lies and steals and lives off the flesh of the dead."

A Raven? Roland thought to himself. Running Brook's mention of a raven reminded Roland of his own dream from earlier. The raven's eyes had bored into him and struck fear in his heart. *That was just a dream,* Roland told himself. He desperately wanted to return to Rebecca's house, but he found himself paying more attention to Running Brook's story instead of chafing his heels impatiently.

"As I flew in my dream, I spied the Raven flying into the forest surrounding this camp. I was disturbed to see the Raven for he is always a messenger of evil. I have seen him before in my dreams but never so close to my people. So I swooped down from the clouds to find him and ask what evil he brought. The trees were thick in my dream, and I couldn't see through their heavy branches. I gave into despair as I lost sight of the Raven, but he called his mocking cry from a distance. Every time I thought I had lost the Raven, I would hear another mocking caw through the trees ahead, and I would fly towards that sound.

"I found the Raven in the middle of the forest. There was a giant oak tree in a small clearing, and you lay beside it. You had been gravely injured. Blood poured from your nose and through your shirt. The Raven sat upon your shoulder and waited for me to arrive. He watched me with his evil, black eyes as I flew to the oak tree, and I knew he meant me harm. 'Why do you sit on this man's shoulder?' I asked the Raven. 'He is injured and needs help.'

"The Raven laughed at my question. 'I need rest, and his shoulder is a comfortable place. It is a soft place, and I can smell his blood. Blood is a good smell.'

"'You are an evil bird. You should help this man. I know him, and he is a good man.'

"'I do not choose to help. Chaos and destruction are to my liking, and I do not wish to impede their progress.'

"'Then fly away, for I wish to aid him. He has done good things for my people, and I do not wish to leave him like this,' I told the Raven and flapped my wings as I prepared to fly to the ground beside you.

"The Raven is an evil bird, and he is also a cowardly one. The Raven feeds upon the dead and off the kills of other animals. It does not hunt its own food for it is frightened of other animals. It shook its wings as I approached and called out to me, 'Come no further, for I have words you should hear.'

"I was hesitant to listen to the Raven, for he is fond of lying. Even when he speaks the truth, it is tainted with foul lies. 'Speak then, or I will drive you away. This man is gravely injured, and I will tend his wounds.'

"'Life slips from this man, and soon he will depart this world. I am the Raven, and I would let him die and feed upon his flesh. That is my way of life, but you are different. You would take this man to your camp and tend his wounds. That is honorable, but if you do so, death will follow.'

"His answer troubled me for the Raven had the look of truth in his eyes. 'What do you mean by that answer? If I tend his wounds, I will cheat death of its prize.'

"The Raven laughed at my answer. 'That is what you think, but great evil lies over this man. He draws near to death, and he can only survive if you aid him. That evil will follow him, and it will threaten your people if you tend his wounds.'

"'You lie. How can aiding this man hurt my people? It is an honorable thing, and my ancestors would approve of this action. They would not unleash evil upon my people for it.'

"'You fool yourself then. You know I speak the truth, and I say this. If you bring this man to your camp, the lives of every man, woman, and child in your tribe hang in the balance, and they could all be destroyed.'

"I was greatly troubled by this answer for I could tell the Raven told me the truth. I wished to aid you, for you have always tried to help my people.

But how could I risk the lives of all my tribe for the benefit of one man? I was caught between two choices. Both answers threatened someone, and I did not know what to do. But then I saw a smile lurking on the face of the Raven. 'Why do you smile?' I asked him.

"'I enjoy pain, and your soul is in torment,' the Raven laughed.

"But his face showed his lie. The Raven had told the truth before, but now treachery and deceit tainted his answers. 'No. There is more. You told the truth before, but you have not shared all of it. What other words have you hidden from me?'

"The Raven drew back and grew worried when I asked this question. His actions spoke clearly that I had caught his lie. 'What do you mean? I have told you all I know of this man and what will happen if you tend his wounds.'

"'You have told me part of the truth, but not all of it. I will hear the rest now,' I told the Raven and swooped down to your side. But the Raven was quick and flew into the air before I reached the ground. I tried to fly back into the air and pursue him, but the Raven flew into the forest and quickly disappeared into the thick trees. I turned back to your body and was greatly troubled, for I still did not know what to do.

"I sat on the ground beside you and watched as blood flowed from your body. It was clear that you would die soon unless I decided to give my aid, and I did not want to leave you to die in the forest. But the Raven's words weighed heavily upon me, and I had no choice but to abandon you. The lives of all my people outweigh the balance of any one man, and I could not risk them. But the Raven had not spoken the whole truth, and I desired to know what he had not told me.

"So I sang, Sheriff. I sang to the spirits of my ancestors to show me the truth that the Raven had denied me. I continued to sing to the sky until a Wolf emerged from the forest and sat down on the other side of your body. The Wolf is a wise animal and knows the answers to a great many things, but he does not share them lightly. The Wolf does not speak with others that are not of his kind, and I knew that I must convince him to help me first.

"'I greet you, Wolf. I ask that you help this man.'

"The wolf nodded in reply. 'I greet you, but why should I help this man? He is not a Wolf. What do I gain from helping him?'

"'He is a good man and does not deserve to die. He has helped my people by keeping the White Man away from our village. It is not right to let him die.'

"'Then help him. Why do you need my aid? You are capable of tending his wounds as well as I.'

"'I spoke to the Raven before you arrived, and he told me that a great evil lies over this man. If I tend his wounds, that evil will threaten my people, and many could die.'

106

"'The Raven is an evil bird, but it spoke the truth. I can feel evil hanging over this man. There is great danger surrounding him, and all who draw close risk their own lives.'

"It pained me to hear the Wolf confirm the Raven's answer. Although I thought the Raven had spoken the truth, I could not be certain. 'But there is more. I could feel it when the Raven spoke to me. When I asked him to tell me the rest of the truth, the Raven flew into the forest. Was I correct? Is there more to this man than the Raven spoke of?'

"'You are correct. The Raven did not tell you the whole truth. He lies by telling half-truths and concealing the rest.'

"I rejoiced at this answer for perhaps there was a way to save you without harming my people. 'Will you tell me the rest of the truth? I wish to help this man.'

"The Wolf looked at me with bored eyes. 'I already told you to help him if you desire, but it will bring danger upon all of your people.'

"'Then there is no way to tend his wounds without bringing danger upon my people?'

"'No. The evil that lies over him is too great.'

"My joy disappeared with this answer for it looked as if there was no way to aid you. I grew saddened for I did not wish to let you die, but I could not risk the lives of my people. 'Then I must leave him here. Can he survive if I do not tend his wounds?'

"'No. He is greatly injured and lies close to death as we speak. If you do not aid him, he will soon die, and his spirit will journey to the Land of Shadows.'

"I bowed my head in grief, for I would miss you. 'Then will you tell me the rest of the Raven's story? I wish to know what he concealed from me.' I did not think the knowledge would help you, but I still wished to have it. The Raven is evil and flew close to my people. Perhaps he would still bring evil upon them.

"'Why should I tell you? I gain nothing from it.'

"I expected this answer from the Wolf and was ready for it. The Wolf does not like to share its knowledge with others, but it will if asked properly. I have spoken to the Wolf before and have always found success with flattery. 'But only you can help. You are the wisest of all animals. I have nothing to give you, but I will sing praises of your name to my people.'

"The Wolf swelled with pride at my answer for he is a vain animal. 'I would be pleased if you sing my name to your people. Do you promise to do so?'

"'By the blood of my ancestors, I will sing praises for the next waxing and waning of the summer moon.'

"'Done then. The Raven spoke truly that you would risk your people's lives if you helped this man, but with his death comes the death of all your people. If he dies of these wounds, every man and child in your camp will die within the next three days,' the Wolf spoke then ran into the forest. I sat beside you for a moment longer, then I awakened from my dream."

Roland listened attentively to Running Brook talk about his dream. His own dream before waking in the teepee had been extremely vivid, and the parallels between his own and the Cheyenne Chief's frightened Roland. He wanted to discount the dream, but he found he couldn't. It sounded as if Running Brook was describing the exact same clearing he had dreamed about. It had been Rebecca that was injured in his dream, but there had also been a raven perched on her shoulder. They weren't exactly the same dream, but Roland still found the two remarkably similar for two different men to have. "I also had a dream," Roland uttered quietly.

Running Brook nodded. "Dreams are often sent out to many, but few realize they have been spoken to. Tell me of your dream."

"Shouldn't we go help Rebecca first?" Despite the parallels between his and Running Brook's dreams, he had no desire to tell the Chief about his own. He wanted to help Rebecca first, and then he would happily discuss whatever Running Brook wanted for days on end. His patience was beginning to wear thin again.

"In time, Sheriff. The Wolf and the Raven were right. I can feel evil hanging over you. It is thick like a cloud of smoke. I have put myself in front of this evil to help you and endangered my people's lives. All of our fates are tied together in this. I will go with you to this house, but first I wish to know about this evil."

"I don't understand. What evil are you talking about? There's something in her house, but I don't know what it is. And I don't know how it can hurt any of *you*. It's in Rebecca's house! Can't we just go help her? Please. She could need our help right now," he pleaded with the Chief. Despite Running Brook's assurances that she would be fine, Roland was anxious to begin the trek to her house immediately.

"I hope to discover who is in her house then we will begin our journey."

"How? I don't know what the hell's in her house. That's why I came to you. Can't you just sing to your ancestors again? Maybe they can tell you something." Running Brook had claimed to sing to his ancestors several times that evening, and Roland didn't know why the Cheyenne didn't just ask them what was in Rebecca's house and why his people were being threatened. It would save time and allow them to begin the ten-mile journey. He didn't really see how the Cheyenne would be endangered from Rebecca's house, but *she* was in plenty of danger.

108

Running Brook shook his head. "No. My ancestors will help me, but they will not fight battles for me. They told me that your Rebecca would live through the night, and they helped me heal your wounds. They even sent the Wolf in my dream, but they will not tell me what evil I face. I must discover that on my own. Please tell me of your dream. Perhaps I can learn more about this evil from you."

Roland shook his head in resignation. He didn't think that telling Running Brook about his dream would help the Chief understand the supposed danger to his people any better, but the Cheyenne didn't appear as if he would back down from his request. *What do a few more minutes matter?* Roland thought then quickly told his tale.

"I dreamed I was running through the forest. Something evil had taken Rebecca and fled, but I chased after it. When I caught her, she was standing against the oak tree you described. There was a raven on her shoulder, but it flew away when I arrived. Rebecca looked horrible, and she called to me for help. I tried to reach her, but I was pushed away from her by some kind of invisible wall. She disappeared in a cloud of smoke, and when I tried to search around the tree to find her, she was gone. I looked up and saw a raven sitting in the tree above me. Then I woke up. Does that mean anything to you?"

"It is interesting, Sheriff. A great evil is at work to send out two Ravens into the land of dreams. If he sat upon her shoulder, the evil is directed towards your Rebecca."

At the mention of evil being directed towards Rebecca, Roland's heart beat wildly in fear. He had bandied enough words with the Chief. "We have to go help her now, damn it!" Roland struggled to rise, but he found his muscles were still too weak.

"Please, do not try to rise. You will only hurt yourself. I told you she will not be hurt any further. There is an evil around her, but it will cause her no more harm until the Sun sleeps. There is still time to talk, and there is more I wish to know from you."

"I don't want to talk any more, Running Brook. What else do you need to know? So I had a dream, and you had a dream. Does that help you any? We've spent enough time talking. I know Rebecca has evil directed at her. Hell, that whole house is evil, and I want her out of there *right now*! You can ask me whatever you want during the ride."

"I am strong in the knowledge of the Cheyenne's traditions, and I do not fear going to this house. But I do wish to know what I am facing. A warrior picks his weapon according to what type of enemy he will fight. My people are in danger, and I want to protect them. I want you to tell me what you saw at this house and how you were hurt so badly. Then I will know what evil I am to fight and can prepare for the battle."

Roland bit his lip to hold back a hot retort. He knew the Chief was right not to rush off to the house blindly. Even though he yearned to ride to her rescue immediately, Roland tried to calm his nerves and nodded in reply. "Okay, you're right. I'll tell you about the house. It all started two nights ago. I went over to Rebecca's house for dinner, and everything seemed to be fine. Then we heard a knocking sound coming from her study, so we went to see what it was. Before we could get there, the knocking sound grew louder and started to beat faster. Then the front door began to open and shut on its own, and the furniture began to shake. Books were flying through the air, and dishes were smashing themselves to pieces in the kitchen."

"An evil spirit," Running Brook commented softly.

"What? An evil spirit? What the hell is that?" Roland broke from his story and asked Running Brook. The Chief had mentioned a spirit before. *A ghost?* Roland wondered to himself.

"I will tell you later."

"No, I want to know what you're talking about now."

"You are the one in a hurry, Sheriff. I will tell you after your tale is finished."

Roland paused for a moment before resuming. He wanted to know what the Cheyenne Chief had meant by his comment, but Roland decided against asking him again. Running Brook would explain when he was ready and not a moment sooner. He didn't like being completely under the power of Running Brook, but he didn't have any other choice than to comply if he wanted to help Rebecca. "I was going to leave the house through the front door, but it kept opening and closing on its own so I decided to leave through one of the windows. Rebecca went through first and made it out of the house safely, then I climbed through the window. I was halfway through, when I heard a voice call out. I—"

"What did the voice say?" Running Brook broke in.

"It kept saying 'mine'. Does that mean anything?"

"Hmm." Running Brook nodded to himself as if confirming something. "Please finish."

"Anyway, the voice called out, and a fire started in the fireplace. I got scared and leapt out of the window. That's how I got some of the injuries you healed. The cut in my side and most of the other cuts on my arms and legs were from the glass in the window. After we escaped, we both returned to town and went to sleep. I returned to the house the next day, and everything seemed fine. The place was one hell of a mess, but nothing was flying around on its own. I thought it was safe, so Rebecca and I went back last night. But it wasn't safe. Whatever's in the house came back and trapped Rebecca in her room. She looked sick as hell. She kept thrashing around on her bed and wouldn't respond to anything I said. I tried to drag her out of the house, but I was attacked. Her quilt wrapped around me, and furniture kept hitting me. I passed out for a while then sought you out. I don't understand what the hell is going on. Is it a ghost or some type of magic?"

"Hmm," Running Brook grunted to himself and stood up. He arched his back to stretch muscles that were sore from hours of sitting. "I will return in a moment, Sheriff. We must hurry."

"What the hell are you talking about? Where are you going? What do you mean 'We must hurry?' I thought you said Rebecca would be fine while we talked in here. I answered your questions, and you can Goddamn well answer mine."

Running Brook looked anxious and seemed to lean towards the entrance to the teepee. "I will do so, Sheriff, but first there are things I must see to." The Chief held up a hand briefly then exited quickly.

"Goddamn it! Don't you leave me here, Running Brook!" Roland shouted at the entrance, but no response came back. "Damn," he swore again and tried his best to rise from the ground, but his body was simply too weak. His exhausted muscles refused to obey any command he gave them, and he gave up trying to chase after the Chief. Exhaustion swept over him, but Roland was too angry to give in to sleep. He had been patient with Running Brook in hopes that the Chief would help Rebecca, but he hadn't expected the Cheyenne to abandon him in return.

Roland let his eyes wander over the interior of the teepee while he lay helplessly. Running Brook's wife had died a number of years ago, and the teepee definitely gave mute evidence that only one person lived inside. Roland rested on the only bedding, and there wasn't much else in the way of living necessities. The only other things Roland could see were a number of jars, pipes, stones, and feathers that had been set into neat piles or hung on the wall of the teepee. The jars and pipes had been painted and elaborately decorated, and Roland wondered what was inside them. The feathers appeared to have come from many different types of birds, and the stones had no particular similarities, although all were colorful. It certainly was more barren than the interiors of other teepees Roland had observed.

A loud cry sounded outside of the tent, and Roland shifted his gaze to the entrance of the teepee. The cry was followed by a few more, and soon Roland heard them coming from all corners of the camp. *What the hell's going on?* Roland thought to himself.

Several voices approached the teepee, and Roland narrowed his eyes as he stared at the entrance. He expected Running Brook to enter and explain what was going on, but he was surprised when Falling Thunder swept into the teepee and knelt beside him. Roland was able to make out his features better than he had in the forest and could see that Running Brook was indeed telling the truth. Red paint had been applied to Falling Thunder's face in a pattern of vertical lines, marking the brave as ready to fight. His long hair fell loosely around his shoulders, and his eyes danced with excitement. "Sheriff, you look much better than before." The brave grinned at Roland mischievously.

"What in Sam Hill's going on out there? And where's your father?"

"My people want to wish us luck. My father is overseeing our preparations." Falling Thunder stopped abruptly when he saw the look of confusion still upon Roland's face. "Did my father not tell you of these things?"

"No. He didn't tell me a Goddamn thing. He's supposed to be helping me. Will you please tell me what's going on out there?" Roland felt anger boiling up inside him. He had been patient so far, but he had put up with enough.

Falling Thunder considered answering then shook his head. "I cannot do that, Sheriff. My father will tell you what you need to know when you need to know it." A look of bafflement flashed across his features. "I do not understand why he did not tell you where we go, but that is between you and my father. Are you ready?"

"Ready for what? I just want to know what the hell's going on. If Running Brook's going to leave me in here, will you please help me to my horse? I have something I need to take care of." Roland was tired of waiting for Running Brook's help. Rebecca was still in danger, and he didn't intend to wait any longer. The Chief had performed some sort of magic upon his injuries and would be a great asset in fighting Rebecca's house, but time was critical. Roland didn't want to waste any more of it.

"That is why I am here. Please be still, and I will lift you, Sheriff," the brave spoke softly and placed one hand under Roland's knees and another under his shoulder. Roland relaxed his body as he felt Falling Thunder pick him up, and he dangled helplessly in the brave's arms until he was slung over one of his shoulders. "It is not far," Falling Thunder commented then slowly exited the teepee, careful not to drop Roland as he ducked through the entrance.

A noisy bedlam greeted Roland as he emerged from the teepee, and he was amazed to see nearly the entire tribe roaming about the camp. It was hard to focus on any particular person or group from his upside-down position, but he managed to cast his tired gaze around and observe most of the tribe. He saw several children wearing wolf skins dance about while others reared back in fear from the fur-covered youngsters. Many of the women participated in a less strenuous manner and simply sat upon the ground, beating the earth while singing to the summer sky. As Roland watched, he noted that a great many of them returned his curious stare. Something strange was going on in the Cheyenne camp, and Roland had no idea what it was. He meant to find out eventually, but whether he got that answer or not, he was riding to Rebecca's house as soon as he was seated upon a horse. Roland had been patient with

112

Running Brook after his miraculous healing, but his patience had come to an end.

He was staring at one of the boys wearing a wolf skin when he was abruptly pulled back over Falling Thunder's shoulder. "I will put you on your horse now, Sheriff." The brave held Roland in front of him and bore him towards his horse. Nearly two dozen other horses stood near his, and a large number of them had a Cheyenne brave atop them. Most of the braves were young warriors with bows slung over their shoulders, making them look very dangerous in such a large group. The braves curiously watched Falling Thunder carry Roland towards them and craned their necks to gain a better view.

Falling Thunder slung him over a horse, and Roland struggled to move his tired limbs into a more comfortable position. The Cheyenne didn't leave Roland folded over the horse for long, and he helped Roland into an uneasy sitting position. He had to lean forward against the horse's neck and wrap his exhausted arms around it to keep from falling out of the saddle. "Thank you, Falling Thunder." Roland breathed a sigh of relief once he was safely mounted.

"You are welcome, Sheriff."

"Where did you find my horse? I thought he was lost after I passed out."

"I found him not far from your body. I thought you would want him back, so I brought him along."

"Thanks again. I was—" Roland broke off as he sensed the silence. Every man, woman, and child had stopped what they were doing and stared towards him and Falling Thunder. He found their quiet scrutiny unnerving, and he shivered once uncomfortably. "What's going on?"

"We have formed a war party, and my people wish to see the man who has caused it."

"A war party? Blazes, you're not attacking New Haven?" Roland's eyes grew wide with fear and surprise. If the Cheyenne were planning to attack New Haven, he had more problems than he could possibly handle. He already felt as if he was juggling a dozen balls of fire with Rebecca and the Dark Riders. If the Cheyenne added to those problems, he would be in over his head.

"No, we ride to your Rebecca's house," Running Brook's voice answered behind him. Roland turned his head and saw the Chief standing by his horse, looking very serious. "We wear war paint on our faces, for the evil we face threatens every life here. We have no desire to hurt the White Man and bring their wrath upon us."

"You're going to Rebecca's house?" Roland asked impatiently. He wasn't going to wait any longer for the Chief to ask more questions. If Running Brook was going to ride with him, Roland would welcome his company, but otherwise, Roland would have to leave. His body was exhausted, but he would chance the journey anyway. Roland had left Rebecca in that house for too long, no matter what assurances Running Brook had made.

"Yes, Sheriff. All these men will ride with us. I do not think we will need them, but we will ride forth twenty-one strong. My ancestors tell us that twenty-one is a powerful number. If you are ready, we can leave now. There is much work to do before this day is through, and we must hurry if we wish to complete it before the sun sets."

Roland nodded in satisfaction. "It's about damn time."

Chapter Six

Running Brook turned back to the people of his tribe and held up a hand. Quietness settled over everyone gathered as they watched their Chief expectantly. He called out something briefly in Cheyenne, and the entire tribe erupted in cheers. Running Brook smiled as he watched them resume their previous activities, then he turned to Roland. "We will leave now," the Chief told him solemnly. Roland watched in confusion as Running Brook slowly climbed atop one of the unoccupied horses. He was relieved that they were finally riding to Rebecca's house, but he still wanted Running Brook to explain why he had left the teepee so suddenly and why all Roland's questions had been ignored. A hand tapped his leg, and Roland looked down to see Falling Thunder.

"Come, Sheriff. I will ride with you. You are too weak to make the journey alone." The brave put his hand on Roland's horse and flexed his knees.

"What do you think you're doing?" Roland was dead tired, but he wanted to ride by himself. He hated to admit that he was fallible. Roland had swallowed his pride in seeking out Running Brook's aid for Rebecca's sake, but he could salvage some dignity if he rode by himself.

"You are nearly falling off your horse. You will not stay on more than five minutes without help," Falling Thunder laughed.

Roland sighed as he realized that the brave was right. His body was indeed too weak to make the journey, and as much as Roland wanted to demonstrate his determination, his top priority was to save Rebecca. It wouldn't help her if he slowed the Cheyenne's trek by falling out of the saddle. "Fine. Get up here." He curled his lip in self-disgust.

"Hold still," Falling Thunder cautioned and nimbly swung a leg over the horse's back. Roland sucked in a nervous breath as he felt himself slowly topple to the left, but Falling Thunder gripped his shoulders and held him in place. "See. This is not so bad."

"I'd rather ride by myself," Roland muttered under his breath.

"What was that, Sheriff?"

"I said where's your damn father. I have a few questions I want to ask him."

A thick finger shot over his shoulder and pointed at the Chief. Running Brook rode a young mare and looked natural on horseback. Roland knew that Running Brook had been a hunter when he was younger and guessed that he had never lost the skill of horsemanship even after all those years. He held up a hand in greeting when he saw Roland staring at him then called out a few brief words in Cheyenne. The braves in their party cried out in response, and Running Brook's horse took off at a brisk pace into the forest. "We ride, Sheriff.

There will be time to talk to my father later on," Falling Thunder explained then tapped Roland's horse into motion.

Roland kept a nervous hand on his horse's neck to maintain his precarious balance, but Falling Thunder held his shoulders firmly. As the horse picked up speed, Roland had to admit that he was glad the brave had ridden double with him. Falling Thunder's support was the only reason he hadn't fallen off the horse so far, and he never would have completed the long trek to Rebecca's house on his own. Roland swore that when he finally returned to New Haven, he wouldn't set foot near a horse for a month. At least his injuries no longer caused him any pain, and he didn't have to cringe with each step the horse took. He wished he had more energy, but riding with exhaustion was much better than having each gait send waves of agony through his body.

As they rode through the forest, Roland tried to catch sight of Running Brook, but the Chief remained at the front of their party. Roland had a great number of questions he wanted to ask Running Brook when he finally had the chance to talk with him again. Normally the Chief would talk his ears off, and it was extremely odd for him to be so secretive about his actions. Other than his brief comment about a spirit, Running Brook hadn't given Roland a hint about what was holding Rebecca captive in her house. With over a dozen braves riding between him and the Chief, Roland would have to wait until later to seek those answers.

The first mile was bad for Roland as his body kept wanting to topple sideways from his horse. The little strength he had when awakening earlier dissipated as they traveled over the bumpy terrain of the forest, and he found himself using Falling Thunder for more and more support. By the time they covered another mile, Roland could barely keep his eyes open and leaned back into Falling Thunder, trusting that the brave wouldn't let him fall. As much as he wanted to contribute to the efforts to save Rebecca, Roland found himself drifting increasingly close to slumber. He dug a fingernail into his palm and tried to keep his eyes open, but his eyelids grew heavier with each passing minute. He caught one last glance of the sun through the forest's leafy canopy before exhaustion finally caught up with him, and he closed his eyes in resignation as sleep stole over him.

Once again the descending darkness ushered Roland into a dream. This time he found himself standing in Rebecca's house as the haunting raged about him furiously. The erratic pounding boomed within the study, and furniture had risen into the air, swirling around in a mad dance. The bedroom door remained closed, but he could hear Rebecca's muted screams for help behind it, and he knew that he had to rescue her or she would perish. Roland grimly drew both of his pistols and strode forward with one in each hand.

One of the chairs stopped its frantic pirouettes and launched itself at Roland. Without hesitation Roland smoothly fired a shot at it and watched in amazement as it exploded in a fiery burst of light. Black spots danced in front of his eyes, and he was momentarily blinded by the brief flash. He cringed as he expected another piece of furniture to attack him, but he remained unscathed as his vision slowly returned. When he could finally see clearly, Roland stared at the glowing remains of the chair he had shot as they slowly drifted to the floor like wounded fireflies. He stood warily with his guns pointed in the air in case more of the furniture chose to swoop towards him, but they continued their dance, seemingly oblivious to him as the last flecks of light flickered out.

Another scream sounded from within the bedroom, and Roland continued his advance. In response to his action, a pair of chairs swooped down from opposite sides of the room and launched themselves at Roland in unison, but Roland was ready for the attack and immediately fired a bullet from each gun, striking true with both shots. As before, each piece of furniture exploded in a brilliant flash, but Roland was wise enough to shut his eyes. When he opened them, Roland had only a moment of surprise before he fired twice more at a pair of chairs that were flying towards him. They also exploded in a fiery flash, and the entire den was filled with swirling flecks of light that slowly floated to the floor.

In the midst of the cascading shower of lights, Roland kept a cautious eye upon the remaining three chairs and the couch. They ignored Roland as they turned pirouettes to the accompaniment of the loud knocking. A terrified scream penetrated the bedroom door. *Rebecca,* Roland thought desperately and quickly darted his eyes in that direction before bringing them back to the furniture. Each time he had tried to approach the door so far, he had been attacked, and Roland decided to remove the threat before another attack could prove successful. The dancing furniture made easy targets, and Roland didn't waste a single bullet as he fired once at each piece. The chairs all exploded in bursts of light, but the couch made a huge boom that drowned out even the loud knocking as it sent an enormous cloud of glowing flecks throughout the room.

Roland stood still as he viewed the fiery remains of the furniture, half-expecting the house to throw yet another attack at him. When none was forthcoming, Roland holstered one of his guns and approached the bedroom door with a lone gun ready for use. He felt the air grow cold around him as he gripped the doorknob. The knocking began to grow frenzied, and the scratchy voice called out, *"Mine!"* The single word reverberated loudly, and another scream from Rebecca immediately followed.

Fear for Rebecca clamped around his heart, and he roughly twisted the doorknob. He nearly yanked the door from its hinges as he swung it open, then stopped as he observed the scene inside. The sheets from Rebecca's bed had wrapped themselves around her and lifted her into the air. A muffled cry emerged from within them as Rebecca struggled and kicked desperately to escape their smothering embrace. "Rebecca!" Roland cried in terror and rushed forward to free her, quickly holstering his gun. The sheets twisted under his grip, and Roland had to struggle to peel them from her writhing body. With great effort, he pulled two of them away and threw them to the floor, breathing easier when only one remained wrapped around Rebecca. That relief turned into surprise and fright as the last sheet returned to inanimateness in his hands and unfolded to reveal nothing inside. Roland gaped at the lifeless sheets then frantically pawed through them as if Rebecca might be hidden somewhere, but there wasn't a single trace of her presence.

"*Mine!*" The voice boomed from behind him, and Roland turned and drew both pistols in a fluid motion. He had to squint his eyes as a brilliant light the size of an apple shone brightly before him. There seemed to be a figure behind it, swathed in darkness. Although Roland couldn't make out any of its features, he knew that the figure was evil and meant him harm. He was certain that it was the cause of the haunting of Rebecca's house, and its nearness frightened him. "*Mine!*" The voice called again as it extended its darkness outward and slowly began to envelop the brilliant light.

"Roland, help me!" Rebecca's voice sounded from within the light, and Roland knew that somehow she was imprisoned within it. Black tendrils wrapped themselves about her shining confinement, slowly extinguishing it, and he was certain that he had to save her from that darkness or she would die. Making sure he wouldn't hit her, Roland took careful aim and fired a single shot at the mysterious figure and squinted as it exploded in a cascade of lights. Rebecca's prison became lost in the swirling sea of glowing sparks, and when the air cleared, it was nowhere to be found. Tiny flecks of light floated throughout the room, but Roland couldn't find a single trace of Rebecca.

"Rebecca!" Roland cried out desperately as the room began to blur, then he was yanked from his dream.

He awakened to find himself laying on grass with Running Brook kneeling by his side and gently shaking his shoulder. The chief's features were hazy to Roland's blurry eyes. Roland shuddered once as the fright from his dream slowly faded. He couldn't remember ever having such disturbing dreams.

"You were talking in your sleep, Sheriff. Did you have another dream?" Running Brook asked solemnly.

"Damn it, don't you ask me any more questions! I have a few for you, and you're going to answer them first," Roland snapped then tried to make his exhausted body sit up. His tired muscles complained loudly and nearly refused, but Roland was too angry to lie on the ground helplessly. He had Running Brook before him at last, and he intended to question the Chief thoroughly, preferring to do so sitting up rather than laying prone before him. Gritting his teeth, Roland planted his hands on the ground and pushed down with a brief burst of energy. After taking a few ragged breaths, he was about to blast Running

118

Brook for abandoning him when he noticed his surroundings for the first time. "We're here," Roland whispered in surprise. The exterior of Rebecca's house was no more than a hundred feet away. He knew that his body had been exhausted, but he couldn't believe he had slept on horseback for over eight miles. It seemed as if he had just closed his eyes a few minutes ago.

"Yes, Sheriff. We are here. It was a quick journey, but Falling Thunder told me you slept for most of it." Running Brook pointed a mischievous finger at him and grinned. "I said your body would be tired, but you did not listen."

Roland shook his head and stared at the house with nervous apprehension. It appeared so peaceful under the light of day. No loud knockings disturbed the quiet air, and no lights flickered behind the windows. If Roland hadn't experienced such harrowing events inside the house, he never would have suspected anything to be out of the ordinary. Yet Roland *had* experienced those events and knew that the innocent-looking exterior was a facade. He just prayed that Rebecca was still alive.

Shifting his gaze to Running Brook, Roland saw that the Chief still watched him with an amused grin. "What the hell are you smiling at? Are you going in to—" Roland broke off as he noticed for the first time that Rebecca was laying on the ground behind Running Brook. "Rebecca," he whispered, but she didn't respond. She was on her back with her head turned towards Roland. Her eyes, however, remained shut tight. "Rebecca," Roland called out again. "What the hell's wrong with her?" He demanded from Running Brook. "Is she alive?" Roland felt his heart tighten in fear as he waited for an answer. *Please, let her be alive,* he pleaded.

"She lives, Sheriff, but she is in great danger," Running Brook explained gravely.

"What in Sam Hill's that supposed to mean? What's wrong with her, Goddamn it?" Roland shouted at the Chief. He couldn't stand to see Rebecca looking so lifeless. Roland tried to move towards her, but his exhausted muscles wouldn't allow it.

Running Brook looked at Roland with sorrow in his eyes. "You are weak like a newborn babe, Sheriff. You should not move so much."

"Help me to her, damn you!" Roland cried and pawed at the ground as he tried to crawl across the grass to her side. Even in his desperation, Roland was only able to move a few scant inches.

Running Brook, however, rose to his feet and wrapped his arms around Roland's chest. Roland breathed a sigh of relief when Running Brook dragged him to her side. He reached out and touched her hair, marveling at how soft it was under his fingertips. "Rebecca," Roland whispered, but she remained silent. "Rebecca," he repeated and grabbed one of her hands, cringing when he felt how cold it was. Her skin was also drained of color, almost completely pale, giving her a sickly appearance. "What the hell's wrong with her?" Roland asked the Chief worriedly.

Running Brook looked at him solemnly before answering. "I believe an evil spirit resides within this house, and it is this spirit that has captured your Rebecca. That is why I must wait until the moon rises, and then I will try to wrest her from this spirit."

"What's an evil spirit? Do you mean a ghost? What's it done to her?" Roland's eyes widened as he listened to the Chief's answers. He had briefly considered a ghost to be the culprit the morning after the first haunting, but he had discarded the idea. Hearing Running Brook offer that suggestion made him reconsider. It was the only explanation that made any sense.

"The White Man calls them ghosts, but the Cheyenne call them spirits," Running Brook answered.

"But she's out of the house. What's wrong with her?"

"Her spirit has been captured, Sheriff," the Cheyenne told him grimly.

Captured, Roland thought numbly. He didn't understand what Running Brook was talking about, but the sight of Rebecca and the Chief's words filled him with dread. *Did it take her soul?* Roland wondered as Running Brook went into more detail.

"The Cheyenne believe that every man, woman, and child has a spirit that continues to live even after the body has died. After death, the spirit journeys to the Land of Shadows, where it dwells briefly with other spirits before it is reborn and lives within flesh again. This cycle repeats itself seven times. After a spirit's body has died seven times, it leaves the Land of Shadows and journeys to the Happy Hunting Grounds where the grass is always green and there are many animals to hunt. The spirits of my ancestors use our time on this earth to judge us, and the greater the deeds we perform, the stronger we will be when we make the journey to the Happy Hunting Grounds. I have died five times before, Sheriff, and after this life, the next time I die, I will go to the Happy Hunting Grounds. I think I have led good lives and helped my people, but the spirits of my ancestors are the judges. Perhaps I will stand high among them, or maybe I will not. Time will tell."

"What the hell does that have to do with Rebecca?" Roland snapped. He couldn't tear his eyes from her, and it was eating at him to see her lay there so lifelessly. She needed help, and Running Brook was talking about his people's beliefs yet again. Right now Roland didn't care what happened to her in the afterlife as long as she opened her eyes. "Aren't you going to help her?" He pleaded.

"I will help, but I must wait. There is nothing I can do until the moon rises. Will you hear my words?"

Roland bit his lip in frustration. He didn't want to hear any more words. He just wanted Rebecca to open her eyes. *Damn it,* he swore to himself and struggled in vain to rise to his feet. He had no choice but to sit and listen to Running Brook speak. Roland was too weak. "Fine," he snapped.

Running Brook pointed a finger at Roland. "Listen carefully, Sheriff, for this spirit threatens you and your Rebecca and the people of my tribe. The Land of Shadows is a place of waiting for the spirits of my people, but sometimes the spirits of the White Man also make this journey. They usually depart soon after, for the Land of Shadows is a dark place not suited for them. But the spirits of my people sometimes choose to remain in the Land of Shadows, and the spirits of the White Man sometimes do the same.

"Spirits may choose not to be reborn or to make the journey to the Happy Hunting Grounds. They do this for different reasons, but they soon grow tired of staying there. It is difficult to watch men and women enjoy the pleasures of the flesh, while they remain in the Land of Shadows. Most journey onward to their next life or to the Happy Hunting Grounds when the temptation to feel earthly pleasures again grows too great. But others have no choice and are forced to remain in the Land of Shadows.

"If a great evil is performed against a man, he may take an oath of revenge to seek justice for these actions. This oath gives him the power to touch our world after death and speak with those who still live in the flesh, but once this oath is taken, he may not leave the Land of Shadows until it has been fulfilled. The stronger the evil that was performed against him, the stronger his power will be. From the words you told me, I believe the spirit in this house has great strength and power. Most spirits that remain in the Land of Shadows have the strength to move small objects, but the spirit in this house must have been angered greatly. It would take great strength for a spirit to move heavy objects or wound another man."

"But what does that have to do with Rebecca? That's an Indian belief. I don't believe in that stuff." Roland stroked Rebecca's hair as he berated the Chief.

Running Brook looked at Roland as if he were a child. "You do not believe after what you have seen? You are looking with your eyes closed." Roland looked away as he realized that Running Brook had a point. He had seen far too many things over the past three days to doubt anything he heard. The Cheyenne Chief continued on. "Have you or your Rebecca angered another man enough for him to seek revenge?"

Roland looked up, still feeling guilty from Running Brook's rebuke. He only wanted to help Rebecca. "I killed a lot of men in my days of gunslinging. I'm sure they're pretty upset," Roland barked out a coarse laugh. "I've managed to piss off a lot of people over the years. There are too many to remember. But Rebecca hasn't upset anybody. She's one of the sweetest people I know and wouldn't hurt anyone." Roland's face turned ashen, and his eyes widened. *Good God,* he thought and gripped her hand suddenly. "You don't think one of the men I killed is coming back to get even?" Roland was horrified that he could be the cause of the haunting. Hurting her would be the perfect revenge for any of the men he had killed. His grip tightened on her cold hand.

"Have you killed any men while you were Sheriff or angered one who has died?"

"No, I haven't shot anyone is years. I've roughed a few people up, but they're all still alive."

"Then this spirit does not remain in the Land of Shadows because of you. And your Rebecca?"

Roland shook his head. "She hardly ever leaves her house. Her husband was killed about six months ago, but he wasn't around enough to be angry at her. Other than him, I don't think she ever really talked to anybody in town except me."

"Did her husband die near this house?"

"What does that have to do with anything? Aren't you going to help her?"

"I am trying to find what is in this house so I can help her. Spirits are bound to the location of their death. They can only touch earthly objects near that location. That is why this spirit could not belong to any of the men you killed. They were all killed outside this area, and you have not killed anybody since you became Sheriff of New Haven. Was her husband killed near this house?"

"No. I found—" Roland paused as he reconsidered his answer. "I found his body in the middle of town, but I think he was killed somewhere else and dumped there afterwards. We never caught the killer. You don't think it's Bryant? He's been dead for nearly half a year. If he was going to haunt the house, he would have done it a lot sooner, right?"

"Time moves differently for a spirit than it does for those who still live. It moves slower in the Land of Shadows, and the moon could wax and wane a full cycle in the span of a day for a spirit. If this spirit belongs to this Bryant, it might seem to him as if only a week had passed since his death. He could have remained in the Land of Shadows to seek revenge upon his killer. Perhaps he grew impatient with his search and attacked you in anger. Perhaps he is jealous of the pleasures of the flesh. I have talked with spirits before, Sheriff, and it pains them to watch the living take for granted what spirits cannot have. Life in the Land of Shadows is barren."

"Blazes, are you telling me that Bryant is doing all of this? He was her husband, Goddamn it! That doesn't make any sense."

"Spirits that remain in the Land of Shadows do not resemble the people they were when they lived in the flesh. They are angry and trapped in a strange world. This man could have been very good while he lived, but anger can consume any man if it is left to fester and grow. It does not take much to provoke the wrath of such a man. Have you or your Rebecca done anything that would upset this man? If I know why this spirit is upset, perhaps it will give me an advantage over him."

Roland took a deep breath and looked at the ground. "Well, Rebecca and I were supposed to get married last night. Maybe he's jealous."

"Hmm," Running Brook grunted. "Spirits are very jealous of the living. If this man is trapped in the Land of Shadows, he could be seeking to stop your union. The Land of Shadows is a lonely, desolate place, and he will miss being with her in the flesh. From what you have told me, I believe the spirit belongs to this Bryant. His spirit surely rages with anger that his killer has not been brought to justice, and he is unleashing that anger upon you and your Rebecca. That is why he has taken her spirit with him."

Fear seized Roland as he listened to the Chief's words. Two days ago, Roland would have laughed at the mere suggestion of a ghost, but after experiencing the terrors inside Rebecca's house, it seemed the only logical answer. He reached out and grabbed Running Brook's arm. "Then what the hell are you waiting for? Get it back for her." Roland didn't know if Rebecca's spirit had been taken or not. He didn't even know what a spirit was, but he could clearly see that Rebecca did not look well. Only the faint rising and falling of her chest indicated she was still alive.

"Do not worry, Sheriff. She still lives. I will try to wrest her spirit away, but I cannot do so while the sun is in the sky."

"Why not?" Roland demanded roughly.

"The Cheyenne believe that the Sun and the Moon dwelled in the sky from the beginning of time, and from their union came the earth and the stars. The Sun is the Father and keeps watch over us during the day by shining his light upon us. He also stands over the Happy Hunting Grounds. The Moon is the mother and tends the night with her children, lighting the dark sky, so that we may always find our way even at night. The Moon Mother also guards the Land of Shadows, and spirits are at their greatest strength when she rises in the night sky. When the Sun Father is in the sky, spirits cannot be touched. I must wait until the Sun sets. The spirit will be at its strongest, but I can reach it while the Moon is in the sky. That is why I must wait. Does this answer your questions?"

Roland looked at Running Brook as if he were crazy. He didn't believe half of what the Chief had just told him, but he didn't know what else to believe. In his weakened state, Roland was in no condition to help Rebecca either. At least it was nearing dark. Judging by the violet shards shooting through the sky, Roland gauged that there weren't more than fifteen minutes until the sun disappeared. He was prepared to wait that much longer even though fear was twisting his stomach into knots. "I guess so. Do you promise you'll go in there as soon as the sun sets?"

"I give my word, Sheriff. Do not fear. I have much power over spirits. I am not the strongest alive, but I am strong enough for this task. Now I wish to hear of your dream, Sheriff. Perhaps there is some meaning in it that will help me in my fight."

He quickly told Running Brook about his dream, rushing so that he didn't have to think about it any more. Its memory still frightened him. Rebecca's danger had seemed so real, and the figure behind her had scared him. Even after waking, he could almost feel the evil emanating from it.

Running Brook nodded as Roland told his tale and stopped to think for a moment when Roland completed it. "Your dream confirms what we already know. The figure in your dream is the spirit within this house, and it holds your Rebecca captive. I am done with my questions and must begin my preparations for this battle. I will leave you here, Sheriff. You have much at stake, and I know you wish to see what occurs when I enter this house. You will not be able to see much, but you are a stubborn man. I know you would be upset if I did not allow you to remain." The Chief smiled in amusement then rose to his feet.

Roland looked around at Running Brook as the Cheyenne stood and noticed for the first time that he and Running Brook were alone. He didn't see any sign of the braves who had ridden with them. "Where's everyone? You didn't send them back?"

"No. Falling Thunder and the other warriors wait in the forest. They can see us from there and will come if needed."

"Why are they out there? I thought you were taking them all inside with you."

"You did not hear my words correctly then. I will go into this house alone. They will wait in the forest while I do so. We do not want any trouble with the White Man. If one came by and saw twenty armed warriors, they would think the Cheyenne came to do battle. Maybe they would attack our village. It is best if Falling Thunder and the other braves hide close by. Nobody can see them, but they are still close enough to see if we need their help. Now I must prepare, Sheriff."

Roland watched curiously as Running Brook ambled over to his horse. He didn't know how the Chief could "prepare" to enter the house, but Roland meant to observe carefully what Running Brook did in case he himself had to enter the house again. The Chief stopped a few steps away and turned back to Roland. "This is yours," he announced and tossed Roland's pistol onto the ground. Roland immediately pulled it to him, grateful to have it back. He had completely forgotten it in his mad scramble from the house.

The Chief walked nearly twenty feet from Roland then stood still. Roland watched closely to see how the Chief would ready himself for the battle. Running Brook, however, didn't do anything that Roland thought would help. Crossing his legs, the Chief sat upon the ground and put a rock on each knee. Then he turned each palm up and held them just above the rocks. As Roland watched in perplexity, Running Brook closed his eyes and began to sing in Cheyenne. He expected the Chief to do something spectacular, but for nearly ten minutes, Running Brook continued to chant, oblivious of Roland's watchful eyes. As he chanted, Roland felt his eyes grow heavy with exhaustion and monotony, and he was nearly ready to lay down and go back to sleep beside Rebecca when Falling Thunder emerged from the forest.

The rest of the braves still hung back inside the forest, out of sight from the stray visitor, but Falling Thunder quickly covered the ground between them. He cast a brief glance at his father then took a seat next to Roland. "Sheriff," he greeted.

"Falling Thunder." Roland nodded wearily. "I thought you were supposed to be out of sight."

The brave shrugged his shoulders nonchalantly. "My father is here. I am here. What difference if a White Man sees one Cheyenne or two?"

Roland barked out a laugh and shook his head in amusement. "That's true." It felt good to laugh again. The past few days had been hellish, and it seemed as if the last time he was happy had been an eternity ago. "I don't suppose you know what he's doing? The sun's about to set, and he's still chanting."

"He is cleansing himself for his fight, Sheriff. The rocks on his knees represent the earth, and his palms face upwards to represent the sky. My father sings to the spirits of our ancestors to send him everything that is good and pure from the highest cloud to the lowest rock. He will take their strength and add them to his own. Then he will be assured of victory."

Roland rolled his eyes in response. He had been willing to accept that Bryant's ghost haunted Rebecca's house, and he no choice but to believe that Running Brook had healed him. He had even accepted Running Brook's stories of the Sun and Moon as a Cheyenne myth, but this explanation was the most far-fetched he had heard yet.

Falling Thunder's expression was serious, and he looked questioningly towards Roland. "What is funny?"

"Nothing." Roland might find Running Brook's ritual absurd, but he wouldn't offend the Cheyenne people by mocking their beliefs out loud when they were trying to help Rebecca.

A tiny smile crept over Falling Thunder's face. "You are a bad liar, Sheriff. Do you not believe the stories of my people?"

The brave's eyes had grown wide with merriment, and Roland had the uncomfortable feeling that he was being baited. "I respect them, but some of them are a bit hard for me to believe."

"But you came to my father for help. You have seen a spirit from the Land of Shadows. My father has even healed your wounds, and you still do not believe?"

Falling Thunder's words shamed Roland. He had indeed been hit over the head with one extraordinary event after another, and he knew that he shouldn't doubt the validity of anything no matter how preposterous the idea sounded. Yet Falling Thunder's explanation sounded ludicrous. "You're right. I've seen some incredible things over the past few days, and I don't understand most of it. I believe and respect you father, and I don't know how the hell he healed me. But singing to the sky with a couple of rocks on your knees seems pretty crazy to me."

The brave considered Roland's answer for a moment then nodded once decisively. "Why do you always wear black, Sheriff?"

The question took Roland by surprise. He had been expecting another rebuke for not respecting the ways of the Cheyenne. "I've worn black ever since my family died," Roland replied quietly.

"How long has it been since their deaths?"

"It was nearly thirty years ago. Why do you want to know?" Roland didn't find the subject particularly enjoyable. Finding his family dead had been one of the darkest moments in his life, and he didn't like to talk about it.

"Thirty years, and you still wear black? Do you still grieve?"

"I'm not grieving for them anymore. It happened a long time ago. Hell, I was just a kid back then. I guess I still wear black because I'm used to it. I wore black the day I was in my first duel, and it just became routine to wear it after that. You could say it's lucky."

"But you do not think black is a magical color?"

"Hell no. It's just a dumb superstition. It doesn't have any meaning."

"You treat it as such. You are no different than the Cheyenne. How is your wearing black different than my father's song? My father's song will make him feel more relaxed and confident. If you do not believe in the power of this song, think of it as a lucky charm."

Roland had no choice but to nod in agreement with Falling Thunder. He knew he still believed in superstitions left over from his days of gunslinging, and almost every man he had known during those years had a few bizarre habits that made perfect sense to only themselves. Doc Holliday had drunk himself to death, but despite what everyone told him, he had actually thought that drinking was good for him. A few people had looked at Roland with arched eyebrows over his constant choice of black clothes, but he had ignored them, thinking there was nothing odd at all about his fashion sense.

The two sat quietly for another five minutes while they watched Running Brook continue his song. Roland grew increasingly tired as he listened to the Chief's chant, but he forced himself to remain awake through sheer

126

determination. He held Rebecca's hand the entire time and drew strength from her. He was staying awake for her. One way or another, Roland would help her awaken. He wouldn't abandon her while she was so helpless.

The air slowly grew cooler, and Roland could see only a tiny fraction of the sun as it disappeared behind the western horizon. Soon Running Brook would finally enter the house to save Rebecca, and Roland had no intention of sleeping through her rescue. He was close to asking Falling Thunder if they should disturb his father when the Chief stopped his singing and opened his eyes. Running Brook straightened his back then removed the pair of rocks from his knees and gently placed them on the ground. He moved slowly as he rose to his feet, as if a lassitude had swept over his body. "Are you going in now, Running Brook?"

Running Brook turned his head at the question, and his eyes narrowed as they passed over Falling Thunder. "I will go in now, Sheriff. Do not follow after me no matter what you hear from inside. You will only endanger your life and hers if you choose to enter. Do you understand?"

Roland was a bit taken back by the severity of Running Brook's voice. He had never seen the Chief look so serious in their previous meetings. Even with a pair of guns at his side, at that moment Roland would have thought twice about getting in Running Brook's way. "Don't worry about me. I don't think I could walk to the house right now even if I wanted to do. Please help her."

"I will do my best." Running Brook answered solemnly then turned his attention to his son. "I told you to stay in the forest."

"Yes, Father, but I thought someone should be here while you were singing. He is still weak, and I can help him flee if the spirit is too great for you."

"You lie badly. You know I will not be defeated. But stay here with the Sheriff. I promised he could stay close to this house, and I charge you to watch over him while I am inside. Do not follow after me," Running Brook cautioned once more in that solemn tone, then turned smoothly and marched with a calm serenity towards the front door. He reached into a pouch at his belt and withdrew some type of powder which he lightly cast over the doorknob before reaching out to turn it.

"Mine!" The scratchy voice echoed from within the house, and Roland flinched as he remembered what had happened the previous night. Running Brook, however, opened the door and proceeded inside as if he had heard nothing.

"You do not lie, Sheriff. There is indeed a spirit from the Land of Shadows within this house," Falling Thunder commented quietly, but his eyes never left the entrance his father had just walked through.

Other than a brief glance at the brave when he spoke, Roland also kept his eyes fastened on the open doorway, his hand gripping Rebecca's firmly. The air seemed to grow quiet as even the crickets became still. For a few moments that quietness continued, and Roland could hear his own heart beat as he waited impatiently for any sign of what was going on inside. Roland flinched in surprise when a loud knock reverberated loudly from the house. It echoed like a bass drum through the morning air, shattering the serene facade.

That first knock was just the beginning. It was followed by a slow steady pounding that was loud even one hundred feet from the house. *He'll get her out,* Roland kept thinking to himself. The deep pounding sounded nearly a dozen times, and Roland found himself tapping his foot to its steady rhythm. Then the voice called from the house again. *"Mine!"* Its scratchy cry drowned out the deep knocking. As soon as its echo faded, the pounding picked up its pace, beating erratically like it was enraged. A bluish light flickered behind several of the windows, giving the house a sinister appearance under the darkening sky.

"Mine!" The voice cried again, and the blue light flared brighter as if to punctuate that single word. The front door slammed shut, loudly striking the doorframe, and just as suddenly jerked back open. Roland had seen that happen twice before, but it still chilled his blood to watch the front door open and shut on its own. *"Mine!"* The scratchy voice called out in an angry tone, and a sudden flurry of frenzied motion exploded within the house. The lights flared so brightly that Roland thought there was a fire inside, and the knocking beat at a furiously chaotic tempo.

In the middle of that sudden bedlam, Running Brook appeared at the door. He quickly walked away from the house as the noise and lights continued to blare and flicker ominously. *"Mine!"* The voice called out again, but Running Brook paid it no heed as he hurried to Roland and his son.

"What happened?" Roland demanded. Rebecca lay motionless by his side, not flinching despite the loud noises echoing from her house. "She still won't wake up."

"I will explain in a moment," Running Brook answered breathlessly. Now that he was closer, Roland could see that sweat beaded along his forehead, and he drew his breaths in ragged gasps. "Help me carry them to the forest," he told his son and knelt by Rebecca's side.

What's going on? Roland wondered before Falling Thunder picked him up. The brave cradled Roland carefully in his arms as Running Brook did the same with Rebecca. "What the hell are you doing?" Roland demanded. He wanted his questions answered.

"Be silent," Running Brook ordered in an exhausted voice, and Roland held his tongue. The two Cheyenne carried Roland and Rebecca an additional fifty yards from the house then set the pair down. Running Brook kneeled down on the other side of Rebecca and looked at the house. The blue lights still flickered, but the noise had died down as they distanced themselves from the house. Then he touched Rebecca's forehead and looked at Roland with a somber expression on his face. "She lives, but her spirit now resides in the Land of Shadows."

"What? What do you mean 'resides in the Land of Shadows?' She's not dead. I thought you said the Land of Shadows was where people went when they died."

The Chief paused to sit upon the ground and rested his palms on each of his knees before answering. "She is alive, Sheriff, but there is much I must tell you. There is a powerful spirit in that house. I have never felt such anger from a spirit before. A great evil was performed against this man while he was still alive."

"Is it Bryant?" Roland broke in.

"I think it is, but I do not know for certain. I tried to talk to this spirit to find out why he is so angry, but he would not answer. I do know it is a White Man's spirit. My people have difficulty talking to the spirits of your people. There is a courtesy among my people, and our spirits will at least speak with those who still live to tell why they remain in the Land of Shadows. This spirit refused to tell me its purpose for remaining.

"When I entered the house, the spirit sought to attack me by throwing objects at me. This is an old trick of spirits and can be very deadly, but I know how to protect myself. I was able to turn every attack this time, but I would not want to face this spirit again. I am considered very powerful when it comes to fighting spirits, Sheriff, but I fear this spirit could destroy me. When I brought you to my teepee, I smelled evil in the air about you. I could tell that a dangerous evil threatened you as well as my people, and I was frightened. That same stench fills this house."

"What the hell are you trying to say? Is she okay or not?" Roland broke in desperately. He wasn't in the mood for a long complicated answer. He just wanted a simple explanation of Rebecca's condition. The excitement of the house was fading, and he felt himself growing drowsier by the moment.

The Chief looked at Roland with a somber expression. "Please listen, Sheriff. I will answer all of your questions, but you need to hear my words. They are for the safety of you and your Rebecca." He paused and waited for Roland to respond.

Roland tried to keep his temper from exploding. His mind was paralyzed with fear for Rebecca. He had thought she was simply asleep or unconscious at first, but Running Brook's words made him fear that her condition was far worse. He would have preferred a brief answer for some peace of mind, but if Running Brook was determined to tell the story at his own pace, Roland had no choice but to bide his time. "Okay. Tell me what you have to, but please hurry if you can. I'm getting really tired."

"I will do my best. As I said, there was great evil in the air around her, and I knew it was the same evil that threatened my people. I do not know why this evil threatens my people or even how it will seek to destroy them. So I opened a window into the Land of Shadows. The Land of Shadows does not exist on this earth, but one can listen or see into it if one knows how. It is a trick I learned a long time ago when I was still a boy. I closed my eyes and focused all of my body, mind, and spirit into looking into the Land of Shadows. It was exactly as you described in your dream.

"At first, I saw nothing, but then I was able to make out the faint outlines of this spirit. It sensed me and wrapped a wall of darkness over itself to hide from me. I was still able to see this spirit, but it appeared as a giant mass of darkness, a pitch black figure without features but exuding a powerful aura of evil. 'Why do you hide yourself from me? I am here to help you achieve peace. If you tell me the reason you remain in the Land of Shadows, I will do my best to help find revenge,' I told it, hoping that it would trust me and reveal its identity.

"Instead it held forth a shining ball of light that was so bright it nearly hurt my eyes. Although it was a simple ball of light, I knew it was the spirit of your Rebecca and that this spirit held her within its grasp. Then it called out 'mine.'"

Roland felt a shiver run up his spine as he listened to Running Brook's tale and found the similarities to his dream. Twice now his dreams had touched upon Rebecca's dilemma. The events tied to the house kept getting more and more bizarre, and he feared going back to sleep. He had no idea what his dreams would reveal to him next.

"'This spirit does not belong to you. Please give it to me so we may both leave in peace. I promise my aid in your search for vengeance,' I pleaded with the spirit. But it cried out 'mine' again. At that point, I had no choice and had to leave the house."

"Wait a minute," Roland cut in. His exhaustion faded away as true fear took hold of him. "Are you trying to tell me that whatever is in that house has her soul?" Running Brook had mentioned that before, but Roland hadn't questioned him on it.

"Yes, Sheriff. It still has her spirit."

"And what does that mean to her?"

Running Brook looked down at the ground before meeting Roland's eyes. "She will live but will not awaken while her spirit is gone."

"Well, get it back, Goddamn it!" Roland cried in frustration. He had sought out Running Brook to help him with Rebecca, not to leave her spirit in the house.

130

"I cannot do that," the Chief answered quietly.

"Why the hell not? You healed my wounds, and you turned back all the house's attacks. Why can't you banish Bryant's ghost?"

"Because the spirit could destroy her spirit if it is angered."

"What?"

"A spirit is a very fragile thing, Sheriff. If this spirit has drawn the spirit of your Rebecca into the Land of Shadows, nothing prevents him from ripping it to pieces. Then your Rebecca would never awaken again and would never live again after this life is over."

"Blazes. If we leave her like this, she'll die. Isn't it better to take a chance? If this ghost really is Bryant, there's no way he would destroy her soul. They were married, Goddamn it."

"There is no way to know what this spirit will do. I already told you that spirits do not act as they did when they still lived. The Land of Shadows changes them, especially if they remain there for too long. You can trust luck, but there is a better way. Actually, there are two."

"Well, what are they? Goddamn it, Running Brook, can't you hurry this up? I'm about ready to pass out."

"As you wish. The first way is to banish this spirit. A spirit may remain in the Land of Shadows if it swears an oath of revenge, but once that oath has been fulfilled, it must move on to the Happy Hunting Grounds or be reborn. This is your mission, Sheriff. I believe that the spirit in this house belongs to the man you call Bryant. If you avenge his death, he will be forced to leave the Land of Shadows and will have to release her spirit. Do you understand?"

"I think so. Are you telling me that if I find Bryant's killer, then Bryant will have to go away?"

"Yes, Sheriff, but it takes more than finding the killer. An oath of revenge requires a balance. You must take the life of the man who killed this Bryant."

"But I don't know who the hell killed him. I've been trying to figure it out for over half a year."

"Then you must try harder. That could be the only way to rescue her spirit without harming her."

Goddamn it, Roland swore. So far, he had encountered nothing but failure when investigating Bryant's murder. "Wait a minute. I thought you said there were two ways."

"Yes, there is another way perhaps."

"What do you mean 'perhaps?' Either there is or there isn't."

"There are two men well known to my people. They are called *Swinazha Ruelena,* or the Ghost Hunters as White Men would call them."

"Ghost Hunters?"

Running Brook nodded. "They are two men powerful in the ways of spirits, especially those of the White Man. One of them even is a White Man, and the other is a medicine man famous to my people. They can make this spirit talk to them and tell them why it has remained in the Land of Shadows. Then they can avenge his death and banish him from the Land of Shadows."

"That's great. Why did you say 'perhaps?' It sounds like they would be able to help." He yawned as a numbing languor swept over his body.

"I must first summon them, Sheriff. That will be my task. I will call to them from my dreams and tell them I need their aid. Hopefully they will come. I think they will. They give their help where it is needed most, and it is needed here."

"When do you think they could get here?" He hoped Running Brook would say soon. Bryant's murder had gone unsolved for over six months for a good reason. There hadn't been any evidence at the time of the crime, and Roland doubted that new evidence would arise out of nowhere. That left only these Ghost Hunters Running Brook had mentioned.

"I do not know, Sheriff. They travel to many different places and could be very far from here. I will try to send a message to them. If one knows how you can talk to others from a great distance through dreams. I know this trick as do the Ghost Hunters. I cannot make any promises, but it could be two days or it could be many moons. In the meantime, you should seek out Bryant's killer. That is a sure way to banish this spirit from the Land of Shadows. Do you understand?"

"I guess so," Roland answered in disgust. Neither was a choice he particularly liked. He didn't want to wait an indefinite amount of time for these Ghost Hunters to show up, but he had no choice. Bryant's killer had remained anonymous, and he really didn't expect that to change. More than likely, the killer was a Dark Rider, but Roland didn't have the strength or the men to take on the entire gang. It looked as if Rebecca would remain in her current condition for a while longer, and Roland bowed his head in despair and exhaustion.

"Sleep, Sheriff. There is no more you can do this night. You should rest. I will see that you both are returned to New Haven safely, and I will send word if I am able to speak with the Ghost Hunters."

Roland didn't have any arguments. He was too exhausted from the horrifying evening, and he wanted to sleep so he could cease worrying for Rebecca for at least a little while. Laying down beside her, Roland closed his eyes, and his hand still held hers tightly when sleep finally overcame him.

Chapter Seven

"Roland, wake up."

Sheriff Black muttered groggily at the voice. Exhaustion still plagued him. His body pleaded for more sleep, and Roland wanted the intrusive voice to leave him alone. But the voice was persistent and wouldn't let him drift away so easily. "Damn it, Roland, would you wake up?" A pair of hands began to shake him roughly, and Sheriff Black opened his eyes in resignation.

His vision was blurred from a long rest, but Roland was able to make out his surroundings. He was laying comfortably in a bed, and the walls were painted a deep shade of burgundy. It was a small room, and the wooden dresser that stood against the wall took up most of the excess space not used by the bed. Roland blinked in surprise and rubbed at his eyes as he realized he was back in The Last Frontier. He was even more surprised when he saw Jack standing over him with an angry expression on his face. "Jack?" He muttered in a hoarse voice and cleared his throat. "How the hell did I get back here?"

Jack stopped shaking Roland and took a few steps backwards, crossing his arms across his chest. His hands were balled into fists, and he clenched a copy of *The New Haven Gazette* in one of them. "Damn it, Roland. Do you want to tell me what's going on?" His jaw was set rigidly, and his eyebrows were lowered.

Blazes, Roland cursed to himself. He had seen that look on Jack's face before. "I don't know what you're talking about. Where's Rebecca?" He didn't know why Jack was so upset, but he looked furious that morning. Normally the deputy would back down when told to, but if Jack was upset enough, he would keep issuing demands until he was satisfied. Roland appreciated the fact that Jack spoke his mind, but sometimes it was inconvenient.

"She's in the next room. Sullivan took a look at both of you and couldn't figure out what was wrong. We tried to wake both of you but didn't have any luck. He was really surprised that all of your wounds were gone." He barked out a laugh. "Amazed is more like it. By now, the whole town knows that you were injured and had some miraculous recovery. At least you've been muttering in your sleep, but Rebecca's been completely silent." His face locked into an angry expression again. "Enough of that, though. What in Sam Hill's going on?" Jack demanded roughly.

Roland nodded silently. Running Brook had told him that Rebecca would keep breathing, but she wouldn't awaken until her soul had been retrieved from the Land of Shadows. He looked up at Jack who stood imposingly beside his bed. Roland didn't feel like dealing with Jack while he was in such an angry mood, and he wasn't ready to talk about the terrifying events of the past few days quite yet. Jack more than likely wouldn't believe him anyway. "That's a private matter, Jack. I said I'd tell you about it later. Just give me a little more time."

"No, Roland. It's not a private matter," Jack replied in a restrained tone and threw the newspaper at Roland.

It landed on his chest, and Roland picked it up warily. He cast a brief glance at the newspaper then returned his gaze back to the angry deputy. "What the hell are you upset about?"

"Read it, Roland. Front page. You can't miss it."

Sheriff Black slowly unfolded the newspaper while keeping a wary eye on his deputy. He had never seen Jack so angry before, and while he could understand Jack being somewhat upset about him not divulging what had occurred at Rebecca's house, Roland didn't expect him to become so bitter and angry. That changed the moment he looked at the headlines. Blood drained from his face, and his anger quickly matched Jack's. "Son of a bitch. What the hell's this? This can't be right."

"Oh, it's right. We nearly had a riot last night. If Alvin hadn't stepped in, we would have had one nice little war on our hands. Go on, read it. Then tell me what's true in there and what's not."

Dragging his eyes back to the front page, Roland slowly began to read scarcely believing the contents.

Sheriff Black and Widow Attacked by Savages

Sheriff Black and Rebecca White were attacked by a band of Cheyenne Indians early Saturday evening. Luckily both survived the attack, but that was only by the fortunate help of Doctor Richard Sullivan. According to Doctor Sullivan, each sustained wounds and had not recovered consciousness by Sunday evening.

Witnesses saw one of the savages approach deputy Jack Logan and boast of the event. The Indian was armed with a bow and arrows as well as a small ax that is typically used to scalp victims. The savage also wore face paint that Indians usually wear when they have killed men.

"I saw one of the deputies take one of those Injuns to Jack, and he said the Sheriff and Miss White had been hurt real bad. He laughed about it and said next time he would scalp the both of them. Then Jack got on a horse and took a few men with him to get their bodies," witness Paul Henderson reported.

Rebecca's husband, Bryant, was killed earlier this year, and several deputies believe the two incidents are related. To this date, his killer has not been apprehended, although an investigation into Cheyenne involvement has begun. Hopefully this act will lead to the expulsion of the Cheyenne from their settlement so that they cannot harm any more citizens of New Haven.

"Is this some type of joke?" Roland wanted to believe that the truth couldn't be so badly warped, but he knew better. *The New Haven Gazette* supposedly reported the news, but its editor Matthew Brady frequently bent the truth to his liking. After Bryant's murder, the paper had printed many articles speculating about his killer, yet only one had pointed suspicion towards Carlos and his men. That was just one of the instances in which *The Gazette* had twisted a story to their desires. There were no laws that said it had to print the absolute truth, and Roland had seen too many articles that struck nowhere close.

"No, Roland. At least ten people saw that brave come into town yesterday, and the rumors they spread nearly caused a riot. After this article, I'll be amazed if they don't form a posse and ride out to the Cheyenne camp to kill them all. Will you just tell me what the hell's going on?"

Roland had known that approaching the Cheyenne was a risky undertaking, but he hadn't thought they would be so maligned. "The Cheyenne didn't hurt me or Rebecca. They were just trying to help us. Hell, Running Brook even tended our wounds. There's no truth to this at all," he told Jack in a numbed tone.

"I know that, Goddamn it. I talked to him when I rode out to Rebecca's house, but he wouldn't tell me anything except that you two had been injured and needed to rest. I want you to tell me why you had to get their help in the first place and what happened to your wounds and what happened to Rebecca's house. That place is a mess!" Jack raged.

Sheriff Black forced his tired body into a seated position and rested his back against the wall. He was still looking up at Jack, but at least Roland wasn't laying on his back. It was more difficult to argue with his old friend that way. He took a moment to consider how to approach Jack. The deputy was furious, but Roland still didn't plan on telling him about the haunting. *Find out what's happened,* Roland told himself. It would be easier to lie to Jack once he knew what had happened from the time he blacked out at Rebecca's house. "How long have I been asleep, Jack?"

The deputy looked like he was about to spit nails, and he rolled his eyes in frustration before answering. "Phillip, Morgan, and I rode out to

Rebecca's house early Saturday night, and you've been asleep for nearly two days. Now will you tell me what's going on, damn it?"

"Are you telling me it's Monday?" Roland couldn't believe he had slept that long. *Two days?* Running Brook had told him that he would be exhausted and would have to rest, but he didn't say anything about sleeping for two days. "Why didn't you wake me sooner?"

"Running Brook told us to let you sleep until you woke up, and Sullivan didn't see anything wrong with that. He's checked on you and Rebecca three times since we brought you back and didn't find anything wrong. I tried calling your name, but it took about ten minutes of shaking you today to wake you up."

"Damn." Roland hated to lose that much time, but there was nothing to be done about it. At least his wounds were gone, and he would hopefully be back to full strength soon. "I'll tell you about me and Rebecca in a minute, but I want you to tell me what's happened here the last few days."

Jack's face scrunched up angrily again. "No, Roland. You tell—"

"Damn it, Jack," Roland cut him off. "I'm still the Sheriff here, and I want you to tell me what happened last night. If people are really upset about the Cheyenne, I need to know. It's my job."

Anger flashed across Jack's face, and for a moment, Roland thought that Jack would refuse to answer his questions and demand his own first. But the deputy fixed him with a glare and acquiesced. "Fine. I'll tell you what happened, but then I want a full report of what happened the past few nights with you." He paused until Roland nodded then continued.

"I was getting worried when you still hadn't shown up at The Frontier by eight o'clock. You're usually on time, and I thought maybe your wound had broken open. I was about to send Ben out to look for you when Alvin dropped by. He's hired some magician all the way from Paris, France to perform for the Fourth of July celebration. You know how big the celebration was last year. Supposedly this guy is famous over in Europe, and half the people in town went out last night celebrating the news. We had more drunk people than we're used to, and by the time things had settled down, it was pretty late." A flush crept up Jack's face, and he coughed once delicately. "I thought you two might have been celebrating on your own and lost track of time." He paused when Roland arched his eyebrows. "Come on, Roland. I thought if you were in any serious trouble, Rebecca would have come back to get help. What else would you two be doing?

"Anyway, when you still hadn't shown up by Sunday afternoon, me and Morgan were starting to get worried. He went to your house to check on you but didn't find anything. It was just before dark at that point. We started getting a search party together to try and find you when Running Brook sent one of his braves into town. Luckily the first person he ran into was Morgan. If it was anybody else, he might have been shot on sight. You know how people are. They don't really think about the Cheyenne as long as they don't see or hear them. If they see one walking in the streets, they think we're being attacked by Indians. A few people did see him, but it was after he was with Morgan. I guess that calmed them down a little bit. Morgan brought him to me, and I got Wade, and the three of us rode out to Rebecca's house.

"When we got there, Running Brook was watching over you both. At first, I thought he might have been the one who hurt you, but he said he had healed you. He said you two needed to rest, and that Rebecca had some illness and might not wake for some time." Jack paused as if just remembering something. "Oh yeah, he also said to tell you the two men you talked about would be here in a week. Do you know who he's talking about?"

Roland smiled at the news. *The Ghost Hunters.* He had begun to worry that the only way to exorcise Bryant's ghost would be to find his killer. Roland would still look for that culprit the best he could, but it was comforting to have a safety net in case his search didn't yield any results. "Yeah, they're doctors who can help Rebecca," Roland lied smoothly.

Jack nodded and didn't ask any questions, but Roland knew that the deputy was dying to do so. "Running Brook and the brave left after that, and we loaded each of you onto a horse. Ben and Morgan rode double on the other one, and I walked back. I took a look in her house after they left. Damn, Roland. That place is a mess. What happened in there?"

"Keep talking, Jack. I'll tell you when you're finished."

"Okay. Sullivan took a look at both of you and couldn't find anything wrong. He tried waking you, but neither of you would stir no matter what he did so he decided to wait and see what happened. The town was buzzing with the whole incident. Everyone kept dropping by The Frontier asking why a Cheyenne had been in town and what had happened to you and Rebecca. Everyone in this place saw Morgan and Ben carrying you two upstairs, and I guess the rumor spread.

"By nightfall, people were up in arms, saying that the Cheyenne had attacked you and that it was time to push the Indians out of the area. A couple of men over at The Snake were drunk. They got their guns and were going to ride out to the Cheyenne camp to kill some Indians. Morgan and I stopped them, and everyone else settled down after that and went home. I thought the whole thing had blown over until I saw that damn article. I tell you, Roland, as soon as people get a little bit of liquor in them tonight, they're going to start talking war again. I think the only way to stop them is to have you tell them that the Cheyenne didn't hurt you. Otherwise, the Cheyenne and this town might have some bloodshed on their hands. We don't need this right now. The Riders are coming back tomorrow, and I guarantee you we'll have our hands full with them."

137

Roland was quiet for a moment as he absorbed all of the information Jack had just told him. He was beginning to understand the danger that Running Brook had risked by aiding him. There was a great chance the Cheyenne people would be attacked after helping him. Roland shuddered to think what would have happened if he had actually died. The Cheyenne would have had serious trouble on their hands if they had been blamed for his death. At least Alvin would help him keep peace. As much as he disliked the mayor, he knew he could count on Alvin for helping him stop any mob from forming. If the Cheyenne were attacked, it would only be a matter of time before the government sent army units to New Haven, and neither Roland nor Alvin wanted that to happen. "Yeah, you're right. If you'll help me downstairs, I'll start spreading the word that the Cheyenne didn't hurt me or Rebecca. Hopefully that'll be enough. I also want to speak with Matthew about this. That son of a bitch has printed some bogus articles before but nothing like this. We can discuss the Riders later on." Carlos and his men would definitely be a problem, but they weren't going to be in town for another day and were low on Roland's list of concerns for the time being.

"I'll send William over to Matthew's house, but I want some answers from you first," Jack stated in a firm voice and puffed his chest out as if expecting to have to drag the words out of Roland.

Roland had hoped he could simply tell Jack that he didn't feel like talking about the subject, but looking at his pugnacious deputy, that apparently wasn't an option. He still didn't want to talk about Rebecca's house, and as much as hated to lie to Jack, that was the only option available. "Calm down, Jack. I said I'd tell you what happened, and I'm a man of my word." Roland paused for a moment while he scrambled frantically to come up with a lie that Jack would believe and smiled when he hit upon one that would appease his deputy.

"Not many people know this, but Rebecca has been sick for a long time. It was something she caught when she lived in Philadelphia," Roland began slowly and picked up speed as the story fleshed itself out. "Most of the time it's not too bad, but sometimes she has fainting spells and won't wake up for quite a while. She's seen lots of doctors and didn't feel the need to see any more once she moved here. No offense to Sullivan, but she's seen some of the finest doctors that Philadelphia had to offer and didn't want to go through any more tests. We were riding back to town the other night, and she had a seizure. I know you don't believe me, but honestly, we got thrown from the horse and that's how I got all those cuts and bruises. Then the next night, we rode out to her house to pick up her wedding dress for the ceremony, but when we got there, the place had been roughed up real good. My guess is the Riders decided to get a little revenge for the other night. It's like you said, everyone knows that Rebecca and I have been seeing each other, and it's just like Carlos to destroy her house to send me a warning. Rebecca had a seizure again when she saw how badly it had been damaged, and I couldn't wake her so I rode towards town. Luckily I ran into Running Brook and a hunting party. I was pretty damn tired and don't think I would have made it all the way back. They helped me back to Rebecca's house, and I passed out right after that. I don't know what happened to all of my wounds. They were still there when I passed out. The next thing I knew, I woke up here. That's the truth, Jack. "

Jack looked at him in disbelief for a second, and Sheriff Black struggled to maintain a straight face. He hated to deceive his old friend, but Jack didn't need to know any of the events that had happened over the last few days. What Roland had just told him would suffice for the time being. "Why do I get the feeling that you're not telling me the truth?"

Roland forced his face into an innocent expression. "Come on, Jack. When have I ever lied to you? I've refused to tell you things, but I've never lied."

Grudgingly the deputy nodded. "Okay, Roland. If that's what you say happened, I'll believe you. But those wounds from the other night didn't look like something that happened from falling off a horse, and I want to know how they disappeared."

"So do I. I was sore as hell when I passed out. I'll have to ask Running Brook the next time I see him."

"You just let me know what he says, and I'm sure Sullivan will want to know as well. How do you feel? Are you up to going downstairs?"

The last thing Roland wanted to do was get up. Sleep beckoned, but he'd have to wait to rest his body. He had been asleep for too long and needed to calm the people of New Haven before anymore serious trouble arose. Besides, Roland wanted to check on Rebecca. He knew she would still be asleep, but he wanted to see her before he went downstairs. "I'm tired, Jack, but I'll do it. Just give me a few minutes to get dressed, and I want to look in on Rebecca as well. Send someone to get Matthew. I don't care if he wants to come here or not. I want to have a few words with that son of a bitch, and I mean to do it tonight."

"Whatever you say, Roland. Here's the key to Rebecca's room. She's staying next door. I'll see you downstairs in a few minutes." The deputy fished in his coat pocket and brought out an iron key which he casually tossed onto the Sheriff's bed. He tipped his hat then turned to exit the room.

"Jack." The deputy paused in the act of opening the door and looked back inquisitively. "Have George rustle up some food while you're at it. I'm starving."

"Sure," Jack responded and stepped out into the hallway.

Roland breathed a sigh of relief when the door shut. He hadn't expected lying to Jack to be so easy, and he was glad that his deputy would at least leave the issue alone for a little while.

The suit he had worn when he proposed to Rebecca was folded neatly on top of the dresser. It was probably still dirty and caked with blood from the previous night, and while he didn't want to wear such soiled clothing, he didn't have any other choice unless he wanted to ride out to his house to fetch something else. Breathing a deep sigh of resignation, Sheriff Black swung his tired legs off the bed, planted his feet on the floor, and forced himself to stand. He trembled for a moment as he bore his weight for the first time in nearly two days, but he was glad to see that a great deal of his strength had returned. Twisting his shoulders, Roland stretched a few times to get rid of the stiffness that had settled into his muscles from laying in bed so long.

He slowly walked over to the dresser, wanting to test the strength of his legs before he pushed himself too hard. They were still a bit weak, but he was confident that he could ride a horse or even venture over to The Snake if he had to. Picking up the suit, Sheriff Black was amazed to see there wasn't a single speck of dirt or drop of blood on it. Taking a closer look, he noticed that it wasn't the suit he had worn on Friday but one of the suits he had left at his house. *Jack must have picked it up for me.* Sometimes he thought that he didn't appreciate his old friend enough.

It felt good to put on clean clothes again. Except for the brief time when he had donned his best suit, it seemed as if lately his clothes had been permanently caked with dirt, blood, and dust. Hopefully he would have a few peaceful days, and this suit would remain clean. Straightening out his coat sleeves, Sheriff Black noticed that the suit hung loosely about his frame. It had fit perfectly the last time he had worn it, and when he glanced in the mirror, he saw why that had changed. The Sheriff had always been lean, but his cheeks had hollowed out, giving him a gaunt appearance. Running Brook has said that his body had to facilitate his healing, but he hadn't mentioned that he would lose weight in the process. He scowled at his reflection before turning away. At least he was healed. Being injured had frustrated him, but he could move about freely once again. He could always gain the weight back by eating a few extra helpings of Rebecca's cooking as soon as she was well.

He pulled the brim of his hat downward and left the room, clutching the iron key that Jack had given him. As he unlocked her door, Roland tried to harden his nerves. Seeing her so lifeless had crushed his spirits before, but he had to remain strong while she was injured. Worry for her, however, gnawed at his heart as he opened the door and gazed upon her pale body. She lay on her back, wearing only her shift and not moving except for the slow rising and falling of her chest. It was hard to believe that anything was wrong with her. She seemed to be sleeping peacefully, but Roland knew that it would be quite a while before she opened her eyes again. Quietly closing the door behind him, Roland carefully sat upon the edge of her bed and took one of her hands in his own. It felt cold in his grasp, and he had to look closely at her chest to make sure she was still breathing. "Rebecca, it's me, Roland," he whispered softly and brushed a lock of hair off her forehead gently with his other hand.

Roland felt a tear form in one of his eyes, and he blinked angrily, turning his head away from her to collect himself. He hadn't cried since he found his family dead during the Civil War and had sworn that he'd never cry again. For thirty years, he had kept that promise, but seeing Rebecca so helpless was tearing him apart. Forcing himself to gaze at her once again, Roland caressed her cheek with a finger. "Rebecca, don't worry. I'll get you out of this, I swear. There are people on the way right now, and I'm going to find whoever killed Bryant. I promise I won't rest until you're awake again. I love you." He bent over and placed a single kiss upon her lips and rose to his feet. Roland wiped away the tears that had collected in his eyes and flicked his fingers angrily at the floor. It wasn't right for her to be like this. She had never hurt anybody. If anyone should be laying on that bed helplessly, it was him. But complaining about it wasn't going to help matters. "I love you, Rebecca White," Roland whispered once more and left the room before he broke down completely.

He stood in the hallway and leaned against the door for a moment as he fought off the tears that wanted to spill from his eyes. *You have to be strong*, Roland told himself. Rebecca couldn't afford for him to fall to pieces. He needed to start searching for Bryant's killer again. The trail had grown cold after six months, but he had promised that he would do everything in his power to help her. If he had to kill someone himself to find out what had occurred the night Bryant was murdered, he was prepared to do so. He might have duties as Sheriff, but Rebecca's safety came first. Blinking a few more times to clear the tears from his eyes, Roland straightened his hat and put on a grim face as he marched downstairs.

There was a lively crowd in The Last Frontier that Monday evening. A silence settled over the customers as all heads turned to stare at him. Roland saw Jack sitting at the bar next to George Wright, and forcing his face into a smile, the Sheriff casually strolled over to join them, nodding his head to people as he passed them by. Socializing was the last thing Roland wanted to do. Rebecca was foremost on his mind, but he needed to put to rest any fears the people of New Haven had about the Cheyenne. He wouldn't be able to spend time helping Rebecca if a war broke out with their Indian neighbors.

"George," Roland greeted the saloon owner as he sat on a barstool and joined them. Even though his spirits were dragging horribly, he forced his voice to sound cheerful as if he didn't have a care in the world.

The saloon owner blinked in astonishment then his chubby face shifted into a smile as well. "Sheriff, it's good to see you. I must say you look a lot better than you did Friday. If you'll forgive me, you looked real bad."

The Sheriff tipped his head back, laughed, and clapped George on the shoulder. "Yeah, I guess I did. Nothing like a few days of rest to heal a few wounds, eh?"

"I guess so. I'm just glad you're okay. Everyone was pretty worried about you. Especially after that mess with the Cheyenne."

The people close enough to hear their conversation ceased talking and looked their way. Roland was immediately aware of their eyes and made sure they got the right impression of the situation. "Don't worry about me. I've never felt better. I'm still a little tired, but I feel fine. I was pretty lucky. Rebecca had a fainting spell the other night when we went out to her house, and I was too weak to ride back to town for help. Luckily a few Cheyenne were hunting in the area and helped us out. God knows what would have happened if they hadn't. I guess somebody would have dropped by sooner or later, but you never know. Hey, Edmund, can I get a shot of whiskey?" Roland casually called out to the bartender.

Edmund nodded and adroitly poured him a full shot glass. Then he slid the glass across the bar into Roland's waiting hand.

He probably shouldn't have had any alcohol that night. Roland was exhausted from Running Brook's healing, but he felt that he had earned the right to a good stiff shot of alcohol. A numbing warmness settled over him as he belted it down, and he sucked in a breath through his teeth before exhaling in satisfaction. *I needed that.* "So, George, how's business been the last few days?"

"It's been good, Sheriff. Real good. After the Mayor announced that magician from Paris was coming for the Fourth of July, everyone in town felt like celebrating." George droned on and on about how great the Fourth of July celebration would be that year, completely forgetting about the entire Cheyenne event, and that's exactly what Sheriff Black wanted. He knew he could go out of his way to deny the incident, but people would always wonder if he was telling the truth or simply trying to cover something up to avoid trouble. By treating it as something trivial, the Sheriff put their worries to rest without vigorously having to defend the Cheyenne.

Over the next hour, Sheriff Black made his way around the saloon, stopping to talk with nearly everyone there. The Cheyenne were on many people's minds, but after fifteen minutes, the word had spread within The Last Frontier that the Cheyenne were nothing to worry about. While Roland was glad that he was allaying everyone's fears, the talk soon turned to his engagement to Rebecca. He had always thought that rumors traveled fast in New Haven, but he was amazed that his engagement was such common knowledge. Jack and Reverend Thatcher were the only two people he had told about it, and he knew that his deputy would have kept his mouth shut. Unfortunately Reverend Thatcher loved to talk, and he had probably mentioned Roland's request for a marriage as well as his failure to show up with Rebecca two nights ago.

Normally Roland would have loved to talk about her, but he found the subject painful with her laying unconscious upstairs. Yet he politely chatted with patrons about Rebecca, his engagement, or whatever else they wanted to discuss. He was trying to deflect any suspicion pointed towards the Cheyenne, and the Sheriff knew he wouldn't accomplish that goal if he was secretive or morose. And so he kept his face locked into the same nonchalant smile and tried to appear optimistic as he talked away and waited for *The New Haven Gazette's* editor to arrive at the saloon.

He was in the middle of defending the end of his notorious bachelorhood for the seventh or eighth time that evening when Jack finally caught his attention and motioned him over. "Excuse me," Roland politely dismissed the men he was talking to and made his way across the tavern. "What is it, Jack? Is he here?" He hated having to play all nice and unconcerned for the saloon patrons, and he was ready to take out his frustrations on Matthew for making him do it. Sheriff Black almost pitied the editor. He had built up quite a bit of anger over the last four days, and he was finally going to unleash it on someone.

"Yeah, William just got back. I thought you might like to question him outside, away from everyone. Good job, by the way. I think everyone in this place has forgotten the Cheyenne. There's no sense in raising their curiosity by yelling at Matthew in front of them. I take it you do plan to yell at him?" His deputy arched an eyebrow inquisitively.

Damn straight, Roland thought to himself. "I'm going to make him sorry he ever printed that Goddamn article, and I'm making damn sure he prints one tomorrow that clears the Cheyenne of any wrongdoing. I think I'll take you up on that suggestion, though. Are they right outside?" Sheriff Black cracked his knuckles in anticipation.

"No, I told William to take him over to the station house. Nobody'll hear you over there."

"Good idea. You stay here and watch the place while I have a word with our favorite editor." People nodded their heads politely to Sheriff Black as he stalked out of the saloon, but he barely noticed them. Roland intended to make sure that Matthew never published such an unfounded article again, and more importantly, he was going to find out why he had linked the Cheyenne attack to Bryant's murder. If Matthew had any knowledge of the crime, Roland was going to drag every scrap of information out of him.

The night air was still warm, and Roland fervently wished the summer heat would lessen sometime soon. That, however, was low on his list of concerns. He crossed the street to the station house with a bounce to his step that he hadn't had in days and opened the door. Roland smiled when he saw William and Robert chatting with Matthew Brady. All three looked up at the Sheriff as he entered and shut the door behind him. "Good evening, gentlemen."

The two deputies tipped their hats politely, and Matthew had a curious expression on his face. "Sheriff, I heard you wanted to talk to me."

"Yes, I do." Sheriff Black grinned a predatory smile and took a seat. "William, Robert, why don't you two wait for me over in The Frontier while I talk with our editor here?"

Robert gave him an odd look. "Uh, Sheriff. I'm supposed to be manning the station house. I thought you didn't ever want me to ever leave while I'm on duty."

Sheriff Black barely heard him. "Don't worry about that. I'll be here, and I'll come get you when I'm finished. Go on, everything's under control."

"All right. We'll see you over there then," Robert replied and quietly left the station house with William right behind him.

"All alone at last. How are you this evening, Matthew?"

Matthew had watched the deputies leave with a nervous expression, and he appeared to be uncomfortable alone in the station house with Roland. The editor was a thin man in his mid-thirties with a pair of thick eyeglasses and thinning brown hair. Matthew had founded *The New Haven Gazette* and had served as the editor and sole writer for over a year, but when the newspaper had grown into a daily publication, he had hired a pair of additional writers. "I'm fine. What's this about, Roland?" Sheriff Black didn't answer and stared at him with a feral grin, waiting patiently. Matthew shifted nervously in his chair as the pause grew before he cleared his throat. "What's this about, Sheriff?"

Sheriff Black clapped his hands together once then folded them and placed them under his chin. "Much better, Matthew. I always said you were a bright man, but I can't figure out why you printed that story this afternoon. I'm sure you had a pretty good reason for it."

Matthew held up his hands defensively. "Come on, Sheriff. I had witnesses that saw the whole thing. I was just reporting the news."

"Why didn't you wait to ask me what had happened or ask Jack? Either of us could have told you the truth. And what's this about an investigation into '*Cheyenne involvement*' with Bryant White's murder?" Sheriff Black placed a sarcastic emphasis on the editor's own words.

"Oh, that. You know how newspapers are. I just guessed that you would be investigating them. It seemed pretty logical." Matthew laughed nervously at the incident.

"Is that so? Because it doesn't seem too Goddamn logical to me. The Cheyenne were helping me and Rebecca, and I'm pretty sure a Dark Rider killed Bryant." He leaned forward and stared at Matthew as he awaited his response.

144

The editor scooted back in his chair without thinking and stared worriedly at Sheriff Black. He had never had any problems with the Sheriff and generally discounted all the rumors that were circulating about him. But alone with Sheriff Black in the station house, thoughts of all those rumors were floating through his head, and he didn't want to anger a man who had reportedly killed over a hundred people. "The Riders are old news. Nobody cares about them, but people still worry about those savages, even though they don't talk about it much."

Sheriff Black casually unfolded his hands then brushed his fingernails on his coat. He looked at them critically for a moment then exhaled upon them before returning his gaze to Matthew. "I really don't give a damn if the Riders are old news. You're going to print an article tomorrow clearing the Cheyenne of this entire thing. You make sure you write that Running Brook helped both me and Rebecca. I don't need everyone taking out their guns and heading into the forest to drive the Cheyenne out."

Matthew's expression changed instantly from timidness to outrage. "You can't do that! *The Gazette* is mine, and I'll print whatever I want to. I'll never print an article defending those savages. We'll all be a lot safer if they move somewhere else."

Shaking his head in resignation, Sheriff Black slowly drew one of his pistols and placed it on his lap, never taking his eyes off Matthew. *Have it your way,* he thought to himself. Roland idly stroked its metal surface as the blood slowly drained from the editor's face. "I don't think you heard me, Matthew. Let's try this one more time. You're going to print a story tomorrow that clears the Cheyenne."

A bead of sweat trickled down the side of Matthew's face, and he took a deep gulp. "You won't shoot me. Everyone will know you did it," he stammered desperately.

"All I have to do is say you attacked me. Who do you think people will believe? Now, this is the last time I'm going to ask so think *real* carefully. Are you going to print that story tomorrow or not?"

"Okay, I'll print the article, now will you put the gun away?" Matthew's voice rose with fear.

"Not just yet, Matthew. I have a few more questions I want to ask you first, and I want you to be *very* honest with me. I've had a really bad week, and I'm sure you don't want to upset me. Do you?" Sheriff Black winked and leaned back casually. He had found over the years that people were more terrified when he drew a gun and acted as if nothing was out of the ordinary.

"No, Sheriff. Oh God, please don't kill me."

"Just answer my questions, and you don't have anything to worry about. I'm curious why you only printed one story blaming the Riders for Bryant

White's death. Everyone in town thinks they killed him, but you blamed the Cheyenne in your article. I want to know why."

Matthew looked at him with a stricken expression his face. "If I tell you that, I'm a dead man."

Sheriff Black smiled nonchalantly and pointed his gun at the blubbering editor. "You're a dead man if you don't." The editor jumped as the Sheriff cocked the gun. Roland felt a momentary pang of guilt, but it didn't last long. He was terrifying Matthew for Rebecca, and he would take on any amount of guilt, pain, or suffering if it helped her.

"Okay, I'll tell you. Just don't shoot me." Matthew paused to inhale deeply. "Alvin paid me to do it and said if I ever printed another article blaming them, Carlos would kill me. Oh God, please don't tell anybody. Alvin said I was dead if I ever told anybody about it."

"Relax, Matthew. We're almost through, and don't worry, this is just between you and me. Nobody else is going to hear about this conversation. One last question. Do you know who killed Bryant White?" He carefully watched the sniffling editor to see if he was telling the truth.

"Alvin didn't say, but I think it was a Dark Rider. I don't know which one, but I'm pretty sure it was one of them. Is that it? Can I go now? Please, Sheriff, I promise I'll print that article tomorrow, and I won't tell anybody about this. "

"Get out of here. I'll read *The Gazette* tomorrow afternoon, and I'd better see that article. If I don't, we'll have another conversation, and I don't think you'll like that," Roland told him grimly, but his heart wasn't in it. *Damn.* He had hoped to gain some insight into the identity of Bryant's killer, but he was no closer than the morning after Bryant was killed.

"Yes, Sheriff. I promise, I'll write it immediately," the editor said and cautiously got to his feet. When Sheriff Black didn't make a move, he shuffled to the door, never turning his back to the Sheriff. He reached behind him to open the door and left the station house.

Roland watched Matthew flee into the street then leaned back and considered what he knew about the circumstances surrounding Bryant's death. Bryant had been out gambling that night and had never returned home. Witnesses had placed him at The Snake playing cards with Mad Dog, Wild Carl, and Curly, but eight other Dark Riders had been in town that evening. Alvin even disappeared for a while the next day as he helped the Riders put together an alibi and bribed Matthew to cease articles laying blame at the Riders' feet. Parts of a train shipment had just turned up missing, and Roland suspected the Dark Riders with Bryant's aid. If that was the case, the Riders had no cause to be angry with him. Bryant had just helped them with a robbery. It didn't make any sense. The few clues Roland had did nothing to shed light on the killer's identity. *Somebody had to know who did it,* Roland thought in frustration.

His eyes opened wide as he reconsidered his last thought. Surely, all of the Dark Riders and Alvin knew who was the guilty man, and if he could drag the truth out of one of them, he could apprehend the culprit. He would have to wait until the following day before the Riders returned to town, but then he intended to drag the truth out of them even if he had to attack all twenty-two of them single-handedly. Roland stood up and nodded in satisfaction. Rebecca was still asleep, but he had finally stumbled upon a way to help her. *The Gazette* was even going to clear the Cheyenne of any wrongdoing. Roland's lopsided grin settled into place as he walked across the street feeling victorious.

The saloon had grown busier while the Sheriff was away, and he knew the crowds would swell even larger as the night progressed. Jack, Robert, and William sat at a table chatting quietly when Roland stepped through the door. They turned in his direction and waved him over. Several newcomers asked him for an account of the previous night, but he dismissed them with a casual smile as he headed towards the three deputies.

"I hope you scared that son of a bitch good after all the trouble he's caused." Jack grinned as the Sheriff pulled up a chair to their table.

Roland cracked his knuckles. "He's going to print a story tomorrow clearing the Cheyenne, and I don't think he'll be writing anymore stories that would upset me anytime soon." He leaned back in his chair and spread his arms wide as he yawned loudly. Roland was glad he had been able to get up and move around, but he was still suffering lingering exhaustion from Running Brook's healing. It was starting to catch up with him, and as much as he wanted to stay downstairs in the saloon for a while, the Sheriff knew it was time he sought his bed.

"Oh come on, Sheriff. Tell us what happened before I go back to the station house," Robert begged. "That little bastard looked scared to death when he saw us walking out of there. I almost felt sorry for him." Robert was a bald-headed man in his mid-thirties with a crooked nose. He had broken it a long time ago, but it had never healed properly, leaving him with a permanent reminder of the incident. Robert had been a fairly excitable youth, and his enthusiasm had never dwindled. That enthusiasm had led him to New Haven and into Roland's service as a deputy.

The Sheriff held up a hand to silence them all. "Listen, I promised him I wouldn't ever talk about it, and I know he won't talk about it either. So let's just leave it at that." He arched an eyebrow and stared at each of them in turn so they got the point. Jack snorted in disdain, although the other two gave their assurances the matter was closed. He expected that from Jack and was sure the deputy would pester him with questions about the encounter later on. "Good. Robert, get back over to the station house. I want somebody there around the clock, especially with all this fuss over the Cheyenne. I don't think anything else will happen tonight, but you never know. Jack, who's riding patrol tonight?"

Jack looked up at the ceiling for a moment and considered the question before returning his gaze to Sheriff Black. "Ben, Morgan, and Wade."

"Good, everything's pretty well covered. Hopefully we'll have a quiet night. God knows, we all need it. When Carlos and his boys ride into town tomorrow, I'm sure we'll need all the rest we can get."

"You're not expecting trouble from them, are you? They should be settled down after the other night," Robert questioned.

"No, I expect them to act tough. Carlos doesn't like to lose face, and that's what's happened. He has a reputation to maintain if he wants people to be afraid of him. I don't think he'll pull another stunt like he did the other night, but we should all be ready for it just in case. Now get back over to the station house. I don't want anybody to go there and find it empty."

"Yes, Sheriff," Robert tipped his hat and left the saloon.

Sheriff Black talked with William and Jack for another five minutes. Their conversation shifted to the Dark Riders after William had expressed his astonishment over Roland's engagement. There were too many women in the world for William ever to consider settling down with one for the rest of his life. From time to time, Jack got that inquisitive look on his face, and Roland knew that the deputy was dying to question him about his encounter with Matthew. It was only a matter of time before Jack started asking questions, and Roland really didn't want to discuss it in front of anyone else. He knew that sooner or later he would have to tell Jack just to get him off his back. "Hey, William, I think Heather's staring at you." He jerked his head in the direction of Madam Sherry's strumpet and waited for the inevitable.

William glanced lecherously at H. "Is that so? Well, I guess I'll have to go talk to her then. If you gentlemen will excuse me, I have some business to attend to." He winked at Jack and the Sheriff, then sauntered over to banter with her.

Jack rolled his eyes in amusement. "God, I like that boy, but he chases after anything in a dress."

Roland chuckled as he watched the deputy strike up a conversation with Heather. "Yeah, but we all have our vices. It's better than some others I could think of."

"That's true, but why did you send him over there? Did you want to discuss something?"

"Not really, but I figured you would ask me about Matthew sooner or later, and William doesn't need to hear that story."

"Why, Roland, what makes you say that?" Jack asked facetiously.

148

"Because I know you. That's why. You always have to know everything, but that's my fault. I should have put you in your place a long time ago." Roland shook his head ruefully.

"You trust me. That's because I'm smarter than the rest of these young 'uns, with the exception of Morgan of course." He grinned impudently at the Sheriff. "Now, why don't you tell me what happened over there with our favorite newspaper writer."

"There's really not much to tell. I told him I was upset over the article and wanted him to print one that cleared Running Brook and his people. He started acting all cocky, so I drew one of my pistols and—"

"You did what?" Jack cut him off loudly, and several people turned in their direction. The deputy glared back at them until everyone turned around and minded their own business. "Blazes, Roland, if he prints that you pulled a gun on him, Alvin will start telling people that you're conspiring with the Cheyenne. You and I know it's not true, but a lot of people will believe it. That weasel isn't good for much, but Alvin knows how to make the people of this town believe every word he says."

"Don't worry about Matthew. He's too scared of me to breathe a word of what happened tonight. I told him I'd kill him if he did." Jack sputtered in anger, but Roland interrupted him before he could start a diatribe. "And don't worry about Alvin. He's a Goddamn snake, but I've known him a long time. He won't do anything that might get me fired as Sheriff. New Haven's a special town, and I'm one of the few men who can help preserve it. By the way, you'll never guess what Matthew told me tonight."

Jack exhaled slowly and looked at Roland with disgust. "What?" He asked in a resigned tone. He wasn't sure that he wanted to know what else Roland had done in the station house. Sometimes Roland had a knack for causing trouble.

"Calm down, Jack. Sometimes you act like an old woman. Matthew told me Alvin paid him a good bit of money not to print any more articles blaming the Riders for Bryant's death. Alvin also told him Carlos would kill him if he ever mentioned their conversation. I'd say that points the finger at the Riders. Wouldn't you?"

"We already know the Riders killed him, Roland. We've known that since the day it happened, but we still don't know which one did it. What were you planning on doing? Arresting them all?" With the way Roland had been acting lately, Jack wasn't quite sure what Roland would do.

"Of course not. I'm not stupid." He wasn't about to tell Jack that he had contemplated the thought very seriously. "I'm just curious who you think did it. I'm not arresting anyone until I can prove it, so calm down."

"I'm calm. You've just been acting strangely lately, and I could see you trying to take on all twenty-two Riders to get the guilty man. Hell, I don't

149

have a clue who it could be. Maybe it's Carlos or Curly or even Mad Dog if he ever sobered up long enough to kill anyone. It could even be Alvin for all I know. Damn, why do you even care? I know he was married to Rebecca, but why don't you just let it die? You two can get married and forget all about him. The trail's too cold to ever catch the killer now. It's been six months, Roland, and nobody even cares anymore. Bryant was a two-bit thief who helped the Riders, and the world's a better place without him."

"Yeah, I know that, but I was just—" Roland broke off as Ben burst through the saloon door. Sweat drenched Ben's clothes, and he looked as if he had just sprinted across the entire town. The deputy looked about the room desperately before his eyes fell upon the Sheriff and Jack. "What the hell?" Roland muttered as The Last Frontier became completely silent.

"Sheriff, hurry, we've got trouble," Ben shouted and waved him towards the door.

"Blazes," Sheriff Black swore and rose to his feet, patting his holstered guns once reassuringly before rushing to the deputy. Jack was right behind him, and even William untangled himself from Heather to join them.

"What's going on out there?" Someone from the saloon shouted, but Roland ignored the question and pushed Ben outside with his other two deputies close behind.

"What the hell's going on, Ben?"

"There's a whole bunch of people about to ride off and attack the Cheyenne," Ben panted.

"Goddamn it. Where are they?" Sheriff Black spat on the ground. It looked like he might just have to use one of his guns that night after all.

"They're over by The Snake. We'd better hurry. Paul Henderson's leading them up, and they sound real angry." Ben bent over and put his hands on his knees, inhaling deeply to catch his breath.

"Let's go. Now!" Sheriff Black barked and pointed at the five horses that were tethered in front of the station house. William, Jack, and the Sheriff rushed across the street and began to untie the horses from the tethering post, while Ben held a hand to his side and ambled behind them. The two deputies quickly jumped into the saddles, but Sheriff Black paused before climbing into the saddle. "Are they in front of The Snake?" He shouted at Ben as the panting deputy finally caught up to them.

"Yeah. Right where the Riders were the other night," he wheezed.

"Get Robert and meet us over there," Roland ordered then forced his tired body to climb onto his horse. He had been ready to retire just a few minutes ago, but adrenaline had taken over, giving him a much-needed boost of energy. "Let's go!" Sheriff Black shouted and spurred his horse into a gallop.

A crowd had walked out of The Last Frontier to watch in amazement as their Sheriff and two deputies galloped around the corner. Roland held on tightly to the reins and pressed his legs firmly against the horse's side, swearing that if Matthew didn't print that article the next day, he would make it his duty to shoot him. Sheriff Black just hoped that the mob was still in front of The Snake and hadn't left already. His fears were put to the rest as they caught sight of the saloon and the crowd that had gathered in front of it. He pulled his horse to a halt to survey the scene before proceeding any further, and the two deputies stopped with him.

"Sweet Mary, mother of Jesus," William whispered in disbelief over the bedlam.

"Exactly," Sheriff Black muttered grimly and spurred his horse forward.

Just over seventy people had gathered in front of The Rattlesnake saloon, and nearly all of them carried guns or rifles. There were even women in the crowd. Sheriff Black wasn't surprised to see that Paul Henderson was the one stirring them up. Paul was one of the most vocal opponents of the Cheyenne, and he continuously unleashed his opinion on anyone foolish enough to listen. Most of the time, the people of New Haven didn't pay him any attention, but after the past few days, public sentiment had turned against the neighboring Indians, making people more susceptible to his diatribes.

Morgan and Wade were also in the crowd and saw the three men approach, but most of the crowd was oblivious to their arrival as they listened to Paul preach. "What else do you need to happen? They've already killed one good man and nearly killed our good Sheriff and an innocent woman. Will it be one of our children next? Perhaps one of your daughters or sons. I say we drive the savages out once and for all," Paul shouted over the crowd, and he was rewarded with a loud burst of applause and shouts of approval.

Sheriff Black watched the crowd with disgust. He had wondered why Morgan and the rest of the deputies hadn't dispersed the crowd, but he could see the reason now. Morgan would have been a fool to draw a gun in such a hostile environment for fear of getting shot, but the Sheriff didn't feel fear. He only felt outrage that the Cheyenne could be so easily vilified by a bogus article and a few rumors. He casually drew one of his pistols and fired it into the air. Heads whipped around to look at the cause of the shot, and Jack, William, Morgan, and Wade drew their own guns as they watched their Sheriff. He was about to speak when Paul broke the momentary silence.

"You see, even Sheriff Black and his men will ride with us to drive the filthy savages away from this decent town. We can't be defeated. Who is with me?" Paul's eyes were wide with an almost fanatic glow.

Roland decided to stop him from speaking before he got even more carried away. He fired his gun into the air again and glared at Paul with contempt. "Paul, you shut your Goddamn mouth!" Sheriff Black shouted over the suddenly quiet gathering. "Nobody is attacking the Cheyenne. Do you people hear me? I said *nobody*. I wasn't attacked by the Cheyenne, and neither was Rebecca.

151

She fell ill two nights ago, and their Chief healed her. Sullivan didn't do anything for us until we returned to town, and the only reason we did so was because of the Cheyenne. They're not to blame for anything. They were only trying to help, and I give my thanks to their people. I swear if any of you so much as tries to attack a single Indian, I will personally shoot you. I hope all of you heard, because the next time I have to break up one of these little gatherings, I'm going to be *really angry*." He cast his glare over the crowd and was pleased to see that many had looked down at the ground with guilt. Many of them might still think the Cheyenne should be driven away, but at least they wouldn't try anything that night. "Good, now all of you go about your business." He turned his angry stare upon Paul and set his jaw. "Paul, you go home. If I see you anywhere after five minutes, I'm going to throw you in jail for a week."

He continued to sit on his horse and glare at the crowd as they quickly dispersed. Paul looked on the verge of defying him, but he saw that the mood of the gathering had shifted and wisely left the area before Sheriff Black made good on his promise.

"Here comes the rest of the cavalry," Jack commented dryly, and Sheriff Black turned his head to see Robert and Ben riding towards them.

"Poor bastards, they missed out on all the excitement." Roland's face shifted into a tight grin, but he set his jaw angrily as he spotted Alvin in the departing crowd. "Jack, William, you wait here. I need to talk to that Goddamn snake." He didn't even bother to see if they obeyed his order. The anger inside of him began to boil as he approached the mayor, and he had an open look of hostility on his face when he reached Alvin. At last, he had somebody who probably knew the identity of Bryant White's killer, and he meant to pull the truth out of the mayor with whatever force was needed.

"Roland, good show. I was going to try and disperse them myself, but I see you beat me to it. They're so easy to manipulate." Alvin wore his customary pressed suit and had assumed his public face, smiling broadly as if he and the Sheriff were the best of friends.

Roland's anger faded a bit as the mayor greeted him. He had thought Alvin was involved with the crowd, but it appeared as if they were both on the same side for once. "You didn't have anything to do with this?" He asked just to be sure.

The mayor tipped his head back and laughed. "Roland, you know me better than that. Why would I want the Indians attacked? The government would send troops here, and neither of us wants their presence. That would bring an end to everything you and I have worked for."

Roland took a deep breath to calm down. "You're right. I talked to Matthew Brady tonight, and he's going to print a story that clears them of any wrongdoing. This should be the last incident we have over the Cheyenne for a while."

"That's good to hear. You don't need any more problems with Carlos and his men returning tomorrow. How do you feel? You look a hell of a lot better than you did the other night."

"I'm fine, Alvin. You just tell Carlos he'd better not have a repeat performance of the other night. I'm in a really bad mood, and I don't think any of you want to push me right now."

Alvin laughed merrily again and looked at the Sheriff with a knowing grin. "Come on, Roland. We both know you won't risk bloodshed over the Riders. You're just angry again. You'll calm down tomorrow. I wouldn't worry, though. I talked to Carlos, and he won't pull another stunt like that. They'll just be loud and threatening, but nobody will draw a gun or they'll have to answer to me. Does that make you happy?"

"You can laugh, but I'm warning you. If any of the Riders draw a gun tomorrow night, I'll shoot first and ask questions later. Don't try my patience." He wanted to ask Alvin about the Riders' role in Bryant's murder, but there were too many people within earshot. There would be plenty of time to question Alvin later when they were alone and couldn't be overheard, and he thought the mayor might not like his method of finding the truth. Matthew had responded well to threats, and he was anxious to see what Alvin would do under the same circumstances.

"Whatever you say. We'll see how you feel tomorrow," Alvin mocked but his face had tightened into a feral grin that showed his true feelings.

Roland spat on the ground, and the mayor had to jump backwards to avoid having his boots struck. He looked up furiously at the Sheriff, and Roland cocked one of his lopsided smiles. "You'd better pray that they don't try a thing, or you'll see how I Goddamn feel tomorrow." Then he turned his horse around and rode back to The Last Frontier to collect on some much deserved rest.

153

Chapter Eight

Roland awakened shortly before dawn on Tuesday morning feeling more refreshed than he had since the ordeal at Rebecca's house had begun. His dreams had been plagued by visions of Rebecca locked in a sphere of light and a dark figure who held it in his grasp. Those dreams still made him shiver, but physically Roland felt better than he could remember. A slight trace of exhaustion still lingered in his body, but it didn't slow him down as he rose out of bed. It was comforting to see the sun rise again. He still couldn't believe that he had slept for nearly two days. When he'd turned in the night before, Roland had been slightly worried that he would sleep through all of Tuesday as well. With the Dark Riders returning that evening, there was too much happening that evening to sleep through the entire day.

He stretched his arms to get blood circulating through his limbs then began dressing. The clothes he had worn the night before were still the only ones he had at The Frontier, but he had managed not to destroy those garments as he had done with his last two suits. He donned the black coat, slacks, and vest then placed his black hat upon his head, straightening it in the mirror. Stubble darkened his face, but his razor lay by the water basin at his house. Sheriff Black rubbed a hand over the prickly growth and decided he could live with it for another day. It gave him a more rugged appearance, and that wouldn't hurt when Carlos and his men returned. Sheriff Black strapped on his gunbelt and donned his silver medal of office, then took one last look in the mirror before leaving the room.

Roland had a lot he wanted to do that morning, but first he wanted to look in on Rebecca. He took a deep breath before unlocking her door and entering the room. The sight of her helpless on the bed tore at his heart. Her skin was paler than the day before, and her hair hung limply around her shoulders. Sullivan had provided a nurse to look after Rebecca twice a day. The nurse gave her chicken broth and cleaned her, but Rebecca's enforced sleep was obviously beginning to take a toll. His mouth curled into a bitter smile as he sat on the edge of the bed and took her cold hand in his. "Good morning, Rebecca. Last night was pretty wild." Roland proceeded to tell her about the previous night's engagement as if they were both sitting at a table, eating one of her delicious meals. He gently caressed her forehead with a callused knuckle, fighting to keep back the tears that were welling up in his eyes. As much as it pained him to sit with her that morning, Roland made himself continue to tell his story. For all he knew, she could hear every word he said, and he wouldn't abandon her to complete silence while she lay there helpless.

"I didn't get to talk to Alvin last night about Bryant because there were too many people around. But I swear I'll talk with him tonight. I should see him later on with the Riders coming back to town. I'll talk to you later and tell you how everything went." He bent over and placed a kiss upon her lips. "I love you, Rebecca White," Roland whispered then left the room.

His face settled into a granite mask of anger as he stalked down the stairs. He wanted to focus all of his attention on helping her, but the events taking place in New Haven were conspiring to steal that time from him. First the mob last night and now the Dark Riders' imminent return demanded his attention, and as much as he wanted to ignore them, he was still the Sheriff and couldn't shirk his responsibilities. He had taken care of the Cheyenne problem. He swore he would do the same with the Riders, and as soon as he had the chance, he would question the mayor thoroughly over the Riders' part in Bryant's death. The Ghost Hunters might be able to help her, but they wouldn't arrive for another week. Roland wouldn't let her spend a needless day in her hellish prison if there was anything in his power to prevent it.

The saloon was empty that early in the morning, and Roland descended the staircase in absolute silence. He fished the key to the front door out of his coat pocket and stepped outside, squinting as the sun shone brightly. The air was still blazing hot, and he wondered if the temperature would ever lessen. Locking the door behind him, Roland walked across the street to the station house.

Phillip looked up from his book as Sheriff Black entered and pushed his glasses upward on his nose with his index finger. He sat behind the desk and gently laid the book down. "Morning, Sheriff. It's good to see you again. How are you feeling?"

"A lot better, Phillip," the Sheriff replied and took a seat in one of the wooden chairs. "Anything exciting happen after I went to sleep?"

"Naw. Things were pretty quiet after you scared everyone off last night." He grinned mischievously. "It's the most peace I've had in a long time. I read a whole book last night and started another one a few hours ago."

"I'm glad someone had a quiet evening," Roland commented dryly. Only Phillip would appreciate peace and quiet because it gave him more time to read. "You know that the Riders are coming back tonight?"

"Yeah, I reckon it'll get pretty noisy."

"That's my guess. Can you show up at six? I want everyone on duty. I don't think Carlos is stupid enough to cause any trouble, but it can't hurt to have everyone ready just in case. He's a lot less likely to try anything against nine armed men."

"Sure. I'll go to bed as soon as I'm off. Do you need me any earlier?"

"No. Carlos and his men won't even be out of bed until late afternoon, and they won't come to town until at least six or seven. It'll take 'em a few hours to get drunk, and that's when I want everyone here."

"Sounds good to me. Are you taking over the watch?"

"Yeah, I'm feeling better. Go home and rest, Phillip. You just might need that sleep later tonight," Roland told his deputy seriously. He hoped that things would be peaceful that evening, but he wasn't trusting his luck too much anymore. If there was trouble that night, Roland wanted everybody ready for it.

Phillip pushed his glasses up and nodded. "I'll do that, Sheriff. See you at six," he commented and walked into the brutal summer heat.

Left alone, Roland contemplated what he would do about Rebecca, the Dark Riders, and Alvin. He hated to see her so lifeless, and he wanted to do anything possible to rescue her. Roland intended to question Alvin quite extensively over the Dark Riders' involvement in Bryant's murder, but he didn't know how effective that would be. Even if he learned who killed Bryant, arresting the guilty man would be tantamount to declaring war on Carlos and his men. As tempting as it was to engage them in a fight, Roland was reluctant to provoke the Riders. There were twenty-two Dark Riders compared to his eight deputies, and any fight between the two would result in a large loss of lives. He was prepared to risk his own life to help Rebecca, but he couldn't ask the same of his men. *Damn,* Roland thought in frustration. All of his problems had become intertwined, and solving one problem only aggravated another.

Time passed by quickly as he thought of his dilemma, and he was surprised when Wade arrived to take over the station house. "Morning, Wade," the Sheriff greeted the deputy as he walked through the door.

Wade's blue eyes widened momentarily. "Sheriff, I didn't expect to see you here. How are you feeling?"

"I'm fine," he replied curtly and wondered if he would have to answer that question to every single person he met that day. "I want everyone to stay on duty late tonight since the Riders are coming back. That isn't a problem, is it?"

The young deputy grinned savagely as if he relished the idea of a confrontation. "Nope. I hope those bastards try something, and then we can teach them all a lesson."

Roland grinned right back at him and narrowed his eyebrows. Shooting a few of the troublesome Riders would probably brighten his mood. He wouldn't do it, but it was tempting nonetheless. "We'll see. I want everyone to leave them alone, but if they start something, I intend to make those sons of bitches very sorry."

Wade's eyes seemed to grow even brighter, and Roland knew he shouldn't encourage the deputy. That type of danger was the sole reason Wade had come to New Haven in the first place, and if he got himself in the mood to fight, Wade just might provoke the Dark Riders. "Sounds good. Are we meeting later on?"

"Yeah, we'll meet over here at six o'clock and talk about how we're going to handle them. It should be pretty slow today, especially after last night, but keep alert. I don't think the Riders will show up until after dark, but you never know." Roland stood up so Wade could take a seat behind the desk. "See you later." He tipped his hat then walked across the street to The Frontier.

When he opened the saloon door, he saw that George had emerged from his room upstairs and stood behind the bar. The saloon owner was busy as always, fastidiously cleaning the bar and anything else he could get his hands on. "Morning, George," Roland greeted him.

"Morning, Sheriff," George stopped his cleaning and took a seat. The two chatted for nearly an hour while they waited for the staff and customers to arrive that Tuesday morning. Roland wasn't in a talkative mood, but he forced himself to stay downstairs with George. Left to his own devices, Roland would have gone upstairs to sit with Rebecca, but he knew that would only enrage him and put him in a foul mood for the rest of the day. He needed a level head that afternoon if he wanted to deal with the Riders and Alvin. Otherwise, he just might ignore his conscience and provoke them, no matter the consequences.

By noon, the staff of The Last Frontier had arrived, and a few customers had filtered in as well. Jack showed up soon after, and George excused himself so Roland could talk privately with the deputy. "Morning," Roland greeted as Jack took a seat next to him at the bar.

"Morning, Roland. Feeling any better?"

"Yeah, I feel a lot better." Roland shook his head in amusement. "You'd be amazed how many people have asked me that already."

"At least they're not talking about the Cheyenne anymore."

"That's true. That son of a bitch had better print that story, though. I want to close this problem out for good. I don't want it creeping up again tonight when the Riders return."

"I wouldn't worry. It sounds like you scared him good. I just hope he doesn't write that you pulled a gun on him. That's all we need." Jack shot Roland a stern gaze.

Roland barked out a laugh. "Matthew won't say a Goddamn thing. He's too scared. Hell, he hasn't said anything about Alvin threatening him."

"I hope you're right, Roland. So how do you want to handle the Riders tonight?"

"I talked to Wade and Phillip this morning. They both said they'd meet over at the station house at six. It looks like we'll have everyone on duty except Simon, but I don't think he'd be any good in a fight with Sarah so close."

"Good. I hope we won't need anyone, but it can't hurt to be cautious."

"That's what I was thinking. I want to put you, Morgan, and Wade across the street from The Snake."

Jack looked at him strangely. "Not inside?"

"Naw. If I put you inside, it'll just piss off Carlos and the others. They'll be drunk, and there's no reason to provoke them. I *do* want someone nearby in case they get out of hand. I'll stay here with William, and the rest can ride patrol and stay close to The Snake. If they don't cause any trouble tonight, I don't want them to see a single deputy. I know Carlos, and if he sees any of us, he'll pick a fight."

"Sounds good to me. Should we just keep a normal schedule until six?"

"Yeah, there's no sense changing anything, but I do want Ben to keep an eye on the south side of town. If he sees any of the Riders coming early, I want to know about it within five minutes."

Jack stayed in The Frontier and kept Roland company for the remainder of the afternoon. Roland was glad he had his old friend to keep his mind from dwelling on Rebecca. A conversation with Alvin would have to wait until that evening, and Roland knew that if he had all afternoon to think about the situation, he would be worried sick.

People kept filtering into The Last Frontier as the day progressed. Simon showed up shortly after Jack. The straw-haired deputy joined their conversation, but he kept silent for the most part. He was an extremely quick gunman, but Simon wasn't the brightest person in the world. Simon did as he was told, and that was good enough for Roland. He didn't need sociable deputies; he needed dependable ones. A decent-sized crowd had assembled in the saloon by two o'clock when Sullivan arrived.

The doctor paused when he saw the Sheriff and walked over to their table. "Sheriff, I see you're up and about," he commented in the nasal tone that irritated Roland so much.

"Yeah, I woke up yesterday and feel fine. Are you here to look at Rebecca?"

"Yes, I am, but I have a few questions for you as well. I was—"

"Let's go take a look at Rebecca first, and I'll answer your questions. Okay?" Roland broke him off in a flat tone. He knew that when he spoke in that dangerous tone, people obeyed his orders instantly. It was just one of the perks of his reputed past.

Sullivan blinked once and acquiesced to Roland's demand. "Of course. Shall we go upstairs?"

"Yeah," Roland answered the doctor and rose to his feet. He tipped his hat to Jack and Simon. "I'll be back in a few minutes. Let's go, Doc." Roland walked ahead of the doctor so he couldn't be peppered with questions. He knew that Sullivan was curious about how his wounds had disappeared, and Roland didn't want to be questioned about it in front of Jack. The deputy was curious enough already about the events that had taken place at Rebecca's house, and Roland had no intention of rekindling any of that curiosity.

He used the iron key to unlock Rebecca's door and opened it for the doctor. "After you, Doc." Roland stepped back and allowed him to enter first.

Sullivan walked into the room and began to examine Rebecca. Once again, the sight of her lying so helpless on the bed tore at Roland's heart, and a smoldering anger over the whole predicament rose within him. As he examined Rebecca, Sullivan asked Roland questions about his vanished injuries. Roland just stared at the doctor with dangerous eyes. Sullivan looked up once at the fuming Sheriff and quickly resumed his examination in silence.

The whole examination only took a few minutes before the doctor finished. "Well, Sheriff, she still won't wake up. I'll make sure she gets water and broth in her system. I talked to Miss Higgins, and she said she could look on her twice a day. It'll cost extra, though."

"Fine," Roland answered and waved a hand negligently. He had enough money that he had saved over the years, and he wouldn't spare a penny to ensure that Rebecca was in the best possible health.

"I was also thinking about bleeding her."

The Sheriff's face grew even stonier as he listened to the doctor's prognosis. "No bleeding."

"But, Sheriff, it could help—"

"I said no bleeding," Roland cut him off in a tone that brooked no arguments.

"Fine," Sullivan threw his arms in the air in exasperation. "I'll give her some more water, but that's about all I can do. I'll go downstairs and get some."

Roland remained silent as Sullivan left the room to get water for Rebecca. She looked so frail to him. The Ghost Hunters might be coming in a week, but Roland wasn't sure that Rebecca would make it that long. She looked worse than when he had checked on her that morning. Faint, dark rings circled her eyes, and her cheeks seemed even more hollow than before. He decided he might just have to force the issue with the Dark Riders after all.

Sullivan returned shortly with a pitcher. He pulled a funnel out of his medicine bag and slowly poured water down Rebecca's throat. Roland watched for a minute then had to leave the room. Watching Rebecca have water forced down her throat sickened him. Only a week before she had been vibrant and full of charm, but she had been reduced to a lifeless shell that needed even its basic functions taken care of. Anger continued to well within him, and he descended the staircase with a furious expression on his face. Jack sat alone at a table, and Roland went to join him. "Where's Simon?"

"I sent him to pick up a copy of *The Gazette*."

"Good. I hope that son of a bitch printed the story or I'll hunt the bastard down and shoot him," Roland snapped.

"You're in a good mood. I take it Rebecca's still not awake." Jack looked at him with concern.

"No."

"Any sign she'll wake up?" The deputy asked hopefully.

"No. I don't want to talk about it anymore, Jack."

"You got it." Jack raised his hands peacefully. (Repetitive; we already know this!) They waited in silence for Simon's return. Sullivan came downstairs a short time later, but after one look at Roland's stormy face, he left the saloon without another word.

Simon returned a few minutes after Sullivan left, and the deputy immediately came to their table. "Here's the paper, Sheriff," he announced slowly and placed it on the table. Even Roland, despite his bad mood, couldn't help but smile when he saw the front page.

Cheyenne Cleared of Attack

The Cheyenne Indians did not attack Sheriff Black and Rebecca White Friday evening. A series of misunderstandings resulted in wrongful blame, and The New Haven Gazette wishes to apologize for the article. Sheriff Black personally vouched for their innocence.

According to the Sheriff, he and Miss White were injured following a fall from a horse. Several Indians were hunting in the area and stopped to render them aid. After tending their wounds, one of them rode into town to summon help for the wounded couple. This was the brave who was witnessed by Paul Henderson, but it appears that Mr. Henderson misinterpreted the events that transpired.

Also, the Indians are not under investigation for the murder of Bryant White. That heinous crime still is unsolved, and Sheriff Black has no new leads on the identity of the killer, although he is certain that Cheyenne Indians were not involved with the killing.

Again, The New Haven Gazette wishes to apologize for the article that was printed yesterday and regrets any trouble this may have caused the Cheyenne Indians. They do not mean us any harm, and no good would come out of attacking them, especially for an act they did not commit.

160

"Goddamn, Roland. You must have scared the living hell out of that boy. I can almost see him shaking in his boots right now. He's so full of himself." Jack slapped Roland's shoulder after he read the article.

"I guess I have a way with words." Roland grinned. The newspaper article had lightened his mood. He had hated to use such intimidation with Matthew, but he wasn't about to let a mob rise up against the Cheyenne. After breaking up the crowd the night before and *The Gazette's* apologetic article, Roland didn't foresee any more problems over the Indians. Now he could focus all of his attention on the Dark Riders' return and discovering the identity of Bryant's killer.

"Is it good?" Simon looked at Jack and Roland with a confused expression. The expecting father couldn't read a word to save his life.

"Sorry, Simon. Matthew apologized and completely cleared the Cheyenne of any wrongdoing. That should keep the Cheyenne off everyone's minds for a little while," Roland summarized the letter.

"Or until Paul gets over his fear of you. If I didn't know you so well, Roland, I could see why people are so afraid of you. You nearly had Paul pissin' in his britches last night." Jack slapped the table and chuckled.

"We'll see. Paul hates the Cheyenne, and I can't see him going too long without starting his preaching again. You can't really stop a man like that short of killing him. The only thing that worries me is when people start listening to him. As long as everyone thinks he's crazy, we have nothing to fear."

"Until tonight," Jack broke in and effectively killed the jocularity of their conversation.

"Yeah. Speaking of the Riders, Simon, I want you back on patrol. I don't expect the Riders until later, but you never know with Carlos. He might just ride into town early to piss me off. You got that?"

Simon considered the question carefully before slowly nodding his head once. "Yes, Sheriff. I'll go now." Simon tipped his hat and quietly left the table.

"He's nice enough, but sometimes Simon's a bit on the slow side." Jack smoothed down the tips of his mustache as he watched the slow-witted deputy leave the saloon.

"But he's quick with a pistol, and he keeps his temper in line," Sheriff Black instantly came to Simon's defense. None of his deputies was perfect, but he had taken his time when he picked them. Despite their flaws, he would confidently stand beside them and take on all twenty-two Dark Riders if he had to.

"I know. I was just teasing, Roland. Congratulations again on that article. I thought you were stupid to pull a gun on Matthew, but it looks like you made the right choice. The last thing we need is a mob ready to declare war on the Cheyenne."

Sheriff Black nodded grimly. "Why do you think I went to all the trouble? We're going to need all of our men ready tonight, not tied up with Paul and a bunch of drunk fools."

Jack looked at him seriously. "What do you think will happen tonight? Do you think Alvin can keep them out of any serious trouble?"

Running a hand across his stubbly cheeks, the Sheriff took a moment to answer. "I don't know. It all depends on how worked up Carlos gets. If he thinks we've hurt his pride too much, he might just make another scene. I hope Alvin talked to him and won't let him get out of hand, but you never know. This is a delicate little game the three of us have been playing for the last year, and it's only a matter of time until it blows up." A tiny part of him wished Carlos would try something stupid that night. It would give him a perfectly legitimate excuse to declare war on the Riders and to kill as many of them as he saw fit. Even if he didn't know exactly which of their number had murdered Bryant White, he was bound to get the guilty man if he shot them all.

"Let's hope it's not tonight. This last week's been a long one, and I just want some peace and quiet."

"I think we could all use some peace and quiet," Roland commented softly, but he wasn't referring to the Riders or Cheyenne. All he wanted was to awaken his beautiful fiancée and to marry her as he had intended. He quickly forced himself to think of something else. Every time he thought of her, Roland seemed to spiral downward into a black mood, and he wanted to keep his mind focused for the remainder of the day. It would do her no good if he got shot while his mind was elsewhere. There would be time after the Dark Riders left town.

Nearly an hour after he jubilantly read *The New Haven Gazette*, his quiet afternoon ended when Morgan escorted a young man into the saloon. Morgan had also fought in the Civil War and had roamed the West as a gunslinger. Like Roland, he had been drawn to New Haven for the atmosphere that came so close to the Wild West. He was nearly sixty years old with long white hair, but he was still quick with a gun and extremely intelligent. Besides Jack, he was the only deputy who ever questioned Roland's orders. The grizzled deputy had donned his stern gaze that he only wore when there was trouble about. Both Jack and Roland instantly caught his mood and slid hands down towards their holsters in case they were needed, carefully watching the pair approach.

The young man who walked in front of Morgan intrigued Roland. He was no more than a few years over twenty, and it looked as if he had grown a beard to make himself appear older. Both his beard and short curly hair were pitch black, and with his grey eyes, the young man reminded Roland quite a bit

162

of himself when he was that age. He wore a loose fitting brown suit and sauntered with an arrogant swagger to show he wasn't afraid of Morgan, Sheriff Black, or anyone else for that matter.

"I thought you might want to talk to this one, Sheriff. He just came into town and was looking to pick a fight. I figured you didn't want any wildcards floating around town with the Riders coming back," Morgan reported with his granite face locked into a severe expression.

Roland examined the young man for a moment. He was putting forth an air as if the entire conversation bored him, but Roland had been around long enough to detect nervousness under his front of bravado. "So what are you doing in New Haven—" Roland trailed his last few words off as he waited for the young man to supply his name.

"My name's Jimmy the Quick, and I'm just passing through town. That's all. If you're done, I'll just be on my way." Jimmy looked them over with disdain, although Roland knew that he was only trying to make a good impression. Once upon a time, Roland had been a youngster traveling the world and trying not to let anyone know how truly scared he was. The young man's answer, however, made him laugh, and even Morgan's face cracked into a smile. "What's so Goddamn funny?" Jimmy's eyes narrowed as he lowered his hand. The young man had a Colt .45 on each hip, and he held his hand poised just above one of them.

The smile instantly left Sheriff Black's face, and he looked at the young man with a dangerous expression. "I wouldn't try to draw that if I were you. I might look old, but I can still take you on the draw. And even if you get me, there are eight other deputies in this town. You try to draw a gun here, and I'll put you down. You understand that?"

"I'm not afraid of you, old man."

"You should be. I've been around a long time and survived a lot worse than you. Jack, Morgan, would you excuse us for a few minutes? I think I'll talk to this fearless gunslinger alone. I have a few things he might want to hear."

"You sure?" Jack kept a wary eye on Jimmy as the young man stood defiantly in front of them. A few patrons had turned their heads in the direction of their table as if they had noticed something out of the ordinary about Morgan's entry with the angry-looking stranger.

"Don't worry about me, Jack. I can handle this one. Just stay over at the bar. If there's any trouble, you'll be close enough."

"Sure, Roland, you're the boss," Jack replied and casually walked over to the bar, keeping an eye on the table.

"Do you need me anymore, Sheriff?" Morgan asked in his gravelly voice.

"No, I can take things from here. Thanks for bringing him by. I appreciate it."

"You're welcome." Morgan nodded once then marched out of The Frontier to continue his patrol.

Roland turned his attention back to the young man, who had taken a seat across the table. Jimmy looked around the saloon lazily with a bored expression, ignoring Sheriff Black. "By the way, the reason we were laughing is because we already have a 'Carlos the Quick' here in town. You might want to pick something a little more original."

A blush crept up the young man's cheeks, then he stared at Roland defiantly. "We'll just see how quick he is. I'd bet I'm a hell of a lot faster on the draw." Jimmy straightened his back, and his chest barreled outwards pugnaciously.

As much as Jimmy was trying to be obnoxious, Roland couldn't help but grin at him. In the past few days, it was one of the few things that had brought a smile to his face. He could almost look back in time at himself when he had just begun his travels through the West and see the spitting image of the young man sitting across the table. Roland had been cocky towards everyone, anxious to prove that he was man enough to survive on their turf. "You're pretty quick on the draw?"

"I'm the fastest you've ever seen, old man. I've killed plenty of men, and I can kill this Carlos just as easily."

"I've seen a lot of fast shots in my day, but I'm curious. How many men have you killed?"

Jimmy appeared flustered for a moment, and he glowered at Roland. "I've killed lots. Eleven was my last count."

"Eleven? That's quite a few. Who was the first person you killed?"

Once again, Jimmy paused for a moment and glared at Roland as if his questions were infuriating. "It was a gunslinger who got in my way. He thought he was quicker than me, so I proved him wrong. I shot him dead in the street."

"A duel then?" Roland arched an eyebrow.

"Yeah, it was a duel. We counted to ten, turned, and fired. He never even got a shot off. I shot him right through the heart and dropped him."

"So where was this duel of yours? I hear about most of the gunslingers that pass through this area, but I've never heard of you."

"It was down in Texas, and you've never heard of me 'cause anyone who crosses my path is six feet under."

"That's an interesting story, boy, but I've been in lots of duels and not a single one of them was like you said."

"Are you calling me a liar?" Jimmy's hands slowly balled up into fists, and he looked like he was ready to pull out his gun and test the Sheriff's speed on the draw.

"Listen, I was just like you a long time ago. When I first headed out West, I couldn't wait to notch my first kill, and I used to brag about things I hadn't done. I killed plenty of men during the War, but I hadn't ever killed anyone in a duel or a fight. Hell, I'd never even seen a duel. A word of advice: duels aren't nearly as fair as they're made out to be. There's no counting down from ten. There's no waiting to make sure the other man is ready. There's just two men drawing their guns and firing. Anyone who says otherwise hasn't seen a duel."

Jimmy's bravado seemed to leak out of him, and his shoulders hunched over as he stared down at the table. "I didn't know that."

"Not many people do until they've actually seen one, and there aren't too many duels these days. So where are you from?"

"Virginia."

Roland nodded and leaned back in his chair. It appeared the fight had gone out of the rambunctious young man, and he trusted that he could keep their conversation friendly. Roland actually liked Jimmy, but he didn't want the young man trying to prove his worth in New Haven. He could remember when he was young, and he didn't want a repeat performance with Jimmy. There was already enough trouble in New Haven without having a young gunslinger trying to put a notch on his gunbelt. "I was stationed in Virginia for a while during the war, but I'm from Mississippi. That was a long time ago, though. I've been traveling all over the West for the past thirty years until I settled down here. Any particular reason you came to New Haven?"

Jimmy looked up at him with an embarrassed expression. "I heard that this town was a lot like how the West used to be. Everywhere I've been so far, it's so crowded with settlers. I always wanted to try my luck with Billy the Kid, Wyatt Earp, or Doc Holliday. I practiced with a gun every day when I grew up, but then when I got out here, everything had changed."

Roland nodded in agreement. "The West isn't the same anymore. There aren't many places like New Haven around, but here's another word of advice: don't go looking to notch your first kill here. This town is a lot like the West used to be. We've got gambling and whores and even a good deal of fighting, but we don't have any gunfights. As soon as people start getting killed, we'll have the government in here trying to settle things down. I don't want any trouble from them. I just want to keep this town like it is. You're welcome to stay here as long as you want, but don't go causing any trouble."

"Is there anywhere you can test your skill anymore?" A wistful look crossed Jimmy's face, and Roland immediately felt sorry for him. The West's death had robbed Roland of his own way of life, but at least he had been able to live as a gunslinger for almost three decades. Jimmy would never know what it had been like to roam the land, free as a bird, with a gun at his side.

165

"I don't think so. The West dried up about five years ago. We all saw it coming, but we never thought it would actually happen. At first, it was just a few people who got arrested, but soon anybody dueling found himself at the end of a rope. Gambling died, and so did most of the bordellos. Pretty soon, there was nothing left. Those weren't fun years, but I found this place. It's not exactly the same as the West I grew up in, but it's as close as I can get."

"So you spent a lot of time in the West?"

"Yeah, I traveled around for about thirty years. I had a lot of good times." Roland shook his head as he looked back fondly on all of his wild adventures. It was still hard to believe sometimes that he was forty-seven and that the West had effectively been dead for nearly five years.

"My name's Jimmy Wilson." The young man surprised Roland by offering his hand.

Roland gripped the hand firmly and shook it. "I'm Roland, Roland Black, and I'm Sheriff here in New Haven."

Jimmy rubbed his forehead for a moment as if he was sifting through his memories. "I've never heard of any Roland Black, and I've studied the West quite a bit. I grew up with stories of Wyatt Earp and Tombstone and all the others, but I've never heard of you."

Roland had to laugh at that comment. For so long, the people of New Haven had been afraid of his dubious past and had gone to great lengths not to provoke him, and now this young man hadn't even heard of him. "That's probably because I usually kept out of the foreground. I had a lot of adventures, though. I was nineteen when I had my first duel. I was playing faro in South Dakota and was winning that night. Some fellow was all liquored up and pulled a gun, and I just got lucky and drew mine quicker. I always thought duels were performed in the streets with a whole bunch of rules, but luck and speed are the only two reasons I'm still alive. Nobody gave much fuss over the whole incident, but I left town the next morning. It was like that a lot. I'd get in a fight over something stupid and would leave town the next morning. I went on some bounty hunts but never killed anyone too famous, so I never had too much of a reputation. I did help kill the Utah Outlaws, but Doc got all the credit for that one."

"*Doc?* You knew Doc Holliday?" Jimmy's eyes had grown wide, and he looked at Roland with a newfound respect that bordered on awe.

"Yeah, I knew Doc Holliday," Roland replied, and his ego swelled with pride.

"What was he like?" Jimmy listened attentively, his face rapt with fascination.

Roland smiled as he remembered the sickly young man he had ridden with that one time. Doc was one of the highlights of his days of gunslinging. All the other people he had met had faded into obscurity, but nearly everyone had heard of the young dentist from Atlanta. "He was a pretty interesting fellow. He'd get up in the morning and drink a pint of whiskey before he'd leave his room. By the end of the day, he'd have downed at least a quart of the stuff, but it never slowed him down. He was the quickest gun I've ever seen in my life. Nobody else even came close."

"And you went on a bounty hunt with him?" Jimmy asked excitedly. "What happened?"

"I met him in Colorado about ten years ago. There were some people in Denver who wanted to put a bounty on the Utah Outlaws, and I had drifted in to find some work. I was at a saloon having a few drinks, and Doc was in there playing cards. Doc's one of the best card players I've ever seen. He had just split off from Wyatt and Virgil Earp while they headed to Tombstone. He must have downed at least ten shots of whiskey while I was in the place. Doc was always a sick man, and when he was drinking, he looked like a corpse. Anyway, one of the men he was gambling with got upset and pulled a gun out of his holster, and before I knew it Doc had shot him, holstered his gun, and was tossing back another shot of whiskey before anyone else could react."

"Damn, and he didn't get in any trouble?" Jimmy asked in wonderment.

"Naw, back then, fights over cards were overlooked as long as the person who got killed wasn't too famous. Doc knew to get out of town soon. Dead people often have friends and family, and sometimes they try to get their own revenge. But nobody was going to arrest him. He was too famous himself.

"I wound up talking to him later on, and we got along pretty well. Doc was extremely polite, a true gentlemen. Even though he was drunk most of the time, he made sure to speak clearly and politely to everyone. I can still see him sitting there, reeking of whiskey and his eyes bloodshot as hell, but he was the perfect southern gentlemen. I guess it came from his upbringing. I heard his parents were wealthy. Maybe he got it from them.

"I told him I was looking to go on a bounty hunt, and he asked if he could join me. I never knew why he wanted to go along. Maybe he just wanted to get out of town after killing that man, or maybe he just wanted some excitement for a few days. But who was I to ask? Doc Holliday wanted to go on a bounty hunt with me, and I would have been a fool to turn him down." Roland wasn't paying attention to Jimmy anymore and had a lost expression on his face like he was in another time. It was hard to believe that he had met Doc over ten years ago. It seemed as if the time had flown by, and all the glorious adventures of his youth had occurred so long ago. Yet he could still vividly remember all of the details of his encounter with the infamous, drunken gunslinger.

"So what happened next? Did you catch the Outlaws?" Jimmy had folded his hands on the table and looked like a child waiting to receive candy.

"It took a few days to get the contract arranged. There's not much bounty work anymore, but if you ever decide to give it a try, remember to get everything agreed on first. My first bounty job, I got promised two hundred dollars to arrest an outlaw, but when I brought him back, they only gave me fifty. It was Doc and me and two other fellows I had ridden with a few times. We set out as soon as the money was all taken care of.

"One of the Outlaws had been bragging to a whore that he was going to Dodge City, so that's where we started riding towards. We all packed clothes and rations, but Doc must have brought at least ten bottles of whiskey along with him. Luckily we caught up with the Outlaws a week later, or he might just have run out. I don't know what Doc would have been like sober. I don't think he would either. He must have spent the last twenty years of his life drunk.

"We found them just after sunset one night. Their campfire was lit up, and we approached it carefully, spreading out so we could attack from several sides. I was just of the mind to shoot them, as were the other two men with us, but not Doc. We had all taken great care to move silently and sneak up on them when Doc shouted out to them, 'Excuse me, good sirs. Please come out quietly, or I'll be obliged to shoot you.' I don't know who was more surprised, the Outlaws or us. He said later he thought it would be rude to shoot them without giving them a fair warning first. They got their warning, and they all tried to grab their guns. None of them got a shot off, though. Doc might have given them a fair warning, but he didn't wait for any of them to shoot first. I hit one of them, but Doc shot the other three on his own. The two men we were with both missed, and that was the end of it. We went back, got our money, and all went our own ways. I never saw Doc after that, but I had one hell of a good time while I got to ride with him."

"He died, though, right? I heard he got shot."

Roland shook his head. That's how Doc should have died. "He died of consumption. That's what drove him to drink in the first place. His lungs were always a mess, and he looked like he was on death's bed for over ten years from what I heard. I never expected him to live more than two months after I met him, but he hung on for another five years. He went through that whole trouble down in Tombstone, and afterwards, he just faded away. Wyatt headed out to California to spend all of his money. I don't know. I think Doc was lucky to die when he did. He was the perfect embodiment of the West, and it would have broken his heart to see it fall apart. Wyatt might have been able to move on, but it would have crushed Doc. Gambling, drinking, and gunslinging were his life."

Jimmy's jaw had dropped open, and he stared at Roland with something close to awe. "I can't believe you really rode with Doc Holliday. Did you know anyone else famous?"

"I met a whole bunch of famous people during my time, but Doc was the only notorious one I ever rode with. I tended to stay in the background most of the time, but I think I had a pretty good run."

"I just can't believe it. I always read about Doc and Wyatt and all the others. I would have given anything to meet some of them."

"You can. I hear Wyatt's still out in California. He's not too friendly from what I've heard, but you could track him down if you really want to meet a legend."

"It's not the same. I want to ride with someone like that. I know I'm quick. I've practiced my whole life with a pistol. Every morning, I'd draw and fire out in the woods. I just want to test my speed once." Jimmy's eyes had grown wide with excitement.

"Not here, though," Roland quickly pointed out before Jimmy got any ideas. "I understand what you mean. I have a deputy named Wade who's just like you. He trained with a gun for over ten years and headed West to make a name for himself. Unfortunately that's frowned upon these days. If you go trying to pick a fight, you're going to find yourself at the end of a rope. And don't go getting any ideas about taking out Carlos. If you try him, you won't have to wait to be hung. He'll put you down. You got that?"

"I don't suppose you need any more deputies here? This place is exactly like all the things I read about the West."

"I already have eight deputies. I picked them out carefully. Wade always wanted to prove his speed with a gun, but I know he won't shoot anyone if he doesn't have to. You seem a little anxious to me, and I don't know if you'd have the same control. You're welcome to stay as long as you want, but I don't want any trouble. We already have enough of that here in New Haven."

"I think I'll take you up on that then. This place is great. I've been traveling all over, and nothing is like this place." Jimmy looked down at the table with a bashful expression. "I don't suppose you'd want to tell me about some of your adventures. I always liked hearing stories when I was a kid, but there doesn't seem to be anyone around who actually lived through much of it. I just want to hear what the West was really like."

Roland leaned back in his chair and cracked his knuckles. He saw Jack looking over his way with a curious expression and waved him off. Jimmy might be anxious to prove himself, but Roland didn't think he would try anything in New Haven. He had already called the youth's bluff, and it seemed that he was more interested in the West than actually getting himself into trouble. As far as telling some of the stories from his glory days, Roland would be happy to oblige. He always enjoyed looking back on his times in the West, but he rarely told his stories to anyone. The people of New Haven feared his mysterious past, and he wanted to keep them off balance. Yet Jimmy at least deserved to hear what it had been like to live in the wild days of the West. Like Wade and others who had missed those years, stories were the only way they could ever experience it. "Yeah, I can tell you about my years in the West," Roland answered and passed the long afternoon by relating his myriad adventures over the last twenty-five years. He talked of the War, his numerous duels and bounty hunts, and a few of the more famous people he had met over the years.

Jimmy listened with rapt attention the whole time, and he reminded Roland a lot of a small child opening presents on Christmas morning as Roland wove his tales. Not many people had heard the true story of Roland's past. He had told Jack, Morgan, and Rebecca but nobody else in New Haven. Normally he wouldn't have told Jimmy either, but he needed to do something to take his thoughts away from Rebecca, the Dark Riders, and Alvin.

Jack dropped by once to make sure everything was okay, but once he heard Roland talking of his past, he left the two alone. Like Roland, he too sensed that Jimmy would be satiated with stories of the West from someone who had lived through so many adventures. They passed nearly two hours. Jimmy had obviously heard quite a few rumors of the West, but most of them had been tall tales. He was amazed at some of the stories that had been blown out of proportion and the less than heroic personalities of some of the West's most notorious figures.

Roland kept an eye on the clock hanging over the bar as more and more people filtered into The Frontier. He enjoyed telling his stories, but it was almost five. Fairly soon, he would have to end his storytelling for the day and prepare for the Riders' return, but that happened a little sooner than Sheriff Black had expected.

He was in the middle of explaining one of his bounty hunts when Ben burst into the saloon. Jack and Roland immediately stopped what they were doing and looked up expectantly at the frantic deputy. Ben's eyes were wide, and he was perspiring heavily. Most of the crowd in the saloon stopped their talking and watched as Ben rushed to Roland's table with Jack hurrying from the bar. They all knew of the Dark Riders' return.

"Sheriff," Ben panted. "Carlos and about a dozen Riders just rode into town from the south. They looked like they're heading over to The Snake. I didn't get too good a look at them, but Carlos looked pretty angry."

"Damn it!" Roland swore and hit the table in frustration. "Sorry, Jimmy, but story time is over." He looked at his two deputies with a serious expression. "Let's go see if we can keep that bastard from killing anyone tonight."

Chapter Nine

Jimmy's eyes had grown wide with excitement over the exchange between Roland and the deputies, and he was nearly hopping out of his seat. "Who are the Riders? What's going on? Is there going to be a shoot out?"

"Shut up, Jimmy. It's nothing you need to worry about. Let's go over to the station house and round up everyone," Roland told his two deputies and stood up. Roland took only three steps towards the door before he turned back to the young man to whom he had just been telling his life story. "I mean it. I don't want any trouble from you tonight. You stay here. If I catch you causing any trouble, I'll throw you in jail for a Goddamn month," he warned then grimly stalked out of The Frontier.

Roland was half-tempted to provoke a fight with Carlos just for the hell of it. He had finally been enjoying himself for what seemed like the first time in ages when the Riders' untimely entrance had abruptly cut it short. He was determined to leave the gang in peace, though, as long as they didn't cause any trouble. But with the way his luck had been running of late, Roland considered the odds of that occurring as being fairly low.

Jack held the door open for Ben and Roland as they gathered in the station house. Robert sat behind the desk. "What's going on, Sheriff?"

"The Riders just rode in. I want you and Ben to gather everyone up and bring them back here."

"Yes, Sheriff," the two deputies chimed in unison and quickly moved out the door.

"What's the plan, Roland?" Jack asked quietly. He had taken a seat in one of the wooden chairs in the office and looked up at Roland with an inquisitive expression.

"Goddamn it. I didn't think they'd show up for another two or three hours." Roland slammed his fist against the wall then took a deep calming breath. "I want you by The Snake. I'll send Morgan, Ben, and Wade over to help you. Keep close enough to hear if any shots are fired, but for God's sake don't let Carlos or any of them see you. If any trouble breaks out, send Ben or Wade back here, and we'll come over immediately."

"Why not bring everyone over there? I'd feel a hell of a lot safer if I had seven or eight men with me. If the Riders see us and start shooting, we'll be dead before you can get there."

"No, I don't think they'll shoot anyone unless Carlos gets pissed off, and I guarantee you, he'll go through the roof if he sees all of us gathered together. Besides Ben said he only saw a dozen of them, and that means there are still ten of them left. For all we know, the rest circled around town and will come in from the other side. I just want to be ready for anything to happen."

"All right. You want me to head over there now or wait for everyone?"

"Head over there now. I want to keep an eye on them. I'll send Ben, Morgan, and Wade over as soon as I'm done with them. Why don't you talk to Sam and stay in his supply shop. It's right across the street from The Snake, and I don't think he'll mind if we use his shop to keep an eye on the Riders."

"I'll do that," Jack replied and stood up. He stretched his arms and flexed his back then looked at Roland with a somber expression. "You just be ready to ride our way. I'm good, Roland, but even I can't hold off a dozen men."

"Don't worry, we'll be ready. You just be careful, Jack," Roland cautioned his deputy.

"You know me better than that, Roland. I'm always careful. That's why I'm still alive." Jack grinned impudently and left the building.

Sheriff Black watched him leave with a dour expression on his face. Talking with Jimmy and reminiscing about his years of gunslinging had buoyed his spirits, but the Riders' untimely return put him in a bad mood. Hopefully Carlos wouldn't start any trouble, but Roland wanted to be ready for anything. He began to pace back and forth in the station house as he impatiently waited for the other deputies to arrive. Nearly fifteen minutes later, five deputies rode up to the station house. Roland watched them dismount through the window then took a seat behind the desk.

"Ben, Wade, and Morgan," he called out immediately. The two younger deputies straightened their backs attentively when he spoke their names, but Morgan simply gazed at Roland expectantly. "I want you to go over to Sam's store. I already sent Jack over there. If any trouble breaks out, I want one of you to get the rest of us. We'll stay here by the station house. I want to be ready in case the rest of those bastards try something tonight." He placed his hands upon the desk and looked at all of them sternly. "I don't want any heroics tonight. We're going to make sure the Riders don't get in any trouble, and they don't need our help. You three just keep an eye on The Snake, and the rest of us will be waiting. Do you understand?"

"Yes, Sheriff," Ben and Wade chimed in unison, and Morgan nodded slowly. Roland was glad that Ben didn't chip in with his normal quota of questions. He wasn't in the mood to deal with Ben's inquisitiveness that night.

"Good, then get over there. I don't want Jack alone for any longer than he has to be," Roland snapped, and the three filed out of the station house, leaving him alone with the other two deputies. "Robert, I want you to stay here in the station house. When Phillip shows up, I want him to wait here with you. William and I are going back to The Frontier. Keep all the horses ready to go at a moment's notice."

Robert looked around for a moment and ran a hand over his bald head. "Aren't you going to wait here, Sheriff?"

"No, I'm not. I want to make everything look like normal tonight. Carlos wants to prove he's not afraid of me, and I want to show everyone in town that I'm not afraid of him. That means I'll do what I do every night: sit in The Frontier. Any more questions?"

"No, Sheriff," Robert replied and spread his hands. All of the deputies knew how much he hated having his orders questioned.

"Good. If there's any trouble, I want one of you to come over and get us. Let's go, William," he ordered and rose to his feet. William waited outside, his blue eyes watching Sheriff Black as he stopped and pointed a finger at him. "You just keep your mind on business tonight. You can play with the women tomorrow," Sheriff Black said simply then turned back to The Frontier.

"Yes, Sheriff," William whispered then rushed to catch up with Roland as he strode across the street.

The crowd inside The Last Frontier was a large one that night. Roland was glad to see it so busy. If that many people were enjoying themselves, it meant they weren't somewhere else causing trouble. Even Jimmy had settled in and was playing a game of poker with some of the saloon's regulars. That one in particular Roland was happy to see pursuing a peaceful recreation. He didn't need a wildcard loose in the streets with the potential for danger that already existed.

"Get us a bottle of whiskey," Roland told William and proceeded to his customary table. It was in the corner by a window, allowing him to look out into the street so he could see if any deputies approached the station house. He watched William go over to the bar and retrieve a bottle and two shot glasses, and his lips curled into a tiny smile in anticipation of a good, stiff shot of whiskey. A few of Sherry's strumpets were at the saloon that night, and William had always been a good customer. His amorous deputy, however, brushed them aside as he darted occasional glances towards the Sheriff.

"Here you are, Sheriff." William placed the bottle on the table and took a seat.

Roland didn't bother thanking him, but simply poured a full glass for each of them and slid one over to his deputy. "Drink it. It's going to be a long night." He tossed the shot down and pursed his lips in satisfaction as a comfortable warmth spread through his body. *I needed that.* He leaned back in his chair feeling more relaxed than he had a few minutes before.

William gulped his down and coughed once as the fiery liquor burned his throat. "Damn, that feels good," he whispered hoarsely and reached for the bottle to pour himself another shot.

"No." Roland grabbed the bottle and pulled it back towards him and out of the deputy's reach. "One shot's enough. We might need to use our guns later, and I don't want us seeing double." Doc Holliday had been the only man he had ever met who could actually shoot better when he was drunk. Over the years, he had seen too many men get themselves killed in gunfights because they had consumed too much alcohol. If he had to fight over a dozen men that night, Roland didn't want to be impaired in any way at all.

"You're right. I'm just anxious." William rubbed his hands together nervously.

"Get used to it, and don't talk so much. I'm concentrating," Sheriff Black grumbled as he watched the empty street restlessly. He knew it could be hours before any trouble occurred if at all. It was all too tempting to go over to The Snake and force the issue, yet Roland had survived the West far too long to allow impatience to disrupt his plans.

William was quick to follow Roland's advice and sat quietly in his seat as the Sheriff watched the street with a stony gaze. A few people started towards their table, but a small, warning shake of William's head encouraged them to take their conversations elsewhere. Even the jovial saloon owner stayed across the room, choosing to avoid Roland.

They sat in awkward silence for perhaps ten minutes, then Roland suddenly arched his back and glared out the window. *You Goddamn snake,* he thought as he watched the figure approach the saloon. "Go over to the bar and wait there," Roland ordered, his eyes never leaving the window.

The young deputy glanced out the window curiously to see what had piqued Roland's interest and whistled as he saw Alvin strolling up the street. "Why's he coming here?" He asked without thinking and winced as Roland turned his gaze upon him.

"I don't know, Goddamn it. The son of a bitch probably wants to talk. Now get over to the bar. I want to talk to him alone." Roland's command found no argument this time as William quickly rose from his seat. "And stay out of trouble. I mean it. No women."

"Yes, Sheriff," William responded immediately and quickly crossed the saloon floor, putting as much distance between himself and the Sheriff as possible.

Alvin disappeared from sight as he walked around to the front of the saloon, and Roland leaned back in his chair. *What the hell do you want, Alvin?* Roland thought to himself as he waited for the mayor to enter. With the Dark Riders' return to town, Roland didn't need any trouble from Alvin.

Most of the crowd had noticed William's flight across the room, and a momentary silence descended over the entire saloon when Alvin entered. As always, he was dressed immaculately. His suit was light grey that night, freshly pressed, and even his black boots were polished. His blue eyes peered about the tavern before they spotted Roland at his table. A well-practiced smile came to the mayor's face as he calmly strode over to the Sheriff, his cane tapping against the floor in a measured beat. He smiled and nodded to people as he passed them, making sure to maintain his public image. "Roland, it's good to see you." Alvin smiled widely as he took a seat across the table. He stared at the bottle of whiskey and the two empty shot glasses. "Getting an early start?" The mayor raised an eyebrow.

Roland ignored him and rubbed his hands together. *What game are you playing?* "Trying to raise a few votes, *Mayor*?" He emphasized the last word with a sarcastic bite.

Alvin's smile slipped a little, but he smoothly resumed the benevolent expression he always wore in public. He looked down at one of the lapels on his jacket and brushed off a speck of dust with the back of his hand before returning his gaze to Roland. "Always, Roland, always. Just remember, you might be Sheriff for the time being, but I'll always be mayor." His eyes narrowed slightly, and Roland knew that he was the only one who could see how evil Alvin really was. To everyone else, Alvin looked like a perfect gentleman having a conversation with the Sheriff. "You're in a pleasant mood this evening, but I didn't come here to exchange insults with you. Carlos and some of his men just rode over to The Snake," he taunted Roland smugly.

"I already know that," Roland answered. He knew the mayor was trying to use the Riders' arrival as some sort of trump card to hold over him, but he would be damned if he'd give Alvin any satisfaction.

"Are you doing anything about it?"

"It's been taken care of." Roland forced his face to assume a lazy expression as if it were the last thing on his mind.

Alvin was taken back by Roland's carefree attitude. It usually only took a few biting comments to enrage the Sheriff. He brushed an errant strand of white hair back across his forehead and nodded. "I'm glad to see that. I talked to Carlos yesterday, and he seemed in an unpleasant mood. Hopefully he won't do anything rash."

Roland shrugged his shoulders as if it didn't matter either way. "It's his funeral if he does, Alvin. I told you, and I told him, don't test my patience. It's awfully thin right now."

"Well, I can see you're not one for conversation tonight, so I think my job here is finished. Good evening." Alvin slowly stood up and shrugged so his coat settled on his shoulders. "Oh, by the way, good job with Matthew. I had a good laugh reading his story today. Just be careful, Roland. You never know when another problem might arise." He left the threat hanging in the air as he walked away from the table.

Roland watched as Alvin went about greeting various people with the fake smile he always wore, and his mood grew darker. He was tired of Alvin always playing off the Dark Riders against him. Roland wanted to keep the town safe, but Alvin always had to push him. He had also been sorely tempted to question Alvin about the Dark Riders' involvement in Bryant's murder, but once again, the circumstances hadn't been right. Alvin would certainly never volunteer that information, and it would take a method similar to the one he had used with Matthew to persuade him to give up the killer. Twice the mayor had unwittingly escaped him, but Roland swore that the next time he would make it a point to corner Alvin in some place where nobody would witness the encounter. *I'll get you soon, you son of a bitch.*

Alvin stayed in The Last Frontier for nearly ten minutes, chatting with a number of people before he finally left. William waited until Alvin had walked out the door and then warily approached Roland's table. Roland sat stone-faced in his chair, glaring out the window. "Uh, Sheriff. Are you all right?"

"Sit down and shut up," Roland growled and settled back into an icy silence.

William heeded his advice and took the same seat Alvin had just been sitting in. He was tempted to ask Roland what he and the mayor had talked about, but the Sheriff looked upset. The deputy knew how to bide his time, and he did just that as the two of them sat in the saloon and waited for word from one of the other deputies.

The crowd inside The Last Frontier grew louder as the sky grew darker. The last train had left shortly before five that afternoon, and by dusk, everyone had finished their work for the day. Some had gone home, but most had wandered into one of the town's saloons to find entertainment. Sherry's girls circulated about the establishment as they solicited customers, and a few men started arguing over their card games as they drank more and more liquor. Of course, they didn't let it get too far out of hand with the Sheriff sitting so close. Roland's mood improved with the mayor gone, but he kept tapping his foot and looking out the window anxiously as he waited to hear from one of his deputies.

It was nearly an hour after Alvin left when their wait finally ended. Ben galloped down the street and stopped in front of the station house. He jumped off his horse and didn't even bother to tie it to the tether post as he rushed inside. "Let's go," Roland stated and rose to his feet, placing a hand on his holster reassuringly. A hush once again descended over The Frontier as the customers and staff watched the pair rush outside, but Sheriff Black and William paid them no attention in their hurry to hear Ben's news. Roland would have been concerned if he had seen the wild excitement that danced in Jimmy's eyes and the mischievous grin on his face as the young gunslinger watched them leave.

They were nearly halfway across the street when Ben emerged from the station house. He stopped short when he saw Roland and William approaching him and looked at the Sheriff with a serious expression. "Jack sent me, Sheriff. He wants you to come over to The Snake."

"What's going on? Has Carlos started anything?" Roland barked. If there was a gunfight about to start, he didn't know why the other two deputies were still inside.

"It's not Carlos, Sheriff. It's the mayor. He just showed up at The Snake about five minutes ago. Jack wasn't sure why he was there and told me to come get you. Why do you think he's there?"

"That son of a bitch," Roland raged and spat on the ground derisively, ignoring Ben's question. He had just about had it with Alvin. For the past year, the mayor had flaunted the Dark Riders' propensity for violence, and Roland was through with their arrangement. His nonchalant attitude in the saloon must have convinced the mayor to take matters into his own hands. He could vividly picture Alvin's thought process. If threats wouldn't bend Roland to his will, he would just have to escalate those threats into something more tangible. It wasn't the first time Alvin had played these games, but Roland was determined to make it the last. If Alvin thought that he could intimidate Roland, the mayor was in for quite a surprise.

William and Ben exchanged a silent glance as they watched Roland clench his fists and struggle to maintain his temper. "You don't think the mayor would tell the Riders to start any trouble, do you? That doesn't make any sense. Why would he do that?" Ben asked when it became clear that William was going to keep his silence.

"I don't know what that Goddamn snake will do." The Sheriff spat again and curbed his temper. "Ben, you stay here." Roland was in no mood to hear any more of the deputy's questions. "You're in charge. Just be ready in case we need you. William, you're coming with me. Let's go see what that bastard's up to." Roland's eyes had gone completely flat, and he stalked to his horse when he finished his instructions without waiting to see if his deputies had any questions.

One of Ben's eyebrows shot up questioningly, but William shook his head and headed over to his horse. Both had seen the Sheriff in one of his bad moods before and knew to stay quiet and follow his orders. Ben could always hear what had happened later on when everything had been settled.

"Come on. We don't have all day," Roland barked as he looked down from his horse to see William untying his own from the tether post.

"Yes, Sheriff," William replied and quickly scrambled into the saddle. Before he could even adjust his balance, Roland had already spurred his own horse into a gallop. Shaking his head, William kicked his own mount and followed after the Sheriff. Their ride was furious as they galloped towards Sam's Supply Store. They circled to the east and came upon the store from the back entrance.

Three horses awaited the pair as they approached. Jack had obviously taken his advice, and they had tied their horses crudely to one of the building's wooden supports. Wordlessly Roland dismounted and left his horse for William to tether. He had more important things to attend to. William didn't offer a word of resistance as he watched the Sheriff throw open the door and stalk inside.

Sam Mitchell owned the town's largest supply store, selling everything from food to tools to ammunition. He had opened it when the town was first founded and had watched it thrive as New Haven grew. The shop usually closed at dusk when people had either settled in for the evening or gone out to carouse. A few lanterns had been lit, and Roland could see the faint outlines of three figures crouched by one of the front windows.

"Roland? Is that you?" He heard Jack's whisper from the front of the store.

"Yeah, it's me," Roland replied as he tried to navigate his way through the dark store. The two lanterns gave enough light to form dark silhouettes of objects, but not much more. He proceeded slowly, keeping his arms extended so he wouldn't bump into anything. Roland cursed as his shin struck an unseen chair, but other than that, he emerged at the front of the store safely. "Blazes, do you have to keep it so dark in here? I can barely see," he muttered irritably.

Morgan and Wade knelt at the edge of the one of the windows, while Jack had withdrawn a bit to talk to Roland. His face was covered in shadows under the dim lighting, and Roland had to strain to make out Jack's shoulders shrugging as his eyes slowly became accustomed to the darkness. "What do you want me to do? Tell everyone we're in here? I thought we were supposed to keep out of sight, not hang a sign on the front of the shop saying 'deputies inside,'" Jack replied.

"Sorry, Jack. I'm just pissed at Alvin. What's going on? Ben said he's at The Snake."

Jack shook his head and sighed in disappointment. "I was hoping you could tell me. He came over about ten minutes ago and has been in there ever since. I don't think he'd tell the Riders to do anything stupid, but you never know." Jack paused, and Roland could see his white teeth as the deputy smiled widely. "Besides, I know how much you like him, so I thought I'd invite you over."

"Thanks, Jack. It's probably good you did, though. I talked to him earlier, and he didn't leave in a very good mood."

Although Roland couldn't see his face, Jack's groan of disgust told him clearly that the deputy had donned one of his disappointed expressions. "Damn it, Roland. What did you do this time?" Jack asked in a voice dripping with pessimism. Alvin was a hard man to anger, but Jack knew that Roland was somebody who could do it without trying.

"Nothing." Roland scowled as he replayed the incident in his mind. He hadn't been overly friendly to Alvin, but he hadn't picked a fight with him either.

"Nothing? Come on, Roland. I'm not stupid. Why did you talk to him in the first place?"

"He came by to warn me that the Riders were in town and to congratulate me on Matthew's story." Footsteps interrupted Roland, and he turned his head towards the back of the store. "We're up front, William," Roland called out to his deputy and turned his attention back to Jack. "Anyway, he was trying to piss me off, but I didn't play along."

"What the hell did you do? Threaten him?" Jack asked incredulously.

Roland paused as William walked by. "Go wait with Morgan and Wade," he ordered and waited for the deputy to kneel down by the window before continuing. "I told him that Carlos had better stay in line and if he caused any trouble, we'd put him down. Alvin got upset and left. That's it. He always did like to get his way."

Jack thought it over for a second then nodded. "Sorry, but you know how you get sometimes. I wonder what Alvin's up to. Do you think he'll cause any trouble?"

"I don't know, Jack, I just don't know. We're going to have to wait and see, but I wouldn't be surprised if Carlos tried to pick a fight later on. But enough of Alvin. Who did Carlos bring with him?"

"The usual. Curly's over there. Mad Dog, Wild Carl, Marshall, and a few Banditos. I don't know who else, but he's got enough men to cause trouble if he wants to. Damn it, Roland. We don't need a fight like this. They've got at least thirteen men over there. They'd kill at least half, if not all of us, in a gunfight."

"Calm down, Jack. We don't know they're going to start a fight, and even if they do, I think you underestimate us. I've survived a long time, and I don't plan on dying by a Dark Rider bullet. Let's just wait and see what happens. Alvin's not stupid. He won't be able to defend the Riders if they kill anyone."

"I hope you're right, Roland. We're all in a lot of trouble if you're wrong," Jack replied dubiously.

"Let's just wait and see," Roland answered and joined the other deputies kneeling by the store's windows. As they crouched in the dark confines of the supply store, Roland hoped that no confrontation would occur. Despite his assurances to Jack, Roland wasn't very optimistic about their chances in a gunfight.

Jack watched the saloon with a worried frown, and each of the other deputies could sense the tension in Roland. Each passing moment, they all grew more and more anxious to see the issue settled one way or another, but they had no choice but to wait. Morgan told dry jokes from time to time as he

179

liked to do, and it seemed to lighten the mood a little bit. Roland, however, paid the old veteran no mind and focused on The Rattlesnake, waiting for something to happen.

Like The Last Frontier, The Rattlesnake was a busy saloon that Tuesday evening. The normal crowd shuffled in and out in their pursuit of entertainment, and a good number of the men who left the saloon stumbled into the street with a drunken gait that Roland saw all too often. Other than that, they had no indication of what was going on inside The Rattlesnake that night and had to bide their time, tensing each time the door swung open.

Nearly an hour after Roland had joined his men in the supply store, the Dark Riders finally left The Rattlesnake. Instantly Roland and his deputies dropped their hands to their holsters and watched the Riders intently to see if violence would be needed. "Nobody do anything stupid," Roland warned needlessly The deputies all knew their orders.

All of the Dark Riders filed out of The Rattlesnake at the same time, led by Carlos and Alvin. The mayor and the outlaw seemed to be having a spirited discussion, and by the slight sway to Carlos's step, he had obviously consumed quite a bit of liquor during his few hours in the saloon. The dozen men with him all had that same arrogant, swaying gait that they assumed when they were drunk and pugnacious. "Damn," Roland swore as he watched them exit the saloon. Just as Jack had reported, Curly, Mad Dog, Wild Carl, Marshall, and a half dozen Banditos were in the party. If that group decided to cause trouble, Roland and his men were in for a very bad evening. "William, go untie your horse. If they pick a fight, we're going to need every gun we can get."

"Do you want me to get help?"

"No, just wait outside. If I want you to get help, I'll signal. Now go," Roland ordered tersely.

William wordlessly obeyed the order and quickly headed to the back of the store. But as Roland watched the mayor and the Dark Riders, he thought he might not need the extra help after all. Alvin had the stern expression on his face that he usually donned when he was ordering Carlos to do something. Carlos, on the other hand, didn't have his customary sneer and seemed to be listening attentively to Alvin's words. A few of the Riders mounted their horses, and Roland smiled as he began to think that perhaps the situation might not result in any violence. He didn't know why Alvin had sought out Carlos, and he was sure it would mean trouble for him at a later time. That, however, would be another night, and he would deal with that situation if it arose.

"I think they're leaving," Jack laughed in relief, and the tension that had been building in the store over the past hour seemed to dissipate.

"I think you're right." Roland smiled in response as he watched the last of the Riders take to their horses. Only Carlos remained on his feet, still talking to the mayor. Alvin told him one last comment, and the outlaw nodded in response then turned to his men. "That's it. They're going to leave." Roland breathed a sigh of relief. The night had been a success, and it looked like he even had a good chance of cornering the mayor by himself. He still intended to drag the truth out of Alvin to determine who had killed Bryant, but he now had the extra incentive of discovering what he had been discussing with Carlos.

"See, I told y'all there was nothing to worry about," Morgan laughed.

"We should have listened to you." Roland chuckled. His chiseled face dropped into a lopsided grin as he watched Carlos approach his horse. But his jaw dropped open, and the blood drained from his face a moment later when Jimmy sauntered into the middle of the street. "Goddamn it," Roland swore as he watched Jimmy approach Carlos and Alvin. He had known that the kid could be trouble, but he had thought that his warning had been severe enough.

Jimmy walked with an arrogant stride, and his chest was puffed out. His eyes held the same defiant glint that Roland had noticed when he first met the young man. Roland had thought at the time that Jimmy was somebody desperately trying to prove his worth, and it looked as if the young man was going to test his skill against Carlos to make a name for himself. "I'm looking for Carlos," Jimmy shouted belligerently, and Roland cringed at the situation which had just exploded with danger.

"Jack, stay in here. I'm going to stop that little bastard before Carlos kills him," Roland snarled in disgust and rushed to the front door, drawing one of his guns as the events outside continued to unfold.

Carlos had turned to Jimmy and looked at him with a mixture of contempt and curiosity. Instinctively his hand drifted down towards his gun as he sneered at the young man. "What do you want, boy?" He asked in his thick accent, puffing out his own chest to match Jimmy's arrogance.

"I've heard you're quick, and I'm here to prove I'm quicker. That is if you're not—"

"Jimmy, shut up. You're under arrest!" Roland shouted as he swung open the shop's front door. He leveled his gun at Jimmy's chest and prayed that nobody started firing. With thirteen Dark Riders and a loose cannon, he was a dead man if a gunfight erupted.

For a moment, it looked as if Jimmy was going to draw his own pistol, but he saw that Sheriff Black could shoot him without a second thought if he did so. With a disgusted grimace, Jimmy put his hands in the air. "Don't shoot. I won't try anything."

Carlos, however, did draw his pistol, and all of the Dark Riders quickly followed suit. A tingle of fear went up Roland's spine as he looked at thirteen guns pointed at him. It wasn't a fear of dying, for he had conquered that a long time ago. It took courage to survive a duel, and if he had been scared for his own life, he would have fallen a long time ago. But he did fear not seeing Rebecca again and, more importantly, abandoning her while she was locked in her perpetual sleep. "I'm not here for you, Carlos. I just want this one," he jerked his head in the direction of Jimmy.

The outlaw's lip curled in contempt. "Why were you hiding over there, Sheriff? You afraid of me and my men? You too much of a coward to face us like a man, or do you have to hide like a little girl?" His voice dripped with scorn, and Roland thought he just might be a dead man. It would only take one of those men to shoot, and there was going to be a blood bath in New Haven.

"I was keeping an eye on you, Carlos. It's my job, but I don't want any trouble tonight. I just want this one. I'm throwing him in jail." He shot Jimmy a stern gaze, while he kept his gun pointed at the young gunslinger. Some of the cockiness had left Jimmy's demeanor as he stood defenseless in the midst of fourteen drawn guns. Alvin watched the ordeal with an amused smile on his face, and Roland cursed inwardly. The mayor looked far more likely to encourage Carlos to shoot rather than stop him.

"What do you want him for, Sheriff? He was challenging me. I say he's mine." Carlos pointed his gun at Jimmy, whose face drained of all color. Carlos smiled mockingly at Roland. Some of the Riders followed Carlos's example and aimed at the young man, although there were still over half a dozen guns pointed uncomfortably at Sheriff Black.

"Let's kill 'em both, Carlos," Wild Carl shouted, and several of his companions answered with similar catcalls.

"Maybe, but I want to hear him beg for his life first. Come on, Sheriff. Maybe I'll let you live, if you ask real sweet for it. Get on your knees."

Roland looked at Alvin, but the mayor simply arched an eyebrow as he watched the Sheriff's predicament. He considered giving in to the outlaw's demands for a moment, but his stubbornness kicked in. Carlos and his men were either going to shoot him or not, and he would be damned if he was going to die on his knees before a piece of garbage like Carlos. "You don't want to shoot me, Carlos. I let you stay in this town, but if you kill me, the government will track you down. The minute I die, you're a marked man, and you know it." He knew that logic was true, but he just hoped that Carlos, Curly, and the rest of the Dark Riders would see it that way. They might be tracked down and hanged later on, but that would be of little solace to Roland at that point.

"Let's shoot him," Mad Dog shouted out, and the rest of them began cheering loudly.

Carlos seemed to consider the issue with a great deal of concentration, and Roland forced himself to keep a level expression despite the fear that had welled up inside him. He just hoped that Jack and the others stayed inside. If any of them emerged from the shop, the unexpected interference likely would decide his fate as well as theirs. A crowd had gathered to witness the event, and Roland suddenly realized that he had a trump card he could play. "You don't want to shoot me in front of all these people, Carlos. They'd never let you come back to town again," he addressed the outlaw, but his words were meant for Alvin.

Alvin glanced at the people who had gathered to watch, and Roland knew exactly what he was thinking. The people voted for him because he was cultured and urbane. They also voted for him because he kept the Dark Riders from getting out of hand. If he allowed Carlos and his men to shoot the Sheriff, his popularity would suffer. As much as he disliked Roland, Alvin would never take a blow to his reputation. There would always be time to get back at the Sheriff at a later date when it would be more convenient. A brief look of regret flashed across the mayor's face, then he assumed his amicable public persona once again. "Let him go, Carlos. You made your point."

Carlos turned his head in surprise, but his gun never wavered from pointing at Roland. "What? I'm gonna kill him this time. You should be happy."

The mayor shook his head, his long hair swinging about his shoulders. "No, Carlos, you're not going to kill him. Why don't you go home now," he ordered in a commanding tone.

Usually Carlos argued for a few moments then gave in to Alvin's wishes. He knew that his men enjoyed a lot of freedom because of the mayor's support, but like Roland, he too was stubborn. "Get out of here. This isn't your concern," he told Alvin, and his men shouted their approval. A few of them fired their guns into the air, causing Roland to flinch nervously. Jimmy looked like he was about to faint, but he kept still with his hands in the air.

Alvin looked completely flabbergasted. He didn't like having his orders disregarded, and his moment of shock turned into an icy rage. "Damn it, Carlos. I said to get the hell out of here," the mayor hissed at the outlaw. Plenty of people could see the events transpiring, but none were actually close enough to hear what was said. Nobody wanted to be that close to the volatile situation, and they all watched from a safe distance. "If you don't, I swear I'll cut you all off."

Carlos sneered at the mayor and spat in his direction. "Shut your mouth, Alvin, or I'll shoot you too." He fixed Alvin with a baleful gaze, while Alvin's jaw dropped open in shock. Roland had never seen the mayor so stunned in the entire time he had known Alvin. If there hadn't been so many guns pointed at him, Roland would have burst into gales of laughter. He had waited a long time to see the wind let of out Alvin's sails, but this wasn't quite the way he had envisioned it. Roland's momentary amusement ended when Carlos turned his head back towards him. "Get on your knees and beg, or you're dead."

Roland had run out of options. His luck had run rather poorly for the past week, so he shouldn't have been too surprised when Carlos finally decided to disobey Alvin. If Carlos was belligerent enough to threaten Alvin, Roland knew that the outlaw was likely to shoot him if he sank to his knees or not, and he intended to die on his feet, defiant to the end. "You Goddamn, coward." He forced his own face into a contemptuous expression, mimicking the outlaw. "Why don't you fight me yourself, or do you need your men to help you?" He forced his voice to drip with disdain for the outlaw to provoke as much anger as possible.

Just as Sheriff Black had desired, Carlos's eyes widened in rage, and he was nearly frothing at the mouth. "I'm not afraid of you, Sheriff," he spat out in contempt. "Put your gun away, and we'll fight."

Roland hated to holster his gun for even a moment, but he had no choice. If he refused Carlos at this point, he knew he was a dead man. *You're a dead man anyway,* Roland told himself, but he planned on taking Carlos out before he died. Spinning his gun twice, he slipped it into his holster and shot Jimmy one last glance of disgust. Jimmy looked relieved to have Roland's pistol off him and quickly darted out of the midst of the explosive situation. Roland watched him leave safely with seething anger. He couldn't believe that he was going to die on account of the young man's actions. "Step out into the street, Carlos, and let's get this over with."

Carlos sneered at Roland and sauntered into the street, his chest puffed out arrogantly. A startled buzz rippled through the crowd as they realized what was about to take place. Carlos's sneer deepened as he came to a stop in the middle of the street, nearly twenty feet from Roland. He set his feet in a wide stance and dropped his hand to his side. "Now you die."

"Tell your men to put up their weapons. This is between me and you. That is if you're not too afraid." Roland's voice dripped with scorn, and once again he successfully needled the outlaw.

"Put your guns away," Carlos shouted at his men, while he continued to glare at Sheriff Black with murderous hatred. "I'll kill him myself." The Dark Riders obeyed his command without question. They weren't worried about being unarmed. There were over a dozen of them, and the Sheriff was by himself. If Carlos did fall, they could still draw and kill him without a problem. Most of them had big smiles on their faces as they holstered their weapons and called out jeers towards the Sheriff. "Happy, you bastard?" Carlos stuck out his chin and leered.

"Perfectly, you son of a bitch." Roland's face curled into a lopsided grin as he dropped his right hand to his side. *Goodbye, Rebecca,* Roland thought forlornly. He knew that he was a dead man in the next twenty seconds no matter the outcome of his duel, but he forced himself to stay calm. He had never lost a duel in his life, and he wasn't about to let Carlos be the first man to best him. He slowed his breathing as he relaxed his body and cleared his mind. Nothing mattered except him and Carlos. Roland had perfected the technique over years of gunslinging. He didn't want nervousness to force his shot astray. "Throw down," he told the Dark Rider in a quiet voice.

184

Both men tensed as the entire street became quiet. Even the Dark Riders ceased their taunting and watched the two men with rapt attention. Roland didn't notice any of that. His focus was solely on Carlos. The outlaw's fingers tapped his gun expectantly as he waited for Roland to draw first. Roland knew that Carlos prided himself on his quickness and would want him to be the first to draw his weapon. Detractors would say he beat Roland by luck otherwise, and Carlos wanted to protect his notoriety as surely as Alvin wanted to protect his popularity. Roland didn't care much about appearance, and he intended to draw, fire, and shoot the Dark Rider right through the heart. He took a deep breath, and his fingers were just about to pull his gun from its holster when Jack's voice broke the silence.

"Nobody move!" Jack's cry pierced the night air, and Carlos drew his weapon instinctively.

As quick as Carlos was, Roland was just as fast, and both men stood rigidly with their guns pointed at each other. Roland didn't dare take his eyes off Carlos as he heard Jack behind him. He had expected Jack to stay safely in the supply shop, but as long as he was outside, Roland intended to use it to his advantage. The stalemate with Carlos wouldn't last much longer. The tension in the air was so thick, he could almost taste it. It wouldn't be long before a gunfight erupted in the street and people were killed. "Jack, is everyone in place?" He hoped Jack was smart enough to play along with his bluff.

"Yeah, they're all in position. You want me to take out these bastards?" Jack sounded like he didn't have a care in the world.

Roland had never been so thankful to have Jack as a deputy, and he grinned at Carlos. "You and your men, put your guns away, Carlos. I've got fifteen men hiding on this street, and they're all aiming at your men. You're not under arrest, and you can come back whenever you want." He threw out the last part to make Carlos more susceptible to agreeing. If Carlos thought that he was being driven out of town or would be punished, he likely would fire just to prove he couldn't be kept out of town. His only reason for coming into New Haven in the first place that evening had been to demonstrate his lack of respect for Roland's banishment.

Carlos took his eyes off Roland for a moment and scanned the street with a bewildered gaze, and the Sheriff knew exactly what he was thinking. Jack had emerged from the supply shop, so maybe Roland wasn't lying about there being more men hidden on the street. *Come on,* Roland thought as he watched Carlos look for more men.

Alvin decided the issue. He had watched the near duel and the events afterwards with something close to shock on his face. Carlos had always given in to his wishes, and he had used that control to gain more power for himself. The outlaw's disregard and threats towards him had shaken the mayor quite severely, but as Carlos tried to decide whether to put away his gun or not,

Alvin took action on his own. The first time Roland had met Alvin, he had just emerged victorious from a duel. Like the Sheriff, Alvin had spent a number of years as a gunslinger, and he still carried a gun at all times. He drew it swiftly and pointed it at Carlos. "Put your gun up, Carlos, or I'll shoot you myself."

Carlos whipped his head around in surprise, and he froze as he realized he was caught between two gunmen. He wanted to protect his reputation, but even he knew the foolishness of taking on two men when they had him dead in their sight. He glared at the mayor then turned back to the Sheriff and fixed him with a baleful gaze. "Next time, you won't be so Goddamn lucky," he growled then clenched his teeth in frustration as he holstered his gun.

The tension left Roland, and he allowed himself to take in the rest of his surroundings for the first time. In addition to Jack, the other three men inside the supply shop had emerged and stood rigidly with drawn weapons. A few of the Dark Riders still held guns in their hands, but most had put them up when Carlos had holstered his own weapon. Curly, Mad Dog, and Wild Carl in particular looked ready to fight, but they had heard the conversation between Jack and Roland. A large portion of the Dark Riders scanned the buildings on the street, looking for the phantom men that Roland had claimed were there. Roland didn't like seeing some of them with drawn weapons and wanted them to leave as soon as possible. If any of them discovered that he and Jack had been bluffing, there would indeed be a blood bath in the street. "You and your men leave, Carlos. You can come back tomorrow, but I want you out of town now."

Carlos spat on the ground and tried to act as if he didn't even notice the guns that were leveled at him. "We'll be back, Sheriff." He swaggered over to his men, and Roland was pleased to see the rest of the Dark Riders holstering their weapons. "Let's go," Carlos shouted to his men and swung his leg over his horse. He shot the Sheriff one last look of hatred then spurred his horse into a gallop. The rest of his men followed his lead, and they rode out of town, crying catcalls and shouting rowdily as they disappeared from view.

"Sweet mother of Jesus," Jack breathed out in relief as he and the other deputies holstered their own guns. He walked over to join Roland and wiped sweat from his forehead. "I thought you were a dead man, Roland."

"So did I," Roland replied. "Thanks for helping, but why the hell did you do it? We should all be dead right now."

"Hell, Roland, I don't want to be Sheriff, so I thought we'd save your ass from getting killed." Jack grinned, but then his expression turned serious. "I don't know. I was just going to watch you and Carlos, but I figured there was no way you'd survive. If he didn't kill you, the Riders would have. The next thing I knew I was out in the street with Morgan, William, and Wade. I guess we just got lucky." He grinned again.

Roland chuckled as well. There was something exhilarating about surviving a gunfight or a confrontation. Roland had just looked death in the eye and not blinked, and he suddenly found himself in a tremendously good mood. "You can say that again. Blazes, if they knew that we were the only ones on this street, I think they'd ride back and shoot us. I can't believe they fell for that, but Carlos never was very smart."

"I'm not complaining."

"Me neither." Roland grinned, but he stopped as he saw Jimmy trying to sneak away. *Son of a bitch.* The young man had very nearly cost him and his men their lives, and Roland intended to scare the hell out of him. There were other things that he needed to see to first, however. "Jack, go get that little bastard and throw him in jail for me. I need to talk to Alvin."

"My pleasure," Jack replied, and his face hardened. Roland almost felt sorry for Jimmy. The young man had upset a lot of people that night, and Roland was sure that Jack and Morgan would have a few words with the gunslinger. Jimmy would be scared to death by the time Roland had a chance to talk to him. "Come on." Jack waved to the three other deputies and stalked towards the fleeing youth.

Roland watched them for a moment and saw that they would easily catch the young man. Jimmy had tried to sneak away, but he hadn't made it very far. Confident that problem was taken care of, he turned to Alvin. The mayor had holstered his own gun but still looked dumbfounded. Roland walked towards him, anger slowly building up inside him. He was looking forward to an informative conversation with the mayor, but once again, there were still too many people around. One way or another, Roland was determined to make it happen that night. "Alvin, I have some business to attend to, but I want you over at the station house in thirty minutes."

Alvin looked at him with a dazed expression. "Can't it wait until tomorrow? It's been a long night, and I want to get some sleep."

"No. There are some things I need to talk to you about. Thirty minutes?"

The mayor waved a hand in submission. "Fine, Roland. Thirty minutes." Roland turned back to the street with a slight grin. He couldn't remember seeing Alvin more flustered, and chuckling to himself, he crossed the street towards Jack and his captive.

The deputies had caught up with Jimmy, and the young man stood between them with a scared expression. Jimmy's eyes widened as he saw Roland approaching, and he began to mutter quickly to appease him. "I'm sorry, I didn't mean—"

Roland's fist cut his sentence off, and Jimmy crumpled to the ground. The Sheriff's blow had taken Jimmy on the nose, and the gunslinger held his hand over his face as blood trickled through his fingers. Roland had been in enough bar fights during his life to know how to hit someone effectively. He

187

knew that Jimmy wouldn't see straight for a few minutes. "You just shut up. I told you to stay in the saloon tonight, Goddamn it," he raged at Jimmy as the young man looked up at him with fear in his eyes. "You nearly got us all killed."

"But—" Jimmy tried to break in.

"I said shut up," Roland cut him off and glared at Jimmy until he was sure that the young man would remain silent. "You're lucky I don't kill you right now. I am throwing you in jail for a week, and if I hear one more word out of you, I swear to God, I'll beat the living hell out of you. Do you understand?" The young man took Roland's words literally and nodded. "Good. William, Wade, take this son of a bitch to the station house and lock him up. I'll be over in a while."

"Yes, Sheriff," they replied and roughly pulled Jimmy to his feet to haul him towards the station house.

"Morgan, go make sure those bastards left town. Meet me at the station house when you're sure they're gone." The deputy nodded and walked back to the supply shop to get his horse.

"I was going to hit him myself, but I thought I'd let you have the pleasure," Jack chuckled.

Roland flashed his lopsided grin. "You could have hit him as well. Hell, as far as I'm concerned, everyone can go over and hit the son of a bitch. With that stunt he pulled, he's lucky I didn't shoot him."

"For a second there, I thought you just might."

"I don't like dead bodies. Otherwise, he'd be dead right now. Jack, make sure that everyone settles down here. We don't need any more trouble tonight."

"No problem, Roland. I don't think anyone wants to start anything after this. Hell, that's two nights in a row we've had to draw guns. I think everyone in this town is scared to death of you."

"Not Carlos," Roland replied in a flat tone. "Do you need anyone else? I can send William and Wade back to help you."

"Naw, I'm fine. Nobody is going to do anything."

"Good, then I'm heading over to the station house. I'll meet you back at The Frontier later on." Roland tipped his hat and went to retrieve his horse. He found himself smiling as he rode back to the station house. Despite the harrowing events that had just transpired, he had lived through them and was finally going to question Alvin about the Dark Riders' involvement in Bryant's death. If all went well, he might even be able to kill the murderer within the next few days and awaken Rebecca. As he considered it, his mood seemed to brighten even more. It had been hell with her unconscious, and he was ready to see her awake again.

Once he reached the station house, he tied his horse to the tether post. Roland looked around and spotted a dark building where he could wait for the mayor to arrive. He didn't want to bring Alvin into the station house. His deputies would be inside as well as their new prisoner, and he didn't want anyone to witness their conversation. Leaning back against the building, Roland cloaked himself in darkness, impatiently watching the street for the mayor.

Alvin rode up sooner than the half hour Roland had told him. He had claimed he was tired, and that was the only reason the Sheriff could imagine for such an early arrival. Normally the mayor kept Roland waiting just to annoy him. Alvin looked a great deal better than he had back at The Rattlesnake. His color had returned, and he appeared to have recovered from his shock at Carlos's disobedience. "Alvin," Roland called and stepped away from the building so the mayor could see him.

The mayor squinted and peered at the dark building until he caught sight of Roland. Even removed from the shadows, Roland was a hard figure to see on a dark night with his black clothing. "Roland? Why aren't you inside?"

"I wanted to talk in private, and this seemed a good place. Come on over." He stepped back and waited for Alvin to step out of public view. There weren't many people out in the streets at that time of night, but Roland didn't want to take any chances. Slowly he drew his gun as Alvin approached him. *Come on, you Goddamn snake,* Roland waited expectantly.

"What's this all about, Roland? I'm tired." Alvin had an annoyed expression as he sat upon his horse.

They weren't completely out of public view, but Roland figured that nobody would be able to see him holding his gun when he was covered by shadows. Alvin, however, would be able to see him just fine. He raised his gun and pointed it at the mayor, grinning as Alvin's jaw dropped open. "I have a few questions for you, Alvin, and I want you to answer all of them. Do you understand?"

"Blazes, Roland. What in Sam Hill do you think you're doing? You can't threaten me like this. I'm the mayor, Goddamn it." He puffed up in outrage, while one of his hands slowly reached inside his coat.

"Don't even try it," Roland barked. "Take your gun out slowly and drop it on the ground, or I swear I'll shoot you right now."

Alvin took a deep breath and stared at Roland malevolently. He looked as if he couldn't believe Roland was threatening him, but one look at Roland's face told him that the Sheriff was indeed serious. He slowly drew his gun, and the Sheriff tensed for a moment until he dropped it onto the ground. "Happy?" The mayor asked sarcastically.

"I'm asking the questions, Alvin, but yes, I am happy." Roland smiled at Alvin, savoring the anger he knew was simmering inside the mayor. "Why'd you go to The Snake tonight? I know you were there for at least half an hour, so don't lie to me." The mayor's eyes widened for a moment, and he looked around as if trying to think of answer. "Answer me now, Alvin, or you're a dead man."

"You won't shoot me," Alvin told Roland.

"Try me and find out. Now answer me, Goddamn it."

Alvin blinked at the intensity of Roland's reply and looked a little less sure of himself than he had a moment before. "Fine. I was talking to Carlos. You pissed me off before, Roland, and I was going to have some of the Riders make a disturbance over the next few days. That's it."

"What kind of disturbance?"

"The usual. Getting drunk, getting in fights, maybe even firing a few shots. Nothing more than that. Just enough to keep you busy."

Roland shook his head. "I should shoot you anyway, you son of a bitch, but it's not worth it. It doesn't look like you control the Riders anymore, so I'll just deal with them however I see fit." He paused for a moment to let Alvin's fear rise. At last, he was going to ask the question he had been yearning to ask for the past two days, and he wanted Alvin as malleable as possible. "One more question, Alvin, and I want you to think *real* hard about this one. Who killed Bryant White?"

Alvin surprised Roland when his face turned completely pale. "I don't know," he stammered.

"That's not what I want to hear. I know it's a Dark Rider, and I want you to tell me which one." Roland closed one eye as he carefully aimed his gun at Alvin's head.

"I'm a dead man if I tell you that, Roland."

"You're a dead man if you don't. This is your last chance, Alvin. Who killed Bryant White?"

Alvin shivered and gulped as he looked at the gun pointed at him. "Curly."

Roland's eyes narrowed as he gauged the mayor to see if he was telling the truth. "Why the hell would Curly kill Bryant? That doesn't make any sense." He knew that Curly had played cards with Bryant the night he was killed, but the Dark Rider had no motive.

"He was drunk, and they got in an argument. That's all I know, Roland. Carlos told me to keep the blame off Curly, and I did." A bead of sweat trickled down the side of Alvin's face.

The mayor's display of fear convinced Roland that he was telling the truth. Roland never would have picked Curly as Bryant's murderer, but it did make some sense. Curly became awfully violent when he was drunk, and Bryant's murder had been brutally violent. Roland was upset with himself, though. Curly had been in his grasp that night, and he had let him go. It hadn't been the ideal setting to arrest the Dark Rider, but it still pained him to see the key to Rebecca's awakening safely out of town. Curly would probably be back the following night, and then Roland intended to kill the Dark Rider and free Rebecca from the Land of Shadows.

"You see, Alvin, that wasn't too painful." Roland smiled and walked towards the mayor, never taking his gun off of him.

"What are you doing?" Alvin drew back as he eyed Roland warily.

"Getting your gun," Sheriff Black replied and bent over to pick up Alvin's pistol. He opened the chamber and tapped the bullets out, letting them spill onto the ground. With a quick jerk of his wrist, Roland snapped the chamber back into place and offered the unloaded weapon to the mayor. "I believe this is yours."

Alvin reached out for the gun with a trembling hand and slowly holstered it. "Are we done here?"

"You can go, Alvin, but I wouldn't go talking about this to anyone. You might piss me off, and I don't think you want that. Remember what I said. If you push me, I'll push back." Roland chuckled and walked over to the station house to check on his prisoner.

Chapter Ten

Roland awoke at dawn the following morning feeling rejuvenated and in a wondrous mood. For the first time since Rebecca had fallen ill, Roland's slumber hadn't been plagued by nightmares. Instead he had dreamed of Rebecca awakening. Her beauty had shone radiantly, and they stood before Reverend Thatcher to speak their wedding vows. Alvin had given him the information that he needed to banish Bryant from the Land of Shadows, and Roland intended to introduce Curly to his maker that evening. It was a shame that Running Brook had already summoned the Ghost Hunters. He planned on taking care of the problem himself, and the mysterious pair Running Brook spoke of would be wasting their time.

He didn't get out of bed immediately, choosing instead to lounge for a few minutes longer as sunlight crept through the curtains. His fortunes were finally taking a turn for the better, and he wanted to savor the feeling for a little longer before he resumed his duties as Sheriff. The previous day had yielded the identity of Bryant's killer, a resolution over the Cheyenne, and the destruction of Alvin's source of power. *Not a bad day*, Roland chuckled to himself. He counted on that Wednesday being just as productive and planned on having Rebecca smiling and laughing in his arms again before he went to sleep.

Finally restlessness set in, and the Sheriff swung his legs out of bed and came to his feet. He stumbled over to the water basin and splashed some water on his face. Four days' worth of stubble decorated his face, and Roland thought about riding back to his house to get his razor. He hadn't worried about it the last few days, but Rebecca would be awake that evening. Roland didn't want to greet her with a scraggly face. *Maybe I can borrow one from George*, Roland thought to himself.

His suit was slightly dirty, but it was still clean enough for him to wear. He put on the black coat, trousers, and boots then pulled the brim of his hat down low. Roland took a moment to polish his badge before pinning it to his coat. Lastly, he buckled on his holsters. He drew one of his guns and opened the chamber, making sure that it was fully loaded, then proceeded to do the same with the other. There was going to be a gunfight sometime that day, and he wanted to be fully prepared. Roland almost felt sorry for Curly and whoever else wandered into town with him. They didn't know what was lying in store for them.

He locked his door behind him then entered Rebecca's room. The sight of her tore at his heart, but Roland entered the room with a bounce in his step. She wouldn't be in that condition much longer. Taking a seat beside her, Roland reached out and took one of her cold, frail hands in his own. "Good morning,

Rebecca. I know who killed Bryant, and I'm going to get him tonight. Soon, you'll be awake again. Soon," Roland told her softly.

Roland sat with her quietly for nearly ten minutes before bringing her hand to his lips and kissing it. "I'll see you tonight, and everything will be better. You'll see." A tear threatened to form in the corner of his eye, but it wasn't from sorrow. His life had been so perfect before she had fallen ill, and he intended to resume that course without delay. He had no doubt that he would bring Curly to justice and Rebecca would awaken. Depending on how weak she was from her four days of slumber, they could even marry within the next few days. "I love you, Rebecca White." Roland placed her hand gently back at her side and left the room, locking it behind him.

Nobody else had risen that morning, and Sheriff Black left the quiet saloon to relieve Phillip of his duties. The air outside seemed to have grown even hotter. Sweat formed on his forehead the moment he left The Frontier. He entered the station house and closed the door behind him in relief. "Damn, it's *hot* out there," he commented to Phillip.

Phillip sat behind the desk and put a book down in front of him. He leaned back and put a hand comfortably on his ample stomach. "Didn't think it would cool down any. I just hope it lets up some before the Fourth."

"You and me both." Roland shook his head ruefully. "You remember last year. The way things have been going lately, I half expect a shoot-out with the Riders," the Sheriff commented wryly.

The deputy laughed, but they both knew that there was the possibility of real danger on the holiday. The Sheriff had only been in town for a month when New Haven celebrated the Fourth of July in 1891. It had been a wild affair with fireworks, and quite a few people had consumed more than their fair share of alcohol. Luckily no guns had been fired, but that had been a close call. A fair number of fights and brawls had broken out, and only the presence of Roland and his deputies had discouraged them from escalating any further. The upcoming celebration promised to be even greater, especially with the magician Alvin had promised to bring.

"Any problems last night?"

Phillip shook his head. "Everything was quiet after the Riders left town. I think you scared everyone. Nobody wants to cross you after that."

A mischievous grin crossed Roland's face. "Good. They shouldn't cross me. And what about him? Any noise from him after I left?" Roland thrust his chin towards the cell room where Jimmy slept.

Phillip shook his head again. "Not a word. I think you scared him worse than everyone else." The deputy squinted at Roland and rubbed his chin. "I thought you were going to kill him. He must've thought the same."

"I should've killed him. He nearly put us all in the middle of a damn gunfight. The last thing this town needs is a shoot-out with a dozen Dark Riders.

But don't worry, Phillip. I won't hurt him. I'm just going to let him serve out his week, then I'll let him go," Roland assured his deputy.

"You're the Sheriff. You need anything else?"

"Not right now, but I want you back on duty a couple of hours early."

Phillip shot him a worried glance. "You don't think the Riders will come back again, do you?"

"You never know. Carlos has a temper on him, and there's no telling what he'll do. It can't hurt to be safe," Roland lied to his deputy. He feared the Riders would return to town, but not to seek revenge from the previous night. The Riders likely would try to kill him to avenge the death of Curly. The Dark Rider had killed Bryant, and nothing would stop Roland from dispensing justice upon him. Carlos, however, would definitely attempt to avenge one of his brethren, putting himself and Roland on a collision course for another confrontation. Despite that danger, Roland had no intention of backing down from his plan. He just wanted to be ready for the fallout.

"Count me in then." Phillip assumed a grave face. The deputy stood up, grunting as sweat rolled down his cheeks. The heat always bothered Phillip. He didn't mind the winter too much, but he wanted to curl up and sleep for three months when the summer blazed through Colorado. "What time do you want me back?"

"Seven." Roland hated to deceive Phillip, but he had no choice. He had to kill Curly to save Rebecca, and he needed to prepare for the Dark Riders' retaliation. At least his men wouldn't be caught unaware when Carlos returned to town with a thirst for vengeance. Roland just hoped that all of his men lived through it. He didn't know how he would feel if one of his men died because of his actions.

"Sounds good." Phillip tipped his battered hat and walked to the door. "Damn, it's hot," he repeated Roland's earlier comment then closed the door behind him.

Roland took a seat behind the desk and waited for William to take over the shift. The Sheriff was in a wonderful mood and just wanted to lean back and savor it. It wouldn't be long before Curly entered town and Roland administered justice. The fallout of his actions might be severe, but it was a risk that Roland had to take. He doubted the Riders would wage a pitched battle in the middle of town if Roland had enough men in position, and he could handle a few loose cannons if they came gunning for him. If worse came to worst, he and Rebecca could move away from New Haven and begin their lives anew somewhere far from Carlos and the Dark Riders.

For nearly half an hour, Roland leaned back in his chair with his feet propped on top of the desk, picturing Curly dying over and over again. Sometimes it was a duel, and the Sheriff calmly put a bullet through the Rider's heart before Curly could even raise his gun. Other times, he simply shot Curly in cold blood. It wasn't a particularly glamorous method of killing someone, but Roland wasn't interested in being stylish. He just wanted Curly dead, Bryant banished from the Land of Shadows, and Rebecca awake once again. *Soon, Curly, you're mine,* Roland kept thinking to himself.

"Hey, I'm hungry," Jimmy's voice broke his concentration, and the Sheriff looked over at the cell room door. One of his hands instinctively dropped to his holster. His fingers lightly tapped the butt of his pistol as he slowly approached the door and swung it open.

Jimmy was the only prisoner in the pair of cells. He stood against the bars, curling his arms about them and lazily watching the main door open. The young man was a far cry from the previous night. His dark hair was tangled, and his clothes were wrinkled. A purple bruise decorated his cheek from a punch one of the deputies must have delivered, and his nose was still swollen from the punch Roland had administered. But the cocky look was even more evident on his face. Instead of flinching from the bars, his back arched defiantly.

"You called?" Roland responded to the arrogant pose by leaning back against the wall as if he didn't notice the posturing. He had wanted to kill Jimmy the night before, but Roland had calmed down since then. Despite the fact that Roland had nearly wound up in a gunfight because of the young man, he couldn't help but like Jimmy. It was a stupid stunt that Jimmy had pulled, but it was no different than something Roland himself might have tried when he had first ventured West. The more he talked to Jimmy, the more the young man reminded Roland of how naïve he had been during his early days as a gunslinger.

The prisoner raised his eyebrows sardonically and cracked his knuckles in a show of disdain. "Yeah, I called. I could use some breakfast," Jimmy stated in a flat tone.

Roland tipped back his head and laughed. He wouldn't have expected any different from the young man. So far, Jimmy hadn't failed to put forth a front of bravado, and he wasn't disappointing Roland that Wednesday morning, Despite his amusement with Jimmy's demeanor, Roland would be damned if he gave in to a prisoner's demands in his own jail. "This isn't some hotel, boy. This is a jail. You'll get some food later on when we decide to give it to you."

Jimmy's face turned red, and he reached instinctively for his belt. Roland only laughed harder, which seemed to make Jimmy even angrier. "Damn it, it isn't funny. I'm hungry," the young gunslinger pouted, but his tone sounded more embarrassed than angry.

Roland cocked his head to the side while Jimmy continued to glare at him. "Have you ever been in jail before, Jimmy?"

A faint blush crept up Jimmy's neck again, answering Roland's question. "No, I haven't. So what?" Jimmy asked belligerently.

Roland shrugged his shoulders and tried his best to wipe the smile from his face. He remembered the first time he had spent a night behind bars, and he hadn't acted much better than Jimmy. "Listen, I just wanted to tell you a few things to make your time here a little easier. Okay?" Roland asked cordially.

Jimmy still looked at Roland with that cocky look on his face, but he had lost some of the edge from it. He appeared grateful, but he nodded grudgingly, unwilling to admit it. "Fine, I'll listen," he answered flippantly.

Thanks for the favor, Roland thought sarcastically, but he didn't reprimand Jimmy for his rudeness. The first day in jail could easily overwhelm people, and Roland was having fun talking to the young man. It was like having a son just like himself. He might not be able to help Jimmy much, but Roland intended to at least teach him a few things about living in the West while he had the young man in his prison. "Good. You get food twice a day, once around noon and once in the evening. The rest of the time, keep quiet. You're in jail, not a saloon. Most of the time, I'd say you could chat with the deputies. Robert and Phillip usually don't mind the company, but you're not too popular with anyone right now. Not after last night." Roland wasn't upset with Jimmy anymore, but he couldn't guarantee that the rest of his deputies would be as forgiving.

"So I'm just supposed to sit here?" All traces of cockiness faded from his face.

"What did you think jail was like, Jimmy? It's supposed to be a punishment."

"Yeah, but it seemed so much better in all the stories," Jimmy muttered and stared at his surroundings, for the first time realizing that he would be spending quite a bit of time in the close confines. The cell was small, a ten foot square. A metal chamberpot and a rickety cot were the only two objects inside. It wasn't glamorous, but like Roland had stated, he wasn't trying to woo occupants.

"I've heard a lot of stories about the West, and most of them don't hit too close to the truth. Just remember that," Roland advised the young man with a rueful shake of his head. He wanted to laugh at the gunslinger; his glorious notions of gunslinging were amusing. Roland had headed West with wool over his eyes years before, but even he hadn't been as naïve as Jimmy.

"I will," Jimmy answered sullenly and looked at the floor. "Are all jails like this then?"

"I've seen a lot of jails in my time, and this one is actually better than most, so count yourself lucky."

"Have you ever been in jail?" Jimmy asked quietly.

Roland barked out a laugh at the question, and Jimmy looked up quickly to see what was so funny. "I'm sorry. Just thinking back," the Sheriff apologized.

He had been arrested in the very first town he had entered in Colorado. Like Jimmy, he had walked about the streets as if he was the quickest, meanest gun ever to brave the West. One brawl and a night in jail later, Roland had lost a lot of that arrogance and settled down somewhat to lead a productive career as a gunslinger. He just hoped the same trick would work for Jimmy and the young man wouldn't get himself into any more trouble. Roland had decided to keep him in jail for a week, but if Jimmy tried a stunt like that in any other city, he would find himself swinging at the end of a rope. "Yeah, I've been in jail before. It was a long time ago." Roland couldn't help but grin as he thought back on the event.

"What for? Did you escape?" Jimmy perked up excitedly, expecting the Sheriff to have lived through one of the daredevil escapes he had read about.

"Escape? Nobody escapes from jail," Roland laughed, and Jimmy's smile disappeared from his face. "I got in a fight, and I spent the night in jail. That was it."

Jimmy looked fairly disappointed as another of his precious myths of the Wild West was debunked. "You mean you never met *anybody* that escaped from jail?"

Roland was about to answer no, but he stopped when he remembered someone. He couldn't believe he had almost forgotten that story. "I met one man who escaped from prison," he answered quietly, and his mouth curled into a lopsided grin as Jimmy's eyes lit up with excitement.

"What happened?" Jimmy folded his hands together tightly and tapped his foot on the floor impatiently.

"I wasn't there, but I heard about it later on," Sheriff Black prefaced his story then quickly resumed as he saw how anxious Jimmy was. "Doc and I—"

"*Doc Holliday?*" Jimmy broke in excitedly. He leaned forward, his eyes growing wide with excitement.

"Yes, Doc Holliday," Roland answered and shook his head. The young gunslinger had loved to hear his tales of the Wild West but had been most interested in those of the famous gambler. "We were out on that bounty hunt I told you about the other night."

"The one where you tracked down those outlaws?" The prisoner interrupted again.

"Yes, damn it. Now will you shut up and let me finish the story?" Sheriff Black paused a moment to make sure that Jimmy would indeed remain silent before continuing. The young man kept tapping his foot with excitement, but he had pursed his lips together tightly. Satisfied, Roland continued his story. "Doc was telling me about this time he was in jail. I can't remember where it was. Somewhere in South Dakota I think." Roland squinted and looked at the ceiling, sifting through his recollections of the event. He shrugged his shoulders a moment later. "It doesn't really matter where. Doc was in jail, and he was going to be hanged the following morning.

"Security was pretty tight around the jail, and there wasn't any way that Doc was going to break out on his own. But he had help that night, or he wouldn't have lived to make such a name for himself. He had a whore he had met, and she was quite taken with him as he told it. Kate was her name, Big Nose Kate, one of the smartest women in the West. Not too pretty, though. She had a big crooked nose, but she and Doc were nearly always together from what I understand. Kate set a fire on the other side of town, and every man guarding the jail rushed to put it out. Only one remained, and Kate sneaked up to the jail and shot him. She freed Doc, and the two of them rode out of town together while everyone else was still busy with the fire. That's about all I remember," Roland finished his tale, his eyes looking through Jimmy to a time that he remembered fondly.

Jimmy had listened with rapt attention, and he waited until the Sheriff was finished with his story before speaking. "I never heard that story before, and I've heard a lot about Doc Holliday. Do you think it really happened?"

Roland shrugged his shoulders. "Who knows with Doc. He was a crazy son of a bitch," Roland laughed. "He'd tell people what they wanted to hear most of the time, but he seemed pretty serious that night. He was quiet when he told the story. Most of the time, Doc liked to brag." Roland shrugged his shoulders. "I'll never know, but if I had to guess I would say he was telling the truth," the Sheriff answered and began to tell Jimmy other tales of the notorious gunslinger and gambler as well as other stories he had heard over the years about other famous figures in the Old West.

Time flew by quickly while Roland entertained the prisoner. Normally he left his prisoners alone to spend their confinement in solitude, but he enjoyed telling the stories to Jimmy. The young man had an enthusiasm for them, and Roland was all too happy to recount things that had happened during that period of his life. He stared off to one side of the cell with a lost look in his eyes as he brought up memories from his glory years. Before he knew it, it was nearly noon and William had shown up to take over the shift. "I'll see you tomorrow," Roland told the prisoner then went to meet his deputy.

"Morning, Sheriff," the rakish deputy greeted him as Roland locked the cell room door behind him.

"Morning, William."

The deputy pointed at the cells. "Is he giving you any trouble?" He asked pugnaciously.

"No, I was just talking to him," Roland answered quickly to head off any trouble. "Let's just make sure he's still alive at the end of the week," the Sheriff commented in a gravely tone and lowered his eyebrows. He didn't want the young gunslinger to get roughed up while he was away, and he reckoned that a few authoritative words should do the trick.

"Sure, Sheriff, no problem. I was just wondering," William quickly acquiesced to Roland. "Should we be on alert today?"

"Yeah, there's no telling what The Riders might do. I don't want any trouble with them if they come into town, though. Carlos isn't stupid. He won't pick a fight unless we piss him off first." Roland paused and cracked his knuckles ominously. "But if anybody sees Curly today, I want to know about it immediately."

William leaned back in surprise. "Curly? What do you want with Curly?" He asked confusedly.

"Don't you worry about it. It's between me and Curly. Got it?" Roland pointed a finger and stared at William intently.

The deputy took a half-step back from Roland's menacing glare and spread his hands wide. "Yeah, Sheriff. You're the boss."

"Good, I'll see you later." Roland tipped his hat and left William alone to keep an eye on the station house. The air had grown considerably hotter while he had been inside, and he rushed across the street before he broke out in a sweat. Sheriff Black took a deep breath once he was back in the shade and fanned himself with one hand as he entered The Last Frontier. *This weather has to end,* Roland thought to himself.

George greeted him as he walked inside, and Roland chatted with the saloon owner for a few minutes before sitting down at his customary table to wait for Jack. Not too much later, the deputy arrived at The Frontier and headed towards Roland's table. "Morning, Jack," the Sheriff greeted as Jack pulled up a chair at the table.

"Morning, Roland." Jack shook his head. "That was some night we had."

"You can say that again. Hopefully things will calm down for a while."

"You don't think Carlos will come back to town?" Jack raised an eyebrow in surprise.

"He'll come back. I'm pretty damn sure of it. It's only a matter of time. Hopefully he won't start any trouble, but I want everyone ready for the worst. It's one week until the Fourth. If we can keep everything calm until then I think we'll be fine." Roland smiled, and his eyes drifted from Jack for a moment. By the Fourth, he planned on having taken care of Curly and being married to Rebecca.

"You're probably right." Jack paused and looked more closely at the Sheriff. Something about the Sheriff's smile struck him as odd. "You're in an awfully good mood today. Is Rebecca doing better?"

Roland felt his spirits darken for a moment, but they quickly rose back up again. Rebecca would soon be awake. All he had to do was catch Curly, and that would be accomplished by the end of the day. "No, she's still sick. I'm just glad to be alive, that's all. Last night was a close one." He hated to lie to Jack so much, but until Rebecca was safely awake, he intended to keep his friend in the dark.

"Sounds like a good reason to me. It's good to see you in a better mood, Roland. Don't worry about Rebecca. I'm sure she'll be healthy again real soon," Jack told Roland with a sincere look on his face.

"I'm sure she will too," Roland replied and smiled a toothy grin back at his deputy. "Jack, I want everyone to keep an eye out for Curly tonight."

"Curly?" Jack looked at the Sheriff strangely. "What do you want him for?"

Roland leaned forward and narrowed his eyes. "This doesn't leave the table."

The deputy looked at Roland curiously and nodded. "Sure, Roland. Whatever you say."

The Sheriff flashed his lopsided grin and leaned back in his chair. He didn't mind Jack knowing that Curly was Bryant's murderer as long as Jack didn't know why Roland was so keen on solving the crime after all the time that had passed. Jack wouldn't blab about it to anyone else either. Curly might just avoid New Haven if he knew Roland planned on arresting him for Byrant's murder. "He killed Bryant."

Jack jerked forward in his chair, his eyes burning into Roland. "Curly? Are you sure?"

"Take my word, Jack. It's him. I have it on very good authority." Roland smirked as he remembered how he'd dragged the information out of Alvin.

"How'd you find that out? He's been dead for almost a year." Jack shook his head as if he couldn't believe it was true.

"I'm gonna keep that one a secret, Jack. The person doesn't want to be identified. Hard to believe, eh?" Roland rubbed his hands together gleefully. *Curly, you are a dead man*, he thought to himself. *Soon, Rebecca, soon you'll be with me again.*

"I just can't believe it. I would have suspected Carlos or any of the other Riders, but Curly? Hell, Roland, all he ever does is get drunk and threaten people. Whoever cut open Bryant was a mean son of a bitch. It just doesn't make sense."

Roland shrugged his shoulders. It didn't make sense to him either, but he didn't really care at that point. Alvin had told him the truth. He had seen the fear in the mayor's eyes, and he was convinced that Curly was his man. Nothing would stop him from putting a bullet between the Dark Rider's eyes. "I agree. Who knows, maybe he got drunk. You know him. He gets crazy when he's drinking. Trust me, though. I'm positive it's Curly. Make sure everyone knows to keep an eye out for him. If he shows his face in town, I'm arresting the son of a bitch." *Then I'll kill him,* Roland added to himself.

"You've got it, Roland. I'll be happy to see the bastard hang if he's the one." Jack shook his head. "Blazes, Roland. Carlos will throw a conniption fit if we arrest Curly. He'll try to show you up to prove he's not scared of you."

"I'll worry about Carlos later. Let's just get Curly and deal with the rest of the Riders if they become a problem. Nobody commits murder in my town and walks away from it."

"I'm not saying let him walk away, Roland. I'm just thinking out loud. I'll let everyone know to keep an eye out for him when I make my rounds." Jack shook his head one more time. "Damn, Curly?" He muttered to himself.

The Sheriff felt his heart beat quicker. *So close,* he thought. With all of his deputies looking for Curly, the Rider wouldn't be in town more than ten minutes before Roland got a hold of him. "Have you seen Alvin this morning?" He asked brightly. Everything was going perfectly so far that day.

Roland's tone of voice instantly put Jack on edge. "No, I haven't. Why do you ask?" Jack kept a close eye on the Sheriff. Roland hated Alvin, and he didn't know why Roland would sound so happy when talking about the mayor.

"No reason, Jack. I was just curious," Roland answered and his grin became even wider. Alvin could usually be seen in the morning, trying to socialize as much as possible. There were business contacts at the train station, visitors to talk to, and voters to keep in his pocket. If he wasn't anywhere to be seen, the previous night must have truly shaken him. Roland wanted to stand up and dance. Curly would soon be dead, Rebecca would soon be awake, and his biggest source of irritation appeared to have lost all of his power.

The Sheriff's answer and his huge smile put fear into Jack. He had known Roland a long time, and when he got that grin, he had usually done something foolish. "You didn't go and do something stupid again, did you?" Jack gave him a withering gaze.

"Me?" Roland put a hand on his chest and tried to look convincing. He didn't want Jack to lecture him and spoil his good mood, but he couldn't make the smile go away. "I didn't do anything, Jack. I'm just happy to be alive. Come on, we've got Bryant's killer, and there's a rift between Carlos and Alvin. You should be smiling too. Why else do you think Alvin's missing?"

"I guess you're right." Jack matched Roland's grin with one of his own. "Maybe we'll get some peace around here for a while. Well, if there's nothing else, I'll go out on my rounds now. I'll be sure to tell everyone to keep an eye out for Curly."

"Sounds good." Roland tipped his hat and rubbed his hands together while Jack left the saloon. "Soon, you bastard, you're mine," he whispered gleefully and began to wait for word of Curly's return.

A short while later, William showed up at The Frontier to help keep an eye on the saloon. Roland wasn't in the mood to chat as he normally did. He was completely focused on finding and killing Curly that evening, and he didn't want anything to divert his attention. After a few words, William caught on that Roland wasn't in one of his talkative moods and took a seat at the bar. The deputy looked much happier at the bar chatting with George and the barmaids, but Roland scarcely paid him any notice. He kept gazing out the window, waiting for one of his deputies to come galloping up, or even better for Curly himself to come into The Last Frontier. The first part of the day dragged by slowly. Plenty of people walked or rode through the streets, but nearly all of them were preparing for the afternoon train. There wasn't a sign of a single Dark Rider.

Shortly after three that afternoon, Sullivan stopped by The Last Frontier to check on Rebecca. Roland immediately went to join the stout, little doctor as he headed upstairs. "Come up and get me if there's any trouble," he called out to William and trudged up right behind the doctor.

Once again, the sight of Rebecca's body nearly brought tears to his eyes, but it was tempered with the knowledge that all would soon be better. *Curly usually doesn't come to town until later,* Roland tried to cheer himself up, *and when he does, he'll die.* Sullivan grabbed one of her frail wrists and gauged her pulse as Roland watched anxiously. *Let her be okay. One more night and you'll be safe again, Rebecca.* "How is she, Doc?"

"She's very weak. I can keep giving her water and broth, but she'll waste away if this goes on a few more weeks. Are you sure you won't let me bleed her? I think it might—"

"No!" Roland broke in loudly, and Sullivan flinched slightly. "I'm sorry," Roland spread his hands peacefully. "I've been on edge lately, but don't cut her. Do whatever you have to, but no bleeding." He was counting on Rebecca awakening that night, and Roland had no intention of letting Sullivan cut her a few hours before that occurred.

"Fine, then let me get back to work." Sullivan turned his back on Roland and quickly finished his cursory examination. He took a few minutes to pour some water down her throat while massaging her neck to ensure that she drank it. After that, he closed his medical bag and left the room.

Roland waited until the doctor left and turned to Rebecca's listless body. "I love you, Rebecca White. Tonight, you'll be free again," he spoke softly then quietly closed the door behind him.

The night slowly dragged on while Roland impatiently tapped his foot and gazed out the window, anxiously awaiting any word of Curly's return. Morgan rode up to the saloon shortly after sunset, and Roland leapt out of his chair and dashed to The Frontier's entrance. The deputy looked up in surprise as Roland burst from the saloon. "Is the son of a bitch here?" Roland's hand anxiously tapped the butt of one of his pistols. He could barely wait to disperse justice and see his beloved Rebecca awaken.

Morgan, however, shook his head. "Naw, Roland. I just came by to see how things were here. I haven't seen a single Rider all night. I guess we must've scared them off after last night."

Roland exhaled loudly in disappointment. "Everything's fine. I just want a few words with Curly. That's all." *Goddamn you Curly, come to town. I'm going to kill you, you son of a bitch, then Rebecca and I can get married.*

"Everyone's looking for him. Don't worry, you'll know as soon as he gets into town. How's Miss White doing?" The grizzled deputy looked at the Sheriff sympathetically, a strange expression for his wrinkled face. Morgan had been married for over twenty years, but his wife had passed away from pneumonia nearly five years before. He usually kept his face a stoic mask, but he understood what Roland was going through.

"She's doing the same, Morgan. Thanks." Roland began to calm down at the deputy's words. *He'll be here soon,* Roland told himself. *Then Rebecca will wake up.* "She'll be back to health soon. I'm convinced of it, Morgan."

"That's good to hear, Roland. If you'll excuse me, I'll be on my way. I want to keep patrolling. They could be back any time, and we want to be ready." Morgan tipped his hat and walked back to his horse.

"Let me know if Curly shows up," Roland called out one more time needlessly.

Morgan turned back to him and shook his head ruefully. "Don't worry, Sheriff, you'll know before the bastard has a chance to get a drink."

Roland scowled at the way he was acting. He had to be calm and patient and wait for Curly to arrive. Running around like a headless chicken wasn't doing anybody any good. He took a seat at his table, but try as he might, he couldn't keep himself from tapping his foot on the floor impatiently as he waited for the Dark Rider to return. With his face locked in a grim mask of anticipation, he ignored the rest of the saloon and sat with his head turned towards the street.

William kept his distance from the Sheriff that night. He saw the scowl on the Sheriff's face and the impatient way he kept staring out the window. William had no intention of trifling with Roland when he was in one of his foul moods, especially when there were so many women to talk to. He kept himself busy bantering with several of Sherry's strumpets that evening. Most of the tavern's patrons also left Roland alone when they saw the look on his face or after a discreet head shake from George. A few went by to say hello, but after a few curt words from Sheriff Black, they quickly found someplace else in The Frontier more interesting.

The hours kept passing by without any word of Curly's return. A few more of his deputies dropped by, but it appeared that all of the Dark Riders had stayed out of town that evening. They soon stopped coming by at all after being accosted by the eager Sheriff before they entered the saloon. Miss Higgins showed up shortly after eight to feed Rebecca, but Roland stayed at his table. He didn't want to watch Rebecca being fed. He was already on edge. She left soon after, and Roland resumed his impatient wait. At ten, Roland had given up hope that the Riders would return and asked George for a bottle of whiskey. His wondrous good mood had soured. He sat at his table in stony silence, calmly downing full shots one after another. By the time Jack showed up shortly after midnight, Roland was feeling the effects of his drinking. He chose to wait for the deputy at his table instead of greeting him outside.

Jack entered the saloon and headed straight for Roland's table but stopped abruptly when he caught sight of the Sheriff. "Blazes, Roland. You look like hell," the deputy exclaimed in surprise. He had seen Sheriff Black drink whiskey before, but Jack had never seen Roland look as terrible as he did that night. The Sheriff's eyes were streaked with red lines, and the blood had drained from his face, giving him a ghastly appearance.

"Tell me about it," Roland slurred and pushed the chair across the table backwards with his foot. "Take a seat, Jack."

Jack paused and looked at Roland, but the Sheriff just sat there silently, staring back up at him with bloodshot eyes. He shook his head once disapprovingly before sitting in the chair Roland had just shoved back. "What the hell are you doing, Roland? You're drunk, Goddamn it," he whispered fiercely.

"Why, I believe you're right, Jack." Roland reached out for the bottle of whiskey to pour himself another glass, but his deputy was quicker and pulled it to the other side of the table.

"I think you've had enough," Jack told the Sheriff in a stern voice.

"Damn it, you always take the fun out of everything, Jack." Roland sighed once in disappointment. He was in the mood for one more shot, but he supposed that he had probably had enough already. "I take it there's no word of Curly?" Roland asked rhetorically.

"No, we would've told you if there was. Is that why you're drunk, Roland? We'll get him tomorrow or the day after. What in Sam Hill's wrong with you? You've been acting strange for the last week."

Roland waved a hand in dismissal. "Don't worry about me. I'm fine. What about Alvin? Has anyone seen that Goddamn snake today?"

"Nobody's seen him all day. It's kinda strange. Alvin's usually out talking to people." Jack rubbed his chin thoughtfully. "I wonder if he's sick."

"Maybe." Roland smiled wickedly, brandishing his teeth. *Alvin, I go you. You're running scared of me.* "I'm going upstairs, Jack. That son of a bitch won't show up tonight. I guess we scared them off. Maybe tomorrow." He pushed his chair back and slowly stood up. Roland had to put his han

204

down on the table for a few moments to gain his sense of balance. "Wake me if there's any trouble, Jack. G'night."

"Good night, Roland. I'll see you in the morning." Jack shook his head as he watched Roland stumble towards the staircase.

Many of the patrons stared at the drunken Sheriff as he made his way across the saloon, but Roland paid them no mind as he slowly made his way upstairs, clinging to the banister. He stopped at the top of the staircase and hunched over to catch his breath and his bearings. The hallway kept spinning and only grew worse when he closed his eyes. Lurching forward again, he made his way down the hall, leaning against the wall comfortingly to keep from falling over. He stopped at Rebecca's door and fumbled inside his coat pocket for the key to her room. But that simple task eluded him, and he pressed his hand against her door. "I love you, Rebecca. Tomorrow. Tomorrow, he'll come back, then everything will be better. I promise," he mumbled and staggered over one door to his own room.

Once again, he fished inside his pocket to find the key to his own room. After nearly a minute, he found it and looked down at it blearily. He glanced over at Rebecca's room one last time and considered going in to sit with her a moment, but he didn't want to visit her in such a drunken state. He would wait and talk to her in the morning after he had sobered up. Roland unlocked his door, entered his room, and managed to take off his hat and his boots before he finally passed out for the night.

Roland awoke the next morning when the sun first started creeping through his curtains. His head felt as if Dennis the blacksmith had been pounding it with one of his hammers, and his mouth was completely dry. Immediately he promised himself that he would never drink as much as he had the previous evening. It wasn't the first time he had paid the penalty for drinking too much, and it wasn't the first time he had made such a promise. He held a hand over his eyes to shield them from the horridly bright sunlight and forced himself to sit up. His entire body groaned at the effort, but Roland stood and shuffled towards the water basin. There was no taking back the drinking that he had done the night before, and he would just have to pay the penalty for his actions.

His hands kept trembling slightly as he dressed, and he hoped that his hangover would pass quickly. Sheriff Black wanted to be ready for Curly when he returned to town, but he wouldn't be effective if his hands couldn't get a decent grip on his pistols. Roland shrugged it off, though. His hangovers never lasted too long, and Curly wouldn't come back to town until well into the evening. After he donned his badge of office and buckled on his holsters, Roland went to see Rebecca.

He was positive that Curly would return that Friday and Rebecca would finally emerge from her slumber. Yet he had thought the same thing the day before, and none of the Dark Riders had shown their faces in town. But he

forced himself to be optimistic as he opened the door. That was the only w
he could deal with seeing Rebecca. She seemed to grow thinner by the d
while the dark rings around her eyes became more pronounced. Her che
kept sinking inwards, and the bones of her skull were clearly visible. Sulli
had been right when he said she only a had a few weeks. *That won't happ*
Roland thought defiantly. *Curly's coming back tonight, Goddamn it, and*
kill the son of a bitch. A scowl crossed his face as he thought of the Dark Ri
but his features softened as he took a seat on the bed. "Good morning, Rebec
I love you," Roland greeted her and ran a knuckle across her pale forehead

For ten minutes Roland sat by her side, telling her of his previous d
but after that short time he finally had to leave. He remembered her vibr
smile and demure eyes, and he hated to have that memory tainted by her sicke
appearance. "I'll see you tonight, Rebecca. Curly will come back, and I'll
him. Then Bryant will leave, and you can come home again. I love you," Rol
whispered softly and placed a kiss on her cold, sunken cheek.

He stood outside her door for a moment and tried to collect his thoug
before going downstairs. *That bastard has to come back. Yesterday was a flu*
The Riders were just scared and taking a day off. They have to come ba
Especially Curly. Roland cracked his knuckles ominously, convinced it wo
come to pass. He was determined that Rebecca would be free that evening

His morning flew by quickly. He took over the shift from Phillip a
spent the next few hours talking with Jimmy. The young gunslinger was anxi
to be released from prison, but he seemed to find it worth the price after hear
some of Roland's stories. The Sheriff didn't mind either. It distracted him fo
few hours. He needed a break from worrying about saving Rebecca and Curl
return, and telling stories of his past always seemed to brighten his mood.
the time Wade showed up to relieve him, Roland was almost disappointec
leave.

He took his usual table at The Last Frontier, and shortly after, Ja
showed up for his customary visit. The deputy looked at Roland wit
disapproving frown as he walked up to the table. "Don't bother, Jack," Rol
irritably cut off the inevitable quip from his old friend. He wasn't in the mo
for any of Jack's humor that morning.

A tiny smile played at the corners of Jack's mouth, and his countena
turned to one of mirth. "Why, Roland, I wasn't going to mention anything,
now that you bring it up—What were you doing last night? I don't think I
ever seen you that drunk." Jack pulled up a chair and joined Roland at
table. He folded his hands and stared at Roland innocently.

Roland sighed and shook his head. "Let's just say Rebecca being s
got to me. Okay? Can we leave it that, please?" Roland tried to make his vo
sound hoarse.

206

Jack instantly looked like he regretted his words, and Roland felt a pang of guilt for manipulating his friend. "I'm sorry, Roland. I was just kidding you. How are you feeling this morning?"

"I'm feeling better. I thought I was going to die when I got out of bed." Roland paused to wipe a bead of sweat from his forehead. Even inside the brutal heat was still scorching the people of New Haven. "So did any of the Riders come into town last night?" Roland thought he would have heard of it if they had, but Jack would be the one to know.

The deputy shook his head. "Naw, I never saw a single one of 'em. Carlos must be scared. That's the only thing I can think of. I didn't expect another show like the other night, but I thought they'd at least show up. You know how Carlos is. He doesn't like to lose face."

Roland rubbed his chin and thought about it. Jack was right. At least a few of the Dark Riders should have returned to town. Carlos always responded to a public defeat by flaunting his strength. He briefly thought that the Riders might be up to some sort of trouble, but he couldn't even begin to imagine how they would strike at him and all his men. Carlos knew if he did that, he would be tracked down and killed. The outlaw was crazy, but he wasn't suicidal. Once he had cooled down, he wouldn't do anything that foolish. Or at least Roland hoped so. "It doesn't make any sense to me either. Let's just keep everyone ready for him to return. We don't have Alvin to keep Carlos in line anymore. Oh yeah, has anyone seen Alvin today?"

"Not today, but Morgan saw him riding into town last night."

"Last night? What the hell was he doing out last night?" Roland looked at Jack with a confused expression.

Jack shrugged his shoulders. "You've got me. I'm just telling you what Morgan saw. Alvin rode into town from the south sometime around one or so. You think he was out making up with the Riders?"

Sheriff Black shook his head. "I don't think so. Carlos has a mean streak in him. I don't think he'll ever forgive Alvin for pulling a gun on him the other night. I don't know what the hell he was doing, and I don't like it when that son of a bitch is up to something I don't know." Roland barked out a laugh. "It makes me nervous."

"You and me both, Roland, you and me both," Jack laughed in response. The two talked a little bit longer then Jack went out for his patrol.

Once again Roland gazed out the window restlessly. He was tired of worrying over Rebecca, and he wanted the ordeal to be over as quickly as possible. Curly, however, was unlikely to return before sunset at the absolute earliest, and even though Roland hated to think of the possibility, the Dark Rider might not even return that day. Sooner or later, the outlaw would unknowingly deliver himself into Roland's hands, but Roland might have quite a wait before that happened. For most of the afternoon, he waited silently at his table. He didn't have a hostile look on his face, and he didn't jump every time one of his deputies approached the saloon. Nonetheless, it was quite clear that he wanted to be left alone, and everyone who entered the saloon that day steered clear of Sheriff Black.

The day passed by quietly. William showed up to help out at The Frontier. The rakish deputy avoided the Sheriff and spent his time chatting with the customers, especially when Sherry's girls started to trickle into the establishment. Miss Higgins arrived after two to tend to Rebecca, but Roland once again remained in his seat. From time to time, Morgan or one of the other deputies dropped by to report to Roland, but other than that, Roland didn't talk to anyone else. Sullivan showed up that afternoon, right after the train had left town, to check up on Rebecca. Roland accompanied the stuffy doctor to her room, and the whole procedure took only a small amount of time. Sullivan had learned not to ask Roland if he could bleed the widow, and he confined himself to giving her water and checking her pulse and temperature.

Business at The Last Frontier picked up at dusk. People kept trickling into the saloon, but no word came of the Dark Riders. Roland was tempted to have a drink of whiskey to help pass the time, but he had learned from his monstrous hangover. As the clock hands slowly spun, Roland grew increasingly more anxious for Curly to return. He tried to calm himself, but it was to little avail. Roland couldn't stand having Rebecca asleep any longer. *Come on, you son of a bitch,* he kept thinking as he stared out the window and waited for word that Curly had come back to town.

Just before nine o'clock, Alvin dropped by The Frontier. As usual, Alvin's hair nearly glowed under the candle light, and he flashed his well-practiced smile for all the customers. Roland didn't know if he was more surprised to see the mayor or by the fact that Alvin immediately approached his table. It took Alvin a few moments to cross the saloon since he smiled or said hello to everyone along the way. Roland had expected Alvin to look harried and upset, but the mayor seemed to be overflowing with cheerfulness. "Roland, so good to see you. How are you this evening?" Alvin proclaimed loudly as he walked up to the table, playing up for all the people watching. His eyes, however, glowed malevolently.

Roland wanted to stand up and knock the smile right off his smug face, but he would look like the fool, not Alvin. "I'm fine, Alvin, and you?" Roland forced his own face into a mask of cheerfulness. *Go on smiling, you bastard. I know you remember what happened the last time I saw you. You can fool them, but not me.*

"I'm doing fine, Roland. I couldn't be better." His smile deepened and for a moment anyone who looked at him carefully could see the hatred etched upon his face. But just as quickly, he resumed his amicable countenance

"How's Rebecca doing? The same I take it. Pity," Alvin said in an obvious show of false sympathy.

A low growl formed in Roland's throat, and he caught himself on the verge of leaping out of his seat to throttle the mayor. *Laugh, you son of a bitch. Your power over the Riders is over, and you won't be mayor much longer.* Roland took a deep breath and regained control of his temper. As much as he wanted to beat Alvin into oblivion, it wasn't the right time or place for it. *Soon, you Goddamn snake.* "She's fine," Roland rasped. His eyes narrowed, and a scowl formed on his face. "I haven't seen you or your boys in town lately." Roland stopped, smacked his forehead, and smiled fiercely at the mayor. "Oh that's right. Carlos isn't talking to you anymore. Pity." Roland waited for the look of disgust or anger to appear on Alvin's face, but the mayor surprised him.

Instead of snapping back another reply, Alvin tipped his head back and laughed. "I'm sorry, Roland. I didn't mean to keep you unoccupied, but I've been busy the last few days. Business is so taxing. Well, I just wanted to stop by and chat. I'll talk to you later." The mayor's eyes narrowed for a moment, but Roland was the only one who could see the hatred in them. Then Alvin turned and began to talk to several of the customers, donning his well-practiced smile once again.

Roland watched confusedly as Alvin socialized for the next hour. From time to time, the mayor turned in his direction and looked at Roland with amusement painted on his face. He had expected Alvin to be upset about his loss of control over the Dark Riders, but the mayor appeared jovial that night. True, he would probably don that same face no matter how bad things were. Nonetheless, Alvin seemed completely unfazed about the Dark Riders, and that concerned Roland. He had hoped that he wouldn't have to worry about Alvin on top of all his other problems. *You Goddamn snake,* Roland snarled to himself as Alvin shook hands and tried to raise more votes. *What the hell are you up to?* The mayor left shortly after ten o'clock, but he shot Roland one last bemused glance and winked before he walked out of The Frontier, further adding to Roland's confusion.

Having Alvin to worry about was the last thing Roland needed. He was still worried sick about Rebecca and anxiously awaited the return of Curly. Despite his persistent glances out the window, no word came that night of the Riders returning to town. The Sheriff stayed up past two that morning, but it was more from being sick with worry than out of any hope that the Dark Riders would return that night. He had hoped that Rebecca would be awake that evening, but it was looking like there could be quite a wait for her awakening.

Roland stopped by Rebecca's room shortly before he went to sleep that night. He wanted to promise her that everything would be better soon, but his confidence was beginning to crack. Every time things had gone well for him lately, the carpet had been ripped out from underneath him. The absolute surety that Curly would be dead was beginning to fade and was replaced by a grim outlook on the whole situation. Roland was sure that he would catch Curly eventually, but he didn't know if it would be in time to help his ailing fiancée. He finally took to his bed, but Roland tossed and turned for quite some time before he could actually fall asleep. The pleasant dreams that had ruled over his sleep the last few days were replaced with grim nightmares of Rebecca's house and a hulking darkness that enveloped her, taking her away from him.

When he awoke Friday morning, exhaustion plagued his body, and his head felt as if it had been packed in wool. The restful sleep he had previously enjoyed had been thrown out the window along with his pleasant dreams, and it was with a scowl that the Sheriff went forth to perform his duties that day. He followed the same pattern that he had established over the previous two days, starting by visiting Rebecca. His assurances to her that all would be well sounded less convincing as his own optimism dwindled. Nonetheless, he tried to sound optimistic as he held her hand and spoke gently to her.

Jimmy was all too willing to listen to stories of Roland's past once again, and Roland tried to lose himself in the glory of his youth for at least a few hours. That time with the young gunslinger proved to be the only moments of peace that Roland enjoyed the entire day. He waited in The Frontier again that Friday evening, anxiously looking out the window for any word of Curly's return. The Riders, however, were conspicuously absent for the third day in a row. His mood became darker and darker as he realized that Rebecca would have to remain in her hellish prison for yet another day. Roland started glaring at the customers and snapping at anyone who tried to engage him in conversation, and soon only a few of his deputies approached him.

Alvin showed up around eight and circulated around the saloon, chatting with patrons. Occasionally he threw Roland a glance, his mouth curling into a smirk. Roland tapped his fingers against the butt of his pistol, but he managed to keep his emotions in check. The mayor didn't speak a word to Roland, but the Sheriff was ready to strangle someone by the time Alvin left an hour later. When he finally went to sleep, he was in such a foul mood he skipped saying goodnight to Rebecca. He didn't think he could face her in such a pessimistic frame of mind. His sleep was haunted by nightmarish visions as he rested poorly for the second night in a row.

That pattern continued as June turned into July. Every morning, it became increasingly harder to tell Rebecca that she would be free when he was no longer certain that was the case. Despite Miss Higgins' visits to feed her broth, Rebecca's condition grew worse every morning as she became increasingly thinner. He told Jimmy more stories as the young gunslinger's sentence crept towards its end. Roland talked to Jack, but everyone else avoided

210

him, including his deputies. Even Morgan stopped dropping by The Last Frontier as Roland's mood grew worse. Sullivan continued to check up on Rebecca, and by July 1, Roland was nearly ready to let the doctor bleed her. He caught himself on the verge of giving that permission, deciding to wait a few more days before letting it happen.

The Riders remained absent, and Roland wondered if they had all packed up and moved to a different town. He wished that he knew where their secret hideout was so he could go and shoot Curly, but he was forced to wait impatiently. Alvin dropped by The Frontier every night, smiling mockingly at Roland, but he never approached Roland's table to speak to the Sheriff. Instead, he shot those derisive glances his way. It took every ounce of willpower not to beat the mayor into a bloody pulp, but Roland was aware of how badly that would reflect upon him and his job. He kept his silence, determined that when things had settled with Rebecca, he would pay Alvin back for the grief that the mayor had caused him.

Only Running Brook's brief words after emerging from Rebecca's house provided Roland any solace during the hellish times. The Cheyenne Chief had promised that he would summon two Ghost Hunters to help Rebecca, and he had told Jack that they would arrive in New Haven sometime around the beginning of July. Roland had scoffed at their help, thinking he could handle everything himself, but that idea seemed less likely every day. By the first of July, Roland was clinging to the faith that they would arrive and be able to rescue Rebecca from the Land of Shadows. He had considered that a preposterous hope a week before, but it was all he had left to believe in. He instructed Jack to keep an eye out for an Indian and a white man traveling together, but other than that, he was forced to wait impassively as his precious Rebecca wasted away.

Book Two:
The Ghost Hunters
July 2 - 6

Chapter Eleven

The sun continued to blaze down upon New Haven on July 2 as the two strangers rode towards the town from the north. Both men were tired from a long journey. They had ridden as quickly as possible from Arizona to reach New Haven, hoping that their talents could be utilized. They were a curious looking pair. One was a white man, and the other was a Navajo Indian. While it wasn't uncommon to see an Indian traveling between towns, it was quite rare to find one traveling in the company of white men.

The white man was a tall, gaunt man named Henry, and he had long white hair that curled down about his shoulders. His mustache was also white and drooped down low on either side of his mouth, as was popular at the time. He was pale-skinned, his pallor so white that he almost appeared ill, and he had pale blue eyes that were ringed by black circles as if he was suffering from exhaustion. Despite his elderly appearance, his face was untouched by wrinkles except for the corners of his mouth and at the corners of his eyes. His clothes were common: a plain white shirt worn under a tan coat and jeans, leather boots, and a wide-brimmed hat to block out the sun. A silver bullet dangled from a leather band worn about his neck, bouncing on his chest as his horse walked towards New Haven.

The Indian was called Singing Rock. The Navajo had long black hair streaked with grey and tied in a braid that hung halfway down his back. Like Henry, Singing Rock wore simple clothing. Other than moccasins, he only wore leather trousers and a light shirt to keep cool in the summer heat. Two streaks of blue paint arced across each of his cheeks, and he wore a string of clinking beads around his neck. He was a short man, standing just over five feet, but he was quite broad, giving him a sizable bulk. Singing Rock rode beside Henry with a serious expression locked upon his face.

"So what do you think we'll find here?" Henry asked the Navajo in a thick, Southern drawl. He had grown up in the South and had inherited the slow, pronounced method of speaking that was so common in the social circles in which he had briefly dwelled.

"I do not know. I only spoke to Running Brook for a short time. He said to seek the Sheriff. There is an evil spirit loose, and the Sheriff will know where to find it." Singing Rock explained, his face never losing its chiseled seriousness.

Henry rolled his eyes. "I already know that, Singing Rock. I'm just wondering what we'll find here, that's all. Arizona was not pleasant," he quipped. The last sentence was an understatement. The ghost of a murdered man had somehow wandered into the Land of Shadows, staying in that desolate place to seek his revenge upon the living. Singing Rock and Henry had entered the Land of Shadows and tried to convince the spirit to leave, but their efforts had proved futile. The ghost killed one man and razed a house before Singing Rock had destroyed his spirit. They didn't like to resort to such an extreme measure for once a spirit was obliterated it was forever denied the chance for rebirth. But sometimes spirits left them no other choice.

"Hmm," Singing Rock grunted. The Navajo spoke English quite well, and likewise, Henry had picked up the Navajo dialect over five years of traveling with Singing Rock. Singing Rock, however, usually chose not to say much at all in either of the two languages. He liked to keep quiet and let Henry do all the talking unless there was something important to say.

"Did anyone ever tell you that you talk too much?" Henry baited his friend and grinned at him. He liked to joke around before they reached their destination, for once they arrived in town there was no telling what dangers awaited them.

Singing Rock turned his head and looked at Henry with a flat stare. "You talk enough for ten men."

Henry chuckled at the joke. "That's only because you're so damn quiet. Besides, you know how much I love the sound of my voice." The Navajo didn't respond to the comment, choosing to stare straight ahead and ignore Henry. They rode in silence after that as they neared New Haven.

The sun was just beginning to set, turning the clouds a deep purple, when Henry and Singing Rock finally rode into town. Henry looked around curiously at the streets. He had been a gunslinger in his youth and had ridden through many towns during his lifetime. Those years had left him with the keen ability of being able to gauge when there would be trouble. Singing Rock was a Navajo, and Indians weren't always welcome in White communities. The two had to be ready to flee if problems arose. The same communities that so desperately wanted their help were often blinded by prejudice, and Henry had found himself fleeing for his life several times while he had worked with Singing Rock. Henry carried a gun for that reason, but he hadn't fired it in five years and had no intention of doing so that evening. That was a part of his gunslinging days, and he had given up his old way of life.

Something about the city tweaked his interest, but he couldn't quite put his finger on it. Henry didn't feel threatened, but there was something vaguely familiar about the town. He had seen many railroad towns come and go, and by the looks of it, New Haven was only a young town several years old. Henry knew for a fact that he and Singing Rock had never ridden through the town before, and it bothered him that a strange town would look so familiar.

"*What is bothering you?*" Singing Rock asked in his native tongue. He never spoke English in White communities. It gave him an extra advantage when people thought he couldn't understand what they were saying. More than once, it had actually saved his life. Singing Rock stared at Henry with a concerned look on his face. He had learned to listen when his partner became suspicious.

Henry hesitated before answering. Something was definitely odd about the town, but he couldn't quite put it into words. He sometimes he got strange feelings of danger, and he and Singing Rock would immediately leave the town they were in. But it wasn't like that. He didn't feel threatened. New Haven just seemed awfully familiar, like he had lived there in his past. *"I do not know. Something here seems familiar,"* he replied in Navajo.

"Do you sense danger?" Singing Rock asked with concern.

"Not danger. It is like I was here before." Henry shrugged his shoulders. He still wasn't used to his whole way of life with Singing Rock. They had traveled together for a long time, but he found it difficult to adjust to a world of spirits and strange feelings.

"Do you think we should leave?" Singing Rock had a tremendous knowledge of Navajo lore, but he respected Henry's abilities, which was why he had rescued him nearly five years ago from death's bed.

Henry shook his head. *"No, we should go on. I do not sense danger, but we should be ready for trouble."* Whatever was bothering him would have to be puzzled out later on. There was business to attend to first.

Their arrival passed unnoticed as they proceeded towards the center of town. All too often, they had to ride deep into the heart of a city before one of the locals pointed them in the right direction. By nightfall, most people were either at home or busy in one of the town's taverns. The further they rode down the main street, the more Henry felt like he had visited New Haven before. He had ridden all over the West when he was younger, but he was positive that he had never been to New Haven. He bit his lower lip in consternation and tried to figure it out when he saw a man stumble out into the street. "Let me do the talking as usual," Henry told Singing Rock needlessly. They had worked out the arrangements in their traveling a long time ago.

The Indian stared at him a moment and frowned as if he hated to be reminded then nodded almost imperceptibly.

The pair rode towards the man as he stumbled along with his head down. The drunken man finally looked up when Henry and Singing Rock were no more than thirty feet away and stared at them with bloodshot eyes. After shaking his head, he rubbed his eyes as if he didn't believe what he was seeing. His mouth curled into a grin and his hands balled into fists. "A Goddamn Injun!" He shouted in excitement and lurched forward. "Get your guns. There's a Goddamn Injun!" He staggered towards Henry and Singing Rock.

They watched the man warily and prepared to turn their horses and flee. They were all too glad to lend their experience where it was needed, but they wouldn't place their lives in jeopardy to do so. It wouldn't be the first time they had been chased out of town. Just two months ago, they had fled a

217

town in Wyoming, two steps ahead of a group of drunken men who were determined to hang Singing Rock. But they stopped on the verge of leaving town as Morgan galloped towards them, his long white hair streaming behind him. He reined in his horse in front of the drunken man with a furious expression on his face. "What the hell do you think you're doing, Stephen?"

"There's an Injun. I was gonna keep 'em from killing us all," Stephen slurred his words, swaying slightly from the effects of a great deal of alcohol. He leaned against the deputy's horse to steady himself.

Morgan looked down at him with contempt. "Stephen, I'm telling you this once. Go home. We don't have any problems with the Cheyenne. Just remember what happened last week. Sheriff Black will get pissed if he hears you started a fight with them. You got that?" The old man asked Stephen in an ominous voice and waited for his answer with an arched eyebrow.

Even in his state of inebriation, Stephen got a very serious expression on his face as it drained of color. "No, sir. I don't want no trouble with the Sheriff. You won't tell him about this, will you?" Stephen's words suddenly sounded very pronounced. Roland's recent dark moods and fiery temper were enough to scare just about anybody from getting on his bad side.

"If you go home and don't cause any more trouble, I won't say a word. Now get out of here, Stephen," the old deputy ordered in a fierce tone. Stephen took his advice and began to stumble his way down the street. Morgan watched him until it was obvious that Stephen was indeed going to continue on his present path and not turn around to cause more trouble. Then the deputy turned his attention to the pair of strangers. The Indian sparked his curiosity, but it was Henry who caught his attention. He had seen plenty of Indians before, but they usually weren't accompanied by white men. "I haven't seen you two before. Who are you?"

"My name is Henry, sir, and my friend here is called Singing Rock," Henry responded politely in his Southern drawl. Singing Rock kept silent and watched Henry deal with Morgan.

"Henry, Singing Rock," the deputy nodded. "My name's Morgan, and I'm a deputy here in New Haven. We've had some Indian problems lately, and I want to know why you're in town. We don't need any trouble right now."

"We're not here for trouble, Morgan. We came to see your Sheriff. He should be expecting us," Henry answered then tilted his head slightly to the side. "You mentioned trouble with Indians. Is it something we need to be concerned with?" If the town was hostile towards Indians, Henry wanted to know.

Morgan shook his head. "I wouldn't worry about it. Stephen was just drunk. Just stay with me, and nobody will bother you. The Sheriff's in a pretty bad mood, and nobody wants to get on his bad side right now." Morgan pointed a finger at the pair. "I don't know what your business with Sheriff Black is, but

218

be warned, he's not in a good mood. Unless it's really important, I'd wait to speak with him."

"No, sir, we cannot wait. We've traveled a long way to get here, and it's urgent we speak with the Sheriff. I believe he's waiting for us," Henry drawled. New Haven made him uneasy. Henry wanted to see the Sheriff, help him out, and leave the town as soon as possible. Singing Rock continued to sit on his horse quietly, looking about as if he didn't care one way or another, but Henry knew that the Navajo was paying close attention to their conversation.

The deputy stared at them for a moment as if he wanted to ask about the urgent matter that had brought them to New Haven, but Morgan kept his silence. He appreciated his own privacy and respected that of others as well. "Fine, I'll take you to The Frontier. Follow me, it's not far," he instructed the pair and turned his horse towards the saloon.

Singing Rock looked inquisitively at Henry, who nodded once before following the deputy. The Indian took his cue from his companion and followed right behind him. As they rode, Henry kept looking at his surroundings, trying to determine why everything looked so familiar. The answer lurked at the edge of his mind and teased him with how close he was to the solution, but try as he might, Henry couldn't put his finger on it.

The three rode quietly, Henry gazing about curiously, Morgan sitting stony-faced on his horse, and Singing Rock peering straight ahead as if he didn't know or care what was going on around him. Finally Morgan broke that silence. Morgan didn't want to intrude upon Sheriff Black's privacy, but he was greatly intrigued by the pair , and if he asked a few questions, didn't think Roland would mind. "If you don't mind me asking, how come a white man and an Indian are traveling together?"

Henry jerked his attention back to his immediate situation. There would be time later on to figure out why New Haven seemed so familiar. He put a finger to his lips and paused to consider how much he should tell the deputy. The story behind how he had met Singing Rock was hard to believe and one that he wanted to keep private. He had led his life of notoriety years before but wanted to live in anonymity now that he had a new purpose. "That's an awfully long story. Let's just say that Singing Rock saved my life about five years back, and I ride with him to repay the favor." Henry felt comfortable with that answer. It wasn't a lie. He had forsaken lying shortly after he met Singing Rock, but his answer only scratched the surface and left a great deal untold.

Morgan nodded and didn't press any further. "Does he speak any English?" The deputy pointed at the silent Indian.

The old traveler chuckled in response, and the corners of his mouth curled into a tiny grin. "He can speak a little bit, but he prefers his own language," Henry explained and once again avoided the question by telling a half-truth. Technically Singing Rock *could* speak a little bit of English, but the

Navajo was capable of much more. Henry didn't think that Morgan really needed to know that Singing Rock could speak and understand English perfectly well.

The deputy nodded at the answer and studied the two carefully. Henry's answers hadn't told Morgan much about the travelers. They were quite a curious-looking pair. Morgan wasn't like Ben, who would have pestered them to death with questions, but one thing about the Indian still bothered him. "Is he a Cheyenne? I don't remember seeing him before."

"No, sir. He's Navajo," Henry responded for his friend, and Morgan left them alone after that.

They got a few stares as they rode down the street. Most of the people in New Haven couldn't distinguish a Navajo from a Cheyenne Indian any better than Morgan. The near riot over the Cheyenne was less than a week old, and many of the people in town harbored a slight grudge against their Indian neighbors. Nobody disturbed the trio, though. Morgan wasn't as feared as Roland, but he did make a stern impression as he rode, stiff-backed at the front of their party.

Henry also noticed the curious stares and the mannerisms of the deputy. He counted himself lucky that he and Singing Rock had encountered Morgan so soon after their arrival. If they hadn't, it looked as if they might have been attacked. Their welcome by Stephen certainly hadn't boded very well. "You mentioned trouble with the Cheyenne before. What kind of trouble was it?" Henry asked the deputy. If he and Singing Rock were walking into a den of vipers, he definitely wanted to be prepared.

Morgan's lip curled in disgust. "We had a few folks that wanted to boot the Cheyenne off their land." The deputy shook his head as if he still couldn't believe the event. "It's nothing to worry about, though. Roland put the fear of God into them. The bastards all went home after that. When Roland gets upset people tread softly around him." Morgan chuckled.

Warning signals instantly went off in Henry's head. *It can't be.* He looked at Morgan intensely. "Roland?" He asked warily. Henry had been a gunslinger in his youth and had met many other gunslingers over the years. One of them had been named Roland. It wasn't a common name, but surely it couldn't be the same man.

"Roland's the Sheriff. I thought you knew him." Morgan's eyes narrowed as he looked at the old traveler.

"*Roland Black?*" Henry exclaimed, and his face momentarily showed his shock before settling back into its calm appearance. For five years everyone had thought he was dead, and Henry wanted to keep it that way. He preferred to remain anonymous, but it would only take one person to spoil his ruse. He had met a Roland Black years ago, and there probably weren't two Roland Blacks living in the West. *Damn it,* he cursed mentally. *Why does Roland have to be here?* He prayed that the Sheriff wouldn't recognize him. After all, it had been years since he had seen Roland, and he had aged tremendously since then.

Henry's outburst surprised Morgan. "Don't you know him? I thought you had important business with him."

The old traveler took a deep breath before answering and tried to keep his expression relaxed. Of all the people to be the Sheriff, it had to be somebody he had met before. "We were sent to meet the Sheriff. It's a private affair," he evaded the issue without lying to the deputy. Hopefully Morgan wouldn't press it any further. Henry wouldn't lie even to save his anonymity and didn't want to have to dodge the deputy's questions all night long. Henry just hoped that the Sheriff wasn't the same man he had met years ago. His work with Singing Rock might not be able to continue if word of his whereabouts became known.

Morgan looked on the verge of retorting, but he held his silence as they approached The Last Frontier. If it was a private affair with Roland, he wasn't about to meddle in it. Henry sat in silence the whole time, his eyes focused straight ahead. He had given up on trying to determine why the town felt so familiar and had concentrated on his more immediate problem. He and Singing Rock would still help the Sheriff, but Henry wanted to be done with the ordeal and out of town as quickly as possible. The less time they spent in New Haven, the less time Roland had to recognize him.

The saloon was crowded that night, and the noise from inside could be heard from nearly half a block away. Singing Rock eyed the saloon warily, but Henry looked up from his contemplation with a sorrowful gaze. He remembered the times when the saloons of the West had been truly rowdy, not just loud. Too many times, he had been in the thick of that rowdiness, gambling, whoring, and fighting, but those times had died long ago.

"Remember what I said about the Sheriff. He's in a really bad mood, so you just make sure you don't upset him," Morgan cautioned. Then the three left their tethered horses behind as they entered the saloon.

Most of the din inside The Frontier died as the three men walked in, and nearly every eye in the saloon focused on Singing Rock. The Navajo was aware of the attention, but he retained his stoic expression and looked ahead with a blank stare, seemingly ignoring everyone. Henry, however, whistled softly as he viewed the inside, finally realizing what it was that seemed so familiar about the town. The Last Frontier seemed to be a place directly out of his past. Sherry's girls immediately caught his attention, as did the rowdy nature of the place. He had visited a number of saloons when he was younger, and he had thought that the rough and tumble nature of his youth had been forever banished. His eyes lit up with excitement when they saw the card games being played. There were several poker games being played that night, but he focused on the faro dealers. *Damn, they're playing faro,* he thought excitedly. Henry had thought faro was extinct. He remembered countless hours spent playing the game of chance, and his hands itched to join one of the games.

His attention was yanked back to the matters at hand as Singing Rock subtly elbowed his ribs. *"Pay attention,"* the Navajo cautioned softly in his native tongue.

Henry forced himself to follow Morgan's gaze. There was too much in the saloon that he wanted to observe, things that he had thought were gone forever. His excitement quickly wore off as he viewed Roland getting up from his table. The Sheriff had a week's growth of stubble on his cheeks, and his eyes had bags under them. But he was obviously the man Henry had met years ago. *Damn, it's him.* Henry wanted to turn around and leave, but they had come too far. He pulled the brim of his hat down low to limit the Sheriff's view of his face and stared at the floor. Hopefully that would be enough to mask his identity.

The Sheriff sat at his customary table in the back corner of the saloon. It was still too early for the Dark Riders to arrive that evening, and he wasn't looking obsessively out the window quite yet. He did, however, look up at the entrance of The Frontier when the noise level suddenly dropped. Roland slowly rose from his seat, his eyes filled with disbelief as if doubting what they were seeing. A smile formed on his face, and he approached the trio quickly. "It's you," Roland whispered excitedly.

"What's that, Sheriff?" Morgan asked and tapped his ear to signal that Roland had spoken too softly. The deputy looked askance at the Sheriff. The smile and sudden enthusiasm on his face were out of character.

Roland ignored his deputy as he fought to keep his emotions under control. He was ready to skip and dance across the floor. "What do we have here, Morgan?"

The deputy shrugged his shoulders, taking Roland's dismissal in stride. "They said they're here to see you, so I brought 'em here."

"I thought they might be." Roland's grin stretched even wider, and he rubbed his hands together in satisfaction. "I can handle it from here, Morgan. Thanks." Roland tipped his hat to the deputy and focused all of his attention on the two men.

"Sheriff," Morgan replied and tipped his own hat, glancing curiously one last time at the pair he had just escorted to The Frontier. Answers about the mysterious pair would have to wait until another time.

Roland scarcely noticed Morgan as he headed out the door. "I've been expecting you. I'm Roland Black, Sheriff of New Haven." He held out a hand to the pair.

Henry had watched Roland nervously, but so far the Sheriff didn't appear to have recognized him. He just hoped it stayed that way. "It is a pleasure to meet you. My name is Henry, and my friend here is named Singing Rock." The old traveler lifted his head for a moment and made eye contact before hastily looking downwards. He had thought that maybe on closer inspection the Sheriff would turn out to be someone else, but that hadn't proved to be the case. Roland's hair had acquired more grey, and more wrinkles decorated his chiseled face. Other than that, the Sheriff was exactly as Henry remembered him. *The Sheriff can't recognize me,* Henry thought. It had been so long since he had met Roland, and his own appearance had aged far more than Roland's. Besides, everyone still thought he was dead.

The Sheriff paused as he shook Henry's hand. Something about the old man struck him as familiar, but he couldn't quite place it. *It doesn't matter.* The Ghost Hunters had finally arrived in New Haven, and Rebecca would soon awaken from her week-long slumber. "Henry," Roland nodded then held out his hand to Singing Rock. The Navajo took the hand in a firm grip and grunted once in greeting. "Does he speak English?" Roland asked Henry.

"He can speak a little, Sheriff. Do you have somewhere to speak in private?" Henry kept his head lowered and smiled once in response. No matter what town he and Singing Rock visited, he was invariably asked if Singing Rock could speak English at least a dozen times.

"Over there," Roland jerked his head in the direction of his table and led the pair across the saloon.

Roland was in the mood to skip the entire way, but he forced himself to calm down. Henry watched Roland from under the brim of his hat, astonished at the smile on his face. The gunslinger he remembered had never smiled. Roland had simply gone about his business with a grim look on his face. The man had obviously changed. He was curious to see why Roland had summoned him. If a spirit was haunting Roland or someone he loved, that might explain why he was acting so differently. Roland took a seat at the table and motioned for Henry and Singing Rock to do so as well.

The Sheriff was about to say something to them when he looked up suddenly. The crowd inside The Frontier was deathly quiet and watching Roland and his two companions. Most of their attention seemed to be focused on Singing Rock. Roland's eyebrows lowered, and he cast a dark gaze about the room. As his eyes passed over each customer, they quickly resumed their own business and stopped gawking at the Navajo. *People are still scared of him,* Henry noticed with interest. Despite the ten years since he had met Roland, the Sheriff still had a frightful reputation.

Roland turned his attention back to the pair of travelers after he was sure everyone was minding their own business. The grim look left his face to be replaced with an excited smile. He rubbed his hands together as if anxious to get down to business. "You're the Ghost Hunters, right? The ones Running Brook sent for?"

Henry put a hand over his mouth and guffawed at the question. He had been called many things, but never a ghost hunter before. It was close to what he and Singing Rock did, but not quite accurate.

"What's so Goddamn funny? Are you or not?" Roland's smile slipped quickly, and he suddenly looked like a man at the end of his rope.

"Nothing's funny, Sheriff." *Don't laugh at him,* Henry thought to himself. He had seen many people stretched to the end of their emotional limits during the course of his travels with Singing Rock, and he had learned not to anger them. People who were walking on the edge could do strange things if pushed over. "I've never heard that phrase before. Singing Rock and I talk with spirits. We don't hunt ghosts. But to answer your question, we are the ones Running Brook sent for. Singing Rock talked to him in a dream. We never found out what exactly the problem was. How can we help you?"

Roland closed his eyes and bowed his head. For a few moments Henry thought that his old acquaintance was about to cry. He didn't actually weep, but when he raised his head, there were tears at the corners of his eyes. His cheeks stretched wide in a relieved smile. The Sheriff took a deep breath before continuing. "Thank you, thank you so much. I've been hoping you would show up. There's a ghost in a house outside of town, and it has the spirit of the woman I love."

Henry sighed and exchanged a long look with Singing Rock. Both men were not pleased with what they heard. Rescuing someone from the Land of Shadows was the most difficult thing they had to do. Banishing a spirit wasn't too bad, but when it held the spirit of a member of the living in its grasp, it could become a much more daunting task. "*Do you want to look at her body first?*" Henry asked in Navajo.

"*Yes, that would be best. If we must fight a spirit, let us be sure that it has this woman he speaks of first,*" Singing Rock answered in his native language.

Roland watched them uneasily as they spoke back and forth. Henry had noticed that most people became very uncomfortable when they couldn't understand exactly what he and Singing Rock were saying. "Is the woman still alive?" Henry asked Roland.

"Yes, she's still alive," Roland retorted in a heated voice. Once again, the Sheriff's frayed nerves came to the surface, and Henry quickly spread his hands wide in a peaceful gesture.

"I mean no offense, Sheriff. We will do all we can to help her, but I'm just trying to gather all the facts. Is she awake?" *Always give people a line of hope,* Henry thought to himself. When people thought there was no hope, they could do irrational things.

"No, she's been asleep for over a week. Can you help her?" Roland asked in a stricken voice. Henry continued to be amazed by Roland. The gunslinger he had known would never act so upset over a woman. Roland had always seemed to personify the eternal bachelor, but time changes everything.

"We should go look at her body and see if it is really captive in the Land of Shadows," Singing Rock broke in and interrupted Henry's musing.

"You are right," Henry answered and turned his attention back to the Sheriff. "Why don't we go look at her body. Then we can go on from there."

Roland looked at them anxiously. "What? Don't you want to go to the house first? That's where her spirit is. That's where the ghost is." He sounded insistent.

"That may be, Sheriff, but we need to look at her body first. We can learn a lot about what we're facing. I don't like to wrestle with a spirit when I don't know something about it first," Henry drawled in response.

"Yes, you're right. I'm sorry. I just want to see her awake again. C'mon, she's upstairs," Roland answered with a downcast expression and came to his feet. He waited for the two Ghost Hunters to rise then led them upstairs. Once again every eye in the saloon watched Roland and his two companions climb the stairs curiously, but Roland didn't even seem to notice them.

Henry noticed them, though, and cast a glance towards Singing Rock. The Navajo shrugged his shoulders as if he didn't know why they were getting so many glances either. *We can talk after we look at the body,* Henry thought as Roland led them down the hallway towards Rebecca's room. Roland pulled the key out of his pocket, unlocked the door, and stood back so Henry and Singing Rock could enter first. "She's in here."

The two walked into the dark room as Roland lit a lantern, casting a pale glow over the room. Henry whistled in surprise when he saw Rebecca's body. It was consistent with what he had seen before, but it still shocked him when he saw the wasted bodies of those trapped in the Land of Shadows. Singing Rock's eyebrows lifted as he peered at the body. *"You look at the body. I'll keep the Sheriff calm,"* Henry suggested to the Navajo.

"Hmm," Singing Rock muttered affirmatively and stepped over to the side of the bed to take a look at Rebecca.

"What's he doing?" Roland asked anxiously.

Henry looked over and saw that the Sheriff's face was a mixture of hope and depression. *He must really love her,* Henry thought. "Don't worry, Sheriff. He's taking a look at her to see if her spirit's in the Land of Shadows. She won't be hurt."

Roland nodded, but he continued to peer nervously at Singing Rock as the Navajo examined his fiancée.

Singing Rock seemed oblivious of the two other men in the room. He pulled a rattle from a pouch around his waist and began to shake it back and forth. Gently he lowered his open palm onto her forehead and sang softly.

"What's he doing?" Roland turned to Henry.

"Shh, he's trying to listen," Henry whispered sternly.

"Listen to—" Roland started to ask, but Henry cut him off.

"Later, Sheriff. Be quiet."

Roland looked like he wanted to retort again, but he kept his silence. For nearly a minute, the two watched the Navajo continue to chant. By then Roland was tapping his fingers nervously on the butt of his gun as if he was dying to ask a question, but the Sheriff followed Henry's request and waited silently. Suddenly Singing Rock cried out in surprise and opened his eyes. He removed his hand from Rebecca's forehead and rubbed his temples.

"What is it? What's going on?" Roland cried out and grabbed Henry's jacket, roughly forcing the Ghost Hunter to face him.

For a moment Henry and the Sheriff looked eye to eye, and a flicker of recognition crossed Roland's face. *Damn, he knows it's me. Damn.* Quickly he pushed Roland's hands off him and pulled the brim of his hat down low. "In a minute. Let us talk first," Henry muttered irritably. If Roland recognized him, his work with Singing Rock was finished, and he still had a debt to repay the Navajo. He stomped over to Singing Rock and frowned as he looked at his partner. The Navajo looked exhausted, which was unusual. Singing Rock had performed the same ritual many times, and it had never left him so spent afterwards. *"How are you?"*

Singing Rock took his hands from his temples and stared at Henry gravely. *"There is great evil around this woman. It fills the air like rotted meat."*

Henry had expected as much. Singing Rock had said that Running Brook had sounded urgent in his summons, and Henry's luck had run poor since arriving in New Haven. Still he didn't know why an evil spirit would be such a cause of concern. He and Singing Rock had faced numerous malevolent spirits and had emerged unscathed from those encounters. *"Evil? Is it an evil spirit we face?"*

"I do not know if the spirit is evil or not. I just know that evil swirls around this woman. All who draw near her or lend aid place themselves in peril's way." Singing Rock had a troubled look on his face. Usually Singing Rock took danger stoically, and this was one of the few times Henry could remember seeing him worried.

"Should we leave? If there is danger, maybe we should avoid putting ourselves in its path," Henry suggested. He wouldn't mind leaving the town anyway. He had a debt to repay his Navajo partner, but his work would come to an abrupt end the moment it was publicized that he was still alive. The Ghost Hunter's word was the one thing in his life that had always been constant. More importantly, Henry had taken many lives over his years of gunslinging and had quite a bit of atoning to do before he found salvation. He would fail on both fronts if Roland recognized him.

Singing Rock, however, didn't hesitate. He immediately shook his head. *"No, we will stay. Perhaps later, if the danger grows too great, we will leave. But for now, it is our duty to help this man and Running Brook. It is a great evil we face, and it will be a great feat if we can beat it."*

Henry sighed. He had expected that answer from Singing Rock. The only times they hadn't completed their mission was when they had been chased away by the very people they were trying to help. Their lives weren't in danger, but there was a real danger to their partnership. Henry was about to retort when Roland cleared his throat loudly.

The Sheriff had a harried expression when Henry turned to face him. Roland immediately held up his hands apologetically, which nearly caused Henry to chuckle despite the seriousness of the situation. He had never seen Roland so amicable. The gunslinger he remembered would never have apologized even if he had insulted someone. "I'm sorry to interrupt, but is she okay?"

Henry had forgotten that he wasn't speaking English and immediately felt bad. He could tell how worried Roland was and hadn't meant to keep him waiting. Holding up one finger to tell Roland to wait a moment longer, he turned back to Singing Rock. *"How is she? Will she live?"*

The Navajo shrugged his shoulders, and his face scrunched up into a puzzled expression. *"I do not know. She is very weak already and will not last much longer. She has one more week. Perhaps a few more days. Tell him she will be well if we can defeat her captor at dawn."*

Roland's face was crumpled up with worry as Henry turned back to him. He had obviously seen Singing Rock's dubious gesturing and had assumed the worst. "Please tell me she's okay," he pleaded to Henry.

"Calm down, Sheriff. She's in bad condition, but she'll be okay if we can banish the spirit that captured her. I wouldn't worry. She should be awake and recovering in the morning," Henry spoke quicker than his normal drawl to allay Roland's worries.

The Sheriff exhaled loudly at the answer and leaned back against the wall as if drained by the whole ordeal. He closed his eyes tightly and savored the moment. "Thank God," he whispered.

"See if he knows who the spirit might belong to," Singing Rock suggested to Henry.

Henry rolled his eyes at his partner. He had done this often enough and knew exactly what to do, but he was going to wait for Roland to finish relishing the good news.

The Sheriff looked up when he heard Singing Rock speak. Roland's face appeared braced for the worst, and Henry guessed that things must have indeed gone badly for Roland of late. "Is there something else?" Roland asked in a hoarse voice.

"Don't worry so much. I just have a few questions for you."

Tension leaked out of Roland, and his shoulders slumped visibly. He took a deep breath and nodded. "Sure, anything you want. I just want her awake as soon as possible."

"That's what we're here for," Henry comforted the Sheriff. He still expected Roland to be the man of iron nerves he had met years ago, but he had seen too many people under extreme duress during his travels with Singing Rock and was not surprised to see even the Sheriff's tough outer wall crack. "You said there was a ghost in her house. What makes you think that?"

Roland lowered his head and barked out a laugh. When he raised his head, Henry nearly took a step back. His eyes appeared haunted by a terrible memory. "It threw furniture around, it threw me around." Roland took a deep breath and closed his eyes before continuing. "Then it grabbed Rebecca. I'd say that's a Goddamn ghost," the Sheriff finished in a defeated voice.

Henry and Singing Rock exchanged a quick glance. It confirmed what they already suspected. "Did it say anything?"

"What?" Roland asked, looking up in confusion.

"The ghost. Did it say anything?"

"It kept saying 'mine' over and over."

The Ghost Hunter paused for a moment and tapped his chin. All too often, the people being haunted by a spirit were deeply involved in the death of that person or had committed a terrible atrocity towards the spirit. He wanted to know if Roland was involved in that death, but he didn't want to come out and accuse the Sheriff. Roland looked on the verge of breaking, and he wasn't about to upset him. "Do you know who the ghost belongs to?"

"I'm pretty damn sure it's Rebecca's husband, Bryant White."

"How did he die?"

"He was killed about six months ago. We found him lying in the middle of the street. Someone slit his throat."

"Do you have any idea who killed him?" Henry asked hopefully. If Roland could kill the guilty person, there would be no need to enter the Land of Shadows. Neither Henry nor Singing Rock were afraid to do so, but if they could avoid it, they certainly would choose to avoid the house altogether. They had a way to determine who had killed a person, but if Roland knew, there was no sense going through the long ritual.

Roland ran a hand over his eyes wearily, and his jaw clenched angrily. "Yeah, I know who it is."

Henry glanced at Singing Rock quickly, and the Navajo raised his eyebrows in interest. "Has he been arrested?"

Roland hit the wall behind him with a loud thud. "No," he answered between gritted teeth. "I can't catch the son of a bitch. I'll get him eventually, but it could take months." He looked at Henry accusingly. "I thought you could help her anyway."

"We can, Sheriff. We can." Henry put up two hands defensively. "But you can't blame us for trying to find the easiest way to help her."

"You're right. I'm sorry. I'm just on edge lately."

"There's no need to apologize."

"Ask him for a room to sleep in. We need to rest before the sun's rising. I am exhausted, and we need to talk," Singing Rock told his partner.

Henry looked at the Navajo lazily. *"Give me some credit. I was going to ask him."* Roland looked at them curiously when they began to speak in Navajo, and Henry quickly shifted back to English. "I guess we have all we need. Is it possible to get two rooms so we could rest before going to the house?"

"What?" Roland looked at the two of them anxiously. "Why can't you go fight the spirit now?" His fists were clenched at his side, not for violence, Henry decided, but out of pure frustration.

"We need to wait until dawn. That's when spirits are at their weakest," Henry told the Sheriff. It was a common question that they were asked. People always wanted him and Singing Rock to dash off and rescue their loved ones, but the Ghost Hunters weren't about to risk their lives needlessly.

"Dawn? Don't tell me you believe that Sun Father and Moon Mother stuff?" The Sheriff asked disgustedly.

Henry looked at Roland in confusion and turned questioningly to Singing Rock. *"Do you know what he is talking about?"*

"The Sun Father and Moon Mother are beliefs of the Cheyenne. They believe that the Sun and the Moon created the Earth. The Moon is the Mother, and the Sun is the Father."

The Ghost Hunter turned back to Roland. "That's a Cheyenne tradition. No, I don't believe that the sun and the moon created the world. But I do know that spirits are at their weakest when the sun first rises. Don't ask me why. I don't know. They just are. An evil spirit holds this woman's spirit, and if we're to fight it, I intend to do so when I have the greatest advantage."

Roland clenched his jaw in disappointment. "Damn," he swore. He took a deep breath and struggled to regain his composure. Roland still appeared tightly wound, but he no longer seemed ready to explode.

"I'm sorry. I wish there was more we could do now, but it's best to wait," Henry offered consolingly. He hated to see the look of depression on the faces of the people he helped. Rebecca's wasn't the first spirit that he had seen captured, and it probably wouldn't be the last. Countless times he and Singing Rock had journeyed into the Land of Shadows to help innocent people, but it never grew easier to see the pain that the ordeal inflicted upon the loved ones they were summoned to help. It was worse when the one who was suffering was somebody he knew.

"I know. She's just been like this for so long. I want to see her like she used to be." Roland put a hand over his eyes, and his shoulders began to shake slightly.

Henry looked at Singing Rock uncomfortably as Roland grieved quietly. The Navajo returned his stare and arched an eyebrow as if wondering how long the Sheriff would continue to cry. Henry shrugged his shoulders and kept his eyes averted.

After a half-minute, Roland cleared his throat raggedly, and Henry turned to face the Sheriff. Roland's eyes were puffy, and he wiped at them furiously to clear all traces of tears. "I'm sorry. I guess it finally got to me." Roland looked at the floor, embarrassed by his tears.

"Please, don't worry, Sheriff. All will be well in the morning. Now if you could please get us two rooms, we would greatly appreciate it." Henry was still worried that the Sheriff would recognize him. The sooner they were in their own rooms, the sooner that danger would pass.

"Sure, let's go talk to George." He avoided eye contact with them after his bout of tears, which was fine with Henry, but the Ghost Hunter kept his hat brim lowered as an extra precaution.

Henry held up a hand. "We'll wait up here if you don't mind. The people downstairs were staring at Singing Rock, and we don't like a lot of attention."

"Sure, that's no problem. Do you need anything else? Food?"

"No, we're fine. We just need sleep."

"I'll be back in a bit," Roland told them. He bumped into Henry on his way out, and the Ghost Hunter quickly ducked his head to avoid eye contact. The Sheriff didn't appear to recognize him and left the room without a glance backwards.

As soon as the door closed, Singing Rock crossed his arms across his chest. He looked at Henry with a disapproving frown. *"What is wrong with you? You are acting strangely this night."*

"I know the Sheriff. I do not want him to recognize me. I want to get rid of this spirit and leave town as soon as possible."

Singing Rock's eyebrows shot up in surprise at Henry's answer, and his frown disappeared. *"You know this man?"*

"Yes. I met him a long time ago and traveled with him for a few days. I do not think he will know me. I look much different than I used to, and everyone still thinks I am dead. But who can tell what lies in the future?"

"Is this what caused you to feel so uncomfortable when we first came to town?"

"I think so. That and the saloon downstairs. Did you see it down there? They were playing faro and poker. What I would not give to sit down there for five minutes," Henry answered wistfully. He could remember the days when playing faro had been as natural as breathing air. Henry had renounced that part of his life once had he fallen in with Singing Rock. He was ashamed of many of the things he had done as a gunslinger, but he remembered the game of faro with a special warmness in his heart.

Singing Rock looked at Henry and could almost read his thoughts. The man he had rescued from death five years before had been reckless and lucky to have lived as long as he did, but Singing Rock had seen the talent and opportunity in him as well. He had rescued Henry to help him in his work and had made the gunslinger swear to give up all his former pleasures. At times it had been difficult for Henry, but so far he had kept his word. *"Remember your oath. That part of your life is over,"* Singing Rock warned just in case Henry's resolve was beginning to crumble.

Henry shook his head and pulled his mind back to current matters. The games downstairs were very tempting, but he had promised Singing Rock that he would never gamble again. If there was one thing Henry valued above everything else, it was his word. *"Do not worry about me. I remember my promises. I do want to leave here as soon as we can. After we help this woman, we should leave town immediately. If the Sheriff recognizes me, it could be the end of my work."*

"You are right." Singing Rock exhaled loudly. He was sore and tired from their long journey and had looked forward to a few days of rest, but their work was more important than a chance to catch up on sleep. *"We cannot let him recognize you. People must continue to believe you are dead."*

"I know, but enough of that. What do you think about her?" Henry pointed at Rebecca's frail body.

"There is evil around her. The spirit does not seem especially strong, but I can smell the evil in this room. I do not know if it is the spirit itself or events around it that cause this stench." Singing Rock almost sounded confused, and that worried Henry. He had never seen his partner unsure of himself before.

"Can you beat it?"

"I can defeat this spirit, but there is something else. This woman's life hangs in the balance, and great danger lies in wait if she perishes. We must not only defeat this spirit but escort her spirit safely back from the Land of Shadows."

"You mean me," Henry muttered. There would only be one person entering the Land of Shadows, and they both knew who it was. For the first six months they had traveled together, Singing Rock had always been the one to enter, but since those days, it was almost always Henry.

231

"That is why I brought you back from the dead. This is a White Man's spirit, so you must make the journey." Singing Rock had no qualms about dealing with the spirits of his own people, but he had difficulty relating to those of White Men.

Henry exhaled loudly. He was beginning to feel uncomfortable about this journey. Over the course of his travels with Singing Rock, he had entered the Land of Shadows numerous times and had grown used to it, but many things about New Haven already bothered him. Why was faro being played downstairs, and what were the odds of Roland being Sheriff of the town? He had already asked himself those questions over and over, but he found the evil that Singing Rock kept talking about even more disturbing. Henry had faced extremely evil spirits, but Singing Rock's cryptic comments on top of everything else put him on edge. *"I just want to know what this danger is that you keep talking about."*

Singing Rock shrugged his shoulders. *"I do not know. I just know it is there. Maybe you will find this out once you enter the Land of Shadows."*

"Why thank you, Singing Rock. I'm glad you could be of such assistance," Henry quipped to his friend in English then lapsed into silence as they waited for Roland to return.

Roland reentered the room a few minutes later without knocking. Henry immediately lowered his head so the brim of his hat nearly covered his eyes, but the Sheriff squinted and tried to get a better view of his face. Henry spoke up quickly to distract Roland from examining his features too closely. "Did you get the rooms?"

The Sheriff blinked and stopped staring at Henry so intently. "Yeah, I got two rooms for you. When do you want me to wake you?"

Henry looked at Singing Rock. *"What do you think? A few hours before dawn?"*

The Navajo considered it for a moment then nodded once. *"That should be plenty of time for us to prepare."*

The Ghost Hunter turned back to the Sheriff and cast his eyes downward. "Wake us up a few hours before dawn. We have to prepare to enter the house, and that should give us enough time."

"A few hours before dawn," Roland repeated softly to himself. "Let me show you to your rooms," he announced and opened the door for the other two men. The Sheriff locked the door behind him then escorted the Ghost Hunters down the hallway. He stopped at a door five down from Rebecca's own room and unlocked it. "Here's one of them," Roland said and held out the key.

Henry grabbed the key and gave it to Singing Rock. *"You take this one. Sleep well."*

The Navajo nodded. *"And you as well."* He entered the room, and a moment later, Henry and Roland heard the lock slide home.

"And your room is next door." Roland walked over to the next room and paused, tapping his chin with the key. He looked curiously at Henry once again, and the Ghost Hunter lowered his head even more. Henry knew it looked suspicious, but he didn't really care. He just wanted to make sure that Roland didn't recognize him. "Are you sure I don't know you? You look real familiar," Roland asked the Ghost Hunter.

Sometimes Henry wished he could still lie, but he kept his word to Singing Rock. "It's possible that we've met. I've traveled all across this great country of ours and met many people. Now if you don't mind, I'd like to get some rest. It is not that long 'til dawn, and it's going to be a busy morning." Henry reached out and plucked the key from Roland's hand. He quickly unlocked his door and entered, anxious to remove himself from Roland's sight.

"Are you sure you can help her?" Roland asked plaintively just before Henry closed the door.

The Ghost Hunter stopped himself from slamming the door in Roland's face. He wanted to keep the Sheriff away, but his old acquaintance sounded desperate for reassurance that his fiancée would indeed be all right. "Don't worry. In the morning we'll go to her house."

"And then?" Roland asked expectantly.

"Then, Sheriff, we'll talk to this ghost and take back Rebecca's spirit from it. Good night," Henry explained and closed the door. He locked it with a great deal of satisfaction. It looked as if Roland recognized his face but couldn't place it. As long as Roland couldn't place his name with his face, Henry was happy. Kicking off his boots and casually tossing his hat onto the dresser, Henry laid down on the bed.

He couldn't believe his luck. For the last five years, he had looked for a faro game. Poker was still played, but Henry had always been more partial to faro. He didn't want to play the game, just watch it. It was tempting to go downstairs and watch the gamblers, but he wanted to limit the amount of time that Roland had to scrutinize his face.

Henry stopped worrying about Roland and gambling. He had bigger problems in the morning. It wouldn't be the first time he had faced a spirit, and it wouldn't be the last. But the Ghost Hunter was on edge. *Nothing some rest won't cure,* Henry thought to himself as he stretched out on the bed. It felt wonderful to be sleeping indoors after two weeks of hard travel, and he fell asleep almost as soon as his eyes closed.

Chapter Twelve

Roland stood outside Henry's door for a few moments as the Ghost Hunter locked it from the inside. There was something oddly familiar about the Ghost Hunter. He knew that he had seen him somewhere before, and the way Henry kept ducking his head made it look like he was avoiding the Sheriff's gaze. Roland didn't know why Henry would want to hide his identity from him. Even if Henry had committed some atrocity in the past, Roland would gladly forgive the Ghost Hunter since he was helping Rebecca. He tried to remember any Henrys he had met during his years of gunslinging, but none came to mind. He finally shrugged his shoulders. The Ghost Hunters were helping him, and if they wanted to be private, he would let them.

Walking down the hallway, he took the key to Rebecca's room out of his coat pocket and unlocked her door. A smile came to his lips as he entered the room. Even her wasted appearance couldn't keep his heart from racing in his chest. He took a seat on the bed and took one of her frail hands in his own. "Tonight, Rebecca. Tonight, you'll be awake. This will all be over soon, and we can get married," Roland whispered, smoothing back an errant strand of hair from her forehead. Tears once again threatened to form at the corner of his eye, but Roland didn't care. He was deliriously happy for the first time since he had discovered who had killed Bryant. Only this time, Roland wouldn't be thwarted. The Ghost Hunters had arrived in town, and he was positive that Rebecca would awaken that very night.

He sat with her for a few more minutes, quietly holding her hand and envisioning what would transpire once she emerged from her slumber. There would be a wedding soon, Roland decided. It seemed an eternity since he had proposed to Rebecca, and he meant to collect on her acceptance as soon as she returned to full strength. At last he rose from the bed and placed a single kiss on her forehead. "Don't worry, Rebecca. I'll take care of everything tonight. I promise," Roland whispered. He took one last look at her before leaving the room and locking it behind him.

Roland put the key in his pocket and straightened his shoulders. His face settled into a lopsided grin as he started down the hallway. He was no longer concerned about Curly returning or Alvin's politics. Rebecca would soon be awake despite what seemed a conspiracy on the part of every enemy he had. The world seemed in perfect order once more, and he would be damned if he didn't smile.

The crowd in The Last Frontier quieted for a few moments as he descended the stairs, but once they saw that Singing Rock and Henry weren't with him, they quickly returned to their own affairs. Making his way across the floor, Roland took a seat at his table and waited for dawn to arrive. Time seemed to drag slowly, but it was much better than the uncertainty of waiting for Curly to return. He looked out the window every now and then, more from curiosity than anything else. Roland still intended to arrest Curly the moment he returned to New Haven, but the Dark Rider was no longer such a pressing concern.

Despite Roland's improved mood, people still avoided the Sheriff like the plague. A few cast glances his way every so often, but other than that he had no contact with anyone over the next hour. Even William was too preoccupied bantering with Sherry's girls to sit down and talk to Roland. Roland couldn't blame any of them. With his dark moods over the last week, only Jack had talked to him. Luckily the deputy entered the saloon shortly after eight to help break up the monotony.

Jack looked tired as he made his way across the floor towards Roland's table. The tips of his mustache seemed to droop, and he plopped himself down in a chair with a loud exhale. He ran a hand across his eyes then through his hair. "Damn, this has been a busy night, and it's not even nine yet."

Roland sat up and propped his chin on his hand. "What the hell happened to you, Jack? You don't look so good."

"No whiskey tonight, eh?" Jack peered at the table for a moment. "Damn, I could use some." He played with the tips of his mustache as he collected his thoughts then continued. "Let's see. We had a fight at The Snake earlier tonight. It wasn't too bad. A few bloody noses, but nobody brought any guns into it. Then you'll love this, Roland. Paul Henderson showed up about fifteen minutes ago and tried to raise another mob to wipe out the Cheyenne." He stopped and smacked his head sarcastically. "Oh yeah, I almost forgot. He was upset because he heard an Indian was in town. Then I talked to Morgan, and he said he left him with you." Jack spat accusingly and glared at Roland.

Taken back, Roland raised his eyebrows and looked back at his old friend. He had thought things would go smoothly for the rest of the evening, but it appeared that he was wrong. "Calm down, Jack. Is everything okay now? Paul went home before he could cause any trouble?"

"Yes, he did, but you're avoiding the question, Roland. Why the hell do you have an Indian visitor after all the trouble we've had the last few weeks?"

Roland ignored Jack's rancor and held up a finger, wagging it back and forth as his mouth curled into its customary lopsided grin. "I'll tell you about it later, Jack. It's a private matter."

Jack glared at Roland as if he intended to stare holes right through the Sheriff. "Like hell it's a private matter. There was nearly a mob tonight. What's going on?"

"I already told you it's private," Roland answered in a gravelly tone and stubbornly dug in his heels. He hated to keep Jack in the dark, but he still wasn't ready to tell what had occurred at Rebecca's house. Once Rebecca was awake, he would tell Jack about the whole ordeal, but not until then. "I'll go talk to Paul and make sure there's not another problem. Don't worry about the Indian. He's upstairs, and he should be gone tomorrow. It's my problem. You let me deal with it. I'm still Sheriff of this town."

Jack stared at Roland for a few moments, and the Sheriff returned his stare without blinking. Finally Jack looked away and swore, "Goddamn it, Roland. You'd better tell me what's been going on soon. You owe me that."

Roland smiled a toothy grin. "Trust me, Jack. Have I ever lied to you?"

"Yes, you have," Jack muttered then looked at the Sheriff. He squinted for a moment as if he didn't believe what he was seeing. "What the hell has put you in such a good mood? You've been storming around for the last week."

Leaning back in his chair, Roland spread his arms wide. "Let's just say life is better today." It was all he could do to keep from laughing out loud and telling Jack the whole story. But things had found a way to go wrong for him over the last few weeks, and he didn't want to jinx his luck.

Jack blinked in surprise at Roland's turn of emotions. He had expected to see the dark-mooded Sheriff who had made the entire town avoid him. "Does this have to do with that Indian Morgan brought over here?"

"Don't worry about it. I'll tell you soon enough," Roland told the deputy magnanimously.

"You'd better," Jack grumbled.

"How's everything else going tonight?"

Jack muttered something under his breath then answered Roland's question. "Besides Paul and the fights, quiet. I haven't seen a single Rider. Everyone's looking, but so far no luck."

Shrugging his shoulders, Roland waved the comment off. "They'll be back sooner or later."

"I thought you wanted Curly arrested. You've been trying to catch the son of a bitch for a week," Jack exclaimed confusedly. Roland wasn't making any sense. He kept waffling back and forth between moods. One minute he wanted Curly arrested, and the next he didn't seem to care.

"I still want him, Jack, but there's no sense getting upset over it. Curly'll return one of these days, and we'll be waiting for him."

Jack shook his head and gave up trying to figure out Roland. "I also came by to see if you're going to release that little bastard."

Who? Roland was about to ask Jack what he was talking about when he remembered his prisoner. In the excitement of the Ghost Hunters' arrival, Jimmy had completely slipped his mind. He had promised to lock Jimmy up for one week, and that Tuesday evening was the end of his sentence. "Thanks for reminding me. I forgot all about him."

"How could you forget, Roland?" Jack looked at Roland strangely. It wasn't as if they had dozens of prisoners. Jimmy was the lone occupant, and he should have been easy to remember.

"It's a long story. Why don't we head on over and let him go?"

"Sure," Jack waved a hand in dismissal.

Roland spoke to William briefly before leaving The Frontier. Once he was sure that the rakish deputy wouldn't go traipsing off with some woman and leave the saloon unattended, he headed across the street with Jack. They walked silently, Roland looking up at the stars and Jack staring at the Sheriff. Roland knew that Jack had questions he wanted to ask, but Roland was in no hurry to answer them. Hopefully his old friend would just back off and wait for Roland to give him answers in time, but the Sheriff didn't know how feasible that was. Jack could be patient, but Roland had already stretched his patience pretty far.

Opening the door, Roland stepped aside and let Jack enter the station house first then shut it behind them. Robert was on duty that Tuesday night. He was leaning back in his chair, his feet propped up on the desk. Robert's hat had fallen low over his face, and from the way he quickly scrambled to sit up straight, Roland guessed that he had just waked the deputy from a nap. "Evening, Robert. How are you?"

"Fine, Sheriff, fine." The deputy rubbed his eyes and squinted at the pair of men who had just entered. "You startled me."

"I can see." Roland smiled mischievously. Normally he would have gone off the handle over one of his men falling asleep during their duty, but he was in a wondrous mood that evening and wasn't going to berate anyone. He was, however, ready to have some fun with his deputy. "You have a good nap?"

Despite his much larger size and years of gunslinging, Robert instantly became defensive. "I'm sorry, Sheriff. I was just dozing off for a little bit. I didn't think those bastards would come back until later this evening anyway." Sincerity was painted across the broken-nosed deputy's face, and Roland had a hard time keeping from laughing at the sight. Robert rarely backed down from a confrontation, but Roland had cultivated his reputation.

"I don't know, Jack," Roland turned to his other deputy. "Didn't we say we'd hang the next person who slept on the job?"

Jack looked at Roland as if he was crazy until he saw the smile on his face and caught on to the act. Jack coughed once and put a hand over his mouth. Roland could get away with that damn smirk of his, but Jack knew that if he tried to kid around with Robert, he'd be grinning from ear to ear. "I think you're right, Roland. Want me to get a gallows ready?" Even with his hand covering his mouth, Jack was sure that Robert could see the large grin on his face.

"But, but—" Robert sputtered in disbelief but lapsed into silence when Roland held up his left hand.

The Sheriff tapped his fingers on his cheek for a moment as if pondering Jack's suggestion, pretending to ignore Robert's startled expression. It was tempting to drag out the scenario a little further, but he had made his point and had his fun already. There was no sense beating a dead horse. "Naw, Jack. He's not worth the timber. I guess we'll let him live." Jack began chuckling, and Roland winked at Robert. "Got ya," he teased the deputy.

Robert put a hand on his chest and breathed a sigh of relief. "Blazes, Sheriff. Don't do that. You about scared me to death."

"Just giving you a hard time. Make sure you don't fall asleep on the job again," Roland commented flippantly.

"Yes sir," Robert answered.

"Good," Roland exclaimed and clapped his hands together. "Any trouble from the prisoner?"

"No, Sheriff. He's been real quiet the whole time. Aren't you supposed to let him out tonight?"

"That's why we're here, Robert. Can I get the keys?" There were two sets of key to the jail cells. One was in the desk, and the other hung on the wall.

"Sure," Robert replied and reached back, plucking the ring of keys from their resting place on the wall. He tossed them to Roland, who caught them in one hand.

"Thanks, Robert. I'll take care of this one. Get his guns out of storage, will you?"

"Okay," Robert answered, but Roland had already turned to the cell room door. He unlocked it and entered the narrow hallway with Jack right behind him.

Jimmy was still the only prisoner in the cells. The young man had been sleeping, but he quickly sprung out of bed when he saw Roland enter. The week in jail had been tough on him. His dark beard and hair were tangled, and his clothes were wrinkled and dirty. He was obviously ready to be released. "Sheriff, can I get out now?"

"That's why we're here," Roland answered. He paused a moment before opening the cell. The Sheriff had enjoyed Jimmy's company over the last week. It had been a pleasant diversion to tell his stories to a willing listener. Roland would actually miss the rascal, although with Rebecca about to awaken from her slumber, he wouldn't be needing to tell those stories as much as before. Turning the key, he pushed open the door and stood back so Jimmy could exit.

The young gunslinger exhaled loudly when the cell door swung inward, and Roland could see the tension in Jimmy dissipate. A broad smile creased his face as he stepped out of his cell. "Thanks, this feels good," he muttered then quickly headed towards the cell room door as if afraid the Sheriff would change his mind. His shoulders flinched once when Roland slammed his cell door closed, but after that Jimmy walked calmly out to the main office of the station house.

Roland locked the cell room door behind him then tossed the keys to Robert. He crossed his arms and leaned back against one of the walls and fixed Jimmy with a stern glare. Despite his good mood, Roland wanted to make sure that the young adventurer left town. Things were going well, and Roland intended to keep them that way. "All right, Jimmy. You're free to go. I'm even going to return your guns to you, but I want you on your way immediately."

Jimmy's smile froze on his face. "Leave? Why do I have to leave?"

"Because you pissed off Carlos. That's why. The next time Carlos comes to town, he'll go out of his way to shoot you. I don't need a gunfight in the middle of town. You also pissed off all my deputies. You nearly got half of us killed, and most of them are still mad," Roland stated in a tone that brooked no arguments.

Nonetheless Jimmy began protesting immediately. "That's not fair, damn it. I served my week, and I want to stay." He set his feet wide apart in a fighting stance, and even though his guns still lay on the table behind him, Jimmy's hands drifted towards his hips.

Robert arched an eyebrow from behind Jimmy, and Roland shook his head slightly. He didn't want his deputy to beat the hell out of Jimmy. He had enjoyed talking with the youth, but Roland was adamant about him leaving. There were too many bad things that could happen if he remained in town, and there would always be the likely chance that the adventurer would do something stupid. "Robert, give me his guns."

"Sure, Sheriff," the deputy replied and carried Jimmy's two pistols in their gunbelt over to Roland.

Jimmy looked a little less sure of himself as he saw Roland holding his weapons. Roland's explanation was still fresh in his mind, and he realized that it wouldn't take much for one of the lawmen to shoot him. He held out his hands in front of him. "I didn't mean any trouble, Sheriff. I was just asking to stay." His voice had lost much of its bluster and sounded more plaintive.

Roland hated to banish the youth from New Haven. He had listened to how much Jimmy craved something from the Old West culture, and New Haven was as close as he would ever come. "Sorry, Jimmy, but you've used up all of your privileges here. I want you on the first train out of here tomorrow afternoon."

The young gunslinger's chest puffed out for a moment as if he was going to argue with the Sheriff, but he quickly backed down after taking one more look at his pistols in Roland's hands. Regret painted his face, and he sighed once forlornly. "All right. I'll be on the afternoon train out of here," Jimmy answered in a resigned tone then reached up and tipped his hat.

Jack snorted at Jimmy's submission. If Roland let his deputy have his way, Jack would have hung Jimmy. Roland couldn't blame him. Jimmy had nearly got Jack killed. Luckily the young gunslinger acquiesced before Jack had lost his temper. "Good, I believe the train's headin' out at three tomorrow afternoon. Right, Jack?"

The deputy nodded. "Last I checked."

"Good, then. I want you on that train, Jimmy. You should be able to get a room at The Frontier tonight," Roland told the youth.

"Can I at least gamble tonight if I promise to stay out of trouble?" Jimmy's eyes widened imploringly as he meekly asked Roland for one last fling in New Haven.

Roland wanted to tell him it was out of the question, but Jimmy's voice sounded so desperate, almost like a child asking for a Christmas present. Even though he knew it would infuriate Jack and some of the other deputies, Roland nodded. "All right, you can gamble tonight, but if I have *any* trouble out of you, I'll run you out of town on foot. Do you understand me?" He asked in a gravelly voice.

"That's no problem, Sheriff. You can trust me," he answered earnestly, a boyish smile coming to his cheeks.

Jack snorted once again. "About as far as I can throw you," he muttered derisively.

Jimmy's smile dropped from his face, and he stared at Jack with a cocky, arrogant glare. Roland stepped in before anything could develop. "That's enough, Jack. Jimmy, you remember what I said. Now take your guns and go over to The Frontier. I don't want you anywhere else tonight. I want to keep an eye on you myself."

He handed the gunslinger his gunbelt and watched Jimmy fasten it around his waist. Jimmy grinned smugly then strutted to the door with an arrogant jaunt to his step. He tipped his hat before he left the station house, and the scared youth Roland had witnessed over the last week was gone. In its place was a cocky, young gunslinger exuding confidence, even though Roland knew most of that was an act. "Gentlemen," Jimmy called out then left the three men behind.

"Son of a bitch," Jack swore as soon as the door was closed. His lip curled into a sneer as he watched Jimmy stroll across the street.

"Calm down, Jack," Roland put a hand on the deputy's shoulder.

Jack immediately jerked it away from Roland and stared at the Sheriff with incredulous eyes. "What the hell's with you? You've been acting strange as hell. You were ready to kill him last week, now you're letting him play cards all night. Blazes, he almost got us killed."

Robert watched Jack and Roland with amazement. Nobody ever talked to the Sheriff like that. Roland's eyes narrowed as Jack finished his diatribe, and his jaw set determinately. "I'm still the Goddamn Sheriff in this town, Jack. Don't forget it."

The deputy was about to retort then threw his hands up in frustration. Jack stomped out of the station house, slamming the door behind him.

Roland shook his head and turned to Robert. The deputy looked as if he was trying to make himself invisible. "Good night, Robert. Don't go to sleep again," Roland chastised and quickly left the station house.

Jack had just finished untying his horse and was about to swing into the saddle when Roland emerged from inside. The deputy's face turned into a scowl when he saw the Sheriff, and he swung himself up defiantly as if he didn't even notice Roland walking his way.

"Jack, will you please stop?" Roland called out as Jack raised one of his feet to spur his horse into a gallop.

The deputy took a deep breath to control his temper and glared at Roland. "What do you want, Roland?" Scorn dripped from his mouth

Roland paused before answering. He had never seen the deputy so mad at him before, and the Sheriff intended to put an end to whatever was causing Jack to act so furious. "I want to know why you're so damn mad. You stormed out of there like Sherry when one of her customers tries to skip out on a bill."

"How the hell can you let him play cards all damn night?" Jack spat, pointing a finger towards The Frontier.

"You're not that upset about him playing cards, are you?" Roland asked skeptically. He could understand Jack not being happy about Jimmy having free reign for the evening, but he didn't expect him to act so angry.

"He nearly got us killed, or did you forget that?"

"No, I didn't, but we all lived. He just wants to see some of the Old West, and he's leaving tomorrow. Let him have one night of playing cards. Is that too much?"

Jack took another deep breath, and much of the anger seemed to seep out of him. "All right, but I'm still pissed about that trouble with Paul tonight, and I want to know what's going on with you. Things are going to hell in this town lately, and you've been acting strange. I know Rebecca's been sick, but you're still Sheriff."

"I said I'd tell you about it soon," the Sheriff reminded.

"Yeah, I know. Sorry about that." Jack genuinely looked sorry for his outburst, but Roland knew that he must have been hopping mad to have been so temperamental.

"Don't worry about it. Let me know if anything else happens at The Snake tonight." He hoped that would do it. Rebecca would be awake the following morning, and everything would be better. Then Roland would tell Jack everything.

Jack tipped his hat and was about to head over to The Rattlesnake when he paused. He stroked his mustache and looked at Roland curiously. "Roland, are you sure those two aren't going to cause any trouble?"

"The two strangers?"

"Yeah."

"Trust me, Jack. I've got it all under control. Now get over to The Snake. I don't want the Riders to come back and only find Wade there."

The answer seemed to satisfy Jack. "You've got it," he called out and tapped his horse's ribs with one of his heels. Roland watched them trot down the street then went back to The Last Frontier to take up his customary spot once again.

Jimmy was at the bar talking to Edmund when Roland entered the saloon. He kept the gunslinger in the corner of his eye as he made his way across the floor to his table. Taking a seat, Roland focused all of his attention on the interior of The Frontier and didn't bother looking outside at all. The likelihood of Curly returning was slim, but he didn't even need the Dark Rider anymore. The Ghost Hunters' arrival took care of that predicament. The only possible problem he had was Jimmy.

Much to Roland's surprise, the young gunslinger behaved himself that evening. After Jimmy finished at the bar, he worked himself into a poker game and seemed to settle in fine. Roland kept glancing towards the table frequently for half an hour but stopped after that. Jimmy appeared perfectly happy to play cards in an almost Old Western setting.

The next hour went by slowly. Customers continued to pour into the saloon, and by nine there was a large crowd inside. More and more card games were struck up, and Sherry's strumpets targeted the clientele in greater numbers. William had begun chatting with them once Roland returned, and he seemed to be having a great time as he flirted with the half dozen prostitutes Sherry had sent over that evening. Everyone left Roland alone. Word hadn't spread that his black mood was over, and nobody wanted to talk if he was still in that state. He wouldn't have minded some company to help the time pass by, but Roland stayed at his table so he could keep an eye on the whole saloon. The Sheriff didn't expect trouble that evening, but he wanted to be ready just in case.

He was beginning to think it was going to be a long, tedious night when Wade burst into the saloon. The deputy quickly scanned the saloon with his pale blues eyes until they settled on Roland. He motioned Roland towards him and moved towards the Sheriff at the same time. Roland didn't know what was wrong, but Wade had a serious expression. Jumping out of his chair, Roland met the deputy halfway across the floor.

"Sheriff, come quick. The Riders are back in town," Wade panted loudly. His voice carried across the saloon, and everyone quieted instantly.

242

William paused in the midst of bantering with one of Sherry's girls and turned towards Roland and Wade. Jimmy's eyes sparkled, but Roland scarcely noticed him.

"How many? Who came? Curly?" Roland barked at Wade and grabbed the deputy's shoulders in a grip so tight it turned his knuckles white. It looked like he might not need to wait for the Ghost Hunters after all. His lips pulled back in an excited grin as he waited for the answer.

Wade looked surprised at Roland's response, but he didn't cower back as some of the Sheriff's other men did. "There's only four. Mad Dog, Carl and two others. Curly might be there." He stared back at the madly grinning Sheriff with a steady gaze. "Jack said to hurry, though."

Roland blinked and let go of the deputy, causing Wade to fall back half a step. "Come on, William, we've got company," the Sheriff shouted to his other deputy and turned back to Wade. "They're at The Snake?"

"Yes, sir," Wade answered in an excited voice. His own mouth curled into a tiny smile, so small that Roland could barely see it, but Wade's eyes sparkled with adventure as if this was the greatest thing that had happened in months.

"Then let's go," Roland barked and pushed Wade towards the door as William scurried across the saloon to catch up with them. The Sheriff paused at the door and looked back once. Jimmy had halfway risen out of his seat as he watched Roland and Wade rush out the door. Roland simply pointed one finger at the gunslinger and glared at him so fiercely that Jimmy immediately took a seat. With that danger hopefully averted, Roland dashed outside.

Wade had already jumped on his horse and sat anxiously atop it, ready to ride. "Are they inside already?" Roland called out.

"Yes, sir. All four of 'em."

"Good, they won't start anything yet." He paused as William rushed out of the saloon then turned his eyes back to Wade. "Wait for us," he ordered and ran across the street right behind William. The two of them quickly mounted a pair of horses then Roland kicked his horse and shouted, "Let's get the bastards!" Then with a loud whoop, the three lawmen galloped down the street past the startled looks of the few who were wandering through town.

Roland's blood boiled through his veins as he raced around the corner with the wind blowing in his face. If there were only four Riders at The Snake and Curly was one of them, he was a dead man. Roland had no doubts that he could kill the Dark Rider if given half a chance. He was confident that the Ghost Hunters could keep their word and help Rebecca, but the Sheriff didn't want to chance it. With his two pistols, he planned on killing Curly that evening and taking destiny into his own hands.

Jack, Morgan, and Ben stood by their horses fifty yards from The Rattlesnake. It was close enough for them to see if any of the Riders left the saloon, but far enough away for them to avoid being noticed by anyone inside. Jack and Morgan watched The Snake with set jaws and serious expressions on their faces. They had been around long enough and knew the danger they might face that night, but Ben stared at it with a mixture of apprehension and curiosity. Roland just hoped that the deputy didn't assault him with questions.

"What's happening, Jack?" Roland asked briskly as he reined in his horse beside the three waiting deputies.

"There are four of them inside. Been in there for about five minutes. Morgan saw 'em go in," Jack reported, flicking only a quick glance towards Roland before he returned his attention to The Rattlesnake.

Roland hopped off his horse and drew one of his guns as he stood by the three men. Wade and William quickly followed suit, making it six armed men ready for the quartet of Dark Riders. Even Ben with all his inquisitiveness looked ready to fight whoever marched out of The Snake. Roland's eyes gleamed as he stared down the street. *Soon, Rebecca, soon this will all be over.*

"How do you want to handle this?" Jack broke his concentration, and Roland quickly jerked his head around.

"What?" Roland had gotten so lost in thinking about shooting Curly that he hadn't heard Jack's comment.

"I said how do you want to handle this," Jack repeated, jutting his chin towards The Rattlesnake.

Roland rubbed his fingers down his bristly cheeks as he thought about the problem. "Is Curly with them?"

"I don't know, Sheriff," Morgan answered. "I saw Mad Dog and Carl. Hell, you can't miss them with that long hair of theirs," the deputy chuckled as he ran a finger through his own long, white hair. "I didn't get a good look at the other two, though. They went inside too quickly. It could be Curly, but it could be any of the Riders."

"Damn!" Roland swore and hit his thigh with his left hand. If Curly had been inside, the Sheriff would have stormed The Rattlesnake with his guns blazing, but things were a little bit trickier without knowing for certain whether or not his quarry was inside. He exhaled and inhaled slowly as he thought about how to approach the situation. If Curly was inside, he wanted the outlaw dead, but if Curly wasn't in town and Roland killed all the Riders inside, Curly might disappear from town for a while or even forever.

"Roland?" Jack called quietly as he and the other men watched Roland expectantly to see what he would do.

"Shut up, Jack. I'm trying to think, damn it," Roland cursed at the deputy. He took one more look at The Snake then exhaled out his nose, his nostrils flaring wide as he turned to his men. "All right, I want all of you to stay outside. Jack, you and Ben stay along the street, and the rest of you, take

244

cover by Sam's supply shop. I'm going inside," he ordered grimly then began to walk towards the saloon.

"Are you crazy?" Jack exclaimed and grabbed Roland's shoulder.

The Sheriff threw Jack's arm off and stared murderously at the deputy. Even Jack shrunk back from Roland's withering gaze. "I told you all to move. Now do it. I don't want to get killed if I have to run outside," he hissed. Roland stalked towards The Rattlesnake once more, not bothering to see if his deputies were actually following his orders. He had a murderer to catch, and he was ready to end the chase. Jack and the others watched Roland march towards the saloon for a moment before scrambling to get in position. Nobody, not even Jack, had ever seen Roland appear so ready to kill a man.

Roland's boots crunched the dirt beneath them as he walked steadily towards the entrance. The warm summer heat and everything else around him faded into the background. Even his breathing slowed as he readied himself for a possible fight. He holstered his gun as he went up the steps. There was no sense provoking a fight if one wasn't necessary, and if he needed his guns, Sheriff Black was confident that he could draw them in time.

The Rattlesnake had a decent-sized crowd that evening. It never drew as many as The Last Frontier, but it had its own steady clientele. The noise died down as Sheriff Black walked inside, and every single eye focused on him. Most of the patrons that night were drunks or rowdy gamblers who at one time or another had drawn the Sheriff's wrath. Roland hardly ever entered The Rattlesnake, preferring to let his deputies keep an eye on it, and the patrons watched him carefully, trying to judge why he had paid a visit that evening.

He stopped at the entrance and let his eyes roam over the inside of the saloon. They widened in excitement for a moment when they fell upon Mad Dog and Wild Carl. The two Dark Riders' hands immediately went to their holsters and held there in case bullets were needed. Roland's excitement was short-lived, though. The two Riders sat at a table shared only by a pair of Sherry's seedier whores. He only had to look two tables over and see two Banditos to know that his trip had been a waste. He was surprised to see the Banditos present without Carlos, but they occasionally came to town without their leader. Bitter disappointment set in his gut, but Roland tried to shrug it off. The Ghost Hunters were still in town, and they would rescue Rebecca at dawn. He would have preferred to help her immediately and all by himself, but it was the result that mattered not the method.

Roland still wanted Curly dead. Even if the Ghost Hunters succeeded, Curly had murdered someone in New Haven, and that marked him as a dead man in Roland's eyes. Roland just had to lure him back to town. He held his hands away from his holsters in an obvious display of peace then walked slowly towards Mad Dog and Carl's table. Cracking his knuckles once, Roland kicked a chair up to the table and took a seat, leaning back nonchalantly as if he wasn't worried about a single thing. "Evening, gentlemen." Roland tipped his hat. "Ladies, could you excuse us a moment? I need a word here with these two fine men," the Sheriff quipped with a lopsided grin, but it didn't touch his eyes. He had come for business, and it only took one look at him to tell that he was serious.

The two strumpets quickly scurried away from the table, leaving the two Riders and Sheriff Black all by themselves. Mad Dog spat tobacco juice into a spittoon and glared at the Sheriff. He had brown hair that ran in tangled knots down to his shoulders. A scraggy beard decorated his face, and his eyes were dark green. His clothes were dirty, but Roland knew that a sawed-off shotgun was under his coat. He usually spent much of his time drinking, and the Sheriff wasn't surprised to see that he was already drunk. "What the hell you doing, Sheriff? We ain't done nothing," he sneered at the Sheriff, showing his yellowed teeth.

Sheriff Black wrinkled his nose as the Dark Rider's pungent breath wafted across the table, but other than that he kept his composure rigid. "I came to check on you boys. Nobody's seen you in a week," he bantered in an almost jovial tone. Roland paused to rub one of his knuckles over his Sheriff's badge, continuing to look at the pair of Dark Riders the whole time. "I just want to know what the special occasion is."

"We wanted to come back. There ain't no law against that, Sheriff," Wild Carl chimed in. Wild Carl had long dark hair and a long drooping mustache. He was cleaner than Mad Dog, but Roland had met pigs that had more hygiene than Mad Dog. Wild Carl had received his nickname from his eyes. The left one was fine, but the right one was lazy and wandered about. When Wild Carl got upset, his stare was supposed to be maniacal and quite unsettling. Nobody was quite sure why Mad Dog had chosen his particular name, but Roland had always thought he was a son of a bitch.

"I never said there was, Carl. I just wanted to make sure you two and those two stay out of trouble." Sheriff Black jutted his chin towards the two Banditos who were watching the conversation. He wasn't aware of any Banditos who could speak very good English, but they watched his hands and more importantly his guns very closely.

"We will. Now why don't you get the hell out of here and leave us alone," Carl slurred and slammed his fist on the table, knocking over a bottle of whiskey. He grabbed it quickly before it could spill too much on the floor.

The Sheriff fought the urge to laugh. Carl was trying to be threatening, but he and Mad Dog looked like a couple of drunk idiots. There was no sense staying around The Rattlesnake any longer. Drunk idiots tended to do stupid things. He wanted Curly, not the two at the table.

"All right, I will," Roland replied flippantly, implying that he was leaving by choice and not because the Dark Riders had told him to. "One last

246

thing. I wanted to tell you the Riders are welcome back in New Haven. I don't want any trouble, and if you don't start any, all of you are welcome in town. Tell that to Carlos," Sheriff Black told the pair then lazily came to his feet. He leaned over the table and smirked at Carl before he left. "You're supposed to drink the whiskey, not pour it on the floor," the Sheriff chuckled, winked once at the Dark Rider, and then turned around smoothly. He walked to the door slowly, sauntering arrogantly to show he didn't have a fear in the world at that moment. Until he made it out the door, he wasn't quite sure that he would be safe. He had provoked Carl and offered his back to the Dark Rider. Over the years, Roland had seen men shot over far less, but he gambled that they would let him leave safely. Fortunately, his luck held true.

When he stepped out of The Rattlesnake and out of immediate danger, Roland's mouth curled into a lopsided grin, and his eyes sparkled merrily. The whole incident had been quite a bit of fun. It had been dangerous, but surviving a dangerous situation always produced a wild, adrenaline rush of excitement. He had even accomplished something. Hopefully Mad Dog or Wild Carl would actually remember his comments and pass them on to Carlos. Soon after that, the Sheriff might even expect to see Curly in town. By then, Rebecca would be awake, but Sheriff Black had justice to dispense to the Dark Rider. All in all, that Tuesday was proving to be an excellent one. The Ghost Hunters had arrived, Rebecca would soon be free from the Land of Shadows, and he had set in motion Curly's appointment with a gallows.

Once he stepped into the street, Roland held his hands up in the air. Moments later, five deputies popped up out of nowhere. Roland pointed at Jack and Ben, who stood in front of a store two buildings over from the saloon. He walked towards the pair, and Wade, Morgan, and William followed his lead. Rubbing his hands together in satisfaction and smiling his lopsided grin, Roland approached Jack and Ben with a slight bounce to his step.

Jack watched Sheriff Black with a raised eyebrow. He had seen that self-congratulating smirk too many times before, and usually it meant Roland had gotten himself into trouble. "I take it Curly wasn't in there?" There hadn't been any gunshots. The way Roland had acted before entering the saloon, Jack had expected him to shoot everyone inside if Bryant's murderer had been in sight.

"No." Roland shook his head, but his smile didn't fade in the slightest. "Just Mad Dog, Carl, and a couple Banditos. Don't worry, though, he'll be back," he stated confidently.

"What makes you say that?" Jack's shoulders straightened, and he looked at Roland with genuine curiosity.

"Trust me, Jack. One way or another, he'll be back soon, then I'll have the son of a bitch," Roland answered as the other three deputies walked up. William appeared relieved to have avoided a gunfight, but disappointment painted Wade's face. The quiet deputy was as bad as Jimmy, who Sheriff Black was glad to see wasn't anywhere near The Rattlesnake. He had meant what he said to the young gunslinger. If Jimmy caused any trouble, he would run him out of town immediately.

Morgan looked relieved to have avoided a gunfight as well, and he grinned as he walked up to the Sheriff. "What the hell happened in there? I expected you to take out all the Riders and anyone who got in your way."

"Nothing much. It was just Mad Dog, Carl, and some Banditos. I told them to behave, and we wouldn't bother them." Roland stopped and stared at all of his men. "I mean it. Nobody picks a fight with them. We don't need any more trouble. Things have been crazy enough around here lately."

"What about Curly?" Jack asked.

"That one's different," Roland answered quietly, and his eyes narrowed. "If that bastard shows up, I want to know about it." The Sheriff shrugged his shoulders as if dismissing the whole subject. "The rest of them I couldn't care less about. Who knows, if all goes well, we could have a peaceful Fourth of July."

That drew laughter from all of them. They remembered the previous year's celebration. There would be trouble on the Fourth no matter what they did, but hopefully they could minimize it as much as possible. After that, everyone headed back to their normal posts except Morgan, who stayed inside the supply shop to keep an eye on The Snake just in case more Riders showed up that evening.

Roland and William went back to The Last Frontier after tying their horses to the tether post in front of the station house. The Sheriff was disappointed that Curly hadn't come to town that evening. Everything was going so well, and he was in such a wonderful mood that killing Curly would have been the icing on the cake. Nonetheless, Roland felt exhilarated. He had faced a potentially lethal situation and emerged unharmed, and Rebecca would be awake in a matter of hours. The wait bothered him. He was ready to see her immediately, not wait patiently for dawn to arrive, but Roland didn't have much choice.

The Last Frontier instantly became silent when he entered the saloon. Every head turned towards him and William curiously as if they could glean what had happened at The Rattlesnake simply by looking at the pair. Roland chose to ignore them and headed towards his table. He wasn't in the mood to repeat the events of the past half hour to every customer in the saloon. William enjoyed socializing so Roland let the deputy explain what had happened. After sitting down at his table, he took a quick look at the clock hanging over the bar and grimaced when he saw it wasn't even ten o'clock yet. There was still a long way to go until dawn as he sat impatiently at his table and counted the seconds until Rebecca would awaken.

The crowd in the saloon grew over the next hour. It was only two days before the Fourth of July, and many had begun to celebrate early. Even with nobody approaching him to talk, Roland still caught snippets of conversation about the upcoming celebration. There was general excitement about the day of dancing, drinking, fireworks, and most especially the magician Alvin had hired. The magician hadn't arrived in town, and some of the patrons were worried that he wouldn't show up in time. Roland hoped that Alvin would deliver on his promise. Ever since he had announced the magician from Paris, the whole town had grown excited about his performance. If he didn't show, Roland could guarantee trouble on the Fourth. He planned on asking Alvin about the magician's arrival when the mayor came to The Frontier that evening. Alvin had come by and cast those damn mischievous glances in his direction the last five days, and Roland didn't really think he would stop that Tuesday.

He watched Jimmy play cards for a while. The young gunslinger seemed to be doing quite well at poker, judging by the smug grin on his face and the somber expressions of his competitors. William told what had happened at The Snake several times to curious onlookers. Several of them glanced at Roland as if wondering if they should get his opinion on the events, but they all decided against it. Luckily for William, the interest died down eventually as the story circulated quickly around the tavern, and he could once again devote his time to flirting with the few unattached women in The Frontier. Other than that, it was a quiet night at The Last Frontier until just after eleven when Alvin showed up.

The mayor was impeccably dressed as usual. That Tuesday he wore a light grey suit with a watch tucked into one of the front pockets of his jacket. His longish white hair had been thoroughly raked over with a comb until each and every hair fell perfectly in place. A well-polished smile decorated his face as he entered the saloon, his cane tapping loudly against the wooden floor. He instantly began chatting with the patrons, shaking hands and socializing with the fake persona that infuriated Sheriff Black to no end. Alvin glanced towards Roland a few times, his eyes sparkling with amusement and his mouth curling into a sardonic grin. Roland was quite sure that he was the only one who saw the mayor for what he really was, but Roland was used to it.

After nearly twenty long minutes of drumming up support for himself, Alvin finally found his way to Roland's table. His smile grew even wider as he approached. His eyes narrowed mischievously as if he knew something that Roland didn't. "Good evening, Roland. How are you?" Alvin asked brightly.

Roland found Alvin's smug charade annoying. He wasn't sure if Alvin was really hiding something or just trying to worry Roland as payback, and when Roland wasn't sure what Alvin was up to, he grew worried. The mayor had a great propensity for trouble, but that wasn't what Roland wanted to talk about that night. There would be time after the Fourth of July celebration to deal with Alvin. "I'm fine, Alvin. Why don't you take a seat?" Roland answered cordially and waved a hand towards the seat across from him.

Alvin's eyebrows shot up in surprise, and he looked at Roland appraisingly. "Awfully friendly of you," he commented suspiciously and slowly took a seat as if expecting some sort of trick from Roland. He rested the cane against the side of the table and leaned forward. "What do you want?" Alvin stared at Roland warily.

"Alvin, Alvin, is that any way to greet an old friend?" Roland answered in that same bright voice which the mayor had used, and his mouth curled into a lopsided grin. He tried to stare back at Alvin with that same smug, knowing expression, and judging from Alvin's response he had nailed it perfectly. "I just had a few things I wanted to talk about."

The mayor had clearly been expecting to rattle the Sheriff, but Roland's flippant attitude that night confused Alvin. He paused before answering, carefully considering his words. "Sure, Roland. What's on your mind?" His eyes narrowed, and he watched the Sheriff like a hawk.

"Is the magician still coming to town for the Fourth? Everyone's expecting him, and they're going to be pissed as hell if he doesn't make it."

"That would make a lot of trouble for you, wouldn't it? Maybe a few more fights? I'd hate to spoil the celebration for you and your men." Alvin's grin became malevolent, and his eyes flashed briefly before settling back to their normal appearance.

Roland stared right back at the smiling mayor with his cocky lopsided grin and indifferent expression. "Hell, Alvin. You're the one who promised the magician would be here. Not me. People are gonna be more pissed at you than me, don't you think? So is he going to be here or not?"

Anger flashed across the mayor's face, and his expression lost all of its friendliness for a moment as he glared murderously at Roland. "He's an *illusionist*, not a magician, Roland. And he'll be here, so you can stop your worrying," Alvin spat out and continued to stare malevolently at Roland.

"Illusionist then. Glad to hear he'll be here. Thanks, Alvin." Roland was having fun goading the mayor, especially since it seemed to be so successful. He decided to place one more barb before Alvin left. "I ran into Mad Dog and Carl tonight. They were at The Snake with a couple of Banditos, and I was wondering if you knew what they were doing in town," Roland commented innocently then drew back as if suddenly remembering something. He hit his forehead with his palm and shook his head a few times, staring at Alvin apologetically. "I'm sorry, Alvin. I forgot. They don't talk to you anymore. Pity." Roland's voice dripped with false sympathy as he tried to push Alvin while he had the mayor upset.

The mayor, however, surprised Roland. Instead of flying even further off the handle, Alvin suddenly regained his composure, and his mouth once again curled into that smug, mocking smile that Roland hated. He looked ready to laugh at the Sheriff rather than hurl more insults. "You're right, Roland. I don't talk with them anymore. Pity." He pushed himself back from the table and cracked his knuckles. Alvin chuckled softly as he grinned even wider at the Sheriff. "Well, take care. I need to talk to George about getting our illusionist a room." He got up from the table and chuckled at Roland one more time before walking towards the bar.

Roland suspiciously watched Alvin make his way across The Frontier. The mayor's behavior both confused and worried the Sheriff. Alvin had been nearly livid with rage over Roland's turning the tables on him, but he had suddenly calmed down after the Sheriff mentioned his lack of influence with the Dark Riders. Alvin had been acting smug as hell for the last week and was especially smug after Roland had brought up Mad Dog and Carl. *Blazes, he can't still be talking to them.* Roland's eyes widened at the thought. *He pointed a Goddamn gun at Carlos. He'd never forgive Alvin for that.* But the more Roland thought about it, the more it made sense. If the mayor was still talking to the Dark Riders, that would explain Curly's absence from town and Alvin's disappearance the night after the near-gunfight a week before. Roland glanced over at the bar only to see Alvin look his way malevolently. *Damn it,* Roland thought, *I need to talk to Jack.* If Alvin and the Dark Riders were communicating again, there could be big trouble in New Haven.

The mayor stayed at The Last Frontier for another hour, casting those mocking glances in Roland's direction. At midnight, Alvin finally left as the customers began to trickle out of the saloon. Those who had to get up early in the morning couldn't afford to be out too late. As the mayor was leaving, he grinned knowingly at Roland, his eyes sparkling with menace. The Sheriff watched him leave and returned the stare with his own lopsided grin and a flippant expression on his face, but Alvin's behavior worried him. The moment the mayor walked out the door, Roland's face turned perplexed as he tried to figure out what game Alvin was playing.

About fifteen minutes later, Jack dropped by The Frontier for his last visit of the night. Roland was glad to see that he appeared to have calmed down from earlier. He needed Jack to help him with Alvin, not act upset over Singing Rock's arrival. The deputy looked tired as he took a seat across from Roland, resting his head on one of his hands. He exhaled loudly and rubbed his eyes wearily. "Damn, this has been a long night."

"Tell me about it," Roland commented drolly. "Was there any more trouble from Carl or Mad Dog?"

"Nah, you know we would have got you if anything else happened."

"I thought so, but I just wanted to be sure. We've got enough other problems."

"What?" Jack's head lifted, and his back straightened as he listened attentively to Roland. "What else happened?"

"Alvin dropped by tonight," Roland began and paused as he remembered the mocking look on the mayor's face as he walked out of the saloon.

"So? He comes by here every night, Roland," Jack pointed out.

"Let me finish. He came in here. That's nothing unusual. He's been doing it for the last week more than ever. Giving me that Goddamn grin of his. I'm telling you he's up to something, and I don't know what it is. That worries me, Jack."

Jack slapped the table and chuckled. "Is that all? Hell, he's just trying to get even with you, that's all. Ever since he lost control of the Riders, he's been itching to get even with you. Don't let him get to you."

"No, Jack," Roland spoke quietly, and his face turned deadly serious. Jack stopped his chuckling and gave Roland his undivided attention. "I know him better than you. I've known him longer than you have, and I know when that son of a bitch is up to something. He was mad as hell at me, but the minute I mentioned the Dark Riders, he got that damn grin of his. I think he might be talking to the Riders again."

"Blazes, that's all we need right now," Jack whispered and whistled in amazement. Then his face became confused. "Roland, that doesn't make any sense. If they're talking to Alvin, the Riders would be coming into town every night. They wouldn't be staying away."

"I know. That's what worries me. It makes sense for Curly not to be in town. Alvin's probably told the son of a bitch I'm looking for him, but I don't know why Carlos and the rest haven't returned. The way that Goddamn snake was grinning, he's planned something. I just want you and everyone else to keep your eyes open. I have a feeling something bad is going to happen soon."

Jack shook his head and stared up at the ceiling for a moment in frustration. "You don't have any idea what he'd do? He didn't give you any hints?"

"No, he didn't tell me a Goddamn thing. Just that smile of his. I don't have—" Roland broke off, and his face turned worried. "The Fourth is the day after tomorrow. You don't think they'd try anything then, do you?"

"No, Alvin's not stupid. He's been planning the celebration for months. He even hired that magician every one is talking about. He won't do anything to cause any trouble."

"Illusionist," Roland corrected absentmindedly.

"What?" Jack asked.

"He's an illusionist," Roland pointed out once more.

"Why the hell do I care about that, Roland?" Jack looked at him like he was crazy.

252

"Never mind," Roland waved the matter off. The memory of his conversation with Alvin was still fresh in his mind. "I think you're right, though. He has spent too much time on this to do something stupid. If I know Alvin, he's going to want everyone in town completely grateful to him for the next year for throwing such a marvelous celebration." Roland rubbed the stubble on his cheeks as he thought about the matter for a few moments then shook his head in frustration. "Hell, I don't know what Alvin's up to, but just let everyone know to be careful these next few days. I don't trust that Goddamn snake."

"Do you want everyone to show up early tomorrow and have them work late to make sure nothing happens?"

Roland briefly considered the idea before shaking his head again. "No, I want everyone rested for the Fourth. We're going to have our hands full that day. Just keep acting as we've been. Keep an eye out for Riders, and let me know if any come into town."

"You've got it. Well if there's nothing else, I'm going to turn in. I'm exhausted."

"That's it. Good night, Jack."

"Good night, Roland," the deputy replied and rose to his feet. He walked across the saloon on tired legs, and Roland envied him. Jack would be resting quite soon, but it would be some time before Roland would find a bed again. Not until sometime after dawn, but at least then he would have Rebecca in his arms once again.

Roland tried to keep his mind preoccupied on Rebecca as the night wore on. He was growing restless for dawn to arrive so he could return to her house with the Ghost Hunters. The night had at least provided some excitement and worry to keep his mind off the matter of Rebecca, but things slowed down considerably after Jack left. More and more customers left the saloon until there were only two tables with people at them. Jimmy was at one of them, playing cards and still winning from the looks of him. The other table also had a poker game going on, but George didn't seem too keen towards the card players.

"All right, gentlemen, time to go," he announced. George didn't mind staying up late, but cardplayers weren't going to be buying much alcohol. If there was no more revenue to be earned, he usually shut the shop down.

"Come on, George. We were just getting started," one of the men complained.

"Then go finish somewhere else. You know I shut down around this time, so get going," George repeated firmly and looked over at Roland. The saloon owner didn't have to say a word further as all of the men collected their money and stood. Despite the fact that Roland had been in a pleasant mood all evening, people still treaded softly around him. The gamblers shuffled out of the saloon, a few of them stumbling clumsily, and tipped their hat respectfully towards Roland on their way out.

Jimmy, however, kept his seat. "You too, young man. It's time to close," George fussed to the young gunslinger.

"I have a room here, old man. I'm going to stay down here a bit longer," Jimmy replied in dismissal and turned his attention to one of the walls, ignoring the saloon owner.

George's cheeks turned red, and he puffed up at Jimmy's flippancy. But he kept his temper in check since Jimmy was a customer. "Sorry about that, I forgot. It's been a long night," he apologized to Jimmy then turned to Roland. "Good night, Sheriff. You'll lock up?"

"I've got it, George. Good night," Roland told the saloon owner and watched as the portly man waddled upstairs to his own bedroom at the head of the staircase. Once George had closed his bedroom door, Roland looked over at Jimmy. The gunslinger sat at his table nonchalantly, watching Roland with a cocky expression on his face. The Sheriff wanted to laugh. Jimmy was still trying his damnedest to make an impression on everyone in New Haven. "Is there something you wanted, Jimmy?" He tried hard to keep the laughter out of his voice.

"Yeah, I wanted to stay another day in town," Jimmy answered in a disinterested voice. He looked around lazily as if he didn't really care how Roland responded.

Roland, however, had already pegged Jimmy. Whenever Jimmy started to act disinterested, he might as well have hung a sign on his chest that read 'interested.' He found the boy's antics amusing, but as much as they reminded him of his own childhood, there was no way the Sheriff was going to let Jimmy stay in town another day. "No, Jimmy. I already told you, I want you on the afternoon train tomorrow," he stated in a flat voice.

His answer seemed to break through Jimmy's facade, and the gunslinger's face became pleading. "Please, Sheriff. Everyone's been talking about the Fourth of July celebration. Can't I stay for that? It's only one more day. I'll behave. I promise," Jimmy pleaded, his eyes widening and the cocky look completely wiped from his face.

The boy's plea gave Roland a slight dilemma. He hated to send anyone away during the Fourth of July. The fireworks display in 1891 had been incredible, and the illusionist coming to town promised to top even that. Roland knew how upset Jack and the rest would be for letting the young gunslinger stay, but he decided that he could withstand their anger. He had been given several second chances in his time, and he would be poorly repaying those who had helped him over the years by kicking Jimmy out. Besides, Rebecca would be awake the following day, and Roland was in a better mood than usual.

He scrunched up his face into a granite mask and stared at the boy as menacingly as possible. "Okay, you can stay," he told the gunslinger, and Jimmy's face immediately got that cocky smirk. He started to say something, but Roland cut him off. "Two things," Roland snapped and pointed a finger at Jimmy. "One, you leave on the first train after the celebration. You stay no longer than that. Two, you behave. No fights, no arguments. If you upset any of my men, I will throw you out of town. Do we have an understanding?"

"Yes, sir," Jimmy tried to sound contrite, but he failed as his eyes sparkled with that mischievous glint that worried Roland so much.

"You just remember that, Goddamn it," Roland swore and began to have second thoughts when he saw the expression on Jimmy's face. Hopefully Jimmy's reprieve of another day wouldn't come back to haunt Roland. Jimmy must have sensed Roland's doubts because he quickly stood up, tipped his hat, and headed up towards his room before Roland could say another word. "Blazes," the Sheriff muttered as Jimmy trudged upstairs. He wanted to give the gunslinger the benefit of the doubt, but he had bad feelings about trusting Jimmy. Roland hoped that he hadn't made the wrong decision.

He rose from his chair on tired legs and shuffled over to the front door to lock it. Roland intended to get some good rest once Rebecca was awake again. He had been running himself ragged for days, and it was finally catching up with him. He took a look at the clock and sighed as he realized he had another three hours to wait for the Ghost Hunters. Roland was ready to ride out to her house and rescue her immediately, but Henry had been clear in his instructions. Two hours before dawn. Resigned, he took a seat at one of the tables and rapped his knuckles on its wooden surface as he watched the seconds go by.

His heart kept beating faster as the clock's hands slowly spun themselves in circles. Every minute brought him that much closer to reuniting with Rebecca. Roland glanced upstairs from time to time, tempted to wake Jimmy and tell him some more stories. He had let the gunslinger go upstairs too easily. It would have taken his mind off the wait if he had an audience to entertain, but he had to wait alone as dawn inched ever closer.

Sleep threatened to overtake him several times, and he caught himself on the verge of laying his head on his arms and giving into its tempting embrace. He shook his head firmly each time and rose out of his chair, pacing around the floor several times until he had banished the immediate threat. Then he'd sit back down and impatiently rap his knuckles on the table once more. It was a frustrating cycle that he repeated several times as he watched the clock continue its slow spiral towards Rebecca's salvation.

When the hour hand finally wound its way past the five, Roland stood up and blinked his bleary eyes several times. He felt like his head was packed in wool, and his reactions seemed to have slowed down, but his heart was beating wildly as he made his way towards the stairs. Despite his weariness, there was a bounce to his step. Rebecca would be awake in a matter of hours, and lack of sleep couldn't curb his enthusiasm. His mouth had curled into a smile, not his customary lopsided grin but a full-blown, ear-to-ear smile as he approached the Ghost Hunters' rooms. He paused on the verge of knocking and cast a glance at Rebecca's room.

Lowering his arm, he reached into his pocket and withdrew the key to her door. Quietly he unlocked it and turned on a lantern. He didn't notice her emaciated body or tangled hair as he knelt by the bed. A tear fell from his eye, but Roland ignored it as he smoothed a lock of hair from her forehead. "It will all be over soon, Rebecca. It will all be over soon," he told her in a hoarse whisper. "I love you, Rebecca. I'll see you soon." Roland leaned over and placed a kiss on her cold cheek. Then he rose on tired legs. He paused before turning off the lamp and stared one last time at Rebecca before extinguishing it.

Roland locked her door then leaned back against it for a moment to collect himself. He rubbed furiously at his eye to clear out any tears, but he only managed to blur his vision even further. He was embarrassed by the tears, even though they were tears of happiness, and wanted to be sure that they weren't evident. Once all traces of them were gone, Roland marched his exhausted body down the hall and stopped in front of Henry's room. With a grin lighting his face, Roland rapped crisply on the door five times and waited for the Ghost Hunter to arise and help the woman he loved awaken once more.

Chapter Thirteen

Henry groaned as the loud knocking on his door resumed again. He had been sleeping so well, and the last thing he wanted to do was get out of bed. Every muscle in his body ached from several weeks of furious traveling, but he sat up in resignation as the pounding continued. "All right, I'm awake," he slurred in his thick accent. He ran his fingers through his hair then rubbed his eyes to wipe the sleep away.

He hopped out of bed and put on his hat and boots. Henry could still remember the days when he could last months with hardly any sleep and be ready to go at a moment's notice, but those days were over. Much had changed in his life since the day he met Singing Rock, and a vastly reduced stamina was one of them. He grabbed his silver bullet pendant and slipped its leather strap over his head. Then he buckled his single holster to his right hip. Henry seriously doubted that he would ever need his gun, but old habits die hard. He had carried a gun for too many years to stop it completely. Singing Rock didn't even like him carrying the single pistol, but the Navajo had relented. Even Singing Rock knew that sometimes they needed protection, and there was a difference between being a gunslinger without a conscience and being armed for self-defense.

The knocking started up again, furiously this time. "Come on, it's less than two hours 'til dawn," Roland's anxious voice came from the other side.

"Just a second." Henry looked at the door in amusement, and a slight smile graced his lips. He had seen many people act irrationally over matters dealing with spirits, but he never would have expected Roland Black to be acting that way. Henry supposed he couldn't blame Roland. The first time that he had encountered a spirit, he had been scared nearly to death, and most people had always considered him to be fearless.

The Ghost Hunter patted his holster one last time then took a deep breath. He wasn't looking forward to being face-to-face with Roland again, and he never particularly liked fighting spirits. Pulling his hat down low again, Henry went to the door, unlocked it, then swung it open. "Good morning, Sheriff," Henry greeted as he dipped his head low so Roland could only view the bottom part of his face.

The Sheriff peered at him closely and even lowered his head slightly to get a better look, but he quickly raised his head again when Henry ducked his own even lower in response. "I take it you had a good rest?" Roland asked politely.

"It was decent enough. I'll go wake Singing Rock and we can talk to this spirit of yours," he told Roland in his thick drawl. Henry wanted his time alone with the Sheriff to end as quickly as possible. Once they were outside, the darkness of night would do plenty to cloud his features.

"Great," Roland gushed enthusiastically and stepped back so Henry could exit the room. The Sheriff still looked as if he was curious about Henry's appearance, but other than that one glimpse, Roland refrained from trying to examine his features again.

With his head lowered, Henry walked into the hall and down to Singing Rock's door. He pounded on it twice with a balled fist. *"Singing Rock. It is time to go to the house,"* Henry called out in Navajo. There was a loud grunt from inside and a faint rustling. The Ghost Hunter stepped back from the door and turned his head slightly towards Roland. "He'll be out in a few minutes. He's a sound sleeper."

"Good," Roland replied anxiously to Henry's first statement.

Henry waited with his back turned to Roland. Usually he asked the people he was helping a few questions or tried to keep them calm before he and Singing Rock entered the Land of Shadows. There was no way, however, he was going to face Roland until they were outside in the dark, summer night.

For nearly two minutes he waited nervously at the door. He could almost feel Roland's desire to be at the house and for them to rescue his fiancée. Henry resisted the urge to knock on the door again. A lantern had been lit inside the room, and he could hear the Navajo moving around. It just took time to fasten all the belts and pouches that Singing Rock liked to carry. Finally the door opened, and the Navajo stepped out. *"What is wrong with you? You look like a child who has just done something wrong,"* he asked from the doorway.

"Nothing," Henry shot back testily. *"Let us get outside before he recognizes me."*

The Navajo nodded, and Henry backed up, turning away from the Sheriff. They let Roland guide them outside, while Singing Rock placed himself between the Sheriff and Henry. Once they stepped out the front door, Henry relaxed as tension drained from him. The moon was bright in the sky that morning, but it was much too dark for Roland to study his face. "So where is this ghost of yours, Sheriff?" He asked in his thick drawl.

"It's about a mile outside of town," Roland replied and pointed east. "Wait here a minute. I need to get a horse." The Sheriff ran across the street to the station house and untied one of the colts. The Ghost Hunters untied their own horses and by the time they had mounted theirs, Roland was already trotting across the street. His horse seemed to feel the anxiety of its rider as it pranced nervously towards the two men. "Come on. Let's go." Roland sounded ready to laugh with joy.

Henry exchanged a quick look with Singing Rock and rolled his eyes. They had seen too many people get all giddy when they thought their problems were about to be solved. Roland, like many others, didn't realize how the Land of Shadows was. More than likely, Henry and Singing Rock would be able to help him, but sometimes it was a cruel place. Nonetheless, it probably did him some good to be in a pleasant mood. It sounded as if Roland had been in foul spirits for the past weeks, and he could use some hope. "All right. Lead the way, Sheriff."

The three men rode towards Rebecca's house. The Sheriff, eager to arrive at Rebecca's house, rode at the front of their party. He kept looking back at Singing Rock and Henry as if encouraging them to ride faster. The Ghost Hunters, however, were quite tired of traveling quickly. It had been a long journey from Arizona, and there was no sense hurrying if speed wasn't necessary. Several times Roland had to rein in his horse when he strayed too far ahead. They finally crested a small hill, and Roland pointed a finger ahead. "That's it. That's Rebecca's house," he announced, and even in the dark, Henry could see the Sheriff's white teeth as he grinned.

Henry looked ahead and saw the house. He tilted his head and peered at it closely for a moment, his face scrunching up in contemplation. Singing Rock looked over at him. *"What do you think? Is this a good place?"* Henry asked Singing Rock, but Roland quickly stepped in.

"Come on, let's go," Roland suggested anxiously and prepared to dart ahead on his horse again.

"No!" Henry shouted out. "We wait here."

Roland reined in his horse abruptly and looked back in confusion. "But the house is up there."

"I know, but we're stopping here. We're not going in before dawn. They're too powerful at night," Henry explained once again.

"But I thought you said you'd help her," Roland accused Henry, his eyes once again filling with worry for Rebecca.

"I did," Henry threw up his hands in an attempt to stave off Roland's anger. "But there's no sense warning it. This is close enough. We can wait and prepare here, and the ghost will never see us this far from the house. Don't worry, we'll go in at dawn," he assured Roland, and it seemed to do the trick. Roland quickly backed down.

The three dismounted and tied their horses to a tree. Henry groaned when he got off his mount. His muscles were still tender from over a week of riding, and even though the ride had been short, it was enough to rekindle some of that soreness. He stretched his legs and arms in an attempt to loosen some of the cramping. That seemed to help his tired muscles , but he still walked over to Singing Rock with a slight limp. *"What do you think?"* Henry pointed at the house.

Singing Rock studied it for a moment. His eyes narrowed, and a thoughtful look formed upon his face. In the dim lights, there weren't many details that they could make out. *It's a large house,* Henry thought to himself. Much larger than the easy-to-assemble homes that were so common throughout the West. Under the pale moonlight, only its large silhouette was visible, a dark monolith that seemed foreboding. The Navajo sniffed the air in front of him and closed his eyes, savoring the aroma for a moment. His nose wrinkled up, and a disgusted expression crossed his face. *"There is evil in this house,"* the Navajo stated simply.

"What type of evil? A spirit?"

Singing Rock looked over with a disapproving frown. *"You know the signs for yourself. What do you think?"* The Navajo chastised.

A faint blush crept up Henry's neck. Even after five years, he wasn't used to sensing ghosts and spirits. Singing Rock had taught him how to do it and fully expected for Henry to be independent. He usually took the initiative and scouted out spirits in the Land of Shadows, but sometimes he preferred to have Singing Rock do the work just to be sure. *"Fine,"* Henry muttered and closed his eyes.

He slowed his breathing and tried to block out all thoughts except the house that stood a quarter mile away. His fear over Roland discovering his identity faded as did his nervousness over entering the house. They were replaced by a single image of the ominous house that they were soon to enter. Like Singing Rock, he took a deep breath and nearly retched at the foul scent of evil. It reeked of rotten eggs and spoiled meat, and Henry had to put all of his energy into maintaining his focus. For a few moments, the vision he had summoned in his mind wavered and threatened to dissolve.

After that brief flickering, it came back into focus, and Henry once more tried to relax. In his mind, he imagined himself rising off his feet and floating towards the house. At first nothing happened, but suddenly the image of the house began to drift closer, allowing him to observe more details. It was still obscured by darkness, but he was able to see the windows and door more clearly as he drew nearer.

Henry looked carefully at each window, but behind every one of them laid more darkness. No matter how hard he tried, he couldn't seem to break through. He was about ready to give up when a flickering behind one of the windows caught his eye. Henry studied the window, but nothing else happened. He was beginning to think it had been a trick of his imagination when he saw it again, a swirling blackness. The window was nearly pitch black, but for a moment a completely dark figure passed in front of the window before settling to rest. Once he saw it move, Henry studied the figure carefully, watching as it lurked by the window. There weren't any features to the darkness he was observing, just a shapeless form that lounged by the window as if keeping an eye on the area in front of it. A brief flash of light twinkled from the middle of the form, but it was quickly extinguished. Henry stared at the area where the light had flashed, but it didn't occur again. He once again imagined himself floating forward, so he could observe the dark figure and mysterious twinkling from a closer vantage point.

260

"Can you get her out?" Roland's voice called from a distance.

The Sheriff's voice broke his concentration, and the image of the house wavered in front of him. Henry struggled to keep if from shattering, but it was too late. In an explosion of tiny colorful shards, the image of the house disappeared from his mind. Exhaling from the effort, the Ghost Hunter opened his eyes and saw the Sheriff standing directly in front of him. For a moment, he was so drained from his recent actions that he stared Roland directly in the eye. Then, suddenly remembering where he was and who Roland was, Henry tipped his hat down to hide his features. It was dark outside, but Roland might recognize him from a few feet away. "What did you say?"

"I said what do you think? Can you get her out?" Roland asked in a tense voice.

"Calm down, Sheriff," Henry replied in his slow drawl then shook his head to shake the cobwebs from it. Gazing into the Land of Shadows always left him dazed afterwards. "We'll get her out. Just wait another hour or so."

Roland nodded. "Okay. Is there anything you need me to do?"

Henry felt sorry for the Sheriff. It was obvious that Roland had been put through an emotional hell and was anxious to end it. The Ghost Hunter also knew how independent Roland was and how waiting helplessly must be grating on his nerves. "No, we've got it from here. Why don't you sit down so Singing Rock and I can prepare to enter the house?"

Roland nodded once more. "All right, let me know if there's anything I can do to help," he responded and walked over to a tall oak. He took a seat on the ground and leaned back against the tree, his knees propped up. Roland tapped a nervous finger on his leg and kept switching his gaze between the house and the Ghost Hunters.

"He looks upset," Singing Rock commented softly.

Henry watched Roland with a concerned look on his face. He hated to see Roland so upset, but Henry was used to seeing people unhappy. It came with his line of work. *"He will be fine once we rescue his woman."*

Singing Rock looked at Roland and nodded, agreeing with Henry's words. *"What did you see in the house?"*

"Did you not look as well?"

"No, I had to watch the white man to make sure he did not approach the house. If there is a spirit inside, we must creep up on it, not alert it to our presence. Is there a spirit inside the house?" The Navajo repeated.

"I am sure of it. There was a dark figure inside, and I saw a sparkling light. I think it was a spirit and a captive spirit," Henry answered then paused as he thought about his vision. *"I think there is great evil around here. It smelled like rotted meat, but it does not make sense. Why would a spirit smell so evil?"* Henry had gained a tremendous amount of experience over the last five years, but he still leaned on Singing Rock from time to time for advice. He had never

encountered evil that powerful during his journeys with the Navajo and wanted to consult with him.

"I do not know. There are many reasons. Maybe this man was killed under evil circumstances. Maybe this spirit intends great evil. I do not know. We shall have to wait and see."

Henry nodded solemnly. He hadn't expected a definite answer from Singing Rock. Over the years, the one thing that he had learned from the Navajo was never to assume anything in their line of work. Spirits were tricky things and never acted the same way from town to town. *"Are you going to prepare now?"*

Singing Rock grunted affirmatively.

Usually the Navajo spent nearly an hour readying himself to combat spirits. It would be Henry who entered the Land of Shadows, but Singing Rock would guard Henry's physical body during his journey. *"Good, I am going to talk to the Sheriff and see if I can calm him."*

"Be sure he does not recognize you," Singing Rock cautioned.

"Trust me," Henry replied dryly. He wasn't about to let Roland learn his identity.

Singing Rock sat upon the ground. He sifted through the numerous pouches attached to his belt, carefully laying a few of them on the ground. Henry watched him for a moment then warily approached Roland. The Sheriff still sat watching the house with a frustrated expression on his face. He looked up as he heard the Ghost Hunter walk towards him. "Are you almost ready?" The Sheriff asked anxiously.

"Not yet. Dawn's still more than an hour away. As soon as the sun's up, we'll get her out. Don't worry," Henry answered consolingly again, confident that it wasn't the last time Roland would ask that same question. Henry could understand what Roland was feeling. A long time ago he had thought he was in love, and if she had ever been in danger Henry would have acted just as Roland was acting now.

Roland pursed his lips in frustration as if that was exactly the answer that he had expected. He looked over at Singing Rock, who was chanting in a soft singsong voice. The Navajo occasionally dipped his hand into one of his pouches and threw a fine powder into the air or sprinkled it in the air in front of him. The Sheriff watched Singing Rock with a confused expression then turned to Henry. "What the hell's he doing?"

"He's preparing himself so he won't be hurt."

"Hurt?" Roland shot worriedly, his eyes widening in fear. "I thought you said this was safe. That you could get her out of there," the Sheriff accused.

Henry put his hands up defensively. "I said we would get her out of there. I never said it was safe. The Land of Shadows and the spirits that live there are dangerous things. You carry your guns every day for protection.

Consider this the same thing. Singing Rock and I have been doing this a long time. We'll get her out."

The nervous tension seemed to disappear from Roland at the answer, and he leaned back into the tree. His face looked exhausted, and it seemed the only way that Roland was still awake was through sheer determination. "Sorry, I just want her awake again."

"Not too much longer."

"So when's the last time he entered the Land of Shadows?" Roland jutted his chin towards Singing Rock. He sounded like he was asking more to keep his mind off waiting for dawn than out of any real curiosity.

Henry cringed at the question. That was one of the areas that he didn't like to talk about. He revealed as little about his past that he could get away with, but sometimes people asked point blank questions that he couldn't avoid. Swearing to himself, Henry cursed the day that he had promised Singing Rock that he wouldn't lie any more. "A while," Henry answered in his thick drawl and awaited the fiery response from Roland.

"What?" Roland exclaimed, leaning forward from his comfortable backrest. "I thought you've been doing this for years, Goddamn it."

"We have been doing this for years, Sheriff. I didn't lie," Henry answered softly and waited for Roland to figure out the rest. He hoped the questioning would stop there. There were too many things that he didn't want the Sheriff to know. Hopefully he could steer Roland away from them.

For a second, Roland looked at Henry as if he didn't know what the Ghost Hunter was talking about. Then comprehension slowly dawned on his face, and his mouth dropped down in surprise. "You? You're going into the Land of Shadows?"

"Yes."

"That doesn't make any sense. I thought this Land of Shadows was an Indian thing," the Sheriff accused.

"It is, but sometimes the spirits of White Men make their way to the Land of Shadows. That's why I travel with Singing Rock. He travels into the Land of Shadows if there are Indians to be dealt with, but I make the journey if it's a White Man causing problems."

"But I don't understand. Why the hell doesn't he go in for white men? What difference is there? Can't he destroy them all?"

"Singing Rock could destroy any spirit he comes across, but we're not going into the Land of Shadows to destroy this spirit. I'm going in to persuade him to let Rebecca go."

"That's it?" Roland looked flabbergasted.

Henry wasn't surprised by the reaction. People generally thought that the only way to deal with spirits was to obliterate them. "That's it. I'm going in to find out who the spirit belongs to, and why he's upset. Then I can use that information to avenge whatever wrong was committed against him, and he will be banished from the Land of Shadows, or I'll convince him to release Rebecca and end this whole ordeal. Singing Rock has better luck talking to his people, and I have better luck talking to the spirits of White Men than he would."

The Sheriff nodded in slow understanding, but then his face became puzzled. Roland looked at Singing Rock again in confusion then back at Henry. "If you're going into the Land of Shadows, how come he's the one doing all the singing and not you?"

Henry rolled his eyes in frustration. He was revealing far more to Roland than he wanted, and he thought of ways to shift the conversation somewhere else. "It doesn't take much preparation to enter the Land of Shadows, but it does take quite a bit to protect yourself against attack. That's what he does. I go into the house and enter the Land of Shadows. Singing Rock goes in to keep the spirit inside from harming me while I make the journey. But enough of that. Why don't you tell me more about the man whose spirit I have to face," Henry suggested needlessly. There really wasn't any compelling reason for him to find out more about the spirit of the man, but it would hopefully divert Roland's attention from asking anything more personal about his background, especially something that might reveal more of his identity.

"Bryant? What do you want to know about Bryant?"

"Why don't you tell me what he was like when he was still alive," Henry suggested, a slight smile playing across his lips. He was glad the sky was still dark so Roland couldn't see the relieved look on his face. It appeared that he had successfully sidetracked the Sheriff's line of questioning.

Roland looked up at the stars as if trying to remember the man. "Let's see. Bryant was a greedy man. He was always trying to find a way to make more money. I'm pretty sure that's why he hooked up with the Dark Riders," Roland began explaining.

"Dark Riders?" Henry broke in. "Who are they?"

Roland spat on the ground. "They're a bunch of Goddamn outlaws. Kinda like the Cowboys in Tombstone."

Henry felt his blood chill slightly, and his hand instinctively reached towards the lone gun he had holstered. He wanted no trouble with a band of outlaws. His days of gunslinging were long over, and Henry had no intention of resuming them. New Haven was turning out to be a town of more than a few surprises for the Ghost Hunter. "Why don't you have them arrested or killed then? You don't want outlaws running your town."

"I wish I could, but it's worth letting them run wild right now. If I arrest them, they're going to wage war, and I'm going to lose a few men. Then I'll have marshals in here trying to clean things up. I like New Haven the way it is, and I don't want the governor deciding this town needs to be more modern like the rest of the Goddamn West. Hell, this is the only place left," Roland answered softly, and his face had a distant look as if he was fondly remembering something from a long time ago.

The Ghost Hunter knew how Roland felt. New Haven was the closest thing that he had seen to his glory years. If he hadn't found a new purpose with Singing Rock, he more than likely would have settled in the small Colorado town. "That makes sense, but why don't you finish telling me about Bryant."

"Oh, yeah," Roland shook his head and came back to the present. "Let's see. Bryant was a greedy son of a bitch. I'm almost positive he was selling the Riders information about train routes. He was getting paid handsomely for it and loved to show off for the whole town. Bought that Goddamn house, and he was always coming into town gambling and drinking. I can't say I was too sorry to see him go," Roland stated then his face took on a softer expression. "At least I got to meet Rebecca through him. That stupid son of a bitch doesn't know how lucky he was to have her."

"Maybe he does," Henry interjected.

"What?"

"Maybe he misses her, and that's why he took her spirit. You never can tell about spirits. So how did he die?"

"Had his throat slit from ear to ear. It was pretty bloody. There was one hell of a crowd gathered around him," Roland shook his head as he remembered the way people had flocked to the death scene. "That was the first murder in New Haven, so it was quite an ordeal."

Henry looked at the house for a moment inquisitively then glanced towards town. He put a hand to his chin as if considering something.

"What's wrong?" Roland asked worriedly.

"Nothing," Henry answered slowly. "Just wondering what that many people would be doing this far out of town. That's an awfully long way to travel to see a dead body."

"His body was left in the middle of town. Running Brook said he was killed here, but I don't know. It was six months ago, and there weren't any witnesses."

"It doesn't matter. We're going into the house soon, and we'll rescue her spirit one way or another. It doesn't matter how he died." Roland grew quiet after Henry spoke, and the Ghost Hunter was uncomfortable in the silence. He didn't like being that close to Roland. If Roland grew bored, he'd start asking questions again, and Henry didn't like where that could lead. "I need to do something so I'll leave you here by yourself, Sheriff." It was a vague statement, but it wasn't lie, Henry thought to himself.

"Okay," Roland replied absent-mindedly as he stared at Rebecca's house with an anxious expression on his face.

Henry left Roland alone and walked over to Singing Rock. The Navajo sat with his legs crossed and his arms outstretched with the palms facing upwards. He continued to chant in that same singsong voice with nearly a dozen pouches spread in a semicircle on the ground in front of him. Taking a seat about ten feet from his chanting partner, Henry crossed his legs and stretched his arms out in imitation of Singing Rock. *Hopefully Roland will leave me alone,* he thought.

Singing Rock had explained the importance of his rituals before. They were a way of communicating with the spirits of his ancestors, but more importantly they relaxed his mind before one of his dangerous encounters. Henry didn't have a problem settling his nerves before he entered the Land of Shadows. Years of gunfights had quickly taught him how to cool his blood and steady his nerves, but the Ghost Hunter wanted Roland to think he was busy chanting. He usually shied away from questions concerning his past, but he felt an even more urgent need to do so with Roland. It would only take the right question for Roland to guess who he really was.

Over the next hour, Singing Rock continued his preparations as Henry sat nearby with his eyes opened just a slit so he could keep an eye on Roland. The Sheriff looked over at the pair from time to time, but Henry made sure that he didn't react. Crickets chirped loudly as dawn inched ever closer, and the Sheriff rose to his feet and paced back and forth along a short line as he grew impatient for the two Ghost Hunters to enter the house. Several times he looked on the verge of interrupting their rituals. Finally as the night sky began to lighten into a dark greyish hue, Singing Rock opened his eyes.

The Navajo blinked a few times as he took in his surroundings. His face was a calm mask of serenity that nothing could crack. Turning his head, Singing Rock was surprised to see Henry sitting so close, although the only reaction on his face was the slightest raising of the eyebrows. *"Why do you sit here?"* He asked slowly as if the answer did not concern him one way or another.

Even though he had seen Singing Rock devoid of emotion before, it still chilled his blood every time the Navajo talked to him in that dead voice. *"The Sheriff. He was asking too many questions, so I left him. But that is for later. Let us enter this house."*

"Are you ready?"

"Yes."

"Then let us enter. Make sure he does not follow, or he will endanger himself and the woman we go to rescue."

"I will take care of it."

"Good," Singing Rock answered as he picked up his pouches and attached them to his belt.

Roland's eyes had widened with anticipation when he heard the two Ghost Hunters talking, and he rushed towards Henry when he saw the Ghost Hunter look his way. "Are you going now? It's nearly dawn." He asked excitedly.

"Yes, we are, but listen closely to me," Henry said as he rose to his feet. His knees were still sore, and he paused for a moment to rub the aching joints. "You must not follow us. You can place yourself and Rebecca in a great deal of danger. Do you understand?" He waited for the Sheriff to nod his head reluctantly. Henry knew that Roland wanted to help out more than anything else in the world, but the best way for him to help was to watch from afar. "Good, we'll be back soon. Remember, don't enter no matter what you see or hear. We know what we're doing."

Henry dismissed the Sheriff and turned back to Singing Rock. The Navajo had finished attaching his pouches and stood stoically, watching the house they were about to enter. As always Henry felt a sliver of fear shoot through his stomach, but he shrugged it aside and slowed his breathing. Quickly that slice of fear was replaced by a cold, icy calm that cast out all of his fear and anxiety. The air around him seemed to grow still and quiet as he turned to Singing Rock with that same devoid expression on his face. *"Let us begin,"* he told his partner in a flat, emotionless voice.

Singing Rock slowly walked towards the house. Roland watched them leave with wild eyes and an anxious grin, but the Ghost Hunters paid him no mind as they focused on the task at hand. They stepped across the dry grass, crunching the brittle stalks underneath them, staring only at the house. Singing Rock moved in front and kept his hands at his sides by his pouches. He dipped into one of them and raised a balled fist as fine yellow powder slowly seeped from his tight grip. Henry followed directly behind him, running his eyes over the windows, looking for some sign of danger.

"Mine!" A loud, raspy voice called out when they were about a hundred feet away. A brief gust of wind rustled through the grass, kicking up dead leaves and a scattering of dirt. *"Mine!"* The voice repeated.

"Be gone!" Singing Rock shouted in his native tongue and cast the fistful of yellow powder into the air. The wind swirled one more time, causing the powder to fall to the ground in a tight spiral, then died down.

The pair continued to approach the house, but after that one incident, they had no more trouble. Everything seemed to grow even more quiet as they stepped onto the porch. Even the crickets ceased their chirping as Singing Rock extended an open hand, palm first, towards the door. He didn't touch the knob but held his hand nearly a foot away and closed his eyes, concentrating intensely. Singing Rock sniffed the air in front of him, then suddenly his eyes shot open. *"Back away,"* he barked at the door and reached into one of his pouches and pulled out a pinch of blue powder. Singing Rock flicked the pale blue powder at the doorknob and stepped back. When the powder hit the door,

267

sparks of electricity shot into the air and danced about the surface of the doorknob.

Singing Rock watched the door with his stoic face until the last few sparks crackled one final time and faded away. Then reaching out his hand confidently, the Navajo twisted the doorknob and swung the door inward. He dipped into his pouches again, and armed with one of his powders, Singing Rock entered the dark house.

Henry followed right behind him, making sure to stay close to his partner. He knew how to enter the Land of Shadows, but he couldn't fend off the attacks that the spirit was sure to throw at them. At first Henry couldn't make anything out in the dark interior, and he nearly bumped into Singing Rock when the Navajo abruptly stopped in front of him. Suddenly a faintly glowing cloud of dust appeared in front of them, and Henry knew that the Navajo had just thrown some of his glowing powder to help them see better.

"Mine!" The voice called again, and this time it sounded truly angry. A dark form shot into the air and twisted there for a moment. Then, without any warning, it shot straight towards them. Singing Rock, however, held out an open hand with his palm facing outwards, and the object halted immediately with a loud wooden thud. Henry didn't even break a sweat in his calm state. He and Singing Rock had been attacked in the same fashion more times than he could remember. In the faint glow, he could see the object was a wooden chair that was now broken from its violent repulsion by the Navajo.

"Are you ready?" Singing Rock asked Henry, not even turning to look at him as he continued to cast a wary glance over the rest of the house. The Navajo withdrew a handful of powder and cast it into the air, leaving another cloud of faint light to replace the other that was beginning to settle on the floor.

"I am."

"Then go quickly. Dawn will come soon. There is no time to waste," Singing Rock told him. He continued his vigilant stare around the house, waiting for the spirit to throw something else at him and Henry.

Henry didn't bother responding but instead looked at the floor. There were tiny pieces of glass littering it so he cleared a space with his foot. Once he had a clear place to sit, the Ghost Hunter took a seat and crossed his legs. He felt his heartbeat lessen its pace, and a peaceful lethargy stole over him. It almost felt like he was falling asleep.

For nearly five years Henry had been entering the Land of Shadows. At first he had slaved at the effort, but eventually it became easier until it was almost second nature. To enter the Land of Shadows, the Ghost Hunter imagined a gate into the desolate place. Singing Rock had suggested a cave, but Henry had chosen a different symbol. Carefully he fashioned an image of a dark lake in his mind. It was nothing more than a gate, and the Land of Shadows awaited on the other side. A large thud echoed around him, but Henry knew it was only Singing Rock fending off another attack. Ignoring the occasional bursts of noise, Henry constructed the image again, building it piece by piece. First he envisioned the water, then he removed the gentle ripples so the surface was perfectly even.

"Mine!" The voice called again, but Henry paid it no mind as he poured all of his thoughts into creating the picture of a lake in his mind. When he was satisfied that it looked perfectly real, Henry imagined floating towards the water. Slowly it drew closer and closer, until he could reach out and touch its cold surface. Clenching his muscles and bracing himself for impact, Henry launched himself mentally at the water. A biting cold hit him when his hands penetrated its icy surface, and he got one last look at the water before his head entered.

Suddenly the house faded away completely, and Henry was falling. He was no longer in water but was instead falling through air. Bracing himself, Henry was ready when he hit the hard ground a few seconds later. He had done this many times and knew what to expect when passing through the gate to the Land of Shadows. The ground beneath him was littered with a light covering of loose dirt that kicked up into a faint cloud when he struck. He stood and absentmindedly brushed off his clothes. Then Henry looked around and tried to see where exactly he was in the Land of Shadows.

He stood in the midst of a bleak landscape, although Henry nearly always found himself in a similar terrain when he traveled to the Land of Shadows. There was scant lighting, leaving the barren world devoid of color. No sun shone in the sky, nor was there a moon to light the way. Instead a pale glow illuminated just enough of the desolate place for him to see. The ground on which he stood was ashen grey, and no matter where he looked, Henry had never seen a sign of anything living. Not a single bush, tree, or animal existed as far as he knew, but Henry expected that of a place that housed the spirits of the dead.

The flat terrain seemed to stretch eternally in every direction without any hills, valleys, or mountains. Just as he had expected, the only thing visible to him was the house that he had just departed. It stood nearly a hundred yards from where he was. Every time Henry journeyed to the Land of Shadows, he found himself a short distance from the place from where he had just left in the world of the living. Squaring his shoulders, Henry marched resolutely towards the house. There was no sense dawdling in the Land of Shadows. He had journeyed here for a reason, and he intended to finish his mission as soon as possible.

His footsteps made an eerie crunching sound that echoed faintly as they thudded on the hard, ashen ground. Other than that, the barren land was devoid of all sound, amplifying the noise of his strides. Henry shrugged it aside. The absolute quiet had disturbed him the first time he visited the Land of Shadows, but he had learned over the years that it was the loud things that were to be feared.

As he approached the house, Henry studied it carefully. Sometimes the Land of Shadows tried to trick him, but he found if he paid close attention, he could usually outwit the spirits that lived there. The house looked very similar to the one he had entered a short time ago in the world of the living, but its walls had been leeched of color, leaving them the same ashen hue as the hard ground. The space behind the windows was completely dark, not giving him the slightest hint as to what lay behind them. It was pretty much what Henry expected. Most houses looked the same in the Land of Shadows, barren, secretive, and ominous. He slowly walked up the steps to the door, trying to soften his footsteps. If all was going well, the spirit was still busy trying to fight Singing Rock and hadn't even noticed that Henry had entered the Land of Shadows. Confronting a spirit was always easier when he had the element of surprise on his side. Henry didn't have any intention of fighting the spirit, but he might not be left with a choice. Putting his ear up to the door, he strained to hear anything inside, but there was nothing except the soft rush of his own breathing. Henry grabbed the doorknob, twisted it firmly, and kicked the door open.

The moment his foot struck the door, the air turned cold, and Henry felt his body lurch forward, causing his stomach to knot up in nausea. Walls sprung up all around him, and when Henry looked around he was definitely inside the house. A much bigger house. He stood in the center of a humongous room that he recognized as the front room of Rebecca's house. Like the outside, the interior of the house was cloaked with a faint illumination that barely allowed him to make out the colorless features. Despite the fact that he was inside, the ground was still hard ashen dirt instead of wooden floors. The open doorway was a good fifty yards away, and he guessed that the walls were a good two hundred yards apart. There was a pyramid of furniture stacked not too far away, but that wasn't what caught his attention.

A dark figure hunched in one of the corners, and when Henry looked at it, he felt a coldness seep into his bones. It was nondescript, just a blob of darkness that barely stood apart from the dark grey walls. *Got you,* Henry thought to himself. He had seen enough spirits in the Land of Shadows to recognize one. They might try to hide, but when he saw the lurking dark shapes and felt that bone-chilling coldness, he knew what he was looking at.

He walked towards it slowly, not hurrying or showing any signs of fear. *Never show a spirit fear,* Singing Rock had told him a long time ago. *They can sense it and will attack you. All spirits fear that which is stronger, and if you show no fear, they will back down from you.* It hadn't always worked, Henry thought grimly, but more times than not, spirits had acquiesced to his demands or simply fled if he approached them boldly. He tried not to be arrogant in his demeanor, but rather tried to assume that stoic, indifferent-to-fear expression that Singing Rock wore so often.

His footsteps continued to echo softly as he approached the figure with his face locked into an expressionless mask. He thought he might actually sneak up on the spirit, but he sensed it turning when he was nearly twenty feet away. It was a black shadow, nearly six feet tall and two feet wide, that pulsed and writhed. It vaguely resembled a human, but it was impossible to discern anything about it. A gust of cold air washed over him, and he felt menacing thoughts directed towards him. Instantly Henry knew that he had the spirit's undivided attention. He stopped in his tracks and planted his feet in a wide stance to show that he wasn't afraid and was willing to fight even though he intended it no harm. "Why do you remain here?" Henry called out to the form, his words echoing as if in a cave.

"Mine! Leave! Mine!" The spirit cried out in a deep, raspy growl that reverberated throughout the house. It appeared to hunch up confrontationally, but Henry calmly stood his ground.

"I'm here to help you," Henry told it peacefully, but it erupted in rage again.

A bone-numbing wave of cold swept over him followed by a shrill cry so loud it nearly buckled his knees. *"Go! Leave! I don't need help!"* It shouted at him.

God, why does it have to be another angry spirit? Henry thought to himself as he struggled to keep a straight composure. His body was freezing cold, but he resisted the urge to shiver or rub his limbs in an attempt to warm them. He was determined to maintain a strong show of will in front of the spirit, and it appeared that it had worked to some degree. The spirit had actually spoken a complete sentence instead of those vague one word calls. "Listen, I can help you get revenge on the one who hurt you."

"Must die!" The spirit bellowed, and that time Henry broke down and rocked backwards from the ear-shattering cry of rage. *"Kill him!"*

Henry cupped his hands over his ears and waited for the echoes to die before removing them. His ears rung, and he felt deaf after the latest explosion from the spirit. He staggered back a step, staring at the dark shadow in front of him, half-expecting it to shriek another deafening cry. "I can help make sure he dies—"

"Must die! Kill! Kill!" The spirit cut him off, wailing in fury. Its form seemed to ripple in the air, as if it was caught in a heated frenzy of anger.

A jagged lance of pain formed at the back of Henry's head as the latest round of cries swept over him and echoed throughout the house. He tried to focus his mind and drown out the pain, but no matter how hard he tried, Henry couldn't make himself focus. Pain and the spirit's deafening cries kept

271

smothering any attempt he made to regain control of his composure. Finally he snapped and shouted back at the spirit, "I can kill him, Goddamn it, if you'll tell me who it is!" He was half-tempted to destroy the spirit right there and then, but that wasn't why he had come. It had Rebecca's spirit, and he needed to convince Bryant to release her before he risked attacking the spirit.

It ceased rippling and floated peacefully in the air for a moment as the echoes of Henry's cry echoed against the walls. The Ghost Hunter thought for a second that it might cease its fierce cries, but that notion was shattered when it began to rage once again. *"Kill! Kill him! Must die!"*

Henry fell to his knees with his hands clasped over his ears. Tears leaked from the corners of his eyes as he tightly squeezed them shut to drown out the pain. Most of the time spirits were willing to talk to him, but it was quite obvious that this one had no intention of telling him why it remained in the Land of Shadows. Henry had the splitting headache to prove it.

Sleep beckoned him. Its sweet lure promised an end to the pain in his head and ears, but Henry knew better than to heed its seductive call. *Fall asleep in the Land of Shadows, and you will not return to the world of the living,* Singing Rock had told him numerous times when they had first begun their travels together. Fighting back the pain, he opened his eyes and stared up at the spirit. It had drawn near him, and Henry knew he should back away. Supposedly a spirit's touch was all it took to draw someone into the Land of Shadows. This spirit already had one prisoner, and Henry had no intentions of becoming a second.

He quickly formed a picture of a door in his mind, just as he had earlier pictured a calm lake. *A lake starts, door departs,* Henry repeated the rhyme in his head. Time was becoming critical. The spirit was slowly drawing nearer, and Henry's strength was rapidly dwindling. If he was going to make it out alive, Henry needed to prepare the way to leave immediately. Piece by piece, the Ghost Hunter constructed a gate to leave the Land of Shadows. Only years of previous experience saved Henry as he drew on that wealth of knowledge to weave together a realistic door in his mind, seemingly hovering only inches from his grasp.

The spirit was a mere two yards from him when he finished the image in his mind. Sure that he had a way out of the Land of Shadows, Henry returned to the reason that he had come there in the first place. He hadn't rescued Rebecca, he hadn't confirmed that the spirit was Bryant, and he hadn't even begun to determine why the spirit was in the Land of Shadows. But he still had one last chance to try and accomplish something.

"Halt!" He yelled in the most authoritative tone he could muster. It was hampered somewhat by a splitting headache, but it seemed to do the trick as the dark shadowy figure abruptly stopped. The spirit continued to float at close proximity, but at least it came no closer.

Henry paused before his next act. Singing Rock had told him long ago that spirits react strongly to the name that they were given in the world of the living. They hated to be called by that name as it reminded them of the times when they still wore flesh and could partake of earthly pleasures. Henry didn't want to risk angering the spirit, but he had to know who the spirit belonged to. So far, he had only been given the name of Rebecca's husband, but Henry wanted to be absolutely sure. Clenching his fists and preparing to flee at the first sign of hostility, Henry tipped back his head and yelled at the top of his lungs. "Bryant White, I bind you!"

He had tried that particular trick before successfully, and he wasn't disappointed with the results. A surprised groan escaped the spirit, and it shrunk back from Henry. Its dark surface seemed to bubble and ripple as it contorted in agony. Pale blue sparks danced about its surface, crackling as they traced the bubbling contours, and a soft groan emanated from the middle of the shadowy form.

Good, Henry thought. *It really is Bryant.* Now that he had confirmed who the spirit was, Henry grimly pushed on. "Bryant White, release Rebecca to the world of the living. She still breathes. Don't condemn her to a life spent in this place," he called out forcefully.

Whatever he had expected didn't happen. The spirit seemed to flinch back in pain when its name was called out, but the mention of Rebecca's name spurned a tremendous anger in it. Henry's hair was blown backwards by a surging burst of cold air, and the spirit swelled up to nearly twice its size. *"Mine! Mine!"* It shouted and stretched out a thick arm of darkness. Gripped with black tendrils, it held aloft a shining ball of white light which erased many of the shadows in the dimly lit room. *"Mine!"* The voice shrieked deafeningly and floated towards Henry again.

The glowing sphere caught Henry's attention immediately, and it was a bittersweet discovery. On one hand, he was glad to confirm that Bryant actually held Rebecca's spirit, but he still couldn't bring his full powers to bear for fear of upsetting the spirit. It would take only one squeeze by those dark tendrils, and Rebecca would be dead. Already Henry had stayed too long. Reasoning wasn't going to work with Bryant, and the spirit wasn't giving him any more time as it floated ever closer to him. Closing his eyes, Henry poured all of his energy into the door he had constructed in his mind. It quickly grew larger and larger until it stood directly in front of him. Henry reached out and turned the knob.

His breath was knocked out of him as he felt his body lurch forward once again. Bright streaks of light flew by him, and the air dipped to freezing temperatures. It lasted only a second, and before he could shiver from the biting cold, Henry abruptly came to a stop. His stomach turned over and over, and his body felt bruised and battered. Even though he knew what to expect upon exiting the Land of Shadows, Henry never emerged completely unscathed.

He rested on his hands and knees with his eyes shut as he waited for his convulsing stomach to come to rest. When at last it had settled enough, Henry opened his eyes. Faint sunlight crept in through the windows as he looked around. The house lay in shambles. Broken glass and splinters of wood littered the floor, and nearly every piece of furniture had been shattered to pieces.

Standing in the midst of the rubble was Singing Rock. He still wore his customary stoic face, but at least Henry's partner showed occasional emotion. When the Navajo went into one of his trances, nothing fazed him. Singing Rock looked at Henry with an arched eyebrow. *"Were you successful?"*

Henry rubbed his eyes and breathed slowly. His head was killing him. Bryant's spirit had nearly deafened him with his loud cries, and even after escaping from the Land of Shadows Henry still felt the effects of it. *"No,"* he answered in a disappointed tone. The Ghost Hunter had hoped to rescue Rebecca that morning, but there had been nothing more he could do. Captive spirits were the most difficult situations that he and Singing Rock had to deal with. It looked as if they had a lot more work to do than Henry wanted.

Singing Rock blew air threw his nose, his nostrils flaring wide. *"Were you able to find out who this spirit belongs to?"*

"Yes, but I do not know why he stays in the Land of Shadows. He refused to speak with me and tried to attack me."

"Hmm," Singing Rock muttered and stroked his chin. *"We must find another way then. You must talk to the Sheriff and see if he can catch the man who killed this spirit."*

The Ghost Hunter felt his heart skip a beat. *"Are you joking, Singing Rock? That man knows me. If he recognizes me, I will no longer be able to help you."*

The Navajo nodded solemnly. *"I know this, but we will stay until he does recognize you. As you said before, everyone believes you are dead."*

"Damn," Henry swore as he rose to his feet. He brushed debris off his trousers and looked at Singing Rock with disgust. "I hope you realize what you're doing," he muttered then turned to look out the window. Even though they had stopped their horses a good distance from the house, he could still see Roland. Shaking his head, Henry walked towards the door and thought about how he was going to continue to dodge the man. More importantly, he wondered how he was going to tell Roland that he had failed to rescue the woman he loved.

Chapter Fourteen

"Roland, wake up!" A voice called from the hallway, followed by a furious pounding on his door.

The Sheriff turned over groggily and stared at the door through bleary eyes. He had no idea how long he had slept since he and the Ghost Hunters had returned from Rebecca's house, but it wasn't long enough. Even though sunlight streamed through the curtains, Roland wanted nothing more than to curl back up under the sheets and sleep for the remainder of the day. His body cried out for more rest, and more importantly he had lost the desire to get up and face anyone. Roland had counted on Rebecca waking that day, but once again his hopes had been crushed. He closed his eyes, determined to grab a few more hours of sleep to replenish his strength and escape the pain of another failure on Rebecca's behalf, but the person at the door was persistent.

"Damn it, Roland. Get up!" Roland recognized Jack's impatient voice on the other side of the door.

Roland sighed. *Damn it, Jack. Leave me alone.* But when Jack used that impatient tone of voice, there was no choice but to listen to him. "I'm coming. Hold on," Roland mumbled onerously. He rubbed at his eyes and rose unsteadily to a sitting position, ignoring his body's pleas for more sleep. Roland wore only his smallclothes, but he didn't bother putting anything else on as he stumbled to the door. He turned the knob and opened it to find Jack with his fist poised to knock yet again. "What's the fuss about, Jack?" Roland asked in irritation.

Jack's face twisted into a scowl. "You look like hell. What happened to you?"

The Sheriff waved a hand in dismissal. He knew that he didn't look good. He felt even worse, but he was in no mood to talk about it with Jack. Roland had counted on having Rebecca awake and telling Jack the whole story that afternoon, but this morning's events had shattered those plans. He didn't really even care about why Jack was so upset. All he cared about was more rest. "I don't want to talk about it. What the hell's so damn urgent you have to wake me up?"

The deputy stared at Roland speculatively for a moment longer before bringing his attention back to the matter at hand. There would be time later to ask Roland about his appearance, but there were more pressing subjects to deal with first. "That magician of Alvin's just showed up, and half the town is already starting to celebrate. I thought you should come down to make sure things don't get out of hand."

"What?" Roland's face curled up in confusion. "The illusionist? Already? What time is it?"

"It's three o'clock."

Roland's put a hand to his eyes and shook his head. "Goddamn it," he uttered. It appeared sleep wasn't an option.

"Are you okay, Roland?" Jack in a concerned voice.

"I'm fine, Jack. Just give me a few minutes to get dressed, and I'll meet you downstairs," Roland answered in disgust and closed the door before Jack could say anything else. He was not in the mood to play Sheriff that afternoon, and he was even less keen on having Jack pester him with questions. Roland was in a foul mood over the most recent failure to awaken Rebecca and just wanted to stay in his room to avoid everyone.

He quickly donned his trousers, coat, and hat. Roland rubbed a hand over his newly grown beard and considered shaving before dismissing the idea. Rebecca still slept, and there wasn't anybody else worth impressing. He pinned his badge of office to his coat then picked up his gun belt. The guns felt comforting as he held them in his hands. He almost hoped that somebody would force him to use one of them. *Especially you, Curly.* After fastening the belt around his waist, Roland stalked into the hallway, locking his door behind him.

The Sheriff marched past Rebecca's room. He slowed for a moment, tempted to sit with her again, but his mood was far too dark that morning. Roland had sat at her side when he returned from the house shortly after dawn and assured her that all would be well, even though pessimism weighted his spirits. The Ghost Hunters seemed to think that she would soon break free of the constraints which bound her in slumber, although Roland was beginning to doubt their word as well. Henry had already failed once. Then there was the fact that the Ghost Hunter tantalizingly reminded him of somebody he had once met. All in all, it made him not want to trust either one of them. The death of Curly kept becoming a more promising solution to the whole ordeal. Until the Dark Rider returned to town or the location of the outlaws' hideout became known, Roland wasn't in the mood to sit with Rebecca. He would just be uttering false words of hope.

He paused outside Henry's door and raised his fist. The Ghost Hunter had promised to talk more that day. After he and Singing Rock had emerged from Rebecca's house, Henry had tried his best to convince Roland that Rebecca would be rescued. It would just take more than the one attempt. He hadn't looked good when he climbed off the porch to meet Roland. His clothes were covered with dust, and his skin appeared even paler than it had been the night before. Once again, Roland had been struck by an uncanny resemblance to someone he had met in his past. He just couldn't remember who. The answer hung just on the outskirts of his memory, teasing him with how close he was. He was positive that sooner or later it would come to him.

The image of Henry stepping out of the house still remained with him. The Ghost Hunter's face had been drained completely of blood, and the man barely looked alive. After answering a few of Roland's questions, Henry had asked to return to town. The entire ride back, the Ghost Hunter kept closing his eyes and putting his hand to his forehead. He said that he was suffering from a headache and wanted to sleep as soon as they returned to The Last Frontier. Henry claimed he would explain everything later but needed to rest after his journey into the Land of Shadows. Roland didn't know whether to believe him or not. The Sheriff half-thought it was another ruse designed to limit the amount of time he had to observe the Ghost Hunter's face.

After contemplating the issue for a moment, Roland let his fist fall by his side. There was business to attend to first. He would give the Ghost Hunter time to awaken, but if Henry hadn't risen by nightfall, Roland intended to rouse the man himself.

The crowd in The Frontier was quite a bit larger than it would have been on any other day. Already there were several tables of card games going on. Two of George's faro dealers were in action, and Roland saw that Jimmy had jumped into one of the poker games. Some of Sherry's girls had come to The Frontier in hopes of landing a customer. From what Roland could see, quite a bit of alcohol had already been consumed. *Goddamn Fourth of July.* The year before, people had been drunk the day before and a good two days after the festivities, and this year promised to be an even grander celebration. Pulling up a chair, Roland joined Jack at his table. "Jack," Roland nodded.

"Roland," Jack answered. "I talked to George, and Alvin's still bringing the magician here to stay. I thought we'd just wait here for him."

"Sounds good," the Sheriff replied curtly. "Is Alvin bringing him straight here?"

"I don't know." Jack shrugged his shoulders. "I just know that the afternoon train should be arriving any minute now. I imagine Alvin will bring him here. What else would he do with him?"

"Who knows with that son of a bitch," Roland muttered. "Fine, we wait here." The Sheriff looked around the saloon, his eyes lighting up when they caught sight of William. The rakish deputy was talking to one of Sherry's girls at the bar. "Send William out there. If Alvin tries to pull something with the illusionist, I want to know."

"You've got it, Roland," Jack answered and rose to his feet. He straightened his jacket then approached William.

Roland watched his deputy like a hawk as he brooded in his chair. *Of all the Goddamn times for the Fourth to fall,* Roland thought bitterly. There was going to be a great deal of work to deal with the revelry that was sure to take place over the next few days. Roland wanted nothing more than to concentrate solely on helping Rebecca, but that seemed impossible. The Sheriff was beginning to think that there was a conspiracy against him. *Hopefully you'll come back, you son of a bitch,* Roland grimly thought of Curly. The safety of New Haven floated somewhere in the back of his head, but Rebecca was foremost in his thoughts. As long as it didn't inconvenience his endeavors for Rebecca too much, Sheriff Black intended to do his job, but if the two came into conflict, Roland knew where his heart lay.

Jack tapped William on the shoulder, and the rakish deputy looked upset for being interrupted during his flirtations. The annoyed expression quickly disappeared after Jack gave him his instructions. William looked at Roland once, saw his thunderous expression, and walked briskly towards the saloon's exit as Jack returned to Roland's table. "William's going to wait for the afternoon train."

"Good," Roland replied gruffly. "Okay, now that that's settled, how do you want to handle the Fourth?" He could come up with a plan on his own, but exhaustion slowed his thoughts. Jack planning the details sounded like a much better idea.

Roland's deputy blinked in surprise. Jack was used to Roland dictating how things would be done. Occasionally the Sheriff asked for suggestions or comments on his decisions, but Jack couldn't remember Roland ever asking for such direct help before. "Don't you have anything in mind, Roland?" He asked in disbelief.

The Sheriff waved a hand in annoyance. *Damn it, do I have to do everything myself?* Roland thought bitterly. He struggled to curb his temper before it could erupt to the surface. There was no sense in blowing up at Jack. The deputy hadn't done anything to inspire Roland's wrath. "I haven't really had much of a chance to think about it with Rebecca so sick," Roland explained in a soft, taut voice.

The deputy nodded and wisely kept quiet. He smoothed down the tips of his mustache as he thought about the problem. "The fireworks are at eight tomorrow. The magician's at nine. Right?" He looked up at Roland.

Roland nodded without saying a word and waved a hand flippantly, indicating for Jack to proceed.

Jack took Roland's apathetic interest in stride. He knew that if Dotty were sick like Rebecca, he too would have been in a foul mood. "The way I see it, we need a full staff on hand about that time. We probably won't need anyone in the saloons. Everyone's going to be out watching the show." He paused and squinted as he thought carefully. "I say you, Morgan, Wade, and I can be up here early. The rest can show up at four or so. We can all stay on 'til at least one or two. Everyone should be home by that point. If they're going to cause trouble, they'll have done it long before midnight. Sound good to you?"

"Yeah, Jack, it does. Thanks," Roland answered his old friend in an uninterested voice. He knew that protecting the people of New Haven was important, but no matter how hard he tried, Roland simply couldn't make himself interested.

278

"Damn it, Roland!" Jack exclaimed and slammed his fist down on the table.

Everyone in the saloon, including Roland, looked at the deputy in surprise. The customers quickly returned to their own business, but the Sheriff looked at Jack like he was crazy. "What the hell's gotten into you?"

"No, Roland. What the hell's gotten into you? You're the Goddamn Sheriff of this town, and you're acting like you don't care if all hell breaks loose. I understand about Rebecca, but blazes, Roland, you've been acting like this for a few weeks. What happens if there's trouble tomorrow? Will you be able to help out?" Jack tore into Roland, unafraid of the Sheriff's response. His shoulders had straightened, and his chest puffed out pugnaciously as if daring Roland to challenge any of the words he had just spoken.

Anger flared through Roland's veins before Jack had even finished speaking, and he leaned forward furiously. His bottom lip curled down in a fierce snarl, and Jack's eyes widened momentarily. Roughly, Roland reached out and grabbed Jack's coat in a tight-knuckled grip. "It's my job, Jack. Don't tell me how to do it, Goddamn it," Roland uttered through clenched teeth.

Jack's heart skipped a beat when the enraged Sheriff leaned across the table, but he held his ground. He slapped Roland's hand away and casually leaned back in his chair as if Roland's actions hadn't bothered him in the slightest. "I'm going to pretend you didn't do that, Roland," he said simply and folded his arms across his chest, calmly watching to see what the Sheriff would do next.

Roland glared at Jack for a moment longer before the deputy's words hit him, and he looked down at his hands in disgust. He leaned back in his chair and closed his eyes in resignation. Taking a few deep breaths, Roland tried to cool his temper down. He couldn't believe that he had just snapped at one of his oldest friends. When he opened his eyes, Jack still sat with that smugly calm expression and his arms folded casually. His pride hated him for it, but Roland cleared his throat and apologized. "I'm sorry, Jack. I've been a bit on edge lately."

"Don't worry about it," Jack replied and waved a hand in dismissal. "I understand things have been rough with Rebecca sick, but we need you Roland. Morgan and I can't handle this town by ourselves. What if the Dark Riders come back? I'm surprised they haven't with the way you've been acting. You and I both know tomorrow is going to be a long day, and it would be nice if you'd help out instead of brooding in here." Jack stopped and put up both hands defensively. "I'm not trying to preach. I'm just trying to get you to do your job."

Guilt quickly took the place of anger as Roland realized how much he had shirked his job over the past few weeks. He had performed adequately, but his heart hadn't been in the effort. Even more so, Roland felt ashamed of the way he had blown up at Jack. His old friend had stood by his side far too many times for him to be treated so rudely. Rebecca's safety was foremost on his mind, but Roland finally admitted to himself that there was nothing more he could do about it by sulking in The Last Frontier. "I know," he responded quietly. "I know. It's been hard with Rebecca being so sick, but I swear I'll be there tomorrow." Roland tried to smile, but he simply couldn't force the muscles of his face. He felt tired more than anything else. For the first time in his life, Roland felt like an old man.

The deputy's face creased back into one of his wide, toothy grins. "That's good to hear. You've been scaring the hell out of me. Don't worry about Rebecca. She'll do fine. Sullivan's one helluva doctor," Jack attempted to cheer up Roland without much luck.

Roland nodded, but a smile failed to grace his lips. He knew that there was nothing more that could be done to help Rebecca. Henry had promised more answers when he awakened, but that was probably still a few hours away. There was nothing else but his job. He just hoped it would help take his mind off worrying. Roland hated to feel so helpless. Not since his family had been slaughtered had Roland felt so little control over his destiny and those of the people he loved. He would just have to place Rebecca's safety in the hands of the Ghost Hunters and hope that they could help her. There was nothing more that he could do. He forced the corners of his mouth into a tiny smile, but no happiness twinkled in his eyes. "We'll see. Why don't you stay here and wait for Alvin to show up with the magician," Roland suggested more to avoid being left alone than out of any necessity.

"Sure," Jack replied and rubbed his hands together mischievously. "I just want to see that son of a bitch upstaged for once. Everyone should be looking at this magician and not Alvin. You know how much he loves to be the center of attention," the deputy remarked dryly.

Despite his dismal mood, Roland couldn't help chuckling. He had never felt so grateful to have Jack as a friend than at that moment. The deputy knew how to drag answers out of Roland, refused to back down, and most importantly had been able to read Roland well enough to realize that the Sheriff needed a good laugh. "I hope it pisses off that Goddamn bastard something fierce," Roland remarked and suddenly felt in a better mood. Nothing would make him truly happy until Rebecca was awake and at his side, but ridiculing Alvin always brightened his day.

They sat there mocking the mayor for another fifteen minutes or so, and Roland was glad that his old friend had helped lift his dark mood. Sheriff Black knew that he wasn't a pleasant person to be around when he was in a bad mood, but he had found it awfully difficult to find a reason to smile lately. He was just about to ask what was taking Alvin so long when he looked out the window and saw a sizable crowd approaching The Frontier. "It looks like we've got company," Roland noted then whistled in amazement.

Roland had expected a crowd on the Fourth of July, not the day before, but almost one hundred people filled the streets, making their way towards The Last Frontier. At the front of the crowd Roland saw Alvin. The mayor was dressed impeccably in a dark grey suit, and a public smile lit up his face as he led the throng towards the saloon. At his side walked an older man with a long white beard, and Roland guessed he was the illusionist. The main thing, though, that caught his eye was the size of the crowd. If they got out of hand, he and Jack would not be enough to quell them. All of his deputies wouldn't be enough.

"Holy Mary, mother of God. Look at them," Jack commented in a stunned voice. He too had been prepared to face large crowds on the Fourth of July, not the day before.

"No time for that," Roland ordered crisply. Something about seeing Alvin with that infuriatingly smug look on his face made Roland push Rebecca behind him as thoughts of ruining the mayor's sunny disposition took control. The thought of Alvin at the head of one hundred people scared him enough to become very interested in the situation at hand. "Go get Morgan, Wade, and Ben. I want as many guns as I can get in here," he told Jack decisively. *Won't do much good, but it can't hurt.* Any problems in The Last Frontier would be over before Jack could return with anyone.

"Got it," Jack replied and was on his feet instantly, running towards the front door. The other deputies were out patrolling the streets and should have noticed the crowd. Hopefully they had followed as well. Simon was home with his wife, but Roland wished the deputy had left her alone that afternoon. He wanted all the help he could get his hands on.

The customers inside The Last Frontier noticed Jack leaving the saloon and saw the crowd moving towards the tavern. Everyone in town knew about the illusionist Alvin had hired, and immediately they were all on their feet, anxiously awaiting his arrival. George's face grew joyous as he watched the large crowd, obviously thrilled at the large number of customers about to enter his tavern. Jimmy also observed the proceedings with a cocky grin and wild excitement in his eyes. Roland barely noticed the customers in the saloon, although Jimmy caught his attention momentarily. He hoped the young man wouldn't do anything stupid, but he didn't have time to think about Jimmy. He focused on the large crowd of people rapidly marching towards the saloon.

Once again he concentrated on the man walking next to Alvin. He was an old man with a white curly beard that reached halfway down his chest. A pair of gold-wired eyeglasses sat atop his nose, and he wore a black tophat that rose a good six inches above his head. He didn't wear a coat but had a red cape draped around his shoulders. His shirt was white with frilly laces along the sleeves, and he wore a pair of black gloves. Roland had never seen clothing like it. *They must dress like that in France,* Roland thought, but he had no more time to ponder the matter as Alvin and his guest walked through the front door. Sheriff Black dropped his right hand to his side, placing it comfortably atop his pistol in case trouble broke out. He didn't trust Alvin any further than he could throw him.

The mayor wore his polished smile as he walked into the saloon. He waved his arm grandiosely before him as if he owned the entire place and looked around the room. His smile became mocking as his eyes passed over Roland, but other than that, the mayor didn't acknowledge Roland's presence. The illusionist appeared even more thrilled with the crowd than Alvin. He puffed up with a haughty expression as he moved towards the bar. The crowd behind them began to pour into the saloon as well, and in a matter of moments the tavern was fuller than Roland had ever seen it. People swelled towards his table as open spaces disappeared.

Roland lost sight of Alvin and the illusionist and rose to his feet to gain a better vantage point. He kept his right hand on the butt of his pistol as he used his height to look over the crowd. The Sheriff didn't like the smirk that Alvin kept flashing. *The son of a bitch is up to something,* Roland thought, but he had no idea what it was.

Alvin stood at the bar and turned to face the people who had packed themselves into the bar. The mayor suddenly held up his hands, and silence instantly spread over the saloon. Everyone from the gamblers to the patrons to the people who had just walked in off the streets grew silent and waited to hear what Alvin had to say. Roland had to bite his lip to keep quiet. It was obvious from the self-congratulatory expression on his face that Alvin intended to milk the popularity of the illusionist for all he could. Roland would have loved to ruin it for the mayor, but even Roland found himself waiting impatiently to hear what Alvin would say next. The silence seemed to last an eternity until Alvin broke it. "Ladies and gentlemen," he announced in his well-polished voice. "I am pleased to introduce from Paris, France, Zoltan the Master Illusionist."

Thunderous applause erupted in The Last Frontier as people clapped, whistled, and shouted their appreciation for the man Alvin had brought to New Haven. Zoltan looked enormously pleased with the pandemonium. He raised his arms to shoulder level, dragging the corners of his cape in each hand. The illusionist kept his back arched stiffly momentarily then made a sweeping bow to the crowd assembled before him. His bow only caused the applause to grow louder, and Roland suddenly found himself unable to hear anything else as the noise grew deafening. As pleased as Zoltan appeared, Alvin seemed even happier. His smile deepened as he watched the crowd with a calculated eye. Roland doubted anyone else saw how the mayor was gauging their emotions, but he knew exactly how Alvin's mind worked.

Zoltan straightened his back after his bow and stood before the people in The Last Frontier with his arms still raised and holding the corners of his cape. His eyes sparkled merrily behind his glasses, and he smiled confidently. He waited for the noise to die down then dropped his arms, making his cape billow out behind him then settle gracefully upon his back. "Thank you very much. I hope I can live up to your expectations," he called out in a thick, French accent.

Whistles and clapping broke out once again in response, and the illusionist puffed up a little more arrogantly every second it went on. *God, he has a bigger head on his shoulders than Alvin,* Roland thought. "Let's see some magic now!" A loud voice called out, and Zoltan blinked a few times and rubbed his chin thoughtfully.

Alvin stepped forward and raised one of his arms. "He would love to perform for you, but the show is set for tomorrow night. Just remember to be in front of the train station by eight o'clock for the fireworks. He'll perform at nine," he told the crowd then smiled his well-practiced smirk.

A sigh of disappointment stole over the crowd, and even Roland had to admit that he had looked forward to seeing a bit of magic. Roland could have used some cheering up, and the illusionist's magic would have been entertaining. Zoltan watched as Alvin spoke to the crowd and noticed how they reacted to his announcement. He tapped the mayor on the shoulder, and Alvin turned towards him. "Actually, I will perform a trick for them right now. It will —how do you say?— whet their appetite for tomorrow's performance." Zoltan turned back to the crowd as thunderous applause showered him again. He smiled and spread his arms wide, basking in the adulation. "Thank you, thank you. Now if you will all back up a few steps to give me room," he requested once the noise had died down.

Roland bumped against the wall as everyone moved backwards to clear more space for the illusionist. Roland looked around the room quickly, but he still didn't see Jack or any of the others. He didn't think it would make much of a difference anyway. If the crowd in The Last Frontier grew rowdy, it would take more than six men to stop them. The crowd grew silent, and Roland returned his focus to the illusionist.

Zoltan waited for a few moments in the silence, letting the anticipation of his show build. "Ladies and gentlemen," he boomed in his thick accent. His voice penetrated every corner of the saloon, and nobody had to strain their ears to hear him. "Let me tell you a story. It is a simple story, but it is one I think you will enjoy. It begins slowly, but it ends with a bang," he started and shot his arms forward suddenly. A loud boom exploded, and a brief flash shot forth from his hands. A cloud of smoke wafted from them as everyone clapped their approval.

"Once upon a time, there was a young man named Pierre. One day he was walking through his village when he saw a beautiful young woman named Marie. He fell in love with her instantly and rushed to her. 'Here, my lady, take these flowers as a symbol of my love,' Pierre told her," Zoltan continued and snapped his fingers. A bouquet of flowers suddenly appeared in his hand.

"'Thank you, you are too kind,' Marie told Pierre and blushed bright red. She found Pierre handsome and also fell in love instantly. 'I will treasure them always.'

"'No, my lady, these flowers will wilt tomorrow.'" Zoltan shook his hand, and suddenly the flowers disappeared. He held his palm open for a few moments to make sure the crowd saw they had vanished. "'But your beauty will remain. You are kind to let your beautiful words fall upon a man such as me.'

"'Speak not that way. You are a handsome man, and words come freely as leaves upon trees.'" Zoltan raised his hand and rubbed his fingers together. Dozens of green leaves fell from his hand and fell to the floor.

The crowd clapped after each of the illusionist's three tricks, and even Roland had to admit that he was impressed. He had seen magicians before, but the way Zoltan blended his story and magic captivated the entire crowd.

"Pierre was even more smitten by her and grabbed her hand, placing a kiss upon it. 'My lady, you are beautiful and fair. My heart is taken with you. Will you marry me?'

"Marie laughed with joy. 'Yes, Pierre, yes, I will marry you.' She looked down the street and saw her father approaching. 'Look, here comes my father. Ask him for permission, and we can be wed tonight.'

"The two ran to Marie's father, and Pierre asked for her hand. 'Sir, I am in love with your daughter, and we wish to marry.'

"Her father was a very wealthy man, and he disapproved of Pierre the moment he saw him." Zoltan removed the tophat from his head and held it right side up. He shook it around then turned it upside down. "'Young man, I will not let you marry my daughter. I am a rich man.'" Zoltan reached into the hat and pulled out several gold coins. "'I have this much gold.'" The illusionist clenched his fist, enveloping the coins and shielding them from the crowd's view. "'You have none.'" Zoltan opened his hand, and the gold coins had disappeared.

"'But, Father, I love this man,' Marie pleaded, but it was to no avail. Her father refused to give his permission. 'If you will not give permission, Father, we will have to run away and be wed.'

"'I will not allow it. You are coming home with me now,' her father told her and tried to grab her arm.

"But Marie was quick and danced back from him. 'Look, Father, over there.' Marie pointed behind her father. He turned around, and the moment he wasn't looking Marie and Pierre ran and hid in a barn nearby." Zoltan put his hat back on and removed his cape from his shoulders. He arched an eyebrow at Alvin and pointed at the mayor's cane. Alvin stared at him for a moment in confusion then handed it over to him. Zoltan wrapped his cape tightly around the cane and held it up for everyone to see.

"They hid in the barn for several hours while Marie's father looked for them. Finally he came to the barn, and he saw two footprints leading into it. He knocked on the barn door and called out. 'Marie, I know you are in there. Come out.'" Zoltan knocked three times on the cane that he had wrapped inside his cape. "But there was no answer, so he kicked in the door.

"When he went inside, they were nowhere to be found. So what happened to Marie and Pierre? How could they escape? All I can tell you is that love finds a way, and the lovebirds lived happily ever after." He grabbed one end of his cape and, with a flick of his wrist, unrolled it. Everyone clapped thunderously as two birds emerged and flew into the air. Zoltan bathed in the applause and took a deep bow.

Roland could scarcely believe his eyes. He had no idea how Zoltan had just performed his magic. The illusionist hadn't even prepared for the performance. Roland expected magic like that to be saved for the following evening. If this was just to whet their appetites, Roland couldn't wait to see what was in store for the Fourth of July celebration. It looked like it was going to be a celebration to remember.

Alvin held up a hand, and the room grew quiet. The mayor had a self-congratulatory look on his face. He knew that everyone had been impressed, and he also knew that he was the one to thank for bringing Zoltan to New Haven. As much as Roland wanted to dislike the illusionist to spite Alvin, he had to give the mayor credit for bringing him in. "Thank you, everyone, for coming over, but there won't be any more shows until tomorrow evening. Our guest has traveled a long way to be here, and he needs to rest up if he wants to perform tomorrow. Don't forget. Fireworks are at eight, and at nine o'clock, Zoltan the Master Illusionist will be performing in front of the train station," the mayor announced, and The Frontier burst into applause once more.

Roland refrained from clapping as he held his hand on his pistol. Everything seemed fine, but that damn smirk on Alvin's face still bothered him. Alvin was up to something, and until the Sheriff found out what it was, he wouldn't let his guard down around the man. A few people cried out for Zoltan to perform more magic, but the illusionist had donned his cape once more and stood talking to Alvin, ignoring the crowd. Eventually people realized that Zoltan wouldn't be performing again that evening. Slowly they trickled out of the saloon, giving Roland more room to stretch. Quite a few people stayed at The Last Frontier to begin celebrating the Fourth of July early. It was still a good nine hours away, but that wasn't about to stop those who were already finished for the day. Once the train was gone, most people had nothing else to do and began their celebration in earnest.

As the crowd cleared, Roland saw Jack, Morgan, Wade, Ben, and William approach his table. Customers in the saloon stared at the five deputies as they walked towards Roland's table. They weren't used to seeing that many deputies together unless there was trouble. "Roland," Jack greeted as he pulled up a chair and took a seat at the table.

Sheriff Black tipped his hat in response then waved a hand at his table. "Have a seat, gentlemen." He looked at them as they took a seat and squinted. "How the hell did you all get here this quickly? The illusionist just walked in a few minutes ago."

"We followed them in, Sheriff. It was kind of hard to miss them walking through the streets," Ben answered.

"So you've been here the whole time?"

"Yeah, we were over by the door. You probably couldn't see us with all the people in here. How do you think he does that stuff? That trick with the birds was incredible."

"You can ask him later, Ben," Roland cut off the deputy. . "I want all of you to know we're on emergency duty from here until tomorrow night. People are already celebrating, and I want to make sure we have enough men to handle any problems. Any questions?"

"You think the Riders are coming into town?" Wade asked coolly, his eyes glowing with excitement.

Even though Wade's hand was beneath the table, Roland could almost picture the deputy reaching for his pistol. He was beginning to wonder who was worse, Jimmy or Wade. Until he actually had a chance to shoot someone, Wade was going to itch to get in a gunfight. "I don't know, Wade. We don't need any trouble with them. If they do come to town, nobody does anything to them. There will be plenty of time to deal with them after the Fourth of July." He hoped that would end any heroic ideas Wade had floating through his head. While Roland wouldn't have minded shooting a few of the outlaws, that type of trouble was the last thing that he needed.

"But what if Curly comes into town?" Wade asked.

Roland's mouth curled into a bitter smile, and he cracked his knuckles. "If that son of a bitch comes to town, he's mine. You get me, and I'll take care of him. Understand?" The Sheriff asked rhetorically in a flat, emotionless voice that brooked no arguments. "Any other questions?"

"Yeah, how are we going to work tonight and tomorrow?" Morgan asked.

Roland rubbed his stubbly chin as he thought about the problem. "We'll keep normal rotations tonight, except I want you, Ben, and Wade working until one. I want everyone here by one tomorrow afternoon. There aren't any trains tomorrow, so people will be getting an early start on the drinking. I don't want to be caught short-handed."

Morgan nodded. "That sounds good, but what about tomorrow night?"

"We'll keep normal rotation again, except I want Jack and Morgan patrolling over by the train station. There'll be some people celebrating over there, and I want somebody to keep an eye on them. At seven, I want everyone except Robert over at the train station. The fireworks start at eight and the illusionist an hour later. Last year, all hell broke out after the fireworks, and I want to make sure it doesn't happen again."

"Sounds good to me," Morgan commented in his gravelly voice.

"Great, anyone else?" Roland waited a few moments, and when nobody answered, he continued speaking. "All right then, everyone get busy. We've got a lot of work over the next two days," Roland dismissed his men.

Each deputy except Jack and William rose from his seat, tipped his hat, and left the saloon. William sauntered over to the bar to resume chatting with the suddenly greater number of female customers. Jack, on the other hand, stayed seated and watched the others leave. Once the last of them had walked out the door and William had struck up a conversation with a woman at the bar, he turned back to Roland. His eyes looked amused, and a slight smile played on his lips.

Roland scowled at his old friend. "What the hell are you smiling at?"

"Nothing. It's just good to see you taking your job seriously, Roland. That's it."

The Sheriff glared at Jack, but try as he might, he couldn't get angry at him. He felt guilty more than anything. He knew that he had ignored his job and hated for Jack to feel he had to remind him. "Trust me, Jack. You don't have to worry about me." He just hoped that he could live up to that promise.

Jack's smile deepened, and he leaned back comfortably in his chair. "I knew I could count on you," he replied sarcastically.

"Son of a bitch," Roland muttered and shook his head ruefully as his mouth curled into a lopsided grin.

"Bastard," Jack quipped back impudently. He looked over at the bar and saw that Zoltan and Alvin were still talking. A few people had joined the mayor and the illusionist, but for the most part everyone was busy minding their own business. The deputy pointed at Zoltan. "So what do you think of the magician?"

"He's an illusionist, Jack, and I think he's pretty damn good. This was performing cold. I imagine he's going to put on a hell of a show tomorrow night when he's ready for it. Could you see him from where you were standing?"

"Yeah, barely. I agree, though. He's incredible. Some of it was common stuff, but that trick with the birds was incredible."

Roland looked over at Zoltan. The illusionist was laughing at something that Alvin had just said. "You've got to give that snake some credit. He's set up a good show this year. Nobody will forget it."

"Probably not. Any idea what he's been up to?"

"No, and it's starting to bother me." Roland stopped and grinned at Jack. "Maybe I should pull a gun on him."

"Please don't do anything stupid this weekend. I don't want any problems with Alvin or the Riders." Jack rolled his eyes. "I swear, one of these days you're going to get you and me both killed with one of those stupid stunts you pull."

"I promise I won't do anything to Alvin. You can relax." Roland stared at the mayor, who continued to chat with Zoltan and a few others with his fake smile. He looked over at Roland, and his eyebrows lowered malevolently. Then he returned to his conversation. The Sheriff hit the table with his fist. His momentary good cheer seemed to have vanished as rage surged through his veins. "What the hell's that man up to?"

"I don't know, Roland. Maybe you should ask him," Jack replied and shook his head in resignation. He had seen the look Alvin shot Roland's way and knew that the Sheriff wouldn't sit by idly.

Roland stayed quiet after Jack spoke and continued to watch Alvin like a hawk. *What the hell are you doing, you son of a bitch?* The mayor suddenly tipped his head back and laughed. Several of the other men he was with also burst into laughter. Roland's hands tightened into fists as he watched the man. *Everyone in this town loves you right now, but they don't know you like I do.* As he stopped laughing, Alvin cast a quick glance towards the Sheriff's table and smirked when he saw that Roland was already looking at him. Then with a withering glance, he turned back to his own conversation again. The Sheriff rose to his feet instantly, one hand clenched tightly in a fist and the other gripping the butt of his pistol.

"What the hell are you doing?" Jack asked in alarm and stood up as well. His face looked worried, and he started to move between Roland and Alvin.

"I'm following your advice. I'll be right back. Hold the table for me," Roland told him in a cold voice and walked towards the bar. His upper lip curled into a sneer, and his eyes narrowed into a slits. People moved out of his way as he moved towards Alvin. Jimmy noticed Roland marching across the saloon and half-rose from his poker table until a murderous glare from Sheriff Black sent him right back into his seat.

Alvin chatted with George Wright, Zoltan, and a few others. They all looked up at the Sheriff as he stalked towards them. George's face became nervous as he saw Roland stomp towards the bar. It was easy to see that the Sheriff wasn't in the best of moods. "What can I do for you, Sheriff?"

288

Roland's face locked into a cocky grin in response. He was furious as hell with Alvin, but he would be damned if he'd let Alvin know it. The mayor looked amused rather than scared of Roland, but that was something that he intended to correct. "Nothing, George. I just came over here to meet our illusionist. Hello, I'm Roland Black, Sheriff of New Haven," he told Zoltan and held out his hand.

The illusionist reached out and shook Roland's hand with a weak grasp. "It is a pleasure to meet you," he replied in his French accent.

From a distance, he had only been able to make out generalities about the illusionist, but now that he was talking to the man, he studied him quickly. Zoltan looked nearly seventy years old. Wrinkles decorated his face, and his hair and lengthy beard were solid white. His clothes were obviously quite expensive. His cape and shirt appeared to be made of silk, and his glasses even had gold frames. "The pleasure's all mine," Roland told him and smiled widely. George backed up a few steps, but the illusionist didn't seem to think there was anything dangerous in the Sheriff's countenance. *Probably because he doesn't know me.* "That was a pretty good show you put on. I'm looking forward to tomorrow."

Zoltan seemed to swell up as Roland paid him a compliment. His chest thrust outward, and his face turned into a smugly self-confident grin of arrogance. He brushed one set of fingernails across his silk shirt and looked enormously pleased with himself. "Thank you. I'm glad you enjoyed it. I promise my show tomorrow will be even more spectacular."

"That's good to hear. Wouldn't you say, George?" He asked the saloon owner.

George nodded. "Yes, Sheriff. I'm looking forward to it."

Roland's mouth curled into its lopsided grin as he turned to Alvin. "What about you, Alvin? What do you think about Zoltan here?" He asked the question with good-natured enthusiasm, but his eyes burned into the mayor hatefully.

Alvin's smile never slipped, but his eyebrows lowered as he returned the Sheriff's glare. They didn't shine with hatred, but rather with the same smug amusement that had infuriated Roland to no end. "I can't wait for tomorrow night. I'm going to love it." Alvin's voice didn't drip with sarcasm or contempt, but Roland had known the mayor long enough to be certain that he meant something more by those words. The Sheriff continued to stare at Alvin, and the mayor returned his gaze. George and the others at the bar appeared incredibly uncomfortable as the tension between Roland and Alvin grew.

Zoltan finally broke the silence. He had swollen up with arrogance as people had expressed their enthusiasm for the following night's performance, but the illusionist looked confused over the exchange between the two men. "Do not worry, gentlemen. It is only a short time before tomorrow night, and I promise I will show you things you have never dreamed possible," he stated grandiosely.

The illusionist's words interrupted the stare down between Alvin and Roland and broke the mounting tension. The mayor's eyes narrowed contemptuously, and his smile briefly turned mocking. Then he turned back to the illusionist. "Really?" He asked innocently as if nothing had just occurred between himself and Roland.

"That is what I do," Zoltan answered arrogantly. "I make the impossible become possible. You will not believe your eyes tomorrow night."

"Sounds great," Alvin replied enthusiastically. "We're all looking forward to it. Eh, Bill?" The mayor clapped one of the men standing next to him on the back.

Like George and a few others, Bill did not look at ease, and he flinched as Alvin struck him on the back. "Uh, yeah. I certainly am."

The Sheriff watched the exchange between Alvin and Bill with a terse expression on his face. The way the mayor kept acting so smugly confident grated fiercely on Roland's nerves. He had enjoyed the skittish way that Alvin had deferred to him after he had pulled a gun on the mayor. Now Alvin acted as if Roland was powerless to harm him, and Sheriff Black intended to show him the error of his ways. "Alvin, I'd like a word with you," he rasped harshly, glaring at the mayor.

Instead of inspiring terror in Alvin, the mayor turned to him in amusement and grinned at Roland pityingly. "Sure, old boy. Anything I can do to help," Alvin responded condescendingly. He turned back to George, Zoltan, and the others and shrugged his shoulders as if baffled by the Sheriff's behavior. "Excuse me, gentlemen. Zoltan, I'll be right back. I trust these men will keep you company." He returned his focus back to Roland. "Where to, Roland?"

Roland's hand leapt towards his holster automatically, and Alvin probably had no idea how close he came to dying right that moment. The Sheriff, however, reined in his temper. Alvin was clearly trying to goad him and was being quite successful at it. "My table," he stated flatly and stalked across the saloon without bothering to see if Alvin followed.

People moved out of his way when they saw the thunderous look of anger on his face. He crushed each boot down on the wooden floor with tremendous force as if he could grind Alvin underneath. *Damn you, Alvin. I will find out what you're up to, and you will be sorry you crossed my path.*

Jack looked up with a cocked eyebrow and whistled as the two men approached the table. He saw both the furious expression on the Sheriff's face and the smug look of content on Alvin's. The combined pair was not a good sign. Normally he would have trusted Roland to handle Alvin all by himself, but Roland hadn't been himself ever since Rebecca had fallen ill. Jack was frightened that the Sheriff would do something stupid and get them all in a pot

290

of boiling water. "What's going on, Rol—" he managed to ask before Roland cut him off.

"Give us a few minutes alone, Jack. I need to talk with Alvin," Roland cut him off as he took his customary seat and glared at Alvin.

The mayor, meanwhile, calmly pulled up a chair and took a seat at the table. He tipped his hat towards Jack and inclined his head. "Good evening, Jack. How's Dotty?"

"Evening, Alvin. Dotty's fine." The deputy looked at both men one more time. He raised both eyebrows and glanced at Roland. "Everything okay, Roland?"

"Everything's fine, Jack," Roland snapped impatiently. He wanted to question Alvin again and didn't need Jack around to mess things up. The situation might warrant him threatening the mayor, and his old friend surely wouldn't approve of such tactics.

Jack appeared skeptical, but he rose from his seat anyway. "I'll be at the bar. Gentlemen." He tipped his hat then slowly crossed the floor, glancing back occasionally at Roland and Alvin.

"So what's this about, Roland?" Alvin asked when Jack was out of earshot. His eyes widened innocently, but his mouth curled slightly in an amused smirk.

"You know what. What the hell's all that Goddamn smiling about?" The Sheriff scowled, and his hand dropped onto the butt of one of his pistols. Nobody could see his guns under the table as he caressed a handle with his thumb, waiting patiently to see if it was needed.

Alvin slapped a hand over his heart as a facetious, innocent expression stole over his face. "Why, Roland, I don't know what you're talking about," he remarked sarcastically.

Roland growled deep in the back of his throat and roughly jerked the pistol from its holster. He jabbed it into Alvin's stomach and cocked it. The Sheriff grinned victoriously at the mayor, and his eyes narrowed menacingly. "Let's try this one more time, Alvin, and this time I want you to answer. What the hell are you up to?" Roland asked contemptuously.

The mayor looked down into his lap with something close to disinterest and saw the gun pointing at his stomach. Then he looked back up at Roland with a bored expression. Roland couldn't believe his eyes. Alvin didn't even look the slightest bit afraid. "Put the gun up, Roland," Alvin uttered as if the gun threatening him was the last thing on his mind.

"Damn it, I'm the one in charge here," Roland hissed and nearly shot the mayor right then and there. His patience was nearly at an end, and Alvin kept trying to stretch it further. If he didn't get some answers out of the mayor soon, New Haven would be electing a new one.

"Whatever you say," Alvin commented sarcastically and waved a hand in dismissal. "I know you won't shoot me, Roland, and you know it too."

Roland's eyes widened. He was pointing a gun at Alvin, and the mayor wasn't even blinking. *The son of a bitch doesn't think I'll do it*, Roland thought incredulously. *He thinks I'm bluffing. Well, he's gonna find out how serious I am.* "Don't underestimate me, Alvin. It's been a bad week."

"Oh, come on, Roland. Tomorrow's the Fourth of July. You're not going to shoot me. You'd get arrested for murder. Then New Haven wouldn't have a mayor or a sheriff on the busiest day of the year."

"This town would be a hell of a lot better off without you around," Roland replied grimly.

Alvin rolled his eyes mockingly and looked at Roland as if he couldn't believe the way that the Sheriff was acting. "Fine. Put the gun up, and we'll talk." The mayor put his hands on the table in a show of good faith.

Roland stared at Alvin silently in response. *Maybe, he'll tell me something if I holster the gun.* As much as Roland hated to admit it, Alvin was right. Shooting the mayor on the third of July would cripple New Haven's celebration the following day. They would lose the organizer of the whole event and the head peace officer. Most importantly, his ability to help Rebecca would be dashed as well. He still didn't trust Alvin, but reluctantly he slipped the gun into its holster. Roland then put his own hands on the table. "All right, start talking then. What the hell have you been up to?"

"Nothing, Roland. I'm just in a good mood. I've been planning for the Fourth of July a long time, and it's nearly completed," Alvin explained sincerely, but the Sheriff didn't buy a word of it.

"I don't believe you. What's with all those Goddamn smiles? I know you're up to something, and I want to know what," Roland insisted again. His breathing slowed, and his hand drifted down towards his holster again. Alvin kept exhausting all of his patience.

Alvin waved a hand in the air nonchalantly. "Oh, that." He wagged a finger at Roland reprovingly, and his smile deepened. His eyes shone with a mocking glint that infuriated Roland. "I can't tell you. I've got a surprise lined up for the celebration tomorrow, and I guarantee you'll never forget it, Roland." He stood up from the table and didn't appear the slightest bit worried that the Sheriff would shoot him as he rose to his feet.

Roland shook his head and looked at Alvin in disbelief. The mayor kept refusing to answer his questions. *Damn it, Alvin. Don't make me have to shoot you.* Alvin smirked at him one more time as he stood over Roland, and he looked at the Sheriff with a pitying glance. Fire shot through Roland's veins, and his face turned into a mask of rage. He didn't fly out of his seat or shoot Alvin as he stood before him. There would be another time and another place to take care of the mayor, but Roland intended to find the information that he wanted even if he had to drag it out of Alvin by force. He pointed a rigid finger at the mayor. "Watch your back, Alvin, or I'll be right there," Roland whispered so softly that it barely reached Alvin's ears.

Instead of acting scared, Alvin's smile deepened, and he looked ready to laugh at Roland. "I'll do that," he replied good-naturedly and turned to leave. He paused in mid turn and put a finger to his lips in contemplation. Then he turned back to the Sheriff, and his eyes widened with sincerity. "Oh, Roland. Watch your back, or you'll be dead," Alvin told him cheerfully, then his face locked back into its social mask. With a fake smile, the mayor turned around and rejoined Zoltan and the others at the bar.

Chapter Fifteen

Henry awakened to a chorus of noise coming from downstairs. He had no idea what was causing the ruckus, but it was too loud for him to fall back asleep. The Ghost Hunter was still tired, but not as exhausted as he had been when they rode into town with the disappointed Sheriff. He didn't want to get out of bed. It felt wonderful to lay on a mattress and relax his weary body after weeks of travel. There was Roland to face as well. His old acquaintance had not been pleased after Henry failed to help Rebecca. Knowing Roland's temper, the Sheriff was not going to be a pleasant man that afternoon.

Grimacing, Henry sat up and immediately pressed a hand to his forehead. A sliver of pain still ran through his head although it wasn't as bad as that morning. Henry had faced many spirits in the Land of Shadows, but the one belonging to Bryant White was the first to hurt him in a long, long time. After emerging from the Land of Shadows, Henry had thought that he would black out and was amazed that he had ridden all the way back to New Haven before collapsing in his own bed. *God, I could use some whiskey.* Most of the time, Henry didn't mind his vow to give up drinking, but his old companion would have certainly alleviated the pain.

He took a deep breath before rising to his feet. Swirls of light swam through his vision, and the room tottered on its foundation. The world seemed to move at half speed as he began dressing. *This damn headache will go away once I start moving,* Henry thought wistfully, although he didn't hold much faith in that. It felt like a bad hangover, and Henry only knew of one cure for that. Unfortunately he had forsaken it.

Putting on his boots seemed to take forever, and he nearly gave up and went back to sleep after pulling one of them over his foot. As he started moving, Henry began to feel a little better. His head still hurt, but it wasn't slowing him down quite as much. Shoving his arms through his jacket, Henry reached for his hat and put it on his head, pulling the brim down low once more. The Ghost Hunter had no desire to leave his room while the sun was still shining, but Singing Rock would probably insist upon it.

Henry nearly left his gun in his room, but he paused in the act of walking to the door. He stared at the weapon for a moment, and his fingers reached up to caress the silver bullet hanging around his neck. *What the hell.* Henry was positive that he wouldn't use the gun, but old habits died hard. He had carried it around far too long to leave it behind. After he had buckled the holster to his belt, he felt much safer. Henry opened the door and stepped into the hallway.

A loud chorus of cheers and applause erupted from downstairs once more as if in response to his presence, and the Ghost Hunter squinted down the hallway. He had no idea what was causing the noise and really wasn't too interested. *It doesn't concern me.* Henry's only interest in New Haven was leaving the town as quickly as possible with his anonymity intact. Ignoring the bedlam, he walked to Singing Rock's room and rapped on the door several times. *"Singing Rock, it is me,"* he called out loudly over the din below.

There was a sound of footsteps on the other side of the door, and suddenly it swung open. Singing Rock looked as if he had just awakened. His grey hair hung loosely around his shoulders, and the skin around his eyes was puffy. He stared at Henry with bleary eyes. *"Come in,"* he muttered in Navajo and turned around.

Henry stepped inside the room and quietly closed the door behind him. He was glad to see that he wasn't the only one who still felt the effects of that morning. The Navajo shuffled over to his bed and plopped onto it, looking up at Henry with a miserable expression on his face. *"You look happy today,"* Henry told him flippantly.

"Hmm," Singing Rock snorted and leveled him with a withering gaze. *"I am tired. Fighting that spirit was exhausting."* He paused as another loud burst of applause filtered through the door. *"What is going on down there? It woke me up."*

Henry shrugged his shoulders. *"It woke me too, but I do not care what it is. We have other things to worry about."*

"I do care. I need my rest as do you. Fighting spirits exhausts the body and mind. Going into the Land of Shadows is twice as bad," Singing Rock lectured, and Henry listened patiently.

"All right," Henry drawled in English and put up his hands defensively. "I'll find out what it is if it keeps up. I want to get some more sleep as well."

Singing Rock nodded and let the matter rest. *"Good. Now, we must determine what to do about this spirit."*

Henry rolled his eyes in frustration. *"I can try to go back into the Land of Shadows and see if he gives me her spirit."*

"Do you think that will work?"

"I do not know, but it is all I can think of. We already know who killed Bryant, but the Sheriff cannot catch him. Next time, I'll have better luck in the Land of Shadows."

Singing Rock shook his head and looked at Henry disapprovingly. *"I taught you better than that. You never should have allowed his spirit to get so close to you. You should have left the Land of Shadows the moment you grew weak. If he had touched you, you would have never been able to return to the world of flesh."*

I know that, Henry thought to himself, but his face never changed expressions. *"You are right, but I am alive so let us not dwell on it. What do you think we should do?"*

The Navajo rubbed his chin for a moment as he thought about the problem. *"Talk to the Sheriff."*

"What?" Henry blurted out in English. "Are you crazy? Roland will recognize me if I go downstairs today. It's broad daylight outside. He's sure to place a name with my face. Do you want everyone to know I'm still alive?" Henry asked Singing Rock accusingly.

"What I want does not matter," Singing Rock told him patiently, and Roland shook his head in frustration because he knew exactly what the Navajo was going to say. *"All that matters is that we do what we were chosen to do. The spirits of my ancestors chose me to help the lost spirits in the Land of Shadows find the Happy Hunting Grounds. I saved you to help with this task as well. We cannot turn our backs on anyone as long as our lives are not in jeopardy."*

"Singing Rock, I will not be able to help you anymore if everyone knows I am still alive. There is bound to be someone who is still upset with me. I will be arrested and hanged. Or somebody will track me down and shoot me so they can brag that they were the one to kill me. Then our work will be done because I will be dead," Henry explained pointedly to no avail. He knew how Singing Rock felt about his mission to help every spirit he could. There were only three times that they had left a town without completing their mission, and all three had been towns run by white people determined to kill Singing Rock because of the color of his skin. Unless that happened in New Haven, they would stay until Bryant White's spirit had been destroyed or moved on from the Land of Shadows.

"You know our mission," Singing Rock replied disapprovingly just as Henry had known he would. *"We must continue even if it means endangering your secret. Only if our help is refused may we leave."*

Damn you, Singing Rock, Henry thought to himself heatedly, but all he did was nod in response. He owed Singing Rock his life, and until he had repaid that debt, he would do whatever the Navajo commanded. "Fine, I'll go downstairs and talk to him," he replied petulantly in English. He knew that Singing Rock preferred to speak in his own native tongue, but Henry wanted to show his disapproval with the situation. It was a petty thing to do, but the Ghost Hunter didn't really care. "Is there anything you want me to ask him?"

One of Singing Rock's eyebrows arched up sardonically, and he stared at Henry reprovingly. *"Just see if you can find out anything about who killed this Bryant. Make him try everything in his power to bring this man to justice. You have done this before. You know what to do,"* Singing Rock answered needlessly. Henry had indeed done this many times before and had only asked to voice his disagreement over not leaving town. *"And see if you can find out what is making all that noise downstairs. I want to go back to sleep."*

Singing Rock stretched his arms and laid back upon the bed as Henry watched. *Damn it, I don't want to deal with Roland again.* The past twelve hours had been rough on Henry. His head still hurt from the encounter with

296

Bryant's spirit, and he wanted to have a quick wit if he was going to talk with Roland. After forsaking lying, Henry had only the option of evasion, and that was rather difficult when his mind was working at half-speed. Despite all of that, Singing Rock had given him a command, and he had no choice but to obey.

He left the room quietly and shut the door behind him. Whatever had caused the ruckus before had died down. There was some noise rising from below but nothing as loud as the bedlam that had awakened him. When he reached the top of the stairway, Henry was amazed to see the tavern overflowing with people. It was a crowd that Henry didn't expect to see until late in the evening. *I can't have slept that late,* he thought in disbelief, but sunlight still poured through the windows. Shaking his head, he slowly walked downstairs, looking at the crowd with curious eyes and searching for Roland. His eyes finally caught sight of the black-clad Sheriff sitting at the exact same table in the back corner. *He likes to see everyone and know nobody can sneak up on him,* Henry observed. He sat with Jack, who Henry remembered meeting the previous night.

The Sheriff's face was locked in a mask of rage as Henry waded his way across the floor. Roland's jaw was clenched, and his eyes seemed to burn holes right through the wall. *Great, I'm glad to see I caught him in a good mood.* Henry just hoped that anger wasn't directed towards him for that morning's failure. Roland didn't notice Henry until the Ghost Hunter had nearly made his way though the thick mass of people. Henry tugged once more on his hat and pulled it low in order to limit Roland's vision of his features. He didn't think it would do much good during the day, but every little bit of caution helped. "Sheriff, I hope I'm not interrupting," he announced as he approached Roland's table.

Roland looked up with a scowl on his face, and his brown eyes stared murderously at Henry. It took Henry by surprise how upset Roland was, but he wasn't frightened. He had faced far worse than Roland Black in his days and lived to tell about it. "What the hell do you want?" The Sheriff rasped thickly.

"I had a few questions I wanted to ask you so I thought I'd come downstairs. What was all that noise if you don't mind me asking? It woke me up." He directed the question more towards Jack than Roland. So far the Sheriff didn't appear to be in a very talkative mood.

Jack smoothed down the tips of his mustache as he looked curiously at Henry. The Ghost Hunter didn't mind Jack staring so obviously at him. He had never met the deputy before his journey to New Haven, and Jack was probably just curious about a white man traveling with an Indian. Roland was the only one in town who could recognize him, but the Sheriff appeared completely uninterested in the Ghost Hunter and kept glancing towards the bar with a look of open hatred painted on his face.

"Our magician came into town an hour ago. He just gave a performance right here in the bar." Jack stopped and swept his arm dramatically. "We had a pretty big crowd as you can see, and they got carried away. Your name's Henry, right?" The deputy asked and stuck out his hand in greeting.

"That's right," Henry replied and reached out to shake the proffered hand. He was about to add something else when Roland broke in.

"I need to talk with him alone, Jack. If you could excuse us for a few minutes," he ordered coarsely. His eyes glowed menacingly, and he looked ready to kill someone.

"Sure, Roland," Jack replied slowly. "I need to go check on a few things anyway. I'll stop by the saloon later tonight. Henry." Jack tipped his hat to the Ghost Hunter and stood up. He took one last glance He looked at the Sheriff with an annoyed expression before walking away from the table, but Roland didn't even glance his way.

The Sheriff focused on Henry and continued to fix him with a flat stare. "What the hell do you want?" He asked Henry, each word dripping with scorn.

Henry paused before answering. He had expected Roland to be upset with him, but he wasn't prepared for the furious man he was facing, especially with his headache refusing to go away. *Be careful with him. He's at the end of his rope.* "I just wanted to ask you a few more questions, Sheriff. That's all," the Ghost Hunter explained and watched Roland carefully to make sure that he didn't do something irrational.

Roland's eyes narrowed, and his mouth curled into a sneer. "Questions!" He whispered fiercely. "Damn it, you said you could get her out of there. Why don't you go out to the house and get her spirit back instead of sitting here asking me *questions,*" Roland hissed the last word vehemently, and his entire body quivered as if he was about to erupt in violence.

Watching Roland carefully, Henry slid his hand towards his holster. The Sheriff looked like a man about to lose control, and Henry intended to be ready to draw at an moment's notice if Roland decided to attack him. He waited a moment to give Roland a chance to calm down. His head continued to throb, but Henry tried to shake it off. He needed to think carefully around the Sheriff, not have his wits dulled by a headache. "Sheriff, I'm trying to help you. I will do my best to rescue her, and I'll go back to the house as soon as possible," he answered peacefully and held his breath as he awaited Roland's response.

To Henry's relief, Roland stared coldly at him for a moment longer, then his face gradually relaxed. He still didn't look happy, but the mask of rage disappeared from his face. Roland glanced down at the table then brought his eyes back up to Henry. "I'm sorry. It's been a bad day. What do you need?" The Sheriff still sounded furious, *but not at me,* Henry thought with relief.

Henry's hand lifted from his holster and came to rest on the table. "I wanted to ask you about Bryant White's death."

Roland's eyes narrowed, and his fist clenched without thought. His jaw muscles flexed under his skin as he ground his teeth together. "I already told you everything I know."

The Ghost Hunter immediately spread his hands wide peacefully. "Yes, you did, but let's just go over it one more time. That way we can both be sure we didn't miss anything," Henry suggested in a more upbeat tone. He wanted to make sure that Roland didn't descend back into an icy rage.

Once again Roland's shoulders lowered, and he appeared to calm down. Henry breathed a sigh of relief. He just wanted his conversation with the Sheriff over as quickly as possible, and that would be easier accomplished if he wasn't so volatile. "What do you want to know?" Roland asked wearily.

Henry breathed a sigh of relief and wiped a bead of sweat from his cheek, grateful that Roland's temper had cooled down once again. He rubbed a tired hand over his aching temples. "How did he die?"

Roland shook his head and looked down at the table as if the subject caused him a great deal of distress. "We found his body in the middle of town about seven months ago. Curly slit his throat and beat him up pretty good."

"But he didn't die there?" Henry asked to confirm the locale of death. Bryant White had to have died near his own house, not in the middle of town. There was no possibility that his spirit could be haunting a house over a mile away.

"Nah," Roland looked back up and shook his head. "There wasn't any blood on the ground around him. Somebody gets cut up like that, they bleed all over. The only blood on Bryant was on his clothes."

"So he could have died by his house?"

"I guess so," Roland answered then rubbed his chin as he contemplated the answer. "I woke Rebecca up the following morning, though, and she had slept through the entire night. If somebody killed Bryant up there, they did it quietly. Else she would've woken up."

Unless she had something to do with it, Henry thought but kept that opinion to himself. Roland was already in a foul mood, and he didn't need Henry accusing his comatose fiancée of committing the crime. "All right, that makes sense so far. Now, who do you think killed him?" He had already asked Roland once before, but he wanted to hear what the Sheriff said after another day to think about it.

Roland's eyes went flat, and he turned his head away from Henry and stared out the window. "I don't think. I know who it is," he answered quietly, his voice taut with anger.

"Who?"

The Sheriff turned back to Henry, and his face was a mask of barely controlled rage. "It's that son of a bitch Curly."

"Are you sure it's him?"

Roland chuckled softly, a cold, evil laugh, not one of joy. "Oh, I'm sure it's him. I have it from a reliable source," he answered, and a faint smile graced his lips. He turned to the bar and stared at a group of men over there.

Henry's headache flared painfully, and he grimaced as he massaged his temples. *Damn, I need to hurry.* "So why haven't you arrested him yet?" Henry asked, distracting Roland from the object of his concentration.

The Sheriff turned his head and focused again on the Ghost Hunter. "Because I don't know where the bastard's hiding out. As soon as I can get my hands on him, I'll kill him, but he hasn't been to town in over a week."

"Do you think he'll come back at all, or has he skipped town?"

"He'll come back. All the Dark Riders stayed away for a while, but they've started coming back. I expect Curly'll be in town soon. He could never go long without getting some liquor in him."

"And the Dark Riders are a bunch of outlaws?" Henry's blood had chilled when Roland mentioned them earlier. He had confronted a band of outlaws once in his life, and Henry had no intention of ever doing so again if it laid within his control. If all went well, he and Singing Rock would be far from New Haven very shortly, and he would never have any dealings with the Dark Riders.

"Pretty much. They do robbery, smuggling, things of that sort. As long as they don't hurt anyone coming into or leaving this town, I leave them alone. There are too damn many of them for me to take out without getting state troops in here, and I don't want any outside help in New Haven."

"Then there's no way to get to Curly in the meantime?"

"Nope, but that son of a bitch will be back." Roland's lips pulled back in a chilling grin. Even though Curly had committed murder, Henry almost pitied the man when Roland finally caught up with him.

"Any idea when that will be?"

Roland shrugged his shoulders. "I don't know, but it should be soon. And when he does, I'll be waiting for him."

Henry was silent for a moment after Roland's answer, but he couldn't think of anything else to ask. Roland had covered everything that he had wanted to know, and he wasn't about to stay downstairs to chat with the Sheriff. Henry wanted to be as far from Roland as possible. Every now and then Roland squinted as if carefully studying the Ghost Hunter's face. It was only a matter of time before the Sheriff figured him out, and his headache was growing worse in the loud saloon. "Thanks, Sheriff. I suppose that's got it for me," Henry answered, but he had barely risen from his seat when Roland spoke up.

"Wait!" Roland called out and held up a hand to signal that even though Henry might be done talking, he still had a few questions on his mind.

Damn! Henry cursed inwardly, but his expression never changed. Careful to keep his head lowered, the Ghost Hunter sat back down in the wooden chair. "What else can I do for you, Sheriff?" His head throbbed painfully, and he found it increasingly difficult to focus on the task at hand. He wanted nothing more than to return to his bed upstairs and sleep for another four or five hours.

Roland leaned forward and quietly stared at Henry. His eyes burned intensely, and the Ghost Hunter found it difficult to sit still. *He knows it's me,* Henry thought as his heartbeat accelerated in a panicked tempo. Roland kept that silence for a few more seconds before breaking it. "Can you really get her out of there?"

Henry exhaled in relief. *Just answer his questions and get back upstairs before he figures out it's you.* "I told you before, Sheriff. We'll do everything in our power to get her spirit back for you."

"That's not what I asked," Roland pointed out bitterly. "I asked if you're going to get her out of there or not. I don't want any of your lies either. You said you'd get her out of there this morning, and you didn't."

It wasn't the first time that Henry had been accosted by the very people he was trying to help. Often if he and Singing Rock failed at their first attempt, they would be rebuked for their lack of success. "I never promised we'd get her back, Sheriff. I said we'd do our best, and I did learn information about Bryant's spirit. I assure you, Singing Rock and I will go back and fight this spirit until she is safe with you or we're dead. That I do promise." It was pretty much the same explanation that Henry had given Roland that very morning after he and Singing Rock had emerged unsuccessful from Rebecca's house. *Hopefully he'll listen this time.*

A brief look of guilt flashed across Roland's face, and he paused to rub at his eyes wearily. He sighed once forlornly, and much of the anger in him seemed to dissipate. "I'm sorry. I just haven't been myself since Rebecca fell ill. I don't mean you any disrespect." His voice sounded half-apologetic as if Roland wasn't use to justifying his actions.

"Don't worry about it," Henry casually waved the matter off. "You've been under a lot of stress lately. I don't hold it against you. Singing Rock and I—" the Ghost Hunter broke off as Jimmy approached their table.

The Sheriff rolled his eyes in frustration as Jimmy sauntered towards them, but Henry noticed a certain wry amusement in Roland's expression as well. The youth had a cocky grin on his lips and a merry glint in his eye that reminded Henry of the years when he first stepped foot in the West. "Sheriff," the young man tipped his hat then nodded at Henry. "I hope I'm not interrupting."

"Actually you are, Jimmy. We're talking about some private matters," Roland pointed out and waited patiently for the young man to leave. Henry was amazed at the manner in which Roland dealt with the young man. So far, he had only seen Roland display his fiery temper, not a patient, amused demeanor.

"Sorry to bother you, Sheriff. I just wanted to thank you again for letting me stay. That magician was incredible. I'm looking forward to tomorrow," he said quickly, and his face lit up with wonder.

"You're welcome. Now, if you'd leave us alone, I need to talk to my friend here," Roland responded.

"Sure," Jimmy answered and turned to leave then stopped abruptly. He stared pointedly at Henry for a moment, and the Ghost Hunter casually let one of his hands drop to his side. Pain coursed through his head, and he didn't think that he'd be much good in a fight. Nonetheless, Henry intended to be ready if Jimmy meant him harm. He didn't care much for anyone looking at him with that much interest. "What's that?" The young gunslinger suddenly asked, pointing a finger at the silver bullet hanging on his chest.

Roland lost the look of wry amusement and glared at Jimmy. "Goddamn it, Jimmy. I said we're busy here. Now leave."

"It's all right, Sheriff," Henry replied when he saw the crestfallen expression on the boy's face. *Damn, he looks like me when I was his age,* Henry thought back to a time long ago. "It's just a good luck charm I like to wear. I haven't fired a gun in years, but I like to keep a reminder," he explained and waited for Jimmy to leave. Roland watched Jimmy through narrowed eyes as he continued to stand in front of the table.

Jimmy rubbed his chin, oblivious to the dark glare that Roland was aiming at him. "*You* were a gunslinger?" He asked in disbelief.

Something about the way Jimmy asked the question irritated Henry, and a brief flash of pride kicked in. "I'm the fastest son of a bitch you've ever seen," he fired off boastfully before he could think a response through. Henry paused in horror after he answered Jimmy and couldn't believe what he had just said. *Oh my God.* For five years, he hadn't given one hint to his identity, then he went and blew it without thinking because of a headache and pride. He was so caught up in shock over his answer that he didn't notice Jimmy staring at him with a great deal more scrutiny. For that matter, even Roland was eyeing him much differently.

"You're *that* fast?" Jimmy asked once again in disbelief.

Henry looked up at the boy with a pale face and a look of bewilderment. *Get out of here.* Henry wanted to get upstairs more than ever. The noise of the crowd was really starting to bother him, and he couldn't believe the slip he had just made. If he wasn't careful, he might say something else that would tell Roland exactly who he was. "Nevermind. I want to finish talking to the Sheriff if you'll excuse us," he answered in a stunned voice.

"Sure," Jimmy responded, but his face clearly showed his interest in what Henry had just said. He tipped his hat to the two men and sauntered to his poker table. The young gunslinger cast a curious stare over his shoulder as he made his way across The Last Frontier. He pursed his lips as he studied Henry one more time as if to evaluate the validity of his boast.

The Sheriff rubbed his chin thoughtfully as Jimmy walked across the saloon, carefully studying the Ghost Hunter's face. His eyes burned into Henry like a hawk. "If you don't mind me asking, are you that fast?" Roland asked.

Get upstairs quick. Far too many people were asking questions about his past, and he wanted to go someplace where he could avoid them all. The Sheriff's scrutiny made him extremely uncomfortable. The Ghost Hunter took a moment and breathed deeply, trying to clear some of the cobwebs from his head. He wanted to be good and sure that he didn't blurt out something else that he wished to keep secret, especially with Roland paying such close attention. "I was in a few gunfights when I was younger, but it was a long time ago," Henry explained and waved his hand as if the whole matter was insignificant.

Roland's eyes narrowed more, and his head tilted slightly as he continued to study Henry. "Is that so? I used to be a gunslinger myself, and I don't remember seeing you about. What did you say your last name was?"

Son of a bitch, Henry swore to himself. Henry straightened his back and returned Roland's stare. He didn't have the chiseled, forbidding gaze of the Sheriff, but he could still look pretty mean when he had to. "I didn't say. Let's just leave it at that. We all have things in our past we want to forget, and this is one I intend to keep that way. I'm here to help with a ghost, not answer all of your questions." Since forswearing lying five years ago, Henry had become quite adept at telling half-truths, and when those failed, he had found that flatly refusing to answer questions also worked quite well.

The Sheriff watched him silently after Henry spoke, his eyes burning intensely. After a few moments, however, Roland leaned back in his chair, and his voice took on a more peaceful tone. "You're right. I'm just curious. That's all." Roland's face looked anything but pacified. Henry knew it was just a matter of time before Roland started digging for more clues to his past. Hopefully he and Singing Rock would be well out of New Haven by that point.

"Good, then if there's nothing else, I'm going upstairs to catch up on some rest." Henry just wanted to flee the scene while he was still able to use a few of his wits. His head was becoming more and more foggy by the minute.

"No!" Roland held up a hand and half rose to his feet in alarm. "I still have some more questions for you."

Goddamn it! Henry had dealt with many people who had pestered him with one question after another as if they could somehow divine how to enter the Land of Shadows and rescue their loved ones all by themselves. It looked as if Roland wasn't going to let him go until he had performed an exhausting round of questioning, and Henry didn't know if he had the strength for it. He sat back down reluctantly, the throbbing at his temples pleading for him to get more rest. "Please make them quick, Sheriff. I need to get more sleep if we're going back to the house at dawn."

Roland's jaw clenched together firmly. "I just want to know why you think you're going to get Rebecca back safely. You already failed once," he accused the Ghost Hunter.

Henry shook his head then rubbed his eyes tiredly. *How many times do I have to tell this to him?* Roland had asked the exact same question that morning after they left Rebecca's house, and Henry had answered it then. The answer hadn't changed since, but Henry responded anyway. Roland had looked like he was about to crack from pressure, and Henry could understand why the Sheriff's mind might not have been completely on the conversation that morning. "When I went in this morning I hoped to get Rebecca and bring her out safely, but Bryant's spirit was too strong. But now I know how strong his spirit is, and I know what to expect the next time I enter the Land of Shadows. I'd prefer it if you captured his murderer yourself, but if you can't, I'm confident I can make him give up her spirit."

That answer didn't seem to completely satisfy the Sheriff, and he leaned forward in his chair and folded his hands together. "Yes, but what I really want to know is—bastard son of a whore!" Roland broke off, and his eyes glowed in fury as he stared at the bar.

Henry glanced briefly in the direction that Roland was staring. A man with long white hair and a cane was walking towards their table. He wore a nice suit and a mischievous grin. Something about the man attracted Henry's curiosity, but he turned his head downward after a moment and stared at the table, running a finger over each temple in an attempt to ease the throbbing. Whoever it was didn't need to talk to him. The man's business was with the Sheriff. *Please, let me go upstairs soon,* Henry thought forlornly as he continued to massage the sides of his head.

"Sheriff," the long-haired man greeted in an overly friendly way that sounded fake to Henry.

"What the hell do you want?" Roland asked in a flat, emotionless tone.

"I just wanted to come over and meet your friend, Roland. This is the one who showed up with an Indian?"

Henry looked up at the question, and it took only a second for shock to penetrate the fog in his head. The pain instantly became secondary, and panic gripped his heart. *Son of a bitch!*

Alvin's eyes grew wide with shock of his own, and he took a step backwards. "*You!*" The mayor hissed in astonishment. His jaw dropped open in utter bewilderment, and the blood slowly drained from his face.

"Alvin," Henry rasped in defeat. The moment he laid eyes on the mayor, Henry had known that his secret was over. Roland might have had some difficulty placing a name with the face, but there was no way Alvin would ever forget him.

Roland twisted his head back and forth a few times as he stared at one man then the other in confusion. "What the hell's going on?" He demanded.

The mayor paid no heed to the Sheriff as he continued to stare at Henry as if the Ghost Hunter was a ghost himself. His right hand reached inside his jacket and rested on the butt of his pistol. From the look on his face, he was prepared to use it at a moment's notice. "You're supposed to be dead," Alvin whispered accusingly.

First Roland, now Alvin. Who next? Wyatt? Henry thought bitterly. His mouth curled into a tight, self-mocking smile. After five years of zealously protecting his identity, he had finally encountered someone who had recognized him instantly. *I should have killed that son of a bitch when I had the chance.* "Sorry to disappoint you, Alvin, but I'm still alive," he responded quietly. Henry tried to force the cobwebs from his mind. He and Singing Rock would have to leave New Haven in the very near future before somebody came trying to kill him. It was only a matter of time before it became common knowledge that he was still alive.

"Goddamn it!" Roland hissed and slammed his fist down on the table, causing both men to stop their contemplation and look at him. He glared at Henry before dragging his eyes over to the mayor. His lip curled in disgust as he looked at Alvin, and his eyes filled with hate. "What the hell's going on, Alvin? Do you know him?"

Alvin turned to Roland, and his face was completely pale. A look of shock had replaced his polished smile. "Blazes, Roland. You know him. It's Doc Holliday."

A flicker of recognition twinkled in Roland's eyes then his jaw dropped in surprise as well. "Son of a bitch," he mouthed silently as he and Alvin stared at Henry. He tried to say something else, but from the look of it, Roland was speechless.

Goddamn it to hell. Henry bowed his head for a moment, acutely aware of the scrutiny the other men were placing upon him. When he looked up, Alvin and Roland still had stunned expressions on their faces. "Hello, Roland. It's been a while," he stated softly. *Damn you, Singing Rock, for making me stay here. They know I'm alive.* The lengths that he had gone to in order to protect his anonymity had all been for naught.

"Good God almighty. It is you," Roland whispered hoarsely. "I thought you were dead," he commented in amazement. "Blazes, Doc, how the hell are you still alive? Everyone thought you've been dead for at least five years."

"Please call me Henry," the Ghost Hunter answered with a pained look. "I gave up that other name a long time ago. That man did die five years ago." Henry's eyes had a haunted look in them. *I can't believe they know it's me. They know Doc Holliday is alive.* He had thought this day would never happen. *I should have stayed in bed a few hours longer.*

"Why Henry?"

"It's my name, Roland. John Henry Holliday."

"Henry, then," Roland repeated himself, but he looked uncomfortable using that name as if it didn't fit the man he was talking to. "What the hell have you been doing, and why does everybody think you're dead?"

Henry's eyes slowly slid towards Alvin and held there. "I don't want to answer that question right now, Roland." He would more than likely have to tell Roland about what had happened to him, but Henry would be damned if he was going to tell Alvin.

Roland didn't hesitate a second. A hand thrust into the air and pointed at the bar. "Get the hell out of here, Alvin. We've got private business," he ordered in a flat tone.

Alvin shook his head and turned to Roland. "It's Doc Holliday, Roland," he repeated to the Sheriff as if he still didn't believe it.

"I know that, and I swear to God if you tell another living soul, I'll hunt you down and put a bullet in you. Do you understand me?"

The mayor's eyes narrowed at Roland's threat, and he appeared to recover from some of his shock. A trace of his polished smile graced his lips, but his face was still pale. He straightened his back and ran a hand through his long white hair. "I'll leave you two alone then," he announced haughtily and turned back towards the bar. Alvin turned and stared at Henry twice as he made his way across the floor, an expression of complete incredulity on his face.

Henry watched Alvin leave their table with mixed emotions of relief and dread. The mayor made him nervous, especially after the last time that they had met. But once again he was alone with Roland, and he wasn't ready to answer the questions that he knew Roland would ask. He rubbed his eyes and steeled himself. There were many things that he had thought buried forever, but it looked as if they were going to be dug up.

"Blazes, Doc—" Roland paused when Henry flinched as if he'd been slapped. "I'm sorry, Henry." The Sheriff stopped once more and shook his head in disbelief. "What the hell happened to you? The last I heard you had died. Hell, everyone thought you had died. How'd you wind up traveling with an Indian and fighting ghosts?"

A long moment of silence passed as Henry put his elbows on the table and rested his head in his hands, casting his eyes downward wearily. A throbbing ache pulsed at his temples, and Roland was asking questions that he didn't want to answer. *Damn, I can't think.* He tried to come up with some way out of the mess that he suddenly found himself in, but his frazzled mind failed to provide him with solutions. Henry didn't think there was any way out of the predicament. Roland and Alvin had recognized him, and more importantly, he had reacted to his name. It was too late to connive his way out. "That's a long story, Roland."

Roland shrugged his shoulders. "I've got all the time in the world." He leaned forward over the table, his face rapt with anticipation of Henry's response.

Raising his head, Henry winced when he saw Roland's expression. *There's no way he'll let me leave until I've told him everything,* the Ghost Hunter thought in resignation. "Fine. What do you want to know?" He asked listlessly in a monotone voice.

"I already told you. I want to know what happened to you. You're supposed to be dead."

Henry sighed once, and his eyes drifted off to the side of Roland as if they were looking off to another time. "About five years ago, I was close to dying. My lungs were pretty bad back then, and it was a miracle I lived as long as I did. I had heard of a hot spring bath here in Colorado over in Glenwood Springs, and I went there to see if it could heal my lungs. They tried the best they could there, but I kept getting worse." His eyes tightened for a moment painfully as he brought that memory back from the dark recesses of his mind. He remembered the weeks spent in excruciating pain, praying for death to deliver him from his lungs' hellish torture.

"I was crazy with pain, and I hadn't had a drop of liquor in weeks. I could barely breathe, and I only wanted one drink to take the edge off the pain. The nurses wouldn't let me, though. They took care of me for over a month, but they wouldn't give me a single drop to drink. Luckily I kept blacking out. I think the pain would have killed me if I had been awake the whole time."

"But what happened?" Roland asked when Henry paused. A haunted expression clouded the Ghost Hunter's eyes, and he seemed to forget about Roland and the entire saloon as he looked to the side.

Henry flinched as if Roland's question had jolted him back to reality. "I'm sorry, I'm a bit tired," the Ghost Hunter explained and rubbed his eyes before continuing. "I think the nurses had given me up for dead. They came by my bed less often, or maybe I was just passed out when they treated me." Henry shrugged his shoulders. "It doesn't really matter. I woke up one night, and my lungs hurt worse than ever before. I kept coughing up blood. I was pretty sure I was going to die that night, but I was saved.

"Some time in the night, Singing Rock came to my bed. I thought I was dreaming when I first saw him. Why would an Indian be by my bed? He told me to close my eyes and relax. I don't know why, but I listened to him. I closed my eyes and fell asleep again in seconds." The Ghost Hunter stopped and looked at Henry with a defeated expression. "The next part sounds crazy, but I swear I'm telling the truth."

Roland spread his hands. "Go ahead. Nothing really sounds too crazy anymore after all the things that have gone on around here lately."

"All right," Henry replied, but he shook his head, and his lips curled into a self-depreciating smile. His eyes turned downward, and he stared at the table as he continued his story. "I woke up in some teepee with Singing Rock standing over me singing. It nearly scared me to death. I had no idea where I was or who Singing Rock was either. I tried to sit up, but I couldn't move a muscle. I couldn't even turn my head. At first I thought it was my lungs, but I was able to breath just fine. I just couldn't sit up.

"Singing Rock looked pleased when I woke up, and he stopped his singing and sat down beside me. I had to strain to make my eyes look at him, and the rest of my body refused to budge an inch. He didn't speak English well, but I was able to understand most of what he said. He told me that he healed me and that my lungs were fine. That was why I couldn't move at all. The Indians have a way of taking health from the rest of your body and using it to fight the unhealthy parts. Anyway, that's what he did to me. I don't suppose that makes any sense, but it's true. I haven't had a problem with my lungs since that day." He looked up to see if Roland was believing any of the words he'd just spoken.

Much to the Ghost Hunter's surprise, it wasn't disbelief on Roland's face but rather a strange look of recognition. The Sheriff placed a hand almost gingerly upon his ribs. "I believe you. Running Brook did the same thing to me. I couldn't move, and I slept for nearly two days afterwards," Roland recounted softly.

Henry's eyes widened with surprise. "Running Brook healed you? What happened?"

Roland scowled in disgust. "I jumped through a window at Rebecca's house and cut up my side. I had passed out and was bleeding pretty good when Running Brook's son found me. He took me back to their village, and Running Brook healed me."

The Ghost Hunter nodded. "At least you understand what I'm talking about. I thought you wouldn't believe me."

"No, I believe you." Roland paused to bark out a laugh. "Hell, I thought nobody would believe *me*. I'm glad to see it wasn't my mind playing tricks on me, but enough about me. Why did he wake you up? That doesn't make any sense. You said you didn't know him."

Taking a deep breath, Henry paused before continuing his tale. His head was still killing him, and he wanted to go upstairs. Roland, however, appeared eager to hear what he had to say. *Not much longer to go, then you can sleep.* He focused on Roland as he continued the story. "I slept for a few weeks afterwards. I guess my body was in a lot worse shape than yours." He stopped to shake his head ruefully. "Hell, my body was in worse shape then just about anyone I've ever met. When I finally woke up, I was hungrier than you could believe. After I got done eating, I asked Singing Rock why he had helped me."

Henry paused and rubbed his chin thoughtfully. He didn't want to share that information with Roland, but he didn't see the harm in it. Roland had already learned more about him than he ever thought he'd have to reveal. What harm could a little more information do? "He told me he sensed something special in me. He called it the 'talent' or 'gift.' I had no idea what he was talking about and asked him. That's when he told me what he did." Henry's eyes once again grew clouded as he drifted back to the day five years ago when Singing Rock had outlined the new focus in his life.

"He told me about ghosts and spirits and things like that for a while. I thought he was crazy, but I listened to him because he had healed me. The man saved my life so I at least owed him that much. You see, Singing Rock believes it's his duty in life to help those in the Land of Shadows find their final resting place, whether it's to take them to The Happy Hunting Grounds or help them be reborn in the World of Flesh. That's why he healed me.

"Singing Rock told me I also had the 'gift' of being able to travel to The Land of Shadows. He even offered to prove it to me. Now, I really thought he was crazy, but I decided to stay one more day with him. My body was still recovering from its healing, and I owed Singing Rock for saving my life. I went back to sleep after that, but he woke me an hour or so before dawn. That was the morning I entered The Land of Shadows for the first time," Henry stated, and his voice was tinged with regret.

"What's it like?" Roland broke in.

Henry stared at the ceiling and idly rubbed his chin as he contemplated Roland's question. "There's no color. Everything is grey, and there's no light. The whole place is as dark as the middle of night with a full moon. There are no mountains or valleys, just hard, grey ground stretching as far as you can see." The Ghost Hunter stopped and shook his head. "There's no way to describe it. You'd have to go there. Singing Rock tried to explain everything to me first, but I never understood any of it until I actually entered that first time.

"That was a little over five years ago. I didn't believe Singing Rock at all. He had healed my lungs, but a land of spirits? It sounded like crazy talk to me. Anyway, sometime around dawn, the two of us entered. I about pissed myself when I first saw the Land of Shadows. That morning, Singing Rock just showed me the place. He showed me how to travel in it and explained some of the rules."

"Rules?"

"There are rules for the Land of Shadows. Never fall asleep there, never touch a spirit, never drink or eat anything you find there. Most of it's common sense."

"What happens if you break any of them?"

"You're trapped in the Land of Shadows forever, without any hope of rebirth." Henry waved the matter off like it was inconsequential. "After that, I had no choice but to believe Singing Rock, and seeing how he saved my life, I've traveled with him from that point on. I also want to make amends for all the people I shot over the years."

Roland's eyes squinted inquisitively. "But why the hell does everyone think you're dead?"

Henry looked up with a look of defeat on his face. "Because that's the only way I can help Singing Rock. He saved my life, and I *owe* him for that. I could never help him if people were still hunting me down for the things I've done. By this time, somebody would've put a bullet in me just for bragging rights. Those were the conditions Singing Rock gave me. No more gunfighting, no gambling, no drinking, and no lying."

"No drinking?" Roland asked in amazement.

"I haven't had anything to drink in over five years, Roland," Henry answered quietly.

Roland appeared more stunned over Henry's sobriety than he did over the notorious gunfighter being alive. "I still don't understand. Why are you helping him? Can't he help people by himself?"

"Singing Rock can help other Indians, but sometimes a White Man gets caught in the Land of Shadows. That's why I ride with him. I have more luck talking to their spirits than he does, and it's easier for him to enter a town or city with me around than by himself. I guess that's all over now."

"What are you talking about?"

"I won't be able to travel with Singing Rock anymore. As soon as word gets out that I'm still alive, there will be bounty hunters and glory seekers tracking me down. I'd endanger Singing Rock instead of helping him."

The Sheriff leaned back in his chair, and his eyes widened with sincerity. He put a hand to his chest. "I swear I won't say anything, Doc," Roland replied earnestly.

Henry winced at hearing his former nickname. "Please call me 'Henry.'"

"I'm sorry. It slipped my mind."

"Sure," Henry waved the matter off, but he still looked defeated. "It doesn't really matter what you do, Roland. Alvin will tell people, and that'll be the end of it."

"How the hell does *Alvin* know who you are? He never said anything about meeting you," Roland asked and glanced over at the bar, his jaw tightening rigidly when he saw Alvin laughing.

"I shot him," Henry answered softly.

Roland snapped his head back around, and his eyes grew wide in amazement. "You did *what?*"

Henry looked at the table again. "I shot him. It was a long time ago. He tried to cheat me at cards, and I was drunk. He reached for his gun, and I shot him in the leg before he could draw. I don't know why I didn't kill him, but I let him live." Henry lifted his head and gazed out the window. "I won a lot of money at faro that night," he commented softly. That night seemed so long ago. *How long has it been?* Henry's life before he met Singing Rock seemed like a blur. He spent so many years drunk that his memories had jumbled together, making it difficult to keep them straight in his head. Henry had lived with more clarity since then, for which he was grateful nearly every day.

"So that's how he got the cane. Blazes, I can't believe you shot him." Roland had a hopelessly stunned look on his face. A tiny, forlorn smile touched the corners of his mouth. "You don't know how much trouble you'd have saved me if you had killed that bastard."

"What's done is done. Listen, Roland. I'm not going to pretend I'm happy you know I'm alive. I've worked a long time on keeping that a secret. I'll still help Rebecca. Singing Rock and I promised, and I keep my word." He stopped and leveled a finger at Roland. "But you see if you can find Bryant's killer. I want to be out of town as soon as possible. Alvin knows I'm alive, and I don't trust him. He's the type to carry a grudge. I want to go somewhere quiet and live out the rest of my life, not get a bullet in the back."

"I promise. I'll look for Curly."

"Good," Henry answered succinctly and rose to his feet a bit unsteadily. The room seemed to spin for a moment, and he grabbed a chair to help balance himself. After a moment it passed, and Henry straightened his back. "Just make sure you do. I want this whole damn thing over with," the Ghost Hunter answered disgustedly. "Wake us a few hours before dawn." Then he turned his back on the Sheriff.

Everything around him seemed to move at half-speed as Henry made his way to the staircase. He couldn't believe that his secret was out. For five years he had traveled with Singing Rock, and Henry didn't know what he would do now. Gunslinging was no longer an option, and he'd only endanger Singing Rock with his notorious reputation. *Don't think about it now,* he thought to himself. He needed sleep more than anything else. He'd think about his options when he wasn't so tired.

Henry stopped at Singing Rock's door as he walked down the hallway. He sighed once then knocked on it. *I can't believe they know I am alive,* he thought as he tapped his foot impatiently.

Singing Rock answered the door a moment later. *"Did you speak to the Sheriff?"*

"I spoke to him. He will look for Bryant's killer," Henry answered sullenly and shook his head.

The Navajo's eyes narrowed. *"What is wrong? You are acting strangely."*

They know I'm alive. Henry didn't know whether he wanted to laugh or cry. *"They recognized me."*

"They know who you are?" Singing Rock asked and blinked in surprise.

"I told you they would. My work with you is finished." Henry paused and rubbed his eyes wearily. Hopefully everything would seem better in the morning. *"I need to sleep."*

Singing Rock reached out and put a hand on Henry's shoulder. His face softened from its typical stoic mask. *"We will work this out. Do not worry. It will be fine."*

Henry snorted. Nothing would be fine. Soon he'd have dozens of glory seekers chasing after him to make a name for themselves, but he nodded quietly. He didn't want an argument. He just wanted sleep. *"Perhaps. I will see you in the morning,"* he told Singing Rock and went to his room to collect on some well-deserved rest.

Chapter Sixteen

Roland watched Henry walk across the saloon, his mind still reeling from what had just transpired. *Blazes, Doc Holliday.* He had never expected to see the notorious gunslinger again and had never begun to suspect that he was one of the Ghost Hunters. Roland still couldn't get used to thinking of him as Henry either. Not once had the Sheriff heard him called anything but Doc. *Goddamn, Doc Holliday.* He didn't know what to think of it. Mostly his wits were numb. Looking out the window, Roland went over all of his memories of Doc Holliday and contemplated what he thought about the gunslinger coming to New Haven to help Rebecca.

Alvin had watched the two men conversing, and a few minutes after Henry went upstairs, the mayor crossed the saloon to talk to Roland. His face was still ashen, and he looked like a man who had just received very bad news. He walked up to the table and stood quietly for a moment as Roland continued to look out the window. Finally he cleared his throat, and the Sheriff instantly turned around.

A sneer formed on Roland's face, and his hand dropped to his pistol. Alvin was the last person he wanted to see that night. His mood was already sour to begin with, and Henry had thrown quite a shock at him. Roland just wanted to sit at his table quietly and collect his thoughts. "What the hell do you want, Alvin?"

The mayor ignored Roland's hostility and took a seat at the table. Roland's eyes narrowed, but Alvin paid them no heed. "That was Doc Holliday you were just talking to."

Roland decided to have some fun with Alvin and shrugged his shoulders. "I don't know what you're talking about."

"What the hell do you mean? You know exactly what I'm talking about."

One corner of his mouth tilted upward as he flashed his lopsided smile. "Really, Alvin. I have no idea what you're talking about. Doc Holliday's been dead for five years. The man we were talking with is named Henry."

Alvin's eyes narrowed, and he glared at Roland. "I don't know what game you're playing, Roland, but you and I both know Doc Holliday is alive and in this saloon. I want to know what you're going to do about it."

Leaning back in his chair, Roland folded his arms over his chest. "What did you have in mind?"

"I want you to arrest him," Alvin demanded.

"Now why would I arrest him? Henry hasn't done anything wrong since he's been here. So I can't arrest him. Can I?"

"But he's done plenty of other things. You know he's wanted for murder in several states. I demand that you arrest him, Roland!" Alvin insisted, and flecks of spittle formed at the corners of his mouth.

Roland's eyes grew wide. He hadn't expected Alvin to get so upset. Henry had said that he shot Alvin, but Roland hadn't thought the mayor would be so livid. *Might as well keep pushing him,* Roland chuckled to himself. "Demand? You're demanding me, Alvin?" His smirk grew larger as he continued to goad the mayor. "I'm still Sheriff in case you forgot, and as far as I can tell Henry's who he says he is. There's no cause to arrest him."

Alvin kept silent for a moment and struggled to regain his composure. It was one of the few times Roland could remember successfully goading the mayor in public. He had infuriated Alvin before, but it had always been in private. Roland just hoped that other people in the saloon were watching the mayor to see his true face. Finally a more collected mask replaced the one of unbridled fury. "What game are you playing, Roland?" Alvin repeated himself and watched the Sheriff with narrowed, calculating eyes.

Putting a hand to his heart, Roland did his best job to look sincere. "How can you say such a thing after all the time we've known each other?"

"Goddamn it, I'm not joking."

"Neither am I. Now why don't you run along, Alvin? I'm busy right now." Roland folded his arms across his chest and waited for the mayor to leave.

Clearly that wasn't the answer that Alvin wanted to hear. He glared at Roland for a few seconds then stood up. "You think you're so damn clever, Roland, but I've got a surprise of my own," he replied ominously.

"Can't wait to see it," Roland replied flippantly, which only seemed to aggravate Alvin even more. The mayor's hands tightened into fists. "Be careful though, Alvin. You wouldn't want to get shot again. Would you?"

Alvin's face turned into a mask of rage once again, and for a moment anybody in the entire saloon could have seen the real Alvin. "You'll get your wish, and your friend too," he announced then left before Roland could say anything else to upset him. Instead of going back to the bar, Alvin headed straight for the exit. His cane struck the floor loudly as he stalked across the saloon. Several people tried to stop him for a few words, but the mayor ignored them all, leaving a trail of surprised-looking people in his wake. He kicked open the door and headed out into the street.

Everyone had seen Alvin talking to Roland and turned to stare at the Sheriff once Alvin was outside. Roland barely even noticed their attention as he looked out the window and saw Alvin angrily stalking down the street. *Got you, you son of a bitch.* After all those damn smirks Alvin had been shooting him, he was glad to get under the mayor's skin. Roland was surprised to find himself in a good mood for a change. *Maybe I should make Doc an offer to stick around. I've never seen Alvin so upset in my life.*

Gradually Alvin disappeared from sight, and the customers in the saloon returned to their own business. A sizable crowd stayed in The Frontier for the rest of the day. With the upcoming celebration, most of the town decided to start drinking a day early. Sherry's women began circulating around the saloon before disappearing with their clients. Numerous card games were played, and as soon as one person stepped out of a game, somebody immediately took their place. Zoltan went upstairs shortly after Alvin left, and the town of New Haven was left with nothing but expectation for the following day's performance.

Roland still couldn't believe that his old acquaintance was not only alive but currently sleeping upstairs. He had thought Doc had long since gone to the grave, but it seemed that the wily gunslinger kept cheating death at every turn. *Henry?* No matter how many times he said it, Roland could no longer think of the Ghost Hunter as anything but Doc. He'd have to guard his tongue if the two were in public, or he might accidentally betray Henry's secret. Between his worry for Rebecca and Doc's surprising resurrection, Roland had quite a few things on his mind the day before the Fourth.

Little trouble broke out that evening as Roland's men patrolled the city. There were a few fights at The Rattlesnake, but that was nothing new. They were quickly broken up before anybody could get hurt, and that was the end of it. A few Dark Riders came to town. Ben burst into the saloon to tell the Sheriff. Roland's blood heated up as he asked for details, but it quickly cooled off when it turned out there were just a few Banditos and Marshall. *I want Curly,* Roland thought to himself as he sat at his table, but the Dark Rider didn't return that night. Sullivan showed up just before dusk to examine Rebecca. Roland accompanied him upstairs and watched stony-faced as he looked her over. After finding no signs of improvement or worsening, Sullivan promised to send over a nurse to clean and feed Rebecca then left the saloon.

Roland spent nearly fifteen minutes in Rebecca's room after Sullivan was through, quietly holding her hand. He didn't utter a single word the whole time. Roland was tired of making Rebecca promises that he couldn't keep. He just wanted to be with her and hold her hand, trying to lend her some of his strength. Finally Roland couldn't take it anymore and rose to his feet with tears starting to form at the corners of his eyes. "I love you, Rebecca," he whispered before leaving her room and returning to his customary table downstairs.

After returning, Roland sat at his table and stared out the window with a rigid jaw. *It's not fair. Why Rebecca?* He thought hopelessly. *God have mercy on you when I finally catch you, Curly.* Roland kept considering grisly punishments for the Dark Rider. Catching the outlaw was the only thing that he had to fixate on. He was tired of dreaming that Rebecca would awaken and they could be married only to have his hopes ruthlessly denied. Catching and killing Curly seemed more substantial. Sooner or later, Curly would return to town, and Roland intended to be waiting for him with a loaded gun.

The hours passed by slowly that evening. Perhaps warned by the other deputies of Roland's sour mood, Jack avoided The Last Frontier for the rest of the night. From time to time a deputy stopped in to report, but any talk was brief. Otherwise Roland watched the slow but steady hands of the clock spin around and around. Customers gradually left the saloon, a great many of them stumbling and slurring from the cumulative effects of alcohol. By two, none of Sherry's girls remained, and most of the card games had long since ceased or moved to a new location.

Just as the night before, Jimmy's table was one of the last to call it quits. The young gunslinger wore his customary cocky smile, and his eyes flashed with arrogance. From the look of him, Roland figured that he'd had another lucky night. "Well, gentleman, I'm calling it a night," Jimmy proclaimed brashly as he scooped his latest earnings towards him.

A few of the men at the table might have tried to cause some trouble, especially with the arrogant way that Jimmy behaved, but nobody was foolish enough to provoke a fight with Roland sitting a few tables away. There was some grumbling and unhappy faces as they left, but everyone left peacefully. Jimmy watched his table clear out as he counted his money with a mischievous smirk. Jimmy's behavior amused Roland, but the Sheriff would be glad when he finally left town. The arrogant expression that Jimmy always wore would eventually anger someone, and Roland didn't need any more trouble in New Haven than he already had.

By the time Jimmy finished counting his money, the saloon had nearly emptied. Only a few men who had passed out, George, and some of his staff remained. The young gunslinger looked around, saw nobody was left, then sauntered over to Roland's table. "Sheriff," Jimmy greeted as he casually took a seat.

Roland smiled as the brash youth joined him. "Jimmy," Roland nodded.

"Sorry about earlier. I didn't mean to interrupt," he apologized, and for a moment, just a brief one, he looked apologetic.

"Don't worry about it." Roland waved his hand in the air.

The cocky glint instantly reappeared in Jimmy's eyes, and his mouth curled into that troublesome grin. "So who was that guy? Is he really that fast?" Jimmy stopped when he saw Roland shake his head dumbfoundedly, and the gunslinger looked at the Sheriff strangely. "You all right, Sheriff?"

It's Doc Holliday. He's supposed to be dead, but he's here in New Haven to help free Rebecca from a ghost. Other than that, everything's fine. He still couldn't believe that the notorious gunslinger was still alive and upstairs, but he had promised to protect Henry's secret and intended to do so. Alvin would probably spoil his efforts, but Roland at least wouldn't tell Jimmy. If Jimmy knew Henry's real identity, then the gunslinger would either challenge him to a duel to make a name for himself, or he would pester Henry relentlessly for stories of his past. Roland didn't know which would be worse. Roland shook his head to clear his mind. "Nah, he was just kidding you. He's never been in a gunfight in his life."

Jimmy looked crestfallen. "Oh, I see," he murmured, and Roland nearly burst out laughing. As interested as he was in the history of the West and making a name for himself, Jimmy wouldn't believe his luck if he knew that he had actually met Doc Holliday that evening. "Well, I just wanted to stop by and thank you one more time for letting me stay. That magician was incredible. I can't wait to see his performance tomorrow."

"You're welcome, Jimmy. Just remember. I want you out of town the following day." Roland fixed the young man with a stern gaze to let him know he was serious.

The cocky smile that was just forming on Jimmy's face quickly disappeared. "You're still going to make me leave? I've been real good, Sheriff. Can't you let me stay here longer? I'll behave. I promise," Jimmy pleaded.

"No, Jimmy. It's only a matter of time before you get an itchy trigger finger. I don't need any trouble in town right now, so I'm afraid you have to leave."

Jimmy sighed in resignation. "I didn't think you'd change your mind, but I had to try." He shrugged his shoulders. "Oh well, at least I got to stay a few extra days."

"It looks like you did pretty well too." Roland pointed at the bulge of money in Jimmy's coat pockets.

"Yeah," Jimmy patted the money. "Nobody can play poker here to save their lives, Sheriff. If only it was like this everywhere, I'd be a rich man. Well, I'm going up to get some sleep. Tomorrow's going to be a busy day." He stood up and patted his jacket one more time just to make sure the money was still there. "Good night, Sheriff."

"Good night, Jimmy. Enjoy the celebration tomorrow," Roland replied and tipped his hat.

"Thanks, I will," Jimmy answered and shot Roland a mischievous grin.

As he watched Jimmy saunter towards the stairs, Roland began to regret his decision to allow the young man to stay in town. *Don't let him do anything stupid tomorrow.* Things were likely to be hectic enough the following morning without having to deal with Jimmy. Roland just prayed that he had scared the young man enough to prevent him from committing a foolish act of bravado, but only time would tell. Looking up at the clock, Roland decided that it was time for him to seek out his bed as well. It was tempting to stay up all night again, but the following day was going to be busy for him, especially with all the festivities, and he had to get up before dawn to help the Ghost Hunters go to Rebecca's house. That only left him three hours to sleep.

He paused as he walked by Rebecca's room, but Roland decided against going in. He needed sleep more than anything, and he didn't feel up to telling her that all would be well. *Please, let them get her out of there tomorrow.* Roland doubted that the Ghost Hunters would be able to help, but that was all he had to believe in. *Unless Curly shows up tomorrow.* After he took off his clothes and laid down on the bed, Roland said a brief prayer for Rebecca's health and awakening. Then he closed his eyes and was asleep a moment later.

Roland didn't sleep peacefully that night. Instead he tossed and turned as haunted dreams plagued him. Roland walked to Rebecca's house with Doc Holliday and Singing Rock at his side. The outlaw's hair was no longer white but the youthful dark black that Roland remembered. His eyes were bloodshot, and his step was slightly unsteady from copious amounts of alcohol. He carried a bottle in one hand, and a pistol in the other. Suddenly, he turned to Roland. "Don't worry, Roland. This ghost will not provide us any difficulties," Doc drawled in a thick, drunken Southern accent.

The Sheriff kept quiet and continued his approach towards the house. The moon shone full overhead, and the night seemed almost chilly despite the brutal summer that had swept through Colorado. A fierce wind lashed against his face, but not a single leaf or blade of grass bent under its pressure. Roland looked at Singing Rock, but the Navajo kept walking, oblivious to the Sheriff. Even in the dark of night, Roland could see Singing Rock's rigid jawline and the blue lines etched along his cheek.

As they passed over another hill, Roland caught sight of Rebecca's house, and his heart beat faster. *Almost, Rebecca.* Each footstep sounded incredibly loud, and Roland expected the house to erupt violently at their intrusion. The house appeared sinister under the full moon. It rose ominously before them, and its windows looked like eyes malevolently watching their every move. Still the house remained quiet as Roland and the Ghost Hunters brazenly approached it.

"Mine!" The loud scratchy voice of Bryant rang out through the cold night air.

Roland jumped, but the Ghost Hunters never flinched in their steady advance. Doc dropped the bottle of whiskey and drew his other pistol. His footsteps wavered from side to side, but his hands never shook once. Singing Rock reached into one of his pouches and brought out a handful of yellow powder. He held his fist forward like a weapon, his pace never abating in the slightest.

A loud gunshot pierced the air, and with a grunt, Singing Rock fell to the ground. Roland quickly knelt beside him and turned the Navajo over. To his horror, a bloody wound marked the center of Singing Rock's chest, and his eyes had already glazed over. The Sheriff looked up to tell Doc, but the gunslinger continued his grim advance.

"Mine!" Bryant called out, and another gunshot rang through the air. Doc didn't hesitate but fired his weapons instantly. Behind a tree, a Bandito fell to the ground, and Wild Carl caught a bullet in the chest as he lay nearly hidden in the tall grass. Shot after shot flew true, and when the barrage ended, nearly a dozen bodies littered the ground outside the house.

Roland drew his own gun and leapt to his feet. Doc Holliday never paused in his deadly outburst and was nearly at the porch. He ran to catch up with the outlaw but stopped dead in his tracks as Carlos stepped out from behind a tree. His eyes glittered evilly, and his teeth shone in a demonic grin. Doc never had a chance, and he collapsed in a heap as Carlos's bullets tore through him. "No!" Roland cried and emptied his pistol into the Dark Rider. Carlos never made a sound as he fell to the ground dead.

Save Rebecca, Roland repeated to himself. He walked to the door, stepping over Doc's body. He averted his eyes as he passed the gunslinger. Doc had been a friend a long time ago, but Rebecca was more important. The doorknob was cold in his palm as he turned it and pushed the door inward. He hissed in surprise as it opened to reveal Alvin standing there patiently with a drawn gun. Tiny red lights glowed behind his eyes, and a hulking darkness seemed to lurk directly behind him. "Mine," the mayor whispered hoarsely and fired.

Pain seared through Roland's chest as he fell to the ground, and the world began to darken rapidly. "Rebecca," he called out, but his dwindling strength forced it into a barely audible whisper. The last thing he saw before everything turned to black was Alvin standing over him with a malicious grin on his face. Then the mayor fired at him one more time, and everything faded away.

Roland jerked into a sitting position, his smallclothes damp with sweat. His breath came in ragged gasps as panic still infused him. Gradually Roland calmed as he realized the whole ordeal had been a dream. *It seemed real enough, damn it,* Roland thought irritably. The dream had scared him terribly, especially the part with Alvin standing over him. *The bastard would do it, too, if I give him the chance.*

He looked over at the window and saw it was still pitch black outside. It was tempting to go back to sleep, but he had awakened with a burst of adrenaline. Roland doubted he could catch anymore rest after the excitement the dream had caused. With an exhausted groan, Roland swung his feet out of bed and stumbled over to his coat, which he had carelessly tossed onto the floor. He went to the window and pulled back the drapes. Squinting, Roland peered at the dark face of his timepiece under the dim moonlight. *Damn, it's five,* he thought in alarm and hustled into action.

Henry had said to wake him a few hours before dawn, but there was just over an hour before the sun rose. Hurriedly Roland donned his clothes, buckled on his holsters, and pinned his badge to his coat. He raked his fingers through his hair once before putting on his hat and dashing out of the room. His footsteps echoed loudly through the silent hall as he sprinted to Henry's room. Roland took a deep breath and pounded on the door three times. He waited impatiently for all of two seconds for a response before repeating the action. "It's Roland. Wake up!"

A strangled groan emerged faintly from the room after Roland's second knocking. "I'm up. Just a second," Henry's sleepy voice came from inside.

Roland scowled at the delay and paced back and forth in front of Henry's door impatiently. A door down the hall opened up, and a head popped out to see what was causing the noise. The Sheriff shot an annoyed glance towards whoever it was, and the door hastily slammed shut. *Damn it, it's nearly dawn. I overslept, and it's going to cost Rebecca another day.* He began to pace again, worriedly chewing on his bottom lip as he awaited Henry's arrival.

Henry took his time emerging from the room. He slowly put on his clothes and paused as he pulled on his boots, staring at the door. *Do I really want to do this? Roland knows I'm alive. Alvin knows I'm alive. My work with Singing Rock is through. Why bother with this last spirit?* It was tempting to leave New Haven behind with his work not completed. The town had brought him nothing but bad luck. He had nearly been killed, his head still hurt from the previous day, and his identity had been discovered. But Henry had given his word, and as much as he hated to do it in this case, he intended to keep it. His word was one of the few things of his that had always been good.

Henry made sure to buckle on his holster that morning. He had been loath to wear it before, but too many people now knew he was alive. It was only a matter of time before someone came gunning for him. He caressed the butt of his pistol. The cold, pearl finishing on the handle felt comfortable. It had been five years since he had fired it, but Henry was confident that he could hit anybody who crossed him. He went to the door and took a deep breath before opening it.

Roland stopped his pacing and looked up anxiously when the door opened, his eyes glowing with anticipation. "Doc—I mean, Henry, it's after five. We'd better hurry if we want to make it in time." He moved down the hall towards Singing Rock's room in an effort to speed the procedure.

The Ghost Hunter frowned at the use of his former nickname but didn't say anything about it. At least Roland had corrected himself. Henry stepped over to Singing Rock's door and rapped on it several times. *"Singing Rock, it is almost dawn. Wake up!"* He called out as he continued to knock.

Finally the Navajo responded. *"Stop making so much noise. I am coming,"* he answered irritably as the sound of shuffling footsteps came through the door.

320

Henry turned to the Sheriff. "He's awake, give him a few minutes." He didn't bother pulling down the brim of his hat when he spoke to Roland. It was too late for that. For the first time, he fully saw the worry and nervousness on Roland's face. Before he had only caught a few glimpses as he kept his head lowered. "Don't worry, Roland. We'll get her out of there," he comforted the Sheriff.

Roland barked a coarse laugh. "People keep saying that. I'll believe she's safe when I see it." His mouth curled into a bitter, self-mocking smile, but his eyes remained haunted.

Biting his lip to keep from saying anything else, Henry turned back to the door and waited for Singing Rock. Roland appeared too upset to be consoled with words, and Henry really didn't want to try. He had enough problems on his mind that morning.

An uncomfortable silence formed while the two waited in the hallway. Neither spoke of the conversation they'd had the previous day. Roland was sick with worry for Rebecca, and Henry's lost anonymity weighed heavily on the Ghost Hunter's mind. The way that Roland looked at Henry had changed since the Sheriff had learned the truth. *He looks at me like I'm a legend.* Henry rather liked the way that his reputation had been embellished, but Roland demonstrated rather poignantly how others would react towards him. *Only not as favorably,* Henry thought darkly.

Finally Singing Rock opened the door, and the Navajo emerged looking groggy. He didn't say anything but simply stared at Henry. The Ghost Hunter turned back to Roland. "All right, let's go," he told the anxious Sheriff then hurried his step to keep up with him as Roland moved swiftly down the hall. Roland rushed down the stairs and out of the saloon, forgetting in his haste to lock the door behind him. Henry and Singing Rock barely had time to make it outside before Roland had untied his horse and mounted it.

"Let's go!" Roland shouted as he cantered across the street.

"Slow down, Roland," Henry cautioned as he moved to the tether post where their mounts were tied. He and Singing Rock untied their horses and slowly climbed atop them. The nearly full day of rest had done Henry a tremendous amount of good, and his muscles barely complained as he settled into the saddle.

Roland's horse sensed its rider's anxiety and pranced nervously in the street. Once the Ghost Hunters had mounted their own horses, the Sheriff cried out, "Let's hurry!" Roland spurred his horse, which rose up on its hind legs and pawed at the air. The horse landed with a thud and then launched into a gallop. Singing Rock arched an eyebrow at Henry, but the Ghost Hunter shook his head. *He's gone crazy,* Henry thought to himself. Then he nudged his horse with the boot of his heel and tried to catch up with Roland.

The three of them galloped through the streets of New Haven and out into the surrounding countryside as they raced to get to Rebecca's house before dawn arrived. The sky had yet to lighten that morning, and Henry prayed that they'd make it in time. He hoped to have the whole ordeal over with that morning if possible, although he had his doubts. Bryant was one of the toughest spirits he had fought, and he didn't think Bryant would easily give over Rebecca's spirit. Fortunately he had a few tricks up his sleeve.

When Rebecca's house finally came into view, Roland threw himself off his horse and quickly tied it to a tree before Singing Rock and Henry could even halt their own mounts. Henry once again rolled his eyes at Roland's impatience, but he couldn't fault the Sheriff. He dismounted his horse much more gingerly as Singing Rock did the same.

"What do you think?" Singing Rock asked as he and Henry tied their horses to a tree.

Henry looked up at the house and shuddered involuntarily. Bryant's spirit had hurt him greatly and had come too close to killing him. He stared at the house for a moment then turned back to Singing Rock. *"I want to finish this once and for all. He will not get the best of me this time,"* Henry answered resolutely.

Singing Rock nodded. *"Good. You seem in a better mood this morning. All will be better,"* he tried to comfort Henry.

The Ghost Hunter snorted, shook his head slightly, then finished tying his horse silently. *Nothing will be better. I'll help Roland, then I'll go off on my own,* he thought bitterly as he pulled the knot tight with a stiff tug. Singing Rock put a hand on his shoulder, and Henry jerked it forward. He didn't like other people touching him. He turned back to Singing Rock and was surprised by the look on the Navajo's face.

Sympathetic eyes stared back at him. Singing Rock had already surprised Henry the night before by understanding his problem rather than taking his customary, stoic approach to everything. *"I know you are worried, but do not fear the future. You are still alive after all these years when you should be dead. All will be well."*

Henry tried to be angry with Singing Rock, but he couldn't do it. He owed the Ghost Hunter and felt horrible about planning to leave him before his debt was repaid. Henry wanted Singing Rock to argue with him and be upset over his leaving. It would have made it easier to walk away. He stared silently at the Navajo for a few seconds then nodded without much conviction. *"We will see,"* he replied quietly. Henry had never witnessed Singing Rock being wrong in the entire five years that he had known him, but he didn't hold much hope for things working out. It simply wasn't worth talking about anymore.

Singing Rock paused in the act of tying his horse as if to say something else, but Henry's demeanor caused him to hold his tongue. He knotted the rope securely then clapped Henry on the shoulder. *"Come, it is time to prepare,"* the Navajo said quietly and began walking towards the house.

"Just make it quick," Henry commented softly. The sun was nearing the end of its slumber, and he wanted to enter the Land of Shadows before that happened.

Roland had watched the two Ghost Hunters quietly, an anxious expression on his face, and his eyes lit up as the two men approached. *Damn it, I don't need this,* Henry thought exhaustedly. Facing Bryant's spirit would be difficult enough without having to deal with Roland. It was so tempting to climb atop his horse and be gone from New Haven and all the troubles that had beset him, but he had promised Roland. "Roland," the Ghost Hunter nodded curtly.

"Doc," Roland replied eagerly, not even noticing that he had once again used Henry's old name. "Are you almost ready? It's nearly dawn," he pointed out the obvious. The air had begun to warm. It was still dark, but the sky was now a dark grey instead of pitch black.

Hearing his old nickname grated on his nerves, but Henry kept his face stoic as if he hadn't heard it. "We'll be ready in a minute. Singing Rock has to prepare himself first." His voice sounded cold. *This is the last time I talk to spirits. Before I die, that is.*

Roland glanced at the ground where Singing Rock had taken a seat. The Navajo had laid numerous pouches around him as he sang in a soft chant. He remembered how long the preparations had taken yesterday and knew that time wouldn't permit such a thorough process that day. "Is it going to take long? The sun'll be up soon," Roland pointed out needlessly once more.

A sarcastic reply dwelled on the tip of Henry's tongue, but he kept it in check. He wanted to be left alone, and Roland's frantic behavior and incessant questioning were stoking his temper. He took a deep breath before replying, "No, it won't take long. He knows how much time is left. We'll go inside in a few minutes."

The Sheriff didn't answer but quietly stared at the Navajo before bringing his eyes up to the house. A deep sorrow haunted them, and Roland's simple display of emotions touched the Ghost Hunter. Reaching out, Henry clapped a hand on Roland's shoulder. "Don't worry. We'll get her out of there."

"Thanks, Henry," Roland answered gratefully, this time getting the name right.

Henry looked at the Sheriff one more time and remembered why he had joined Singing Rock in the first place. *I've killed enough men in my time. Maybe I can save one more person before I'm done.* Then he turned around and marched towards Singing Rock. Each boot stomped on the morning soil with a determined crunch. For the time being, Henry had found some absolution in his life, and he meant to follow through with it. *"Singing Rock, it is time,"* he called out loudly. Sometimes the Navajo got so involved in his chants that he ignored everything around him.

Singing Rock opened his eyes and looked up the moment Henry raised his voice. *"I am ready,"* he replied in the flat, emotionless voice to which Henry had grown accustomed. He methodically gathered up his pouches and fastened them to his belt. Then he rose to his feet and waited for Henry to speak.

"Good, then let us begin," Henry responded and started across the grass towards the dark house that awaited them. As he walked, he cloaked himself in the distanced shield that Singing Rock had already assumed. The troubles with Roland, Alvin, and his lost anonymity weighed heavily on his mind, but Henry had practiced assuming that stoic trance for years before he even met Singing Rock. All his worries faded away, and all that mattered were himself, Singing Rock, the house, and Bryant. The house rose ominously before them, but neither Ghost Hunter slowed his calm, deliberate march.

At forty yards the air seemed to shimmer in front of them. *"Mine!"* The voice called out, its single cry shattering the quiet morning air.

Singing Rock reached into one of his pouches and withdrew a handful of yellow powder. Some sifted through his fingers as he held it front of him like a talisman. Henry followed quietly behind as the Navajo led them to the porch.

"Mine!" Bryant screamed at them in fury, sounding like nails scraping over rusted metal.

"Be still!" Singing Rock cried out and threw the powder at the front door. It spread out in a wide cloud, and sparks leapt from the door handle in a blue cascade the moment it made contact.

Bryant's voice wailed painfully from inside. *"Mine! All Mine! Kill! Kill!"* The metallic, shrieking voice of Bryant rose deafeningly into the sky, but neither Henry nor Singing Rock wavered.

Singing Rock grabbed the door knob without the slightest hint of doubt on his face and turned it. Through the murky darkness of the house, a knife streaked through the air straight towards the Navajo, but Singing Rock simply held up his hand with the palm facing outwards. *"Stop,"* he commanded, and the blade bounced back as if it had struck a wall. It snapped in two pieces as it fell to the floor. Singing Rock paid it no heed and stepped into the house with Henry right behind him.

The inside of the house was in shambles. *Spirits wreck great destruction when they are angered,* Singing Rock had told Henry many times, and they had most certainly upset Bryant the previous dawn. As he had the day before, Singing Rock reached into one of his many pouches and pulled out a handful of glowing powder and hurled it into the air. It grew brighter as it billowed outward, forming a faintly glimmering cloud around them.

"Mine! Leave! Mine! Mine!" Bryant screamed at them, but it sounded as if fear had crept into his voice. Several pieces of wood rose into the air as he shrieked his last word. Not a single piece of whole furniture remained in the house, but the remnants of furniture were deadly enough. Wooden shafts and fragments of broken glass lazily spun in the air for a few moments then flew towards the Ghost Hunters.

Singing Rock already stood prepared for the deadly barrage. He clutched a handful of red powder in his right hand and cast it into the air. *"Be gone!"* He shouted. Another cloud formed around them, dimming the glowing sphere that Singing Rock had already created. Each shard of glass and splinter of wood bounced off the slowly settling dust like it was a steel shield.

"Mine!" Bryant's voice echoed through the house.

Without pause or worry, Singing Rock cast another handful of the glowing powder, providing light once more for the two Ghost Hunters. *"It is time. Go quickly,"* the Navajo commanded as his eyes slowly scanned the dark corners of the room, wary of another attack.

Immediately Henry sat upon the floor. A piece of glass cut his leg, but he never felt it as he constructed a doorway to the Land of Shadows in his mind. As he had for the past five years, he envisioned a perfectly still lake with crystal clear water. When every detail had been perfected and the lake appeared real enough to swim in, he pictured it rushing towards him. Closer and closer it came until his hands knifed through the surface. A biting cold penetrated bone-deep, and a shiver coursed through his body as the water rose above his elbows. Once his head shattered the surface, the entire lake faded away, and he fell through the air. Even though he braced himself for the impact, his breath rushed out of him when he hit the hard, ashen ground. He laid on the ground, gasping for air as he replenished his lungs. A cloud of dust rose into the air when he landed, and Henry coughed as he sucked in some of it.

After a few moments of wheezing and hacking, Henry caught his breath and rose to his feet. He cleared his raw throat a few times as he surveyed the land around him. Nothing had changed since his last visit there. A dismal, pale light provided just enough illumination for him to see that Bryant's house stood a quarter-mile away, and Henry quickly marched in its direction.

His footsteps echoed like he was walking on stone. Henry had never dug into the dirt in the Land of Shadows. He wouldn't be surprised if stone did lurk beneath the surface, but he had always imagined that it was Hell instead. None of those thoughts, however, crossed his mind as he approached the house. All of his attention was focused on the dark home rising before him and the spirit inside. Everything else had faded from his thoughts, and all that remained were Rebecca and Bryant White.

Henry didn't hesitate when he reached the door. He leaned back and kicked the door in, wood splintering away at the hinges as it flew inward.

Without missing a step, he continued his steady march inside. His stomach instantly knotted up with nausea as he felt himself lurch forward. He struggled to keep his stomach from bringing up the previous day's lunch. The nausea passed quickly as it always did, and when he looked around, he stood inside the towering walls of Bryant White's house.

No broken furniture littered the floor, just that dull, ashen ground that extended everywhere in the Land of Shadows. Patches of shadows blanketed the inside, providing a break from the monotonous grey. He took his time scanning the room, careful to examine every dark crevice and shadow before moving on. Even with his deliberate scrutiny, Henry nearly missed Bryant. The dark shadow hunched against one of the walls, almost perfectly blending in with the shadows already there.

Henry took his time as he approached Bryant. His last encounter had taught him the consequences of rushing in without pause, and he had no intention of repeating his mistake. At first he thought Bryant would huddle amidst the shadows quietly, but the spirit rose from the ground when Henry drew near. A formless darkness climbed the wall and seemed to hulk nearly ten feet in the air as the Ghost Hunter halted. "Give her to me," he commanded Bryant. Henry had no intention of negotiating with Bryant. His last visit to the Land of Shadows had taught him the folly of that approach.

His demand only enraged the spirit, and black, shadowy tendrils shot from Bryant, waving erratically in the air. *"Never! Mine! All Mine!"* Bryant shrieked at him and floated towards him.

"Bryant White, halt! I bind you!" Henry shouted with all his energy the moment Bryant started moving towards him. His ears rang with the force of Bryant's shrieking, but he wasn't going to let his guard down for even a second.

Bryant's spirit stopped instantly, and the dark tentacles writhed as the spirit tried to move forward. *"Leave! Kill!"* Bryant shrieked, and Henry nearly put his hands to his ears.

Even though the interior of the house was cold, a bead of sweat formed at his temple and slowly rolled down his cheek. Henry let it continue down his neck as he kept his hands poised in front of him. "Bryant White, I command you to release her," Henry repeated, using Bryant's name again. Now that he had confirmed the spirit's true identity, he planned on using it to his advantage. He wouldn't give Bryant the chance to hurt him this time.

The spirit flinched backwards with a deafening shriek. *"Mine! Will kill! Die! All mine!"* Bryant wailed at Henry, but despite its claims the spirit continued its retreat from the Ghost Hunter. It shrunk in size and huddled against the wall, slowly shifting away from Henry.

Henry kept his hands raised and moved towards the spirit. His feet rose and fell in an almost lackadaisical manner. The Ghost Hunter possessed the ability to hurt or even destroy Bryant's spirit, but that wasn't why he had journeyed to the Land of Shadows. "Bryant White, I command you to release her!" He shouted at the spirit as he continued his methodical advance.

Bryant wailed a terrible cry of pain then made a high-pitched humming sound as if he were weeping.

The Ghost Hunter wasted no time pitying the spirit. "Bryant White, I command you to release her! Bryant White, I bind you! Bryant White, I command you to release her! Bryant White!" Roland barked, and the shadow seemed to flinch every time he spoke the name.

"Mine! Leave!" Bryant shouted, but the words sounded more pleading than threatening.

Henry paid the plea no mind and continued to barrage the spirit with sentence after sentence containing the name Bryant. *A spirit's true name can be a powerful thing,* Singing Rock had told him many times, and that point had never been illustrated so well. He did keep some distance between himself and the shadow. Henry could shout Bryant's name from ten feet effectively without risking a freakish accident. All it took was one shadowy tendril to touch him, and he would never be able to leave the Land of Shadows again. "Bryant White, I command you to release her! Bryant White, I bind you!"

That steady stream finally took its toll on Bryant. With a whining howl it rose up, and a faint glow appeared in the middle of its dark form. The darkness around that tiny source of light seemed to fold away to reveal a shining sphere of light floating in the middle of Bryant's spirit. Bryant's voice echoed softly through the house, whimpering like a scared dog.

The Ghost Hunter's eyes lit up when the sphere was revealed. A faint ringing, almost like wind chimes blowing in a gentle breeze, filled the gaps between Bryant's wailing, and Roland knew without a doubt that it was Rebecca's spirit. *A lost spirit in the Land of Shadows sounds like beautiful music,* Singing Rock had told him before. It wasn't the fist time that Henry had seen one either. Still, Bryant did not surrender the glowing ball of light. "Bryant White! I command you to release her! Now, Bryant White!" Henry shouted at the top of his lungs.

The shadowy mass cringed back with a keening whine, and the glowing sphere shot into the air supported by a dark tendril. It hung there for a moment as the shadowy tentacle wavered erratically underneath it. Slowly it drifted towards Henry as Bryant prepared to surrender Rebecca's spirit.

"Put it on the ground, Bryant White! Put it on the ground and back away, Bryant White!" Henry had no intention of letting those dark tendrils get anywhere close to him.

Bryant's voice whined again pitifully as Henry called out his name. The sphere lowered to the ground on the tip of the shadowy tendril. Henry watched carefully, his body tense with readiness. If that dark extension came

327

anywhere near him, he was ready to jump back and shout Bryant's name until his throat was hoarse, but the tentacle continued to lower the glowing sphere. Henry's eyes glowed with victory. Rebecca would be back with Roland in a matter of minutes, and then he could put the entire business behind him. *Almost there. Just a little—*

With a sudden hiss, tiny streams of smoke rose from the dark mass. *Goddamn! Dawn!* Henry cursed as Bryant screamed triumphantly. *"Mine! Mine! All Mine!"* It exulted as the smoke grew thicker and thicker. Quickly the tentacle withdrew, pulling the glowing sphere back into its dark embrace.

"Bryant White, I bind you! Bryant White!" Henry screamed at it, but it was too late.

Smoke and steam covered the shadowy form like a blanket. The spirit underneath rolled and bubbled with a sinister hissing. *"Mine!"* Bryant cried out one last time then the writhing under the smoke ceased. The cloud of smoke slowly dissipated, but Bryant's spirit was gone.

"Goddamn it!" Henry shouted and slammed his fist into the wall. His knuckles swelled painfully, but he barely noticed as his calm cover fell by the wayside. He had been so close only to have the sun cheat him. It wasn't the first time it had happened, but it always frustrated him. The line between dawn and that time just before was drawn quite finely. If he wanted to encounter spirits at their weakest, he had to pay the price when the Sun came sooner than he expected.

He hit the wall another time, finding some small satisfaction in the simple act. Then he took a deep, calming breath. As angry as he had been, it only took several breaths before he reached a calm state. He blocked out Bryant's escape and all his other worries. Even his concerns over Roland drifted away until his thoughts reached a peaceful plateau. Slowly he constructed an image of a door in his mind, carefully envisioning every last detail: the wood, the shiny brass doorknob, the splinters on the rough surface. When each of these had been etched in his mind, Henry pictured his hand reaching out to twist the doorknob. With a lurch he rushed through the door, and bright lights seemed to fly past him. His body felt like it was in the middle of a great windstorm as his stomach convulsed, and then he stopped.

The Ghost Hunter found himself still seated on the littered wooden floor of Bryant's house. Tiny pinpricks of pain ran up and down his legs and buttocks from small shards of glass. During the conflict he hadn't even noticed them, but now that he was firmly rooted back in the real world, they stung quite a bit. His entire body seemed drained of energy, and he wanted nothing more than to catch some more sleep. At least his head wasn't threatening to split in half this time. Bryant had hurt him pretty severely the last time he had journeyed to the Land of Shadows, but Henry had gained the upper hand in the contest.

328

Singing Rock stood nearby, looking just as weary as Henry felt. Heavy bags had formed under his eyes despite the amount of sleep that he had garnered over the last day. He didn't ask if Henry had succeeded in his mission. Singing Rock had been in the house and noted how the sun's rising had coincided with Bryant's disappearance. He leaned against one of the walls and sighed. *"Are you hurt?"* Even in his exhaustion, the Navajo sounded more concerned for Henry's well-being than his own.

"I am fine." Henry waved a hand in the air, and then he stood up. He swore as a splinter of wood pierced his palm. With a lurch he joined Singing Rock and leaned against the wall. Every muscle in his body protested his movement and cried for rest, but the Ghost Hunter ignored them. "Goddamn!" He swore again in weary frustration. "We're never going to get her out of there. I was so close. So Goddamn close. He was giving her spirit to me when the sun came up."

"Patience," Singing Rock answered and put a hand on Henry's shoulder. *"All will be better. Now, let us go outside. You need to speak to the Sheriff. He will be waiting for word of our failure."* The Navajo began to stagger towards the doorway on tired legs.

Henry sighed again. He didn't look forward to facing Roland. The Sheriff had been cordial since discovering his identity, but that might not last after a second failure. With an exhausted groan, Henry followed Singing Rock. It appeared that he would continue to work with Singing Rock for at least another day. The muscles in his legs protested when he moved to the front door, and the lacerations burned like wasp stings. *You can sleep soon,* Henry told himself. The sooner he finished talking to Roland, the sooner he could go back to New Haven and rest.

As soon as Singing Rock and Henry limped out the door, Roland accosted them. His eyes shone with a nearly fanatical anxiety, and tempered hope etched every line in his face. "Is she safe? Did you get her out of there? What happened, Doc? Goddamn it," Roland assailed the two.

My name's Henry. Taking a deep breath, Henry looked Roland straight in the eye. "I almost had her, Roland. Bryant was just about to give her to me when the sun came up. There was nothing I could do," he replied quietly.

That wasn't the answer that Roland wanted to hear. He surged forward and grabbed Henry by the front of his coat. Henry tried to dodge him and break Roland's grip, but either he was too weak from his journey or Roland was too enraged. "What the hell do you mean you didn't get her out of there? You promised, damn you," Roland accused bitterly.

Don't make him any madder, Henry thought to himself. Roland was walking a fine line. He kept waffling back and forth between anxiety and fiery rage. "Roland, listen to me. There was nothing I could do. Bryant—"

329

"No!" Roland cut him off. "You promised you'd get her out of there, but that son of a bitch still has her."

"Listen to me!" Henry barked at the Sheriff. Singing Rock looked at him curiously, but Henry waved his hand slightly. He knew what he was doing and didn't need any help. "I promised I would get her out of there, and I will. Bryant was giving me her spirit when the sun rose. He was lucky it rose when it did, or she'd be awake right now. Don't worry. I'm going back in tomorrow morning, then we'll get her out for sure."

That answer seemed to appease Roland somewhat. He released Henry and stepped back. Henry brushed off the front of his coat and kept a wary eye on Roland. He didn't trust the Sheriff not to react violently again. "I'm sorry, Doc. I know you're trying to help." The Sheriff put a hand over his eyes and sighed forlornly. "But nothing's going right. She'll never get out of there." He looked past Henry into the house, but his eyes appeared lost.

Henry ignored Roland's use of his former name and spoke up immediately. "Stop it!" He snapped, and the Sheriff stopped his lost stare into the house, turning his gaze to the Ghost Hunter. "She's going to get out of there, and then you two can get married. We'll go back in tomorrow, but you can help too."

"Me?" Roland asked softly in a dazed voice.

"Yes." Henry resisted the urge to slap Roland. The Sheriff needed a good stiff jolt back into reality. "I already told you. Find the bastard that killed Bryant, and you can get rid of his ghost. Then you don't even have to wait until tomorrow."

Recognition flickered in Roland's eyes, and a grim smile formed at the corners of his mouth. "Curly," he whispered ominously. "Thanks, Doc. Hopefully that son of a bitch will come to the celebration tonight, and I'll put him down once and for all."

"Good," Henry replied, and he was so relieved to see Roland smile that that he didn't chastise him for repeatedly calling him Doc. He needed to get used to that name again anyway. Rumors would spread quickly, and Roland wouldn't be the only one to call him by his old moniker. "Then let's get back to town. I'm exhausted."

"Sure," Roland replied. His face still looked lost, but his jaw was set determinedly. Rebecca might still be in the Land of Shadows, but he meant to do everything in his power to rectify that situation before dawn. He marched off the porch without looking to see if the two Ghost Hunters followed. He appeared preoccupied with his own thoughts, and Henry had no intention of interrupting them.

"You handled him well," Singing Rock complimented Henry as they gingerly followed the Sheriff.

They moved sluggishly on tired legs, and Henry dreaded the ride back to town. Riding horseback seemed particularly unpleasant, especially with the lacerations decorating his legs, but sleep awaited at the end of their ride. Henry couldn't wait to rest his tired body. "Hurry up, old man. I'm tired," he teased Singing Rock.

The Navajo looked at him with an unamused expression and raised an eyebrow, grunting in response. He didn't speak a word, but his gait quickened.

Henry chuckled. Poking fun at his stoic partner always seemed to bring out a laugh. With his soft laughter echoing across the still morning air, they rushed to catch up with Roland and find the sleep that awaited them back at The Last Frontier.

Chapter Seventeen

Roland sat at the desk inside the station house, grateful for the quiet. Jimmy's presence the previous week had provided an enjoyable way for him to pass the time, but on the morning of the Fourth of July, Roland simply wanted some quiet to collect his thoughts. Pandemonium and mayhem awaited just around the corner. With Zoltan the illusionist, fireworks, and copious amounts of alcohol, tranquility was the last thing he expected. So he made the most of his time that morning and relaxed peacefully.

He stared out at the empty streets and let his mind drift aimlessly, thinking of happier times when he and Rebecca had been able to be together. Sometimes he swore that he could hear her laughter, and he expected to turn and see her dazzling green eyes. The memories of her tore at Roland, making him ball his fists in frustration. He was tired of waiting for her to wake up. Roland loved Rebecca, but more importantly he needed her. She made him whole, and he had felt broken and out of control ever since she had been taken prisoner in the Land of Shadows.

Soon, Rebecca, Roland thought to himself and closed his eyes. He kept imagining Rebecca finally awakening from her slumber over and over again. Sometimes she would leap out of bed, and they would dance through the streets. Other times, they stood joyously before Reverend Thatcher, or Rebecca simply laid in bed, looking up at him with the dazzling smile and radiant eyes that melted his heart.

Then Roland opened his eyes, and his face became grim. He wished that he could sit in the station house all day and daydream about Rebecca, but his job wouldn't allow that. More importantly, Rebecca wasn't just going to wake up out of the blue. She needed help, and Roland intended to be the one to provide it. Doc had told him that his best chance would be to capture Curly, and that's what he planned to do. *Henry. Call him Henry now,* Roland reminded himself.

It was still hard to believe Doc Holliday was alive and well in New Haven, and Roland was glad to have the gunslinger on his side. Nothing had ever beaten the crafty outlaw. Henry had even found a way to cheat death. The Ghost Hunter had all but guaranteed that he would rescue Rebecca the following dawn, and Roland felt inclined to believe him. He had cooled down since leaving Rebecca's house. Frayed nerves and a fiery temper had caused him to blow up at Henry, which he had regretted afterwards. It seemed that his temper had caused him to do many things of late that he regretted, but hopefully it would all be over soon. If Curly didn't show, Roland put his faith in Henry and his Navajo partner. Somehow Rebecca would awaken.

Roland also felt especially guilty about the way he had treated Jack lately. Jack was probably the closest friend he had had over the years. Not many people had stuck by his side through his many exploits. Then again, not many had survived either. He had shirked his duty and left Jack in the dark about a great number of things. Roland intended to turn that around on the Fourth of July. Despite the setback that morning, he felt confident that Rebecca would awaken and that he could resume performing his job with the diligence to which everyone was accustomed. Roland was sure that Jack would be glad for the change of heart.

He had expected Ben to relieve him on the holiday, but Jack came trotting down the street shortly before eight. The deputy hopped off his horse, carefully tied it to the tether post, and then walked up the stairs with a wary expression on his face. "Morning, Jack," he called out brightly as soon as the door opened. "How's Dotty?"

Jack stopped in the middle of walking through the doorway and stared at Roland as if the Sheriff had just grown a third eye. "Morning, Roland. Dotty's fine. How are you?" He asked warily. The deputy stepped inside the door, but he kept staring at Roland as if the Sheriff was up to something.

"I'm fine. Sit down, Jack." The Sheriff smiled broadly and motioned to one of the chairs in front of the desk.

The deputy took a seat, squinting as he scrutinized Roland. Finally his patience ended as Roland kept smiling silently. "What the hell's gotten into you this morning?" He stopped abruptly, and his eyes widened. "Did Rebecca wake up?"

"No," Roland answered, and the thought of her laying in bed so fragile tore at him. But he kept his smile. *Rebecca will be awake tomorrow. Doc told me.* "Not yet, Jack, but I think she'll be awake soon. There have been some good signs lately."

"That's great, Roland." The deputy smiled back at Roland and truly looked happy for him. "I know how hard it's been for you. So when's the wedding going to be?" The deputy's eyes narrowed impishly.

"Don't rush it. She's not awake yet, but as soon as she's healthy enough...assuming she hasn't changed her mind, that is," Roland joked.

"God can only hope she does." Jack rolled his eyes then his face turned serious. "Congratulations, Roland. I wish you both the best. Let me know if there's anything Dotty or I can do to help out."

"Thanks, Jack. I will. Now what the hell are you doing up this early? I didn't expect to see you for another few hours."

"I wanted to get here early. I guess I'm just nervous about the celebration. Kept tossing and turning all night. Dotty finally kicked me out. I thought I'd join you and make sure everything goes well."

"Sounds good to me. Let's go over the plans one more time," Roland suggested. The two discussed the placement of men and what they thought would happen for the next few hours. Neither really needed to hear the plans again, but it was a way to pass the time. Besides, Roland still felt that he had shirked his job, and he enjoyed going over the plans. It made him feel that he was actually the Sheriff. After a while, their talk drifted to Rebecca and Dotty, what Roland planned to do about the wedding, and finally wound up on Zoltan. By the time they had finished debating how good the illusionist's performance would be that evening, people had begun to emerge into the streets. Soon afterwards Ben appeared, striding by everyone else on his long legs.

Roland and Jack headed over to The Last Frontier after the inquisitive deputy had taken over manning the station house. Unlike most mornings, The Frontier already had a large number of customers. The Fourth of July only came once a year, and the town of New Haven liked to milk the celebration for all it was worth. Roland wasn't even surprised to see a few men already drunk. Their number would only grow as the day wore on. A poker game had begun as well. Jimmy sat at the table with his customary mischievous grin. The young man looked up when Roland entered the saloon and nodded, the cocky smile only deepening. The Sheriff scowled but left him alone. Jimmy had promised to behave, and Roland trusted his word. He only hoped that it wouldn't come back to haunt him.

They approached the bar as soon as they entered the tavern. George sat on a stool, chatting with Edmund. The tavern owner looked at Roland and Jack, smiling as he rose from his seat. George looked happier than most days. He remembered the business his saloon had done the previous year, and with the fireworks and Zoltan, George expected to do even better this time around. "Sheriff, Jack. How are you this morning?"

"George," Roland replied and looked around. "I'm fine. I see it's busy already."

The saloon owner's broad smile deepened as he looked around The Frontier. He rubbed his hands together in anticipation. "It's going to be a busy day. Do you expect much trouble tonight?"

"Hell, you know the answer to that as well as I do," Roland answered and shook his head ruefully.

"You're right. So are you ready for everyone?"

"As ready as we can be, George," Jack replied seriously.

"Good. New Haven's safe in your hands then. Can I get you gentlemen anything?"

"Not today," Roland answered with regret. He wouldn't have minded a strong shot of whiskey. The Fourth promised to be a long, tense day, and the Sheriff wouldn't have minded taking some of the edge off. "I'll take you up on that tomorrow," he laughed and clapped the saloon owner on the back amicably.

"Anytime, Sheriff. Just let me know if you need anything."

"Sounds good. I'll talk with you later." Roland tipped his hat then moved towards his table. Jack nodded to George then quietly followed Roland.

The two men took a seat at Roland's table and watched as the saloon's crowd grew over the course of the afternoon. The rest of the deputies trickled in during that time to let the Sheriff know that they were on duty before going back out to patrol the streets. Roland and Jack intended to join them, but there wasn't much cause for them to leave yet. It was still early in the day. Most of the trouble wouldn't occur until far later. For now, there was little excitement. Jimmy looked their way from time to time, but the young gunslinger never approached their table, opting to stay out of the Sheriff's way lest Roland change his mind and kick him out of town.

Doc Sullivan showed up just before three, and Roland accompanied him upstairs to watch him tend to Rebecca. Most traces of his pleasant mood went out the window when he entered her room. The sight of her laying so gaunt and helpless on the bed made Roland want to pound his fist into the wall. He instead watched stony-faced as Doc gave her a brief examination. Roland hoped that Curly would come to town that afternoon. Anger seethed through his veins, and he looked quite forward to taking it all out on the Dark Rider.

Finally the doctor looked up from his patient. He blinked in surprise as he saw the rage on Roland's face. "She's the same as she was yesterday, Sheriff. I don't know how much longer she can hold on like this. Now, if you'd let me bleed her—"

"No," Roland cut the doctor off firmly. He wasn't going to let anybody else hurt Rebecca. One way or another, Rebecca would awaken the following morning. Either Henry and Singing Rock would rescue her from the Land of Shadows, or Roland would find a way to kill Curly. The Dark Rider couldn't hide from him forever.

"But, Sheriff. She needs—"

"I said no," Roland interrupted him once more then folded his arms across his chest pugnaciously.

"All right." Sullivan shook his head in resignation then packed up his medical bag. He looked at Roland before he left. "I'll send Miss Higgins over to attend her later as usual."

"Fine." Roland waved a hand in dismissal. The doctor stared at Roland for a moment, but the Sheriff didn't even notice him as he looked at Rebecca's listless body. His steady gaze never faltered as Doc Sullivan left the room and shut the door behind him.

The rigidness in his stance softened when the door shut, and Roland knelt by the bed. He rubbed a rough knuckle gently across her cheek, cringing at how emaciated her face had become. The cheek bones jutted out grotesquely, and deep black rings circled her eyes. But she still looked beautiful to Roland. "I love you, Rebecca," he whispered softly. Tears welled at the corners of his eyes, and his other hand clenched into a tight fist. The hand gently stroking

Rebecca's cheek, however, never gave the slightest hint at the rage that coursed through Roland's veins.

For five minutes, Roland continued his vigil with Rebecca. He told her about how close they had come to rescuing her and pledged once more that she would soon be free. He talked of his surprise and shock that Doc Holliday was not only alive but was one of the Ghost Hunters trying to wrest her away from Bryant's spirit. Roland kept talking to Rebecca patiently as if she could hear every word. After five minutes, though, Roland couldn't take any more. He was torn between grief for Rebecca and a fiery rage at Bryant and Curly for putting her in her predicament. Leaning over, Roland placed a single kiss on her forehead. "I'll talk to you later. I love you, Rebecca." Then Roland stood with tears in his eyes and left the room.

He stood outside the door for a few minutes, rubbing his eyes and trying to collect himself. Everyone in town knew that Rebecca had fallen ill, but he didn't intend to make a spectacle out of himself when he went downstairs. He stalked down the hallway, his face locked once again into a rigid mask of fury. He slammed his fist against the wall out of frustration, barely noticing the pain, and continued his march.

People immediately noticed the change of expression on Roland's face. He had walked upstairs with his lopsided smile and returned with a look of burning anger. Jack's eyebrows shot up as he saw Roland approaching the table. He didn't say a word as the Sheriff roughly pulled back a chair and took a seat. "You all right?" He asked with concern as soon as Roland sat down.

"I'm fine," Roland replied abruptly. He didn't look at Jack but gazed around the saloon with furious eyes.

Jack studied Roland carefully for a few moments. "What did Doc have to say?" He asked finally.

Roland turned to Jack and for a second there was complete surprise on his face. *How does he know Doc's still alive?* That thought ran through his head briefly before he realized that Jack was talking about Sullivan. He scowled at nobody in particular. "Nothing new. She's still the same," Roland answered bitterly.

"So do you still think she'll wake up soon?" Jack asked quietly.

Roland's eyes began to burn intensely. "You're Goddamn right I do," he spat between clenched teeth.

Jack was taken aback by the harshness of Roland's answer, but he kept his face calm. "Good. Have you talked with Thatcher about when he could marry you two?"

For a moment, Roland's face stayed locked in a stony mask of rage, then gradually it lost its harshness. Roland closed his eyes and took a deep breath, the tension seemingly leaving his body. "No, Jack, I haven't. I should probably get around to that one of these days," he replied softly. Roland was glad that he had Jack for a friend. Sometimes the deputy knew just the right thing to say to take his mind off his worries.

"Yeah, you should." Jack's lips curled into a tiny smile when he saw Roland relax.

The Sheriff silently let the subject drop. He was in a better mood, but he didn't want to think about Rebecca anymore until Curly came back to town or Henry and Singing Rock were ready to return to her house a third time. He looked around the saloon. So far things were peaceful for the holiday. Jimmy looked like he was winning again, but no trouble was breaking out at his table. The rest of The Frontier appeared peaceful as well. There were quite a few drunks already, but he could handle drunks. Violent drunks were what bothered him, and most of those visited The Rattlesnake. He was glad that he had sent Ben and Wade over there earlier. Hopefully they would head off trouble before it even started, although he had small hopes for a completely peaceful evening. *Oh well, that's why they hired me.* One thing, however, caught his eye. "Where the hell's the illusionist?"

Jack glanced around The Frontier then shrugged his shoulders. "I don't know. Probably still sleeping. I imagine he had a long trip to get here."

Roland nodded, but his expression was still suspicious. "I guess you're right, but I thought Alvin would be parading him around town all day. And where's that son of a bitch? I don't like it when I don't know where Alvin is."

"Don't worry too much, Roland. He'll show up sooner or later, and then you'll want him to leave," Jack chuckled.

Roland looked at him for a moment then joined in the laughter. Jack was right. As soon as Alvin showed his polished smiling face, Roland would be ready to see him leave. He just liked knowing exactly what the mayor was up to, especially with the way that Alvin had been acting recently. "You're right, Jack." He looked out the window and saw that the number of people in the streets had increased. They weren't just the typical men working at their jobs but a large number of women and children as well. "Why don't we go out now? The crowds are starting to pick up. There should be quite a few over at the railroad station."

"Sounds good. Let's go." Jack pushed his chair back from the table and rose to his feet.

Roland joined him, and the two left The Frontier. The sun beat down on them as they headed for the railroad complex, and they were soon sweating in the hot summer air. The official part of the Fourth of July celebration didn't begin until eight (, but that didn't stop the people of New Haven from starting earlier. The previous year people had gathered at the railroad station to engage in a pre-celebration festival. There had been dancing, games, and a great deal of drinking. Roland had expected something similar for the current celebration, but even he was surprised by the number of people already gathered. The Sheriff whistled. "Blazes," he muttered.

Jack simply shook his head as they approached the celebration.

The railroad station was the largest construction in New Haven. It was a two-story building with several add-ons connected to it. The top story was used for clerical purposes and for storage of material that needed to be shipped via the railroad. The bottom story was a lounge for people either awaiting shipments arriving on the train or riding it somewhere else. It also housed the local post office. Several business and warehouses had seen the opportunity inherent in the railroad and had attached themselves to the building to be closer to the locomotive. Will's Tavern was a few buildings down the street, obviously hoping to attract travelers and businessmen just stepping off the train. Even Sherry had set up her house close by.

None of that massive collection of structures was what caught their eyes. Several local musicians had banded together and were playing music in a roped-off area where people danced to the simple ragtime melodies. A few enterprising men had set up games nearby, and children swarmed to them with their reluctant parents in tow. Next to the games area, a large stage had been constructed for Zoltan to perform on, and several men worked diligently behind it setting up the fireworks display. Roland hadn't expected anything that grand to take place. Overall, there must have been at least two hundred people already celebrating in front of the station. The Sheriff had expected maybe fifty or sixty at the early hour.

"I guess Alvin's magician did the trick this year," Jack commented quietly.

The Sheriff didn't answer but continued to study the throng of people. They were a varied bunch, from young to old. Some were drunk, while others appeared completely sober. A platoon of Sherry's girls were out in force, hoping to lure a few customers before nightfall. He wasn't even surprised to see Sherry herself mingling with the crowd. Some people shunned her, while others greeted her with a smile, obviously having patronized her bordello before. "Damn, I'm glad we came out now." Roland squinted as he caught sight of a familiar figure walking their way. "There's Morgan," he announced and pointed at the deputy.

"Good. We need all the help we can get," Jack commented in a relieved tone. The wily, old deputy would be a boon in controlling the Fourth of July crowd.

Morgan met them just outside the roped-off dance area. He shook his head in bafflement. "Can you believe these people?" He asked, jerking a thumb towards the thirty or so people dancing.

"Damn it, what the hell are they thinking? Dancing in this heat?" Sweat already rolled down Roland's neck from the hot temperatures, and he didn't understand how anybody would want to dance in the brutal summer heat.

"You've got me." Morgan shrugged his shoulders then wiped his forehead, which was damp with sweat. "I was about to send someone after you two. This just started up about an hour ago. At this rate, we'll have the whole town here soon." He paused to spit on the ground. "I'm all for a good celebration, but mark my words: there will be trouble before the night is over."

Jack nodded. "I think we all counted on it, Morgan, but we should be able to keep it under control. Where's everyone right now?"

Morgan tapped his chin for a moment and squinted as he tried to remember. "Let's see. Wade and Simon are at The Snake. William is riding around somewhere in this mess, and Ben and Simon are keeping an eye out for Riders. I take it Phillip's still at the station house?"

"I didn't check on him, but he's always there," Roland answered. With the large number of people already celebrating, Roland quickly reconsidered where he wanted his deputies. "Jack, go get Simon and Ben. I want as many people here as possible."

"Are you sure about that, Roland? What about keeping an eye out for Carlos?" Jack asked, his eyes concerned.

"I'm not too worried about Carlos or the others. If they do come to town, they'll go straight to The Snake, and Wade can get help. Tell Wade I want him here by seven though. There might be trouble at The Snake later on, but the whole damn town will be here to see Zoltan tonight," the Sheriff answered.

Morgan nodded slightly as Sheriff Black answered, obviously glad that he was enthusiastic about his job again. The grizzled deputy never complained like Jack did, but he could still disapprove silently. "Sounds good to me. Jack?" Morgan asked the other deputy.

"I guess so. I'd still like to have a look out for the Riders. If they come to town to pick a fight, we won't have any warning."

"You know them better than that, Jack," Roland waved a finger at the deputy, and his mouth curled into a lopsided grin. "If they come to town, they'll get drunk before they do anything. Sound good?"

"All right, you convinced me. I'll go get them now." Jack tipped his hat to both deputies then turned towards the station house to collect a horse.

"I'm going to walk around and talk to some people, Morgan. Get me if there's any trouble," Sheriff Black told the deputy. The deputies could control the crowd more effectively by splitting up to cover more area than banding together in groups. Morgan nodded and turned back towards Will's Tavern, which was across from the dance area. Roland watched him leave then went to mingle with the crowd. He had just entered the fray when he spotted a welcome face. "Dennis," he called out.

The hulking blacksmith turned at hearing his name, and his broad face broke into a smile when he spotted Roland. "Sheriff, it's good to see you. It's been a long time," he greeted and held out a hand.

Shaking the proffered hand, Roland nearly grimaced as Dennis crushed it within his massive grip. Dennis didn't intend it. Roland doubted that the blacksmith had a violent bone in his body, but sometimes Dennis forgot how strong he was. "It's good to see you too. How's Betty?"

"She's good." He stopped and looked around carefully. "Just wanted to make sure she wasn't around," Dennis whispered. "I'm almost finished with her sculpture. It should only be a few more days. You should come by and see it."

"I'll try to come by, Dennis. I've been busy lately," Roland explained and realized how long it had been since he had last visited the blacksmith. For most of his tenure as Sheriff, Roland had stopped by the smithy every morning on his way to the station house. It had been part of his morning routine. His grief over Rebecca falling ill didn't only pertain to her. To a lesser degree, he also wanted to have the rest of his life back on track again. "So, did you shut the shop down for the day?"

The blacksmith chuckled and slapped a hand on his knee. "Didn't have no choice, Sheriff. All the boys wouldn't stop talking about the celebration. I had to give them the day off." He stopped and looked a bit bashful. "Besides, Betty wanted to come out today."

"I understand," Roland commented softly and clapped the blacksmith on the shoulder. "Well, I need to get going. There are a lot of people I need to talk to."

"Sure. Don't let me keep you. I just wanted you to know Betty and me pray for Miss White every night. She's a fine woman. I hope she gets better soon," Dennis told Roland before he could leave.

"Thanks, Dennis. That means a lot. Talk to you later." Roland tipped his hat and wandered back into the crowd. He made a mental note to himself to stop and see the blacksmith sometime soon. Roland hadn't noticed how much he missed his morning visits with Dennis. It seemed like he was missing a lot of things in his life that he used to enjoy.

Sheriff Black stopped and chatted with quite a few people over the next hour. He received a few apprehensive and nervous reactions when he approached some, but everyone quickly overcame their fears as soon as they spoke a few words with the Sheriff. Roland sometimes enjoyed having people frightened of him, but he didn't want to overdo it. He stopped in Will's Tavern, visited with a few people standing in the comfortable shade offered by the railroad station, and even ventured over to the game area.

After competing at a game that involved tossing a wooden ring around a spike ten feet away, Roland had finally had enough. The summer heat was killing him, and he needed to find some respite in the shade. He waded his way through the increasing crowd towards the comfort of the railroad station. Stepping into the shade, Sheriff Black exhaled in relief. His shirt was damp with sweat, and he felt slightly woozy. He was having a great time, but Roland would be greatly relieved when the weather turned cooler.

"Sheriff," a sultry voice called out, and Roland turned towards the speaker already knowing who it was. He cringed a bit, but it was too late to avoid her.

Madam Sherry, owner of New Haven's only brothel, stood just behind him. She wore a low-cut red dress and an ornate silver necklace. Rings adorned each of her fingers, and a pair of earrings dangled from each of her ears. Roland had never spotted Sherry without her full regalia of jewelry, but in addition to those decorations she was a stunningly beautiful woman. Lustrous black hair hung down to her shoulder blades in think ringlets. Her eyes were a deep blue and, in Roland's opinion, came in second only to Rebecca's. She was in her early thirties but had kept herself in marvelous shape over the years, unlike many of the madams he had met during his years of gunslinging.

"Sheriff Black, it's wonderful to see you again. My heavens, how long has it been?" Sherry claimed to have come from the South. The Sheriff doubted many of the stories that she told him, but her thick accent more than proved that she was telling the truth on that account.

"Sherry." Roland tipped his hat, and his mouth settled into its customary lopsided grin. He made sure to keep his eyes focused on her face and not allow them to dip towards her plunging neckline. "It's been a while. How have you been?" He couldn't help smiling around her. It was hard not to around Sherry.

"Fabulous." She leaned towards Roland and whispered to him conspiratorially. "This weather has been driving the men in like wildfire. You wouldn't believe how many have been in."

"I'm not too surprised by anything anymore." Roland knew exactly how much business was going on at her place. He had seen her women attracting business at The Frontier. Furthermore, he had visited a few establishments like Sherry's in his youth and was well aware of how busy they could be at times.

Sherry ignored his flippant remark and put a finger to her lips. She looked at him speculatively, her eyelids lowering seductively. "Are you sure you don't want to come see personally how busy things have been? I'd be all too happy to show you."

Roland shook his head. He had told Sherry many times that he wasn't interested, but he guessed that was part of the allure. Maybe if he hadn't met Rebecca, he might have succumbed to Sherry. "No thanks, Sherry. I'm sure you'll find someone, though. You always do."

"You're no fun," Sherry replied and pouted. She blinked a few times and looked up at him demurely. "Are you sure? I can show you a good time."

"I'm sure. Enjoy the celebration. I need to keep an eye on things." He tipped his hat to her and went outside to join the festivities. The scorching air hit him like a furnace as he once again stepped into the summer heat, but Roland couldn't help chuckling. For too many days he had holed himself up in The Last Frontier and ignored everyone else. In the span of a few hours he had seen Dennis, Sherry, and a great deal of the rest of the town. For Roland it seemed as if his life had paused for the past few weeks, and he could finally start living again. Rebecca would be awake shortly after dawn, and then Roland could truly begin celebrating. His chuckle deepened into a hearty laugh as his mood brightened considerably.

As he circulated among the crowd, Roland spotted a familiar couple by the dance area. Still grinning, he made his way towards them. "Jack, Dotty," he called out.

"Roland," Jack replied. He stood by his wife's side with an arm wrapped around her shoulders. Dotty smiled as Roland walked up, and it was a welcome sight for the Sheriff. It had been too long since he had seen her. Dotty was a good woman and perfectly suited for Jack. She was attractive, but unlike so many of the other women that he had met Dotty had a rough edge underneath her features. She was completely at ease being married to a deputy and never seemed bothered by the danger associated with his job. The two had been married for over twenty years, and Roland had seen few couples better matched.

"Hello, Roland. How are you today?" Dotty asked. Like her husband, she rarely called him Sheriff, preferring to use the name she had always called him.

"I'm doing fine," Roland answered with a mischievous twinkle forming in his eye.

Jack look at him suspiciously. Roland typically had that smug expression after doing something incredibly stupid. "What the hell's gotten into you?"

"I ran into Sherry," the Sheriff answered drolly and shook his head ruefully.

Dotty and Jack exchanged a quick look, then Jack stared at Roland inquisitively. "Really. How is she?"

"She's the same as ever." Roland suddenly noticed the expressions on their faces and realized what they were thinking. "Nothing like that happened. We just talked for a while, that's all." He straightened his shoulders. "Give me some credit, Jack," Roland told his deputy with a faint air of dignity.

"Sorry. Forget I asked," he apologized then cast his gaze over the gathered people. "It's getting pretty crowded out here."

The crowd had swelled to over five hundred people, and it would nearly triple by the time Zoltan performed. "It's almost six. It'll be dark soon, and everyone'll be out by then. Alvin will be happy with himself. Goddamn snake," Roland added.

The deputy barked out a laugh, and even Dotty smiled in amusement. She had been around the two long enough to know their feelings about the mayor. "Actually, I saw him at Will's about fifteen minutes ago. He was trying to put more votes in his pocket," Jack commented.

"Son of a bitch," Roland swore. The lopsided grin faded from his face, and a sneer replaced it for a few moments as he gazed at the saloon. When he turned back to Jack, his expression was serious. Quickly he ran through his deputies in his head. "Where's Wade?"

Jack smoothed down the corners of his mustache. "He's keeping an eye on The Snake. Why?"

"I want him to keep an eye on Alvin tonight," Roland answered in a gravelly voice. His head turned back to the saloon. He was still in a good mood, but something about the way Alvin had acted the last few days grated at him. Roland just couldn't shake the suspicion that the mayor was up to something that night.

"What?" Jack looked surprised over the Sheriff's answer. "Roland, we're spread thin enough as it is. We don't have any men to spare watching Alvin." He paused for a moment and looked at Roland speculatively. "Do you know something I don't?"

"Nah," Roland waved his hand. He turned away from the saloon, and his mouth curled into its trademark grin. "Don't worry about it. It's the Fourth of July. Even Alvin won't cause any trouble tonight." Alvin was probably just trying to scare him. Despite some misgivings, Roland shrugged off the issue.

"Good then. If you'll excuse us, Roland, my husband owes me a dance." Dotty usually kept quiet when Roland and Jack talked about work, but as soon as they were done, she jumped in with her two cents' worth.

"Sorry, Roland, but duty calls." Jack leaned over and kissed Dotty on the forehead. "Shall we?" He extended an elbow to escort his wife into the dance area.

"Have fun. I'll see you later," Roland bade farewell to the pair then circulated among the crowds again. The dance area was filled, as were the games and contest sections. Already he spotted quite a few drunk men and cringed when he thought about how many more he and his men would have on their hands later. As much as he was enjoying the day, Roland was ready for the fireworks and magic show to begin. The sooner they were over, the sooner he could deal with the inevitable trouble that would follow and the sooner he could return to Rebecca's house with the Ghost Hunters. But Roland took it one step at a time. A return to Rebecca's house was quite far off, and it would do no good to start brooding over it again. Continuing to make his way through the celebration, Roland stopped to chat with a number of people as he passed the time away, waiting for the big acts of the night to start.

The sun finally began to lower, providing the town with a much-needed respite from the brutal heat. Roland's shirt was damp with sweat, and he breathed a sigh of relief as the sun disappeared behind the Rockies. His satisfaction was short-lived, however, as the celebration truly began in earnest. Over the next hour, the amount of alcohol consumed went through the roof, and a few isolated events took place. Wade had left the Rattlesnake and relocated at Will's Tavern. He hauled away two men who got into a fight inside the saloon, and Morgan escorted a man to the jail for firing a pistol into the air. The older deputy had a serious, businesslike expression on his face, while Wade had a jubilant expression like he was happy to be involved with something even remotely dangerous. The gunshot had frightened Roland. The last thing they needed was a shoot-out on the Fourth of July. Roland was convinced there would be injuries during the celebration, but as long as he could prevent any deaths from occurring, he would be happy. As much as Wade would love to have someone to test his skills against, Roland would be quite content to have a peaceful evening.

After those two events, people acted a little more sensibly, but Roland knew that was only temporary. There were too many drunks in the streets of New Haven. They all wanted to be on their best behavior until the magic show was over. This was New Haven's greatest celebration ever, and nobody wanted to miss any of it. The real trouble would begin the moment Zoltan completed his performance. Hopefully it would scare a few people out of doing anything stupid for a while.

Roland kept patrolling the area with his dour face, nodding as he passed people. All of his deputies continued to patrol as well, and there were no further incidents as everyone waited impatiently for the fireworks to begin at eight o'clock.

At half past seven, Roland ran into Alvin. The mayor was busy chatting with several men, and his customary political grin was locked firmly on his face. Even in the summertime Alvin seemed unfazed by the hot weather. Not a single bead of sweat dotted his forehead, and his hair remained perfectly combed, a white mane that seemed impervious to whatever the elements threw at it. His grip tightened on the pommel of his cane as Roland strolled up to him and his guests, but that was the only sign of displeasure that he exhibited.

"Evening, gentlemen. Alvin." Roland tipped his hat. The Sheriff had been tempted to ignore Alvin and continue circulating among the crowd but decided against it. He hadn't seen Alvin the entire day, which bothered him slightly. Alvin had been acting far too strange lately, and Roland wanted to make sure that no trouble was laying in wait.

"Roland," Alvin stated flatly. His smile never slipped an inch, but Roland could tell that the mayor was clearly not happy to see him. "What can I do for you?" He asked politely. Alvin would never be rude in front of so many people.

"I just wanted to check on a few things with you. If you gentlemen don't mind." Roland's eyebrows rose inquisitively. The six men nodded and moved away from Roland and Alvin.

Alvin watched the men scatter away then turned back to Roland, the smile dropping from his face. "What do you want, Roland? I'm busy tonight. I don't have time to deal with you."

"I wanted to see how everything was going. Are the fireworks on time?" He asked innocently.

"Don't worry about the fireworks. They're taken care of," Alvin replied condescendingly.

Roland's lip curled into its lopsided grin almost automatically. *Play it that way, you son of a bitch.* The mayor's tone grated at him, but he was determined to avoid making a scene with Alvin. He had been in too good of a mood all day to let him ruin it now. "Good. What about the magic show? I haven't seen Zoltan all day long." The illusionist's costume was too flamboyant to miss, and if Zoltan had shown up at the celebration area, he would have been mobbed by the people there.

"It will be on time," Alvin pointed out insistently. "Zoltan's been busy preparing for the performance. Leave all that to me. I know what I'm doing."

"I just wanted to be sure, Alvin. I mean, this is all your planning. I wouldn't want any of the celebration to be less than perfect." Roland forced his voice to sound cheerful. It was too easy to let Alvin get under his skin.

Alvin leveled him with a withering gaze. "Trust me. Everything will happen tonight *exactly* as I planned. If that's all, I have other business to attend to." A smirk formed on Alvin's face again, and he watched Roland with a knowing expression.

Damn, what the hell are you up to, Alvin? Roland was tiring of that knowing smirk. He knew Alvin was up to something, and he was growing weary of trying to guess what it was. Sooner or later, Alvin would spring his little surprise, and Roland would feel a lot better if he knew what to expect. He seriously doubted, however, that he could drag it out of the mayor unless he pulled a gun on him again, which wasn't a particularly unpleasant idea either. Roland's eyes narrowed as he stared back at Alvin. "Fine, I'll see you later. Just remember, I've got all my men out here tonight, and everyone in town knows this celebration is your affair. I wouldn't do anything to mess it up."

"Like I said, I know *exactly* what I'm doing." He flashed that smirk a moment longer then almost magically donned the polished, oiled smile that he customarily wore. In the blink of an eye, Alvin had resumed his suave, debonair demeanor and looked ready to mingle with the voters again. "Bye, Roland," the mayor dismissed Roland then waved a hand at him derisively. He turned and sought out voters to put in his pocket, striking up a conversation almost immediately.

Roland watched him curiously. *What the hell are you doing, Alvin?* He still wondered if the mayor was trying to scare him or was actually plotting against him. Finally he shrugged his shoulders. There was nothing more that he could do short of pointing a gun at Alvin to drag the truth out of him. He would just have to stay alert and be ready for whatever trouble Alvin tried to cause. He decided to stop roaming the celebration area and chose a good vantage point for the firework display. It also allowed him to keep an eye on Alvin.

As it grew closer to eight o'clock, the mayor ended his chatting and headed behind the stage. Several men had worked the majority of the day to set up the fireworks. Roland had stopped by to watch but had no idea what they were doing. It seemed to involve tying a bunch of strings together and pouring powder into paper cylinders. The mayor conferred with the men for a few moments then climbed onto the stage.

A quietness instantly rippled through the crowd as they realized the real celebration was about to begin. Everyone had enjoyed the singing, dancing, and playing, but that had only been the appetizer before the main course. Alvin stood on the stage with his arms raised dramatically and a self-congratulatory grin on his face. He seemed to savor the rapt attention being lavished upon him. Roland had never seen Alvin look smugger than he did that night. *I hope the damn things won't go off.* Roland would hate for the town not to have a perfect celebration, but it would look bad for Alvin. It would certainly take some of the wind out of the mayor's sails.

"When are the fireworks gonna start?" Someone yelled from the crowd.

Alvin's face curled into a polished smile. He was completely in his element. Roland knew that he was relishing every moment in front of the large crowd. He had their undivided attention and was providing them with something that they desperately wanted. "In just a moment, friend," the mayor answered and paused once more. He folded his hands together and assumed his earnest expression. "Ladies and gentlemen, I know how much this town loves to celebrate the birth of our great country, but tonight I've tried to make it the best celebration that New Haven has ever seen. Is everyone out there having a good time so far?"

A loud cheer arose from the crowd. Alvin basked in the brief adulation before continuing. "Up first, we have a fabulous firework display." He stopped and raised both hands in front of him. "I want to warn everyone here to stay back from the stage. There will be a great deal of smoke, and somebody could accidentally start a fire. I don't want anyone hurt tonight. After the fireworks, Zoltan the Illusionist will be on stage to perform acts of magic and illusion." A loud burst of applause greeted Alvin's second announcement. He looked even more pleased with himself and could barely contain the smirk on his face. As much as Roland disliked him, Alvin was probably the most popular man in New Haven at that hour. "All right then, without anything further, let the fireworks begin." He bowed once to the crowd and was rewarded with a thundering ovation.

Roland hated to see the mayor's ego get stroked so heavily, but he had to admit that Alvin had done a masterful job setting up the celebration. Even he was awaiting the fireworks with a great deal of anticipation, and he wanted to see Zoltan even more. Alvin stepped down from the stage and took a safe vantage point nearly fifty feet away. An uneasy hush fell over the crowd as they all waited for the fireworks to begin. For nearly a full minute, there was silence. Gradually a buzz of conversation rose over the crowd as people speculated on what was delaying the fireworks. Then without warning a loud hiss came from the stage, and an immediate silence rippled from the front to the back of the crowd. Roland's hand came up and rubbed his chin anxiously as he watched the stage along with nearly every other person in town.

Suddenly there was a shrill whistle, and something shot into the air from behind the stage. Roland found himself holding his breath as he looked up at the sky. For nearly two seconds he waited until he was rewarded with a flowery cascade of blue light nearly two hundred feet in the air. A quiet muttering of approval and applause rippled through the crowd as more and more fireworks were launched. Sometimes as many as four bursts filled the air at one time, all of a different color. Some flared out like giant sunflowers, while others shimmered downward in a cascade of sparks. One after another exploded in the summer sky, never giving the audience a chance to catch its breath. Roland was stunned by how spectacular it was, but his enjoyment wasn't complete. He wanted Rebecca by his side to see the fiery bursts in the sky. Rebecca would have loved the display. He could see her staring up with her dazzling smile and laughing joyfully at each explosion. *I love you, Rebecca White.* Roland liked the fireworks, but he wasn't fully able to enjoy them as half of him rested with a sick young woman wasting away at The Last Frontier.

After nearly ten minutes of the presentation, the last of the fireworks detonated in a gigantic burst of red light. The crowd waited until the last ember faded before giving it a thunderous ovation. Alvin turned to watch the crowd, breathing in their adulation. Despite his disdain for Alvin, Roland continued to clap. The mayor had brought in all the fanfare only to keep votes in his pocket, but Roland had to give him credit. So far, it was one of the best celebrations that he had ever attended, and the best was yet to come. Even after the applause died down, Alvin still had a smugly satisfied expression on his face. Roland had a quick urge to knock the smile right off his face, but he decided to leave

347

the mayor alone. He was in a good mood, and Alvin *had* conjured up a marvelous celebration.

Turning back to the crowd, Roland let his eyes roam over all the people, looking for signs of trouble. All of his deputies were present, which was a welcome sight. Later on, he would need all the help that he could muster. Morgan looked grim and ready to stop anyone from getting into trouble, while Jack appeared almost giddy as he stood smiling next to Dotty. Wade had a lazy smile and anxious look in his eyes that gave Roland some slight cause for worry. He didn't need Wade to start a fight. William was naturally chatting to one of Sherry's girls, while Ben seemed engaged in an animated conversation with a few townsfolk who looked like they would rather be anywhere else. Robert watched the proceedings with a stern look on his face, appearing like a hawk with his crooked nose. Even Simon had stayed. Roland hadn't been sure about him; Sarah still hadn't given birth and was due any day. But the wide-eyed look of wonder on Simon's face clearly demonstrated what he thought of the fireworks.

It was a relief having his full complement of men on duty, but that wasn't what he was looking for. It was the rest of the people in the crowd who interested Roland. They were the ones who would be causing trouble, not his deputies. His eyes ran over the crowd, but nothing gave him cause for alarm. The sight of Jimmy made him pause briefly to study the young gunslinger. Jimmy wore a huge grin, not the typical cocky smirk that he usually flashed about. Roland kept forgetting that he was really just a kid, a kid who wanted to make a name for himself, but still just a kid who smiled like an idiot after watching fireworks. He decided that Jimmy wasn't going to cause any trouble and quickly moved on. Everybody else seemed fine. He did see Sherry flirting with numerous men, Dennis watching the festivities with his wife and children, and Matthew Brady taking notes for the following day's *New Haven Gazette*. It seemed that for at least the next hour there would be no trouble for Roland and his men.

There was a sudden burst of applause and nearly every head in the crowd turned towards the back edge of the gathering. Roland craned his neck to gain a better vantage point as the clapping grew louder, but he couldn't catch a glimpse of what everyone was cheering about. Neither could several people around him, judging from the baffled expressions on their faces, but they continued to applaud with the rest of the crowd. A ripple made its way through the center of the crowd until Roland finally saw what had drawn everyone's attention, and then he too began to clap along with everyone else.

Zoltan the Master Illusionist strode through the center of the crowd like a king. He wore black trousers and a white silk shirt with the same red cape billowing out behind him. A black top hat sat on his head, and his white hair and beard glowed. Roland could see that Zoltan obviously loved the attention being lavished upon him. Like Alvin he puffed up self-importantly, feeding on the cheers of the crowd.

Roland turned his head to look at the mayor, and the familiar lopsided grin appeared on his face. Alvin wanted to gain popularity from the evening's events, and he had certainly done so. Yet still, he didn't look happy. Roland was happy to see that the mayor had a look of unhidden envy painted on his face as someone else received all of the attention. *Ha, ha, you son of a bitch. If only everyone else knew you like I do.* Alvin eyes suddenly shifted and stared at Roland, and almost instantly the look of envy was replaced with a broad smile, which bothered Roland. It wasn't Alvin's polished, public smile, but rather he seemed to be smiling evilly like he knew something that Roland didn't. The mayor held the stare for a few more seconds, and then the familiar public expression once again adorned his face as he turned and applauded Zoltan.

The illusionist continued to parade himself regally through the crowd, nodding politely to nobody in particular as he made his way towards the mayor. Once he stood by Alvin, the two began to converse quietly as the applause gradually died down. Roland saw Zoltan's assistant busily sliding props around the stage, but he wanted to make sure that the show was going to start on time. There were too many people gathered in front of the stage, and Roland didn't want to see how rowdy they would act if the show was late. He rubbed at his prickly chin for a moment then approached the spot where the mayor and illusionist were talking.

A small number of men, mostly richer businessmen, also chatted with Alvin and Zoltan, but Roland paid them no mind. "Alvin," he called as he neared the gathering. "Will the show still go on time?"

Alvin looked at him in annoyance. "Yes, Roland. It will. Now if you'll excuse us?"

Roland ignored Alvin's dismissal and continued speaking. Most of the men standing with Alvin and Zoltan looked uncomfortable hearing Alvin and Roland exchange words, and Zoltan simply looked upset for not being the center of attention anymore. "Are you sure? The stage doesn't look ready yet." He fished his timepiece out of his coat and peered at it. "It's supposed to start in half an hour."

The mayor's jaw clenched, and he appeared to struggle for a moment to regain his composure. "The show will be ready at the top of the hour. Now if you will *excuse* us," the mayor dismissed.

"Sure, Alvin, whatever you say," Roland replied insultingly and smiled as he saw Alvin's eyes narrow angrily. He tipped his hat. "Gentlemen. Zoltan, good luck. I look forward to your performance."

The illusionist didn't appear to understand the undercurrent of animosity. He puffed up immediately at Roland's compliment, and a wide smile lit up his face. "Thank you. I promise you will not be disappointed."

Roland walked away from the group, chuckling quietly. Once again, he seemed to have gotten the better of Alvin, but toying with Alvin grew tiresome.

Thoughts of Rebecca kept creeping into his mind, but Roland quashed them every time. It was the first day that he felt like his old self in over two weeks, and if he gave into worrying over Rebecca, he'd be right back where he started. He just wanted to watch the magic show, make it through the night safely, and then return to her house at dawn with the Ghost Hunters. *Don't think about it,* Roland kept telling himself as he tried to avoid looking at his watch every two minutes to see how much further away dawn was.

In the meantime he tried to enjoy himself. The fireworks had been a great deal of fun, but Roland had hated watching them by himself. He didn't want to observe Zoltan's magic show the same way. Scanning the crowd, Roland quickly spotted the pair that he was looking for and walked their way. If he couldn't be with Rebecca, he would watch the show with his best friend.

"Roland," Jack greeted as the Sheriff waded through the crowd towards them.

"Jack, Dotty," Roland called out in return and smiled. He was glad that he had persuaded his old friend to come to New Haven. The last few weeks had been difficult enough. Without his old friend around, Roland wasn't quite sure how he would have made it.

"Roland, what did you think of those fireworks?" Dotty burst out. Her eyes were wide with excitement, and a huge smile spread across her face.

"I thought they were incredible," Roland answered quietly. *You should have seen them, Rebecca. They were beautiful.* "What did you think?"

Dotty clapped a hand to her chest. "I thought they were the best thing I've ever seen. I can't wait for the magic show," she gushed enthusiastically. From the appearance of the rest of the crowd, she wasn't the only one who had thoroughly enjoyed the first part of the celebration.

"Yeah, Alvin's outdone himself this year," Roland commented dryly then chuckled to himself. He and Jack knew that the mayor had brought the celebration to New Haven only to buy himself the election, but either nobody else recognized that or they simply didn't care.

Jack smiled briefly then glanced at the stage. "Do you think it will start on time?"

"It should. I just talked to Alvin, and he said it would." Roland squinted at the stage, and his expression became wistful. "I can't help wanting it to start late or for the performance to be horrible. It would ruin Alvin's little show."

350

"Roland!" Dotty exclaimed in surprise. "That's not nice. Everyone's been looking forward to this celebration for the past two weeks."

"I know. I was just kidding," Roland answered then flashed his lopsided grin. "So how good do you think Zoltan will be?"

"If he's as good as those fireworks, this place will go crazy," Jack answered.

"No," Dotty answered firmly. "Nothing can top the fireworks. They were incredible."

"I don't know about that. You didn't see him perform at The Last Frontier," Roland pointed out. The three of them continued to argue over how impressive Zoltan's performance would be as the time approached nine. Not once did Roland's mind drift to thoughts of Rebecca as he talked with his old friend.

As the time reached nine o'clock, a hush spread over the crowd as they watched the final preparations taking place on stage. A red curtain hung over the back half of the stage, and Zoltan's assistant was busily moving something behind it. In front of the curtain, a large wooden box and a chair sat upon the stage. Other than those three things, the audience had no idea what to expect when the illusionist took the stage. Roland glanced towards the mayor and was surprised to see Zoltan wasn't with him. The mayor, however, seemed pleased with everything and watched the stage with a self-satisfied smile on his face.

Roland leaned over towards Jack to comment on the mayor's expression when Alvin approached the stage. He quickly climbed on top and looked out over the impressive crowd. Alvin breathed deeply, savoring the absolute attention that he received. His eyes roamed over the crowd, his smile growing deeper every second. They stopped when they fell on Roland, and his smile turned wicked for a few moments. *What the hell are you up to?* Roland thought to himself, but Alvin's eyes had already moved on.

"Ladies and gentlemen. I hope you've enjoyed the festivities this evening." He paused and rubbed his hands together as a thunderous cheer erupted from the crowd. Roland rolled his eyes, but nearly everyone else clapped enthusiastically. "Thank you, thank you," Alvin beamed when the applause finally died down. "There's one more treat in store for you tonight. From Paris, France, I present Zoltan the Master Illusionist!" He yelled loud enough for everyone in the entire crowd to hear.

Once again a huge ovation answered Alvin's announcement. He smiled deeply and let his eyes roam over the crowd one more time. His eyes paused on Roland again, and the mayor's eyebrows lowered hatefully as he stared at the Sheriff. After leveling Roland with that brief malicious stare, he exited the platform.

For a few moments, complete silence covered the assembled crowd. Even Roland found himself holding his breath in anticipation of Zoltan's performance, but the illusionist did not appear. An expectant buzz spread throughout the crowd. Jack tapped Roland on the shoulder, and the Sheriff turned his head towards his old friend.

"Where the hell is he?" Jack looked just as anxious as everybody else.

"I don't know. I'm sure—" Roland broke off as a loud explosion erupted on the stage.

When Roland turned his head, Zoltan stood in the middle of a dissipating cloud of smoke. The illusionist kept his back rigid as the smoke drifted away, seemingly oblivious to the cheers that greeted his entrance. Finally he took a deep bow, sweeping the corners of his red cape upwards, causing it to ripple impressively. "Thank you!" He cried to the audience, and like Alvin he wore a self-satisfied smile. Roland didn't mind that one quite as much.

Zoltan basked in the applause until it died out, and then he began his show. "In Europe, we have heard many stories of the great gunfights of the Wild West." Zoltan's voiced echoed over the crowd as everybody kept silent, raptly listening to the illusionist's every word. "Many people feared gunfighters. I have seen women faint from the gruesome stories of skilled gunfighters. But I have never feared a bullet. For I am invincible." Zoltan held his hands up high, and Roland lifted an eyebrow in amusement.

"Let me show you what I mean." Zoltan stepped back and held both arms towards the red curtain behind him. Moments later, his assistant walked through carrying a small, wooden box. The illusionist took it from him and opened the box, keeping its contents hidden from the audience. He waited as everyone craned their necks, anxiously waiting to see what was inside. "I will prove I am invincible with the contents of this box," he announced and put his hand inside.

The box itself was only four inches deep and about a foot long, but Zoltan reached his arm nearly up to the elbow within it. His face scrunched up as he appeared to rummage for something at the very bottom of the box. "Ahh, here it is!" He cried and pulled out a dove. "No, that's not it." He released the bird as the crowd clapped. "Here it is," he announced after searching the box again and pulled out a red scarf. He pulled at both ends and suddenly was holding a red and a blue scarf. Zoltan then grabbed both ends of each scarf and pulled again. This time, he held red, blue, green, and yellow scarves. He looked at the four scarves in annoyance and threw them up into the air. With a bright flash, each disappeared in a cloud of smoke while Zoltan reached into the box a third time and the audience roared their approval.

Once more it appeared as if his arm was buried up to the elbow in the shallow box as everyone waited to see what he would bring out this time. "Aha, this time I have it!" He cried and pulled out a silver-plated Peacemaker.

"Ladies and gentlemen, I will prove to you that I cannot be killed by a mere bullet. First, let me show you that this gun has bullets in it." The illusionist threw the wooden box into the air and fired a single shot at it. Splinters shot outward and the box spun as the lone shot flew true. Without a word, Zoltan's assistant snagged it out of the air and presented it to the illusionist.

"Look at the box, ladies and gentlemen." Zoltan held it out for the audience to see. Roland peered at the box and saw that a single bullet hole now pierced the lid. After giving everyone a chance to view it, Zoltan held the box over his head. An explosion boomed from the stage, and another cloud of smoke appeared above Zoltan. He pulled his arms down and held a rabbit instead of the wooden box. Roland clapped along with the rest of the crowd. *Damn, he's good.* Roland had never seen anything close to this level of magic before and waited dumbfounded with the rest of the crowd to see how the trick played out.

Zoltan handed the rabbit to his assistant and turned back to the audience. "As you can see, this gun contains real bullets. Now I will show how I cannot be killed by a mere bullet." He turned back to the assistant and gave him the gun. The assistant walked to the far side of the stage as Zoltan faced the crowd. "My assistant will now fire a bullet straight at my heart," Zoltan stopped and wagged a finger at the audience. "But I won't be hurt a bit."

He paused as applause burst out in response to his proclamation. "Thank you, but I will also show you that my assistant's bullet is on target." Zoltan twisted his hand, and a piece of paper suddenly appeared in his fingers. "I will hold this piece of paper so the bullet will pass through it just before it strikes me. Now, if I can have silence please." Everyone kept their mouths shut as they eagerly watched the spectacle on stage. Roland found himself biting his lip as Zoltan calmly held the paper over his chest.

The assistant pulled the trigger and nearly everyone jumped as Zoltan fell backwards. *Oh my God, he's dead,* Roland thought briefly before the illusionist bounced back to his feet. "I told you it takes more than a mere bullet to kill me," he announced and held the paper out for all to see. Like the wooden box, a single hole cut through the center of the sheet. Zoltan bowed deeply as the entire audience applauded loudly for the miraculous trick that he had just performed.

"How the *hell* did he do that?" Jack asked in disbelief.

"I don't know," Roland replied, just as bewildered. He'd have given a pretty penny to know how that trick had been accomplished, but he'd never known a magician to give away secrets. The Sheriff didn't think that Zoltan would be any different unless he was paid handsomely.

"My next trick is one that has been banned in France. The last six magicians to try it have died. It is called the Coffin of Death." Once again, he held his hands up in the air. A loud explosion sounded from the side of the stage, and Zoltan looked towards the noise with a confused expression.

Roland craned his neck to see what the illusionist was up to when Jack leaned against his back. "Jack, watch out," Roland barked to his friend as he kept his eyes locked on the magician. He never knew which happened first: Dotty screaming or Roland noticing the wetness on his back. Turning around, Roland nearly fell backwards as Jack tumbled into his arms. The deputy's face was completely ashen, and his shirt was drenched with blood. His eyes rolled back as he labored to take in each breath.

A bullet struck the ground just next to Roland, and the Sheriff hopped involuntarily. He struggled to hold onto Jack, but the deputy fell through his arms and to the ground. Roland stared at the deputy for a half-second before turning towards the stage, drawing both pistols in one fluid motion. A Bandito stood by the side of the stage, aiming his lone gun at Roland. He never got the chance for another shot as Roland fired twice, striking him in the shoulder and throat. With a bloody gurgle, he fell to the ground.

Chaos erupted through the crowd as they realized what was happening. Quickly the stage became obscured to Roland as panicked celebrators rushed every which way to get out of the path of gunfire. The Sheriff craned his neck to see if there were any more Dark Riders behind the stage. Roland didn't even know where the rest of his deputies were. *Please let there only be one of them.* The Sheriff didn't know if he could handle many Dark Riders by himself. Gunfire erupted from several different parts of the celebration area, and Roland looked up to see two different gunfights taking place. Several deputies were engaged in a shootout in the middle of the games area, and another was being waged in front of Will's Tavern.

Dotty continued to scream as she knelt by her wounded husband. Blood welled from Jack's chest, and a tiny trickle leaked from the corner of his mouth. The sight of his best friend injured so badly tore at Roland, but there was nothing to be gained by getting shot himself. "Dotty," he called to his friend's wife. "Dotty, get out of here!" She didn't even hear him as she cradled Jack's head in her lap and pleaded with him to stay alive. "Damn it," Roland swore. He wanted to stay with Dotty and Jack, but he had to join the closest gunfight.

He ran towards the games area and was nearly killed as two bullets were fired his way. Roland instantly dived for cover, not even trying to see where his enemy was. He took in a few deep, ragged breaths as he crouched behind one of the stands that had been set up for the Fourth of July celebration. *Goddamn Dark Riders.* Roland had no idea how many of the outlaws were in New Haven. He especially wanted to know where all of his men were, but aside from the gunshots, he had no idea who was where.

A flurry of motion caught Roland's attention not more than fifty feet away. Behind one of the other stands, Morgan and Wade crouched down, holding their weapons and waiting. Roland wanted to join them, but the distance between the two stands was too great. He had chosen his cover poorly, and now he had to accept his isolated position for the rest of the gunfight. Roland watched the pair of deputies rise and fire a quick barrage of bullets towards a copse of trees. They struck one of the trees, but a second later Carl emerged from behind the tree to fire another volley of bullets.

Morgan and Wade quickly ducked again and waited for the Dark Rider to cease his fire. Carl didn't retreat behind the tree but stayed uncovered with his pistol pointed directly at the deputies' shelter. *No! Don't do it!* Roland started to scream at his deputies to stay under cover, but it was too late. Thinking that they were safe to fire another few shots, Wade and Morgan rose from their crouched position. The blue-eyed deputy never saw what hit him. Wade Hampton had always wanted to be a gunslinger, and he found the fate that awaited most gunslingers as Carl's first shot struck him in the neck. Morgan was luckier. Carl's second shot grazed his shoulder, and the Dark Rider never got off a third one. New Haven's oldest deputy shot Carl right between the eyes. Blood spouted from the Dark Rider's forehead as he toppled to the ground.

"Get out of there, Goddamn it!" Morgan hollered towards the trees. He didn't stop to help Wade. Morgan had been around for too long and knew a fatal injury when he saw one. The deputy stayed behind his cover but didn't crouch back down. Instead he kept his gun pointed directly at the clump of trees which had provided cover for Carl moments before.

Roland didn't know how many more men were back there or where the rest of his men were, but he intended to help Morgan however he could. Taking a deep breath, Roland sprinted towards the stand which Morgan was standing behind. He nearly died before he made it. His deputy turned at the sound of footsteps and came extremely close to firing. Only time-tested nerves kept Roland from joining Wade and Jack among the day's victims. *No. Jack's not dead. He's just hurt,* Roland kept telling himself, but he had seen the wound in Jack's chest. He knew that he was deceiving himself. Morgan didn't say a word as Roland crouched behind the stand and tried to catch his breath. "How many?" Roland gasped between breaths.

The deputy didn't take his eyes off the trees or waver his gun hand as he answered. "Two. David and Mad Dog. I think they have a woman back there. I heard her scream before."

"Son of a bitch," Roland swore. He had hoped that Curly would be with them. The Sheriff prayed that Morgan had heard wrong. Dealing with the Dark Riders was bad enough, but if he had to worry about killing an innocent citizen, it became doubly so. His next question was cut off as a single bullet was fired from the trees.

Morgan immediately crouched down beside Roland. "Goddamn cowards," he muttered. "Took that shot from behind the tree. Too scared to take me on." The old deputy's eyes burned with anger, and his jawline was rigid with barely controlled fury. Roland was glad that Morgan was on his side.

Roland had caught his wind and breathed slow, even breaths as he calmed himself down. He had to stay cool and detached to fight at his best. The Sheriff had nearly three decades of practice at drowning out everything but his enemy. When he felt that he was ready to continue the fight with the Dark Riders, he spoke. "On three, we go get 'em," he told Morgan in a level, detached voice.

Morgan had heard that monotone voice before and had used it himself. He nodded and calmly finished reloading his gun. The sound of gunfire continued to echo from the other side of the celebration area, but the two men ignored it. Their fight was with the men behind the trees. There would be time for the rest of them later.

"One," Roland said the first word slowly, and it seemed the pause before the second number lasted forever. "Two." He braced his knees to spring to his feet and relaxed his shoulders so he could aim better.

"Put your guns down, or I'll kill her," Mad Dog's harsh voice snarled from behind the trees.

"Bastard son of a whore," Roland swore and closed his eyes in frustration. He wasn't going to let any of the Dark Riders go even if it meant casualties for the citizens of New Haven. The Sheriff had hoped to avoid those, but it appeared that Mad Dog was going to force the issue. "No chance, Mad Dog. How do I know you have anybody back there?" He yelled from behind his makeshift cover and rose to his feet. *Come out, you bastard, and I swear I'll kill you.* Roland expected Mad Dog to emerge any second, and he'd fire the moment that he had a shot. He just hoped that he didn't kill anyone else in the process.

Mad Dog emerged from the trees just as Roland had anticipated, but the way that he did made Roland pause before he fired. The Dark Rider had an arm wrapped roughly around Sherry's neck, and the other hand arm held a gun pointed directly at her head. Tears streamed down the brothel owner's cheeks as she scrambled to keep up with her captor. "Put them down, Sheriff, or the bitch dies."

Roland squinted but didn't lower his guns. *Why Sherry?* Naturally it was somebody he knew personally. Still, he had no choice. The Dark Riders had gone too far this time. He wouldn't stop until every last one of them laid under a tombstone. "You're not going anywhere, Mad Dog. Let her go, and I'll kill you quickly," Roland answered quietly. *The left side of his face is open. Hit him in the forehead, and he won't get a shot off at Sherry.* Carefully the Sheriff began lining up his gun with the small target. He wanted to make sure that his shot was on target, or Sherry would die.

He never took that shot. Before Roland could squeeze his trigger and before Mad Dog could utter another word, the left side of Mad Dog's head exploded in a wash of blood, hair, and brains. Roland wheeled around to see Henry holstering his pistol. His face was pale, and he looked as if he couldn't believe that he had fired a gun. At the Ghost Hunter's side stood Jimmy. The young gunslinger's face was flushed, and his eyes glowed with excitement. *What the hell's he doing here?* Roland thought in amazement at the sight of Henry, but he never got to ask the question as Jimmy leveled his gun. "Get down," Jimmy shouted and fired once.

Roland flopped onto the ground beside Morgan and waited as Jimmy walked forward, his pistol never wavering. "You can get up now. I got him," Jimmy told the Sheriff as he passed their stand. His voice sounded cockier than ever, and Roland could have sworn that Jimmy actually strutted by them. When he rose to his feet, Roland immediately forgot about Jimmy's arrogance. The young gunslinger had his gun pointed directly at a Dark Rider named David. Jimmy's bullet had struck him in the stomach, and he writhed on the ground, clutching the bloody wound. David's gun lay three feet away from his sprawled arms where he had dropped it after being shot, but from the looks of him, he wouldn't be using it anyway. Roland just hoped that the Dark Rider lived. He had quite a few questions that he wanted answered.

Quickly sprinting to the Dark Rider, Roland scooped up his pistol and tossed it nearly a dozen feet away. *The son of a bitch can't hurt anyone now.* "Morgan, get over here and keep an eye on this bastard." He quickly looked to the other side of the celebration area and spotted a group of six men fleeing the scene on horseback. *Run, you Goddamn cowards.* Everything had grown quiet, and Roland knew that the fight was over. *Please let everyone else be all right.* "Good job," he told Jimmy as he ran away from the scene.

"Thanks," Jimmy answered, and his grin grew even wider. It wasn't a kill, but it was still a first step for the gunslinger. At least now he had something to brag about.

But Roland never heard him as he raced across the street towards his wounded friend. Dotty still hunched over her husband as Roland approached them. She looked up at Roland with a blank expression. Her cheeks and eyes were red and puffy, and tears streamed down her face. "Roland," she cried softly as the Sheriff knelt beside her.

He had hoped that his memory was wrong and that Jack had taken a serious but not deadly wound. Unfortunately he had remembered all too well. The Bandito's shot had taken Jack square in the chest. Blood soaked all of his shirt and jacket and had begun to pool under him. Roland looked for any sign of life, but Jack's eyes stared vacantly at the night sky above them. Roland bowed his head and took a deep breath. *Jack, I'm sorry. Rest in peace.* Then the Sheriff wordlessly put a hand on Jack's forehead. He wrapped an arm around Dotty's shoulders as he closed Jack's eyes.

Dotty hugged Roland's body and began to cry in choking sobs as Roland patted her back awkwardly. He couldn't tear his stunned eyes from the body of his old friend laying dead in the street. For so long Jack had been there for him as a source of advice, a steady backup, and most importantly a good friend. "It'll be all right, Dotty," Roland whispered even though he knew in his heart that it would never be the same all right again.

Chapter Eighteen

"From ashes to ashes and dust to dust, in the name of the Father, the Son, and the Holy Spirit. Amen," Reverend Thatcher spoke quietly to the assembled crowd. Roland sat next to Dotty with his arm protectively around her shoulders. Like Roland, Dotty wore all black, and her face appeared lost as if she didn't even know where she was. She didn't cry once during the funeral. Her tears seemed to have dried up during the long night before. Roland had never thought that he would have to console Dotty. Jack seemed a far likelier candidate to outlive him, but the West often played by a different set of rules.

The crowd gathered at the church was a large one. Jack had been a popular man, and quite a few of the town's stunned citizens came to pay their last respects. It had been decided to bury Wade and Robert with their fellow deputy. Roland had thought that things were bad enough when Jack and Wade had died, but then Ben had reported that Robert had been shot by Carlos. The crooked-nosed deputy had always wanted to go out in a blaze of glory, and he had found just that fate. The Sheriff had shaken with rage at the news. In addition to Carlos, Curly had been with the other group of Dark Riders. If Roland had only known, he would have made sure that Bryant's murderer died, even if it meant taking half a dozen bullets himself. Rebecca continued to waste away at The Last Frontier. It still gnawed at his stomach that the key to her awakening had been within his grasp, and once more it had slipped through his fingers. He hadn't even been able to return to her house with the Ghost Hunters this morning as he had made arrangements for the three funerals.

He had been shocked to find Henry in the gunfight. The Ghost Hunter had stayed in his room at The Frontier almost the entire time he had been in New Haven. It had been several hours after the gunfight before Roland had tracked him down. Henry claimed that the fireworks had awakened him, and he had simply gone outside to see what was causing the ruckus. Drawn by the colorful demonstration, he had made his way to the celebration area. Roland was just glad that he had joined them. He didn't know if he could have made that shot to put down Carl. Sherry had been grateful as well and asked about the man who had saved her life. Roland told her that Henry was a traveler and that he would pass along her gratitude. The last thing Henry needed was Sherry dogging his every footstep.

Despite his frustration and sorrow over the previous night's events, Roland was proud of his decimated troop of deputies. Ben, William, and Simon had effectively held off Carlos, Curly, and four other riders from inside Will's Tavern. Robert had fallen next to them, but the rest had survived without a scratch. Simon had even killed a rangy Dark Rider in the beginning moments of the gunfight, proving that Roland's confidence in the deputy was not misplaced. Morgan had also fought brilliantly, but Roland expected exactly that from the grizzled war veteran. Roland had wanted a smart band of tough deputies who could handle the violence and responsibility of protecting New Haven, and that's exactly what he had assembled. He only wished all of them could have survived to see the success that they had achieved.

Even more impressive had been Jimmy's actions. Roland had thought that the youth would cause trouble after his foolish behavior with Carlos the week before. His deputies had been furious with his decision to allow the young gunslinger to stay in town an extra day. Jimmy's lone shot of the gunfight, however, had probably saved Roland's life. Roland had hoped that David would live, but despite Doc Sullivan's best efforts, the Dark Rider had died. In a change of emotions, the rest of the deputies had treated Jimmy with camaraderie ever since the gunfight. Morgan had told the story of how he had saved Roland's life, and the other deputies took him into the fold as a fellow gunslinger. He sat next to Morgan, Ben, and William, looking somewhat sorrowful. Considering the size of his grin after the gunfight, it must have taken a Herculean effort to display some semblance of grief.

All of that mattered little to Roland as he sat next to Dotty and listened to Thatcher finish his eulogy for Jack. The Reverend had already given one for Wade and Robert, and Roland had felt sorrow for each of those men who had worked hard as deputies and died for the safety of New Haven. But Jack's loss hit him much harder than he ever could have thought. Rebecca still laid in her bed at The Last Frontier, but Roland steadfastly believed that she would soon emerge from her hellish slumber. Jack, on the other hand, was gone forever, and Roland couldn't believe it. For years Jack had been a good friend, and Roland had depended on him heavily during their time in New Haven. Never again would they sit and chat at The Frontier, never again would Jack chide him for losing his temper with Alvin, and never would Jack stand at his side while he married Rebecca. Numerous memories, both good and bad, of his time with Jack floated through Roland's mind as he sat with a lost look on his face.

When Reverend Thatcher finished the services, Roland blinked in surprise. It seemed that the funeral had just begun, but everyone rose to their feet. *Damn, Jack, why'd you have to go and die? I'll miss you, old friend.* Dotty hunched in her seat next to him, still with that far-away look in her eyes. She had barely spoken a word since Jack died, and Roland worried about her. He knew how he had been with Rebecca sick. His mind hadn't been able to focus on anything else for almost two weeks, and he didn't want Dotty caught in a downward spiral of depression. Despite having to worry about Rebecca, finding and punishing the Dark Riders, and trying to strengthen his troop of deputies, Roland fiercely intended to help out his old friend's wife however he could.

"Dotty," he spoke softly to her. She continued to stare straight ahead as if she hadn't heard him. "Dotty," Roland repeated and gently shook her shoulder. Her head slowly turned to him with a vacant expression. *Damn,* Roland thought in resignation. It hurt him to see her so devastated. Her eyes were red and puffy with blackened rings encircling them. "Come on, it's time to go," he told her gently.

He stood and helped Dotty to her feet. She held onto Roland's elbow as he led her out of the church. A number of people greeted the pair as they walked outside and offered their condolences. Roland wasn't sure if she even understood what half the people were saying, but she nodded silently as if to thank them for their words. Her eyes, however, still looked into a far-off place.

Morgan caught Roland's eye as he walked by. "Meet at The Frontier in an hour?" He asked quietly. Roland and his deputies needed to discuss how they would keep New Haven safe. Three deputies had died, and the Dark Riders were still on the loose. Everyone was tired and angry, but they'd have to band together until times became easier.

Roland nodded and took Dotty away from the church so she could grieve in peace. Jack had set up his house on the north end of town fairly close to the church. Roland led Dotty on the short walk back to her house. He wished that she had relatives in town who could sit with her for the next few difficult days. She would always grieve over Jack, but the next few days would be the worst by far. Roland would have had Rebecca spend time with Dotty, but that wasn't an available option either. The best he could do was to stop by as much as his schedule allowed, and the way things were looking, that wouldn't be much. *Talk to Thatcher,* Roland thought to himself. The Reverend would have more time to visit the widow and make sure that she was doing all right. He'd try to stop on the way back to The Last Frontier.

Dotty turned to him at the doorway and looked up with those sorrowful eyes. "Thank you, Roland," she said in an emotionless voice. He hoped that she would snap out of that catatonic state. It was bad as seeing Rebecca after that first hellish night at her house.

"You're welcome, Dotty. I'll be back with dinner later on. You just get some sleep and don't hesitate if there's anything I can do for you." Roland looked her directly in the eye to make sure that she was paying attention. He didn't know if she even heard what he said or would remember any of it, but he had to try.

"Uh huh," she mumbled indecisively.

"All right then." Roland sighed. *She didn't hear a damn word I said.* He wished things weren't so chaotic in New Haven so he could have more time to spend with Dotty, but whatever the circumstances, Roland would make time. It just wouldn't be as much as he would have liked. Roland opened the door and stood back as she entered her house. "Take care, Dotty. I'll see you later."

Roland stood by the door after he closed it and shut his eyes. He couldn't believe how bad Dotty looked. It was still hard to fathom that Jack was dead. Roland had finally started to get back into his normal routine, and then one of the largest foundations in it got ripped away. He wanted to drift out of reality for a week or two like Dotty, but he couldn't. Grieving for Jack would have to come after he had taken care of everything else. *Goddamn, Jack. How could you die on me?* It was exactly the sort of time when Jack would lend a helping hand to ease Roland's job as Sheriff, but he would just have to accept that Jack would never be able to help out again.

Clenching his fists, Roland stalked back to the church. Questions flew through his mind, but the answers all eluded him. It was a shame that Jimmy had killed David. The Dark Rider would have been quite helpful in determining where his brethren were hiding and what else they had planned. Regardless, Roland intended to find out where the Dark Riders were and deliver justice to each and every one of them even if he had to shoot Alvin to do so. His patience was at an end.

As he stormed down the street, people shied away from him as if he had the plague. His eyes bored straight ahead, glaring murderously, and his jaw clenched into a rigid line of fury. *Why?* The Sheriff asked himself over and over. The previous night's ordeal made absolutely no sense. He didn't know why the Dark Riders had carried out the bloody carnage. Roland had wounded Carlos's pride, but the outlaw hadn't done anything for weeks. Why did he choose the Fourth of July? Nothing had been gained, and they had finally committed an atrocity to turn public sentiment against them. Even Alvin couldn't help them out of the mess they had wrought for themselves.

Alvin was an even more puzzling predicament. The mayor had hinted for over a week of a surprise, and the gunfight at the Fourth of July celebration would certainly qualify. Roland wanted to question Alvin and had tried to find him in the hours after the last bullet had been fired, but the mayor was nowhere to be found. Roland still had no idea where he was. *Probably sulking in his house.* Alvin had exerted a tremendous amount of effort to plan the celebration, and the Dark Riders had destroyed it. Whether Alvin was joking or not, Roland couldn't believe that he would willingly let Carlos and his men wage a gunfight in the middle of New Haven. He had always gained power and prestige by keeping them in check. Furthermore, after Jimmy's foolish escapade with Carlos, Alvin had shown no authority over them.

Alvin, you'd better be ready to talk, Roland thought. A grim smile touched his face, and his eyes continued to stare dead ahead, warning all to avoid him. The summer heat continued to scorch New Haven, but he barely noticed the sweat beading on his forehead. Whether Alvin was involved in the gunfight or not, Roland intended to question him at great length about a number of things. As soon as he talked to Morgan, that would be his first order of business. *You can't hide forever, you son of a bitch.*

Reverend Thatcher was still in the church when Roland returned. He looked tired and upset, a far cry from his customary cheerfulness. Funerals were what he hated most in the world, especially those for good people like the three deputies. "Roland," he greeted softly.

"Reverend," Roland inclined his head. "It's been a long morning," he commented quietly. His anger fell by the wayside, replaced by a strong feeling of sorrow. It seemed unreal that his best friend had just had his funeral in the very halls in which he stood.

"That it has. That it has," Thatcher replied wistfully then clapped his hands together. He put on his happy face even though he felt little joy that morning. Thatcher preferred to be upbeat in the face of adversity. It made it that much easier to make it through the day. "Now what can I do for you?"

Roland didn't answer the smile with one of his own. There were too many things dragging his spirits down for him to find any joy. "It's Dotty, Reverend. She looks awful. She's going to need someone to help her out over the next few days, and I don't know how much time I'll have. I was hoping you could help." At least Robert and Wade weren't married. It was difficult enough trying to help one widow, let alone three.

"Of course," Thatcher chimed in immediately. Roland had once commented that the Reverend would walk a hundred miles to help someone in need, and he held true to form. "I'll be glad to check in on her. I had planned on going by this evening."

"Thanks, I appreciate it. Well, I'll be seeing you." Roland tipped his hat, but Thatcher held up a hand.

"Wait. I wanted to ask about Rebecca. I haven't heard anything in over a week. Is she doing any better?"

"Yes," Roland replied then exhaled loudly. He pushed all thoughts of her to the back of his mind. Things were too chaotic in New Haven, and he didn't have the luxury of brooding over her. "I think she'll be awake soon."

"Good!" Thatcher clapped his hands together once more. "That's good to hear. I've been praying for her. I look forward to performing your wedding once she's healthy." He took a closer look at Roland's drawn face, and his eyebrows furrowed together in concern. "Are *you* all right?" He asked pointedly.

"Don't worry. I'm fine." He didn't have time for Thatcher to fuss over him. Roland respected the Reverend quite a bit, but his schedule was too full to dwell at the church any longer. "I need to be going. Thanks again for helping with Dotty. I'll talk with you soon."

"Take care, Roland, and don't hesitate to come by if you need anything."

The moment Roland stepped outside, his thoughts instantly returned to the puzzling circumstances surrounding the previous night's events. By the time he reached The Last Frontier, a scowl had formed on his face again, causing people to stay clear of him as he stalked through he streets. He entered the saloon to find a paltry crowd. Usually, by two there were at least a dozen men at the tavern, but the gunfight during the magic show had obviously tainted most of the town's thirst for revelry. It seemed as if the streets were less crowded than normal. *They're all just scared.* Roland smiled bitterly as he stalked to the bar.

George grabbed a bottle of whiskey and placed it on the bar as he saw Roland crossing the saloon. "Sheriff," he greeted quietly.

The Sheriff didn't answer him but simply swiped the bottle up with his left hand and marched to his table. He kicked a chair back from the table and plopped himself in the seat, placing his feet on the table. Uncorking the bottle with his teeth, Roland took a deep swig of the fiery liquid, sighing as its comforting warmth spread throughout his body. *Rest in peace, Jack.* He chased that down with another deep sip from the bottle then slammed it down on the table. Whiskey splashed out of the top, but Roland didn't care as he sat stony-faced at his table waiting for Morgan.

He wanted nothing more than to hold Rebecca at that moment. Everything in his life was falling to pieces, and the one person who could make everything better remained locked away in the Land of Shadows. Roland wanted to go up to her room and sit wordlessly with her, but he feared that it would just worsen his already dark mood. Everybody in New Haven, from Dotty to Rebecca, was relying on him, and he had to try to keep some semblance of order. *First talk to Morgan, then see to everything else. One thing at a time.* Roland repeated those two sentences over and over to himself. They helped him maintain focus among the chaotic mess that his life had become.

For nearly half an hour Roland sat at his table. A few patrons came into the saloon during that time, but they ignored the Sheriff after one glance in his direction. He took one more sip of whiskey then let the bottle sit on the table. Roland savored the numbing sensation rolling through his body, but he couldn't afford to get drunk. He was already exhausted after sleeping only a few hours over the last two days. For all he knew, the Dark Riders would return to New Haven, and Roland wanted to be ready for them. *God help them if they do.*

By the time Morgan arrived at The Last Frontier, it was nearly three o'clock. The veteran deputy wore his usual blue jeans and tan overcoat, and his long white hair streamed down around his shoulders. His left arm was held in a sling, but Morgan still had one good arm. That was all he needed. As they did with Roland, the saloon's customers gave Morgan only a cursory glance before minding their own business. They wanted nothing to do with Roland or his deputies that afternoon. Morgan took a seat across from Roland and stared at the bottle of whiskey for a moment before looking up. He didn't say anything about it to Roland, but his expression clearly showed his disapproval.

"Morgan," Roland greeted. A forlorn little smile formed upon his lips as he pictured Jack's disapproving frown. His old friend would have lectured him for even taking a few sips of whiskey.

"Roland, how's Dotty?" Morgan avoided talking about the bottle on the table. It was Roland's business, and he had no intention of butting in unless he was invited.

"Not well." Roland scowled and gazed at the bottle. It was tempting to have just one more sip, but he suppressed the urge. He needed to keep his wits about him over the next few days. "She's going to need someone to look after her for a while. I talked with Thatcher, and he said he'd drop by her house."

"Good. Let me know if there's anything I can do to help. What about everyone else?" Morgan folded his hands together and leaned back in his chair, raising an eyebrow inquisitively. Unlike Jack, Morgan rarely offered his opinion. He preferred to let Roland do all the thinking, and he'd chime in if asked.

"Who are you talking about?"

"Me, Ben, Simon, and everyone else. How are we going to patrol the city?"

Jack, why can't you be here? Roland missed his old friend helping out with the placement of all the deputies, but he would have to handle the situation all by himself. "Phillip can run the station house during the day."

"What about at night?" Morgan broke in.

"To hell with the station house. We're short handed. Until we get more deputies, we'll leave the station house empty at night. I'll be here at The Frontier so people will know how to find somebody if there's trouble. I want you and Simon riding patrol together, and William and Ben doing the same." Roland help up a finger in warning. "No splitting up," he cautioned. "The Riders might come back, and I don't want anybody caught all by himself. We're also going to need some volunteers for citizen deputies. If all the Dark Riders come back, I don't know if we can hold them off." Neither deputy mentioned the possibility of calling in outside help. New Haven's problems would be handled internally. The unique atmosphere of the town would be jeopardized if they asked for help from the governor.

Morgan nodded his approval. "Sounds good. How late do you want us patrolling?"

Roland shrugged his shoulders. "Until everyone goes home. We don't have enough men to cover all the shifts so we'll all have to work some longer days."

The deputy nodded again. Roland couldn't tell if Morgan minded the longer hours or not. He knew that William and Simon would loathe them.

Simon wanted to spend every waking moment with his pregnant wife, and William would hate the decreased amount of time that he could spend wooing the women of New Haven, but Morgan stoically accepted the longer hours without uttering a word of complaint. He did look at Roland cautiously. "What about Jimmy?"

"Don't worry. I'll make sure he's out of town on the next train." Roland made a mental note to check that the young gunslinger was on the afternoon train. He wanted Jimmy out of New Haven like he had originally intended. In all the confusion of the gunfight and Jack's funeral, it had completely slipped his mind.

Morgan held up a hand. "No, Roland. I don't want him to leave."

"What are you talking about?" He knew that Jimmy had gained some popularity with the deputies after he had shot the Dark Rider, but a week ago his men had been ready to throttle him.

"I think you should make him a deputy."

"*Deputy?*" Roland laughed out loud, and several customers looked over their way. He made sure to lower his voice. "Are you out of your mind? You want me to make him a deputy? He's crazy. We don't need someone like him right now. Hell, he'd be more likely to start a Goddamn fight than stop one."

"We need him," Morgan responded calmly. "We don't have enough men, Roland. He's a good shot. He's just young. You already said we need more deputies. Why not him?"

Roland rubbed his chin and thought for a moment. Morgan had a point, but his gut told him not to trust Jimmy any further than he could throw him. "No, Morgan. I can't trust him. The last thing I need is for him to start dueling in the streets. He'd kill someone within a day if I let him stay. At half past four, I want him on that train and out of New Haven."

"You're the Sheriff," Morgan stated, and Roland knew that he wouldn't hear any more about Jimmy from the deputy. "It's a shame about David," the deputy commented.

The Sheriff sighed. "I wish Jimmy had aimed for his shoulder. I wanted him alive, Goddamn it." *Stay calm. It's all done.* If he could have dragged the location of the Dark Riders' hideout out of the wounded outlaw, Roland wouldn't have hesitated to gather a posse and destroy them once and for all. More importantly, he wanted to know if another attack was planned. Roland was short-handed with only five deputies, and another surprise attack could be even deadlier than the Fourth of July carnage.

"Is there any other way to find out what they're up to? If they're declaring war on us, I'd like to know."

"Me too," Roland muttered and rubbed his chin as he stared at the bottle of whiskey. *Just one more sip,* he thought wistfully. "I'll try talking to

Alvin later. He might know what's going on, and he's likely to tell us after Carlos pulled that gun on him at The Snake."

"Who do you want me to get to organize a citizen watch?"

"Talk to Paul Henderson. He's a dumb son of a bitch, but he knows how to gather a big crowd. Tell him—" Roland broke off as William rushed into the saloon with Jimmy and Ben on his heels. "What is it?" He asked worriedly and rose to his feet, both hands immediately reaching for his guns.

William had a curious expression on his face, and Jimmy's grin reached nearly ear to ear. Ben nearly hopped up and down as he waited to ask a question. "This just got printed," William reported and placed a copy of *The New Haven Gazette* on the table.

Roland looked down and cringed the moment he saw the headline. It looked as if his day had just gotten worse. With a sickening feeling in his stomach, the Sheriff made himself read on.

Doc Holliday Saves the Day at Fourth of July Gunfight

Poor planning and the ineptitude of Sheriff Black led to the deaths of three of his men and the halt of the Fourth of July celebration. Jack Logan, Wade Hampton, and Robert Douglas all were killed by members of the Dark Riders gang. The fight was provoked by several deputies who had been drinking heavily during the day.

Madam Sherry herself was nearly killed, but the fortunate intervention of Doc Holliday spared her from becoming a fourth New Haven victim. The outlaw was believed to have died five years ago in Glenwood Springs, but he has been staying at The Last Frontier for the past few days with a Cheyenne Indian. "He's the fastest gun I've ever seen," Sherry reported after the fight was over.

It was unfortunate that it came to such a bloody confrontation, but if Sheriff Black had prepared his men better, none of this would have happened. Carlos and his men deserve their own share of the blame, but the majority should be cast at Sheriff Black. It was he and his men who caused the stopping of Zoltan's magic show and also the deaths of nearly a dozen men.

Sheriff Black is lucky that Doc Holliday was on hand, or the carnage would have been much worse. The notorious gunslinger killed a half dozen Dark Riders all by himself while the rest of Sheriff Black's men watched uselessly.

Roland read the rest of the article, but all of it was the same. It barely scratched the truth while telling horrible lies to make him and his men look bad. *Matthew Brady, you're a dead man.* The Ghost Hunter would have to be told soon. Everybody and their brother would be at The Last Frontier to catch a glimpse of one of the West's most famous gunslingers. *How did he figure— Alvin!* Roland's jaw clenched in fury. Alvin was the only other one who knew that Doc was alive and here in town. That was just one more thing Roland was going to ask him about if he ever tracked down the mayor.

"Is it true?" Roland tore his eyes from the newspaper and stared at Jimmy. "Well, is it?" The young man seemed nearly ready to bounce through the ceiling with joy.

"Is what true?" Roland asked slowly. He was imagining what he would do to Matthew Brady and Alvin.

"Was that Doc Holliday last night?" Jimmy's eyes glowed with excitement, and the rest of the deputies looked just about the same. Even Morgan had an eyebrow raised curiously as he watched the Sheriff.

Blazes. Roland had planned on letting Henry slip out of New Haven with his anonymity intact, but that seemed out of the question after the damning article. The Ghost Hunter had only asked him to keep his identity secret in return for his and Singing Rock's help with Rebecca.

"Hell, no," Roland spat out vehemently after a brief pause.

Jimmy's bright-eyed enthusiasm waned at Roland's denial. "But the article said it was," he protested, wanting it to be Doc Holliday. After telling the story of his adventure with Doc Holliday to Jimmy, Roland could hardly blame the young man.

"That article also said the Dark Riders were innocent. I swear to God when I get my hands on Matthew Brady, he'll wish he was dead," Roland growled, half-acting and half-seriously. He had quite a few questions for *The Gazette* editor as well as for Alvin.

"Then who is it, Sheriff? Jimmy was telling us about his shot. He said it was the best shot he'd ever seen. Didn't he come to town with that Cheyenne?" Ben piped in.

Roland nearly groaned. He was just amazed that Ben had kept quiet as long as he had. "It's none of your business, Ben, but he's here to help me. His name's Henry, and his friend is a Navajo, not a Cheyenne," Roland answered flatly and glared at the deputy. The deputy took it in stride and nodded amicably.

Roland had no intention of letting Jimmy and his men pick at him with questions for the next few hours. "Damn it. You should all be out patrolling the streets right now. We've all got better things to do," he snapped at them.

"Yes, Sheriff," they all responded in unison. Ben turned towards Jimmy. "You coming with us?"

Jimmy's eyes brightened for a moment then he looked at Roland, and they narrowed cunningly. "No, I'm going to stay here for a while and play cards," he answered.

Roland watched the young gunslinger suspiciously as he headed for one of the card tables. Jimmy was up to something, and Roland had no intention of turning his back on him for more than a minute. The last train of the afternoon left in ninety minutes. He had to run a few errands, but Sheriff Black planned on returning in time to see the troublesome young man out of town.

Morgan rose as well and leaned over to Roland before he joined the rest of the deputies. "Doc Holliday's middle name was Henry," he whispered conspiratorially then followed the rest outside.

Son of a bitch, he knows. Roland had underestimated Morgan. He felt that he could lie fairly easily to the rest of his men, but he forgot how long Morgan had been around. Sometimes the crafty old deputy surprised him with the amount of knowledge that he had picked up. For a second, he was worried that Morgan might tell the other men what he had learned, but Roland banished that worry from his mind. If that was Morgan's intention, he would have already done so.

He cast his eyes around the saloon and paused as they rested on Jimmy. The gunslinger had joined a game of poker, but he appeared more interested in what Roland was doing than in the card game. *What are you up to?* Roland gave up. In just over an hour, he would never have to worry about Jimmy again. He wished Jimmy could have come to New Haven at a different time. Roland liked the young man, but he wasn't about to put up with any more of his shenanigans. He shifted his thoughts to the more pressing issue at hand. *Alvin, Matthew.* Roland almost drooled when he thought of what he wanted to do to those two men. One way or another, they were going to answer every single question he had for them. He could picture Jack's disapproving frown over the method he planned to use. Smiling wickedly, Roland returned the bottle of whiskey to George. He made sure to tell the saloon owner where he'd be in case one of his men stopped by, and then the Sheriff gathered a horse and sought out the mayor and Matthew Brady.

Roland decided to pay a visit to Matthew first. *The little bastard will tell me anything I want.* Roland nearly laughed out loud. Alvin would take some intimidation to make him talk, but Matthew would probably piss his pants at the first sight of Roland entering his office. He had warned Matthew after the article about the Cheyenne, and now the editor was about to see what his temper was like when he got really upset.

The New Haven Gazette had a small office near the train station. During the previous year, it had nearly outgrown its tiny space. Through the front window, Roland could see the giant printing press that occupied nearly all of the interior. A few desks had been set up around it. Stacks of paper littered the desks as well as the floor. Roland didn't know how Matthew put out a new edition every day among all the clutter, but as far as he knew, *The Gazette* hadn't missed a single issue ever since it became daily.

Most days Matthew could be found slaving on an issue or out collecting news. That Friday afternoon, Roland only saw one of Matthew's associates named Richard Jackson inside. Richard looked up in surprise as the Sheriff barged into the office, and his face slowly drained of color. He had obviously read the article, and Roland was the last person in the world who he wanted to see. "Sheriff," he whispered.

"Hello, Richard. How are you this afternoon?" Roland made sure to don his lopsided grin. He didn't want to scare Richard. He wanted to find out where Matthew was.

"Fine," he answered in a louder voice. Richard began to look a little more relaxed in response to Roland's pleasant demeanor, but his face was still pale.

"Good. I don't suppose you know where Matthew is? I really need to ask him something."

Richard shook his head. "No, Sheriff. I haven't seen him in a few hours."

Roland's hands balled into fists, but he kept the smile on his face. "Can you tell him I want him to come over to The Frontier when he gets back?"

"Yes," Richard nodded in that same quiet voice.

"Thanks," Roland told the writer and walked out into the street. The smile disappeared from his face. *Son of a bitch.* He didn't have the time to track Matthew down wherever he might be. *I'll be back. You can't hide forever.* Inevitably Matthew would return to the office or show up at The Last Frontier, and then Roland intended to make him very sorry for that article.

After that, Roland rode his horse to Alvin's house. The mayor had constructed his house on the northern outskirts of New Haven. Roland tied his horse to a tree then knocked loudly on the door. When no answer came, Roland was tempted to kick in the door and see for himself if nobody was home, but he decided against it. He wouldn't give Alvin the opportunity to impugn his character before the citizens of New Haven. "Goddamn it," Roland swore aloud and punched the door in frustration. The two men he wanted to see were nowhere to be found. There were too many questions that Roland wanted answered, and nobody was giving him any hints.

Sheriff Black returned to The Last Frontier after his frustrating excursion. Morgan had promised to report as soon as he had rounded up a few citizen deputies. Roland had nothing else to do except wait for either dawn or the Dark Riders to return. There were so many things to take care of but nothing that he could do at the moment. With a scowl on his face, Roland rode through the streets, returned his horse to the station house, and walked across the street to The Frontier. *At least I'll get Jimmy off my back soon,* Roland thought with relief. Nothing else seemed to be going his way.

A loud crowd greeted the Sheriff as he walked through the door. Roland was stunned by the number of people. When he had left the saloon, there had been a small crowd. *What the hell's going on?* He tried to see what the fuss was about, and then he spotted the focus of all the attention. Two men stood at the bar, and everyone in the saloon craned their necks to get a better view of them. One was Zoltan, who beamed at the attention being lavished upon him, and the other was Henry, who looked like he wanted to be anywhere else in the world. *I'm going to kill Matthew,* Roland thought darkly as he pushed his way towards the pair. "Let me through, Goddamn it," the Sheriff barked roughly. People took one look at the fury on his face and quickly stepped aside.

When he finally made it to the bar, Roland wasn't surprised to see Jimmy standing right next to Henry. *That son of a bitch didn't believe a word I said. No wonder he wanted to stay here.* Sheriff Black clenched his jaw and reaffirmed his intent to see Jimmy out of town no matter what, but that was for later. First he needed to help Henry, and that meant clearing out the crowd. "Goddamn it, everybody get out of here!" He yelled at the top of his lungs and assumed an angry scowl. George's eyebrows shot up in surprise. The saloon owner didn't look too happy with Roland's proclamation, but he didn't utter a syllable to counter him.

"It's Doc Holliday, Sheriff," a voice at the back of the crowd yelled back.

Roland glared towards the source, but he couldn't make out who had shouted. He wasn't surprised that it was someone at the back of the crowd. Nobody was brave enough to stand up to his face. "No, it's not. I've known this man for twenty years, and he's not Doc Holliday. His name's Henry. He's a gunslinger from Tennessee. *The Gazette* was wrong. Now everybody go home or start drinking. Leave him alone. I mean it, Goddamn it!" The Sheriff let one of his hands casually drop towards his holster, and people instantly began to file out of the saloon. "I need to talk to you," Roland leaned over and told Henry.

The Ghost Hunter nodded. His face was pale, and sweat had formed at his temples. "Thanks, Roland. I appreciate it."

"Don't mention it." Roland waved a hand in dismissal. "Let's go talk at my table. Give me a second." He turned towards Jimmy and leveled a finger at him. "I want you packed and ready to go. The afternoon train leaves at half past four, and you're going to be on it," he ordered in a tone that brooked no argument.

Jimmy didn't even bat an eye. If anything, his smirk grew larger. "All right, Sheriff. Whatever you say."

"Good," Sheriff Black muttered fiercely. He was a little surprised that Jimmy had acquiesced without a single argument, but he was due for something to go his way.

"Sheriff," Zoltan called out as he turned away from Jimmy.

"Zoltan," Sheriff Black greeted. "What can I do for you?"

"I am leaving soon. I wanted to thank you for bringing me here." He shrugged his shoulders. "I wish it would have been better, but I still want to thank you." The illusionist held out a hand.

Roland shook it. "You're very welcome. I enjoyed the first part of your show. I'm sorry those bastards ruined it for everyone. Where's Alvin? I thought he'd be here to see you off."

Zoltan shrugged his shoulders again. "I do not know. I haven't seen him since last night. Give him my thanks as well. I wanted to thank him in person, but I have another performance to give. I need to catch the next train."

"I'll be sure to track him down," Roland replied grimly. "Do you need any help carrying your baggage to the train station?"

"No. It is already there. If you will excuse me, I need to attend to a few more things. Farewell, Sheriff, and good luck catching those men. I think you'll need it."

The Sheriff nodded as Zoltan headed back upstairs, then he turned to Henry. "Blazes, this place is busy. Let's go sit down," he suggested and stalked across the saloon. He kicked his seat back roughly and sat down. Roland fiercely wanted a sip of whiskey to soothe his frayed nerves. He was close to exploding at someone if he didn't calm down soon.

"Thanks again," Henry said as he took his own seat. The Ghost Hunter looked rugged. Even when he had taken such a beating that first night at Rebecca's house he hadn't looked as bad. "I don't know how everyone found out, but I was beginning to run out of answers for them."

"That son of a bitch Matthew, that's how they found out," Roland spat out cantankerously. "He printed an article in *The Gazette* that said your name and where you were staying, but what the hell are you doing down here anyway? I thought you'd stay up in your room all day."

"Oh," Henry replied and sighed softly. It appeared that his five years of anonymity were at an end. Soon word would spread all over the country that he was still alive. Roland expected him to mope about the article, but the Ghost Hunter answered Roland's question instead. "I wanted to congratulate Zoltan on his performance. He came downstairs so I followed him. That's when everybody came in here." The Ghost Hunter shook his head. "For a moment there, I thought they weren't going to let me go until I admitted who I am."

"I swear I'm going to take it out of Matthew's hide when I catch him." The Sheriff took a deep breath to calm his nerves. Getting upset over *The Gazette* editor wasn't going to accomplish anything. There were far more important matters to take care of first. He leaned forward, his eyes glowing intensely. "So are we going back to the Land of Shadows tomorrow?" Roland asked anxiously. He hadn't even had a chance to visit Rebecca in her room since Jack had been shot. The previous dawn had been wasted, but Roland had no intention of sitting idly during the following one. He would get Rebecca out of there the next morning, and then all of the chaos swirling around him wouldn't seem as bad.

"Have you caught Bryant's killer yet?" Henry asked calmly.

"No, Do—Henry. That son of a bitch was lucky I didn't see him on the Fourth. I wouldn't have let him go." Roland shook his head tiredly. "Hopefully they'll be stupid and come back tonight. Then I'll kill Curly, and this will be over once and for all!" He snapped and slammed his fist down on the table.

Henry nodded nonchalantly as if he hadn't noticed Roland's outburst or the near use of his former nickname. "The first plan should be to capture Curly, and if that doesn't work, we'll go back to the house. We should get him this time," the Ghost Hunter stated confidently.

"Is that a promise?" Roland asked enthusiastically. His brief expression of irritation was replaced by his lopsided grin and a glint of hope in his eyes.

"Roland, you know I can't promise that," Henry stated slowly. "I think we'll get Bryant out of there and free Rebecca, but I can't predict anything in the Land of Shadows." He stared away for a moment, his eyes looking lost. "Strange things happen there, and you never know what it will be like when you enter."

"So you're saying she might be trapped like this forever?" The Ghost Hunter's statement deflated his hope before Roland could get too excited.

"No," Henry jumped in quickly. "This will be over one way or another very soon."

"Are you sure?"

The Ghost Hunter's face stretched into a crafty grin. "Trust me," he declared with panache.

Roland stared at Henry for a moment then chuckled. *I'm acting like a Goddamn baby.* "Thanks, I appreciate it, Henry." He was more grateful than the Ghost Hunter could ever know.

"Don't mention it." Henry looked around the saloon. Most of the people had left after Roland's diatribe, but those who remained continued to stare at their table. "I'll never be able to live in peace again," he observed morosely.

"You don't know that. You can always live up in the mountains. Nobody would bother you up there." Roland wished he could tell Henry that everything would be all right and that his anonymity would continue, but he would be lying.

"No, I'll be dead soon. People from all over the country will try to kill me, Roland, and you know it."

Roland barked out a laugh. "Nobody can kill you. You're the fastest I've ever seen, and after that shot yesterday, I'd say you haven't slowed down at all."

Henry rubbed the bullet hanging around his neck between his thumb and index finger. A sad little smile formed on his face as he looked at Roland. "Do you know why I wear this bullet?"

"No," Roland answered and shrugged his shoulders.

"After Singing Rock rescued me, he told me I had to give up my guns forever. I managed to convince him to let me keep one pistol for protection only." The Ghost Hunter continued to rub the bullet between his fingers as his eyes appeared lost in memories. "I wear this bullet as a reminder of how I used to live. I killed a lot of men, Roland. I can't even remember all of them I was so drunk, and I want to make amends. Traveling with Singing Rock is the only way to find redemption, and now it's over. If I travel with Singing Rock, I'll just endanger him and his mission."

Roland had no idea what to say to Henry. He didn't think anything would ease the Ghost Hunter's worries. "I'm sorry," he responded awkwardly.

"Don't worry about it." Henry smiled that small, tired smile again. "Maybe I'm not supposed to make amends. I'm going upstairs. Wake me a few hours before dawn," he instructed Roland then got up from his seat. He didn't go upstairs immediately but went to the bar first where he struck up a conversation with Jimmy.

Roland watched the two with a curious eye. Both Jimmy and Henry were acting strangely, and he didn't know why the two of them would be talking to each other. His attention, however, was diverted as Zoltan emerged from his room upstairs. He walked down the stairway with an almost regal grace, his cape draped behind him. The magician didn't leave the saloon but instead approached his table. "Zoltan," he greeted the illusionist.

Zoltan stood before Roland, shielding his view of the bar. "Sheriff," he greeted and rippled the edge of his cape. "I wanted to thank you one more time for letting me come to your city."

"You're very welcome. Maybe you can come another time and finish your performance."

Zoltan raised his eyebrows. "You never know, Sheriff. Life moves in mysterious ways. Peace and fortune to you. Farewell," he finished and twirled about, causing his cape to fan impressively behind him.

Roland watched him walk towards the door with a tiny smile. If he had ever met someone who was more conceited than Alvin it would have to be the magician, but unlike Alvin, Roland didn't want to throttle Zoltan. Roland frowned as he saw a rush of people leaving the saloon with the illusionist. He swept his gaze back to the bar and blinked in surprise. Jimmy and Henry were no longer seated there. He looked around the bar and noticed how empty it had suddenly become. *What the hell?* George scurried out from behind the bar and ran towards the door. Roland had no idea what was going on, but he meant to find out. He rose from his seat and ran after the saloon owner. Pushing open the door, Roland's breath caught in his throat as he looked over the crowd lining the street.

Jimmy and Henry stood in the middle of the street, twenty feet apart. Each had a hand poised on the butt of his pistol. *Goddamn it,* Roland thought to himself. This was the last thing that he needed to happen. "Stop!" He shouted at the two, but they ignored him as they both drew their weapons and fired.

Henry's shot flew wide and missed Jimmy completely. The young gunslinger's shot struck on target, and the Ghost Hunter spun around then fell to the ground. Roland pushed his way through the crowd and rushed into the street to check on Henry. *Damn it. Let him be all right.* Henry was Rebecca's only chance at survival, and he continued to lay motionless.

"I did it!" Jimmy shouted and danced about. A smile of joy stretched across his face from ear to ear.

Roland ignored Jimmy and sank to his knees by the wounded Ghost Hunter. Henry's breath came in long, ragged gasps. He lay on his side, his hands held protectively over his chest, which was stained with blood. "Roland," he whispered then closed his eyes. "Somebody get Sullivan!" The Sheriff called out. "Don't you die, Goddamn it," Roland told Henry, but the Ghost Hunter's wheezing became more frenzied.

"I'm already here," Doc Sullivan's nasal voice responded from the crowd, and Roland looked up to see the stuffy little doctor scrambling towards them.

Sheriff Black rose to his feet and moved away from Henry to give Sullivan room to work. He couldn't believe the luck of having Sullivan right there. Henry actually had a small chance of surviving. *Hold on, Henry. You'll make it.*

Sullivan sank down beside the Ghost Hunter and put his hand on Henry's neck. Suddenly Henry took in a deep, hacking breath, and his chest rose in a brief spasm. Then he breathed out a long sigh, and his body became still. Doc Sullivan rose to his feet. "I'm sorry, Sheriff. He's dead."

The words seemed to pass right by Roland. He couldn't tear his eyes off the body. For the second day in a row, somebody he knew had been killed in New Haven. Rebecca's best hope had rested with Henry and Singing Rock, and now even that had been ruthlessly taken from him. *Rest in peace, Henry. Rebecca, I love you.*

"I did it!" Jimmy shouted joyously again as he watched Sullivan pronounce Henry dead. He barely had time to react as Roland's right fist struck him soundly beneath the eye. His head snapped straight back, and the young gunslinger fell to the ground and laid still.

"You son of a bitch," Roland swore and wondered how he was going to straighten out the mess that his life had become.

Chapter Nineteen

Sheriff Black left the barely conscious gunslinger at the station house. Jimmy had awakened while the Sheriff roughly dragged him into the jailhouse, and Roland had belted him again, leaving him woozy. Roland had wordlessly grabbed the ring of keys off the wall then shut Jimmy inside one of the cells. "Rot, you son of a bitch," Roland had growled at him then spat on the young man's chest. He then stalked out of the station house, leaving Phillip only one instruction. "You keep that little bastard quiet," he told the deputy in a chilly voice, and then he gathered a horse and returned to the church much sooner than he had anticipated.

He couldn't believe Doc Holliday was dead. Everything had happened so quickly. One moment he was talking to Zoltan, and the next, Jimmy and Doc were dueling in the street. It made even less sense than the Dark Riders' bloody rampage. At least Carlos and his band of outlaws had reason to dislike Roland, but Jimmy and Henry had barely ever spoken to each other. It wasn't out of character for Jimmy to challenge someone to a duel, especially if he thought his opponent was a notorious gunslinger. But Henry's behavior completely baffled Roland. The Ghost Hunter had just explained how he had given up gunslinging and his quest for redemption. Then minutes later, Henry had exchanged shots in the middle of the street. The most unbelievable part of it was that Doc Holliday had lost. Roland would have sworn up and down that Doc was the fastest gun alive even if he was five years older and going by a different name.

With Henry dead, Roland only hoped that Singing Rock could brave the Land of Shadows all by himself. Otherwise Roland had no choice but to find Curly and bring him to justice. He just didn't know how long it would take or, more importantly, how much time Rebecca had left before her dwindling strength ran out. He hadn't even told the Navajo that his partner was dead. There were too many other things to attend to first, and Roland needed to get them out of the way. *One thing at a time.* After he had arranged for Henry's funeral, he could return to The Frontier and tell Singing Rock of his friend's death. Henry's partner didn't speak English, but Roland would just have to find a way to communicate with him. He had left George with explicit instructions not to allow anyone to disturb the Navajo until he returned. He already had William seeing to the construction of a gallows. As soon as it was completed, Roland intended to hang Jimmy. Roland was willing to overlook some reckless behavior, but he had never allowed killing in his city. *I hope you suffer, Goddamn it.* Roland's fist clenched so tightly his knuckles turned white as he rode down the street with his face locked in a mask of barely controlled fury.

For the second time in two days, Roland had to arrange a funeral. Not since the Civil War could he remember so many people dying in such a short timespan, and unfortunately, he knew the count would rise. One way or another, Roland would bring the Dark Riders to justice, and that would likely bring the deaths of several more men, possibly even his own. At that point, Roland barely cared if he survived. As long as Rebecca awakened and all the guilty found their just reward, Roland could accept dying. He just wanted to ensure that those two conditions were met first.

Thatcher sat in one of the pews reading the bible as Roland stormed into the church. The small preacher looked up, and his face crinkled with surprise at seeing Roland in such a state of anger. "Roland," he greeted quietly and waited for Roland to speak.

"Reverend." Roland didn't even tip his hat or nod. He just stood rigidly with his hands planted on his hips, his entire body shaking with rage. "I've got a dead body at Sullivan's office. I need you to say a prayer for him then bury him for me," he stated in a flat tone. *Jimmy, I hope you burn in Hell.*

The preacher's head drew back in surprise. "Another one. Good God, who is it?" Thatcher put a hand to his chest, his eyes looking worried. "It's not Rebecca?"

"No!" Roland snapped roughly. "It's someone else. An old friend from another state. Can you come over to Sullivan's office?"

Thatcher breathed a sigh of relief. He didn't want to bury somebody else he knew. The Reverend hated to see anybody die, but if God was going to call someone home, he preferred them to be somebody outside his flock. "Certainly. I'll be right over." He paused for a moment as if he was going to say something else then held his tongue. "I'll be there in a few minutes."

"Thank you," Roland answered simply and stalked out of the church. He climbed atop his horse and headed to Doc Sullivan's office by himself. Thatcher knew where it was, and Roland didn't want to accompany him. He didn't feel like talking to anybody. Hopefully he could finish up the details for Henry's funeral then plan what to do about Rebecca. *One thing at a time.*

Doc Sullivan had set up his shop in the middle of town next to Dennis's smithy. It was a large building, serving as both his living quarters and an office. Sullivan had taken Henry's body to his office immediately after the fight. Roland usually would have let Joseph Wilson collect the body for burial, but the doctor had been insistent. Roland had cared little about the location of the body and had let Sullivan do as he wished while he dragged Jimmy to the station house.

The doctor waited inside the building for Roland's arrival. "Sheriff," he greeted in his stuffy voice.

"Doc," Roland replied in a raspy whisper. He didn't want to talk to anyone. It seemed impossible that Henry had died, and he wanted to be as far from the body as possible. The proximity made Roland uncomfortable as he waited for Thatcher to arrive.

Sullivan picked up on Roland's need for silence and kept his mouth shut. He sat down and nervously played with the buttons on his jacket while keeping a cautious eye on Roland. When the door to the office opened and Thatcher walked in, the doctor bounced to his feet looking relieved. "Reverend, why don't you come with me," he greeted and opened the door to the room where Henry's body lay.

"Sure," Thatcher replied. The small man looked tired from the short walk to the office. Sweat had beaded along his forehead and temples, dripping down his neck. Roland couldn't blame him. The summer heat continued to hammer Colorado ruthlessly.

Roland rose to his feet as well, but Sullivan held up a hand. "Why don't you wait here, Sheriff? I don't think you want to see your friend. He was wounded pretty badly," the doctor told Roland.

"All right," Sheriff Black muttered and sat back down. He didn't think that he could be shocked by violence anymore. In twenty years of roaming the West, Roland had seen more than his share. He watched with narrowed eyes as Thatcher went into the room with Sullivan. The door shut behind them, and Roland was left to stew alone in the office. He couldn't wait to pass the body off to Joseph so he could return to the station house. *Jimmy, you're a dead man.* Roland was almost to the point of making a list. There were too many people lately who had crossed him. He would get around to dispensing justice to every one of them, but Jimmy was first. The young gunslinger might be proud of killing Doc Holliday, but his joy would be short-lived.

What the hell's taking so long? Roland thought irritably. They had been with Henry's body for nearly five minutes. It didn't take that long to say a prayer over someone's body. He was in a hurry. There were a number of things that he had to do before he could visit Jimmy, and Roland was looking forward to seeing the young man in jail. He was about to check on the pair when the door opened and Thatcher and Sullivan came out of the room. Sullivan looked as stuffy as ever, but Thatcher's face had gone completely white. "Are you all right?"

Thatcher looked his way and blinked once in confusion. "Yes. Yes, I'm fine, Roland." He sounded dazed and lost.

"Did you bless his body?"

"Bless? Oh yes, I blessed him and said a prayer. Yes."

Roland peered closely at the Reverend. He wasn't acting normal. "Are you sure you're all right, Reverend?"

"He's fine, Sheriff. Your friend took a nasty wound. It just shocked the Reverend to see it. He'll be fine. He just needs some air. Right?" The doctor pushed Thatcher's shoulder, propelling him towards the door.

The Reverend blinked again and seemed to regain some of his focus. "Yes, I'm sorry. I need fresh air. I'll do the funeral tomorrow, Roland. Come talk to me later," he instructed the Sheriff then walked outside, still with a dazed look on his face.

Sheriff Black watched him leave, and more questions formed in his head. Both Thatcher and Sullivan were acting strangely, but he pushed all those questions to the back of his mind. There were too many other things that he needed to attend to, and two men's strange behavior didn't make the list. He stared once at the door leading to Henry's body. It was still hard to believe that Doc Holliday lay dead on the other side of the door. Sullivan had been right in telling him not to look at the body. He didn't want his last memory of Doc to be him laying dead and bloody on a doctor's table. Tearing his eyes from the door, he looked at Sullivan. "Thanks for taking care of him."

"You're welcome. I'll talk to Joseph and arrange it from here. Is that all right?"

"Sure," Roland answered and waved a hand in farewell. He was glad to have Henry's funeral out of his hands. Roland would attend, but he didn't have time to plan all the details. He had only just completed Jack's. It seemed unreal that only a few hours ago he had witnessed his old friend's funeral, and now he had another friend dead as well. *Sullivan can take it from here. You've got other things to worry about.* His eyebrows lowered, and a scowl spread across his face as he stepped into the street. Quickly mounting his horse, Sheriff Black galloped towards The Last Frontier where his next item of business waited.

Roland tied his horse to the tether post outside the station house. He stared at the door and contemplated going inside. Hitting Jimmy a few more times would certainly raise his spirits, but Roland had other things to attend to first. Once he began hitting the gunslinger, he didn't know if he could stop. *I'll get you later,* he thought menacingly then crossed the street. He didn't hesitate as he entered the saloon but headed straight to the bar. A crowd had gathered since he left, and they all drew silent as he stalked towards George. Nearly every eye focused on Roland, but he barely noticed. "Whiskey!" He barked at the saloon owner and slammed a hand down on the bar.

"Yes, Sheriff," George answered and quickly put the same bottle in front of Roland. He didn't say anything else but drew back with a wary look on his face. Roland paid him no heed as he grabbed the bottle, pulled the cork out with his teeth, and took a deep swig of the fiery liquid. It burned his gums and throat as it went down, but he sighed in satisfaction as it hit his stomach. Roland was beyond caring how slow his reflexes became. He had just left his fourth friend to be buried in two days, and now he had to go upstairs and tell Singing Rock what had happened. *Please let him understand some English.* Otherwise Roland would have to summon Running Brook or Falling Thunder, and that could take an entire day. He drank one more mouthful of whiskey then slammed it back on the bar. "Don't move it. I'll be back," Roland told George in a hoarse voice then went to the stairway.

His step was a bit unsteady as he climbed the stairs. He hadn't consumed that much whiskey, but coupled with his exhaustion, it was enough to slightly impair his balance. Roland wasn't looking forward to talking to the Navajo. The news that he brought would not be welcome. *Please still help Rebecca.* Singing Rock's aid was critical in helping Rebecca out of the Land of Shadows. He just prayed that the Navajo was able to assist and would still be willing.

He stopped in front of the Navajo's room and gazed down the hallway. Rebecca's doorway beckoned to him. It had been nearly a day since he had last seen her with the chaos surrounding the gunfights. *In a minute.* Roland wanted to get his conversation with Singing Rock over with before he talked to Rebecca. Then his eyes rested on Henry's door. Jack's death had been hard enough to swallow, but Henry's still seemed impossible to believe. Roland shook his head. *Get it over with and talk to him.* He took a deep breath, then knocked loudly on Singing Rock's door. "Singing Rock," Roland called out. No answer came from the room so the Sheriff knocked another time.

The door suddenly swung open, and Singing Rock stared at Roland. He looked as if he had been up for some time. Roland hadn't spoken with the Navajo and didn't know what to expect of him. He was surprised by the intensity of his gaze. Singing Rock didn't simply glance into the hallway but stared Roland right in the eye. He stood at the doorway quietly and continued to watch Sheriff Black.

Roland found the intense gaze rather intimidating. He wasn't looking forward to the conversation. "Singing Rock, I have bad news," the Sheriff spoke each word slowly as if talking to a small child. He waited for any reaction from the Navajo, but Singing Rock continued his silent stare. *Damn it, he doesn't understand me.* Roland really didn't want to seek out Running Brook, but the Cheyenne chief was likely the only person who could communicate with Henry's partner. *One more time,* Roland thought to himself pessimistically. "Singing Rock," Roland said slowly and pointed a finger at the Navajo. "I." Roland tapped his chest. "Have something to tell you." He pointed at the Navajo one more time. *This is useless.* Roland felt stupid, but at least he had tried to talk with Singing Rock.

"Hmm," the Navajo grunted, and the corners of his mouth turned upwards in the tiniest of smiles. "Then come in, Sheriff," he told the stunned Sheriff and turned around.

Roland entered the room and shut the door behind him as Singing Rock took a seat on the bed. *The son of a bitch can speak English.* Sheriff Black didn't know whether to be glad or angry. *At least he can understand me.* Roland was upset about looking like a fool, but the important thing was that he could talk to Singing Rock. It was much better than summoning an intermediary. "You can speak English?" He asked warily, and his eyes narrowed.

The Navajo grunted again and nodded. "I can speak the White Man's tongue."

"Good," Sheriff Black replied and took a deep breath. This was the part he wasn't looking forward to. *Please let him stay and help Rebecca.* "I've got bad news for you," he repeated his earlier comment. *Just get it over with.* He took one more deep breath. "Henry died about an hour ago," Roland told Singing Rock and waited for a response.

He had barely seen the Navajo display any emotions since his arrival in New Haven, but even Roland was surprised when Singing Rock nodded calmly. After that brief acknowledgement, he crossed his arms across his chest, and continued to stare silently at the Sheriff.

Roland kept quiet for a few more moments. He didn't know if Singing Rock was in shock or hadn't heard him properly. "Do you understand what I said?" He asked in disbelief. No matter how much he hid his emotions, surely Henry's good friend would be upset over his death.

"Hmm. I heard you, Sheriff," Singing Rock answered.

"That's all you have to say?" Roland was stunned. He had taken the death of Doc Holliday far more seriously than the Navajo. *Henry. His name is Henry.* Singing Rock had traveled with the gunslinger for over five years. Surely they had built some semblance of camaraderie in that time.

The Navajo shrugged his shoulders. "What else do you want me to say?" One of his eyebrows raised slightly.

"I thought you'd be upset. Henry's dead," Roland told the Navajo in a bewildered voice. He hadn't looked forward to telling Singing Rock of Henry's death, thinking that the Ghost Hunter would be angry, but Singing Rock's stoic behavior proved him completely wrong.

"All men die, Sheriff. The spirits of my people work in strange ways. Henry was a good man, and he will be reborn as a greater man. This is not my first life, nor is it my last. Each life gives the opportunity to accomplish greater feats. After the seventh death, the spirit may journey to The Happy Hunting Grounds where the grass in green, the sky is blue, and there is always game to be hunted." The Navajo's eyes glazed over with a lost look, and a smile crossed his stoic face. "One day I will journey there, Sheriff, but first I must work hard in this life."

Roland listened to the Navajo and remembered the speech Running Brook had delivered. It seemed months ago rather than only two weeks, but the Cheyenne Chief's words had been nearly identical. Even with the events surrounding Rebecca's illness, Roland still had difficulty believing their lore, but whatever Singing Rock wanted to believe was fine with him. A few of the

Ghost Hunter's words bothered Roland, though. "But Henry's not Navajo. Hell, he's not even an Indian. He doesn't want to go to the Happy Hunting Grounds."

The Navajo was silent for a few moments before he continued. "What do you believe happens to a man after he dies?"

Singing Rock's words took Roland by surprise. He hadn't considered that question in some time. His parents had raised him as a Christian, but that time in Mississippi seemed more than a hundred years in the past. After his family's deaths, Roland had abandoned most of his faith in God. During his years of gunslinging, he had placed all of his faith in his two guns and his speed on the draw. Those were the main things that kept him alive during those tumultuous years. Roland had seen many men buried in that time. They had all received Christian burials, but he had never stopped to think what that meant until Singing Rock posed his question. "You go to heaven," he replied slowly. He didn't know if he believed it or not, but that was the doctrine that had been repeated at every funeral he had ever attended, including Jack's that morning.

"And what is heaven?" Singing Rock asked. He displayed no emotion while he asked questions of Roland, and his arms never once budged from his chest.

Roland flung his arms wide. "How the hell should I know? I haven't been there." His voice rose angrily. He had expected Singing Rock to yell at him and possibly leave New Haven, but Roland hadn't expected to defend Christianity to the Navajo. *What the hell does this have to do with Henry?*

The Navajo's expression didn't change in the slightest at Roland's outburst. Instead he continued his barrage of questions. "How do you know you do not go to The Happy Hunting Grounds?"

"I don't believe in that stuff," Roland scoffed in an almost scathing tone. *What is he talking about? Henry's dead, and he's talking about the Happy Goddamn Hunting Grounds.*

"You do not believe?" Singing Rock actually sounded surprised. "Your woman is trapped in the Land of Shadows, and you do not believe? You have never seen this heaven of yours, but Henry went to the Land of Shadows many times. He knew what to believe in, Sheriff. For five years, he has studied the ways of my people and adopted them. Perhaps you should take a better look at your own beliefs," he pointed out to Roland then fell silent, his arms crossed across his chest and his eyes continuing to bore through Sheriff Black intensely.

"All right, I will," Roland snapped back quickly. He didn't really intend to think about where he would go when he died. It didn't figure very prominently in his list of important things in life, but he wanted Singing Rock to abandon the topic. There were far more important issues that Roland wished to talk to him about. "What about Rebecca?" He asked and held his breath involuntarily as he awaited the answer. One way or another, he meant to free her from the

Land of Shadows, but the task would be much easier with the Ghost Hunter's aid.

"What do you wish to know?" The Navajo looked confused over the question.

"Will you help her?" Roland snapped impatiently.

If Singing Rock was offended by Sheriff Black's tone, he didn't show it. "Yes, Sheriff. I will help. That is why I came here. Henry might be dead, but I will journey to the Land of Shadows in his place. Do you still wish my help?"

Roland blinked in surprise. *Do I still want his help?* He thought incredulously. "Of course I do. I want her out of there."

"Good, then we will go to the house tomorrow at dawn. Wake me two hours before the sun rises, and I will try to rescue her."

"Thank you," Roland told Singing Rock gratefully. He breathed a huge sigh of relief and fought the tears that threatened to form at the corner of his eye. Roland was nearly overcome with relief that Singing Rock would stay in New Haven and help. Rebecca still had a chance to awaken the following morning, and then all his pain and suffering would come to an end. Jack, Henry, Wade, and Robert would still be dead, but at least he would have Rebecca to help him through the troubled times.

"You are welcome, Sheriff. Now let me sleep. I will need my rest if I am to enter the Land of Shadows."

"Sure," Roland answered quickly and backed towards the door. He didn't want to do anything that might upset Singing Rock. His hand gripped the doorknob, and he opened it behind him. "Thank you again. I appreciate it," Roland thanked the Navajo one last time and jumped back into the hallway, anxious to leave the room before Singing Rock changed his mind. He closed the door and collapsed against one of the hallway walls. *Yes!* Roland exulted. He closed his eyes and breathed several sighs of relief. Singing Rock's decision to stay and help was the best news he had heard in days. It almost eclipsed the sorrow of all the deaths that had recently occurred. *Soon, Rebecca. Soon.* A tear spilled down his cheek, but Roland didn't care if anyone saw him or what they thought. Rebecca would be awake soon, and that was all that mattered.

He rubbed at his eye to wipe away the tears and looked down the hallway. His mouth curled into its customary lopsided grin as he strode towards Rebecca's room. Over the past two weeks, Roland had made empty promises to her, but he felt more confident than he had since the terrible ordeal had begun. *Tomorrow, Rebecca. Just hold on until tomorrow.* He opened the door to her room and walked inside. This time the sight of her so weak didn't pain him as it had before. Her cheeks were still hollow, her hair hung in tangled knots, and a faint odor of sickness permeated the room. But Rolland ignored those things. *Soon, Rebecca. Not much longer, then you'll be awake.*

Kneeling beside the bed, Roland took one of her frail hands in his own. His other hand gently caressed her forehead. The skin under his fingertips was cold, but to Roland it was the most beautiful thing that he had ever touched. "Rebecca, it's me, Roland," he told her softly. "I talked to Singing Rock, and he said we'll get you out of there tomorrow." Once more tears rolled down his cheek, but his voice never broke. He wanted to be strong for Rebecca and show her just how confident he was that she would indeed escape her prison this time.

Roland told her what had happened to him since his last visit and was amazed at how much had occurred. It had only been a day and a half since he had discovered that Doc Holliday was alive. In the time between, the town had celebrated the Fourth of July, three deputies had died, and Jimmy had bested Henry in a duel. He painted a vivid story as he told of each event in close detail. Jack's death in particular was difficult. It seemed so unreal that his old friend had died. So much pain and suffering had swirled about Roland for the last two weeks, but Jack's death had struck him harder than the rest. He squeezed her hand tightly as he recounted how he had closed Jack's eyes once and for all. More than anything, he wished Rebecca was awake to help him through the grievous time.

Henry's death was not as difficult to report. Doc Holliday had been one of the legends of his lifetime, and it had been a wonder to find him alive and well in New Haven. But the two of them were not close friends. Henry had aided Rebecca, and for that Roland would be eternally grateful. His death saddened Roland. He hated to see such an important figure die, especially after he had leant a helping hand. Roland would get over it in time, though, especially since Singing Rock had agreed to return to the house. The grief over Jack's death would be much slower to dissipate.

He spoke of his anger at Jimmy. Only circumstances had prevented him from returning to the station house and beating the gunslinger to within an inch of his life. Roland still felt angry at him for the senselessness of the act, but he no longer burned with rage. Singing Rock's decision to stay and seeing Rebecca had lightened his mood. Regardless of his change of heart, he intended to hang the youth. Murder was not permitted in New Haven. He couldn't let Jimmy's crime go unpunished even if he had wanted to. It would set a bad precedent if a murderer didn't pay the ultimate price for his crimes.

He switched to more pleasant topics after telling Rebecca about Jimmy and Henry. "I talked with Thatcher today, and he said he's ready to perform the wedding. As soon as you wake up, we can be married." Roland's eyes glazed over and seemed to stare right through Rebecca. It seemed so long since he'd proposed to her. *Stop it!* He shook his head. Rebecca would be awake the next morning and then they could be married when she regained enough strength.

"Maybe it will cool down. Clouds have to come out sometime, and then it'll finally rain."

Roland continued to talk about the weather, plans for their wedding, and anything else that crossed his mind. He had no idea how long he spent with Rebecca, but the time seemed to fly by. Roland wanted nothing more than to spend the rest of the night by Rebecca's side and then ride to her house at dawn to wrest her spirit away from Bryant once and for all. Unfortunately there were too many things to take care of, and Jack wasn't around anymore to help pick up the slack. He bent over and kissed her forehead tenderly. "I have to go now, Rebecca. I'll be back later, and we'll get you out of there at dawn. Don't worry. It'll all be over soon. I love you, Rebecca White," Roland whispered and kissed her forehead once more. After taking one last look at Rebecca, Roland stepped into the hallway and locked the door behind him.

He marched down the hallway at a brisk pace. Seeing to the gunslinger's funeral, talking to Singing Rock, and sitting with Rebecca had taken a great deal of time. There were still many things to take care of before he and Singing Rock returned to Rebecca's house. He needed to find Morgan. The veteran deputy was functioning as Jack's replacement, and Roland wanted to see if he had recruited any citizen deputies. The Dark Riders were out there somewhere, and until Roland knew where they were and why they had started the gunfight, he wanted the town on alert. William had overseen the construction of a gallows so Jimmy could be hanged. *Hopefully some Goddamn Riders too.*

Roland didn't even pause at the bottom of the stairs and headed straight towards the door. He needed to talk to his deputies, and the station house was the best place to start. Sheriff Black was also looking forward to paying Jimmy a visit. The summer air hit him like a hot fire as he stepped outside. *Blazes.* It seemed as if the temperature had gone up in the past two weeks. Even though he was just walking across the street, sweat formed on his forehead and trickled down from his temple in that brief time. He pushed open the door to the station house and entered, breathing a sigh of relief to be out of the brutal heat. "Damn, it's hot," Roland swore.

Phillip sat behind the desk, a book open in front of him. Black rings encircled his eyes, and his bushy beard seemed more wild and unkempt than normal. *We've all got to get some sleep,* Roland thought wistfully. He had only slept a few hours in the past two days, and his deputies hadn't fared much better. William stood in front of the desk and looked up as Roland entered the station house. The rakish deputy also looked exhausted. Sweat had dampened patches of his grey jacket, and his face was flushed. "You can say that again," William replied dryly, a smile creasing his tired face.

"Is the gallows almost ready?" Roland asked William in a very businesslike manner.

"Yes, Sheriff." The smile disappeared from the deputy's face, and he stood straight as he reported to Sheriff Black. "I talked to Lewis, and he said he'd have it ready by noon tomorrow."

"Good. We'll hang him tomorrow." Roland smiled. He had hoped to hang Jimmy before sundown, but he would settle for the following day. Tomorrow was going to be the day that Rebecca awakened, but Roland wouldn't let Jimmy dodge justice any longer than he had to. "William, I want you to find Morgan and tell him I want to see him. I'll be here or at The Frontier."

William's eyes rolled up in his head, and he breathed a tired sigh. The last thing he wanted to do was go back into the summer heat. "All right. I'll see if I can find him. You don't know where he is, do you?"

Roland tapped his chin. "I think he was talking to Paul Henderson. You might want to start there."

The deputy nodded and headed back outside with a resigned look on his face.

Phillip sat behind the desk with a wry smile on his face. The deputies had often given him and Robert a hard time about always staying in the station house, but lately they had all been envious of the constant shade Phillip enjoyed. Roland's gaze switched to the deputy once William closed the door. "Sheriff," Phillip greeted.

"Phillip." Roland walked over to the desk and took the key ring off their peg. He leaned back against the wall. "Has he made any noise?" Roland jutted his chin towards the cell room door.

"No, Sheriff. He hasn't made a sound since you brought him in. I looked in about twenty minutes ago, and he didn't look too good."

Roland had hit Jimmy hard and expected the young man to have quite a headache. After seeing Singing Rock and Rebecca, Sheriff Black had decided not to beat Jimmy further, but he still felt some pleasure in having taken those two shots at him. *He'll be dead soon enough anyway.* "I'm going to talk to him. I don't want anybody coming in there," he warned Phillip then walked to the door without waiting for a response.

He swung the door open with a metallic creak. As always, his nose wrinkled at the smell of the cells. Roland had been in and presided over numerous jails through the years, and every single one of them had a stench to them. Ignoring the smell as best as he could, Roland approached Jimmy's cell. The gunslinger rested nearly exactly where Roland had left him a few hours before. He lay in the middle of the cell on his stomach, resting his head on his arms as he tried to sleep off the punches. "Jimmy!" Roland called out and dragged the key ring along the iron bars, creating a loud metallic staccato burst.

Jimmy groaned at the noise and wearily lifted his head from the floor. A large purple bruise had formed under his left eye, and his lower lip was swollen. The young gunslinger blinked a few times as he tried to focus, and then he flinched as he made out Roland's face behind the bars.

"I'm not going to hit you, Jimmy," Roland told the frightened young man scornfully. All the sympathy and camaraderie that Roland had felt towards the gunslinger had disappeared the moment Jimmy killed Henry. "Get up. I want to talk to you." Jimmy continued to huddle on the floor and didn't make any move to rise to his feet. "Damn it! I said get up!" Roland barked and dragged the key ring along the bars again. He continued to sweep it left and right.

Finally Jimmy held out a hand. "All right," he said groggily. "I'm getting up." He pushed himself onto his hands and knees then slowly stood up. He rubbed a hand over his swollen cheek and squinted at Roland. "What do you want?" Jimmy asked. All the cockiness and arrogance had left his voice, and he sounded like a tired, beaten man.

"We're hanging you tomorrow," Roland stated matter-of-factly. "They're building a gallows right now." He waited to see if Jimmy had anything to say, but the gunslinger just nodded slowly as if it was what he expected. *You little bastard.* Roland still couldn't believe that Jimmy had killed Doc Holliday. *Jimmy!* He thought in disgust. The young man looked pathetic. Henry should have died by the gun of a real gunslinger not a two-bit pretender who had made only a pair of kills in his lifetime. "I just want to know one thing," Sheriff Black rasped. "Why?"

Jimmy blinked again. "Why what?"

"Why'd you kill him?"

Despite his split lip, swollen eye, and imminent death, a tiny smile crossed Jimmy's lips, and his shoulders straightened proudly. "He was Doc Holliday. I killed the best that ever lived." It sounded more as if he was congratulating himself than bragging to Roland.

Stupid son of a bitch! Rage briefly bubbled up within Roland, and his fists clenched tightly. All Doc had wanted was to be left alone so he could help Singing Rock. He had wanted his name kept secret, but Roland hadn't been able to prevent it. *Alvin and Matthew, you're both dead too.* Roland knew that he couldn't hang the mayor and *Gazette* editor, but he intended to put the fear of God into both of them. If not for their telling of Henry's secret, the Ghost Hunter would still be alive. *I've at least got you,* Roland thought menacingly as he stared at Jimmy. He got himself under control with a great deal of effort then gave the young man a withering gaze. "Yeah, but you'll be dead tomorrow," he said coldly and stalked out of the cell room before he lost his temper and killed Jimmy.

He slammed the door behind him and made sure he locked it before returning the key ring to the wall. Phillip looked up from his book and quickly resumed reading after taking one look at Sheriff Black's expression. "Phillip."

The deputy looked back up with an apprehensive expression. "Yes?"

"I'm going back to The Frontier. No food for him." Roland jutted his chin towards the cell door again. "Let the bastard starve the rest of the night." Roland's mouth curled into a sneer. "Got it?"

"Sure, Sheriff. It's no problem," Phillip answered quickly.

"Good," Sheriff Black replied then left the station house without another word. Roland couldn't believe that Doc Holliday had died because of a stupid kid. The senselessness of it all made Roland want to hit something. First Jack, Wade, and Robert had died for no apparent reason, and then Doc died for even less of one. With Rebecca about to awaken, Roland wanted to celebrate, but events had made his job difficult beyond belief. He still needed to get more deputies, track down the Dark Riders, and execute Jimmy. Besides that, he wanted to find Alvin and Matthew. *Damn it to Hell.* He just hoped some peace, quiet, and maybe a good strong shot of whiskey would calm his nerves.

The Last Frontier was crowded by six o'clock. The afternoon train had come and gone, and nearly everyone was done with their day of work. News of the duel between Jimmy and Henry had spread like wildfire through New Haven, and the town was abuzz with gossip over the event. Everyone knew what had happened the night before, and they had all heard or read the *Gazette* article that claimed Doc Holliday was alive. When Roland stepped through the door the saloon grew quiet, and every eye instantly turned towards him. Roland scowled and ignored their stares as he marched towards the bar.

George looked apprehensive. Roland had a fierce scowl on his face, and after the events of that afternoon, George didn't want to anger the Sheriff inadvertently. The pudgy saloon owner rubbed his hands together nervously. "What can I do for you, Sheriff?"

"Whiskey," Roland answered simply and leaned against the bar as he waited for George to fill his order.

"Right away," George quickly replied and fetched Roland's bottle. He placed it on the bar and took a step backwards. "Is there anything else?"

Roland shook his head but didn't say another word as he turned around and headed towards his table. People continued to stare at Sheriff Black as he stormed across the floor, but everyone quickly moved out of his path. He took a seat and slowly swept his gaze across the room, glowering at every eye that he met. The noise picked back up as more and more people stopped staring and minded their own business. Everyone was still curious about what had happened that afternoon, but nobody wanted to bother Roland about it or draw his ire. After shaking much of the attention, Roland opened the bottle and tossed back a large mouthful of whiskey. It burned his mouth, but the warm, numbing sensation in his belly more than made up for it. He sighed contentedly then put the bottle on the table, leaned back, and waited for Morgan.

Within the next fifteen minutes the grizzled deputy arrived at The Last Frontier. He attracted a fair amount of attention as he walked to Roland's table. The entire saloon didn't grow silent as it had when Roland entered, but almost everyone inside at least glanced at Morgan. He looked tired as he took a seat across from Roland. His face was flushed, and his forehead was damp with sweat. "Roland," he greeted.

"Morgan. Did you get Paul to help?" Roland asked abruptly, getting straight to the point.

"Yeah. He said he'd get another twenty men for us. I also got a few volunteers over at Will's Tavern. If Carlos decides to come back to town, there'll be at least two dozen men waiting for him," Morgan answered and chuckled dryly. "I bet it'll drive him crazy."

Roland grinned as well. If he knew Carlos, the Dark Rider would definitely want to come back and finish business. The presence of those extra guns would certainly dissuade him. Carlos had a temper, but Morgan was right; the Dark Rider was not a stupid man. It was one more thing that he didn't have to worry about. Now he could focus on Rebecca. Once she was awake he would seek out the Dark Riders, but that was for another day. "That's good to hear. Let's make sure we've got somebody keeping an eye out for them all night. I don't want to wake up with a gun in my face."

"I already took care of it." Morgan leaned back in his chair and rubbed at his eyes. "Damn, I'm tired."

"You already have a patrol lined up for tonight?" Roland asked incredulously. He forgot how effective Morgan could be. Morgan knew what needed to be done and took care of it. Sheriff Black was glad he had him around.

"Yeah. I've got Paul and two others watching on the north side and Ben, Simon, and a few volunteers watching on the east side of town. I thought I'd have William and a couple of men keep an eye on the south end of town. That leaves you, me, and Phillip."

"Go home and get some sleep. At midnight, you can take over for the other three." Roland knew how tired his men must feel. He hadn't slept in nearly two days, and slumber kept beckoning him. Nobody else had slept during the long night after Jack, Robert, and Wade died, and they all had to be feeling the same lethargy. They needed sleep, or they'd be no good in a fight even if they had enough guns.

Morgan didn't argue. He knew as well as Roland how much they needed sleep. "What about you?"

Roland glanced at the stairway and sighed. Now that he thought about resting his weary body, it was all he could do to keep his eyes open. It was going to be a long night, and he wanted to have some energy for the following day when Rebecca woke up. "I guess I'll get some sleep as well. I'll have

390

George wake me at midnight. I'm about ready to fall over. We'll meet here at midnight and take over for the others."

"Sounds good. I'll go tell everyone else and go home. See you later, Roland." Morgan rose to his feet, tipped his hat, and walked out of the saloon.

Grabbing the bottle of whiskey, Roland told George to wake him later then headed directly for the stairs. He had made it through the past two days on adrenaline alone, and it was beginning to desert him. The next few days would be exhausting, and he needed to rest while he could. Still Roland hated to sleep while his men were patrolling. He felt that he should be awake in case something happened. It was his job as Sheriff. *To hell with it,* Roland thought sleepily. If he didn't get rest soon, he'd be no good to anyone if a problem did arise.

Bypassing both Singing Rock's and Rebecca's rooms, Roland went straight to his own and entered. He tossed his hat on the floor and took a seat on the bed. After tossing back one more shot of whiskey, Roland set the bottle down. He remembered taking the boots off his aching feet and laying down, but as soon as his head hit the pillow he was sound asleep.

He dreamed that he stood by Rebecca's house in the moments just before dawn, watching the front door anxiously and holding his breath. Singing Rock emerged moments later, cradling Rebecca against his chest. Her arms hung limply by her side, but her dazzling green eyes were open and staring at Roland. *Rebecca,* he thought joyously. Rebecca was finally awake again, and the two of them could finally get married and begin the rest of their lives together. He called out to them, a huge smile lighting up his face. Laughing out loud, Roland ran towards them.

His joy was short-lived, however. Figures in tattered clothes began to rise from the earth, tearing their way through the soil. Singing Rock stopped in his tracks as six of them formed a crude semicircle, pinning him against the house. Roland shot one of them, but the dark figure shrugged the bullet off like it was insignificant. "Rebecca!" He cried and rushed forward, desperate to help the woman he loved.

As he rushed past the first figure, a hand reached out and grabbed his ankle. Roland tried to keep his balance, but he fell to the ground, knocking most of the wind out of him. He tried to scramble back to his feet, but another hand reached out of the soil and pulled his shoulder back to the earth. Roland kicked and fought for all he was worth, but it was to no avail as the figures rose fully out of the earth. With a shuffling gait, they moved towards him. Their faces became clear as they descended upon him, and Roland screamed as he recognized each one. Jack's face was gaunt and lifeless with grey eyes. Jimmy and Henry were right by him. Their skin was darker, but they each grinned malevolently. The other three were Alvin, Curly, and Carlos. Each of them had glowing red eyes and that same evil grin as Jimmy and Henry. All six of them had broken, ragged teeth and long nails sharpened to a point.

"Mine!" Bryant's voice echoed through the morning air as the six figures fell upon Roland.

He nearly catapulted into a sitting position as he awakened from the nightmare. Sweat covered his forehead, and his heart raced. At first he didn't notice the knocking on his door as he calmed down from the frightening dream. "Sheriff," a voice called urgently from the hallway, and Roland tiredly swung his legs out of bed. He had no idea how long he had slept, but it wasn't long enough. Rubbing at his eyes, Roland shuffled to the door, anxious to stop the knocking. "Sheriff," the voice called again. Roland opened the door, squinting at the sudden light. Through his blurred vision, he could make out the pudgy form of George. "George?" He didn't know why the saloon owner was waking him up. *It can't be midnight already!* Roland's entire body screamed for more rest.

"Sheriff, come quick!" George hissed urgently.

The saloon owner's tone was like cold water splashing across Roland's face. A million different scenarios quickly ran through his head. *The Riders? Alvin? Is everyone all right?* Enough trouble had been caused in New Haven over the last few days, and Roland immediately expected the worst. "What is it?" He grabbed George by the shoulders and demanded. Tears formed from the light stabbing at his sleepy eyes, but Roland barely noticed.

"There's a fire," George explained. His eyes had widened nervously when Roland grabbed his shoulders.

"I'll be right down." Roland jumped back into his room and quickly donned his boots and hat. Grabbing his holsters, he ran back into the hallway. If there was one thing that scared him more than the Dark Riders it was a fire. He had seen a few towns destroyed by fire. It didn't take a very big one to set an entire town ablaze. George stood anxiously against the opposite wall. "Where is it?" Roland demanded from the frightened owner.

"The other side of town, by the train station. They sent word for you to come," George explained in a rush.

Roland nodded tersely then ran down the hallway with his holsters in his hands. *Son of a bitch, not the train station,* Roland thought worriedly. The train stop was the most lucrative thing in New Haven. Without it, Roland didn't know if the town could continue to thrive. He rushed down the stairs, through the empty saloon, and out into the street. A number of people were running towards the train station, and Roland joined them. A fire was something that everybody worried about. All of them wanted New Haven to have continued prosperity, but that would all disappear if a fire spread. He buckled on his holsters as he raced down the main street.

George had said that the fire was by the train station, and he was obviously right by the size of the crowd gathered around it. A makeshift line of people passing buckets back and forth stretched to a nearby well. Luckily George had also been wrong. The train station stood unharmed from fire, but the gallows that had been constructed and the stage that Zoltan had performed upon lit up the night sky. *I guess there won't be a hanging tomorrow,* Roland thought with relief. He'd have preferred to get Jimmy's execution over with, but a delay was much better than having the train station go up in ashes.

The blaze was a small one. It wouldn't take much, however, to make it spread, and with its proximity to the train station everyone did their best to ensure that it didn't. Running to the front of the line, Roland quickly joined the men already there. Grabbing one of the next buckets to be passed down the line, Roland hurled it onto the mass of burning wood. He immediately began to sweat under the hot conditions, but he stayed at the front the entire time.

It only took forty minutes to extinguish the fire completely, but by the time it was done Roland was drenched in sweat. His shirt clung to his chest, and several blisters had formed on his palms. He rested his hands on his knees and looked at the blackened wood as he tried to catch his breath. "Sheriff," a voice called behind him, and Roland sighed as he straightened his back. He just wanted to rest for a few more minutes, but duty beckoned. Like many of the men helping near the fire, William's face was red from the heat and had several black smudges on it. His clothes were a complete mess from the smoke, water, and sweat they had been subjected to. *Do I look that bad?* Roland thought but didn't really care. The fire was out, and that's all that mattered. "William," he called out tiredly as he saw the deputy.

"Damn, that was scary there for a minute," William commented breathlessly.

"Yeah, it was. Does anyone have any idea how this thing got started?" It had been dry in New Haven for weeks, but Roland found it odd that the gallows and the stage had caught on fire. Why nothing else? Somewhere in the back of his mind, a tiny voice told Roland that he should remember something.

"I don't know. We saw the fire, and all started helping out. Maybe someone saw it start, though."

"We'll see." Roland shrugged his shoulders. "At least nothing else caught on fire. It's time to get back to your position. I don't want the Riders coming while we're standing around." He still had two hours to go before his shift started, and Roland planned on going back to The Frontier and getting some more rest. The fire had provided a rush of adrenaline, but it was already wearing off.

"Sure," William replied reluctantly. He had to be as tired as Roland, but he only had two more hours before he got a full night's rest. "I'll go tell everyone else to return to the watch."

"Good," Roland replied. He saw Simon and Ben talking in the distance. They hadn't been away from their post for too long, but Roland didn't want the borders of town unwatched any longer than they had to be. He was about to speak to William when he noticed something for the first time and instantly remembered what had eluded him. His heart began racing faster, and the blood drained from his face. "Where's Phillip?" He asked urgently.

"I don't know. I haven't seen him. He might be somewhere around here," William answered.

"Goddamn it," Roland swore as he looked at all the people gathered. Phillip's large frame and bushy beard were hard to miss, and when Roland didn't spot him after a cursory glance, he turned back to William. "Meet me at the station house," he ordered briefly then sprinted ahead.

He panted breathlessly as he raced around the corner. His body was exhausted and sore from his recent excursion, but he hurried on as he focused on returning to the station house as quickly as possible. *Goddamn, let him still be there.* Roland had almost forgotten the stories he had told Jimmy during the young man's week in jail, but he remembered one of them all too well. *Big Nose Kate set a fire on the other side of town, and then she broke Doc Holliday out of prison.* The similarities were too close for Roland's liking, and his fears wouldn't be put to rest until he saw for himself that Jimmy was still in his cell.

He rushed to the station house with a gun in hand. Kicking open the door, he rushed inside and swore as he saw the office sitting empty. "Son of a bitch." The set of keys was missing from the wall, but luckily the second set was still in the desk. Roland yanked open the drawer, pulled them out, then hurried to the cell room door. He put the key in the lock and pushed the door open with his shoulder. Rushing inside with his gun still drawn, Roland's jaw clenched in anger at what he saw.

"Sheriff," Phillip exclaimed in relief when he spotted Roland. The deputy stood in one of the cells, his arms wrapped around the bars. He didn't seem happy, but he wasn't hurt.

Roland, however, barely noticed Phillip as he quickly scoured the rest of the cells. "Goddamn it!" He swore and punched the wall in frustration. With all his other worries, the last thing that he needed was an escaped murderer on the loose. *I should have killed that bastard when I had the chance.* Phillip stood in the one cell, but Jimmy was nowhere to be found.

Chapter Twenty

An array of different emotions coursed through Roland as he listened to Phillip tell what had happened. Sheriff Black hadn't been in the best of moods when he opened the cell door for his deputy, and it only worsened as he heard more details. He sat with a clenched jaw and burning eyes, trying to resist the urge to go outside and shoot someone. *Why?* He thought in frustration. It seemed that he had been asking himself that question far too often of late.

Phillip had seen the crowd rush out of The Last Frontier and had even gone outside to ask someone what they were hurrying towards. His heart had skipped a beat in fear when he heard that the train station was on fire, but he remained at his post. He would have rushed to join in the effort to stamp out the blaze, but Jimmy was in one of the cells. He wasn't about to abandon a prisoner, especially when he was to be hanged the following day. It was frustrating to watch all the people scrambling down the street, but Phillip made himself take a seat. A book lay on the desk, but he was far too nervous about the fire to read anything. Tapping his fingers on his leg, he anxiously waited for word of the fire and how much damage it had caused.

After the initial rush of people, the streets had emptied. He had watched Roland hurry towards the station house a few minutes later, and then there was complete silence as the town battled the fire that consumed the gallows and stage. Nearly five minutes after Roland's frantic race out of the saloon, Phillip had been surprised to see an Indian calmly walk across the street towards the station house. The deputy put a hand on the butt of his pistol and leaned forward in the chair as the Indian entered.

Roland listened in amazement. Phillip's story made no sense, but the deputy had no cause to lie. Singing Rock's arrival in New Haven had been noticed by nearly everybody after the problems with the Cheyenne, and Phillip had been one of them. The deputy recognized the Navajo as he crossed the street and half-expected trouble as he entered the station house. Much to Phillip's surprise, Singing Rock spoke perfect English. The Navajo wanted to see Jimmy, which Phillip quickly disallowed, but Singing Rock was persistent, explaining that Jimmy had killed his partner and how he wanted to see him before he was hanged. Reluctantly Phillip agreed, seeing no harm in allowing a quick peek at the prisoner. If nothing else, it would take his mind off the fire on the other side of town.

Jimmy had looked up groggily from the cot in the cell. At first he wore the look of a frightened young man, but on seeing Phillip escort Singing Rock into the cell room Jimmy instantly smiled. Without warning, the Navajo threw a red powder at Phillip's face. The deputy reached for his pistol, but it was too late. His arms and legs grew heavy, and a deep lethargy swept over him. He fell to the floor as sleep overcame him.

"Then I woke up with him standing over me. I don't know how long I was asleep. That Indian didn't say anything else, just walked out with Jimmy. I had to wait until you came back. There was nothing else I could do," Phillip insisted. He looked relieved to have survived the encounter unscathed, but he also appeared apprehensive. Roland's eyes burned with fury , and Phillip clearly was in the path of that ire. He wanted to assure Roland as quickly as possible that he had no blame in the incident.

Roland didn't say anything at first but stared at the floor. *Why?* He kept asking himself. None of the story made any sense. Why would Singing Rock help Jimmy escape? The gunslinger had just killed Henry. Singing Rock had taken a stoic approach to Henry's death, but helping his killer escape from prison was a completely different story. *Are they in on it together?* It seemed implausible that Singing Rock and Jimmy were co-conspirators, but that was the only answer that made sense to Roland. Why else would the Navajo help Jimmy? He had already sent William to tell everyone to keep an eye out for the pair. Roland had many questions for the Navajo. As for Jimmy, he intended just to shoot him this time around. Building another gallows would take too long, and he wanted the gunslinger dead as soon as possible before something else could go wrong.

Among the confusion, Roland also felt a profound sense of grief. Once again, it appeared that the key to Rebecca's safety was slipping through his fingers. After speaking to Singing Rock, Roland had felt positive that Rebecca would awaken the following morning. His spirits had been low after Henry's death, but the Navajo had convinced him that she would indeed awaken. Now her situation was right where it had been before the Ghost Hunters had even come to town. Henry was dead, and Singing Rock was a wanted man. Roland didn't know why the Navajo had helped Jimmy, but he certainly didn't expect Singing Rock to enter the Land of Shadows to help Rebecca after the Navajo's actions that night. He was confused over the events and angry at both Singing Rock and Jimmy, but mostly Roland's spirits plunged as he had to come to grips with the fact that Rebecca would remain in the Land of Shadows for at least another day.

Waving a hand in dismissal at Phillip, Roland stood up. He had no desire to talk to anyone until he knew more of what had happened. Singing Rock had to show up sooner or later. A Navajo Indian stood out like a sore thumb. As soon as he learned why Singing Rock had aided Jimmy, Roland would have a better handle on the situation. For the meantime the events made absolutely no sense. "I'm going outside," he commented darkly and stepped out into the hot air.

Roland paced back and forth in front of the station house as he waited on any news of Singing Rock or Jimmy. He fleetingly wished that Jack was still alive. Roland could have talked to Jack about Jimmy's escape. His old friend had been the only deputy in whom he could confide his worries. Morgan was a distant second, but the veteran deputy still slept in his bed. For a moment, Roland had been tempted to wake him, but he let Morgan continue his rest. The night promised to be another long one, and Roland intended to have at least one of his men catch up on sleep.

When no word came after ten minutes of frustrated pacing, Roland finally gave up and stalked across the street. His table in The Last Frontier would give him just as much solitude, and it wouldn't be nearly as hot.

Why? He thought again as he walked through the door. Nearly everyone in the saloon was busy drinking heartily, celebrating the successful extinguishing of the fire. At least nobody knew of Jimmy's escape yet. Roland had been adamant with his deputies that he wanted it kept quiet. He hoped that he would catch Jimmy and Singing Rock before they had a chance to flee New Haven, and then nobody else would ever have to know about it.

Roland forewent his bottle of whiskey and waited in the saloon impatiently. *Come on. They can't be hard to find.* He wanted them found soon. Roland's nerves weren't up to much more waiting. He got his wish after fifteen minutes of sitting at his table when he saw William galloping towards the station house. The deputy jumped off his horse and ran inside the station house as soon as he arrived there. Roland just as quickly followed suit and ran out of The Last Frontier, leaving a trail of curious people in his wake. He was halfway across the street when William burst out of the office.

The deputy only took two steps before spotting Roland. "Sheriff," he called and stopped in his tracks.

"What is it?" Roland asked when he reached the deputy.

William took a deep breath and backed up slightly. "Paul saw them leaving town," he reported quietly.

Sheriff Black reached out and grabbed William by the front of his jacket. He pulled the deputy towards him until their noses almost touched. Roland's eyes glowed madly, and his lips curled into a sneer. "What did you say?"

The deputy's eyes darted from side to side, looking for somebody to come to his aid, but he was all alone with the Sheriff. He took another deep breath. "Paul saw them leaving town during the fire, Sheriff. Said it was two people riding north. One of them was an Indian," William said quickly. He had never seen Roland so angry.

"Goddamn it," Roland swore and pushed William away in disgust. He wasn't angry at the deputy, but his blood boiled with fury. *I'll kill him. I swear to God, I'll rip Jimmy's Goddamn heart out.* All hopes of Rebecca awakening the following day left town with Singing Rock. It felt like a knife twisting in his gut. The more that he thought Rebecca would awaken, the more the fates conspired to keep her away from him. He would also look like a fool before the whole town. A prisoner had escaped from a jail cell right under his nose. Alvin and Matthew would crucify him with that fact. *Not if I catch Jimmy first,* he thought grimly. "Get a posse," he told William coldly.

William looked at him like he was crazy, which wasn't far from the truth. Roland wouldn't have recognized himself in the mirror at that moment. A toothy grin spread across his face, and his eyes continued to burn madly. The deputy made sure to keep as much distance as possible between himself and Roland. "What about the Riders?" He pointed out to Roland and cringed as if he expected Roland to explode angrily.

Roland's hands balled into tight fists, and he hissed in frustration. *Goddamn Riders!* Then he took a deep breath and tried to calm down. He knew that he wasn't thinking rationally at the moment and had to be scaring the hell out of William. Roland would have given anything to have Jack there to help out. His old friend could always calm him down and help him see the problem from different sides. He finally settled into a simmering anger instead of an explosive rage. "Go wake Morgan. Then you, me, Morgan, and Simon are going to track that son of a bitch down. Everyone else stays here," he explained between clenched teeth.

"Yes, Sheriff," William replied and immediately sprinted towards his horse, obviously glad to have an excuse to put more distance between himself and Roland. Moments later William was galloping towards Morgan's house.

As soon as William was on the horse, Roland punched the side of the station house in frustration. He felt bad about losing his temper in front of the deputy, but he couldn't help it. After the Fourth of July gunfight, Henry's death, and Rebecca's continued illness, Roland's nerves were frayed too thin. He had no intention of letting Jimmy escape his clutches, and Roland wanted to track down Singing Rock even more. Somewhere in the back of his mind, he still held out the slightest of hopes that the Navajo would help Rebecca. It wasn't likely, but it was better than the progress that he had made on his own.

Roland didn't go back to The Frontier but continued a tense, hurried pacing in front of the station house. He kept looking down the street for William and the other deputies to return as he endured the frustrating wait. At least the Dark Riders wouldn't be able to sneak into the city. Roland had assembled a small group of deputies while leaving Paul and the other volunteers to guard New Haven's borders. Roland and three deputies would be more than enough to track down and capture the two fugitives. If all went well, Roland would be back in New Haven shortly with his recaptured prisoner, and nobody would ever know that Jimmy had escaped.

Nearly ten minutes into his wait, a horse pranced down the street. Roland's jaw clenched as soon as he saw the rider. Alvin Buckner sat atop his horse regally, his long white hair perfectly combed. He wore a light grey suit that night without a smudge of ash or sweat upon it. Roland had wanted to talk to Alvin but not at that particular moment. He still had questions for the mayor, but Roland was more likely to rip his head off than get any answers out of him. Unfortunately Alvin rode his horse straight towards the Sheriff. "Roland," he greeted haughtily, flashing the polished smile that Roland hated so much.

"Where the hell have you been?" Sheriff Black snapped back, and his hand lowered towards his holster. He wasn't about to draw it on Alvin, and they both knew it. Too many people could see them, but old habits died hard. Roland felt safer with his hand comfortably resting on the butt of his pistol.

"I've been around. I heard Doc Holliday got shot. Where's the man who killed him?" The mayor sounded smugly happy about that one.

"He's in jail. We're hanging him tomorrow," Roland stated flatly. *What the hell are you playing at, you son of a bitch?* The mayor seemed to be playing another game with him, and Roland wasn't in the mood for it. *Keep pushing me, Alvin, and you'll regret it,* he thought as he caressed the butt of his pistol.

"Really?" Alvin's eyebrows raised, and he tapped his finger against his chin. "I just heard he escaped. That makes it hard to hang him. Doesn't it?" His smile became mocking as he taunted the Sheriff.

Roland growled at the back of his throat and nearly drew his gun on the spot. Alvin had no idea how close he was to dying at that moment. Roland still didn't know whether or not Alvin had anything to do with the gunfight at the celebration. He wanted to question him with a lot more privacy. They were in too visible an area for him to drag answers out of the mayor. Roland couldn't wait to see Alvin squirm again like he had two weeks ago. "We're going to catch the bastard, and we'll hang him tomorrow. Does that make you happy?" He spat out vehemently.

Alvin put a hand to his chest and looked at Roland with a hurt expression. "Roland, I'm not the one who shot Doc. Don't take it out on me."

"Go to hell, Alvin. Why are you so Goddamn happy? Your little celebration got ruined by Carlos. I thought you'd be mad as hell right now. Or did you tell your whipping boy to start that fight?" Roland watched Alvin closely. He swore that if Alvin confessed to having a part in the gunfight, he'd shoot him right there. Roland didn't care if people saw him or not. Alvin was pushing him way too far. *You'd better pray you had nothing to do with it, you Goddamn snake.*

"Give me some credit, Roland." Alvin's eyes narrowed angrily, and the smile slipped from his face. "Do you think I'd ruin that celebration? I planned it for *months*. I don't know where Carlos is or why he pulled that damn fool stunt of his, but I want him brought to justice as much as you do," he hissed at Roland then straightened his posture and assumed his polished smile again. He pulled his jacket down tightly across his chest as if he regretted his quick outburst.

Roland smiled as he saw Alvin briefly lose his composure. He had known Alvin long enough to know when he was genuinely upset. If the mayor had anything to do with the gunfight, he was doing a remarkably good job of hiding it. "Don't worry, I'll catch every last one of them."

"You're not calling anyone else in, are you?" Alvin asked worriedly.

Roland gave him a withering look. "You know me better than that, Alvin. I can handle it myself. We've got patrols waiting for the Riders to show up. If Carlos even thinks about coming to town, he's a dead man."

"Good," Alvin smiled widely. "And this prisoner of yours? Were you going to track him down tonight?"

"As soon as Morgan and William get back, we're tracking the son of a bitch down," Roland stated. He wished that the three deputies would hurry. The more time they took, the larger the lead that the fugitives put between them.

"Just the three of you?" Alvin piped up, suddenly looking very interested in the conversation. His smile turned slightly mischievous, the same smile that he had flashed at Roland for the past week.

"And Simon," Roland answered warily. He didn't trust that smile of Alvin's at all. The mayor put him on edge when he did it. *He's playing some Goddamn game,* Roland thought again, but he didn't know what sort of game it was. *After I catch Jimmy, you and I are talking, you son of a bitch.*

Alvin appeared not to notice the wariness. "Good." He rubbed his hands together. "Don't let me keep you any longer then. Good luck to you, Roland," he wished the Sheriff and turned his horse around. Roland expected him to go to The Last Frontier. It had been a long time since he had seen the mayor in the saloon, but Alvin returned the way he had come and rode back down the street.

Roland watched him vanish into the distance with narrowed eyes. He still had no idea what Alvin was up to. The mayor continued to hint at something bad happening to Roland, but the Sheriff couldn't decide if he was bluffing or telling the truth. *I will find out what you're up to, Alvin.* As soon as Jimmy and Singing Rock were captured, he intended to pay a nice little visit to Alvin and drag out every answer that had eluded him the past two weeks. *We'll see how much you smile then.*

His thoughts stayed on Alvin only briefly before returning to Singing Rock and Jimmy. *Hurry up, damn it,* he thought in frustration. He wanted to begin their pursuit soon. Even if the fugitives didn't know the area around New Haven, they'd likely escape Roland and his deputies. They had too large a lead, and tracking them down at night would be even more difficult. Roland thought for the briefest of moments about issuing a statewide reward for Jimmy, but that would attract too much attention to New Haven. He hoped to catch the two, but he would rather let them go than endanger the unique culture that had formed in the town.

Luckily for the anxiously waiting Sheriff, William soon returned with Morgan and Simon in tow. The veteran deputy looked quite surprised over the turn of events. Morgan likely could have used a few more hours of sleep, but Roland needed his help. Morgan knew the forests and trails around New Haven probably better than anyone except the Cheyenne. Even with his wounded shoulder, he would be an asset for their party. "Roland," Morgan greeted when the three rode up.

Roland tipped his hat briefly and rushed on. "Paul said they were heading north. Let's ride." He quickly swung his tired frame into the saddle then tapped the horse's ribs with his boot. "Hya," he cried, and then at a quick pace he led the three deputies out of New Haven. There were still a fair number of people milling about that evening. The fire had brought many out of their houses. They looked at Roland and his men galloping through the streets with curious stares, but the Sheriff ignored them. He was focused on their quarry.

At least the air had cooled slightly as they made their way out of town. It was still hot, but Roland didn't find himself instantly drenched in sweat as he had that afternoon. Morgan took over the lead of the party as they left the lights of New Haven. All the men except Morgan drew one of their pistols and kept one hand on the reins of their horses. Jimmy had taken down two men already, and nobody wanted to add himself to the gunslinger's growing number of kills.

They rode quickly at first. There was only one major path to the north, but once they were on it, they slowed down. Roland hated to waste the time. Every minute that they rode at a slow pace increased the distance between themselves and the fugitives, but it was necessary. It would be too easy for Jimmy to wait in concealment and shoot them as they rushed by. Roland hoped that they went a safe distance outside the town and then stopped for the night. Spotting their fire was really their only hope of catching the two. Jimmy had timed his escape perfectly. Even Morgan couldn't track them in the dead of night. The moon was only a quarter full, further damning their pursuit by providing scant lighting.

The men rode in silence to avoid inadvertently warning their quarry. Voices carried far at night, and Roland's men were at enough of a disadvantage in the chase. Roland stewed in the silence, thinking about what he would do to Jimmy when he finally caught the young man. The gunslinger wouldn't look forward to being a prisoner again when Roland was through with him. He also thought of Rebecca and Singing Rock. Every second of their chase brought them closer to dawn and the realization that Rebecca would spend yet another day trapped in the Land of Shadows. That — more than Jimmy, Matthew, the Riders, or Alvin — made Roland furious.

For nearly three miles they continued at that slow pace. By that time they had no idea if they were on the right trail or not, but there was no other choice. It was impossible to find any mark of the fugitives' passage. All the deputies became increasingly more pessimistic, and Roland kept shaking his head in frustration. Nothing else had gone his way the past two weeks; why should they be able to find Jimmy and Singing Rock?

Roland was contemplating calling the search off when Morgan stopped abruptly. The deputy peered out into the darkness while the rest of the deputies waited anxiously. William bit his lower lip, and Roland impatiently tapped his fingers on the butt of his pistol. *Does he see something?* Roland thought earnestly. The laborious chase was growing quite old. He looked in the same direction as Morgan, but he saw nothing of interest. *Please let him see something.* Finally the silence grew too great for Roland to stand it anymore. "What is it?" He asked quietly.

Morgan turned his head and put a finger over his lips. Carefully he dismounted and motioned for the others to follow suit. Quickly Roland swung a tired leg out of the saddle. His muscles protested the sudden exertion, but Roland was far too excited to care. He drew near Morgan and tapped his foot impatiently as he waited for the other two. When Simon and William dismounted and drew near Roland and Morgan, the veteran deputy leaned forward, cradling his wounded arm against his chest. "There's a fire up ahead," he whispered quietly.

Roland immediately whipped his head up and peered carefully into the distance, but he still couldn't see anything. He didn't doubt Morgan's word, though. Morgan was a proven hunter and woodsman. If he claimed he saw a fire, Roland trusted him. "How far away?" Roland asked just as quietly.

The deputy squinted as he thought carefully. "Maybe half a mile. No more than a mile away," he judged.

"Good." Roland rubbed his hands together. Nobody else would have a fire. Travelers would have sought out the refuge of New Haven. Only those who wanted to stay away from the town and its law enforcement would choose to set up camp for the night. In the dark his mouth curled into a lopsided grin. *I've got you, you son of a bitch.* Jimmy was about to be very sorry for ever crossing him. "Let's tie up the horses, then we'll go in on foot." Horses would be too loud for sneaking up on the two fugitives. By approaching on foot, Roland would be able to surprise Jimmy before the young man could reach for his gun. As furious as he was with Jimmy, Roland couldn't belittle the gunslinger's speed, accuracy, or skill with a pistol. Sheriff Black wanted the cards stacked in his favor. He had already lost three deputies and an old friend. Roland had no intention of losing anybody else.

The four men quietly led their horses towards a copse of trees. Roland recognized the area. They were on the northern outskirts of the forest between

402

New Haven and the Cheyenne. He shook his head as he remembered the last time he had entered the woods. Half-conscious and sick with worry, Roland had sought the Cheyenne's help for Rebecca after being attacked by Bryant. That seemed like two months ago, not two weeks. *Keep your mind on Jimmy,* Roland thought disgustedly. It wasn't the time to be thinking about Rebecca or any of the problems surrounding her. If he died, so did all chances of her escaping the Land of Shadows.

Roland tied the horse to a tree then drew one of his guns. All the others followed suit except Morgan. He kept his gun holstered so he could have his one good arm free. There would be plenty of time to draw and fire if it came to that. Sheriff Black looked carefully at the other three men. They were about to enter a dangerous situation, and he wanted to make sure that everyone was ready. He barely glanced at Morgan. The veteran deputy had been in more gunfights than Roland and knew what was required. William stared back at Roland with a set jaw and narrowed eyes. The rakish deputy looked determined and ready for a gunfight, not flirtatious and poised to bed one of New Haven's women. Simon appeared as ready as he could be. His eyes were wide and earnest. He might not have the intensity of William and Morgan, but he would follow their lead without question. "Simon, are you ready?" Sheriff Black asked just to be sure.

Simon nodded steadily several times. "Yes, Sheriff. I'm ready," he affirmed.

Wordlessly he clapped Simon on the shoulder. *Please let him live.* Of all his remaining deputies, Roland would hate to lose Simon the most; he had no intention of letting Simon's unborn child grow up without a father. "All right, let's get this over with," he told the others quietly and slowly walked in the direction that Morgan had pointed.

The cautious approach towards the fire was even more frustrating than the ride out there. Roland wanted to have the whole ordeal over with. If there was going to be a gunfight, he wished that Jimmy would step out in front of them. They could exchange fire, and then everyone could go home. It was made even worse by the fact that he couldn't see the fire they crept towards. Morgan, however, continued to lead them quietly, walking carefully at the front of their party. They all placed each foot gingerly, making sure they didn't accidentally snap a twig or cause any other noise which might give away their presence.

Thoughts of Rebecca, Alvin, and his anger at Jimmy faded away as they drew closer to the campsite. Roland coldly achieved the mindset that he assumed before a gunfight. His breathing slowed, and his senses became heightened as he focused solely on the task at hand. Morgan also took that approach as he looked ahead for danger. William and Simon had never learned the tactic, but each was ready for the trouble awaiting the group.

Roland caught sight of the fire as they crept closer and had no idea how Morgan had spotted it. It was hidden at least forty feet into the forest, and even from their closer vantage point Roland was barely able to see it. The deputy turned his head and looked at Roland expectantly. Roland nodded and took over leading the group. Now that the Sheriff knew where they were headed, he was much more suited to lead them. With his wounded shoulder, Morgan needed to be at the back of the party so he would have more time to draw his gun.

Once they were settled in their new formation, Roland began creeping forward again with William directly behind him. Simon followed the rakish deputy with Morgan at the back. They were still too far to make out any details through the trees. Roland half-expected Jimmy to jump out at any moment. The flickering light came and went as the four men wound their way between trees. After each step, Roland gazed ahead carefully before taking the next one. He knew that he wouldn't go to sleep by a fire without a lookout, and he doubted that Jimmy was a fool either. Hopefully he could sneak up on them and spare Singing Rock's life. If he had to shoot the gunslinger, Roland would happily do so, but the Navajo could still help Rebecca escape the Land of Shadows.

A twig snapped behind Roland, and he wheeled around, drawing his other pistol in one fluid motion. He held his fire as he saw William shrug his shoulders and look guiltily at the ground. *Damn it,* Roland thought in annoyance and quickly turned back around, hugging his body up against a tree. If anyone else heard the twig break, they could enter a gunfight a lot sooner than they expected without the advantage of surprise. For over a minute, all four men stayed close to a tree with their guns pointed towards the campfire. Roland could almost swear that he saw figures hiding among the trees, but he held his fire. He knew it was just his imagination playing tricks on him. Roland preferred fighting in a bar or in the street over sneaking through the forest. Fighting in a city was over quickly. He hated the sneaking and hiding involved with forests.

After that brief pause, Roland turned back to the other men. He held up a hand with the palm extended. *Wait here, I'll see what's ahead,* he thought wordlessly, but his deputies knew what he meant by the gesture. Roland didn't know if anybody had heard the twig, but he wasn't going to risk his neck anymore. One person would be enough to scout ahead, and Roland thought he could take down Jimmy all by himself if needed. Four of them marching through the forest would just increase the chances of Jimmy hearing them. He took a deep breath then left the cover of the tree, stepping back out into the open with both pistols drawn and ready. His heart skipped a beat as he waited for a bullet to strike him, but the forest remained silent. Quietly Roland began creeping forward again.

He placed each foot softly, testing the ground beneath it before putting his full weight down. The campfire was looming close, and he didn't want to risk stepping on another twig. Perhaps Jimmy hadn't heard William, but Roland wasn't going to press his luck. He craned his neck, trying to peer through the trees to see who slept around the fire and who was a lookout, but the foliage was too thick. *Damn it,* Roland thought in frustration as he moved closer to the campsite. By the time he found out who was awake, he'd be on top of them.

The fire cast flickering shadows among the trees, making it appear as if men lurked between them. Roland paid them little attention. He focused on the fire ahead of him. That was where his quarry waited. He ducked his head under a branch and stopped instantly when he saw a figure laying on the ground. His view was limited, but he was able to see part of the campsite between two bushes. Roland stared carefully at the figure, but his back was turned to Roland. *Who is that?* It didn't look like Singing Rock or Jimmy.

Carefully he took another step forward, keeping his guns aimed at the sleeping figure. Whoever it was made no move to offer Roland a better look, and Roland continued to inch closer to the edge of the campsite. His breath came in slow intervals, and his grip tightened upon his guns. *Who are you? Goddamn it.* The closer he came to the sleeping figure, the more it looked like someone else other than the two fugitives. Roland's eyes narrowed. He didn't like surprises.

Roland was five or six steps from the edge of the campsite when he caught his breath suddenly. *Son of a bitch!* He thought and froze as he realized how loud his exhale had been. Ten feet away from the sleeping figure, two Dark Riders lay on the ground, obviously asleep. *Riders!* Roland had thought that the sleeping figure didn't look like Jimmy or Singing Rock, but he had never expected to encounter Dark Riders. He had no idea how many of them were in the forest, but the small band that he had brought wouldn't be enough to take them on in a fight.

He stood still for a few more seconds, making sure that he hadn't been heard. A trickle of sweat ran down the side of his neck as he waited for an alarm to be raised, but none came as Roland's heart raced furiously. Slowly he began to back away from the edge of the campsite. He wanted to put a great deal of distance between the camp and himself. Morgan would remember how to find the campsite again, and Roland planned to return with a larger number of people backing him up. With each step Roland's fear lessened. *Almost there,* he thought to himself. A tiny lopsided smile formed on his face. Roland was just beginning to think that he would make it out alive when he was tackled from behind.

"Help!" Someone above him cried as the Sheriff hit the ground roughly. Roland's two guns flew out of his hands, and the wind was knocked from him. He tried to rise to his feet, but the person who tackled him quickly wrestled him back to the ground. Roland heard a great deal of commotion coming from the campsite, and he twisted his body desperately, trying to shake his attacker off his back. But it was too late.

Two Dark Riders burst through the bushes with guns drawn. "What is it?" Marshall Drake cried out. Roland instantly recognized the Dark Rider. The tall, dark-haired outlaw carried two pistols and looked ready to use them. The other was named Bill, and he was as dirty as Mad Dog. A scraggly beard covered his face, and his balance was a bit unsteady from the obvious consumption of alcohol.

"We got us a visitor," the man above Roland bragged and crawled off his back. Roland's jaw clenched in anger, but he didn't make a move to attack or escape. *Goddamn it!* He raged. There was nothing that he could do, and Roland knew without a doubt that he was a dead man. Carlos had promised to kill him and had tried at the Fourth of July celebration. The outlaw certainly wouldn't spare him now.

"Blazes, it's the Sheriff," Marshall gasped then his face split into a wide grin. He let out a loud bellow of joy. "Hey, boys, we got the Sheriff over here!" He yelled loudly enough for everyone to hear him clearly. "Bring him," he pointed at the man behind Roland and walked backed into the campsite.

"Get up," Roland's captor ordered and kicked him in the ribs. The Sheriff grunted but didn't make any other sound as he rose to his feet. He gazed longingly at the trees where Morgan and the others hid then turned his attention back to his present situation. Bill quickly picked up his two pistols and smiled a snaggle-toothed grin at Roland as he held the Sheriff's pistols tauntingly just out of reach.

"Let's go," the man behind Roland ordered and roughly pushed him from behind.

Roland stumbled forward and nearly lost his balance as his feet got tangled up, but he caught himself from falling over. He gazed at the trees around him once more and sighed. *Goodbye,* he wished the other three deputies. He hoped they weren't stupid enough to try to rescue him. They were far enough from the fire. If Morgan was smart, the three men would be far away from the site before the Riders could send out a search party, but Roland didn't have any more time to spare thinking about his deputies as he stepped past the bushes and into the campsite.

Nine Dark Riders had made their camp in the forest. Roland recognized most of them. Two were Banditos, and there was Bill. Danny was the Rider behind him, and he had already seen Marshall. Three others had names that eluded him. He had always had difficulty remembering names and had found it impossible to memorize all of the Dark Riders' names, but the outlaw who immediately caught his attention stood on the opposite side of the fire with a large grin on his face and laughing as Roland was led into the campsite.

Curly! Roland nearly snarled his name out. He wanted to cry in frustration. After two weeks of waiting for Bryant's murderer, Roland had finally stumbled upon him. Unfortunately it was himself, not Curly, who would be killed that evening. Roland didn't even have the luxury of sacrificing his own life to end Curly's. *Rebecca, I'm sorry.* Roland just prayed that somebody took down the Dark Rider. He didn't want Rebecca to waste away at The Last Frontier. Even if he couldn't be with her, Roland wanted Rebecca to find happiness one day without him.

"I said move," the Rider behind him commanded, and he pushed Roland into the center of the group.

Roland's feet tangled up again, and he couldn't keep his balance that time. He fell on the ground as all nine Dark Riders laughed uproariously. Scowling, Roland quickly rose to his feet and glared at his captors. He'd be damned if he'd cower on the ground. If he was going to die, he intended to do it standing on his feet, staring death defiantly in the eye.

"What the hell are you doing out here, Sheriff?" Marshall asked him. In his brief glance at the Riders, Roland hadn't noticed Carlos. It looked like Marshall was in charge with Carlos absent.

"Go to hell," Roland snapped back and flashed his lopsided grin. His moment of defiance lasted only a few seconds as Marshall stepped forward and swung a punch that caught Roland under his left eye. The Sheriff spun in a half-circle, putting one hand to his cheek. It didn't feel too swollen, but it hurt more than he was willing to show the Riders. Casually he turned back to Marshall. *Come on, you son of a bitch. You can do better than that.*

"I'm going to ask again," Marshall repeated. Like the rest of the Dark Riders gathered around the fire, Marshall's mouth was stretched wide in a grin. "What are you doing out here?"

"I said go to hell, you son of—" Roland's outburst was cut short as Marshall's second punch caught him square in the mouth. The force of the blow caused him to fall backwards, landing painfully on his tailbone. Tentatively his tongue touched his split lip and tasted blood. Roland spat on the ground and stared defiantly at his captor.

Marshall shook his head and drew a pistol. "All right, Sheriff. We'll try this one more time. What are you doing out here?"

Roland smiled up at the Dark Rider, even though it pained his bottom lip. "Go ahead and kill me," he laughed at Marshall. His death was inevitable, and Roland didn't see any advantage in waiting around for it.

The Dark Rider shook his head once more. "I'm not going to kill you. Carlos'll do that, but if you don't answer me right now, I'll shoot you in both knees," Marshall promised. He aimed his gun at Roland's right knee and squinted one eye to line up his sight.

The Sheriff looked at the gun then nodded. Roland was beyond caring if he lived or died at that point, but he had no desire to spend the last few hours of his life with a painful injury. If appeasing Marshall would hold his fire, then he'd just have to play along. Hopefully Morgan and the others were using the time wisely. Roland had bought them more than enough time to make it back to the horses. "I'm tracking someone down," he told the Riders sullenly.

"Well, you found us," Marshall laughed and spread his arms wide.

"That's right," Curly added as the Riders joined in the laughter. The Banditos didn't seem to understand what was being said, but they watched the events with excited grins.

"I wasn't looking for you," Roland pointed out quietly.

"What was that?" Marshall asked over the din and held up one of his hands. Quickly the Riders grew silent in response.

"I said I wasn't looking for you," the Sheriff repeated and spat blood on the ground again.

Marshall stared at Roland intently for a moment then pointed his gun at him once more. "Then who were you looking for?"

Roland's eyes shifted from one side of the camp to the other. He hated to tell the Riders anything at all, but he didn't see any harm in letting them know his reason for being in the woods. "I'm looking for a prisoner."

"What prisoner?" Marshall watched Roland curiously. As far as the Dark Riders knew, they were the only ones who ever got into any trouble in New Haven. They either were intrigued by the existence of another outlaw, or they didn't believe him.

"His name's Jimmy. He killed a man, and I was going to hang him," Roland answered and shook his head. *You little son of a bitch.* He still couldn't believe that Jimmy was going to get away. After Roland died, New Haven would concentrate all of her efforts on bringing the Dark Riders to justice. Jimmy would be an afterthought, and the two fugitives would happily move on to another town.

Marshall studied Roland to gauge his honesty then shrugged his shoulders. He leaned forward, and for the first time his expression grew serious. "Now, where are the rest of your men?"

"I came by myself," Roland answered quietly and tried to keep his face downcast. *Play this right.* If he didn't, the Riders might send a few scouts into the woods, and one or more of the three deputies could die. Roland just hoped that they were long gone.

The Dark Rider pointed his gun at Roland's knee again and smiled. "Don't lie to me, Sheriff. Where are they?"

"I swear I came by myself," Roland cried quickly and held up one of his hands. "Blazes, it's only one man, and we couldn't spare anyone else. Tha damn gunfight you started killed three of my men. I was the only one who could leave," Roland burst out in a rush. *Please let them believe me.*

Marshall stared at Roland for a long moment with narrowed eyes. Finally he nodded and holstered his gun. He stepped back from Roland and looked at Danny. "Tie him up. We'll let Carlos have him when he gets back," he ordered then picked up a bottle of whiskey and took a deep swig.

Danny kicked Roland's back then walked around to face him. The Dark Rider had short black hair, and a full beard. He held his pistol no more than a foot away from the Sheriff's face and sneered, "Don't move. I'll be right back," he commanded.

Roland had the briefest urge to try to grab the gun, but he held himself back. Hopefully there would be another opportunity for escape. He doubted it, but it was still a faint hope. Even if he had taken Danny's gun, there were eight other Dark Riders still watching him closely as Danny sought out some rope. His eyes landed on Curly. The blond Dark Rider still boiled the blood in his veins. *Let me kill him.* Roland was resolved to die that night, but he wanted to take Bryant's killer with him. It made him ball his fists tightly to watch the murderer. Curly didn't seem to notice Roland's hostility. He was drunk as usual, and he found more entertainment drinking with his fellow outlaws than watching Roland.

Danny cut two short lengths of rope which he used to bind Roland's hands and feet tightly. Roland's last hope for escape faded with the tying of those knots. He wouldn't have a chance to escape even if one presented itself now. With his hands and feet bound, Roland sat stony-faced and waited for his death.

The Banditos went back to sleep after the commotion, but the rest of the Riders began to drink from bottles of whiskey they had strewn about the campsite. Danny took a seat behind Roland with a bottle in one hand and his pistol in the other. He wasn't the most efficient guard, but it didn't take much to keep an eye on a bound man. The rest lounged around the fire, passing a few bottles back and forth. Even Marshall, who seemed to be in charge, drank heavily. They called out insults to Roland every couple of minutes, which would send them all into gales of laughter. Each time Danny kicked Roland in the back. "What'd ya think, Sheriff?" He'd ask. Roland wished that he had tried to grab Danny's pistol. He'd be dead at the moment and wouldn't be subject to any more of the hellish waiting.

Curly took a bottle from Marshall and tossed back a deep swig of whiskey. He wiped his mouth with the back of his hand and looked at Roland. "Hey, Sheriff," he called out. Roland just stared at the ground. He had given up trying to glare at them. "So what'd you think when we killed all your men? I think we might have to go back and kill the rest. Huh, Sheriff? How does that sound?" He taunted Roland and laughed.

I hope you choke on that, you Goddamn son of a whore, Roland thought bitterly as the Dark Riders burst into laughter. "What'd ya think, Sheriff?" Danny asked then nudged Roland's back with his boot. Roland would have given anything for a gun. He just wanted to put one bullet right between Curly's eyes. *Or maybe his stomach.* A gutshot was fatal and could linger for days before finally killing the victim.

Danny suddenly grunted and grew silent behind Roland. For a moment, the Riders continued to laugh, but then Marshall rose to his feet as Roland heard Danny fall to the ground. Marshall drew his gun quickly, his hands just a shade unsteady from all the alcohol, but he never got to fire it. An arrow streaked from the forest and took him through his forearm. The Dark Rider dropped his gun and clutched his wounded arm, crying out in pain.

What the hell? Roland thought in amazement as over a dozen figures emerged from the edge of the campsite. *Cheyenne! They're Goddamn Cheyenne!* His face broke into a large smile as he watched them cover the Dark Riders with drawn bows. Each brave had red streaks of paint slanting down his cheeks and looked ready to fire arrows without a second thought. The Dark Riders froze, putting their hands to their holsters but not drawing. They weren't foolish men even with the liquor they had been drinking. The Cheyenne had them covered and could kill them all without much effort. Except for Marshall's yelling, the campsite grew silent.

Falling Thunder calmly walked from the forest. Roland had never been so glad to see the brave in his entire life. He had no idea where they had come from or why they were in that part of the woods, but he didn't really care. It was looking like he would survive his capture after all. "Do not move. We have you surrounded. Throw down your guns, and we will let you live," Falling Thunder commanded in English. He waited, but the Dark Riders made no move to comply. Roland could feel the tension growing around the fire. The Cheyenne brave held up a hand, and one of the braves let an arrow fly. It struck the ground a foot from Curly, and the Dark Rider flinched to one side. "Throw down your guns, or the next arrow will kill you," Falling Thunder ordered again.

Reluctantly the Riders tossed their weapons towards the fire. For a moment it looked like a few would try to go down in a blaze of glory, but after one glance at a dozen bows aimed at them, they quickly changed their minds. Falling Thunder watched as each man disarmed himself and nodded when the last had complied. Even Marshall took a seat and waited silently to see what the brave would do next. Running Brook's son gazed at Roland and pointed towards him. "Untie the Sheriff," he called out.

Yes! Roland thought excitedly. He planned on making a special visit to thank Running Brook and his tribe personally for saving his life. In a million years Roland never would have thought that he would survive being captured by Dark Riders, but it certainly looked as if he was going to walk away safely.

That moment of glee turned into complete and utter shock, however, when Jimmy emerged from the forest. *What the hell's he doing here? You son of a bitch.* Jimmy approached the Sheriff as Roland watched him with stunned eyes. The young gunslinger had his typical cocky smile, and his eyes shone with excitement. He untied Roland's feet then knelt behind the Sheriff and untied his hands.

Roland rubbed each of his wrists slowly to get the blood circulating as Jimmy stood to one side of him. He looked over his shoulder to see Danny laying on the ground with an arrow through his neck. *I hope you burn in hell. What'd ya think, Danny?* When he turned his head, Falling Thunder addressed his men in Cheyenne. The Sheriff had no idea what the brave was talking about, but shortly afterwards a few of the braves began to bind the Dark Riders' hands behind them. His eyes narrowed as he looked up at Jimmy. Roland's jaw tightened, and his mind burned with anger. He was grateful to Falling Thunder, but that didn't extend to Jimmy. The young man had killed Henry, and Roland had no intention of letting the crime go unpunished. He could sort out why Jimmy was with the Cheyenne later. Calmly he waited for the Cheyenne to bind all of the Dark Riders, and then he made his move.

Quickly he rose to his feet and rushed at Jimmy. Roland's hand reached for Jimmy's holster and drew the young man's pistol before he had time to react. He backed up a step and pointed the gun at Jimmy, his mouth curling into a lopsided grin despite the split in his bottom lip. *I've got you, you little bastard,* he thought gleefully. "Put your hands in the air, you son of a bitch, or I swear to God I'll shoot you right now," he ordered, his voice threatening to crack with joy. He couldn't believe the way Lady Luck had smiled upon him. Not only had he survived the Dark Riders, but Jimmy had been personally delivered to him.

Jimmy quickly raised both his arms, his eyes growing wide with fear. He shook his head vigorously left and right. "Don't shoot, Sheriff. I didn't do it. He's—"

"Shut your Goddamn mouth!" Roland shouted at the young man, cutting him off. His grip tightened on the handle of Jimmy's gun until his knuckles were white. Jimmy had killed Henry and vanished with Singing Rock. Roland had planned to hang the fugitive the following day anyway and didn't see the harm in carrying out the sentence immediately. The entire campsite grew quiet as the Dark Riders and the Cheyenne watched Roland brandish the weapon. Roland paid them no attention. His face was locked in a mask of fury as his finger began to squeeze the trigger.

"Damn it, Roland, put the gun down," a thick drawl came from Falling Thunder's direction.

Sheriff Black glanced in that direction, and the gun nearly fell from his fingers in surprise when he saw the man standing next to Falling Thunder. His jaw dropped as he stared at the figure. *It can't be,* he thought in wonder. "B-but, you're dead," he whispered.

Henry shook his head with a rueful smile. "You wouldn't believe how many times I've heard that in the last five years."

Book Three:
Salvation
July 5 - 13

Henry grinned as he watched Roland stand gape-jawed. *He looks like he's seen a ghost,* the Ghost Hunter thought with a chuckle. He couldn't blame Roland. All of the deputies looked just as stunned to see him breathing and even more surprised to find him in the forest. Roland especially, though, kept staring at him as if he expected Henry to disappear at any moment. *Not too bad,* the Ghost Hunter congratulated himself. Henry wasn't one to pat himself on the back, but he had to admit that his plan had worked almost to perfection.

On the night of July the Fourth, Henry had heard the booming fireworks as they detonated in the sky. After looking out his window and seeing the colorful explosions, Henry had quickly left the saloon for a better view. He usually would have remained in his room, especially after being recognized by Roland and Alvin, but it had been over ten years since he had last seen fireworks. Figuring it would do no harm, he had wandered over to the large crowd gathered for the festivities.

By the time he arrived the fireworks were dying down, but instead of abating, the crowd seemed only more excited by the performance to come. Henry had decided to wait for Zoltan's performance. He was too wide awake to go back to sleep, and he saw no harm in watching. Henry had worked too hard lately, and his spirits needed uplifting after Alvin had unmasked him. When Zoltan finally stepped onto the stage, Henry clapped and cheered with the rest of the people, happy to blend in with everyone else. It wasn't the first magic show he had seen, but it certainly impressed him. Zoltan seemed to possess a flair for drama, and Henry couldn't help being drawn into the brief display of magic.

His jaw had dropped open when Zoltan was shot by his assistant and rose to his feet unharmed moments later. The crowd had erupted in applause, but Henry only clapped half-heartedly as he contemplated the possibilities that the trick could open to him. Five years before, he had fooled the world by staging his own funeral. It had worked flawlessly, and he had been able to live an anonymous life until meeting up with Roland and Alvin. He didn't worry about Roland divulging his secret, but Alvin was an entirely different matter. The mayor still walked with a cane from their disagreement a dozen years ago. Sooner or later, Alvin would tell someone else that he still roamed the West, and then he'd constantly have to look over his shoulder for a gunslinger who wanted to put down the notorious Doc Holliday. After watching Zoltan, the solution seemed so obvious. The best way to hold Alvin's tongue would be to fake his death again. As he clapped for Zoltan, Henry thought what better way to stage his death than to be shot.

Less than a minute after his revelation, the celebration was broken up by the Dark Riders, and Henry soon found himself in the middle of a real gunfight instead of the made-up one that he had just envisioned. He had hoped to stay well out of everyone's way. Guns made him uncomfortable , but his skill apparently had not deserted him. He had hesitated for a moment before pulling the trigger. Henry wasn't sure if he could still hit such a small target, but his bullet hit Carl safely and missed the Dark Rider's captive. As soon as he took that one shot Henry fled the scene, anxious to leave before he had to fire his gun again. Even though Carl had held a gun to Sherry's head, Henry felt guilty over firing his lone shot. He had tried to make amends for all the deaths he had caused, and now he had one more to atone for.

The saloon was nearly empty when he returned, but he did see one figure making his way up the staircase. With his long black cape and top hat, Zoltan was a hard person to miss no matter where he went. Henry grinned when he saw the illusionist and called out to him .

Zoltan refused to help him at first. He had puffed up indignantly when Henry suggested that he share the secret of his illusion. Henry had chuckled at the seriousness of his refusal. Zoltan looked more like a mother bear guarding her cubs than a magician protecting a magic trick's secrecy, but with a great deal of persuasion Henry convinced the illusionist to share it. Even if Henry possessed a huge sum of money he doubted he could have bought the secret from Zoltan, but the way he planned on using the trick piqued the illusionist's interest. Once he explained his plan, Zoltan had readily agreed and even looked excited about the prospect. Zoltan always performed in front of crowds who knew his tricks were illusions, but when Henry offered a challenge to fool unsuspecting observers, Zoltan willingly became the first to join his conspiracy. After thanking the illusionist, Henry went back into the streets to collect his next conspirator.

Enlisting Sullivan became his next order of business. The stuffy doctor was a busy man that night, attending to all of the wounded from the gunfight. Several deputies and civilians had been injured, and Sullivan was the only one to help them. Henry discreetly asked a few people where he could find the doctor, and once he had directions to Sullivan's office Henry waited for him to return. After the doctor had seen all of the injured, he tiredly headed towards his office. He was surprised to find Henry waiting for him, but his face quickly lit up when the Ghost Hunter explained his intentions. Sullivan's aid was critical to the plan. With Zoltan's help, Henry could stage his own death, but Sullivan would have to pronounce him dead. Even with fake blood and a good performance, Sullivan could foil the charade. Henry was amused by the doctor. He seemed so fussy and practical, but he had jumped aboard as soon as the plan had been laid out. Sullivan seemed drawn by the danger, and Henry barely had to do any persuading to make the doctor agree.

After securing both Zoltan's and Sullivan's aid, Henry's thoughts then turned to who would pretend to kill him. Jimmy's name sprang to mind immediately. He had only met the young man once, but Jimmy seemed drawn to excitement. During the gunfight, he and Jimmy had charged into the fray, and rather than looking worried or nervous the gunslinger had an excited grin stretching from ear to ear. Henry thought briefly about one of Roland's deputies, but he feared that none of them would want to be part of fooling the Sheriff. That left only Jimmy. Unfortunately Jimmy was busy celebrating his first kill that night, and Henry never had a chance to talk with him.

He had headed back to his room and stopped at Singing Rock's door when the final part of the plan fell into place. The Navajo was awake at that hour. Unlike Henry, he couldn't go about the city without attracting attention so he had remained in his room. While the Navajo had slept, he talked with Running Brook in his dreams. The Cheyenne Chief had reported that a band of nearly twenty men were hiding in the forest by their camp. Roland had told Running Brook that a Dark Rider had killed Bryant White, and the Cheyenne had recognized the men as outlaws.

Henry's first thought was to tell Roland about them, but he hesitated. If he told Roland, the Sheriff would run off half-crazed trying to find them immediately. In all likelihood he'd either run them off or get himself killed. Henry wanted them captured and, more importantly, wanted to find Curly and let Roland kill him. Then Rebecca would awaken, and he and Singing Rock could finally leave New Haven. It would be easy to have the Cheyenne attack the Dark Riders in the forest, but Henry didn't think that they would do so. They'd certainly help capture the outlaws, but killing them was a different story. The relationship between New Haven and her Cheyenne neighbors was tenuous at best. Word that the Cheyenne had murdered people would quickly circulate through town, and it could have damaging repercussions. The fact that they were Dark Riders would do little to spare the Cheyenne from blame. Most people would consider it an atrocity committed by savages, not helping to catch a band of outlaws.

The Ghost Hunter had smiled at the thought of having the Cheyenne capture the Dark Riders and letting Roland stumble upon the prisoners. It would look as if Roland had done all the work, and everything would work out for the best. The Cheyenne wouldn't be impugned, Curly and all his brethren would be captured, and Henry could leave town. At that moment, the plan was finalized in his head. Jimmy could pretend to shoot Henry. Afterwards Roland was bound to throw the gunslinger in jail. Henry knew of a safe way to break him out, and then Roland would follow their trail in the morning to the Dark Riders. He considered telling Roland about the plan, but he knew that Roland wouldn't play along. The very second that he told Roland where Curly was, the Sheriff would be on his horse to kill him. That fact crystallized everything. With a grin on his face, Henry outlined everything for Singing Rock, and the Navajo agreed to the plan.

Roland had come by to talk to him later, and Henry made sure to keep his face straight and not give a hint as to what he had in mind. He had pled exhaustion as an excuse to avoid returning to Rebecca's house at dawn. The Land of Shadows was always risky, and there was no sense journeying there if another way to help Rebecca existed. Roland didn't look happy about not returning to her house, but he grudgingly gave in. He had too many things to attend to already. As soon as Roland walked down the hallway, Henry closed the door and went to sleep for the night. The following morning he awakened and went to Zoltan's room. After waking the magician, Zoltan gave him a small leather bag filled with chicken blood to use during his charade. Then the two went downstairs together and found Jimmy sitting at the bar. Convincing the young man was the easiest part of the entire plan. As soon as he finished outlining his plan, Jimmy took one look at Henry and then Zoltan before eagerly agreeing to help. Henry had second thoughts as Jimmy grinned excitedly. The young man might well cause trouble instead of helping, but it was too late to turn back at that point.

Henry was beginning to feel a swell of egotism when people flooded into the saloon. He was surprised when they rushed towards him. *They want to see Zoltan,* Henry thought, but instead they had all come to see him. His heart fluttered nervously when they called him Doc Holliday. Even though he had a plan in place to make everyone think he was dead again, it was frightening to have his secret exposed to the world. He was close to panicking when Roland returned to the saloon and broke everything up. Right behind him came Sullivan, conveniently checking up on Rebecca. At that moment, Henry decided to proceed with his plan immediately.

After talking with Roland briefly, he returned to the bar and told Jimmy and Zoltan to get ready for the beginning of his plan. Jimmy blinked in surprise, but he nodded and grinned mischievously. As soon as Sullivan walked down the stairs, he and Jimmy hurried outside while Roland was distracted by Zoltan. From that moment on, the plan rushed forward. He and Jimmy quickly exchanged shots, both of them firing well above the other's head. Henry, however, spun in a circle and punctured the bag of chicken blood as he fell. It spilled all over his shirt, making it look as if he had indeed been hit by Jimmy's bullet. The most difficult part of the whole plan had been coughing and wheezing while Roland fretted over him. Henry kept waiting for Sullivan to come to his side so he could pretend to die, and when the doctor arrived Henry nearly ruined the charade by smiling in relief. Instead he had choked out a gasp then laid still while Sullivan pronounced him dead.

Sullivan had taken him back to his office after Roland left. Being slung over a horse and carted across town wasn't pleasant, but Henry kept reminding himself of the rewards that awaited. When they were safely inside the office both men breathed a sigh of relief. He laid down in one of the back rooms and waited for night to fall so he could break Jimmy out of prison and leave New Haven, but Roland had surprised both Henry and Sullivan by showing up with Thatcher. Sullivan had said Roland was arranging a funeral, but he hadn't mentioned anything about someone blessing his body.

Fortunately Sullivan persuaded Roland to remain outside, but he couldn't stop Thatcher from entering the room where Henry played possum. The Reverend nearly had a heart attack when in the middle of blessing Henry's body, the Ghost Hunter coughed. Henry swore quietly and sat up as Thatcher backed away from him in fear. It had taken some very quick talking to convince Thatcher to stay quiet and go along with their plan. In the end it was only Henry's assurance that the whole idea was going to help not only Roland but Rebecca as well that convinced him to agree. Thatcher still looked shocked and bewildered as he left the room, casting one last glimpse at Henry before shutting the door.

When Roland left the office, Henry closed his eyes and took a nap. He couldn't do anything else until nightfall, and sleep would be hard to come by that evening. Sullivan woke him when the sun finally set, and the Ghost Hunter buttoned his coat up tightly. It didn't completely cover the blood stains, but hopefully nobody would notice too much about him in the dark. Pulling the brim of his hat down low Henry stepped nervously into the street, afraid someone would recognize him. But nobody paid him more than a single glance, and he walked through town without any trouble.

The idea of how to break Jimmy out of jail had been an easy one. His escape from jail with the aid of Big Nose Kate remained one of the more memorable moments in his life. He had spent over five years with the woman out of gratitude for saving him , and it only seemed appropriate to use the same method again. If it worked once, he saw no reason to change it. Originally he had planned on setting fire to the stage that Zoltan had performed on, but when he saw the gallows next to it, he quickly decided to ignite both. Sullivan had given him some kerosene and matches, and in the dry summer heat it didn't long for both of them to go up in flames.

He rushed towards the station house as most of New Haven surged towards the fire to extinguish it. By the time he reached the station house, Singing Rock had just unlocked Jimmy's cell door. Henry hopped on his horse and raced ahead of the other two, anxious to flee town before someone noticed him. Minutes later, Jimmy and Singing Rock joined him while New Haven busied itself dousing the two fires. The three had no idea where they were going, but Singing Rock had told Running Brook to have someone waiting for them outside of town. Once they met Falling Thunder, he led them to a party of sixteen Cheyenne braves carefully watching the campsite. Henry had smiled at the sight. It would be easy to capture the Dark Riders in their sleep. If he knew outlaws, Henry was convinced they'd be drunk by midnight, and then it would be simple to silence their lookout and tie up the rest. In the morning when Roland followed their trail to its conclusion, he'd find the Dark Riders neatly trussed up for him, but two things took him by surprise.

Henry couldn't understand a word of Cheyenne, but Singing Rock seemed at ease talking with the braves. He reported that eight Dark Riders had left the camp over an hour ago. The Ghost Hunter held his tongue and didn't swear. The main point of the excursion had been to capture Curly, and Henry had no idea if the Dark Rider was at the camp or riding with the rest. Henry relaxed, though. Inevitably they'd come back to the camp, and then the Cheyenne would capture the whole lot, including Curly.

That never happened as Roland surprised Henry by tracking them down in the dark. That had been the other contingency Henry hadn't planned for. Roland wasn't supposed to find them until the morning when they had captured the Dark Riders. He had no idea what to do as he watched Roland creep forward. His indecisiveness became panic when the Dark Riders discovered Roland and dragged him into the camp. Henry nearly drew his gun and fired, but he made himself wait to see what the Dark Riders did next. If he moved to rescue Roland, the Dark Riders might shoot the Sheriff before they could put all of the outlaws down. Furthermore, the other Dark Riders would return with a lot more caution if they heard gunfire.

Watching as Marshall pointed a gun at Roland had been difficult, but Henry kept his own gun ready and prayed for the best. Luckily they only roughed up Roland then resumed drinking. Henry decided to capture the ones he could and rescue Roland rather than wait. It would be easy to swarm the nine drunk men in the clearing without jeopardizing Roland, but with nearly twenty, it would be close to impossible. He told Singing Rock to pass that on to Falling Thunder, and the Cheyenne brave told his men.

The moment the first arrow flew, Henry rushed to where the three deputies were hiding and called out to them, making sure that they wouldn't accidentally shoot one of the Cheyenne, thinking the braves were harming Roland. He nearly got shot for his troubles, but Morgan quickly reached out and stopped William from firing at him. The veteran deputy began laughing when he saw Henry, but William's eyes nearly popped out of his head. By that time Falling Thunder and his men had effectively captured the Dark Riders, and Jimmy had untied Roland. When he heard Roland threatening the young gunslinger, he had rushed to the edge of the clearing and shouted at him to stop.

William had been surprised to see Henry alive, but Roland nearly fell over in shock. He kept shaking his head as if he couldn't believe what he saw. Henry was a little upset that so many people knew he was still alive, but the results were all he could hope for. Morgan, William, and Simon watched over the captive Dark Riders while Jimmy stood off to the side all by himself. He wasn't in trouble anymore, but nobody seemed to know what to think of him at the moment. Jimmy appeared oblivious, though. His face was lit up with a huge grin, and his eyes still shone with excitement. The gunslinger had enjoyed the past twelve hours immensely, and the deputies' distrust of him couldn't darken his mood. Henry had pulled Roland aside and quickly explained his plan, but the Sheriff kept shaking his head in disbelief.

"But why didn't you tell me?" The Sheriff asked. Henry thought that Roland's feelings were genuinely hurt for not being included. He seemed to have problems accepting what had taken place.

Take it easy on him. He's been through a lot, Henry thought. "I told you already, Roland. You had to act surprised. Nobody would have believed I was dead if you didn't arrest Jimmy. Besides, what would you have done if I told you the Dark Riders were out here?"

Roland shifted his feet uncomfortably. "I would have waited until morning and come after them with a posse," he answered lamely. Henry didn't respond. The Ghost Hunter stood silently with a small, knowing grin on his face. Roland scowled at Henry and spat on the ground. "All right, I would have come after the bastards tonight, but you still should have told me," he accused Henry.

"There's no sense going over this anymore. You know I was right. Let's just leave it at that. You have Curly, and Rebecca will be awake this morning."

"You're right," Roland answered quietly and looked up at the Dark Rider. A large bruise decorated Curly's cheek. Roland had struck the Dark Rider immediately after being rescued. Henry thought for a moment that Roland would actually kill Curly right there in the clearing, but the Sheriff had reined in his temper. Grimly Roland cracked his knuckles and stared at Curly with murderous eyes. Henry almost felt sorry for Curly. It was going to be a rather unpleasant evening for him. "You're right. I think I'll have another word with that son of a bitch. We have some catching up to do."

"Are you going to kill him out here?" Henry asked curiously. The sooner Roland killed Curly, the sooner Rebecca would be free from the Land of Shadows. It would also mean that he and Singing Rock could finally leave New Haven.

Roland continued to glare at Curly with a set jaw. He turned his head towards Henry, and his face softened slightly, but the Ghost Hunter would not have crossed Roland at that moment for all the money in the world. "I should kill that bastard now," he answered fiercely. The Sheriff's entire body quivered with rage, but once again he got his fiery temper under control. "But I can't. I'll wait 'til we get back to town," Roland commented regretfully.

"Why?" Henry raised one of his eyebrows.

"I can't kill him out here. Alvin'll make everyone think I killed him *unfairly*." Roland's lip curled into a sneer at the mayor's name. "I hate that Goddamn snake." He took a deep breath and got himself back under control. "I'll just have to wait 'til we're back in town."

Henry rubbed his chin for a moment. "How long do you think that'll take?"

Roland shrugged his shoulders. "A couple of hours. Why?"

"I want to make sure Rebecca's awake before we leave town," Henry answered tiredly. He was ready to leave immediately. The end of their mission was right there in front of him.

"Leave?" Roland's eyes widened in surprise. "You can't leave yet. What if something goes wrong?"

Henry quickly put his hands up. "Don't worry, Roland. We're not leaving yet. As soon as Rebecca's *awake,* we'll leave town."

"Sorry," Roland apologized and put a hand to his chest in relief. "I just want to make sure she wakes up this time."

"Me too," Henry replied. He wanted to leave New Haven, but he planned on seeing his obligation to Roland through to the end. "We're going back with Falling Thunder. Send word as soon as she's awake or if there's trouble."

"Why? Come to town with me and make sure she wakes up," Roland protested.

Henry sighed. He thought that the world would be a happier place once Rebecca awakened. Roland was nearly crazy with worry for her. "Think about it, Roland. Everyone in town thinks I'm dead. That was the point of the duel with Jimmy. Who's going to believe I'm dead if I ride back into town?" He asked pointedly.

Roland's shoulders slumped. "You're right. I didn't think of that." Then suddenly his eyes flared wide with excitement. "I know. You can sleep at my house tonight. It's close to town, and nobody will see you there."

The Ghost Hunter nearly refused, but he changed his mind when he saw how much Roland wanted him close by. "All right, we'll stay there tonight, but tomorrow we're leaving," he promised.

"Good," Roland answered. "I'll let you know as soon as I kill that son of a bitch." The Sheriff smiled evilly and stared at Curly again. Roland's hand drifted towards his holster almost of its own accord.

"Are you sending anybody back to town for more men?"

"Yeah, probably Morgan." Roland shrugged his shoulders. "I hadn't really thought about it."

"Well, I'd start thinking about it." Henry glanced at the surrounding trees. "There are still eight Dark Riders out there somewhere. They might decide to rescue your prisoners." The Ghost Hunter pointed at the captured

422

outlaws. The first thing that Henry had done was to have four or five Cheyenne acting as lookouts. Henry had no intention of letting the other Dark Riders sneak up on him, but Falling Thunder and his men couldn't stay to help forever.

"You're right. I'll send Morgan and Simon. They can get more men." Roland rubbed his chin and looked at the Dark Riders speculatively. "And a wagon. We'll need something to carry them in." He turned towards his deputies, but Henry grabbed his arm. Roland's eyebrows raised. "What?"

"What about Jimmy?"

"What about him?" Roland asked confusedly.

"He can't go back to town either. Everyone thinks he killed me."

"Blazes," Roland swore and kicked the ground. "And I can't just let him go. Everyone will think I let a murderer go free." He rubbed at his eyes then smiled suddenly. "I know. I'll tell everyone he was involved with the Riders, and we killed him."

"What are you going to do about him now?"

Roland rubbed his chin again and looked at the trees. "I can't turn him loose out here. If Carlos caught him, he'd be a dead man. I guess I can let him stay at my house."

Henry's eyebrows shot up. "How big is this house?"

"Not too big," Roland answered and grinned. "Two of you'll have to sleep on the floor, but at least you won't be in town or out here."

"I guess," Henry answered sullenly. It wouldn't be a bed at The Last Frontier, but Henry would make do. At least he'd have a roof over his head. *You've done a lot worse.* Besides, Henry was so exhausted he could probably fall asleep in the middle of a thunderstorm. "I'm going to talk to Falling Thunder and see if he can stay here for a while longer. You're going to need at least four or five more men until your deputies return."

"All right. I'll get Simon and Morgan on their way as well," Roland replied and headed towards the veteran deputy.

Henry approached Singing Rock and Falling Thunder, who stopped chatting when they saw him approach. He nodded politely at each of them.

Singing Rock returned the nod with an almost indiscernible bob of his head. He held his arms folded across his chest, and his face held its typical stoic mask. "*How is the Sheriff?*" Singing Rock asked in Navajo.

"*He is fine. He is summoning more men.*"

"*Good.*" Singing Rock then turned to Falling Thunder and spoke to him in Cheyenne. The brave answered in his own native tongue. Henry tried to listen to the two talk, but he could only understand a few of the words. Falling Thunder was the first Cheyenne he had ever met, and while some of the words were the same, Cheyenne and Navajo were very different languages. Finally Singing Rock turned back to Henry. "*It is time to go then. Falling Thunder wishes to leave.*"

"I told the Sheriff we would not go to their village but would sleep close to town," Henry explained. He knew that Singing Rock still expected to travel to the Cheyenne village. It wasn't often that he got to spend time with his own people.

Singing Rock frowned at Henry, and his eyebrows lowered. *"Why did you tell him this?"* Henry had known that Singing Rock wouldn't be happy with his decision.

"He wants us close if something goes wrong," Henry answered.

The Navajo kept silent and stared at Henry disapprovingly for a few moments before turning to Falling Thunder. Once again they spoke in Cheyenne, inadvertently shielding Henry from their conversation. Falling Thunder's eyebrows rose as Singing Rock spoke, and he looked at Henry. Then the brave nodded. *"Falling Thunder will go back to his people. We will go as you promised,"* Singing Rock explained, sounding none too happy about it.

"Can he leave some men? The Sheriff will need protection in case the others return," Henry asked and pointed towards the Dark Riders.

"Hmm. I will ask," Singing Rock answered then turned towards the brave a third time. After a brief conversation in Cheyenne, Falling Thunder nodded. *"He will leave five men in the forest."*

Good, Henry thought to himself. The other Dark Riders worried him. Hopefully there wouldn't be a need for the Cheyenne braves, but Henry liked to prepare for everything. *"Give him my thanks,"* Henry told Singing Rock.

Singing Rock turned back to Falling Thunder and conveyed the message in Cheyenne. Falling Thunder listened then grinned suddenly. "You are welcome," he answered in English, and his eyes glowed with amusement. Then the brave began gathering his men.

Son of a bitch, Henry swore to himself when he heard Falling Thunder use English. He scowled at Singing Rock and was rewarded with one of the Navajo's rare smiles. *Damn it, he knew too,* Henry thought angrily then shook his head ruefully. He guessed that was fair after all the times that he had kidded his partner. *"Are you ready to leave?"*

"Are you?" Singing Rock answered, and the grin remained on his face.

Henry bit his lip to keep himself from uttering something rude. He hated when Singing Rock answered a question with a question, and the Navajo was well aware of that. *"I am ready. Let me talk to the Sheriff before we leave."*

Roland was still with his deputies when Henry approached. "Morgan and Simon are about to leave. Are any of the Cheyenne going to stay?" The Sheriff asked as he worriedly watched Falling Thunder gather the braves in the clearing.

"Yeah, there are five of them in the forest. They're all staying until you have more men," Henry answered.

"That's good to hear," Roland breathed a sigh of relief. "I started worrying for a second there."

"Don't worry. You can't see them, but they're out there, Roland," Henry replied then turned to Morgan. "If you don't mind, we'd like to travel with you."

"I thought you didn't want to go back to town?" Roland asked.

"I don't. I don't want to travel by myself, though. There are eight Dark Riders out there, and they could take care of two men fairly easily."

Roland's jaw clenched. "Let me see if I can find where the bastards are," he replied ominously and looked at the captives. His eyes glowed when they passed over Curly, but they moved down the line until they rested on Marshall. Without a word, Roland marched towards the wounded Dark Rider.

Marshall looked up at Roland with a worried expression. He knew that Roland carried a grudge, and he had angered the Sheriff a great deal that night. "What is it, Sheriff?" The Dark Rider asked immediately, clutching his injured arm to his chest. The ends of the arrow had been broken off, but the wooden shaft was still embedded in his arm.

"Where's Carlos?" Roland asked simply. After the Cheyenne had rescued him and captured the Dark Riders, Roland had asked Marshall that same question. The Dark Rider had pled ignorance, but Roland didn't intend to accept that answer again.

"I told you I don't know," Marshall answered in a frightened voice. He flinched back from the Sheriff to put more distance between them.

Roland leaned over and smiled as Marshall leaned back further. *You'd better be scared, you Goddamn bastard.* "I'm going to ask you one more time," Roland told the Dark Rider in a quiet voice. "Where's Carlos?"

"I said I don't know, Sheriff. I'd tell—" he broke off and screamed in pain as Roland grabbed his wounded arm.

I hope it hurts, you son of a bitch, Roland thought as he licked his split lower lip. Marshall had given him that, and he was only repaying the favor. The Sheriff gripped one end of the broken shaft and pulled on it with a fierce tug. Marshall shrieked and writhed in agony. Roland grabbed the front of Marshall's shirt in his fist and pulled him forward until their faces were only inches part. The Dark Rider's breath reeked of alcohol, but Roland barely noticed as he grinned at Marshall. His eyes were wide and shone with a near maniacal glint. "Where the hell is he, Goddamn it?" Roland whispered quietly, inspiring far more terror than yelling at the top of his lungs would have accomplished.

"I don't know," Marshall cried and began sobbing. He pressed his wounded arm against his chest and tried to break free of Roland's iron grip to no avail. "He left earlier to meet somebody. That's all I know. I'd tell you if I knew more," the Dark Rider proclaimed once again.

Roland was surprised to see tears spill down Marshall's cheek. He had meant to frighten the Dark Rider, but he hadn't thought that Marshall would bawl like a baby. With a sneer of disgust, he pushed Marshall away and turned back to the others. He would have bet his life that the Dark Rider had no clue where Carlos was at the moment. Marshall had looked ready to sacrifice his own mother if it would have made Roland leave him alone. *Damn it,* Roland swore to himself in frustration. He would have preferred to know where Carlos was lurking, but hopefully it wouldn't matter. As soon as Morgan returned with more men, they'd be safe from the Dark Riders. "He doesn't know where Carlos is," the Sheriff reported curtly to the Ghost Hunters and Morgan.

The veteran deputy grinned slyly. "I think he would have told you if he did."

Henry shrugged his shoulders. *Hopefully we're lucky then.* "Well, I think we should start towards town," Henry suggested.

Roland nodded and looked at Morgan. "Hurry up, Morgan. I don't like being out here all by myself."

"I'll go as fast as I can. Good luck, Roland," Morgan replied.

"Thanks, you too," Roland answered and pulled Henry aside as Morgan gathered Jimmy and Simon.

"What is it?" Henry asked.

"All I have to do is kill him. Right?" Roland looked at Henry pleadingly.

"What?" Henry looked at Roland in confusion.

"If I kill Curly, Rebecca'll wake up. Right?" Roland asked insistently, and his eyes burned with excitement.

"Of course. I told you that a week ago, Roland. If you kill Bryant's murderer, he'll be banished from the Land of Shadows, and Rebecca will be free." Henry didn't know what all the confusion was about. He had told Roland that exact same thing at least half a dozen times already.

"That's it? Nothing else?"

"There's nothing else," Henry explained patiently, trying to put Roland's fears to rest.

Roland breathed a sigh of relief and smiled his lopsided grin. "Good, I was beginning to worry there was something else I'd have to do." He paused and took another deep breath of relief. "I'll send word as soon as she's awake then."

"That sounds good, Roland. Good luck with Curly and congratulations about Rebecca," Henry replied and clapped the Sheriff on the shoulder.

"Thanks, Henry. I'll see you later," Roland answered. "Morgan," he called out.

"Yeah?" Morgan approached with Simon and Jimmy in tow.

"Take these three back to my house on the way home," Roland told his deputy.

Morgan looked at Roland curiously but didn't ask why the Sheriff was sending them to his own house. He simply nodded. "All right. It's on the way. Anything else?"

"Be careful," Roland advised.

"I'll do my best," Morgan answered dryly, and the corners of his mouth turned upwards in a grin. "Gentlemen, let's go," he told the others and led them out of the woods.

The five men moved silently as they first collected Singing Rock, Henry, and Jimmy's horses then headed towards the trees where the deputies had tethered their own. Singing Rock stared ahead stoically, and Morgan walked at the front of the party, his wounded arm cradled against his chest. Simon simply followed along, but Jimmy stepped with a lively, cocky grin on his face. Henry wished that Roland hadn't told Jimmy to sleep at his house as well. The gunslinger had the look of someone who was always getting into mischief, and Henry had had more than his fair share and was looking forward to some quiet, peaceful times.

"It's just over here," Morgan whispered just loud enough for the others to hear. There were still Dark Riders out in the forest so everyone made sure not to make any extra noise. Roland had waked the entire forest with his interrogation of Marshall, but the Sheriff had five Cheyenne braves waiting in the forest to protect him. It was just the five men heading back to New Haven, and despite the skill that four of them possessed with a gun, it wouldn't be enough to turn back eight men in the woods.

They found Morgan and Simon's horses at the edge of the forest, and after the two deputies had climbed into the saddle, the five men cantered towards town. When they first left the protective shelter of the trees, Henry's shoulders tensed as he looked around, expecting to see Dark Riders waiting for them, but no bullets were fired and nobody was lying in wait. He took a relieved breath and fell in line with the other four.

None of the men talked during the first half of the journey. If the Dark Riders were anywhere nearby, it wouldn't take much to alert them to the five men's presence, but after riding several miles the tension in the group began to ease as they neared their destination. Finally Jimmy broke the silence. "Do you think he'll let me stay in town?" He asked Morgan in a rush as if he had been waiting to ask that question for the last two miles.

Morgan glanced over at Jimmy with an amused look and shook his head ruefully. "I wouldn't count on it," he answered quietly. Jimmy might be speaking loudly, but Morgan knew that they weren't safe until they made it back to town.

Jimmy's shoulders slumped, and the wild grin finally left his face as he frowned in disappointment. "Why?"

"Because he already said you couldn't. Sheriff doesn't like to change his mind very often. Besides, everyone thinks you killed him," Morgan pointed out and jerked a thumb towards Henry. "He can't let you stay after that. Roland said he'd hang any man who dueled in his city, and people wouldn't fear him if he let you stay."

"Oh," Jimmy answered. From the look on his face, the gunslinger knew that all those reasons made sense, but he still wanted to stay in New Haven. After that, they rode in silence the rest of the way.

Henry wasn't surprised to hear the gunslinger speak. Jimmy had been jumping up and down with that excited grin of his ever since Henry had proposed his plan. The entire time they had ridden to join Falling Thunder, Jimmy refused to be quiet. Henry had been glad to arrive at the Dark Rider camp because it finally made Jimmy hold his tongue for a few hours. He did feel sorry for Jimmy, though. New Haven was unlike any town he had ever seen. He was anxious to leave because of all the horrible things that had happened there, but it was still a unique place that Henry knew he'd never find a duplicate of in his travels. The Last Frontier, the faro tables, and ambiance of the town had been a welcome sight. Once Jimmy left town, he'd never find anything close to the Old West culture.

Morgan led them over a hill, and when they had crested it they all saw the lights of New Haven. *It's about time,* Henry thought in relief. He was glad to see their destination. Sleep and safety lay in store for Henry, and he was eager to collect on both. Morgan led them forward, but he didn't go directly to town as he branched off towards Roland's house. "That's it, over there," he pointed towards a house in the distance.

The Ghost Hunter looked in that direction and nodded when he spotted the house. "I see it."

"Good," Morgan replied then held out his hand. "It was a pleasure riding with you, Henry," the deputy said, a knowing smile hovering over his lips.

Henry shook the proffered hand and looked curiously at Morgan. *He knows who I am,* he thought worriedly then banished the thought from his mind. He'd just have to trust the deputy not to divulge his secret. "The same to you. Good luck," Henry told Morgan, and the two parties went their separate ways as Simon and Morgan headed towards town

"Damn, that was fun," Jimmy exclaimed wistfully after Morgan left.

Henry looked at him and felt sorry for the boy again. Jimmy had thoroughly enjoyed all of the evening's events, but Roland's decision to expel him from New Haven was bringing his spirits down. Henry agreed with the Sheriff's decision for personal reasons. He wanted Jimmy as far from New Haven as possible. The sooner people forgot about Jimmy and his gunfight, the better the chance of Henry's ruse working. "Yeah, it was," Henry replied tiredly. He had thought he was exhausted when they began the journey, but now that the end was in sight, Henry's body complained loudly about its need for rest.

The three men tethered their horses then wearily stepped into Roland's house. Even Jimmy's typical exuberance seemed overshadowed by a profound exhaustion. Henry could barely keep his eyes open as he kicked off his boots. Roland's house wasn't large, but it had enough room for two men to sleep comfortably on the floor. "I'll take the bed," Jimmy quickly volunteered and looked at the other two men.

"Fine," Henry replied and waved a hand at the young man. The floor didn't look too comfortable, but Henry was sure that it would do well enough. He didn't care at that point where he went to sleep as long as he could finally rest. With a satisfied groan, he stretched out on the floor and closed his eyes.

Singing Rock laid down on the other side of the room. He grunted at the hard floor, but the Navajo didn't seem to mind the accommodations either. Singing Rock's day had been just as long as Henry's, and he was just as tired. *"Are you feeling better?"*

Henry turned his head and peered at Singing Rock through bleary eyes. *"What?"* He asked in confusion. Henry had been on the verge of falling asleep and struggled to fight it off for a few moments longer.

"Do you feel any better? Your trick worked and everyone thinks you are dead again," the Navajo clarified.

"We will see what happens," Henry answered. He was extremely happy with the day's events, but he wasn't going to rush to any conclusions yet. New Haven had brought nothing but bad luck so far, and Henry had no reason to believe it would change.

"Do not worry. Everything will work out," Singing Rock pointed out in an almost upbeat tone.

"I hope so," Henry muttered quietly. He wanted to continue his work with Singing Rock if at all possible. *"I hope so,"* he whispered wistfully then closed his eyes. Despite his worries about Roland, Alvin, and his elaborate ruse, exhaustion quickly overtook him, and in moments he was fast asleep.

Chapter Twenty-Two

Roland watched as the five men left the camp and most of the Cheyenne braves disappeared into the forest. As soon as they were gone, he turned his attention back to Curly with a wicked smile. *You son of a bitch,* he gloated. The Dark Rider had consumed a great deal of alcohol and didn't know how much trouble he was in. Most of the outlaws knew that things weren't looking good for them, but Roland had special plans for Curly. The Sheriff didn't plan to spare any of their lives, but he was going to end Curly's in the next few hours.

Despite the rage that filled him, Roland felt a lightness in his heart and a spring in his step. Things had seemed bleak when Henry had faked the duel with Jimmy, but fortune had finally smiled upon Roland. Rebecca's awakening was in his immediate sight. There was no more waiting for Henry and Singing Rock. *Not this time,* he thought joyously. With Curly's death would come Rebecca's awakening, and Roland had a hard time keeping from laughing out loud. But he held himself in check. After they returned to town and he could execute Bryant's murderer at long last, then and only then would Roland allow himself to celebrate.

He looked around the campsite, noticing how quiet everything had become. William stood ten feet away from the group of captives, diligently pointing his gun at them. Roland would have preferred more deputies guarding the Dark Riders, but he felt comfortable with the Cheyenne braves hiding in the forest. He couldn't see them, but Roland was certain that they would alert him and come to his aid if Carlos returned. The Sheriff had wanted to keep Simon as a safety measure. Unfortunately Simon's wife still waited to give birth to their child, and Simon had obviously wanted to be with her. Roland shook his head. Maybe he was growing softer, or maybe thoughts of Rebecca awakening had made him more lenient. He knew that he intended to spend every moment with Rebecca as soon as she was awake.

Roland gave up his quick study and turned his attention back to Curly. *You Goddamn bastard,* he snarled mentally and stalked towards the Dark Rider. A few of the outlaws cringed when they saw Roland bearing down upon them. They had captured him, beat him, and threatened to kill him. Everyone had seen what he had done to Marshall and had to think the same was in store for them. Marshall flinched, cradling his wounded arm against his chest. Roland smiled at the Dark Rider. *Don't worry, you'll get what's coming to you later,* he vowed then focused solely on Curly.

Ever since Alvin had given up Curly's name, Roland had dreamed of catching the Dark Rider. Curly had been lucky that he hadn't shown his face in New Haven in almost two weeks, but his luck had finally run dry. It was tempting to kill him immediately, but Roland knew that he had to wait despite the eagerness that made his fingers itch to pull the trigger. Alvin would find a way to turn the killing against him, and Roland wouldn't let anyone spoil his triumph. He wanted the day Rebecca awakened to be perfect. Nothing, however, prevented Roland from putting the fear of God into the Dark Rider. *Not much longer, Curly, then you die.*

He stopped at Curly's feet and spit on the Dark Rider's chest. Curly had watched Roland approach with as much trepidation as the rest of his brethren, but he sat up in alarm when Roland spat upon him. "Hey, what the hell?" He slurred, and even from a few feet away Roland could smell the liquor on his breath.

"Get up," Roland commanded in a taut voice.

"What?" Curly looked up at Roland with bleary eyes and a confused expression. From the looks of him, he had consumed more alcohol than Roland had first thought.

"I said get up!" Roland repeated himself in a louder voice and kicked Curly's thigh with the point of his boot.

The campsite had been relatively quiet, but it became completely silent after Roland's outburst. William held his pistol in a tight grip, intently watching the captives. The rest of the Dark Riders looked at Roland with wide eyes, obviously fearing that the same would happen to them. Roland barely noticed any of it. His only concern was the Dark Rider sitting at his feet. He owed Curly quite a bit of payback, and Roland intended to start collecting on some of it.

Curly immediately put his bound hands to his thigh and groaned in pain. "What'd you do that for?" Roland could barely understand the slurred question.

He kicked the Dark Rider again without hesitation. "I said get up, Goddamn it," Roland answered in a quiet voice.

"Ow!" Curly yelped in pain and cringed backwards as Roland's foot lifted off the ground again. "All right, I'm getting up," he pleaded quickly in an attempt to ward off a third attack. Curly awkwardly rose to his feet. He held his hands to his chest and looked at Roland with a frightened expression. Curly had angered Roland on many occasions, and the Sheriff had thrown him in jail a few times. But he could never remember Roland looking so enraged.

Roland leaned towards the Dark Rider, ignoring the smell of alcohol that emanated from him. Curly immediately flinched back and nearly fell over as he tried to put more distance between himself and the Sheriff. *Scared, you little bastard?* Roland thought with a chuckle. His lopsided smile grew as he leaned forward again, savoring the terror that he was inspiring in Curly. "I know what you did," he whispered just loudly enough for the Dark Rider to hear but nobody else.

Curly looked at Roland with a bleary, confused expression. "What?" He asked bewilderedly.

"I said I know what you did," Roland repeated, and his tone grew harsher. He resisted the urge to shoot the Dark Rider on the spot. *Just wait. He'll be dead soon enough. Rebecca.* He couldn't wait to see her awake once more. In no more than a few hours he'd be reunited with her, and then he could resume his life. It enraged him that the pathetic outlaw in front of him was the ultimate cause for her suffering. For over two weeks Rebecca had suffered due to the actions of a cheap, two-bit drunk.

"I don't know what you're talking about," Curly whined and cowered as Roland's eyes glowed in fury and his nostrils flared.

Roland holstered his gun in one fluid motion then reached out and grabbed the front of Curly's shirt. He pulled the Dark Rider's face up to his own and stared at Curly from no more than six inches away. The smell of alcohol turned his stomach, but Roland was too enraged to care. His lip curled in disgust, and a deep growl formed at the back of his throat. *Bastard son of a whore,* he thought as anger surged through his veins. "I know about Bryant, you son of a bitch," Roland whispered so softly he wasn't even sure if the other Riders heard it.

The Dark Rider's jaw opened, but he never got a chance to say anything else as Roland pushed him backwards. Curly arched his back and tried to regain his balance, but the Sheriff punched the Dark Rider squarely in the nose. Crying out in pain, Curly landed unceremoniously on his backside, blood streaming from his nose. Tears formed in his eyes as he stared up at Roland in terror. He kept scooting back on the ground as Roland stood over him, glaring at the Dark Rider murderously.

"You just sit there. I swear to God, if you cause any trouble, I'll shoot you dead. You got that?" Roland yelled, his words echoing through the still forest. Somewhere in the back of his mind, a tiny voice told him that he shouldn't make so much noise. There were still Dark Riders prowling somewhere in the forest, but Roland didn't care as he quivered with rage.

He knew it would only cause more trouble if he killed Curly in the forest, but he was beginning to rethink his position. *What's the harm?* He reasoned, but Roland knew how Alvin would spin the story if he killed Curly now. Roland didn't think anybody in town would care, but he wanted to play it safe. Once he had Curly at the station house with no witnesses around, Roland could do whatever he wanted. *It won't be that much longer,* he tried to convince himself.

Everyone in the clearing was deathly quiet. The Dark Riders stared at Roland with fear in their eyes, afraid that he intended to beat each of them as well. They quickly looked down at the ground when his gaze met their own, not wanting to provoke the Sheriff in the slightest bit. Marshall especially looked frightened and cradled his wounded arm to his chest as if the Sheriff might hurt it again.

Before he could change his mind Roland stalked to the other side of the clearing and took a seat on the ground, resting his back against a tall oak. From that vantage point he could see everyone at the campsite, but he wasn't so close to Curly. Even from the other side of the clearing, Roland was sorely tempted to draw his gun and shoot Bryant's murderer. Fuming silently, Roland sat impatiently and waited for Morgan to return with more men. He almost hoped that Carlos and the rest of the Dark Riders would show up. Killing a few Riders would brighten his spirits tremendously. After a few minutes, he did draw one of his guns. He held it in his lap, idly stroking the barrel as he stared at Curly. *Enjoy the next few hours, you son of a bitch. They're your last.* It was a small comfort, but it helped pass the time during his frustrating wait.

The wait seemed to drag forever in the quiet campsite. The Dark Riders were too frightened to make any noise, and William kept silent as he watched the captives. Waiting was bad enough, but the absolute silence made it even worse. Every cricket or squirrel that made a sound caused everyone to jump as the sound was magnified. Although it wasn't mentioned, everybody was aware that there were more Dark Riders somewhere in the forest. *Hurry up, Morgan,* Roland wished. Despite his brief wish to the contrary, Roland had no desire to see Carlos that night.

Roland would have given just about anything to talk to Jack at that moment. He had buried his old friend only that morning, but to Roland it seemed like a week had passed with all the chaotic events that had unfolded. Roland didn't know what to think about half the things that were happening. It had been less than twenty-four hours since he promised to look after Dotty, and with a pang of guilt the Sheriff realized that he hadn't even checked on her that evening. In all fairness, he had been busy with Henry's ruse, but he still felt that he should have checked on her. Roland added visiting her the following morning to his growing list of tasks.

In a way, Roland was almost glad that his life had been so tumultuous over the course of the day. It had barely allowed him to grieve for his friend. Roland was sure that once things slowed down, it would affect him a lot more, but at least he would have Rebecca at his side. *I miss you, Jack,* Roland thought wistfully. It would take quite some time before he stopped instinctively wanting Jack around to discuss New Haven's problems. Roland almost felt like he had had lost a hand and kept expecting to find it there even though it was gone.

Roland's expression became increasingly angrier as he thought of Jack and what he would do with the Dark Riders. His lip curled into a sneer, and he ground his teeth together. He hoped that Morgan would hurry up with the reinforcements. Roland kept eyeing the outlaws and pictured firing a few bullets at them. Curly, in particular, caught his attention. Every time Roland's eyes rested on him, the Dark Rider flinched and hastily looked away. Curly's fear only made Roland smile as he stroked the butt of his gun. *Hurry up, Morgan,* he kept repeating to himself as he waited for the deputy's return.

Between bouts of anger, Roland spent his time thinking of Rebecca. It was still hard to believe that she would finally awaken in a matter of hours. Roland yearned to see her smile again and her beautiful green eyes sparkling in the sun. He was tired of always being angry and needed her to help calm him down. He kept picturing her sitting at the dinner table, laughing and smiling. He imagined standing before Thatcher as the Reverend pronounced them man and wife. Those thoughts made him smile and his heart warm with anticipation, but they also caused him to tap his foot nervously on the ground. *Hurry up, Morgan,* he repeated the thought over and over.

Just over two hours after Morgan had left, Roland heard the distant snap of a twig. He flinched then relaxed as he expected it to be another squirrel or raccoon making noise in the forest, but then he heard the soft rumbling of human voices. Instantly he rose to his feet, drawing his other pistol and facing the treeline with two drawn guns. He waited for the Cheyenne to signal him if it was Carlos, but the braves remained hidden in the trees. William turned towards the sound and held his gun in a steady grip, ready to fire if needed. *Please let that be you, Morgan,* Roland thought fervently.

Roland breathed a sigh of relief when the veteran deputy appeared with five men behind him. *It's about Goddamn time,* he thought irritably, but he was glad that Morgan had finally shown up. He wanted to get back into town and as far from the campsite as possible. His heart was racing with excitement. It wouldn't be much longer before Rebecca awakened.

"Sheriff," Morgan greeted as he rode into the campsite. He looked at the prisoners and shook his head as if he still couldn't believe what had happened. Roland recognized the five men with Morgan as some of the volunteers guarding the town's borders.

"Morgan." He approached the deputy and pulled him aside from the others. "What took you so long?" He asked quietly.

"It's a long ride," Morgan answered and shrugged his shoulders.

"Did you get the wagon?" Roland asked anxiously.

"Yeah, it's back about half a mile." Morgan turned and pointed back the way they had approached the clearing. "I left Jared Amsden and five others with it."

"Good," Roland breathed a sigh of relief. Not only did they have a means to transport the Dark Riders back to town, they also had enough men to guard them. "What about the others?"

"They're at your house," Morgan answered and looked at him with a curious grin. Roland knew that the deputy wanted to ask him why they were all sleeping at his house, but Morgan would never voice the question unless Roland brought it up.

"Well, let's get going then," Roland replied. He holstered his guns and rubbed his hands together in anticipation. *Soon, Rebecca. Soon,* he thought, scarcely able to believe that she would finally awaken from her hellish slumber. *Soon, you son of a bitch,* Roland thought menacingly as his eyes passed over Curly. The Dark Rider had no idea of the fate that awaited him in New Haven, or else he would have tried to escape.

Roland, Morgan, William, and the five men who had traveled into the forest surrounded the Dark Riders in a tight circle. The nine captives looked nervously at the men guarding them but made no move to escape. They might have been captured, but Marshall, Curly, and the others weren't stupid men. They saw the futility of trying to escape at the moment. If they were to find a way, they'd have to bide their time and wait for a better opportunity. Besides, none of them wanted to risk drawing Roland's ire that night. He obviously intended to kill them, but the Dark Riders held out a slim hope that their lives would be spared.

The brief walk through the forest was a tense one. Roland was glad that they didn't have to sneak through the trees. His approach to the campsite had been a tenuous one as he carefully placed each foot to avoid making noise. This time they didn't have the same worries, but they still moved at a snail's pace. Guiding nine captives while walking through a dark forest wasn't an easy task, and it took some time as Roland made sure not to allow any of the Dark Riders an opportunity to escape. As they slowly made their way towards the wagon, Roland kept expecting Carlos or another Dark Rider to leap out from behind the trees, but they emerged safely from the forest into the plains that covered most of the northern side of town. Roland grinned when he saw the wagon. *It's about Goddamn time. Not much longer,* he thought gleefully. Within the next two or three hours, Rebecca would awaken, and then everything in his life would be better.

Morgan had indeed brought reinforcements with him when he returned. Six more men waited by the wagon to carry the captives. Roland also recognized them from their help with guarding the edge of town. They all had blackened clothes and streaks of soot lining their faces, mute testimony to their assistance in extinguishing the fires that Henry had set. William and Morgan herded the Dark Riders towards the wagon, careful to keep guns trained on them. The men Morgan had brought formed a crude ring around the Dark Riders, effectively cutting off any hope of escape.

"Get in," Morgan ordered gruffly and waited for the outlaws to obey. The Dark Riders reluctantly crawled onto the bed, grumbling in soft voices. A pair of outlaws had to help Marshall climb onto the wagon when he had trouble with his wounded arm. He cried out in pain as he briefly put weight on it, but then he rolled over into the back of the coach with relief. After that the rest quickly followed suit, and soon all nine Dark Riders were safe in the back of the wagon.

Roland waited for some comment from the outlaws, and he was almost disappointed when none came forth. *Scared them,* Roland thought. He would have liked an excuse to hit or even shoot one of the prisoners, but he knew that his display with Curly had convinced all of them to stay quiet and out of his way. A lopsided grin formed on his face as he walked towards the back of the wagon. He peered inside and saw faces quickly looking away when his eyes met theirs. *You're Goddamn right, you'd better be scared.* Roland's chest swelled up haughtily as he turned from the wagon.

"I want four men behind and two on each side. Morgan and I will ride up front. You," Roland called out and pointed his finger at William. "Ride on the wagon and shoot anybody who makes a Goddamn sound. You got that?"

"Yes, Sheriff," William answered quickly. He looked at the Dark Riders with a hardened face. All of the them stared down at the wooden bed, too wary to utter a single word.

"Good. Let's go, gentlemen," he ordered then clapped his hands. *Not much longer,* he thought to himself anxiously. Everyone wordlessly obeyed his brief command. Casting one last glance at the prisoners on the back of the wagon, Roland's smiled deepened when none of the Riders looked up at him. *Bunch of pathetic sons of bitches*, he thought derisively then joined Morgan at the front of their party.

Leon Hirst sat at the front of the wagon with Richard Howell. William joined them, and once they saw Morgan and Roland at the front of the party, Leon flicked his reins. The four horses pulling the wagon strained their legs to move, but once its wheels began to roll the wagon quickly picked up speed. In no time at all, the party was moving along at a brisk pace towards New Haven.

"About Goddamn time," Roland muttered under his breath. He looked back over his shoulder to make sure that everyone had followed his instructions. His eyes lit up when they passed over Curly, and he tapped his fingers on the butt of his pistol. *You Goddamn bastard,* he thought fiercely.

"Calm down, Roland. We're almost there," Morgan commented quietly.

"What?" Roland jerked his head around and looked at the veteran deputy.

"I said calm down. You look like you've got a bur in your britches." The deputy grinned after his comment.

"You're right. I'll try," Roland replied, but he knew that he had no intention of following through on that promise. If Morgan knew the facts, he wouldn't tell Roland to calm down either. *Not much longer,* Roland agreed with Morgan. As soon as they returned to town, he killed Curly, and Rebecca awakened, Roland's impatience and worries would end. *Soon, Rebecca.*

Morgan gave him a long look that showed he doubted Roland's sincerity, but he kept silent.

The two rode in silence for a while. Roland's mind kept alternating back and forth between malicious thoughts about Curly and joyous thoughts of Rebecca awakening. There were a few conversations among the men Morgan had gathered, but the Dark Riders continued to sit silently in the wagon. Whether it was from fear of Roland or realizing that no good would come out of upsetting their captors, Roland didn't know. When they finally saw the lights of town off in the distance, Morgan turned towards Roland.

"I think you should let Jimmy stay," Morgan stated quietly.

Roland scowled and rolled his eyes in frustration. *Not this again.* He thought that when he had told Morgan to drop the subject the deputy would do so. Morgan had always been good about not pestering him. "I already told you, he can't stay," Roland answered somewhat harshly. He preferred to ride in silence. Visions of Curly's death and Rebecca's awakening kept running through his head, and he'd rather think of them than talk about Jimmy.

Morgan surprised him by pressing on. "I think you're making a mistake," he insisted.

Roland stared at Morgan curiously. He couldn't remember Morgan ever disagreeing with him. The deputy usually made his comments then let Roland make his decision. He had never tried to contradict Roland. That had always been Jack's role. "Why is that?" Roland asked slowly.

The deputy shook his head and smiled good-naturedly. "You need more men, Roland, and that's one of the best deputies you're going to find."

"No," Roland answered flatly and set his jaw. No matter how much Morgan tried, he'd never convince Roland to hire Jimmy as a deputy.

"Why?" Morgan asked, unfazed by Roland's staunch refusal.

"Because he'd cause more harm than help. You know that as well as I do. Blazes, he's nearly caused a gunfight, and there was that stunt he pulled this morning," Roland pointed out angrily. He didn't feel like debating the issue any longer. Roland had told both Jimmy and Morgan that the gunslinger was leaving town.

"That stunt helped catch nine Dark Riders," Morgan commented, and his grin stretched a little wider. He looked over at Roland, but the Sheriff didn't have anything to say. "Just think about it, Roland. That's all I'm asking. He's quick with a gun, and he caught nine Dark Riders. That's more than you or I ever caught. He might be reckless, but he's no worse than I was at that age." The deputy's eyes sparkled mischievously. "Or you."

Roland kept his eyes focused on the lights ahead. He knew that Morgan had a point, but Roland still couldn't make himself trust Jimmy. As soon as the nine Dark Riders were executed, Roland was looking forward to a long, peaceful rest with Rebecca. He wasn't about to let Jimmy spoil that. Roland had promised to run the young man out of town the following day, and that's exactly what he intended to do. "I'll think about it," he told Morgan in a rather dubious tone to keep the deputy off his back.

The last mile passed by without any more words from Morgan, and as they crept closer to New Haven Roland completely forgot about the deputy's request. Curly was Roland's primary focus as they rode into town, and he didn't want to think about Jimmy any more. In a matter of minutes, Roland was finally going to question the Dark Rider about the murder of Bryant White. He had waited an awfully long time to have the outlaw in his clutches, and Roland anticipated his death keenly.

A group of eight men guarded the northern side of town, and they all cheered loudly as the wagon rolled past. "Kill 'em all, Sheriff," a few of them shouted and heckled the Dark Riders. Carlos and his men had killed deputies and ruined the Fourth of July party, and they wouldn't find any sympathetic people in town this time. Even if they had still been in Alvin's good graces, the mayor wouldn't have been able to save them.

They seemed to pass every building and house at a snail's pace. Roland's foot kept tapping anxiously against his horse's side. The horse looked back at Roland a few times and started to gallop forward, but the Sheriff quickly reined it back in. *Damn it, stay calm. You're almost there,* Roland told himself only to tap his foot once more. When he saw the station house ahead, Roland launched into a gallop and nearly leapt out of the saddle. He tethered his horse then drew one of his guns as he waited for the wagon to finish the trek.

Morgan looked at Roland with an amused grin as he approached the station house. Roland barely noticed him or any of the others. The prisoner in the wagon was the only one in the entire party who mattered to Roland. *Now you're mine,* he thought grimly and rubbed his thumb along the edge of his gun.

He stalked to the back of the wagon and joined the other four men who had guarded it on the way back to town. The nine Dark Riders peered out nervously. Not one of them made a sound, but Roland knew that they were all scared to death. In the forest justice had seemed far away, but now that they had arrived in town their fate was not only awaiting them but staring them in the face. Roland's face stretched into a lopsided grin at the sight of them. He was enjoying their capture more and more by the minute. *Especially you, Curly.* "Let's go, you sons of bitches," he called out roughly to the outlaws.

They all looked at him, but nobody moved. Instead they backed up, afraid to be the first one off the bed. Roland stared at Curly, nearly bursting out into coarse laughter when the Dark Rider flinched. He was amused by their fear, but he soon grew irritated. There would be plenty of time to scare the living hell out of the Dark Riders, but Roland wanted to get Curly into one of the cells. He was looking forward to dragging answers out of the Dark Rider before he finally ended his life. Roland lifted his gun and pointed it at Curly's head, snorting a brief laugh when the Dark Rider closed his eyes and waited for the worst. "I said get out. Now, Goddamn it!" He shouted at the top of his lungs.

The Dark Riders scrambled forward as if there were a fire behind them. Even Marshall moved forward, cradling his wounded arm against his chest. One by one they scrambled off the wagon, only to be pushed towards the station house. Morgan, William, and the other men had formed two lines towards the station house, and each Dark Rider marched between them towards the jail cells. Curly was the sixth one off the wagon, and Roland couldn't help giving him a rough push when he stumbled by. The outlaw lurched forward a few steps but caught his balance. He looked up angrily at Roland then turned around and continued his march when he saw the maniacal look of glee on the Sheriff's face. *That's right, you bastard. Your time's up. I'm going to kill you this time. No more escapes.*

Roland stood still as the other three Dark Riders got off the wagon, but his eyes followed Curly. He couldn't believe that he was finally going to bring Bryant's murderer to justice and free Rebecca from her prison. Several times Roland came close to pinching himself. It seemed as if his good luck had to be a dream. Everything else had gone so poorly for him lately, but Roland was confident that things had finally turned around. He tried to keep from dancing with joy as his heart beat rapidly in excitement. *Soon, Rebecca. Soon.*

Marshall was the last to climb off the wagon. One of the Banditos helped the wounded Dark Rider, then Roland fell in behind them and followed them to the station house. Marshall glanced over his shoulder at Roland once, but that one look was enough to convince him to face forward. Roland's lips were stretched wide in an evil grin, and his eyes burned murderously. The men Morgan had summoned stared at Roland curiously as he marched by with a crazed look, but he paid them no attention. Roland's business was with Curly, and he was ready to see that the Dark Rider finally paid the price for his crime.

"Roland," a voice yelled as he was about to step inside the station house. Turning his head, Roland scowled in disgust as he saw Alvin awkwardly hurrying down the street. He hadn't expected to see Alvin still awake. The rest of the town had long since gone to sleep as dawn drew near.

The mayor was dressed impeccably as normal. He wore the same suit from earlier that evening, and his hair was perfectly combed, but Alvin had a worried expression instead of his typical smug grin. His eyes darted towards Marshall and the Bandito as they entered the station house then returned to the Sheriff. "Roland," Alvin gasped breathlessly as he stopped and leaned on his cane. Sweat had formed at his temples, and his face was red.

Roland smiled briefly at Alvin's less than perfect appearance. It was so seldom that he got to see the mayor without his suave, cocky public persona. "What do you want, Alvin?" He asked curtly.

Alvin swallowed hard and took a deep breath then straightened his back. "I see you caught some Riders," he panted.

"Why do you want to know?" Roland asked, his eyes narrowing suspiciously. He crossed his arms across his chest and watched the mayor closely. Roland didn't like it when Alvin did unexpected things, and he had never expected to see Alvin at the station house. *What are you up to?*

"I was just curious." Alvin's face grew hurt as if he was surprised that Roland would question his judgment. "Carlos did threaten to shoot me. Remember?" He pointed out crossly. "So who did you catch?"

Roland stared at Alvin wordlessly for a few moments as the mayor fidgeted with the end of his coat. "Yeah, I caught a few of them," he answered finally, toying with Alvin.

"All of them? Did you kill anyone?" The mayor stared at Roland intently as he leaned forward.

"I don't remember," the Sheriff replied, the corner of his mouth tipping upwards in a lopsided grin. He was beginning to enjoy himself. Curly waited inside, but it was fun to bait Alvin. It was like an appetizer before the main meal.

"Goddamn it, Roland. What the hell happened?" Alvin asked again, his eyes burning intensely. The men standing outside the station house looked at Alvin curiously. None of them had ever seen the mayor lose his composure.

Roland stifled a laugh but continued to smirk at Alvin. "I caught nine of them, Alvin. Nobody died."

"Who'd you catch? Carlos?"

"Nah. Not Carlos, but I did catch Curly." Roland's lopsided smile turned into a deep malicious grin as he mentioned the Dark Rider's name. *Not much longer, Curly.* "I'm going to execute that son of a bitch for killing Bryant White," he informed Alvin.

Alvin's face became deathly pale, and his eyes widened in surprise. "You caught Curly," he repeated quietly. Then he quickly regained his composure, donning a pale shadow of his polished smile. He tried to look at Roland with his customary arrogance, but he looked more shocked than anything else. "You should definitely kill him, Roland. As soon as possible," he insisted.

"Don't worry, I will," Roland answered slowly. Alvin was acting too bizarre, and that worried Roland.

"I have to go," Alvin said abruptly.

"All right, Alvin, but I want to talk to you tomorrow." Roland wanted a few words with the mayor, and he also planned on tracking down Matthew Brady. He owed both of them for spoiling Henry's secret. *What the hell are*

440

you up to, you Goddamn snake? Roland thought bewilderedly. He'd have to ask Alvin about his strange behavior the next day.

"Sure. Just make sure you kill him," Alvin told Roland in an almost demanding tone of voice. Then the mayor turned around and walked away.

Roland frowned as he watched Alvin limp down the street. The whole conversation with Alvin seemed wrong. The only time that Roland had ever seen Alvin lose his composure to such a degree had been with a gun in his face. Roland hadn't even come close to threatening him. *Why were you so upset, Alvin?* It couldn't be the capture of the Dark Riders. Alvin had every reason to hate the Riders after their confrontation. *Worry about it later,* Roland told himself and turned towards the station house. There would be plenty of time to deal with Alvin later on, but Roland was ready to question Curly. He cracked his knuckles and smiled. *Now you die, Curly,* he thought as he walked inside.

Phillip stood behind his desk with a gun in his hand and a nervous expression on his face. A book laid facedown on the desk, telling Roland that the deputy had been reading only moments before the prisoners had arrived. Morgan had told Phillip to expect prisoners, but obviously the well-read deputy hadn't expected quite so large a number. Morgan and William also stood in the crowded room. Each hugged his back against one of the walls and pointed his gun at the outlaws.

Roland wasted no time as he entered. "Phillip, keys," he greeted, holding out his hand and tapping his foot impatiently as Phillip took the ring off the wall. The deputy frowned at the Riders then tossed the ring of keys towards Roland. The Sheriff smoothly snatched them out of the air with one hand, his gun never wavering. He selected the correct key then made his way towards the cell room door.

The Dark Riders watched him nervously. Nearly every one of the outlaws in the station house had been locked up at least once in their career, but they all knew that this would likely be the last time. Unless Carlos made a miracle rescue, every one of them would die, and Roland intended to carry out their sentences quickly to prevent anything bad from happening. He inserted the key into the door and slowly pushed it forward, the hinges screeching as it swung open fully. He walked inside and opened both cell doors. Then he went back into the main room. "Everybody inside," he announced and stepped back from the door to allow plenty of room between himself and the prisoners.

They quietly shuffled into the cell room and split up, four in the left cell and five in the right. Marshall cringed as he walked by Roland, still cradling his wounded arm. Roland supposed that he should have Sullivan look at it, but seeing how he planned on executing Marshall as soon as possible, it would be a waste of the doctor's time.

Curly also flinched as he walked by Roland, and the Sheriff grinned in amusement. Roland couldn't wait to hang the Dark Rider. *Unless I shoot him first,* Roland thought and chuckled out loud. Curly looked up at him then quickly stared straight ahead when he saw the expression on Roland's face. Roland watched as he quickly scurried by and into the left cell with Marshall and the two Banditos. Roland gave the Dark Rider a withering glance as the last two prisoners shuffled into the right cell. All the prisoners stood well back from the door as he locked the right cell. Then he slammed the left door with a loud metallic clamor and twisted the key in it. "I'll be back for you, you son of a bitch," he promised Curly and stalked out the cell room. He found himself smiling almost uncontrollably. *Not much longer, Rebecca.* As soon as he cleared all the men out of the station house, he could begin his interrogation of Curly.

"You look happy," Morgan commented as Roland walked out of the cell room.

Roland shrugged his shoulders. "What do you expect? We caught nine of those bastards. The Dark Riders are finished for good," he grinned at the deputy and kept his real reason hidden. *You're a dead man, Curly.* He felt like singing and dancing in joy.

Morgan grinned, and his eyes sparkled merrily. "It's a shame. Isn't it?" He asked facetiously then his face grew somber. "Don't forget about Carlos, though," Morgan warned.

"Don't worry about him. We'll catch Carlos, but at least now he doesn't have twenty men. It's just a matter of time before all the Dark Riders are dead," he gloated.

"I suppose I could live with that," Morgan replied then glanced at the door leading to the cell room. "What do you want to do about them?" He asked and pointed at the door.

I thought you'd never ask, Roland thought and nearly burst into laughter. "We'll build another gallows then hang 'em. We'll need some extra men around this place in case Carlos decides to break them out. I think six more men out on the street should do it. Don't you?"

Morgan tapped his chin for a moment then nodded. "Yeah, I guess so. We should keep the patrols out, though. That way we'll have plenty of men on hand."

"That sounds great to me," Roland exclaimed and clapped his hands together. "Phillip, William, go home and get some sleep. Morgan and I can take over from here."

Phillip rubbed a hand over his ample stomach and looked at Roland curiously. "You sure you don't want me to stay here and keep an eye on the Riders for you?"

"I'll stay here, Phillip. Don't worry about it," Roland answered and smiled his lopsided grin. *As soon as they leave, it's just you and me, Curly.*

"Sure," Phillip replied. William nodded in relief. Both men had to be tired. Roland knew that he was exhausted, but adrenaline flowed through his veins and would keep him awake for a while longer.

"Where do you want me?" Morgan asked.

"Keep an eye on the patrols out there. I want you two up here by noon tomorrow," Roland ordered and looked at William and Phillip sternly.

"Yes, Sheriff," they responded.

"Good. Then let's get moving," Roland declared and took a seat behind the desk. He propped his feet on the desk and waited anxiously for the deputies to leave the office. Phillip and William were out the door in a hurry, eager to get some rest. Morgan took his time walking out the door and tipped his hat before he stepped back outside.

Roland leapt out of his seat the moment the office was empty and paced around nervously. He wanted to wait a few more minutes in case anybody else had to return. Once he started with Curly, Roland didn't want to be stopped. He kept looking out the window at The Last Frontier. Roland knew that just across the street Rebecca laid in her bed, and in a matter of minutes she would awaken. Finally he couldn't take the waiting any longer and rushed to the door. Locking it so he wouldn't be disturbed, Roland grabbed the set of keys off the wall and approached the cell room door with an eager grin on his face. He unlocked the cell room door then kicked it open with a quick surge of energy. *Now you die, Curly. Soon, Rebecca. Soon.* Drawing his gun, he stepped inside.

The prisoners all came to their feet when Roland kicked open the door and stared at the Sheriff with apprehensive expressions. Roland stood in the doorway for a moment and took a deep breath, savoring the terror he had inspired. Then he stalked to the left cell and stared at the occupants. The Banditos stood against the back wall, pressing themselves against the wall as if it was a shield. Marshall held his injured arm and cringed away from Roland. Curly, however, was the only one who Roland cared about. He also looked scared as he moved back when the Sheriff opened the cell door. Roland let the Dark Riders stand there as they shifted uncomfortably in the quietness. He let the silence hold for a few moments then drew one of his guns. "Curly," he proclaimed. "Get out here," Roland ordered. He aimed at Curly's head as he stepped away from the doorway.

Curly's jaw dropped open in fear and surprise. "B-But, Sheriff. Why c-can't I stay in here?" He pressed his back against the wall, his face scrunching up in terror.

"Get out here," Roland growled. He closed one of his eyes and took closer aim at the Dark Rider.

"All right," Curly answered in a voice that shook with fear. He stepped away from the wall and walked nervously towards the open door. The Dark

Rider watched Roland as if he thought that the Sheriff was going to shoot him dead any second.

Roland thought about doing just that as Curly slowly exited the cell. "Turn around and stand against the wall," he ordered. Curly looked at him with a frightened expression, and the man nearly cowered away from Roland. "Do it now, Goddamn it!" Roland shouted at the top of his lungs and grinned as the Dark Rider hastily responded. He backed up against the wall and stared at Roland as if he expected to die at that moment. *Goddamn it. Is he that stupid?* "I said turn around and face the wall. Do it, or die," Roland told the Dark Rider.

With a sob, Curly obeyed. He took one last look over his shoulder, then pressed his forehead against the wall. "Please don't kill me, Sheriff," he begged tearfully.

"Shut up!" Roland barked as he holstered his gun and closed the cell door. Hastily he locked it then drew his weapon again. *Finally!* He thought in relief. At long last, he could begin his interrogation and execution of Curly. "Turn back around," he ordered the Dark Rider and waited for Curly to face him. Tears streamed down Curly's cheeks, and his lower lip trembled. "Let's go," he ordered and backed up. "I said to move!" Roland shouted when Curly stood still, trembling in fear. With another sob, the Dark Rider took a few faltering steps forward, turning his head to the side as he waited for a bullet to strike him. "Hurry up, or I swear to God I'll shoot you," Roland shouted in frustration. He wasn't going to put up with the Dark Rider dragging his feet much longer.

Curly wiped at his eyes and picked up his pace. The rest of the Dark Riders stayed as far back in their cells as they could and watched Roland and Curly with numb expressions. For all they knew, Roland intended to drag them out of the cells next. Roland backed out of the cell room, keeping his gun aimed at Curly as the two stepped into the office. "Sit in that chair." Roland pointed at one of the chairs with his other hand and waited for Curly to take a seat. In that same cringing shuffle, Curly crossed the office and sat down, folding his hands nervously in his lap. Roland closed the door behind him and locked it. Then he turned towards Curly and smiled a wicked grin of exhilaration. *Now you're mine!*

The Sheriff nearly shook with excitement as he crossed the room towards the frightened Dark Rider. He had waited so long for the whole ordeal to end, and he finally had his wish. There were no witnesses. Just him and Curly. Nothing could stop him this time. "You little bastard," he swore quietly as he stood before Curly. He caressed the hammer of his gun with the ball of his thumb almost lovingly. *So soon,* he thought of Rebecca awakening. *So soon.* "I know about Bryant," Roland told the Dark Rider.

"I promised not to tell," Curly cried out and burst into tears. He stared up at Roland with a pleading look in his eyes. "Please don't kill me," Curly begged.

"Goddamn it!" Roland shouted and hit Curly in the head with the butt of his gun. Curly put a hand to his head and continued to cry as he tried to cover himself protectively with his arms. "I know you killed him! Tell me why you did it, you son of a bitch!" Roland raged at the top of his lungs. Flecks of spittle flew from his mouth, and his lower lip curled into a snarl.

"I didn't—" Curly cried out before Roland cut him off with another crushing blow with his gun.

Roland shook in rage one more time then got his temper under control with a great deal of effort. He looked at the Dark Rider in disgust. Roland had wanted a confession before he executed Curly, but he was growing impatient with the Dark Rider. "This is your last chance. Tell me why you did it," the Sheriff whispered.

"Carlos killed him," Curly whimpered and covered his head as he waited for Roland to strike him again.

"You're lying." The Sheriff pointed his gun at Curly's head and closed one of his eyes as he lined up his sight. Roland had had enough. He was going to end the ordeal once and for all.

"No, Carlos killed him!" Curly shrieked. He uncovered his head and looked up at Roland with teary eyes. "Carlos did it, not me. Please don't kill me!"

The Dark Rider's passionate plea made Roland pause for a moment. Curly looked too frightened to lie, but Alvin had told him that Curly killed Bryant. *Alvin!* Roland thought in disgust. No wonder the mayor had been acting so strangely in front of the station house. *You son of a bitch!* The Sheriff tightened his grip on the pistol, imagining what he would do to Alvin when he caught him. He pressed the barrel of his gun against Curly's head. Roland wanted to make sure that the Dark Rider was telling the truth. *"Who. Killed. Bryant?"* Roland growled.

"Carlos did. I swear to—" he stopped and tried to cover his head, but it was too late.

"Goddamn it!" Roland shouted and swung the gun at Curly's temple. It hit him with a satisfying crunch and knocked the Dark Rider unconscious, but it wasn't enough to curb Roland's temper. *Alvin, you Goddamn snake. This time I'll kill you,* he raged and looked around for something to hit. His eyes lit up as they rested upon the cell room door, and his mouth curled into a murderous grin. He stalked across the room and nearly broke the key as he savagely opened the door.

All the Dark Riders jumped back when he entered. Roland ignored the cell on the right and went straight to the door on the left. He believed Curly's story but was going to get corroboration before he acted on it. The Banditos and Marshall pressed against the back wall in fear. They had all heard Curly's screams and Roland's threats.

Roland knew that he shouldn't go into a cell with three prisoners, but he was beyond caring as he stalked inside and grabbed Marshall's shoulder. He roughly spun the Dark Rider around and threw him to the floor. Roland shot a menacing glance at the Banditos to dissuade them of any foolish heroic notions. Looking back down at Marshall, Roland smiled at the look of terror on the Dark Rider's face. He reached out and yanked on the arrow that was still embedded in Marshall's arm. Marshall screamed as fire coursed agonizingly through his arm.

Letting go of the arrow, Roland put his gun to Marshall's forehead. "You listen to me good, Marshall. I'm going to ask this once, and if you lie I swear I'll kill you. You understand?"

Marshall pressed his wounded arm to his chest, his face still cringing in pain and fear. He nodded once and braced himself for whatever Roland intended.

"*Who. Killed. Bryant. White?*" Roland asked in a fierce whisper.

The Dark Rider's eyes widened for a moment in surprise, but he didn't hesitate to answer with Roland's gun against his head. "Carlos did," he croaked out fearfully.

"Goddamn it!" Roland swore and hit the Dark Rider out of frustration. He stalked out of the cell before he shot someone and locked the door behind him. Then he entered the office and slammed the cell room door on its hinges. He looked at the unconscious body of Curly and gave him a satisfying kick in the ribs. "Alvin." Roland clenched his fists tightly and thought about what he would do to the mayor when he saw him next. Once again, Rebecca's salvation had cruelly slipped through his fingers, and Roland wondered if he was ever going to see her awake again.

446

Roland galloped furiously towards his house. The temperature was beginning to rise as dawn approached, and a light sweat beaded on his forehead. Every jolt in the horse's gait sent tremors of pain shooting through his exhausted body. Every muscle screamed at him to rest, but Roland fought it off with pure adrenaline. Roland's mind was a chaotic mix of rage, frustration, and sorrow, but it helped supply him with one last surge of energy.

Morgan had acted surprised when Roland told him to watch over the station house. The deputy hadn't asked why Roland was abandoning the station house, but the unspoken question had been written in his eyes. Roland was beyond caring at that point. He had dragged Curly's body back into the cell and left him on the floor. The Dark Rider had started to regain consciousness, moaning groggily as Roland moved him. Roland was tempted at that moment to shoot Curly, but he held back. He wanted to kill all the prisoners in one fell swoop. Carlos was another matter.

For days Roland had focused all of his hate and energy on Curly. Alvin hadn't been able to inspire his wrath like Curly had, and even after the Fourth of July gunfight, Roland had wanted to catch Curly far more than Carlos. Before Rebecca had fallen ill, Carlos had been a far larger thorn in Roland's side than Curly. Since he had learned that Carlos was Bryant's killer, his hatred for the Dark Rider dwarfed that for Curly. It felt strange to switch tracks suddenly and focus all of his hatred towards Carlos. Roland didn't want to shoot him. Instead he wanted to beat Carlos to within an inch of his life then leave him to rot in one of the prison cells. It would be a fitting end for the Dark Rider.

It might have taken him all that time to discover the identity of Bryant's killer, but at least Roland finally knew who it was. Unfortunately it wouldn't do Rebecca any good. She'd still waste away in the Land of Shadows another day. Roland knew that he wouldn't catch Carlos any time soon. If the Dark Rider had one ounce of intelligence, he'd flee New Haven as quickly as he could. Half of his men had been captured, and Carlos had to know that Roland was trying to catch him. Carlos was brave, but he wasn't stupid. With a sickening feeling in his stomach, Roland started to realize that he might not ever catch Bryant's murderer.

That left him only one choice. *Henry,* Roland thought hopefully as he neared his house. The Ghost Hunter had almost rescued her, and Roland hoped that Henry would make another attempt. Luck, however, was frowning upon him. Despite the frantic pace of his horse, the sky was beginning to lighten. *Goddamn it,* Roland swore as dawn approached. If Henry decided to return to the Land of Shadows, it would have to wait another day. There just wasn't enough time left before sunrise.

When he arrived at his house, Roland leapt off his horse and didn't bother to tether it. He pushed the door open roughly, causing it to bang loudly as it struck the inside wall. Henry and Singing Rock immediately sat up at the intrusion, looking at him with bleary eyes. "Henry," Roland whispered and approached the Ghost Hunter.

Henry rubbed his eyes and looked up in confusion. "Roland, is that you?" He asked hoarsely.

"It's me," Roland answered and knelt down by Henry. "I need to talk to—" he cut off and dropped his hand to his holster. Roland held his breath and slowly tapped his fingers along the butt of his pistol, waiting to see if he'd have to use it.

Jimmy stood in the doorway of Roland's room wearing only his smallclothes and holding a pistol in his hand. He casually aimed it at Roland, squinting as he tried to make out Roland's features in the early morning. His eyes suddenly grew wide, and he lowered his gun. "Sorry, Sheriff. I didn't know it was you. Just wanted to be sure," he apologized and shrugged his shoulders.

Roland exhaled slowly and moved his hand away from his holster. *Damn, that was close,* he thought in relief. Roland had never considered that he might be in danger bursting into his own house. Luckily Jimmy had paused before shooting. If the gunslinger had decided to shoot first and ask questions later, Roland would have been a dead man. "Don't worry about it."

The gunslinger looked at Roland curiously. "What are you doing here, Sheriff? I thought you wouldn't be by until later."

"That's a good question," Henry muttered groggily.

"That's between me and him, Jimmy." Roland pointed at Henry and then looked back at Jimmy. "Go back to sleep. I'll talk to you later."

Surprisingly Jimmy shrugged his shoulders instead of arguing. "All right, good night," he wished everyone then went back into Roland's room.

Roland glanced at the doorway to make sure that Jimmy wasn't listening, then turned back to Henry. Singing Rock was awake, but the Navajo kept silent and watched the two men. *He doesn't matter. He works with Henry.* "There's a problem," he reported quietly, and his hands curled into frustrated fists.

"What is it?" Henry asked in alarm, shaking off the last vestiges of sleep.

"Curly didn't kill Bryant. Carlos did," Roland answered and felt the brief urge to hit someone. Every time he thought of how Alvin had lied to him and forced Rebecca to spend another day in the Land of Shadows, Roland wanted to destroy something. Carlos had been in New Haven three different times since the haunting had begun at Rebecca's house, and Roland could have killed him if only he had known that the Dark Rider was Bryant's murderer.

"What?" Henry's face wrinkled in disgust. "I thought you were sure. Damn it, Roland, you were positive Curly killed him. What happened?"

"Alvin," Roland answered and clenched his teeth together. After Rebecca was awake, he intended to pay the mayor a long visit. He wasn't sure if Alvin or Carlos was going to die the more horrible death. "That son of a bitch lied to me."

Henry put a hand over his eyes and exhaled deeply. "Roland, what's the matter with you?" He shook his head slowly. "I could've told you not to trust Alvin. Hell, I shot him fifteen years ago because he tried to cheat me." Henry pulled his hand away from his eyes and looked up at Roland in disbelief. "Are you telling me you thought Curly killed Bryant because Alvin told you?"

"Yeah," Roland whispered. His fingernails dug into his palms as he clenched his fists even tighter. *Alvin, you're a dead man,* Roland promised to himself. Carlos was at the top of his list, but Alvin's name followed directly after. *You stupid son of a bitch,* he berated himself. He was almost as upset with himself as he was with Carlos and Alvin. It was his gullibility that had allowed Alvin to pull the wool over his eyes.

"Calm down," Henry told the Sheriff and slowly rose to his feet. "Damn, I'm tired," he commented. The Ghost Hunter stretched his arms to either side and yawned loudly. "Let's go outside. We need to talk."

"Sure," Roland answered, still unable to believe how everything had turned out. He was supposed to be coming to the house to tell Henry that Rebecca had awakened. After Henry's elaborate ruse, it had all been for naught. He turned towards the door but stopped when Henry began speaking in Navajo. Looking back, he saw Henry talking to Singing Rock. The Navajo nodded once and pointed towards the door.

Henry spoke one last time to his partner and glanced at Roland. "Let's go," he suggested.

The two men stepped outside into another hot morning. The sun had crested above the eastern horizon, sending out pink swathes of light through the sky. Even in his chaotic frame of mind, Roland instantly noticed the clouds. There were only a few in the sky, but they were all dark and bloated. Whether or not it rained, the town would at least get some well-deserved shade, but he hadn't come outside to talk about the weather. He looked at the Ghost Hunter nervously and took a deep breath. "Are you still going to help her?" He asked worriedly. Roland wouldn't have blamed Henry if the Ghost Hunter rode off that morning after the way he had botched things. *Stupid, stupid, stupid,* he criticized himself again.

"What?" Henry looked at the Sheriff in surprise. "I told you I'm not leaving until she wakes up. Would you calm down?" The Ghost Hunter chastised.

"Sorry," Roland apologized and looked down at the ground. "What do we do then? Are you going back to the house?" He didn't know how else to help Rebecca. As much as he wanted to believe that Rebecca would awaken, Roland was certain that he wouldn't catch Carlos anytime soon.

"Yeah, we'll go back, but not until tomorrow." He looked at the sun and shook his head. "If I had known this is how it would turn out, we could've gone directly to Rebecca's house." Henry shrugged his shoulders. "I guess that's how it goes."

Thank God, Roland thought in relief. His biggest fear had been Henry and Singing Rock riding to the next town. Rebecca was still imprisoned in the Land of Shadows, but at least the Ghost Hunters were going to stay to help. "Thank you."

"I said I'd help, and I will. I just wish I had known Curly wasn't the murderer. We would've done things differently." He paused and scratched his chin. "Are you sure Carlos is the killer?"

"Pretty sure," Roland answered slowly. He had questioned Curly and Marshall. *They had to be telling the truth,* Roland reasoned. Both had feared for their lives and wouldn't have risked lying to him.

Henry looked at Roland skeptically. He had seen doubt cloud the Sheriff's face momentarily. "Are you *absolutely* sure?"

Roland closed his eyes. *Goddamn it. It has to be Carlos.* "I *think* it is. I scared those sons of bitches good. They were telling the truth. They had to be," he insisted. If the killer wasn't Carlos, Roland didn't know what he would do. He could shake down Alvin and the Dark Riders, but that still might not identify the murderer. *It has to be Carlos. Damn you, Alvin,* Roland cursed the mayor again. Alvin could shed light on the matter, but that would take time. He stared at the sparse clouds in the morning sky wistfully. New Haven finally had a faint promise of rain, and he couldn't enjoy it with all the trouble swirling through his life. *Rebecca, I love you,* Roland thought and longed to be able to tell her that one more time and have her hear the words.

"Do you know any artists?" Henry asked, interrupting Roland's thoughts.

"What?" Roland turned his head towards Henry in confusion.

"Do you know any artists?" Henry repeated. "Painters? Or do you have any pictures of Bryant?"

"Dennis draws sometimes," the Sheriff replied. *Have you lost your mind?* "Any picture of Bryant is in the house, and that's been destroyed. Why?"

Henry ignored the question. "Good," he commented softly and rubbed his hands together. "Can he draw people?"

"Yeah. I saw a picture a few weeks ago of his wife. It looked just like her. What does this have to do with Rebecca?"

"Why, Roland, don't you trust me?" Henry asked in his thick drawl and grinned at the Sheriff.

"I just want to know what you're talking about," Roland pointed out. He was grateful to the Ghost Hunter, but his temper was flaring up almost of its own volition. He was exhausted, frustrated, and angry, and Roland knew that it wouldn't take much to spark rage within him.

"Calm down. I'm talking about how we can find out who Bryant's killer is," the Ghost Hunter pointed out.

"What? That doesn't make any sense," Roland snapped bitterly. "You're talking about artists, not finding his killer."

Henry held up a hand. "Will you give me a second to explain?"

Roland took another deep breath and tried to calm his nerves. "Go ahead. I'm listening," he replied and brushed his hand through the air, signaling Henry to continue.

The Ghost Hunter rolled his eyes. "Thanks," he replied dryly. "Singing Rock knows a way to identify someone's killer."

"What?" Roland exploded, his moment of calmness melting away. "You mean you knew how to do that all along, and you never said anything? Why not, Goddamn it?" His voice echoed loudly through the morning air. *I can't believe it,* he raged. He thought of all the time they could have saved. Roland could have known days ago that Carlos killed Bryant.

"Because you said you knew who killed him. Would you listen?" Henry responded angrily. His eyebrows lowered, and he stared at Roland with a fed up expression.

"Oh," Roland replied guiltily. "I hadn't thought of that. I'm sorry. Go on." *Damn it, calm down,* Roland told himself and took a deep breath.

"Thank you," Henry said and took a deep breath of his own. "We would've done it when we first arrived, but you said you knew who the killer was. There didn't seem any point."

"What does this have to do with artists, though?" Roland forced his voice to stay calm. He didn't want to snap at the Ghost Hunter again.

Henry looked at the sunrise for a moment before answering. "A month after I met Singing Rock we went to a town in Arizona. It was pretty similar to what's going on here. The ghost of a murdered man destroyed a house, and we needed to catch his killer to banish the ghost. But nobody knew who did it. That's when Singing Rock told me the solution. He found a picture of the man and put it in a bowl of water. Then he started singing and chanting over it, and the face of the killer appeared on the surface of the water. It turns out it was the ghost's brother. He was hanged, the ghost disappeared, and we moved on to the next town."

Roland stared at the Ghost Hunter in disbelief. *He's got to be kidding.* "You're not serious. Right?" Roland waited for the punchline, but Henry didn't crack a smile.

"I'm completely serious. I know it sounds crazy, but most people would say the same thing about ghosts and the Land of Shadows until they experience them. Listen, Roland. We'll go back to the house in the morning, but do me a favor and have this Dennis draw a picture of Bryant. Then we can find out who really killed him. Maybe it won't do any good, but it can't hurt."

"You're right." The idea of discovering a killer in a bowl of water seemed ludicrous to the Sheriff, but the Ghost Hunter was right. He had seen more bizarre things over the past three weeks. If it would help Rebecca, he was willing to stretch his imagination a little further.

"What are you going to do with the Dark Riders you caught?"

"Kill them," Roland answered flatly. "I'm having a gallows built, then I'll hang every one of the bastards." His intense hatred of Curly had abated, but he still wanted to make the Dark Riders pay. Maybe his prisoners didn't have anything to do with Bryant's murder, but they had played a part in the Fourth of July gunfight. The people who caused Jack's death deserved to pay the maximum price for their crime.

"Kill them before dawn," Henry replied grimly.

"What?"

"Kill them before dawn." The Ghost Hunter paused and put a finger to his chin. "Let me ask you this. How long do you think it will take for Dennis to draw that picture of Bryant?"

"A few days probably. He worked on Betty's picture for over a week, but that's because he wanted it perfect. Why?"

"Because for all you know, you've already arrested Bryant's killer. It could still be Curly. If you're going to kill them, do it tonight. That way, you might wake Rebecca up by blind luck," the Ghost Hunter pointed out.

That's a Goddamn good idea, he thought excitedly. Seeing the Dark Riders hang might even brighten his spirits. He still believed that Carlos killed Bryant, but Henry was right. It made sense to kill all the Riders immediately. Nothing was gained by prolonging their sentence. "I'll hang the bastards tonight. Lewis should be able to build a new gallows today."

"Good," Henry replied and clapped Roland on the back. "Well, Roland, if that's all, I'm going back to sleep." The Ghost Hunter rubbed his eyes and yawned once more.

Seeing Henry yawn prompted Roland to do likewise, and he was reminded of just how tired he was. He had barely slept during the past two days, and it was finally catching up with him. Roland looked at New Haven with regret. He wanted nothing more than to lay down in his own house and go

452

to sleep, but he was needed in town. There were still a few more things to take care of before he got to rest. "Do you want me to meet you sometime later?"

"After the sun sets. I'm sleeping all day. Good night, Roland," the Ghost Hunter wished.

"Good night," Roland answered and walked to his horse as Henry returned inside. The adrenaline that had carried him back to his house had worn off, and Roland faced a trip back to town when he could barely keep his eyes open. Pulling himself into the saddle, Roland groaned as his tired muscles complained. *Not much longer,* he tried to motivate himself.

He rode at a slow pace, nearly toppling from the saddle several times when he started drifting towards slumber. If he wanted to do anything else that morning, he knew he'd better do it quickly before exhaustion finally overtook him. The heat was brutal, but Roland could have sworn that it was actually a little bit cooler than it had been the past month. *Maybe it's the clouds. Just let it rain,* Roland wished. He was due for something good to come his way.

The same group of men guarded the town's southern border, and they all looked as tired as Roland. "Sheriff," a few of them called out as he passed by, while others only nodded their heads. Roland opted for the latter and nodded as he passed them by. He wanted to find Dennis then go to sleep, and he smiled when he saw the smithy.

Dennis the blacksmith sat on the steps of his shop whittling a piece of wood and whistling a tune that he made up as he went along. He looked up at Roland and blinked in surprise. "Sheriff," the blacksmith greeted.

"Dennis. How's Betty?" Roland stopped his horse but didn't dismount. He was afraid that once he got off the horse, he wouldn't be able to get back on.

"She's fine. How are you? I haven't seen you here in a long time," Dennis commented. He set down his block of wood carefully then placed the knife beside it.

"It's been a long time," Roland answered with a touch of regret in his voice. He remembered when he used to visit Dennis every morning before going to the station house. Those days seemed like forever ago. He yearned for the day his life would return to normal.

"It has. Did you ever figure out how that fire started last night? It scared me and Betty to death."

"No, I never did," Roland answered with a straight face . "Listen, I actually have a favor to ask you."

"Sure. What is it?"

"Do you remember what Bryant White looked like?" Roland felt foolish asking Dennis to draw a picture of Rebecca's dead husband, but if it would help her, it was worth it.

"Sort of. He's been dead for over six months, but I still remember. How's Miss White by the way? We've been praying for her," he told Roland earnestly.

"She's getting better, but that's why I'm here." Dennis's eyebrows rose curiously. "I need you to draw a picture of Bryant."

"What does that have to do with Miss White, Sheriff? That won't help her get any better." He looked at Roland as if the Sheriff wasn't quite right in the head.

"Trust me," Roland tried to assure the blacksmith. "It really will help. I promise. Would you please do it?" He took another deep breath. "Please?" *Damn it, let something go my way.*

"I suppose so," Dennis replied slowly. He looked confused about the request.

Thank God, he thought fervently. The morning had begun on a horrible note, but at least something had worked out. "When do you think you can have it ready?"

Dennis scratched his head and thought for a moment. "Probably sometime tomorrow. I'll start on it later today, and I can finish it up after work tomorrow."

Roland frowned at the estimate and considered asking the blacksmith to begin working on it immediately. He knew, however, that Dennis didn't have the time. He had his own business to take care of first. Besides, if all went well Roland wouldn't need Dennis's help. It was just insurance in case Henry and Singing Rock failed the following morning. "That sounds great. Bring it by The Last Frontier when you finish."

"That's not a problem. You take care of yourself, Sheriff. You look tired," Dennis commented as he leaned over to pick up his block of wood and carving knife.

"I'll try," Roland muttered dryly. "Thanks again, Dennis." The Sheriff then clucked at his horse and headed towards the station house. He couldn't believe how heavy his eyelids felt. *Damn, I'm tired,* Roland told himself and yawned loudly. Once he had Lewis begin the construction of another gallows, he could return to The Frontier and collect on some much-needed rest.

There was still a large group of men standing outside the station house when Roland returned. He greeted them then covered his mouth as he yawned yet again. Looking over the group, Roland quickly noticed that Morgan wasn't among them. *Damn it,* he thought wearily. He wasn't going to dismount until he found out where the deputy was. His legs nearly trembled with exhaustion. "Where's Morgan?" He asked one of the men.

"He's inside, Sheriff," Samuel Howe quickly answered and pointed at the station house door.

454

Roland's lips stretched into a tired smile. "Good," he replied in relief. At least he wouldn't have to ride all over town to track down the deputy. He looked at the ground with mixed feelings of loathing and longing. *Just get off the horse, then you can sleep,* Roland tried to convince himself, but it was hard to make his exhausted muscles move. He closed his eyes and took a deep breath. Then he swung his leg over the horse and landed on the ground. For a moment Roland thought his knees would buckle, but he managed to stay on his feet. *Do it,* Roland told himself and stared at the door, wondering if he really had to talk to Morgan. Sleep sounded so much better, but Roland made his weary legs move forward.

Morgan was sitting at the desk, his hands folded and resting on the surface when Roland entered. The white-haired deputy looked up at Roland and instantly rose to his feet. "Damn it, Roland. Where have you been?" His eyebrows lowered, and his face stretched into a disapproving frown.

For a moment Morgan was the spitting image of Jack. Roland could see his old friend with that same disapproving frown, berating him for doing something stupid. "I had to take care of something," Roland answered, hoping that Morgan would leave it at that.

The deputy glowered at Roland for another few moments then sat back down. "How do you want to split up the men today?" He asked, completely switching topics.

Roland fought the urge to smile. That's how Morgan differed from Jack. His old friend would have gone on for an hour about how he shouldn't have left town. *Jack, I miss you.* "I want somebody in here at all times, and we should probably have some extra people on the borders. I don't think Carlos will come back."

"I don't either, but I don't want to get caught unaware," Morgan pointed out.

"Don't worry. As long as we have a dozen men on duty, Carlos can't do anything. He's got eight men at most by now, probably less." Roland knew that if he was riding with Carlos, he would have found another band of outlaws to join. Losing half your men reduces the power the group wields. "Morgan, I need a favor." The deputy nodded but didn't say a word. "Talk to Lewis and tell him to build another gallows. I want to hang these sons of bitches tonight."

Morgan's eyes widened slightly. "You're hanging all of them tonight?"

"Yeah." Roland smiled his lopsided grin. He couldn't wait to see the Dark Riders at the end of a rope. They had caused him enough pain to last a lifetime. If Roland could only get Matthew Brady and Alvin up there as well, he could rid himself of even more of his troubles.

"All right," the deputy answered. He looked a bit shocked that Roland would execute them in such a hurry. They hadn't had a trial yet, but everyone knew they were guilty. "I'll go see him now."

"I'm going to The Frontier to sleep," Roland told his deputy. Morgan looked at Roland in surprise again. The Sheriff was always the last one to go to sleep and one of the first to show up every morning. Roland wanted to stay on duty until the afternoon, but his body was simply too worn out. "Come get me if there are any problems, and wake me when the gallows is ready. I want to see them hang."

"All right, Roland. Sleep well. You need it." Morgan tipped his hat to Roland.

The Sheriff tipped his hat in return then headed across the street to The Last Frontier. He looked at the interior of the saloon and smiled. It seemed as if ten years had passed since he last stepped foot inside George's tavern. *Stop looking around. Go to sleep.* Shuffling across the floor, Roland looked at the staircase and grimaced. He slowly made his way upstairs, his legs tiredly protesting the effort. When he reached the top of the staircase, he breathed a sigh of relief then continued down the hall.

He glanced at Rebecca's doorway for a moment then walked past. Roland wanted to see her, but he was too exhausted. *After I wake up,* he promised. He unlocked his door and entered the room, staring at the bed with longing. Roland threw his hat onto the floor and sat on the bed. He took his boots off, sighing as his sore feet were allowed to feel the air again. Then Roland laid down and was asleep almost before his head touched the pillow.

He dreamed that he was in the middle of town and could see a large gallows next to the train station. *They're hanging the Dark Riders,* he thought gleefully and ran through the streets, eager to watch the spectacle. The town was empty and quiet as he rushed to see the Dark Riders die. His breath caught in his throat as he approached the structure. Eleven figures in black robes stood around it. Eight circled the gallows, and three figures stood on the platform. But they weren't what grabbed his attention. Rebecca stood on top of the platform with a noose around her neck. She reached out a hand and looked at him imploringly. "Rebecca!" Roland shouted and rushed towards her, drawing both pistols in one fluid motion.

A figure standing on the platform held one of Rebecca's arms in his grasp. When Roland began running towards her, the figure threw back the hood of his cloak, and Roland stopped in his tracks as he saw Alvin smiling evilly at him. The mayor's eyes glowed red, and he drew a gun as well, pointing it at Rebecca's head. "Stop right there, Roland," he mocked and threw back his head as he laughed.

"Goddamn you, let her go!" Roland shouted in frustration. His feet were entrenched in the dirt, but his legs yearned to continue his mad dash towards the gallows.

"I don't think so, Roland," Alvin replied, the grin never slipping from his face. "Say goodbye to her," he advised. Then he let go of her arm and snapped his fingers.

Instantly the other black-robed figures pulled their hoods back as well. Roland flinched as he saw the faces of all the captive Dark Riders and Carlos. Marshall smiled the same grin decorating Alvin's face. Even more disturbing were the two men on the platform. One was Curly. The Dark Rider drew a gun and pointed it at Roland, laughing the whole time. Carlos stood at his side, sneering and with a gun in each hand.

"Let her go!" Roland shouted.

"See you in hell," Alvin smirked then snapped his fingers again.

"Rebecca!" Roland shouted out as the Dark Riders all fired at him. Bullets ripped painfully through his body, and he fell to the ground, stretching his hand out towards Rebecca.

He awoke instantly, covered in sweat and breathing heavily. Roland put a hand to his chest and tried to catch his breath as the memory of the dream faded away. There were hundreds of reasons why he wanted Rebecca to awaken, and his incessant nightmares were one of them. It seemed that ever since she had become trapped in the Land of Shadows, he hadn't had a peaceful night of sleep.

Roland peered at the window and saw only faint light coming in through the drapes. *Damn, it's already sunset,* he thought in alarm and sat up before he could go back to sleep. Roland couldn't believe that he had slept the entire day away, but he had to admit that the rest had done him wonders. His eyes were still bleary and sleepy, but his body felt refreshed. He just wished that he hadn't slept so long. There were several things he needed to do, and he still had to visit Henry at his house.

Quickly putting on his boots and hat, Roland hurried out of the room. He paused at Rebecca's door and put a hand on the surface. "Rebecca, I love you," he whispered then continued down the hall. He had promised to meet Henry right after sunset, and he was going to be late as it was. The Sheriff also wanted to check on the gallows. If all went well, he'd be hanging the Dark Riders sometime in the next few hours. All in all, he had a busy evening ahead of him.

Roland took a deep breath as he walked outside and looked up at the sky. *Blazes, it's cooling down,* he thought gratefully. He had seen a few clouds that morning, but they now covered half the sky as the sun faded into the western horizon. Roland just hoped that it would rain.

As he had ordered, a group of six men stood outside the station house. They were chatting idly, but their backs straightened when Roland stepped outside. "Sheriff," a few greeted as he walked by.

Roland nodded at the men. He was grateful for their help, but he had more pressing concerns at the moment. Rushing by them, he entered the station house.

Phillip sat behind the desk. The large deputy clutched a book in his hands as usual and hastily laid it face-down on the desk when Roland entered. "Good evening, Sheriff," the deputy greeted.

"Phillip." Roland nodded. "How are they?" He jutted his chin towards the cell room.

The deputy glanced at the door then shrugged his shoulders. "Quiet. They haven't made a sound all day," he answered.

I scared the sons of bitches. Roland's mouth curled into a lopsided grin. "Good. Do you know where Morgan is?"

"He said he'd be on the north side of town, but that was a few hours ago."

At least he knew where to find Morgan, and after he talked to the deputy he could return to his house. "All right, I'll see you later," he told Phillip, who nodded in reply, and then Roland was back outside. He took one of the horses at the tether post and climbed into the saddle, amazed at how much difference sleep had made. After a full day's rest, his legs were only slightly sore. He tapped the horse with his boot so that it trotted down the streets of New Haven.

Roland stopped his horse as he turned the corner and whistled. He had hoped that Lewis had started working on the gallows, but he was surprised to find it almost completed. *Soon,* he thought and shivered. The gallows looked exactly like the one from his dream. His nightmare had seemed awfully realistic, and it had only been a few minutes ago. He pushed those thoughts from his mind. It had only been a dream. Roland clucked at his horse and resumed a canter.

Just as Phillip had told him, Morgan stood on the northern edge of town with three other men. Roland didn't think they'd be enough to stop the Dark Riders if Carlos came back to town, but at least they could give an advance warning. The veteran deputy saw Roland approaching and met him a short distance from the other men. "Roland," he greeted. "How about this weather?" Morgan looked at the clouds and held up both hands, the palms facing the sky. "I think it might rain," he observed.

"I think you're right, but we'll see. Who knows with how everything else has gone," he muttered darkly. "How about you? Has it been quiet tonight?"

The deputy looked at the men behind him and rolled his eyes. "Hell, Roland. It's been more quiet than church on a Friday evening. I don't think Carlos is stupid enough to come back to town."

"I'd rather have people ready just in case."

"I'm not going anywhere. Just commenting," the deputy answered drolly.

"All right. I've got a few things to check on. I'll be back in a while, then we can hang those bastards once and for all." Roland grinned wildly. Dawn was a long ways off, but at least he'd have something to occupy his time that evening.

"Sounds good to me," Morgan responded with a grin of his own.

Roland turned his horse around and rode towards his house after visiting with Morgan. He needed to check on Dotty, but visiting Henry and Singing Rock came first. Henry had told him to come back to the house that evening, and Roland intended to do whatever the Ghost Hunter told him. He also wanted to speak to Jimmy. The young man had done him a service by helping catch the Dark Riders, but he had overstayed his welcome. Roland intended to see Jimmy on his way before the gunslinger found some other method to get into trouble.

By the time the Sheriff reached his house, the sun had set. Roland was enjoying the weather immensely. Not only were clouds in the sky, but the temperature seemed to be dropping. It was never as hot at night, but Roland felt a trace of coolness in the air that had been absent for over a month.

He tied his horse to a tether post and walked to the front door when Henry and Jimmy came outside. Roland stopped in his tracks and tipped his hat. "Henry, Jimmy." He paused when Singing Rock followed the other two. "Singing Rock."

The Navajo's eyes looked up at him briefly but kept quiet except for a single grunt of acknowledgement.

"Roland," Henry greeted. "I didn't expect to see you until later."

Roland shrugged his shoulders. "It was a quiet night. I talked to the blacksmith, and he'll have that picture ready by tomorrow night. Are you still going at dawn?"

"That was the plan. If all else fails, we'll have that picture. Are you hanging the Dark Riders?"

"In a few hours," Roland answered and smiled a toothy grin. "I can't wait to see those sons of bitches die." His hands clenched into fists as he thought about all they had done. *But now you die,* he thought with a gruff chuckle.

"Well, that's all I need from you, Roland. Why don't you just meet us back here a few hours before dawn."

"That's it?" Roland asked in confusion. He had expected a long conversation with the Ghost Hunters, not a thirty second exchange.

"What else do you want?" The Ghost Hunter's eyebrows raised in surprise. "I just wanted to see if that picture had been finished or if you had hanged the Dark Riders. Come back if the picture's done or if you hang them and Rebecca wakes up. Otherwise, I'll just see you before dawn."

Blazes, Roland thought in frustration. He could have taken his time and visited Dotty if only he had known that. *Don't worry. Nothing bad came of it.* At least he'd be able to talk to Jimmy. He was about to address the young man when the gunslinger spoke first.

"Sheriff. I'm going to move on. There's nothing for me to do here—" He paused and took a deep breath. "Unless you change your mind and let me stay," Jimmy finished in a rush. He looked at Roland pleadingly, almost begging Roland to let him stay.

Roland was slightly moved by the display but not enough to change his mind. "No, Jimmy. I already told you to leave. Everyone thinks you killed Henry, and I can't let you stay now."

"I thought you'd say that," Jimmy answered glumly. He smiled, shook his head ruefully, then held out a hand. "Good luck to you, Sheriff. I had fun while I was here."

"I'll bet you did," Roland replied dryly and shook the proffered hand. "Be careful out there, and don't cause any trouble. You go waving a gun in any other town, you'll get yourself hanged."

Jimmy flashed his cocky grin at Roland, and his eyes sparkled mischievously. "I'll try," he laughed. "Well, I'm getting my stuff, and I'll be on my way." He nodded and turned back towards the house.

Yeah, I bet you will, Roland thought in disbelief. Jimmy was bound to find trouble wherever his travels took him. Roland just hoped the young man lived through all of it. The Sheriff leaned towards Henry. "How long do you think it'll be before he gets into more trouble?"

"Not too long, I imagine," Henry replied with a grin.

"I think you might—" Roland broke off as he heard a gunshot in the distance. Jimmy froze in his tracks as well, and Henry and Singing Rock looked around warily. Roland's hand dropped towards his holster. "Did you hear that?" He asked and strained his ears. Henry nodded silently. *Probably somebody drunk,* he thought in relief and began to move his hand when a flurry of gunshots echoed through the morning air.

"Goddamn it," Roland swore and ran towards his horse, but as quickly as the Sheriff moved, Jimmy was even faster. The young man sprinted towards his own horse, and before Roland could shout at him, Jimmy was in his saddle. "Jimmy, stop!" Roland yelled, but the young man spurred his horse into a gallop. "Son of a bitch!" Roland swore and raced towards his own horse. If there was trouble in town, he wanted Jimmy as far from it as possible. He leapt into the saddle. "Hya!" He shouted at his horse and thumped it with his boot. The horse whinnied and launched into a gallop, leaving Henry and Singing Rock behind as they watched him chase after Jimmy.

Faster, Roland tried to will his horse on as he flew through the night. He knew Jimmy wasn't far ahead of him, but he wasn't making up any ground on the gunslinger. Roland was even more nervous about who had fired the gunshots. If it was Carlos, Roland wanted to make it back to town before the Dark Rider had a chance to escape.

He still couldn't see Jimmy as they approached town. He flinched as he heard another barrage of gunshots and slapped his horse's side to spur him on to greater speeds. Even with the cooler air, a sweat broke out on Roland's forehead as he rushed onward. His muscles tensed in anticipation of a fight. He wanted to draw one of his pistols, but Roland stopped himself. There would be plenty of time when they reached New Haven. He'd more than likely drop it at the speed he was traveling.

Roland rode into New Haven, scowling as he passed the border. The patrol of five men had abandoned their post. *What the hell's going on?* Roland slowed his horse down as a precaution and drew one of his pistols, holding his horse's reins in the other hand. He looked around, but he didn't see a sign of anyone, not even Jimmy. *Damn it,* he cursed.

Another flurry of bullets thundered through the night air, and Roland's jaw tightened as he realized they were coming from the station house. He jumped off his horse and ran the rest of the way as gunshots began to ring one after another. He had no desire to enter a gunfight on horse. Roland preferred to have his feet on the ground and two guns in his hands. He inched towards the corner as a steady stream of bullets were fired. Quickly he drew his other gun and paused for a moment, readying himself for a gunfight.

Roland took a deep breath and turned the corner. He didn't know what he expected, but Roland was surprised by the size of the gunfight being waged in front of the station house. Smoke filled the air, and eight or nine men and at least a dozen horses already lay dead in the middle of the street. The front of the station house was riddled with bullets, and guns were fired from within. Roland also saw two pockets of men shooting a steady stream of bullets at the station house. One group took refuge in The Last Frontier, and the other hid behind a wagon.

"Blazes," Roland whispered in amazement. He had expected a small gunfight, but he counted six men behind the wagon, and there had to be at least that many inside the saloon. Roland assumed it was the Dark Riders inside the station house, and that meant maybe as many as seventeen armed men if Carlos had brought guns for his brethren. He looked closely at the group behind the wagon and spotted Morgan there. Roland wanted to stay in his safe vantage point, but he needed to know what was going on. *You're a Goddamn fool,* Roland told himself as he looked at the wagon that Morgan was hiding behind.

Taking another deep breath, Roland holstered both his guns and sprinted towards the wagon. His heart pounded in his chest as he ran, and he half-expected a bullet to hit him. Shots continued to fly through the air, but luckily none hit him as he sprinted to Morgan's side. When he was close enough, Roland dove for cover and laid on the ground, gasping to catch his breath.

"Damn, Roland. Are you crazy?" Morgan asked the Sheriff, never taking his eyes off the station house.

Roland chuckled at the deputy's words. *Yeah, I am crazy,* he thought and rose to his feet. He drew both his pistols again, and leaned back against the wagon. "Who's over there?" He asked the deputy.

Morgan looked at him briefly with a withering gaze. "Riders. Who else? I don't know how many are alive, but I know they've already put down at least six of our men."

Our advantage, Roland thought. The Dark Riders' horses all lay dead in the street, and the outlaws had to be running out of bullets. Sooner of later, they had to come out of the station house, and then Roland would kill them all. "Stop shooting," he ordered his deputy.

"What?" Morgan looked at him like he was crazy.

"Save your bullets until we need them. They're not going anywhere," Roland told him with a tight grin.

Morgan nodded. "I should've thought of that," he commented then whistled loudly. "Stop shooting!" He yelled at his men. "Save your bullets!" He turned his head towards The Last Frontier. "Will, stop shooting!" He shouted at the top of his lungs. No answer came from the saloon, but the gunfire from behind the windows ceased.

"Good, now let's see what they do." Roland ducked his head around the wagon and peered at the station house. A few more bullets were fired after Roland's men ceased their own fire, but then the station house grew quiet as well. *Now you're scared.* Roland knew it was only a matter of time before the Riders ran out of bullets and had to make a run for it. The streets grew eerily silent for nearly twenty seconds before Roland turned to Morgan. "Have everyone hold their fire," he told his deputy and casually leaned out and fired a single bullet at the station house.

Gunfire immediately erupted from inside the station house as several Dark Riders returned Roland's lone shot. A few bullets were fired from inside The Last Frontier, but they quickly followed Morgan's lead and held still after the initial volley. Roland repeated that same pattern four times with the same results. His men wasted only a few bullets, but the Dark Riders fired several dozen times. "They should be running out of bullets soon. A few more times like that, and they'll make a run for it," Roland told his deputy.

"You want to wait here or wait for them across the street?" Morgan asked.

Roland leaned back out and took another look at the terrain. It wouldn't be hard to wait on the same side of the street as the station house and hug up against the buildings. They'd have the perfect location for ambushing the Riders

462

when they exited the building. "Let's do it." He looked at the men hiding behind the wagon and frowned. They were all volunteers. He'd have rather had Simon, William, or Ben with him, but Roland would have to make do with just Morgan. "You and me."

"All right. Whenever you say," Morgan replied grimly and leaned forward, ready to sprint as soon as Roland gave the word.

"Now!" Roland shouted, and the two men raced across the street. There were a few moments of silence, and then a smattering of bullets were fired from the station house. Roland could have sworn he heard one whistle by his head, but he and Morgan made it across the street safely. They leaned against the wall of a building, huffing and wheezing as they tried to catch their breath. "Blazes, that was close," Roland commented and put a hand to his heart.

"We're getting too old for this," Morgan quipped dryly.

Roland grinned in return. "You know you love this," he bantered then returned his gaze to the station house. They were two buildings down from it and would have the perfect angle on anybody leaving the building. Roland just hoped it didn't take much longer. He hated waiting.

Come on, you bastards, Roland thought anxiously. In a matter of minutes, Carlos would be dead, and Rebecca would finally be awake. He just wanted to be the one to shoot the Dark Rider. Carlos had caused more than his share of trouble over the last year, and Roland wanted to be the person to issue the payback.

"How much—" Morgan broke off as a flurry of gunfire erupted from the station house.

They both watched the door, carefully aiming their guns. "There they are!" Roland shouted as Dark Riders rushed out the door. Instantly the street exploded with bullets as both sides unleashed an onslaught of gunfire. The Riders quickly split into two groups. One ran east, away from Roland and Morgan, and the other defiantly stood in front of the station house firing bullets.

Roland wasted no time sniping off shots. He quickly put down two Riders, and Morgan dropped a pair as well. Roland almost felt guilty at the ease in dispatching the Dark Riders. The group that stood its ground melted under the heavy barrage of bullets. One by one, they fell to the ground, but they took a few men with them. Roland saw a couple of men fall behind the wagon, and he was sure that somebody had been hit inside The Frontier as well.

In the middle of that group, Carlos stood defiantly. He sneered as he fired both his pistols. A bullet had struck his shoulder, but the Dark Rider ignored the wound and kept firing. Another man fell behind the wagon as Carlos shot him in the forehead, and then the Dark Rider moved onto the next target.

Carlos, Roland hissed and aimed at the Dark Rider. He was going to end Rebecca's imprisonment and the outlaw's reign of terror once and for all. His first shot whistled by Carlos's head, but the next shot hit him in the side. *Got you,* he thought triumphantly. The Dark Rider grimaced in pain and fell to his knees, blood trailing from the corner of his mouth. One of his guns dropped out of his grasp. Carlos looked at Roland, and there was a moment of recognition as their eyes met. With a last burst of strength, the Dark Rider raised his gun and fired at Roland. The shot missed by more than a foot, but Roland heard a grunt as it struck Morgan. *Die, you son of a bitch.* Roland squeezed both triggers. The first bullet struck the outlaw in the chest, and the second hit his throat. Carlos's second gun fell from his hand, and the Dark Rider collapsed. Roland quickly fired two more bullets at Carlos's still body, and they each struck his back. He waited for any sign of movement, but it was obvious that Carlos was dead.

Roland looked up to find that the gunfight was pretty much over. The group standing with Carlos had been obliterated, and the other group had fallen as well. "Burn in hell," he cursed every one of them. At least they would never bother anyone in New Haven again. Roland just hoped it was worth the price. He turned to Morgan and stopped as he saw how pale the deputy had become. "Morgan, are you all right?" He asked in concern. Sullivan would hopefully arrive soon, but Roland knew that the doctor would have a great number of people to see.

"I don't think I'm going to make it this time," Morgan answered in a weak, shaking voice. His hand clutched his stomach, and the deputy's face twisted in pain.

"Shut up! Sullivan'll be here in a minute. You're gonna live," Roland snapped at the deputy and leaned over him. He hissed as he saw the blood soaking the bottom of Morgan's shirt. Roland had thought that Morgan had taken a minimal wound, but he knew that a gutshot did not bode well.

"Not this time, Roland," Morgan whispered and coughed. Blood began to drip from his mouth and run down his chin, staining his long white beard. "Tell Doc Holliday it was good to ride with him. I always wanted to meet that son of a bitch," the deputy told Roland and smiled weakly. He coughed violently and shook as pain ran through his body. Morgan doubled over and looked up at Roland with teary eyes. "Damn, this hurts."

Roland was about to tell him that it would be all right, but Morgan coughed once more and fell silent. Roland looked for any sign of movement, but the deputy laid still. *No!* Roland wanted to shout in frustration. He had lost his fourth deputy in less than two days. "Rest in peace, Morgan." Roland reached out and closed the deputy's eyes.

He had finally gotten his wish. Carlos and the Dark Riders were dead, and Rebecca should be awake. But he had never expected the price to be so high. Instead of feeling elated, Roland felt the bitter taste of defeat.

Chapter Twenty-Four

Roland didn't know how long he stood over Morgan's body, staring numbly at the deputy. He kept thinking that if he waited another few seconds, Morgan would start breathing. *You can't be dead, Morgan,* Roland told himself over and over. First Jack, then Morgan. Roland wanted to hit something in frustration, but he finally turned away from the body with a stunned expression on his face.

The gunfight had been one of the most violent ones that Roland had ever seen in all his days of gunslinging. Nearly a dozen Dark Riders lay dead in the street, and New Haven had lost almost that many as well. Besides Morgan, at least eight more volunteers had lost their lives. Roland made a point of not looking at their faces. He was having a hard enough time and didn't want to know the names of every person who had died. There would be time to check on that later. Sullivan had arrived at the site and was busy looking at people who had been injured. Ben and William stood with the doctor and looked at Roland, but the Sheriff shook his head. *Later,* he thought. He still wanted to check on a few things before he talked to his deputies.

He went inside the station house to view the carnage and closed his eyes in resignation. Roland had expected to find Phillip dead, but he had held a tiny hope that the deputy survived. Seventeen Riders had captured the station house, and he would have been surprised if they left the deputy alive. Phillip's body had been riddled with a dozen bullets, and blood stained his clothes. Roland's lips curled into a sad little smile when he saw a book laying face-down on the desk. He would have been disappointed to find Phillip any other way. There were also six Dark Riders in the station house, including Marshall, but he didn't find much satisfaction in seeing the Riders' corpses. The price had been far too steep.

Roland walked out the door with a dozen things spinning through his stunned mind. They'd have to clean the carnage off the street, he'd have to organize funerals for Morgan and Phillip, and the list went on. But they would all have to wait. He had checked on Phillip, but the next person he wanted to see hadn't been involved in the gunfight at all. *Rebecca,* Roland thought hopefully. Seeing her awake was the only thing that could even hope to brighten his spirits. He wanted something good to come out of all the destruction that had been wrought.

"Sheriff," William called out, but Roland held his hand up and rushed right by.

Later, he thought to himself. He could deal with everything after he saw Rebecca. Roland entered The Last Frontier and headed for the stairway. He trembled as he climbed the stairs. *Rebecca,* he thought again. After three weeks of hellish waiting she would finally be awake. He fumbled around in his pocket as he struggled to get a grip on the key with his nervous fingers. A lopsided grin stretched wide across his face almost involuntarily as he opened the door to her room.

Instantly the grin evaporated as Roland stared at Rebecca's body with shocked eyes. He had expected to see her awake and smiling when he entered the room, but she looked exactly the same as she had every other day for the past three weeks. *She's just resting,* Roland tried to convince himself as he entered her room. He gently shook her frail body, hoping to see her awaken, but her eyes stayed firmly shut. "Rebecca," he whispered and shook her again. "Rebecca!" He yelled, but she remained fast asleep.

Goddamn it! Roland fumed. His fists clenched tightly in frustration. Once again he had been thwarted in his attempt to help Rebecca, and the gunfight had been for nothing. The Dark Riders were destroyed, but that was a small consolation. *Henry!* He thought desperately. *Henry will know what to do.* Roland knew that he needed to stay in town to oversee the aftermath of the gunfight, but he had to visit Henry first. His mind was going to be incapable of thinking about anything else until she was awake. "I love you, Rebecca," Roland told her and forced his voice to be soft despite the bitterness and frustration seething through his body. He placed a single kiss on her forehead then stalked out of the room, down the staircase, and onto the street.

William and Ben still stood outside with Sullivan as he attended to several men. "Sheriff," William called out again.

What the hell does he need? Roland thought sourly, but he turned and approached the deputy. He could go see Henry in a moment. As long as William did all the talking and not Ben, it wouldn't be a long conversation. "What?"

William looked much like Roland felt. His blue eyes were stunned, and his hair was wild. It was a far cry from his customary rakish appearance. "I can't find Curly," he reported.

"What?" Roland repeated angrily. He hadn't checked any of the bodies. He had noticed Marshall, and he had shot Carlos. Roland hadn't thought about looking for Curly's body. He just assumed that the Dark Rider was dead.

"We can't find Curly's body. I looked at everyone but couldn't find him."

"Get a posse together and find the son of a bitch," Roland ordered. He wanted to see all the Dark Riders dead and wouldn't rest until it was accomplished. *Especially you, you Goddamn bastard.* Roland knew that Curly hadn't killed Bryant, but it was still difficult to let go of all the hatred he had felt for the Dark Rider.

William looked at him as if he was crazy. "With what men? There aren't enough people alive to track him down."

"You're right," the Sheriff replied. *Calm down,* Roland told himself. Both Jack and Morgan were dead, and he would have to get by without any help. "Are you sure he's not dead?"

"I counted 'em, Sheriff. There are sixteen dead bodies, and there were seventeen Dark Riders left. That means one of 'em is still alive."

"Goddamn it," Roland snapped irritably. *Think, damn you,* Roland berated himself. "What if—" he broke off as he looked down the street. "What the hell's that?" He asked and drew one of his guns.

William drew his own gun in response, and everyone grew quiet around them as Curly marched down the street. To Roland's surprise, Jimmy walked directly behind him. He had almost forgotten about the gunslinger in the flurry of activity, but the young man apparently held Curly prisoner. "Wait here," Roland told his deputy and approached the pair. He didn't holster his gun but kept it drawn and ready to be fired. It looked as if Jimmy had captured Curly, but he still didn't trust the gunslinger any farther than he could throw him.

Jimmy wore his typical cocky grin, and his eyes narrowed almost condescendingly as he escorted Curly towards Roland. "I caught this one for you," Jimmy announced to Roland as he reached out and grabbed Curly's shoulder. The Dark Rider stopped instantly.

"I didn't do anything, Sheriff. It was all Carlos's idea. Please don't kill me. I swear I'll leave town and never come back. Please!" The Dark Rider begged. His eyes were wide with fear, and he seemed on the verge of tears.

"Shut up!" Jimmy barked and slapped the back of Curly's head. The Dark Rider's head snapped forward, and he held his tongue. "What do you want me to do with him?" Jimmy asked.

"Put him back in prison. There's a gallows waiting for him," Roland answered and rubbed his hands together. He had been furious at Jimmy for racing ahead of him, but he was prepared to forgive the gunslinger. Jimmy had brought him Curly, and with his death, the Dark Riders would be destroyed. *This time, you die, you son of a bitch.* Curly looked ready to faint when Roland stated his intentions. He shook violently but stayed quiet. Roland was sure that the Dark Rider would blubber and beg for his life later on, but at least he didn't start whining in the street. Roland was already tempted to shoot him on the spot and didn't need any further encouragement.

"Let's go," he told Jimmy and turned towards the station house. For a moment he was concerned what people would think of Jimmy. As far as everyone knew, the gunslinger had killed Henry, and Roland had not only allowed him to live but was speaking to him. Then he banished it from his mind. He had Curly and would deal with the consequences later. Roland looked back over his shoulder and saw the pair following him. He wanted Curly in a cell, then he could visit Henry. Roland had quite a few questions he wanted to ask the Ghost Hunter. Carlos was dead, but Rebecca still remained in the Land of Shadows.

Roland closed his eyes briefly at the sight of Phillip and the other dead bodies strewn about the station house. The key ring was missing from the wall, and Roland had to retrieve the set from the desk. His jaw clenched angrily as he stood next to Phillip's body. Too many of his men had died at the hands of the Dark Riders, and he was glad to see them gone. "I've got him from here, Jimmy," Roland told the young man and grabbed Curly's shoulder. Jimmy stepped back from the captive and let Roland have him. "Let's go," Roland told the Dark Rider and propelled him towards the cell door, which stood wide open.

Curly started crying when they entered the cell room. Roland knew that Curly was certain of his doom this time. There was nobody else to rescue him. "Please, Sheriff. I didn't hurt anybody. Please let me go. I swear I'll leave the state." He grabbed Roland's shirt, and his eyes widened pleadingly. "I'll go to California. Just don't kill me, Sheriff," Curly sobbed.

Roland placed his gun against Curly's forehead, and the Dark Rider stopped his blubbering. Tears still streamed down his cheeks, but he stopped his pleas for mercy. "Shut your Goddamn mouth. If I hear one more word out of you, I'll kill you. Now get in there!" Roland shouted at him.

The Dark Rider looked pleadingly at Roland one more time, but he wisely kept his mouth shut. Even in his desperation, Curly understood the futility of trying to change Roland's mind at that point. He turned wordlessly and went into his cell. He cringed when Roland shut the door behind him, signaling the final end to his freedom. "I'll be back in a while. Enjoy your stay." Roland barked out a laugh, loving every minute that Curly dreaded his upcoming sentence. It was small repayment for all the hell that the Dark Riders had wrought, but it was something.

He slammed the cell room door behind him and sighed. It had felt good to torment Curly, but he had other things he needed to do. After locking the cell room door, he turned back to Jimmy. The gunslinger still wore his cocky grin, but his eyes were slightly apprehensive. Jimmy had returned to town against Roland's orders and had to think that the Sheriff would be furious. "Thanks for catching that son of a bitch."

Jimmy blinked in surprise. He clearly had expected a fierce lecture from Roland. The apprehensiveness left his eyes and was replaced with a mischievous twinkle. "It was nothing, Sheriff. Do you think I can stay now? I caught him for you and all. I won't cause any more trouble. I swear I—" Jimmy asked before Roland cut him off.

"Not now!" He interrupted roughly. Jimmy's begging sounded as bad as Curly's. Roland was in no mood to discuss the matter. It was a possibility that he would change his mind later, but that wouldn't be until everything in

New Haven had settled down. There were too many things to oversee, and he didn't want Jimmy underfoot. "We'll talk about it later, but not now. If you want to leave town, that's fine. If not, you're going back to the house," Roland ordered.

The gunslinger thought about arguing for a moment, but the tone of Roland's voice convinced him otherwise. His shoulders slumped in defeat. "All right. I'll go back to the house." He paused for a moment as if he was going to say something else but wisely held his tongue.

"Good. I'll go with you," Roland answered. *Now, Henry.* Roland fought the urge to gallop immediately to his house.

"I said I'd go. You don't have to follow me," Jimmy replied in an insulted tone.

"I trust you, Jimmy, but I need to talk with Henry."

Roland and Jimmy stepped outside, and the Sheriff immediately headed towards William. He needed to put somebody in charge, and Ben would ask too many questions. "I've got something to take care of. I'll be back in an hour. You're in charge."

The deputy nodded and gathered himself together. William's back straightened, and his chest puffed out. "All right. I'll see you in a while," he replied, trying to sound confident.

"Make sure that gallows gets built. I want to hang that son of a bitch tonight." Roland turned around, satisfied that things would be under control until he got back. He missed Morgan and Jack immensely at that moment. Normally he could have put them in charge without a second thought. William wasn't his ideal choice, but he had nobody left. *Don't think about it,* Roland told himself. He could consider how to replace his decimated core of deputies later.

"Meet me on the south side of town," Roland told Jimmy and walked towards his horse. He was glad he had taken the horse before the gunfight. Every other horse had been killed in the deadly exchange of bullets. At least he had one left. It was another small consolation, but Roland had to find those tiny victories. He climbed into the saddle and groaned. Despite his full day of rest, Roland felt exhausted, but he set his jaw as he rode to meet Jimmy. The young man was waiting when Roland reached the southern end of town, and the Sheriff wordlessly started riding towards his house while Jimmy followed behind. The two men didn't speak as they rode through the summer night, which suited Roland fine. He didn't want to talk about whether Jimmy could stay in town when there were so many other issues on his mind.

Roland didn't understand what had happened. He had killed Carlos, Carlos had killed Bryant, and Rebecca should be awake at that very moment. *Unless Carlos didn't kill Bryant,* a tiny voice at the back of his head spoke, but Roland refused to believe that. A Dark Rider had killed Bryant, and every one of them was dead. Curly was still alive, but Roland was going to hang him that evening. Bryant's killer had to be dead. His teeth ground together, and he clenched his fists tightly. It just didn't make any sense.

The trip back to the house was a quick one. Roland swung his tired legs out of the saddle and tied his horse while Jimmy lazily dismounted. Then he turned to the house but stopped as he saw two figures walking out from behind a group of trees. He instantly drew his gun then paused as he made out their faces in the dark night. "Henry? Is that you?"

"Yeah. Didn't mean to scare you," the Ghost Hunter answered and chuckled softly. "I thought you were going to shoot us both there for a few moments."

"I almost did." Roland scowled and holstered his gun. He wasn't in a pleasant mood, and being surprised didn't brighten it. "What are you doing back there?"

"I didn't know who was coming back. You or some Dark Rider. What happened out there? We heard all the shots."

"It was the Goddamn Riders," Roland snapped then exhaled deeply. "They tried to rescue everyone else, and there was a fight. At least those bastards are finally dead."

Henry's eyebrows raised in surprise. "All of them?" He asked in amazement.

"Every one of them except Curly. I killed Carlos, and Rebecca's still asleep. You said she'd wake up. What's going on?" He demanded.

Henry and Singing Rock exchanged a long glance at Roland's tone, and Jimmy went inside. He decided that he didn't want to brave another one of Roland's angry rants. "You killed Carlos?" Henry asked.

"You're damn right, I killed him. The son of a bitch is dead, and Rebecca's still sleeping. What do we do now?" He wanted to hit something. He knew that he should keep his temper, but Roland just couldn't. He was tired of having things go against him.

The two Ghost Hunters exchanged another long glance, and then Henry put his hands up defensively. "Calm down, Roland."

"Goddamn it, I am calm!" Roland exploded.

Henry's eyebrows shot up in amusement, but he comment. "Roland, listen to me. If Carlos killed Bryant, and he's dead, then Rebecca should wake up. I know that's true because I've seen it happen myself to other spirits." He paused and rocked back in his stance. "If she's not awake, then somebody else killed Bryant."

"No they didn't!" Roland hissed and closed his eyes. He took several deep breaths and tried to calm himself down. *It isn't true. Carlos killed Bryant. It has to be him,* Roland insisted to himself. Curly had been scared to death and wouldn't have been capable of lying. Marshall had even corroborated the story.

Goddamn it, who the hell killed him then? He tried to rack his brain for an answer.

"Roland," Henry called, but the Sheriff stood silent with his eyes closed in frustration. "Don't worry about it. We'll go back to her house at dawn, and if you get that picture of Bryant, we'll figure out who killed him. She's not awake tonight, but she will be soon."

Damn it, not again. He was tired of always having another setback every time it seemed Rebecca was going to awaken. Roland hated to think the unmentionable, but it didn't seem so far-fetched that she would never emerge from her slumber. He had always taken her awakening as a certainty, but with the way his luck had run, Roland wouldn't be surprised if she continued to languish in the Land of Shadows until she died. He would just have to wait and see what happened next. "All right. When do you want me back out here?" Roland asked tiredly.

Henry shrugged his shoulders. "I guess a couple of hours before dawn. That'll give us plenty of time to go back to the house."

"I'll see you then," Roland replied.

Henry looked over his shoulder at Roland's house then turned back to the Sheriff. "Is Jimmy staying here?"

"Yeah," Roland answered in an exhausted voice. He didn't want to think about Jimmy or anything else the rest of the night. "Is that a problem?"

"No." Henry shook his head. "I thought you were going to kill him earlier. If that's all, I'm going to rest up some more. The last few nights have been busy," he told Roland wryly.

"Tell me about it. I'll see you in a few hours." All of the anger and adrenaline had left his body, and he walked to his horse feeling exhausted. He looked at his horse for a moment before tiredly swinging up into the saddle. Roland looked at Henry and Singing Rock and tipped his hat to them. "Good night," he wished them and prodded his horse into a trot. Henry tipped his hat in return. Then the pair went back inside as Roland rode towards town.

Even though the ride to town was a short one, it seemed to drag on forever to Roland. Alone in the quiet summer night, Roland had time to dwell on how badly his luck continued to run. He couldn't believe that Rebecca still languished in the Land of Shadows. So many times, it had seemed that her salvation was within his grasp but had been cruelly snatched away at the last second. Roland wanted to believe that Henry and Singing Rock would rescue her, but deep inside, he had serious doubts. Even the memory of her glorious smile and sparkling eyes, which he had always found so beautiful, were beginning to fade. He had a hard time picturing her without summoning up images of her lying emaciated on the bed at The Last Frontier.

Roland also lamented the loss of Morgan and Phillip. It hadn't sunk in yet that Morgan was dead, but he still hadn't come to grips with Jack yet either.

472

There would be funeral arrangements to take care of when he returned, and then Roland was sure that grim realization would take hold. He didn't even know who all had died that night. The latest gunfight seemed like a dream to Roland. He had participated and killed several men, but so many other things ran through his mind that it was hard to remember all of the details.

The only thing that brightened Roland's mood was Curly. Roland couldn't wait to kill the Dark Rider. It was the only way he could strike back at all the things that had gone wrong for him. Curly hadn't killed Jack, Morgan, or Bryant, and his death wouldn't free Rebecca from the Land of Shadows. But he was the only person who Roland could take out his frustration on. He didn't feel any guilt over it, though; Curly's hanging was warranted, and Roland grew more and more excited about Curly as he crept closer to town.

Roland half-expected to see men guarding the southern side of town, but there was no more need for them. The Dark Riders had been obliterated, and New Haven was safe from attack. Several men of the citizen watch had been killed in the gunfight. Roland felt guilty over their deaths, but there was nothing he could have done differently. Carlos had been foolish to attempt the rescue and had paid for it with his life. Roland never would have guessed that the Dark Rider would commit such a brazen, stupid act. *Don't think about it,* Roland told himself harshly. It would do no good to dwell on the fallen. He didn't have time to grieve for anyone. There would be time for grieving once everything had settled down. *If it settles down,* Roland thought pessimistically.

Ben and William still remained at the scene of the gunfight, although it had been mostly cleaned up. Roland was glad there weren't still bodies laying on the ground and wounded crying in the street. The gunfight was over, and he wanted the town to move on as soon as possible. "William," he called out.

The rakish deputy turned around, and Roland was stunned by his appearance. William had always seemed so vibrant and full of energy, but he still looked stunned by the turn of events. "Sheriff," he answered in a dull voice. "I talked to Thatcher, and he said he'd perform the funerals when everything was ready."

"What about the gallows?" Roland asked anxiously. *You're dead this time, you son of a bitch,* Roland thought grimly and darted his eyes towards the station house.

"I don't know," William replied tiredly. He put a hand over his forehead and closed his eyes. Breathing a deep sigh, he shook his head slightly.

Blazes, he thought to himself at the sight of William. He looked like he was standing on his last leg. Roland put a hand on William's shoulder. "Don't worry, Will. I'll check myself. Why don't you go home," he suggested.

"What?" The deputy dropped his hand and looked at Roland. "I can't leave. We don't have enough men."

Roland snorted. "I don't think we need anybody on duty right now. All the Goddamn Riders are dead, and I guarantee you, nobody'll cause any trouble tonight. Besides, I've got Ben and Simon." Roland would have preferred to have William around, but the deputy obviously needed a good night of rest to clear his head.

William looked off to the side. "I sent Simon home already," he confessed to Roland somewhat guiltily. "He wanted to be with Sarah."

"Don't worry," the Sheriff responded immediately. *We all need a good night of rest,* he thought wistfully. He knew that his night would be another long one, but there was no sense having any of his three remaining deputies up all night as well. "Go home. I'll send Ben home after I check on a few things." He was confident that New Haven wouldn't need her few surviving deputies that night.

"Thanks, Sheriff. Do you mind if I leave now?"

"No. I'll take care of everything from here," Roland answered and waved the deputy away.

After William left, Roland went to Ben. The deputy was standing in the street, not accomplishing anything as far as Roland could tell. Ben looked just as stunned and tired as William. Roland wanted to get Ben off the street and home as soon as possible. "Ben, go wait in the station house," he ordered and waited expectantly for the deputy to bombard him with questions.

"All right," Ben answered and followed Roland's order.

Roland watched Ben cross the street and shook his head. It was the first time that he had ever seen Ben not pester someone with questions. Roland actually wished the deputy would have asked him something. It seemed unnatural for him to be so quiet.

He turned away from Ben and went to his horse. First, he wanted to see Lewis and the gallows, and then he wanted to check with Thatcher. Roland sighed as he looked at his horse. The train station wasn't that far away, but he was tired. His body was sore, and he would have loved a good shot of whiskey. But he had to take care of his tasks before he could get a bottle from George.

When he arrived at the train station, Roland was pleased to see the gallows nearly completed. Lewis hammered a nail into the structure as Roland rode up. The carpenter was a tall man with a short scraggly beard and crooked teeth. Lewis wasn't the most handsome man in New Haven by a long shot, but he was the best carpenter. He paused and wiped sweat from his brow. "Damn, that was some fight," Lewis commented needlessly.

The Sheriff dispensed with greetings. He had no desire to talk about the gunfight. "How much longer?"

Lewis scratched at his beard and looked at the gallows behind him. It was no different than the one he had built the night before. There was a small wooden platform six feet above the ground which could hold four men, and a wooden beam five feet above it. It would be a simple matter to tie a rope around the beam and the other around Curly's neck. Then Roland only had to push the Dark Rider off the platform, and that would be the end of the outlaws. "Give me a few more hours, and I'll be done."

"Good." Roland tipped his hat to the carpenter. "Good work. I'll see you later."

The streets had quieted completely as the Sheriff rode towards the church, where Thatcher was preparing funerals for men who had fallen. Normally there would have been people visiting one of the town's saloons, but the gunfight had caused everyone to stay in their homes. Roland didn't particularly mind. It was good not to have to worry about any drunken revelers. He wanted a quiet evening after the trouble that had already occurred.

Roland stopped in front of the church and scowled. It still seemed unreal that he was taking care of two more deputies' funerals. Even though Morgan was the oldest of the deputies, Roland had always thought that he was invincible. The crafty veteran had survived so many gunfights over the years. *Don't think about it,* Roland thought to himself and walked into the church. He just needed to get the details taken care of. There would time for grieving later on.

Reverend Thatcher was busy at work in the church. The tiny bald man scribbled on a piece of paper, writing his sermons for the following day. He was always hard at work on Saturdays to prepare for Sunday's service, but there was extra work to be done that night. Thatcher looked up when Roland opened the door and set his paper aside. "Roland," he called out tiredly and rose to his feet.

"Reverend," Roland greeted and removed his hat. *Just get this over with quickly.* "I need to talk with you."

"Of course, have a seat." Thatcher waved his arm at the pews around him and took a seat in one.

Roland eyed the pew dubiously. He wanted a short visit, and Thatcher was likely to keep him if he sat down. *I don't have time for this,* he thought but took a seat anyway. "Reverend, I just wanted to talk with you about Morgan and Phillip." Roland's jaw clenched together in frustration. *I shouldn't have to do this.*

Thatcher shook his head. "Such a shame and a waste. Too many deaths lately, Sheriff. Too many."

"There won't be after tomorrow," Roland answered grimly. He couldn't wait for noon so he could hang Curly and be done with the affair. *One thing at a time.* "Is there anything you need?"

"No. I'm fine. Joseph is going to bury them, and I'll say a blessing for all of them tomorrow. That should be it," the tiny man answered. His face looked so sorrowful that night. Roland was so used to seeing Thatcher energetic and excited about life, and it was strange to see such a morose expression on his face. Then again, there hadn't been much reason to celebrate lately.

"Thank you," Roland said quietly and breathed a sigh of relief. He was glad that the funeral was out of his hands. "How's Dotty? I haven't been able to see her since Jack's funeral," Roland admitted guiltily.

"She's fine. I visited her earlier and brought her dinner. She's taking it hard, but that's how it always is." Thatcher's face seemed to grow even more sorrowful.

Roland promised himself that he'd visit Dotty once things had settled down. "Well, that's all I needed to ask you. Thanks for your time," Roland moved on quickly and rose to his feet. He wanted to get back to the station house.

"Are you all right, Roland?" Thatcher asked with concern before Roland could get away.

Roland forced himself to don his lopsided grin. "I'm fine. It's just been a long day."

"And Miss White? Is she any better?"

"She's doing better. I'll let you know when she wakes up." *She will wake up, Goddamn it,* Roland told himself half-heartedly. "I need to go, Reverend. Thanks for the help. I'll talk with you later." Roland turned towards the door.

"Roland, whatever happened to that friend of yours?" Thatcher called before the Sheriff could take two steps.

He turned back around. Roland thought Thatcher was a great man, but sometimes he talked more than Ben. "What friend?"

"You know," Thatcher's voice dropped conspiratorially. "The one who faked his death." The Reverend put a hand over his chest. "He nearly scared me to death when he sat up. I thought he was rising from the dead," Thatcher laughed.

Even Roland had to smile at that. He could see Henry scaring the Reverend to no end. Roland himself had nearly had a heart attack when he saw the Ghost Hunter was still alive. "He's doing fine. I'll tell him you said hello. Good night, Reverend." Roland nodded, and this time he was able to make it out of the church without another word from Thatcher.

Roland breathed a sigh of relief when he stepped back into the summer air. He had taken care of everything that he could think of, and now he only had to wait for dawn. It was going to be a long time, but at least he would be able to sit down for a while and not have to worry about anything. Roland's nerves were pretty frayed, and he craved an evening of solitude. He rode back to the station house, enjoying the cooler air. The clouds that appeared that morning had cooled the sweltering heat. *Just let it rain,* Roland wished but doubted it would come to pass. Nothing else had gone his way lately.

As he rode up to the station house, Roland was amazed by how much the building had been damaged. All the windows had been shattered, and shards of glass littered the ground. Bullet holes riddled the front wall, and there were several patches of blood staining the hard dirt. But the inside looked even worse. It would take several days to clean everything, but somebody had to keep an eye on Curly that night. Roland wanted to make sure that the Dark Rider was hanged the following day, and everyone else needed a night of rest.

After Roland tethered his horse, he headed across the street for a bottle of whiskey. It was going to be a long night, and Roland didn't intend to pass it entirely sober. There was no danger with Carlos and his brethren dead, and he could use some of the mind-numbing liquid. When he stepped inside the saloon, Roland whistled as he saw how empty the place was. Normally The Last Frontier was nearly full by nine. A few regulars sat at the bar or played cards, but everyone else had chosen to stay home that evening. Damage from the gunfight had spread to the saloon as well. Every window facing the station house had been broken, and several tables had bullet holes in them. Roland could also see the bloodstains where men had fallen during the fight. He headed straight for the bar where George was sitting. "George," he called out to the saloon owner and slapped a hand down on the bar. "Whiskey."

George quickly brought his bottle of whiskey off the shelf and placed it before Roland. "There you are, Sheriff."

"Thanks. So did you make it through the fight all right?"

"Yes. Yes, I did." He laughed nervously. "I just hid behind the bar until it was all over."

"That was smart. Thanks again for the whiskey. See you later." Roland didn't feel like making small talk. He tipped his hat and turned towards the door. Roland stared at the staircase and paused for a moment as he decided whether or not to visit Rebecca. *No, not now,* he decided. Roland was in a foul mood already, and seeing Rebecca would only make it worse. There would be time to see her later on, and if all went well, she'd be awake in the morning. *I love you,* he wished her then left the saloon.

Ben sat at the desk in the station house with his feet propped up. He had his eyes closed, but he bounced forward the moment Roland walked in the door. The Sheriff shook his head as he viewed the carnage. He had seen the inside of the station house just after the gunfight had ended, but it still shocked him how badly it had been damaged. Bullet holes decorated the walls, and both chairs were little more than splinters. The desk was riddled with holes, and bloodstains covered the floor. *At least they took the bodies out,* Roland tried to look at the bright side of things. "Ben," he greeted his deputy.

"Sheriff," Ben replied sleepily then covered his mouth as he yawned. "Are you still hanging him tonight?"

Roland shook his head. It was tempting to hang Curly earlier, but he wanted the whole town to witness his execution. "I'm hanging him at noon tomorrow. Now go home and get some sleep," Roland ordered the deputy. He was reassured by Ben's inquisitiveness, but Roland had absolutely no desire to answer a rush of questions.

Ben nodded tiredly. "All right. Good night, Sheriff."

"Good night, Ben." Roland watched as Ben slowly stood up and rubbed at his eyes. He tipped his hat towards Roland then left the Sheriff alone in the station house.

Roland took a seat on the desk and shifted uncomfortably a few times. It felt strange to be sitting in the same room in which Phillip had been killed. He uncorked the bottle of whiskey with his teeth then took a large swallow. Roland coughed as it burned his throat then sighed in satisfaction as a tingling warmness spread throughout his chest and arms. He quickly took another sip then leaned against a wall and waited for dawn.

The next six hours passed slowly for Roland. It was a quiet evening with nothing to take his mind off the wait. Even Curly remained quiet in his cell. Roland's mood bobbed up and down the entire night. Sometimes he could barely sit still as excitement coursed through his veins. *Rebecca will wake up,* he'd think with absolute determination and daydream of them getting married. He also had serious pangs of doubt. Nothing had worked to help Rebecca so far, and Roland didn't see why that would change at dawn in spite of Henry's promise. At times, he got up and paced around the small office, but the hands on his watch kept circling at that same unbearably slow pace.

From time to time Roland took a hefty swig of whiskey. He didn't drink too much. Roland wanted to be sober when he returned to Rebecca's house and for her possible awakening. Finally, as it reached four o'clock, Roland went outside. He was leaving Curly unguarded, but Roland had the only key. *He'll be safe,* Roland thought confidently. Roland cast one last glance at The Last Frontier and considered going inside to see Rebecca. Then he shook his head and swung a leg tiredly over his horse. He would see her after he returned from her house, and hopefully she would be awake then. *I love you, Rebecca,* he thought then galloped towards his house.

Even though the journey took only a few minutes, it seemed to drag forever for Roland. *Henry has to get her out this time. He promised,* Roland kept thinking. The cynical voice telling him that it wouldn't work again was also present, but Roland was beginning to believe that Henry would succeed with dawn approaching. He jumped off his horse when he reached his house and rushed to the door. Opening it roughly, he called out, "Henry, wake up. It's almost dawn."

Henry awakened and sat upright immediately. "I'm awake, Roland." He twisted about a few times, trying to stretch out the kinks in his back. Sleeping

478

on the floor hadn't done his back any good. *Is it dawn already?* Henry thought in amazement. It seemed that he couldn't get enough sleep lately. If all went well, it would be his final day in New Haven, and then he and Singing Rock could leave the town. He saw Singing Rock sit up as well. *"Are you ready?"*

The Navajo shrugged his shoulders in the dark. *"Are you?"* He asked in return.

The Ghost Hunter nodded and grinned slightly. *"Yes. Let us finish this,"* he answered and stood up. "Give us a few more minutes to wake up, Roland, then we'll go."

"Fine," Roland answered then went outside.

The two Ghost Hunters woke up from their deep sleep, and then Singing Rock gathered his collection of pouches. Henry waited for the Navajo and stepped outside to join Roland.

"Are you ready?" The Sheriff asked excitedly.

"Yes, Roland. Calm down," Henry told the Sheriff to no avail. He knew that the only way he could keep Roland from bouncing around with nervous energy would be to tie him to a tree. *With one thick rope,* he tacked on. He looked over at Singing Rock with an amused grin. *"I think he is excited."*

"Hmm," the Navajo grunted and folded his arms across his chest. *"You are a wise man,"* he replied, and the corners of his mouth curled up slightly.

Henry chuckled. "Let's go, Roland," he told the Sheriff, then the three men mounted their horses. With Roland leading the way, they began what Henry was sure would be the last trip to Rebecca's house.

It was a quick journey, especially with Roland leading the way at a rapid pace. The Sheriff rode at the front of the party and kept turning in his saddle to look back at the two Ghost Hunters in exasperation. Henry and Singing Rock exchanged glances several times but didn't speak. They simply obliged Roland and picked up their pace as they rushed to Rebecca's house. Henry didn't see the need. Dawn wasn't going to arrive any earlier. When they finally reached her house, Roland scrambled out of his saddle and grabbed the reins to his horse. "We're here," he called out to the Ghost Hunters.

Henry shook his head at Roland's mention of the obvious but held his tongue. "It's still a while 'til dawn, Roland. Tie your horse. We have to wait before we can go in," the Ghost Hunter instructed and dismounted his own horse. He tied it to a tree and looked over his shoulder to see Singing Rock doing the same.

"Is there anything I can do?" Roland asked earnestly.

"Not right now. Just go wait over there." Henry pointed at a tree a good hundred yards from Rebecca's house.

Roland looked at the tree then back at Henry. The Ghost Hunter could see that Roland wanted to find a way to help, but the Sheriff held his tongue. "All right," he replied sullenly and trekked towards the tree.

Henry watched him for a few moments then turned to Singing Rock. *"I wish it was dawn. He is going to be trouble until then."*

"Keep him quiet. I must prepare first," the Navajo instructed.

Henry pursed his lips. He didn't want the aggravation of dealing with Roland, but Singing Rock was right. Roland needed to leave the Navajo alone so Singing Rock could prepare to enter the house. Henry's own preparations didn't take nearly as long. He could calm himself down and focus his thoughts in a matter of seconds.

Roland sat with his back to a tree and his hands folded tightly in his lap. He rocked back and forth slowly, but the moment that Henry approached, he jumped to his feet. "Are you ready?" He asked anxiously.

"No, Roland. Not yet. You know it takes Singing Rock some time to prepare," he chastised Roland and exhaled deeply. It was just under an hour before dawn, and Roland was likely to talk his ear off while they waited. Roland nodded then sat back down. Much to Henry's surprise, Roland kept quiet while they waited for Singing Rock. The Sheriff tapped his finger anxiously on the butt of his pistol, and he swept his gaze between Singing Rock and the house. But Roland didn't utter a single word as he and Henry waited for dawn to arrive.

"Is he going to be ready in time?" Roland finally asked after nearly half an hour of silence. Singing Rock had laid out his pouches on the ground in front of him and was chanting quietly over them.

"Yes. Don't worry about it. We'll get her out this time," Henry assured Roland. He hated giving a guarantee like that to the Sheriff, but he felt confident that this time he would wrest Rebecca away from Bryant. Henry had nearly succeeded the last time, and only the rising of the sun had prevented him from success. They had plenty of time that morning.

Roland nodded and looked at the house, but Henry knew that he was far from convinced. He joined the Sheriff and stared at Rebecca's house. Under the moonlight they could only see its dark silhouette. It rose ominously from the ground, and even though the air was silent, Henry knew that Bryant lurked inside with Rebecca's spirit. His spirit kept a watchful eye on the house and was ready to strike out at anybody who drew near. *Not for long,* Henry thought with determination.

Another ten or fifteen minutes passed, and Henry could tell that Roland was growing more worried by the second. Several times the Sheriff rose to his feet and paced. He kept glancing at Singing Rock, the house, then back to Henry over and over. When Singing Rock ceased his chanting, Roland immediately froze in his footsteps. "Is he ready? Are you going in?" He looked up at the sky, which had had lightened to a dark grey. "It's nearly dawn," he pointed out to Henry.

480

"I know, Roland," Henry answered exasperatedly. He looked at Singing Rock. The Navajo had risen to his feet and was tying a few pouches to his belt. *"Are you ready?"* He called out.

Singing Rock paused and stared at Henry. *"Let us end this,"* he answered in a monotone, lifeless voice.

"Stay here," Henry instructed Roland in a firm voice. So far, Roland had remained safely away from the house, but Henry hadn't seen Roland so agitated in their previous journeys to the house. He leveled a finger at the Sheriff. "I mean it. Stay right here. We don't need any more trouble. Understand?"

Roland nodded, but even in the dark, Henry could see that Roland longed to go into the house with them. "I understand," he whispered. "Good luck. Please bring her out," Roland pleaded softly then stepped back and watched as Henry joined Singing Rock.

Henry felt a moment of anxiousness as he approached Singing Rock. He was more than ready to leave New Haven, and in a matter of minutes, he would finally be free to do so. As he joined his partner, Henry pushed those thoughts from his mind and assumed a focused attitude. All his worry and anxiety fell by the wayside, and the house was the only thing that mattered. *"Are you ready?"* Henry asked Singing Rock in a cold, distant voice.

The Navajo nodded. *"Let us begin,"* he answered and started marching towards the house.

At first the morning air was nearly silent. Only a few crickets chirped to break the silence, but Henry could feel tension in the air. When they were fifty yards from the house, Henry thought the air seemed colder and thicker, but the two men marched on resolutely. Henry could see the broken windows and bits of wood and glass that had been expelled from the house. At forty yards, Henry heard a deep humming that was barely audible. Still the Ghost Hunters approached the house, determined to confront Bryant one last time.

"Mine!" Bryant shrieked, and his cry echoed loudly. Blue light flashed behind two of the windows to punctuate Bryant's single outburst, but Henry and Singing Rock ignored his cry. *"Leave! Mine! All mine! Kill! Kill! Mine!"* Bryant continued to berate them. Henry didn't know if it was anger or desperation. The last time he had met the spirit, Henry had caused Bryant a great deal of pain.

Bryant stopped his wailing after it was apparent that the two Ghost Hunters wouldn't be deterred. The morning air grew silent again as the last of Bryant's echoes faded. Singing Rock continued his march towards the house without pausing, and Henry followed directly behind him. The Navajo walked to the door and reached into one of his pouches. He withdrew a handful of yellow powder and cast it at the door. *"Leave!"* Bryant screamed at them as blue sparks leapt off the doorknob, but Singing Rock ignored his plea. He reached out and twisted the doorknob, pushing the door open.

Singing Rock reached into his pouches and took a handful of powder in each hand. He threw the powder in his left hand and waited as the specks began to glow, casting a dim illumination over the interior of the house. Then he stepped inside and braced himself for a confrontation. Henry followed right after him, trusting his partner to ward off any attacks.

They didn't have to wait long as the house exploded in a flurry of activity. "*Mine!*" Bryant yelled, nearly deafening the two men with his loud cry. At the same time objects rose into the air. The tattered remains of furniture and their splinters hovered and began to turn chaotic pirouettes in mid-air. Blue light flickered from the bedroom, and the front door began to open and slam shut loudly. Singing Rock stood calmly amidst the bedlam and reached into one of his pouches for another handful of powder, waiting for an attack.

Without warning, a battered chair hurled itself towards the pair, and countless splinters and shards of glass followed in its wake. Just as quickly, Singing Rock threw a handful of red powder into the air above them, and the objects bounced harmlessly away. He threw the other handful and spread more illumination throughout the room as the first casting began to wane. "*Go now,*" Singing Rock told Henry as he brought out two more handfuls of powder.

Henry didn't answer but sat on the littered floor, ignoring the shards of glass and bits of wood that pressed against his skin. He closed his eyes, trusting that Singing Rock would protect him, and formed the picture of a lake in his mind as he had hundreds of times before. Quickly he crystallized the image then envisioned himself diving into the water. Henry felt himself break the surface, and his body shivered at the cold water. Then his head broke the surface, and he found himself falling towards the grey, barren dirt of the Land of Shadows.

Henry had the wind knocked out of him as he landed roughly on the hard ground. He sucked in a few breaths and looked around. Rebecca's house stood in front of him, and Henry could hear a deep, humming noise coming from within it. Rising to his feet, he marched towards the house, determined to end the battle with Bryant.

He kicked open the front door and held his breath as he felt his stomach lurch. His feet remained planted on the grey dirt, but he felt the air rush by him like he was hurtling forward. Walls sprung up around him, and he shivered as he was buffeted by a cold wind. Then the motion faded, and Henry found himself in Rebecca's house. He looked around his suddenly larger surroundings and locked onto Bryant. It was hard to see his spirit, but Henry noticed a dark shadow that shifted about in one of the corners. He moved towards it, preparing himself to battle the spirit.

Bryant noticed him approaching, and his spirit rose into the air. Black tentacles writhed in several different directions, and it growled a deep, menacing sound. *"Mine! Leave! Kill! Kill! Mine!"* It shrieked at him, but Henry never slowed his approach.

"Bryant White, I bind you! Bryant White!" Henry shouted at the spirit, encouraged by Bryant's reaction. The spirit keened shrilly, and the tentacles folded back into the shadowy mass. It hunched back down, cowering in the corner, but Henry didn't let up. He was going to force Bryant to surrender Rebecca, and he wasn't going to let up on the spirit until he did. "Bryant White, I bind you! Bryant White! Bryant White, I bind you! Bryant White!" Henry continued to shout at Bryant, and each time the Ghost Hunter spoke Bryant's name, the spirit cried out in pain.

Henry stopped twenty feet away from the shadowy mass, not foolish enough to draw any closer. The temperature dropped the closer he got to Bryant, and he was shivering by the time he stood his ground. Nonetheless he continued his barrage at the spirit. "Bryant White! Bryant White, I command you to release her spirit! Bryant White! Bryant White, I command you to release her spirit!"

Bryant whined with each mention of his name and squirmed against the walls. Finally a tentacle extended from the dark mass, clutching a glowing sphere of light. A faint noise like chimes blowing in a gentle wind filled the air. Henry's eyes lit with victory, but he didn't let his guard down. It would be too easy for Bryant to strike if he ceased his attack for even a moment. "Bryant White, I command you to release her! Put her down, Bryant White! Bryant White!"

The ball of light hung in the air for a moment then the tentacle gently began to lower it. Henry waited for Bryant to place the sphere down, but it stopped several feet above the ground. "Bryant White! Bryant White! Bryant White, put her down! Bryant White, I command you to release her! Bryant White!" Henry shouted at the top of his lungs, expecting Bryant to give in to one last barrage.

Bryant surprised Henry, however. The shadowy form hissed in fury and raised the sphere into the air. The tentacle poised rigidly, tightly gripping the sphere that held Rebecca's spirit. *"Leave! Go or she dies! Kill! Kill! Leave now or kill!"* Bryant shrieked agonizingly despite Henry's shouts. The spirit continued to whine, but it held Rebecca's spirit threateningly.

Henry didn't stop his barrage. He feared for his own safety, and he didn't believe Bryant's threat. Rebecca had been his wife, and he didn't think that Bryant would destroy her soul. "Bryant White! Bryant White, put her down!"

Bryant surprised Henry again. *"Die!"* He shouted and the tentacle began to slam downward.

"Wait!" Henry cried and backed away as he stopped shouting Bryant's name. He danced back far enough to be safe from the spirit's tentacles.

The sphere stopped mere inches away from the ground, and then Bryant raised it back into the air. *"Go or she dies! Leave! Mine! Mine! All mine!"* He cried triumphantly and held Rebecca's spirit aloft like a trophy.

Henry continued to back up slowly, keeping a wary eye on Bryant. He didn't know what to do. Bryant should have given the spirit up, but his determination surprised Henry. The Ghost Hunter never would have guessed that he'd brave all that pain and use Rebecca as a hostage. There was nothing else he could do. He could shout out Bryant's name until the sun rose, but if Bryant shattered that glowing sphere, Rebecca would never awaken again.

"I'm leaving," he told the spirit and formed an image of a door in his mind. Once he had every detail of the door drawn in his head, he closed his eyes and imagined reaching out and opening it. Henry felt his stomach convulse as he rushed forward, hurtling out of the Land of Shadows. Then it was over, and he was back in Bryant's house.

"Mine!" Bryant shrieked exultantly as several pieces of furniture shot towards the Ghost Hunters.

Singing Rock stood over Henry, casting powder and chanting as he rebuffed Bryant's attacks. Henry didn't think that Singing Rock was aware of his return. The sun wasn't up yet, and the Navajo's attention was occupied with Bryant. He stood up and leaned over. *"Leave now!"* Henry told Singing Rock urgently.

The Navajo didn't reply, but he began to back towards the front door. It continued to slam open and shut, but as soon as they moved to leave, it swung open and stayed motionless. The rest of the objects floated in the air, but they ceased their perpetual attacks at the two men. Carefully they inched their way towards the front door. Henry half-expected the door to slam on them, but it didn't budge an inch as they passed through. Once they were on the porch, they quickly back-pedaled until they were a safe distance from the house.

"What happened?" Singing Rock asked as soon as they stopped, but Henry never had a chance to respond.

Roland rushed up to him the moment they left the house. The sky had lightened as dawn approached, and Henry could see the excitement etched on the Sheriff's face. "Is she awake? What happened?" He shouted at Henry. Henry paused a moment and looked at Roland, wondering how to break the bad news. Roland instantly saw him shift his eyes and grabbed Henry's shoulders in a rough grip. "You didn't get her out, d id you?" He hissed between clenched teeth.

"No," Henry answered and waited for Roland to blow up.

"Goddamn it," Roland swore. "You promised. What the blazes happened this time?" He asked in an accusatory tone.

Henry took a deep breath and looked at Singing Rock. The Navajo's eyes had widened slightly, but he made no move to interfere. "Bryant wouldn't give her up. I tried, but he threatened to kill her," he answered quietly.

"Damn it, how many times are you going to say that?" Roland shouted.

"Listen to me. Bryant was going to kill her. Do you hear me? I could've tortured him all day, but he would have killed Rebecca. Is that what you want?" He asked roughly.

Roland stopped and took a deep breath before answering. "There was nothing you could do?" He asked stubbornly.

"No, Roland. There was nothing I could do. I thought Bryant would give her up. He was in a lot of pain, but he could've killed her if he wanted to. I had to leave." Henry felt badly over how things had turned out. He had been so confident that he could rescue Rebecca.

"So what do we do now?" Roland asked in a tired voice.

"Get that picture of Bryant," Henry answered. He wanted to know who had killed Bryant. That was the safest bet to banish Bryant. Henry just hoped that the killer was still in New Haven.

Roland shook his head and stared up at the sky. "And what if that doesn't work?"

"I don't know, Roland. I just don't know."

Chapter Twenty-Five

The three men rode silently towards Roland's house. Henry looked at Roland, but one glance at the Sheriff's face quickly convinced Henry to stay silent. Roland's jaw was locked once again in a rigid mask of fury, and his eyes stared straight ahead as if they would set the grass on fire. He couldn't believe that everything had fallen apart again. He had steeled himself against that possibility earlier, but Roland had let his emotions get out of control once they reached Rebecca's house. Roland had believed that Henry and Singing Rock would emerge victoriously, and the sting of defeat left a bitter taste in his mouth. Rebecca would have to spend another day imprisoned in The Land of Shadows, and Roland didn't know if he could cope with it. All of his friends had been killed. Morgan's funeral was in a few more hours, and Roland didn't even want to attend. Roland wanted nothing more than a bottle of whiskey and a day of sleep. Even Henry's assurance that Dennis's painting of Bryant would yield the murderer's identity gave Roland little solace. Henry had promised many things, and precious few of them had come to pass.

Only Curly's imminent demise gave Roland the slightest reason to feel good. Every time Roland began to despair too heavily for Rebecca, he shifted his thoughts to the Dark Rider. His fingers balled up into tight fists, and his lips curled into a tiny smile. He avoided looking at the two Ghost Hunters. Roland knew that they were trying to help Rebecca, but he was angry and frustrated. *You just need to calm down,* Roland told himself to no avail. He had the feeling that he would burn with rage until he was able to sit down with a bottle of whiskey. Roland wasn't even sure if that would take the edge off his anger, but it certainly couldn't hurt.

The sun had risen above the horizon by the time they reached Roland's house. The previous morning there had been a few scattered clouds, but that Sunday they nearly filled the sky with their bloated grey bodies. From the look of them, Roland was positive that it would rain sometime in the next few days. But he barely cared about the weather and only noted it automatically. Rebecca was his only concern. All the rain in the world wouldn't make up for the fact that she continued to waste away at The Last Frontier.

Henry and Singing Rock dismounted in uncomfortable silence as Roland stared rigidly ahead at New Haven. Singing Rock seemed unfazed by Roland and calmly tethered his horse. Henry, however, appeared bothered by Roland's anger. He looked up at Roland a few times and paused as if to speak before turning back to his horse. When Singing Rock finished, he walked towards the house, leaving Henry alone with Roland. The Ghost Hunter took a deep breath then finally broke the uncomfortable silence. "We'll get her out eventually, Roland," he told the Sheriff softly.

Roland didn't speak. He nodded as he fumed silently. *You said you'd get her out last night,* he raged.

"Just get that picture, and we'll see what we can do," Henry spoke when it became apparent Roland was going to stay quiet. He looked extremely uncomfortable and finally tipped his hat. "Good night, Roland. I'll talk to you when you have Bryant's picture."

"Thanks," he muttered curtly. Roland was grateful that Henry was going to continue his aid and knew it wasn't Henry's fault that Rebecca was still imprisoned in the Land of Shadows, but Roland didn't feel the need to be polite. The day had already started off on the wrong foot. Henry went into the house, and Roland turned his horse around. He tapped its side and rode towards town.

New Haven was silent that Sunday morning. Even Dennis slept a little later on Sundays. Roland rode down the street, envious of everyone for their slumber. He was tired after his long vigil during the night, but he didn't have time for sleep. Even if he had the time, Roland didn't know if he could fall asleep. His stomach was turning in knots over Rebecca. Roland kept feeling stabbing pains in his side, and he knew that he needed to relax. Making himself calm down was unfortunately much more difficult than knowing that it needed to be done.

He headed straight to the station house. Roland wanted to check on the gallows first, but he had left Curly alone for too long. It would do no good to have a gallows if the Dark Rider had found a way to escape from his cell. Roland didn't think it was likely, but he wasn't going to leave anything else to chance. There would always be time to check on the gallows after Ben or William had shown up.

Roland shook his head, and his teeth ground together angrily when he approached the station house. The damage had looked bad enough at night, but it was worse in the sunlight. He wished that he could resurrect Carlos just to kill him again. The Dark Riders had caused him and New Haven so many problems that even death wasn't a fitting punishment. *Stop it!* Roland told himself and thought of Curly instead. He rubbed his hands together in anticipation of the big event. There was much to be done that morning, but Curly's hours were numbered. *Soon, you son of a bitch.*

Seating himself behind the desk, Roland waited for the other deputies to arrive. Roland again felt uneasy sitting in Phillip's chair and squirmed his back trying to find a comfortable position. Uncorking his bottle of whiskey, Roland took a deep swallow and leaned back, impatiently passing the time and attempting to forget all of the people who had fallen recently. His eyes felt heavy after staying up all night, but Roland was too angry to sleep. He kept thinking of Henry promising that Rebecca would awaken and how he had emerged in failure. Even more troubling was Bryant's killer. Henry said that

Dennis's portrait would unmask the murderer, but Roland doubted it. Every Dark Rider except Curly was dead, and Rebecca still remained asleep. Roland didn't know what or who to believe anymore. He just knew not to get his hopes up. Roland was tired of having them dashed to pieces.

Over the next few hours, more and more people began moving about the streets. Steady traffic trudged towards the church as a large number attended Thatcher's service. Roland even saw Dennis, but Roland stayed in the station house. He could talk to Dennis when William arrived to take over the watch.

The deputy arrived at eleven. William looked much better after a night of rest. His hair was combed again, and he had a rakish glint in his eyes. "Sheriff," William greeted as he stepped into the station house. "I think it's going to rain," he commented.

"I think you may be right," Roland answered bleakly, his eyes shifting to the shattered window for a split second. "Take over here for me. I need to check on a few things," Roland ordered curtly as he rose to his feet.

"Be careful out there. Everyone wants to talk about the gunfight," William cautioned.

They won't want to talk to me, Roland thought grimly. "I'll try. Morgan's funeral is at noon. I'll be back after that."

"Oh," William responded in disappointment.

Roland looked at the deputy and noticed immediately that the smile had vanished from his face. William sat glumly behind the desk and waited for Roland to leave. *What the hell is his—He wants to go to the funeral,* Roland quickly surmised. *Blazes, I don't have time for this.* Somebody had to watch the station house, and it wasn't going to be him. Roland knew Morgan better than any of the other deputies, and he would be there even though he was in no mood for a funeral. *Simon. Simon can watch him.* "Have Simon keep an eye on Curly, and I'll see you there," Roland told his deputy.

"Yes, Sheriff," William replied and straightened his back.

The Sheriff walked outside with a scowl on his face. Immediately Roland noticed how much cooler the air had become. The blanket of clouds cast a shadow over most of town, and it wasn't nearly as hot without the sun blaring down on them directly. Roland just wished that the improved weather had come at a better time.

He climbed onto his horse and went to check on the gallows. When he reached the railroad station, Roland smiled in satisfaction. Lewis had indeed finished the structure as promised. Roland had planned on using it for nine Dark Riders originally, but it would do just fine for a single victim. *After the funeral,* Roland told himself. There wasn't that much time before the funeral took place. He also wanted more people to be out on the streets to see Curly hang. The Dark Riders had caused the entire town of New Haven grief, and they all deserved to watch Curly's punishment.

488

Good, Roland thought as he turned his horse around. That was one thing less he had to worry about. He looked at his timepiece and saw that church service was over. He had enough time to visit with Dennis before the funeral. The blacksmith wasn't on his porch that morning. On Sundays the smithy was closed, and after church Dennis usually spent the day inside with his wife. Roland dismounted and went to the door. He knocked three times and waited impatiently for an answer. The funerals started in less than an hour, and Roland wanted to arrive with plenty of time to spare. He was about to knock again when Dennis opened the door. The blacksmith blinked once in surprise then smiled warmly. "Sheriff," he greeted.

"Dennis," Roland replied. He wished that he had more time to chat with the blacksmith, but his time was limited so he got right to the point. "Have you had a chance to work on that picture of Bryant?"

Dennis shrugged his shoulders. "I started it last night and was going to work on it some more after the funeral. I thought you said tonight would be fine," Dennis answered and looked at Roland strangely.

Roland knew that the request was a bizarre one, but he kept telling himself that he was asking for Rebecca. "Tonight's fine, Dennis. I just wanted to know if it would be ready," he assured the blacksmith.

"Are you going to tell me what this is for?" Dennis asked and looked at Roland with a skeptical expression.

You wouldn't believe it, Roland thought bitterly, but he forced himself to smile good-naturedly. "It's for Rebecca. I can't say any more than that." Roland had no intention of ever telling the blacksmith anything else. He liked Dennis, but Roland didn't think anybody would believe what had happened to him over the last three weeks.

Dennis left it at that even though he still looked curious. "We say a prayer each night for Miss White, Sheriff. I want you to know that," the blacksmith told him somberly.

You already told me, Roland thought. Rebecca didn't need prayers. He didn't know what she needed, but it definitely wasn't a prayer. "Thanks, Dennis. When do you think you'll have that picture ready?" Roland pressed on.

The blacksmith pursed his lips as he speculated. "I can have it ready by four if I work all afternoon."

"Four would be great. Thank you, Dennis. You don't know how much this means." Roland tried not get excited. He could deliver the picture to Henry before sunset if Dennis finished on time. "I need to go, but I'll be back at four. Thanks again, Dennis."

"You're welcome, Sheriff. I'll see you at four." Dennis didn't sound too happy about painting on his day off.

Roland tipped his hat and climbed onto his horse before Dennis changed his mind about the schedule. He knew that as soon as the funeral was over,

Dennis would start working on the picture immediately. The blacksmith's word was as good as his skill. Pangs of doubt went through Roland's mind as he rode away. He was glad that he could deliver the picture, but Roland had no confidence that Henry's method would actually work. The whole idea sounded crazy, and the Ghost Hunter had already failed several times. He had to try it, however. Roland didn't know how else Rebecca would ever awaken.

By the time he reached the church it was approaching noon. Roland hated funerals, and he was in a bad mood as he entered the church. He'd rather spend the day drunk than go to Morgan and Phillip's funeral, but he owed it to the men. A large number of people had gathered for the ceremony. Besides Ben and William, the relatives of the other eight men killed also were in attendance. Roland tried not to look at their faces as he took a seat next to his deputies. Morgan and Phillip had lived full lives as gunslingers, and both had always been prepared to take a bullet. The volunteers and innocent bystanders had never expected it. Roland felt an obligation to their relatives. It was his duty to make New Haven safe for everyone, and he had failed. He couldn't deal with it that Sunday. Maybe if Rebecca was awake, Roland would have had the courage and energy to look them in the eye.

Thatcher began the service shortly after noon. The Reverend dreaded funerals, but he always made sure that he did the dead justice. Despite the large number of bodies, Thatcher made sure to detail the qualities of all the men, which made for a long service. Roland's attention was only partially on the service. His thoughts kept drifting towards Rebecca and the picture Dennis was drawing. *It has to work,* Roland insisted to himself, but the argument rang hollow. He just couldn't make himself believe it would result in Rebecca's awakening.

When everyone began standing around him, Roland blinked in surprise and rose to his feet as well. He couldn't believe the funeral was over. It seemed as if it had just started, but Thatcher was obviously through with the service. *Morgan, Phillip, rest in peace,* he wished the two deputies before he left the church. As he walked outside, Roland shook his head in disbelief. He still found it difficult to contemplate that five of his eight deputies were dead. Only three days before, Roland had felt confidence in his strong group of deputies, but two gunfights had decimated them to the bone. As with Jack, Roland knew it would take some time before the finality of Phillip and Morgan's deaths sunk in. He'd miss the gruff veteran and the book-loving deputy. Hopefully their deaths would buy New Haven some lasting peace.

Roland fled the church before he could get dragged into any conversations with the victims' relatives. It was another three hours before Dennis would finish the portrait, and Roland didn't need his spirits any lower. *Curly,* he thought grimly as he rode his horse back to the station house. He had planned on hanging the Dark Rider that afternoon, and he saw no time better than the present. It might even take his mind off Rebecca for a short time. He knew it would help the afternoon go by more quickly.

Simon sat at the desk when Roland stormed into the station house. The deputy looked up, his back straightening when he recognized Roland. "Good afternoon, Sheriff," he greeted.

"Simon." Roland scowled but tried to take the roughness out of his voice. It was difficult to be rude to Simon. "How's Sarah?"

"She's getting close, Sheriff. We'll have a baby any day now." The deputy swelled up with pride, flashing his teeth in a wide grin.

"That's good to hear. I'm getting Curly. Why don't you stay here?" He couldn't wait to hang Curly, but Simon didn't need to see that. Roland fished the key out of his pocket with an eager grin on his face and opened the cell room door. The final end of the Dark Riders was at hand, and Roland found himself almost trembling with excitement.

Curly had been sleeping in the left cell, but he awakened the minute that Roland opened the door with a shrill metallic creak. Instantly his face twisted up in fear, and he came to his feet in a hurry. "Sheriff, w-w-what are you d-doing here?" He stuttered as he backed up from his cell door. His back pressed against the wall as he tried to push through the brick to the other side.

Roland unlocked the cell door, chuckling when he saw Curly's eyes stretch wide with terror. *Finally, you son of a bitch.* Roland couldn't believe that he was going to hang Curly at long last. He had paid a steep price for that honor, but Roland intended to enjoy it. "Get out here," Roland told the Dark Rider quietly.

"I w-wanna stay in here," Curly blubbered.

The Sheriff didn't hesitate and drew one of his pistols. He took careful aim and pointed at Curly's stomach. "Get out here now, or I swear to God, I'll shoot and let you bleed to death." He didn't raise his voice but continued to give orders in a cool, calm voice.

Curly knew that he was going to die either way, and he stumbled forward. Any death was better than a gutshot, which could last days if it didn't hit a vital organ. "Don't kill me, Sheriff. I swear I'll leave town and never come back," he begged as he shuffled his feet with great reluctance.

Roland lunged forward and swung his pistol at Curly's head. The Dark Rider grunted and collapsed when Roland struck him soundly. "Shut your Goddamn mouth, Curly, or I'll kill you right now. Now get up!" He shouted the last sentence at the Dark Rider and pointed his gun at him again.

Slowly Curly rose to his feet, rubbing one hand against his head. He looked on the verge of speaking, but after one look at Roland's gun, Curly kept his mouth shut. Wordlessly he stepped out of the cell and followed Roland into the main room of the station house.

Simon had risen to his feet and drawn his pistol when he saw Roland escorting Curly out of the cell room. "Put the gun down, Simon," Roland instructed the deputy and took a relieved breath when Simon holstered his gun; he didn't want to get shot accidentally.

The Sheriff turned back to Curly. "Hurry up, Goddamn it! I don't have all day." Roland flicked his eyes briefly towards Simon and saw that the deputy was still on his feet. "Simon, you wait here," he ordered the deputy once more.

The two men received some curious stares when they stepped outside. Roland knew that people's interest had to be at a critical high after the two gunfights, and nearly everyone had to know about the gallows. He expected a large crowd to gather as he hanged Curly. *The whole town deserves to watch him die.* Roland propelled Curly forward and stayed behind the Dark Rider, keeping his gun pointed at Curly's head. Leaning forward, he whispered, "If you say one Goddamn word, I'll kill you. Understand?" Quickly Curly's head nodded up and down. Roland smiled. "Good, now walk," he ordered roughly and pushed the Dark Rider again.

As Roland had expected, a crowd began to gather as he escorted Curly towards the gallows. It was a curious mix of people, from volunteers who had participated in the second gunfight to women and children. The crowd grew larger as they made their way down the street with more people joining when they saw the procession go by. Some shouted to Roland and jeered Curly. Roland's lips remained locked in a tight grin as they shouted their approval. He didn't care how Matthew and Alvin tried to spin this story. For once the entire town was behind his actions, and there was nothing the mayor and his flunky could do to stop it. Curly flinched every time someone called for his death, but he never slowed his pace. The gun pressed against the back of his head ensured that.

Curly did come to an immediate halt when he first saw the gallows. "No," he cried softly, but Roland shoved him forward.

"Move, Goddamn it!" He barked at Curly and debated shooting the Dark Rider on the spot. Roland didn't think that anybody would mind, but he held his fire. Hanging Curly seemed more dramatic for the town. He wanted everyone to witness and enjoy Curly's death. It wasn't supposed to be fun only for him.

The Dark Rider reluctantly shuffled towards the gallows. With each step Curly seemed to wilt, hunching down as he realized that he wasn't going to escape death this time. The crowd around him howled with appreciation as they neared the gallows. Roland was surprised by the size. He had expected a fair turnout for the hanging, but several hundred people followed him. Roland wondered how large the crowd would be if he had announced the time of Curly's execution.

"Hang the son of a bitch," a voice called out from the crowd, and Curly's knees locked in fear.

They were only twenty feet from the gallows, but Curly appeared unable to go any further. He turned to Roland desperately. His eyes bulged with terror, and his bottom lip trembled. "Please, Sheriff. I promise I'll leave town. I'll be good. I promise I'll never—"

Roland silenced him with a blow to the head with his gun. Curly fell to his knees, and everyone in the crowd yelled their approval. Sheriff Black looked up and smiled in satisfaction at the people gathered around him. He had been so worried that public sentiment would turn against him, but the crowd looked like they hated the Dark Rider almost as much as Roland did. "Get up, you son of a bitch," Roland told Curly over the loud cheering.

Tears streamed from Curly's eyes as he looked up at Roland pleadingly, but he saw the fierce expression on the Sheriff's face. He knew that his time was done. Sobbing quietly, Curly rose to his feet and stumbled forward when Roland gave him a rough shove.

Finally, Roland thought as they reached the steps of the gallows. The crowd continued to clap and cheer loudly, and Roland found himself enjoying the gathering. He knew how Zoltan must have felt when the entire town had applauded his performance. "Hurry up, Goddamn it," Roland had to shout over the din, and he pushed Curly towards the stairs.

Curly tripped on the first stair and stumbled forward. He caught himself with his hands, but the crowd laughed at the Dark Rider and lashed out with more insults. The Dark Rider looked up at the angry mob with teary eyes and rose to his feet looking stunned. He shuffled up the stairs with that defeated expression as Roland followed behind with an anxious grin.

This if for you, Jack and Morgan, Roland thought to himself. He missed Phillip, Robert, and Wade as well, but he especially missed the other two deputies. Curly's death would do little to ease their loss, but it was the best that Roland could do. "Go on," he snarled at Curly when the Dark Rider froze at the top of the steps. Curly hesitated for a moment then walked out onto the platform. Roland quickly followed him and smiled as he saw the crowd from an elevated position. Everyone looked frenzied, raising their arms and shouting at Curly.

Four nooses hung from a beam above the platform, and Roland grabbed one. Curly flinched when Roland tried to place it around his neck, and the Sheriff dropped the noose and struck him with his gun. "Hold still, Goddamn it!" He shouted and reached for the noose again. This time Curly didn't move other than a nervous tremble as Roland slipped the noose over his head and pulled it tight. Roland grinned as he looked out at the crowd and held up both hands. They quickly grew silent and waited for him to speak. He let the pause hold dramatically for a moment as Alvin had done before beginning a speech.

"This is the last Dark Rider, and I sentence him to death for his crimes against New Haven!" Roland shouted, and the entire crowd erupted in applause and catcalls.

"Die, you son of a bitch," Roland whispered to Curly and stepped back from the Dark Rider. Curly looked back at Roland pleadingly one last time before the Sheriff kicked his back. Curly lurched forward and fell off the platform. His body bounced with a sickening crunch as the rope broke his neck. He twitched twice, his legs kicking spasmatically, and then Curly was still. His body swung backwards and forwards in complete silence as the crowd watched with rapt fascination. The silence lasted for a few moments, then the crowd roared their approval.

Roland watched Curly swing at the end of the rope. He heard the deafening cheers of the crowd and wanted to share their jubilation, but he couldn't. Roland had hoped that Curly's death would help his other problems, but he knew that they were still there and just as horrible as before. Jack and Morgan were still dead, Rebecca was still asleep, and Curly's death wouldn't change that. After all his anticipation, Roland found Curly's death quite underwhelming. *At least the Dark Riders are dead,* he thought with some satisfaction. With Curly dead, there was nothing to do but wait for Dennis to finish the portrait and hope that Henry could save Rebecca this time. Roland doubted that Curly had killed Bryant, but he wanted to be positive. He was going to check on Rebecca just to be sure

He left the body and walked down the stairs, trying to ignore the congratulations that were heaped upon him. Roland didn't want to talk to anyone. He just wanted to return to the station house and continue his wait for Dennis in peace. Wading through the crowd proved difficult, however, as everyone tried to shake his hand or offer their congratulations. Roland forced his lips into a tight grin and moved through the mass of people. He didn't understand why they seemed so happy. *Jack's dead. Morgan's dead. Rebecca.* Curly was dead, but it seemed such a small repayment for all the trouble New Haven had endured.

When Roland was finally past all the people, he walked towards the station house at a brisk pace to outdistance the crowd. He stopped, however, as he saw someone he had been seeking for a few days. *Matthew.* Roland nearly salivated when he saw *The New Haven Gazette* editor standing at the back of the crowd. There was the man who had exposed Henry's secret to the entire town and caused numerous other problems, and Roland intended to teach him a lesson.

Matthew scribbled on a piece of paper, looking up from time to time at the scene around the gallows. He didn't notice Roland at first as he jotted down notes, but when the editor saw Roland bearing down on him, his face twisted in fear. "Sheriff," Matthew greeted with trepidation.

Roland grabbed the editor's arm with an iron grip. "Let's go for a walk," he told Matthew and walked down the street, pulling the unwilling editor along with him. His eyes stared straight ahead and didn't turn towards Matthew once.

Twisting his arm, Matthew tried to break Roland's grip, but Roland's hand didn't budge as it held on tight. Matthew glanced back at the crowd in alarm. He wasn't going to let Roland get him alone somewhere. He took a deep breath to yell for help, but Roland stopped him. "If you yell, I'll kill you," Roland stated quietly in a matter-of-fact tone. Matthew took one glance at Roland's face and held his tongue. Roland's jaw was locked rigidly as he ground his teeth together, and his eyes burned holes in the ground before them. Matthew knew that crossing the Sheriff wouldn't be a smart thing to do.

The office for *The New Haven Gazette* wasn't far from the gallows, and when Roland dragged Matthew there, he was pleased to see it empty. *The Gazette* was shut for business like most of the town on Sundays, but first thing Monday, Matthew and his two employees would be hard at work on their next edition. Roland didn't care about any of that. He just wanted a place where he could scare the hell out of Matthew in privacy. Roland twisted the doorknob, but it was locked. "Open it," Roland ordered flatly.

"Listen, Sheriff. I just—" Matthew broke off.

"I said open it, damn it!" Roland hissed in frustration and tightened his grip on Matthew's arm. Matthew took a deep breath, swallowed, and then pulled a key from his pocket. Roland roughly snatched the key and unlocked the door himself. "Get inside," he commanded and dragged the reluctant editor into the office.

The Gazette office was a chaotic mess of stacks of paper and ink. Roland wondered how they ever printed a newspaper in the midst of such disarray, but he wasn't there to critique the tidiness of the office. Roughly he pushed the editor against a wall and drew one of his guns. *Now we have some fun, you son of a bitch.*

All the color drained from Matthew's face the moment he saw Roland's gun. He was all too aware of what the Sheriff was capable of, having just witnessed Curly's execution. He began shaking violently, and his eyes grew wide with fear. "W-what are you doing?" Matthew asked in alarm as he tried to back up.

Roland didn't answer immediately. At first he only stared at Matthew while idly stroking the hammer of his gun with the ball of his thumb. He waited as Matthew grew increasingly more terrified. Roland planned to put the fear of God into Matthew once and for all. "Do you remember what I told you?" He asked quietly.

Matthew looked at him in confusion. "What are you talking about?" He asked nervously. Beads of sweat ran down his forehead as he stared at the gun less than a foot from his head.

"You know Goddamn well what I'm talking about!" Roland barked, and Matthew flinched against the wall. The editor closed his eyes and turned his head, preparing to be shot. *You Goddamn coward,* Roland thought loathingly. "Look at me," he told the editor, but Matthew kept his head turned away. "I said look at me!" Roland shouted at the top of his lungs. Matthew began to sob, his bottom lip quivering and tears running down his cheeks, but he obeyed Roland's order. "I told you if you printed any more lies you were a dead man. Do you remember that?"

The editor nodded. "It wasn't my fault. Alvin made me do it. He said—" he broke off as Roland held up a finger.

"I don't care about Alvin. What in Sam Hill was that Fourth of July paper? You know that was a lie. They started the fight. And what were you thinking with that story about Doc Holliday? Did you think I wouldn't get mad? Are you a Goddamn idiot?" The Sheriff's rant began softly, but by the time he was finished it had grown into a roar.

Matthew flinched each time Roland fired off a question. When Roland was finally done, the editor tried to answer. "Alvin threatened me. I promise I'll never do it again," he begged. Roland remained silent and kept caressing his gun with the ball of his thumb, waiting for Matthew to grow more desperate. "Did you hear, Sheriff? I promise I'll never do it again," Matthew insisted in a frightened voice.

Roland pretended that he didn't hear Matthew's plea. "I don't know whether I should kill you or not." Roland made it sound like he was talking to himself and trying to make up his mind.

The editor fell to his knees instantly. "Please don't kill me, Sheriff. I won't ever cross you again. I didn't mean it, I swear. Please don't kill me."

"Get up," Roland told the editor disgustedly. He was proud of the fact that when the Dark Riders held him captive, he had stared them defiantly in the eye. When Matthew reluctantly rose to his feet, Roland put the gun to his chest and pushed him back against the wall. Matthew looked down at the gun in stunned silence. "You listen to me. This is your last warning. If you ever print another story like those last two, I'll kill you. Do you understand?" He waited for Matthew to nod his head before continuing. "You're going to print two more articles. One is going to say you made everything up about Doc Holliday. He's really dead. The other is going to say you were wrong about the gunfight. The Dark Riders started it all. If I don't see it tomorrow, I'll kill you. You got that?"

Matthew nodded again, and Roland smiled his lopsided grin. He had planned to put the fear of God into the editor, and it looked like it had worked

In a smooth motion, Roland holstered his gun and walked out of the office without saying another word. Matthew was already scared to death, and there was nothing more he could say to put any more fear into the editor.

Never again would Roland have to worry about *The Gazette*. He had thought the same before, but Matthew would be a fool to thwart him now with nobody to back him up. The Dark Riders were destroyed, and Alvin could no longer use them as a bargaining tool. *Alvin!* Roland thought venomously. Alvin had caused Rebecca to remain in The Land of Shadows for weeks by lying to him about Bryant's murderer. He had time to track down Alvin and have a few words with the mayor. Roland planned to put a hell of a lot more fear into Alvin than he had into Matthew. Grimly he stalked towards the mayor's house. Thoughts of killing Alvin ran through his mind, but Roland only planned on scaring him. *You deserve to die,* Roland thought bleakly.

Roland pounded on Alvin's door when he reached the mayor house. "Alvin!" He shouted, but there was no answer from inside. Roland growled and hit the door again, but the house remained quiet. The Sheriff stared at the door for a few more minutes, debating whether or not to break it down. He wasn't entirely convinced that Alvin wasn't inside. *To Sam Hill with it,* Roland thought disgustedly and waved his hands up in the air. Alvin would turn up sooner or later, and Roland planed to be there waiting.

He stomped to The Last Frontier, fuming that he couldn't find Alvin. Roland opened the door to the saloon roughly, causing it to bang against the door frame. There was a small crowd gathered that afternoon, but Roland paid them no heed as he stalked upstairs. Roland paused outside Rebecca's door and took several deep breaths. *Let her be awake,* he thought hopefully. Opening the door, Roland went to the side of her bed and looked down at her. *Damn,* he thought. Rebecca still remained asleep.

Kneeling beside the bed, Roland took one of her hands in his own. Roland hated seeing her like this every day and was even more tired of not making any progress towards freeing her. "I love you, Rebecca," he told her. He was quiet after that as he held her hand and stared at the wall. For nearly ten minutes Roland stayed by her side until he couldn't take it anymore. He rose to his feet and placed a kiss on her forehead. "I love you, Rebecca. I'll get you out of there if it's the last thing I do." Then he stalked downstairs and out of the saloon.

His thoughts kept churning from rage to sorrow to hope to despair. He couldn't take seeing Rebecca in her weakened state anymore. Henry had to find a way to free her from Bryant. It was eating away at him. He couldn't get a handle on his temper. Every time he saw Rebecca it seemed that fate was laughing at him, telling him there was nothing he could do to help her. He yearned desperately for her to awaken from her hellish slumber. If only she was free, everything else that happened would be easier to handle. He walked to the station house and pushed open the door. In addition to Simon, Ben and William were also in the station house. Roland nodded to the three men.

"Sheriff," Ben replied, and Roland scowled when he saw the deputy's eyes light up with curiosity. "What were you doing with Matthew? We were at the hanging. Boy, was that crowded. I couldn't believe how many people showed up. We were going to talk to you afterwards, but William saw you with Matthew. You looked pretty mad. So what happened?" He asked in a rush.

Roland blinked at the onslaught of words. He was glad that the deputy had recovered from his shock, but sometimes Ben was a bit too much for him. *Hell, Ben's a bit too much all the time.* "I had a few words with him about those stories he wrote," Roland answered flatly and cracked his knuckles. He was in no mood to talk to any of his men at the moment, least of all Ben. Roland needed time to himself to cool his temper before he exploded in anger.

"Was he scared?" Ben asked, leaning forwards as he listen enthusiastically.

"Yes, he was scared, Ben. No more questions," he told the deputy roughly, and Ben nodded amiably as if Roland hadn't just barked at him. "William, I want you at The Snake tonight, and Ben, I want you on patrol. I don't think we'll have any problems, but we should be out just in case," he ordered curtly.

"Sheriff?" Simon asked when Roland paused.

"Yes, Simon?" Roland looked at the deputy.

"Where do you want me?"

"I want you to go home. Stay with Sarah. We don't need any more men. The town should be quiet after last night." Roland knew that he probably didn't need William or Ben that night either, but he wanted at least two men on duty. He could live without Simon. Besides, the deputy would be sick with worry over his wife. Roland intended to let Simon stay at home until Sarah gave birth.

Simon's face slowly stretched into a smile as he realized what Roland had just given him. "Thank you, Sheriff," he said happily.

"You're welcome. Now let's go, gentlemen. I'll be here or on patrol if you need me." Roland watched as the three men left the station house then took a seat behind the desk to begin his wait. When the men left, Roland let out a deep breath and tried to calm down. His stomach was in knots with anger and frustration. All the enjoyment that he had found by seeing Curly hang and threatening Matthew had been wiped out when he visited Rebecca. He kept looking out the window at The Last Frontier, knowing that Rebecca lay in one of the beds there, inching closer to death.

Finally he sat at his desk and counted the seconds until four o'clock. To pass the time, Roland drank a few sips of whiskey periodically. He began to pace around the office, checking his timepiece every five minutes or so. Roland stared at the timepiece's face intently as if he could speed the hands in their slow turnings. It seemed unlikely that Rebecca would awaken with the way his luck had been going, but Roland tried to believe that she would indeed emerge safely. There was nothing else for him to do. If Henry's plan failed this time, Roland was facing the very real possibility that she would never awaken from her slumber. *She will wake up,* Roland told himself fiercely then began his impatient pacing again.

When the time neared four, Roland headed straight to the door and mounted his horse. He tapped its side and quickly rode to Dennis's house. His heart beat furiously with excitement. Roland felt guilty for getting his hopes up yet again, but he simply couldn't help himself. He had to believe that this time Henry would find a way to save Rebecca. *Let it work,* Roland kept telling himself over and over. He leapt out of his saddle when he reached Dennis's house and rushed to the door. Roland knocked three times and waited impatiently for an answer. His foot tapped anxiously as he held back the urge to shout for the blacksmith.

"Sheriff," Dennis greeted when he opened the door. "I just finished it a couple minutes ago. Let me go get it for you."

The blacksmith disappeared into the house while Roland waited impatiently outside. His back straightened the moment the door opened, and he stared anxiously at the picture Dennis held. "Is that it?"

"Sure is," Dennis answered and turned it around for Roland to view. It was a small portrait, only a foot on each side, but the details were perfect. Dennis had used ink to sketch Bryant and had drawn the wrinkles under the eyes and scraggly mustache that had characterized him. Even the haughty, selfish expression that Bryant had always assumed was clearly displayed.

Roland whistled. "It's perfect," he whispered in amazement. He had seen other drawings by Dennis before, but this one seemed to be his best. Roland didn't know if his judgment was biased, but he didn't care. He had what Henry had requested, and now Roland would see if the Ghost Hunter could help Rebecca.

"Is that what you needed?" Dennis asked, breaking Roland's obsessed stare.

Roland looked up at the blacksmith. "It's perfect," he repeated. "Thank you again, Dennis. I appreciate it."

"You're welcome," Dennis responded and handed the portrait to Roland. "Sheriff," he called out as Roland quickly turned away. "You will tell me what this is about one day, won't you?"

I don't think so, Roland thought. "We'll see, Dennis. Tell Betty I said hello," Roland told the blacksmith and tipped his hat. He had a difficult time getting into the saddle as he tried to juggle Dennis's picture. Now that he finally had it, Roland didn't want to ruin it. His horse turned its head and stared at Roland curiously as he scrambled into the saddle then struggled to sit comfortably while cradling the picture. When he was settled in, he nodded to Dennis one more time and tapped his horse with his boot. Slowly the horse walked towards Roland's house.

It was a long, frustrating ride. Roland had made the trip countless times and knew it was only a short distance, but that's what made it so frustrating. He was forced to hold the horse to a slow, almost lackadaisical pace, as he held the painting carefully so it wouldn't be damaged. Roland didn't know if the ink would smear easily. He held the picture along the edges and made sure that it didn't get folded or creased. He looked up at the sky and frowned. The clouds were dark and bloated, threatening to rain on New Haven at any moment. For over a month Roland had wished for that very event, but he found himself hoping fervently that would hold off for a little while longer. Rain would destroy the portrait that he had waited on for two days.

When he arrived at his house, Roland gingerly swung his leg out of the saddle and hopped to the ground. He smiled the moment his feet struck the earth, grateful that the picture hadn't been damaged. *Now let's see if this works,* Roland thought hopefully. Holding the picture carefully, Roland walked to the door and entered the house.

Jimmy, Henry, and Singing Rock all sat in the main room. Henry and the young man seemed to be in a conversation, while Singing Rock sat quietly and watched the pair. They all looked up the moment Roland opened the door. Roland barely paid attention to the other two men. His business was with Henry. "I've got it," he proclaimed and held out the portrait for Henry to view. "Is this what you wanted?"

Henry peered at the portrait and looked up at Roland. "Does that look like Bryant?"

"Exactly like him. Dennis outdid himself," Roland answered. "So what now?" He asked anxiously.

"Give us a few minutes, and then we'll go to the house," Henry answered and started to turn around.

"*The house!*" Roland exclaimed. "You never said anything about to going back to the house."

"Calm down, Roland. I'll explain it on the way there. Now wait for us outside," Henry told the Sheriff and turned to his partner.

Roland stared at the Ghost Hunter then stormed outside. He wasn't used to waiting outside his own house, but Roland didn't want to offend Henry. *Just let it work,* Roland hoped as he paced in front of the door. When it opened moments later, Roland turned expectantly. His spirits sank when Jimmy walked outside. "Jimmy," Roland greeted and began pacing again.

"Sheriff, can I talk to you for a minute?" Jimmy asked Roland.

Blazes, not this again, Roland thought in exasperation. He didn't want to hear Jimmy ask if he could stay again. Roland looked at the gunslinger and was surprised by the look on Jimmy's face. He didn't have a cocky grin or mischievous eyes. Instead Jimmy appeared serious and determined. "What is it?"

"You said to talk to you later. Well, I want to know if I can stay in town. I know I did some stupid things, and I promise I'll behave this time. Sheriff, I really like it here. Please let me stay," Jimmy stated in a slow, dignified voice. It wasn't the pleading, desperate tone he had used before. The young man's back straightened as he awaited Roland's response.

Hell no, Roland thought immediately, but he was struck by the manner in which Jimmy had asked. The pleading and whining had grated on his nerves, but Roland appreciated the dignified manner Jimmy had just used. It calmed his fragile nerves. If Jimmy was going to ask calmly, Roland would give him a rational answer. "I can't let you stay," Roland told Jimmy and waited for an outburst, but the only sign from Jimmy was a small exhale and an almost imperceptible nod as if he had expected that answer.

"I appreciate you helping catch the Dark Riders and getting Curly after the gunfight, but I just can't let you stay. There are too many other things going on right now, and I can't risk you causing any more problems. Maybe if it was another time, I'd let you, but I'm afraid you're going to have to head on." Roland was actually going to miss Jimmy when he left, but with Rebecca still ill, he wasn't going to chance anything else going wrong. The Dark Riders were dead, and Matthew wasn't going to write any more bogus articles. Roland wanted to keep things peaceful.

Jimmy nodded again. "That's what I thought, but it was worth one more try. I'm going to head out in the morning. Thanks again for letting me stay a few extra days. Good luck, Sheriff." Jimmy held out a hand.

Roland grabbed it and shook hands with the young man. "Good luck to you as well. Stay out of trouble," he told Jimmy.

"I will," Jimmy answered, and suddenly his cocky grin was back in place. His eyes sparkled mischievously.

Liar, Roland thought and felt sorry for the sheriff of whatever town Jimmy wound up in. He'd be in for a fair amount of trouble. *But at least it's not me,* he mused with his lopsided grin. His grin disappeared instantly as the door opened and the two Ghost Hunters walked outside. Henry held the portrait in his hands, and Singing Rock carried a large wooden bowl. "Are you ready?" He asked anxiously.

Henry rolled his eyes. "Calm down, Roland. We're going to the house."

"Sorry, I'm just nervous." *Be quiet. You sound like a baby. Everything will work this time.*

"What's all this about?" Jimmy asked, watching the three men curiously.

"Can't tell you, Jimmy. If I don't see you later, good luck," Roland wished the young man and rushed to his horse. He looked guiltily at the Ghost Hunters who were making their way to their mounts a more slowly. He knew he was acting recklessly again, but he didn't care. The key to Rebecca's salvation could be in his hands shortly. Quickly he threw a leg over his saddle and waited impatiently as the Ghost Hunters mounted their own steeds. "Let's go!" He shouted and launched into a canter the moment they were in their saddles.

"Roland!" Henry barked, and the Sheriff turned around with an embarrassed grin. "Slow down. I don't want the picture to get damaged," he chastised and followed at a slower pace. Henry cradled the portrait carefully in his hands.

"Sorry," Roland muttered and forced himself to go at a walk. It was a long trip to Rebecca's house as the three men moved at a slow pace. Roland kept resisting the urge to dig his heels into the side of his horse and take off at a gallop. He wanted to hurry and have the whole ordeal over with. *Rebecca,* he thought wistfully before yanking his attention back to the matter at hand. Roland didn't want to get his head up in the clouds. Even if Henry's ritual worked, it would only identify Bryant's killer, who Roland would still have to capture. *Just ride your horse,* Roland thought to himself. There would be time for contemplation after the Ghost Hunters had finished their ritual. He spoke to Henry briefly, asking him why they had to return to Rebecca's house. The Ghost Hunter told Roland that they had to return to the scene of Bryant's murder for the ritual to work. Other than that, the three men rode in complete silence.

It appeared much darker that evening. Even though he knew dusk was over an hour away, Roland kept expecting night to fall at any moment. The dark clouds had shielded New Haven from the sun's heat the entire day and had absorbed most of its light as well. *At least it's cooler,* Roland thought gratefully. Roland's heart raced excitedly when Rebecca's house appeared before them. *Finally,* he thought with relief and had to fight the urge to gallop towards it. Henry and Singing Rock were the ones doing all the work, and there was no sense leaving them behind. *Calm down,* Roland told himself again. He knew that he was getting worked up again and was putting himself in position for another disappointment.

They dismounted their horses a hundred yards from the house, and Roland looked at it in disbelief. It looked so innocent during the day. He was so used to approaching it in the dark of night when it rose ominously from the earth. It was hard to believe that the house had caused him and Rebecca so much hell during the past three weeks. *Please let this work.*

"You ready?" Henry asked, the hint of a smile forming at the corners of his mouth.

"Yes, hurry up," Roland answered, completely missing the Ghost Hunter's sarcasm. *Please, let this work,* he repeated to himself.

"All right," Henry replied and shook his head. "Then let's go." The Ghost Hunter marched towards the house, carrying the picture, while Singing Rock followed with the wooden bowl he had brought.

Roland marched directly behind them but stopped about twenty yards from the house. "Henry," he called out uncertainly. The Ghost Hunter turned around and looked at Roland curiously. "I thought you told me not to go into the house." Roland wanted to watch their ritual, but he wasn't going to do anything to disrupt them.

Henry shook his head again. "The sun's still up. Come on. We have to hurry. We don't have much longer 'til sunset."

The Sheriff didn't need another word of encouragement and was back on the pair's heels immediately. Roland watched as they opened the door and stepped inside. He had bad memories of the last time he had entered the house. It seemed like years ago that Rebecca had been trapped in the Land of Shadows, but it had only been three weeks since his mad scramble for Running Brook's help. Roland took a deep breath and stepped inside the house.

He whistled when he saw the absolute destruction that had been wrought. "Oh my God," Roland whispered. Bryant had done a fairly good job three weeks ago, but the spirit had obviously decided to finish it. Roland remembered the crude pyramid of furniture that had formed in the middle of the room, but all that remained were splinters and fragments of the furniture. "Oh my God," he repeated in that same stunned voice.

Henry leaned over towards Roland. "I've seen a lot worse," he told the Sheriff quietly.

Roland looked at him in amazement. He wondered what could be worse than the mess he was looking at, but it wasn't the time for those sorts of questions. *Please let this work,* Roland thought again and pushed all thoughts of the house out of his mind. It was time for the ritual, and hopefully he would finally know who killed Bryant.

Singing Rock cleared a space with his foot, sweeping splinters and shards of glass away, then knelt on the ground. He placed the wooden bowl in front of his knees then looked at Henry. "Hold this," the Ghost Hunter told Roland and handed him the portrait of Bryant. Henry unfastened a waterskin from his belt and gave it to the Navajo. Singing Rock poured the water into the bowl. He pressed the palms of his hands together then began to sing over the water.

"What's he doing?" Roland whispered.

"Shh," Henry whispered right back.

Damn, Roland thought in frustration. He was going to have to wait until the Navajo was done to understand everything, and Roland's patience was extremely thin.

503

The Ghost Hunter continued to chant and sing over the bowl of water for nearly five minutes. Occasionally he reached into one of his pouches and sprinkled a bit of powder into the bowl. Suddenly he reached out a hand and looked at Henry. "Give him the portrait," Henry told Roland, and the Sheriff quickly responded. Singing Rock grabbed the picture and folded it in half twice then tossed it into the bowl of water. He pushed the paper all the way to bottom of the bowl then leaned back and glanced at Roland. "Look," the Navajo explained.

Roland heeded Singing Rock's words and stood over the bowl of water, staring at it intently. Henry ambled over and stood next to Roland as he waited impatiently. At first nothing happened, and Roland started to get a disappointing feeling in his chest. *Not again,* he thought to himself in resignation when the surface of the water suddenly glowed bright blue. "Blazes," Roland exclaimed and took a step backwards involuntarily.

"Watch," Henry told him, and Roland cautiously stepped forwards.

The bright blue light slowly faded away, and Roland watched in amazement as it waned. Quite clearly on the surface of the water, Roland could see the outside of Rebecca's house. It was night in the scene that he watched, but he was still able to see the details clearly. *Blazes,* he thought as Bryant appeared, walking towards the door. Rebecca's husband stopped and turned around. He began talking to somebody, but Roland couldn't see who it was. *Come on,* he thought excitedly. Bryant's killer stood tantalizingly off to the side, just far enough so as not to appear in the bowl. Bryant's face flushed angrily, and even though he couldn't hear what was being said, Roland knew that Bryant was arguing with the killer.

Roland watched in stunned silence as a figure suddenly rushed at Bryant. *Oh my God,* Roland thought as he saw who it was. Quickly the figure struck out and hit Bryant's head with a cane. Bryant stumbled backwards dazed, and he clutched at his head. The figure moved quickly and put Bryant in a headlock while he was stunned. A knife was in the murderer's hand a moment later, and then it was dragged across Bryant's throat with deadly force. The figure held Bryant for a moment then let him fall to the ground where he laid still, obviously dead. "Are you sure this is how it happened?" Roland whispered, completely shocked by what he saw.

"Yes," Henry answered, sounding just as stunned.

The figure turned towards the surface of the water, giving the three men their first clear view of his face, but Roland didn't need it. He had already recognized the cane and the long white hair. "Alvin, you Goddamn son of a bitch." The mayor grinned at the surface of the water with his polished oily smile, seemingly mocking Roland and boasting of all the trouble he had caused

"Oh my God," Roland uttered in bewilderment. His eyes had seen the events play themselves out in the bowl of water, but he couldn't make himself believe it. *It has to be a mistake,* Roland told himself. Why would Alvin kill Bryant? It made no sense at all. "Are you sure?" He asked Henry again.

Henry stared at the bowl of water. He shook his head in disbelief then tore his eyes away to look up at Roland with a serious expression. "It's Alvin, Roland. You saw how it happened," he answered solemnly. Henry squinted curiously at the Sheriff. "You had no idea it was him?"

That Goddamn son of a bitch, Roland cursed to himself and nearly kicked the bowl of water across the room. A powerful urge to break something welled up within him, and he had to take several deep breaths to calm himself down. "No," he answered and clenched his fists into tight balls. *Alvin, you're a dead man, you Goddamn snake.* Roland thought of all the times he could have killed Alvin over the last few weeks and saved Rebecca. He recalled them tantalizingly, each of the memories mocking him. Every time he remembered Alvin giving up Curly's name, Roland's lip quivered in rage. Alvin hadn't only killed Bryant and indirectly locked Rebecca in the Land of Shadows. The mayor had also made Roland run in circles for weeks and waste valuable time searching for fool's gold. *Alvin!*

What frustrated Roland more than anything else was the senselessness of the whole ordeal. As far as Roland knew, Alvin had no quarrels with Bryant, and cold-blooded murder seemed out of character for the mayor. Alvin had always preferred to work behind the scenes and seemed to disdain committing physical violence. Carlos or even Curly had made sense as Bryant's killer, but Alvin seemed so illogical. Singing Rock's ritual with the bowl of water, however, had been quite convincing. The scene he had witnessed seemed so lifelike, Roland had almost forgotten that he was staring into a bowl of water. Alvin did meet some of the criteria. The bruises on Bryant's head had obviously been caused by Alvin's cane, and it certainly explained the mayor's absence the night of the murder. "Goddamn it," Roland swore aloud, and the veins along his neck began to rise.

"Calm down," Henry told Roland softly but stood well back from the Sheriff. Roland's face was twisted into a grotesque mask of fury and rage. He was just going to stay out of harm's way until Roland calmed down. Singing Rock stayed even further away, silently watching the two men. The Navajo appeared completely ready to let Henry handle Roland once again.

Roland fixed Henry with a baleful gaze for a few moments, his teeth grinding against one another as anger seethed through his veins. He pointed his index finger rigidly at the Ghost Hunter and took a deep breath. "Let me get this straight. If I kill Alvin, Rebecca wakes up," he stated rather than asked.

Henry darted his eyes towards the bowl. The scene of Bryant's death had started over and showed Bryant approaching his door while Alvin remained just out of sight. The Ghost Hunter looked at Roland and nodded. "He killed Bryant. If you kill him, then Bryant has to leave the Land of Shadows. Then Rebecca will wake up."

"Good," Roland whispered fiercely and cracked his knuckles. "That son of a bitch is dead this time." *You Goddamn snake,* the Sheriff raged. Death wasn't good enough for Alvin. Roland wanted to skin him alive and let him linger in pain for a few days. Even that was too good. Rescuing Rebecca was at the front of his thoughts, but his hatred for Alvin ran a close second. Roland intended to pay him back for everything bad that had happened over the last three weeks. *You Goddamn bastard.*

"Roland, why don't we continue this outside," Henry told Roland and peered out the windows. The sun was still up, but with the dark overcast it almost looked like night. "It's starting to get dark, and I don't want to get caught in here at sunset."

Roland glanced at the window but didn't even notice the dimming light. He barely even paid attention to the Ghost Hunter. His attention was focused solely on Alvin. Roland kept replaying the image of Alvin smiling his polished, oily grin at the surface of the water. It seemed like Alvin was smiling just for Roland, mocking and laughing at him. Roland wanted to hit something when he thought of how easily he had been deceived. *You fool. You let Alvin trick you,* Roland cursed, almost as angry at himself as he was at Alvin. The mayor had given up Curly's name the night Roland had pulled a gun on him. He thought that Alvin had been in the grip of fear, but the mayor had deftly steered him in the wrong direction and forced Rebecca to spend several weeks in the Land of Shadows.

But she won't be there much longer, Roland thought grimly. He had worried that Bryant's killer would be somebody from out of town or one of the Dark Riders. Roland felt some relief that Henry's theory still held true. If the killer had been one of the Dark Riders and Rebecca was still trapped, it would have meant that Henry was mistaken about what was required to banish a spirit from the Land of Shadows. Roland knew exactly where to find Alvin. The mayor would have quite a surprise waiting for him the next time Roland saw him. Roland couldn't wait for Alvin to flash his polished grin only to have it wiped clean when Roland arrested then executed him for Bryant's murder. *Smile while you can, Alvin. I'm going to kill you this time.*

"Come on, Roland," Henry told Roland crossly. "It's getting dark." He glanced out the window anxiously.

Roland looked at the Ghost Hunter and jerked his attention back to the world around him. He took a deep breath and nodded. Standing in the house wasn't going to accomplish anything. "All right. Give me a minute," he replied and took several more breaths, trying to cool his temper. It would only be a few hours before he tracked down Alvin, and then Rebecca would finally awaken. A tiny voice in the back of his head told him not to get his hopes up again, but Roland didn't listen. This time he felt that the path to Rebecca's salvation was laid out before him. *Soon, Rebecca. Soon,* he thought with grim determination. He wasn't going to let anything deter him from rescuing her. She had spent enough time in the Land of Shadows already.

"Are you all right?" Henry asked, breaking Roland out of his reverie again. The Ghost Hunter looked concerned for Roland, but he kept his distance.

The Sheriff blinked then shook his head. He simply couldn't stop his thoughts from drifting to either Rebecca or Alvin as rage and elation kept alternately flowing through him. *Soon, Rebecca. Soon, my love,* Roland thought then tried to push all thoughts of her away. She was clouding his judgment. He needed to focus on Alvin. "I just want her to wake up. Goddamn, Alvin! When I find that son of a bitch, he's going to wish he'd never been born," Roland cursed, and his eyes flashed with rage once more.

Henry nodded quietly and exchanged a quick glance with Singing Rock. The Navajo barely shrugged his shoulders and kept quiet. Henry didn't want to say anything to Roland at that moment, but the ominous silence was worse. "Can you find him? He won't try to run, w ill he?"

Roland chuckled evilly. *You won't get away from me this time, Alvin.* After all he had been through, catching Alvin would be too easy. There was no way he would let Alvin slip through his fingers. "I'll find him. Alvin can't hide from me forever. He doesn't know I'm onto him yet, and that bastard won't leave town while he's mayor. Alvin Buckner's a dead man. By this time tomorrow, I'm going to kill him," Roland answered fiercely and clenched his fists as he imagined shooting Alvin and sending him straight to Hell.

"I don't think so," a voice replied smugly from the doorway to the bedroom.

What the hell? Roland barely had time to think before the first shot was fired. Henry grunted in pain as the Sheriff wheeled around, dropping both hands to his holsters. But Roland froze as he saw the gun pointed directly at his chest; he was quick on the draw, but not that quick. He closed his eyes in frustration, wanting nothing more than to blast away the man standing before him. "You son of a bitch," Roland whispered loathsomely.

"It's good to see you too, Roland," Alvin replied and smiled a contemptuous grin. "Put your hands up, Roland, or I'll shoot," the mayor instructed Roland and sounded as if shooting Roland would be the preferable option. Alvin didn't have his normal impeccable appearance. His hair was disheveled and tangled, his clothes were wrinkled, and his eyes gleamed with a paranoid shine Roland had never seen before.

"Goddamn it," Roland whispered in disgust and raised his arms. "What the hell are you doing here?" He asked in amazement. Rebecca's house was the last place he had expected to find Alvin. Roland looked for a chance to attack Alvin, but the mayor kept the gun pointed at him, never wavering as his eyes firmly locked on Roland.

Alvin laughed again, his trigger hand never moving. "Poor Roland. I was actually out here to hide from you. It was the one place I thought you'd never come. I was there when you came to my house earlier. You should have killed me then. To think I was actually worried about you, then you fell right into my hands." His smirk grew even wider as he taunted Roland. Even though his appearance was disheveled, Alvin still knew how to flash the arrogant smile that made Roland's blood seethe with rage. "Now back up against the wall," Alvin ordered.

Son of a bitch. Roland couldn't believe his stupid luck. It should have been trivial to kill Alvin and free Rebecca, but now Roland would be lucky if he even survived the encounter. Roland looked at Henry and grimaced. The Ghost Hunter laid on the ground, clutching his stomach as blood spread through his shirt like a crimson bloom. His eyes were closed, and his face was pale. *Blazes,* Roland thought. Gutshots were the worst. The wound looked fatal, but it could take Henry a long time to die. *Damn it, Doc,* Roland thought.

"I said up against the wall!" Alvin barked.

The Sheriff looked at Alvin and raised his eyebrows. "What about Henry?" Roland didn't think that there was anything he could do to help, but he had to make an effort. Henry had risked his life to help Rebecca, and Roland owed him for it.

"Let the son of a bitch rot. It's what he deserves," Alvin spat out and glanced at Henry with hatred burning in his eyes. Roland began dropping his hands slowly towards his holsters, but Alvin's glance was brief. "Get back against the wall and put your hands up! Now, Goddamn it!" Alvin yelled wildly and took a step forward.

"All right," Roland said quickly and raised his arms again. *You Goddamn bastard,* he seethed inside as he backed against the wall. If Alvin lived, it meant that Rebecca would remain in The Land of Shadows. That was bad enough, but he couldn't believe he was going to die like this. He had always thought that he would die at the wrong end of a gun. Roland could have accepted dying at the hands of nine Dark Riders, but the thought of Alvin killing him made Roland sick. He looked at Henry again then averted his eyes as the Ghost Hunter continued to writhe on the floor.

As Roland backed up, he noticed Singing Rock. The Navajo had stood quietly when Alvin emerged. He caught Roland's eyes then glanced once towards the window. After that brief acknowledgement, Singing Rock backed up with Roland until they were both against the wall. Roland stood still, watching Alvin intently and trying not to think of Henry as the Ghost Hunter laid bleeding on the floor.

Alvin moved forward with them and stood just over ten feet away from the pair and a scant yard from Henry's body. He smirked as he glanced at the Ghost Hunter then turned his gaze towards Roland. "Throw your gun on the floor, Roland. Slowly!" He barked the last word. Roland carefully reached for the gun on his right hip and slid it out of the holster. He threw it onto the floor and then put his hand back up in the air. *Come on,* Roland hoped that Alvin would miss his other gun. "Both guns, Goddamn it. I'm not stupid, Roland. Do it now!" Alvin's thumb caressed the hammer of his pistol as he watched Roland.

The Sheriff decided not to push the mayor. *Son of a bitch,* Roland raged as he reached down for the pistol on his left hip. He threw that one onto the floor as well and let his hands fall by his side, feeling completely helpless. Roland fired off a quick prayer. He was going to need a miracle to save himself this time. Nobody was going to ride by, and Henry wasn't going to emerge from the forest to rescue him this time. His eyebrows lowered as he watched Alvin to see what would happen next.

Alvin's shoulders relaxed once Roland was disarmed, and he tipped his head back and laughed. "Roland, I can't believe what a day it's been. First you fall out of the sky, and I get to kill Doc Holliday. You'll have to tell me how he's still alive. I thought he was already dead." He grinned at Henry's body then looked up at Roland. "It's better than he deserves, but it's the best I could come up with on such short notice." Alvin chuckled again, a dry throaty laugh. "Still, I must say it's fun to watch that son of a bitch die."

"What the hell do you want?" Roland snapped and interrupted Alvin's mocking. *Rebecca,* he thought in frustration. Roland knew that his only hope for escape was to make Alvin angry. If the mayor was calm, he wouldn't make any mistakes. Roland would consider it a fair trade to trade his life for Alvin's. At least Rebecca would awaken. It was a small chance, but Roland didn't know what else he could do.

"Shut up," Alvin snapped right back, and his eyes narrowed dangerously. "I can kill you two ways. A quick shot through the heart, or like him," the mayor told Roland and pointed at Henry's body.

Damn, Roland thought when he glanced at the Ghost Hunter. Henry continued to bleed, and a small pool of blood had formed under him. His face was completely drained of color, and if not for the almost imperceptible rising and falling of his chest, Roland would have sworn he was dead. *Not much longer,* he thought. Henry only had another five or ten minutes before he bled to death. This time Doc Holliday would not make one of his miraculous escapes from the jaws of death. He nearly had to bite his tongue, but Roland kept silent and stared at Henry with blazing eyes. *I'm sorry, Henry. Rest in peace.*

509

"Good," Alvin stated when he saw that Roland would be quiet and listen. "Now why don't you tell me what you're doing out here. And what happened to this place. Did you lose your temper again, Roland?" Alvin laughed.

Roland's fists clenched tightly, and he felt the blood boil in his veins every time Alvin chuckled. It took all of his restraint not to rush the mayor on the spot. He'd be shot instantly, but he might get lucky and tackle Alvin. Hopefully Singing Rock could finish Alvin at that point. *Stay clam,* Roland told himself. *Think about Rebecca.* Getting himself killed foolishly would abandon Rebecca in The Land of Shadows. He was her only hope for escape, and he couldn't act recklessly even though he expected Alvin to shoot him and leave him for dead.

"Answer me, Roland, or I'll shoot the Injun," Alvin threatened when Roland fumed silently. The Navajo continued to alternate looking at Henry and Alvin. His face was calm as if he wasn't worried and expected the danger to disappear.

Goddamn you, Alvin, Roland raged, but he quickly began speaking. He had already gotten Henry killed, and Roland wasn't about to jeopardize Singing Rock any more than he had to. They would all likely die, but he wanted to keep a small hope alive. *Calm. Stay calm.* "We just needed a quiet place to talk. That's all," Roland answered in a contemptuous whisper. "I don't know what happened here. I figured it was Carlos. That son of a bitch knew how I felt about Rebecca," Roland lied in that same even tone, his face never budging an inch. Alvin had lied to him with absolute conviction, and Roland could certainly return the favor. *Two can play at that game.* Roland didn't know how much good would come out of lying, but Alvin would never believe the real reason why they had come to the house.

Alvin's eyes narrowed again as he studied Roland's face. "I think you're lying, Roland," he accused.

"Why would I lie?" Roland asked immediately. *Be careful,* Roland thought cautiously. It wouldn't take much to make Alvin shoot him. "Everyone thinks he's dead," Roland stated and pointed at Henry. "And who else would destroy the house? I sure as hell didn't. Why would I?" Roland asked indignantly.

The mayor studied Roland carefully then finally nodded. " Now tell me how you found out I killed Bryant."

You son of a bitch. Roland had still doubted that Alvin was the murderer, but the mayor's question confirmed it. "Why, Goddamn it? You had no reason to kill him."

Alvin laughed derisively at Roland. "You don't know what you're talking about. That son of a bitch was stealing from me. I caught him taking money from one of Carlos's heists so I killed him. It was all business, Roland. Nobody crosses me. You should have learned that a long time ago." He laughed again. "Now tell me how you found out it was me. I thought I had covered it up pretty well."

A deep growl formed at the back of Roland's throat as Alvin mocked him, but there was nothing he could do. *Damn it,* he raged. He gladly would have sacrificed his own life at that moment to see Alvin die, but he didn't have the opportunity. Roland quickly calmed himself and hesitated only a moment to think of a lie before answering Alvin's question. He didn't think that Alvin would believe Singing Rock's ritual had yielded the answer. "Curly told me," Roland lied again.

Instantly Alvin's face contorted in rage, and he fired a bullet above Roland. It struck the wall and showered splinters onto Roland's head. "Don't lie to me, Roland. The next one hits your Injun friend. Curly thought Carlos killed Bryant. I told the stupid son of a bitch to take credit for it, and Carlos bragged about it to all the Riders. Now tell me how you found out."

Blazes, he thought in amazement. He had thought that Curly was lying about Carlos, but the Dark Rider had been as clueless as himself. "Henry figured it out," Roland answered before Alvin fired another bullet. "He used some Indian trick. I don't know how it works, but he figured out it was you. I know it's hard to believe, but it's true." He couldn't think of anything else to say without the risk of setting the mayor off.

Alvin stared at Roland loathsomely for a moment then his eyes narrowed to tiny slits. "You're right. I don't believe you," he told Roland and fired his gun again.

Singing Rock grunted in pain as the shot struck him in the shoulder, and he fell to his knees. "Blazes," Roland whispered. He had expected Alvin to kill them all, but he had hoped that he would be shot before the Navajo. Roland had dragged the Ghost Hunters into his affairs, and he felt guilty that they were going to die first. He looked down at Singing Rock in concern. The Navajo's jaw was clenched, and his right arm hung uselessly by his side. Quickly he looked up at Roland. "Dark," he mouthed silently. *What the hell?* Roland thought to himself before Alvin interrupted.

"I told you not to lie to me, Roland, but I don't really care how you found out." Alvin waved the matter off as if it was of no consequence even though he had just shot someone over it. His eyes flitted towards Singing Rock and barely rested on him before they returned to Roland. "I can't let that little secret get spread over town, can I? Who else knows, Roland? Did you tell anyone else? I'll kill him this time, Roland. Don't push me," he warned. Alvin's eyes glowed with a paranoid sheen.

Roland took one look at Alvin and knew that he couldn't tell him the truth. Alvin looked insane as he pointed his gun at Singing Rock, and Roland didn't think that Alvin would believe nobody else was in on his secret. "Morgan," Roland answered safely. "Morgan knew, but he's dead. That's it."

He knew that signed his death warrant. The only reason he was alive was to provide answers for the mayor, and he had just outlived his usefulness. At least Alvin wouldn't go after anybody else. If he had used William or Ben's name, Roland had no doubt that Alvin would try to kill them as well.

Alvin tipped his head back and laughed. His eyes lost their paranoid sheen and turned maliciously gleeful. "Perfect," he cried out exultantly then looked at Roland with false sympathy painted on his face. "Oh, Roland. I believe that makes you expendable. Sorry, but I'm going to have to kill you."

"Go to hell," Roland snapped. He knew that he was going to die this time, but Roland straightened his back and looked at Alvin with contempt. He intended to go out defiantly

"Not before you," Alvin chuckled. "I just want to know one thing. How is he still alive? I thought he got shot two days ago." Alvin pointed at Henry's body, never taking his eyes or his gun off Roland.

Roland glanced at Henry's body and paused when he saw the Ghost Hunter. Henry's eyes opened for a brief moment, and he looked at Roland dully. "Dark," he mouthed, and then his eyelids slowly closed. *Dark. What the—Blazes, they mean nightfall,* Roland thought excitedly. Roland looked out the window and saw how the light was dimming. The sun would soon sink on the horizon, and things would become much different in the house. *Not much longer.*

"Have it your way then," Alvin stated.

Roland looked at Alvin and quickly held out his hands. "I'll tell you. Just don't shoot," he implored the mayor pleadingly. Roland hated to make his voice sound so weak, but if he could pull the wool over Alvin's eyes for just a little bit longer, Roland would have the last laugh.

Alvin's grin spread even wider as he watched Roland beg for a few more minutes of life. "Roland," he muttered condescendingly and shook his head. "Fine, tell me how he's still alive."

Just a few more minutes, Roland thought in relief. "Zoltan showed him how to fake his death like in his performance," Roland dragged out his words, trying to stall as much as possible.

"And that gunslinger was in on it?"

Roland nodded. "And Thatcher and Sullivan. They also set the fire to break Jimmy out of jail. I didn't find out about it until later. It was a ruse to catch all the Dark Riders. I followed them out into the forest and straight to Marshall, Curly, and some of the others. We caught half, but Carlos was somewhere else. Then the second gunfight happened."

"Carlos was with me," Alvin told Roland tauntingly. His eyes watched Roland predatorily to see how he would react.

"What?" Roland burst out in surprise. "I thought you wanted him dead."

"Oh, I did, Roland. Thank you for taking care of that for me. I wish it could have been me pulling the trigger, but the results are what matters. It's a shame about the Fourth of July. You were both supposed to die that night. I tried to shoot you, but I missed. It's a shame. I always liked Jack. It took a few extra days, but I've finally got you both." Alvin smiled cruelly as he watched Roland's face twist into a mask of rage.

"You Goddamn bastard son of a whore," Roland spat out venomously, completely forgetting his tactic of stalling. He nearly charged the mayor at that moment, and only a tremendous amount of restraint made him hold still. *Remember Rebecca,* he told himself. Rushing into a confrontation wouldn't help her. *Stall him,* he reminded himself and cooled his nerves for at least the moment. "Why the hell did you do it, Alvin? It was your celebration." Roland didn't understand Alvin. He had been the most popular man in New Haven that night, and he had sabotaged it for no reason.

"You two shouldn't have pulled guns on me, Roland. I always get even. It might take me a while, but I always get even eventually. You, Carlos, and Doc. It's been a good week." Alvin oozed with a contemptuous mocking that made Roland's blood seethe, then the mayor shrugged his shoulders as if he was tired of bantering words. "It was good knowing you, Roland." The mayor closed one eye, and his arm tensed as he prepared to fire.

"Wait!" Roland cried out. He looked out the corner of his eye and saw it was nearly dark outside. *Damn it, not much longer,* Roland thought desperately. He was so close. Roland didn't want to fall short with only seconds to go. "Please don't kill me," he begged and dropped to his knees. Roland put his hands together and looked up at Alvin with the most pathetic expression he could muster.

Alvin looked at Roland in amazement. "Oh, Roland," he said pityingly. "I thought you'd die on your feet, but I guess I was wrong." He shook his head ruefully one more time. "Goodbye," Alvin told Roland then stopped as a loud creak echoed throughout the house. "What's that?" He asked in surprise and looked around warily, trying to find who or what had caused the noise.

About Goddamn time, Roland thought excitedly as he watched Alvin cautiously. Night had finally fallen, but Roland wasn't out of danger yet. Alvin still held his gun, and it would only take one bullet to kill him. *Hurry up,* Roland thought anxiously. *Attack him.* Cool air swept through the house suddenly, and Roland felt goosebumps rise on his arms and neck. He looked longingly at his guns lying on the floor while Alvin peered around. The guns weren't far away, but they were still far enough.

The mayor shivered as cold air brushed by him. "What the hell's going on?" He muttered then turned back to Roland. His eyes narrowed when he saw Roland staring at the pair of guns. "Go ahead, Roland. Try it," Alvin taunted. "You're not that quick."

Damn! It wouldn't be much longer now. Alvin had no idea about what was about to happen in a matter of seconds. *Hurry up, Bryant!* Roland looked at Alvin contemptuously and smiled his lopsided grin. He didn't say a word but knelt quietly with his mocking grin and waited for Bryant to fully emerge.

Alvin stared at Roland and scowled at the grin on the Sheriff's face. He raised his gun, pointing it at Roland, but a loud knock boomed from the center of the room. Instantly Alvin's eyes grew wide with fear, and he looked around nervously. "What the hell?" He repeated and took a step backwards involuntarily. "What's going on, Roland? Who else is here? Goddamn it, I'll shoot." Alvin stared at Roland with a paranoid gleam in his eyes, and his feet kept shuffling as if he expected to have to turn around and shoot.

Roland felt the air grow thick around him as the sun disappeared over the horizon. He remembered that feeling all too well from the last time he stepped foot inside the house. A low hum buzzed through the house like several bees in the distance. *Just a few more seconds,* he thought desperately.

The mayor looked at Roland with wide eyes. The gun nearly shook in his hand as he pointed it at Roland. "I said what the hell's going on, Roland. Answer me, Goddamn it!" He shouted. Roland held his breath as he waited for Bryant to make his full appearance. *Please,* he thought and scrunched up his eyes as he waited to see if Bryant or Alvin would act first. Alvin's bottom lip curled in hatred as Roland stayed silent. "Fine, die then, you son of a—" he broke off in shock as a spark of blue electricity jumped through the air in front of him. It crackled over the humming noise momentarily, and then another loud knock boomed through the house.

Yes! Roland exulted. A few more sparks leapt through the air, casting a faint blue light over the room. It gave Roland just enough light to see how truly terrified Alvin's face had become. Alvin took another two steps backwards, and his jaw dropped open in fear. His gun was pointed at the ceiling in a weak grasp. Alvin seemed to have forgotten Roland completely in his terror. The mayor's eyes shifted from side to side, looking at the blue sparks with a cross between wonder and fear. Roland had seen enough of the house to be prepared. His heart still raced in his chest, and the sparks leaping through the air made him scared as hell. But he wasn't as stunned as the mayor. "Goodbye, Alvin," Roland whispered.

"What?" Alvin exclaimed and swung his gun nervously towards Roland. He jumped again as another knock sounded in the middle of the room. "What the hell's going on?" He screamed at Roland. The blood drained from his face as a cascade of blue sparks leapt through the air directly in front of him. He jumped back from them and put his hands up defensively.

"*Die!*" Bryant's raspy voice echoed through the air, and the house exploded with activity. Alvin's gun slipped from his numb fingers as the tattered remains of furniture rose into the air and danced about. Sparks of blue light

514

crackled throughout the room, casting a faint glow over the house. Splinters and shards of glass swirled into the middle of the room and formed a twisting funnel with sparks of electricity leaping through the air around it. The front door began to open and close frantically, and the faint hum grew into a loud buzz that drowned out nearly all other sounds. *"Die!"* Bryant roared again.

Roland watched as Alvin was lifted into the air. "No!" The mayor screamed and flailed his arms and legs frantically, but that didn't seem to deter Bryant. Slowly Alvin was twisted until his feet pointed at the ceiling and his head was a foot above the floor. His long white hair hung down in a tangled mess, and his eyes were wide with fear. He stretched a hand out, trying desperately to touch the floor, but he was roughly hurled across the room before he had any success. Alvin hit the far wall with a sickening crunch then bounced off and fell to the floor. *Blazes,* Roland thought as he remembered his own assault at the hands of Bryant. It was safe to get his guns, but Roland made no move as he watched Bryant attack Alvin.

"Die!" Bryant shouted over the loud buzz, and Alvin looked up weakly. He barely had time to react before a battered chair ceased its lazy pirouettes and hurtled towards Alvin. It struck Alvin with a bone-crunching thump and bounced off the mayor. Alvin reeled back and cried out as blood streamed from his nose and a cut over his eyes. *"Die!"* Bryant shrieked, and Alvin only had a few seconds before the chair flew at him again. This time Alvin was hit in the ribs, and he curled into a ball as he tried to protect himself from the furious onslaught. Objects began a relentless assault on the mayor, hurling themselves at him one after another. Roland watched as broken furniture, books, and pots launched themselves at the prone mayor.

Alvin stayed balled up, wincing each time he was hit but not budging from his protective position. *"Die!"* Bryant's voice echoed through the house, and Alvin was raised into the air one more time. Roland felt another cold gust of air blow through the room, making him cradle his arms and shiver. Alvin tried to stay curled in a protective ball, but his body began to spin about violently. Alvin flailed his arms wildly, trying to grab something to stop him, and Bryant hurled Alvin across the room again. The mayor bounced from the wall and laid still on the floor.

Roland stared at Alvin carefully as the house grew quiet. *Is he dead?* He wondered. Objects continued to float in the air, and sparks of blue light crackled. Roland began inching towards his guns. *"Die!"* Bryant shrieked, and Roland leapt back, huddling against the wall. At least a dozen cascades of light flared to punctuate Bryant's cry. *"Die!"* Once again Alvin was raised into the air. Alvin didn't put up a fight that time, his arms and legs dangling weakly as Bryant lifted him. His eyes opened, and the mayor looked up at the ceiling exhaustedly. Alvin didn't appear frightened, but rather stunned, tired, and ready for the whole ordeal to end.

The funnel of splinters and shards of glass spun its way towards Alvin. It tore into Alvin with a spray of blood, and Alvin twisted about, trying to escape. His arms rose defensively to protect his face, and he cried out as splinters and glass ripped into and became embedded in his flesh. "Stop! Please, help me!" Alvin shrieked over the loud buzzing. "Make it stop!" Roland could see blood dripping onto the floor and covering nearly every stretch of skin on the mayor's body.

Now, Roland thought and dove forward for his guns. *"Mine!"* Bryant yelled over the din, and sparks of light flared all around the room. Roland ignored it all and breathed a quick sigh of relief as his fingers wrapped comfortably around one of his dependable guns. He was scared out of his mind with all the calamity swirling around him, but Roland suddenly felt much safer with a gun in his hand. Roland had felt naked when he was unarmed, but he rose confidently to his feet and pointed the gun at Alvin. *Now you die, you son of a bitch.*

"Mine!" Bryant shrieked). The entire room flashed with blue light, and a gale of cold air rushed through the house.

Roland shivered and blinked his eyes to clear them of the flash of light. He took careful aim. "I don't think so," he whispered and squeezed the trigger three times. The first two bullets struck Alvin in the chest, and the third hit in the middle of his forehead. Blood spurted from all three wounds, and Alvin gave one last sigh before his head fell forward and rested against his chest. Roland stood numbly and stared at Alvin, hardly able to believe that the mayor was finally dead. He wanted to dance for joy, but the whole ordeal had left him numb with shock. *Rebecca,* he thought with tired relief. At long last she would finally awaken. *Rebecca, my love.* Roland gave a tiny prayer that he would survive and see her awake once more. He stood his ground and tensed his body, waiting for Bryant to lash out at him for killing Alvin.

The buzzing, however, began to wane as soon as Alvin took his final breath. *"Mine!"* Bryant shrieked, but his voice was softer and didn't even cause an echo in the house. Roland put his hands up defensively as a broken chair wobbled awkwardly through the air at him, but it fell to the floor nearly six feet away. "What the hell?" Roland whispered as more and more objects fell to the floor. The door stopped its incessant noise as it slammed shut then remained motionless.

A sudden flash of blue sparks caused Roland to jump, but they quickly faded. The last of the furniture fell to the floor with loud thumps in the darkening room. Only splinters, books, and shards of glass lumbered in lethargic, jerky motions through the air, and even they began to fall like wounded flies. *"Mine!"* Bryant whispered as the humming noise completely waned. *Oh my God,* Roland thought in amazement as Bryant's power disappeared before his eyes. There was one last flare of blue light in the middle of the room, and Bryant's voice

516

rang out through the house one last time. *"Mine!"* He wailed, but it was a far cry from his previous bellowing. Then the air grew warm around him, and Roland felt the tension leave the room as the last few objects fell to the floor.

"Good God," Roland whispered. He blinked several times and tried to make out details in the suddenly dark house. The blue sparks had scared the hell out of him, but they had at least provided light. A bright yellow glow suddenly covered the room, and Roland wheeled around with gun in hand. He stopped as he saw Singing Rock casting a handful of yellow powder into the air. "Blazes, you scared me." Roland put a hand over his heart, relieve to see it was only the Navajo and not Bryant. "Is that it? Is he gone?"

"He is gone," Singing Rock answered. "Please move," he told Roland and rushed past him to Henry's side. Blood covered Singing Rock's shoulder, but he moved as if the wound didn't bother him.

"Damn," Roland whispered as he looked at Henry's body. Even in the faint light, Roland could see the blood that had soaked his shirt and formed a large pool under him. The Ghost Hunter had no color in his face as he laid still with his eyes closed. "Is he dead?" Roland asked quietly. Seeing Henry doused his jubilation over killing Alvin. *Please let him be all right,* Roland thought even though he knew that the wound was fatal.

Singing Rock didn't answer for a moment as he knelt over his partner. Suddenly he turned to Roland, and the Sheriff was surprised to see the Navajo's eyes burn intensely. "He still breathes. Get me light. I cannot see," he told Roland and leaned back over Henry. Singing Rock chanted over his wounded partner.

Roland didn't hesitate. He ran outside and towards the trees where their horses were tied. His chest burned by the time he reached Henry's horse, but he wasted no time as he quickly looked through the saddlebags for a lantern. As soon as he found one, Roland dropped the saddlebag and rushed back into the house. He paused at the doorway and lit the lantern so that light filled the inside of the house. "Here you go," Roland told Singing Rock as he placed the lantern beside Henry's body.

"Hmm," Singing Rock grunted as he put his hands on Henry's chest. He placed his head just above Henry's shirt and held it there, listening intently.

"What is it?" Roland asked worriedly. It was killing him to look at Henry and all the blood on the floor. He had seen corpses that looked better than Henry did. Bryant's murderer was dead, but once again somebody close to Roland had paid a steep price. *Damn it, it's not fair,* Roland thought bitterly.

Singing Rock didn't answer but started to chant and sing in Navajo over Henry's body. Roland watched in frustrated silence. *Rebecca,* he thought hopefully but made himself stay right where he was. He could check on her once he knew what Henry's condition was. The Ghost Hunter had risked his life to help Rebecca, and that's the least that Roland owed him. His fingers tapped anxiously along his thigh, though. Henry had said that Rebecca would awaken once Bryant's murderer was dead, but Roland tried not to get his hopes up too high even after everything he had seen. *Please, let her be awake,* Roland kept repeating over and over as he dreamed of finally seeing her awake again. Roland was so busy with thoughts of Rebecca floating through his mind that he didn't notice Singing Rock at first. "Sheriff," the Navajo repeated.

"What?" Roland shook his head and looked at Singing Rock. "What is it? How is he?" Henry still looked awful. He was drenched in blood, and his face was ashen. But Roland had seen firsthand how well Running Brook could heal, and Singing Rock had cured Henry of tuberculosis five years before. Even though a lifetime of gunslinging told him that Henry's wound was fatal, Roland wasn't going to discount Singing Rock's skill.

"He is weak, but I will try to save him," Singing Rock reported as if he was discussing the weather.

Try? "Can you save him?" He asked insistently.

"We will see. His body must heal itself. I can only encourage him. You should go, Sheriff. Your woman is waiting. I will do what I can," Singing Rock told Roland and turned back to Henry. He placed his hands on the Ghost Hunter's chest and began to sing again.

Roland watched the Navajo silently for a few moments. He couldn't understand a single word Singing Rock chanted, but he assumed that he would help the Ghost Hunter. Roland felt guilty leaving the house, but the moment Singing Rock had told him to leave, he felt his heart race in excitement. *Rebecca,* his thoughts kept turning to her over and over. "Are you sure?" He asked Singing Rock dubiously, but the Navajo ignored Roland as he chanted over his wounded partner. Roland waited a few moments for an answer, but when none came, he took one last look at Henry and rushed from the house.

A tiny voice of guilt remained at the back of his head, but Roland tried to push it as far away as possible. *Rebecca.* He wanted Henry to live, and he would return soon to check on him. Roland, however, had to know if Rebecca was awake or not. *Rebecca. Rebecca.* Blood raced through his veins as he sprinted towards his horse. His legs were tired, and his chest burned. Yet he pushed beyond his body's exhaustion, barely noticing it as he rushed towards the trees. Seeing Rebecca was all that mattered. He finally had reason to believe she would actually awaken. *Rebecca.*

The knots on the rope tethering his horse were frustrating as Roland hastened to undo them. His fingers kept fumbling in his haste, and he shouted a cry of victory when he unfastened them. *Rebecca.* He swung his legs over the saddle and catapulted himself onto his horse. "Hya!" Roland yelled and dug in his heels. Quickly the horse took off at a gallop, and the two were flying towards town. Roland was forced to slow down a few times as they raced in the dark. The last thing that he wanted was to fall from the horse and ge injured. It was agonizing to slow down to even a canter, but once he was on the main road to town, Roland dug in his heels again. "Hya!" He yelled again, and they galloped the rest of the way.

It took less than ten minutes to return to The Last Frontier, but it seemed an eternity to Roland. The lights of town seemed to hover just over the next hill, and even when he rode into town, Roland couldn't gallop down the street fast enough. *Rebecca.* Her face was burned into his mind, and he had to see her. *Please, let her be awake. Rebecca.* People watched Roland as he raced past, but he didn't notice any of them. His focus was only on Rebecca.

He leapt out of the saddle when he reached The Last Frontier. Roland didn't even bother to tether his horse as he rushed inside. Nearly every eye in the saloon turned towards the Sheriff, but he ignored them all as he ran to the stairs. Most people quickly stepped out of his way, and Roland brushed aside those who weren't that smart. He got a few rude stares, but by that time he was already climbing the stairs, taking them two at a time as he rushed to Rebecca's room. *Rebecca,* he thought wildly. *Please, let her be awake. Please.*

His hand trembled as he reached into his pocket and withdrew the key to her room. He had to try three times to put it into the keyhole with his shaking hands before he succeeded. When it unlocked, Roland flung open the door. Once again the smell of sickness hung in the air, but Roland didn't pay it any heed. *Rebecca.* He quickly lit a lantern, and his spirits sunk to rock bottom as he saw Rebecca. Her skin was still pale, and her cheeks were hollow. The lustrous curls he had always loved hung in tangled snarls. Roland hadn't expected that to change. She had been bedridden for over two weeks. But Roland wanted to punch a wall in frustration as he saw that her eyes were still closed.

No! He wailed to himself. Roland stood quietly in the center of the room for a few moments, wanting to cry. Once again, he had been denied Rebecca's salvation, and Henry had been injured for nothing. *No!* Roland opened his eyes and gazed at her tearfully. He saw past the weakened body and remembered the vibrant woman he loved. It tore at his heart to see her in the bed another day. He crossed the room and knelt by her side.

"Rebecca," he whispered and brushed a knuckle across her forehead tenderly. Her skin felt so cold. He closed his eyes as he felt tears well at the corners. *No!* He thought again. *It's not fair. Rebecca!* Roland longed to see her smile and her sparkling eyes again. It had been so long, so awfully long. He had no idea how he'd ever free her from The Land of Shadows. *Rebecca!*

"Roland," a weak voice called out falteringly, and Roland instantly opened his eyes and pulled back from the bed with a gasp. His lips curled into a tremulous smile as he looked at Rebecca. She stared at him with her marvelous green eyes. They were clouded and bleary from nearly three weeks of sleep, but they were the most beautiful thing Roland had ever seen. Her own lips curled into a pale shadow of its usual brilliance, but Roland thought it could set the world on fire.

"Rebecca," he whispered and wrapped his arms around her, burying his face in her dark hair. He closed his eyes and held onto her as if he would never let her go. "Rebecca," he whispered again in her ear. "Roland," she answered and wrapped her arms weakly around him, and he knew that everything would be all right once more.

Chapter Twenty-Seven

"Are you sure you're up to it?" Roland asked worriedly for the fifth or sixth time, his face scrunched up with concern.

"Roland Black, if you don't stop asking that, I'm going to get cross with you," Rebecca answered and put her hands on her hips. She fixed him with a facetious glare then ruined it by smiling. "For the last time, I feel fine. I need to get out of this room." Rebecca looked disapprovingly at the walls around her. "I've been here for too long."

"All right," Roland responded and put his hands up defensively. He was worried for her but had to admit that she looked fit enough to survive a short walk. "You win." He opened the door to her bedroom and stepped aside, sweeping an arm out dramatically. "Shall we?"

"I thought you'd never ask." Rebecca walked towards the opened door but stopped as Roland wrapped an arm about her waist. "Roland?" She asked in confusion before his head descended, and he placed a single kiss on her lips. "What was that for?" Rebecca asked and looked up at him demurely.

"I just felt like it," Roland answered, grinning like a boy with his hand in the cookie jar. "Now I'm ready," he told her. Roland escorted her into the hallway then locked the door behind them. "All right, let's go see him." He held out an elbow, and she inserted her arm in the proffered opening.

Rebecca didn't say anything as they walked down the stairs, but her smile spoke volumes. It had been one week since Rebecca had awakened from her long slumber, and she still bore signs of her three weeks in the Land of Shadows. She had, however, made remarkable strides in the last seven days. Her cheeks, which had been so hollow, were almost as full as before her encounter with Bryant, and her hair was washed, combed, and looking as lustrous as Roland could remember it. Most importantly, her emerald eyes had regained their former sparkle, and she smiled so brightly that Roland's heart nearly melted every time he saw it.

It was her first trip outside the saloon in nearly a month, and Rebecca looked anxious. She smiled uncontrollably at the large crowd in The Last Frontier that Sunday afternoon, her eyes sparkling merrily. Roland beamed as he walked beside her, happy to see her in such a good mood. The memories of her sojourn in the Land of Shadows were beginning to fade the more time passed.

She wore a green dress that afternoon, one of the dresses Roland had fetched from her house before proposing to her what seemed like years ago. The rest of Rebecca's dresses had been destroyed during Bryant's rampage, but Dotty had volunteered a few from her closet. . Shortly after Rebecca had awakened, Dotty left town to live with her sister in Georgia. Roland hated to see her go, but he knew it was best for her.

The Last Frontier was loud that afternoon as a sizeable crowd gathered to drink and play cards. Roland spotted the customary card players and Sherry's girls trying to attract a few customers. William sat at one of the tables, supposedly keeping an eye on the saloon, but he looked busier flirting with Heather than anything else. George was also busy that afternoon, bustling about the saloon to chat with customers, keeping the saloon tidy, and making sure that everything ran smoothly. He paused in the midst of a conversation as Roland headed down the stairs, quickly excused himself, and approached the couple with a wide grin on his chubby face. "Sheriff, Miss White, how are you this afternoon?"

"We're fine, George. How are you?" Rebecca asked before Roland could answer, which still took Roland by surprise. One of the first things that Roland had noticed after Rebecca awakened was her outgoingness. Rebecca had always been shy on her few trips to town, but that had changed. Ever since her time in The Land of Shadows, Rebecca was feistier and would regularly talk to people other than Roland. He loved every minute of it. They had always been limited to visiting at her house before, but now she seemed eager to sit downstairs at The Last Frontier.

"I'm doing fine, Miss White. I just wanted to say hello. Do you two need anything?"

"Nah, George. We're going for a walk. I'll talk with you later," Roland told the saloon owner.

"All right, Sheriff," George answered and went back to scurrying around the bar.

"What a lovely day," Rebecca commented as they walked outside, and Roland had to agree. It was a cool day that afternoon, and there was a fair amount of cloud cover. The day after Rebecca awakened, rain had finally fallen on the town. Ever since then the temperatures had dropped, and New Haven began having pleasant weather once more.

"That it is," Roland agreed and escorted Rebecca towards the church. He had a hard time looking at the station house even though it was being repaired. New glass had been installed in the windows, and Lewis was working on fixing the bullets holes. Still, it looked like a disaster and served as a grim reminder of all the trouble that the Dark Riders and Alvin had wrought. Roland just looked forward to the day it was fully repaired. He didn't know how much need there would be for a station house with the Dark Riders destroyed, but Roland wanted one. It was a symbol of his and the deputies' authority, and one never knew what further troubles could hit the town.

For now, though, Roland just wanted to enjoy his walk with Rebecca. They chatted as they ambled across town hand in hand. They talked about their upcoming wedding and various other topics, but they avoided discussing The Land of Shadows or the fallen deputies. Roland had told Rebecca about Jack,

Morgan, and the others the day after she had awakened, but he chose not to drudge up those memories anymore. He still missed all of his fallen deputies, but Roland wanted to move on and not dwell on all the bad things that had happened recently. With Rebecca awake, there were much happier things to think about. Rebecca didn't want to talk about her time in The Land of Shadows at all. Roland had asked her once what it had been like to be trapped there, but Rebecca had shuddered and cried. After that incident, Roland let the subject drop. Perhaps one day Rebecca would want to speak of it just as he would lose his reluctance to discuss Jack and the others, but until then they left those subjects alone.

The streets were crowded that afternoon, and several people waved or greeted the pair as they walked by. Roland tipped his hat each time, while Rebecca flashed her dazzling smile and waved in return. It was good to see everyone again and have that interaction. Roland had missed Rebecca the most during her slumber, but he had missed his rapport with the people of New Haven a great deal as well. "Uh oh," Roland muttered as he saw Ben riding towards them.

"What is it?" Rebecca asked worriedly, the smile slipping from her face as she looked at Roland.

Roland just shook his head ruefully. "It's nothing," he answered and waited for the onslaught to begin.

True to form, Ben approached them with his wide-eyed look of curiosity painted across his face. "Sheriff, Miss White," he greeted then launched into a flurry of questions before either of them could respond. "My, it's a nice day we're having. It hasn't been like this in a while. I guess you're feeling better, Miss White? I haven't seen you leave The Frontier since you were sick. Where were you two going? Are you just out on a walk?"

Rebecca stared at Ben incredulously. She had met Ben once before but had never been subjected to his incessant questions. Roland had told her several times what Ben was like, but that wasn't quite the same. "We're doing fine, Ben, but we're in a hurry. I'll talk with you later. Good afternoon," he dismissed the deputy and tipped his hat. Rebecca was feeling better and had become more talkative, but Roland didn't think she was ready for Ben.

"Oh, all right. Good afternoon, Sheriff. The same to you, Miss White," Ben responded and looked as if he wasn't the slightest bit offended for being cut off.

Rebecca appeared a bit overwhelmed as they moved on. She looked over her shoulder at the deputy and shook her head. "You told me about him, Roland, but I never quite believed you. Oh my," she commented.

"You had to see him before you'd understand. Don't worry, though, he's harmless. He'll just talk your ear off," Roland laughed.

They found Thatcher in the church as Roland had expected. Sunday services were over, and other than the Reverend the church was empty. He sat at the front, reading from the bible as he so often did. As soon as they entered, Thatcher looked up from his reading, and his eyebrows rose in surprise. "Roland, Rebecca, how are you? Come in, come in," he greeted enthusiastically and rose to his feet to meet them.

"We're fine. How are you?" Rebecca greeted him in return as she and Roland walked to the front of the church.

"I'm doing great. I've got that baptism next week. I love baptisms," Thatcher answered and rubbed his hands together in satisfaction. He loved baptisms almost as much as he loved weddings. It was a welcome relief after all the funerals he had performed lately. The baby he was baptizing was Simon's newborn son, Jacob. Sarah had given birth two days after Rebecca had awakened, and Roland had told Simon that he didn't want to see him for another week. New Haven was quiet for the moment, and Roland and the other three deputies could more than adequately protect the town. Simon had smiled at the order and thanked Roland before rushing home.

"Good. We wanted to talk to you about our wedding," Roland told the Reverend and squeezed Rebecca's hand. She gripped his in return and smiled up at him.

"Wonderful," Thatcher beamed, and his face lit up in excitement. "Have a seat, please." He sat down on the front pew and motioned for them to do the same. "So when did you have this wedding in mind?" He asked anxiously as soon as the pair had seated themselves.

"As soon as possible," Rebecca spoke up immediately.

Thatcher clapped his hands then rubbed them together. "You just tell me the day, and I'll perform the ceremony."

Roland looked at Rebecca. "What do you say? Tomorrow?" He asked her and felt his heart accelerate. He had waited for so long to marry Rebecca, and now he could actually do it within the next twenty-four hours.

"Yes," she answered. A tear welled at the corner of her eye, and she brushed it away. "Yes, tomorrow. I don't want to wait another day." She looked at Roland, and for that moment the two of them forgot Thatcher and everything else as they lost themselves in the other's gaze.

"Wonderful," Thatcher repeated, breaking the couple's rapture. "I'll get started tonight. Will it be a large service?"

Roland shook his head to clear his mind. Rebecca's eyes were so beautiful. He wanted to spend the rest of his life looking into them. "No. Just the two of us."

Thatcher frowned. The Reverend liked big ceremonies, but he was still happy to perform a wedding no matter the size. "All right. How does three o'clock sound?"

"Perfect," Roland answered and grinned suddenly. *Finally,* he thought excitedly. This time, nothing would stop them from carrying out their vows. "I guess that's it. Rebecca?" She shook her head. "All right, we'll see you tomorrow at three," Roland told the Reverend and rose to his feet. "Thank you."

"No, thank you, Roland. I love weddings." Thatcher grinned back at them.

Roland chuckled as he and Rebecca walked outside. Thatcher was a funny man sometimes. "Not too much longer," Roland commented to Rebecca. His smile didn't diminish as they left the church. He felt foolish walking around with such a huge grin, but Roland didn't care. Everything in the world seemed perfect that afternoon, and he wasn't going to let anything spoil his joy.

"I know. I can't wait," Rebecca giggled and squeezed Roland's hand tightly. She wore the same shameless grin as Roland, and he found it absolutely adorable. *I don't deserve her,* Roland thought to himself. She was the most beautiful woman he had ever seen.

They both received a couple of stares as they walked back to The Last Frontier, but neither one of them minded. They nodded or waved back to everyone they encountered and kept grinning like lovestruck fools. Roland was truly enjoying himself again. He was getting married, and New Haven was safe.

By the time they returned to The Last Frontier, they had been gone just over half an hour. The crowd inside had grown larger while they were away, and they had to wade their way to the staircase. Quite a few people called out to Roland, but he only waved in return. He wanted to take Rebecca upstairs so she could rest.

The noise faded as they reached the hallway and approached Rebecca's room. "Whew, I'm tired," Rebecca commented then yawned to demonstrate the point. "I guess I'm still not as strong as I was."

"I think you're doing fine. I'm glad you could come with me," Roland told her. He leaned against the wall and stared at her as she opened the door. Roland still couldn't believe that he was going to marry such a beautiful woman.

"What?" She asked self-consciously and lowered her eyes to the floor.

"I just wanted to look at you." He leaned over and kissed her. No matter how many times he had kissed her since she had awakened, Roland couldn't get enough of it. It wasn't a brief kiss, but quite a lengthy one that left both of them breathless when he finally pulled back. "I love you, Rebecca."

Rebecca blushed at the words, but her face lit up at the sentiment. Bryant had rarely said those words to her, and she couldn't hear them often enough from Roland. "You're not so bad yourself," she mocked and laughed when Roland's eyebrows raised. "I'm just teasing."

"I know." Roland was enjoying their banter and wished that he didn't have to leave, but he had an obligation to fulfill. He should have left a few hours ago. Reaching out, Roland grabbed a lock of her hair and rubbed it gently between two fingers. "Are you sure you don't mind if I go out there?"

"You need to go, Roland," Rebecca chastised. "You owe it to them, and I do as well. Wish them well for me, and tell them I said thank you."

"All right." He had asked her more for the sake of doing so than anything else. Roland had every intention of going. Rebecca was right, t hey both had an obligation. "Are you sure you'll be all right?" He asked worriedly.

"I'll be fine," Rebecca answered patronizingly. Roland had been worrying and fussing over her for the last week. "I can take care of myself. I think I'm going to take a nap. That walk exhausted me. Don't worry about me."

Roland nodded. He knew that Rebecca was right again, but he couldn't help himself. Ever since Rebecca had been trapped in The Land of Shadows, he worried constantly that something else might happen to her. He was sure that it would fade in time, but Roland knew what life was like without Rebecca. He never wanted to experience it again. "Sorry, I'll try," Roland told her without much conviction.

He pulled her towards him and looked down into her eyes. Roland had a hard time breaking his concentration from those pools of emerald green, but he reached up a hand and cupped her chin. "I love you, Rebecca." He leaned down and kissed her one more time, losing himself in the moment for what seemed like an eternity.

Rebecca's face was flushed when he pulled back, and she had a smile stretching from ear to ear. She pushed him away, though. "Now go. I need to sleep." Rebecca waved Roland away good-naturedly, her eyes still sparkling merrily.

"All right," Roland answered and stepped back from the doorway. He shut his eyes as soon as Rebecca closed the door and savored the memory of her. *I love you,* he thought as he pictured her dazzling smile and sparkling eyes. Roland stood there with his eyes closed for nearly ten seconds before he finally shook his head and came back to reality. He had things to do and didn't have time to daydream. "I love you, Rebecca White," Roland whispered to the door then headed down the hallway.

Rebecca Black. He rolled the name pleasantly over his tongue several times as he walked towards the staircase. It was hard to believe that they'd be married the following day. He had first proposed just over three weeks before, but it seemed as if an eternity had passed since that fateful day. His heart raced inside his chest, and he knew that he would be deliriously happy and a nervous wreck until they were married. *Rebecca Black,* he thought once more. He liked the sound of it. *Not much longer.*

He paid more attention to the crowd at The Frontier as he came down the staircase without Rebecca at his side. It was a busy Sunday for George and the saloon. Normally Sundays were a bit slower, but Roland guessed that with all the trouble New Haven had gone through, people were anxious to celebrate no matter what day of the week it was. He scanned through all the revelers, gamblers, and strumpets until his eyes found William. Roland headed across the floor and interrupted his deputy, who was busy at work as always. "William, I need to talk with you. Heather, do you mind?"

The blond frowned and ran a fingernail over William's chin. "Only if it won't be long."

Roland rolled his eyes. "Not long at all," he told her. "Excuse us." He nearly had to drag William away as he watched Heather strut across the saloon to find another customer. "Come on, William. She'll still be here when we're done." Roland wanted to laugh. He didn't know which was more certain: Ben asking questions, William flirting with Sherry's girls, or the sun rising each morning.

William nodded, but his eyes followed Heather for a few seconds before he turned them towards Roland. "Afternoon, Sheriff. What can I do for you?"

"I have to run an errand. I just wanted to let you know. You're in charge tonight if anything happens." He pointed a finger at the rakish deputy. "None of Sherry's girls. I want you to stay here until I get back. You can go visit Heather tomorrow," Roland lectured William

"All right," William responded and looked glum over the news. His eyes darted towards Heather, and he exhaled once in frustration. "When will you be back?"

"I don't know. It might not be until midnight. I'll see you when I get back. Good luck," he told the deputy, tipped his hat, and walked out of the saloon. He looked over his shoulder once before he left and saw William already engaged in conversation with Heather again. Roland shook his head. He hoped that William would stay at The Frontier. *Don't think about it,* Roland thought to himself. William had always obeyed his orders before, and he didn't think that would change.

Roland crossed the street to get a horse. He stared at the bullet-ridden walls of the station house for a few moments before he untied the horse from the tether post. The shootout with the Dark Riders had taken place eight days before, but Roland could remember it vividly. Phillip and Morgan were just two of the men who had died that evening. The Dark Riders had also been obliterated, but Roland often wondered if it had been worth the price. He missed Morgan's silent leadership and Phillip's ever present books laying face down on the desk. Roland hadn't considered them as much when the two were alive, but he missed them both tremendously now that they were gone.

Don't think about it, Roland thought to himself. The past was the past, and he needed to keep his head in the present. There would be other times to mourn the dead, and Roland had a long journey ahead of him. He climbed onto his horse and tapped it lightly with his boot. "Hya," Roland called out, and they began a slow canter across town. It was definitely a cooler day, Roland noticed appreciatively. He had to ride a good ten miles, and it would be much easier with the cooler air and the clouds overhead.

The railroad station was quiet that afternoon. No trains came through the station on Sundays, and it was appropriately deserted. Even Sherry's business was slow. Roland had told Lewis to take the gallows down the day after Rebecca awakened. It served as a grim reminder of all the troubles New Haven had endured, and Roland wanted the town to begin healing. All of the charred wood from the first gallows and the stage had also been carted away. Roland had to chuckle at that memory. People still wondered how those fires had been started, but Roland intended to let that secret go with him to the grave.

Roland did look around and think about the Fourth of July. That night seemed like an eternity ago. It had begun as New Haven's greatest celebration and ended as her greatest disaster. He wistfully wondered what Wade would have been like had he lived another ten years. Roland had half-expected Wade to meet his death at the wrong end of a gun but not so soon. The Sheriff realized sadly as well that he missed Robert's gruff personality. Sometimes he had taken his deputies for granted, but he certainly missed them now.

The memory of Jack dying was the worst. Jack's death was bad enough, but Alvin's confession that it had only been a poor shot that hit Jack instead of Roland made the Sheriff sick with guilt. It should have been him in a coffin, not Jack. He hadn't told Dotty about Alvin's admission. There was no reason for her to know, and it had been hard to face her after he had learned. In that way only, he was relieved that she had left town. It made dealing with that painful subject easier without Jack's widow there to remind him constantly.

Roland coped much better with Jack's death now than he had the first few days after the shooting. Immediately after, Roland kept turning and expecting to find Jack there. He missed Jack's advice and friendship and always would, but he didn't feel the loss as keenly as he had during those first few hellish days. Roland remembered Jack's enthusiasm and congratulations when Roland had announced his plan to marry Rebecca. It felt strange getting married without Jack by his side, but Roland had to move on with his life. Jack would have wanted it that way. *I miss you, Jack,* Roland thought as he left the railroad station and all of those painful memories behind.

At least he got to chuckle as he rode by *The New Haven Gazette* office He looked inside the window, but the office was empty much to Roland's disappointment. It would have been amusing to see Matthew flinch in fear at the mere sight of Roland. *Not bad,* Roland congratulated himself once again He was quite proud of the effectiveness of his threats to Matthew. Ever since the day Curly was hanged, *The Gazette* had printed nothing but friendly article:

not only towards Roland but all of the deputies as well. As Matthew had promised, he had written articles absolving the deputies of all blame in both shootouts and casting blame squarely on the shoulders of the Dark Riders. He had also written that Doc Holliday was truly dead and the dead traveler had been a gentleman from Arizona. Roland guessed the ruse had worked. Nobody had mentioned Doc's name in over a week. Matthew had even published an article vilifying Alvin after the mayor had been killed. It had laid Bryant's murder as well as connections to the Dark Riders at Alvin's feet.

Alvin, Roland thought loathingly. Carlos, Curly, Marshall, and Matthew had all caused Roland trouble over the last month, but Alvin was the one Roland truly hated. Alvin had taken away his best friend out of wounded pride and brought about the deaths of four other deputies with his manipulation of Carlos. And of course there was the fact that Alvin had killed Bryant and indirectly brought about Rebecca's imprisonment in The Land of Shadows. (her case couldn't be worse than the men who died!!!) Roland often wondered how much of that trouble he could have prevented if he had just shot Alvin a long time ago. Death was too easy a punishment for the mayor. Roland believed in an afterlife after his ordeal with Bryant's spirit, and he just hoped that Alvin was being punished for all his sins. *Rot in Hell, you son of a bitch,* Roland thought vindictively.

Roland pulled his thoughts back into the real world and stopped reminiscing on the past. He had a long ride ahead of him and couldn't afford to be daydreaming. *Let's get going,* Roland thought and was about to urge his horse into a gallop when a voice called out to him. "Sheriff!" Roland turned his head around and sighed in frustration. He was ready to begin his trip and didn't want another interruption. "What is it?" He asked as the other rider approached.

"I just wanted to see where you want me tonight. At the Snake again?" Jimmy asked and flashed his cocky grin.

Roland had to chuckle at the young man. Jimmy was almost infectious with his arrogant smirk. "Yeah, that sounds good to me. It's probably going to be a quiet night, though. I put William in charge so if you need anything, talk to him. He'll be at The Last Frontier," Roland commented. *He damn well better be.*

"I didn't expect there to be any trouble," Jimmy replied and only sounded the slightest bit disappointed.

Just don't cause any yourself, Roland thought. It still surprised him that he let Jimmy stay. He had been prepared to make the gunslinger leave, but Roland had changed his mind after all the events that happened the night Rebecca awakened. He liked the young man and his cocky arrogance. Roland still smiled almost every time he saw Jimmy and remembered when he was a young gunslinger out in the West.

With Rebecca awake, Roland had reconsidered letting Jimmy stay. The Dark Riders were dead, and all of his attention was monopolized with trying to help Rebecca regain her strength. Roland knew that he owed the gunslinger for his help in capturing half the Dark Riders in Henry's elaborate ruse. It had been a simple choice to allow Jimmy to remain in town on the condition that he stay out of trouble. Roland had been forced to concoct a story to justify Jimmy killing Henry, and people had readily believed it. The young man surprised Roland by behaving admirably. He gambled from time to time, but other than that, Jimmy seemed happy just to be in town and immersed in all of its culture that he had waited his entire life to experience.

Roland had been stunned by his next move, but it had made sense at the time. Morgan had told Roland to make the young man a deputy the night he died, but Roland had balked at the idea, thinking Jimmy would do more harm than good. He had changed his mind once again after Jimmy's third day back in town. Roland desperately needed more deputies for the town, and he had little time to look for one while he hovered over Rebecca. It was peaceful for the moment, but three deputies weren't enough. Roland also wanted to find the right type of deputies. All of the fallen had been gunslingers who appreciated New Haven for her culture, and Jimmy possessed those same traits. Roland shook his head sometimes when he saw Jimmy riding through New Haven on patrol, but he had to admit that so far, the young man was working out fine.

"Just remember to get William if there's trouble," Roland told the deputy. New Haven had been absolutely peaceful ever since Alvin's death. Everyone seemed anxious to keep it that way after the violence that had raged for weeks. Roland was enjoying the tranquility while it lasted , but he knew it wouldn't last forever.

"I will. So where are you heading off to?" Jimmy looked at Roland curiously. The Sheriff obviously meant to leave town. He looked ready for a long ride, and his house was on the other side of New Haven.

"I've got something to take care of. I'll be back later tonight," Roland answered. He didn't want to talk about where he was going. He missed Jack. Roland could have told Jack where he was going, but he didn't quite trust Jimmy that much. He liked the young man, but Jack had been his friend for over twenty years.

Jimmy nodded, but he still looked curious. "How's Miss White doing?"

In spite of his hurry to leave town, Roland's mouth stretched wide in a grin. "She's doing fine, Jimmy." His horse pawed at the ground and looked back at Roland. *All right, I know.* He didn't have time for anymore chitchat. Roland had spent far more time with Rebecca than he had intended. He had to hurry if he was going to make it in time. "I need to go. I'll talk to you later."

"Sure, Sheriff. Be careful," Jimmy warned then turned his horse around to continue his patrol.

Roland looked over his shoulder at him and then tapped his horse with his foot. "Hya!" Roland shouted, and the horse reared back, neighing and pawing at the air. Its front hooves then hit the ground, and they took off at a gallop. Cool air rushed against Roland's face as he raced away from New Haven. *Finally,* he thought. Roland had meant to leave much earlier. Falling Thunder had journeyed to New Haven to summon Roland, and he only had until sunset to make it to the Cheyenne village. He still had enough time to complete his journey, but Roland couldn't afford to dawdle.

Henry's health had greatly worried Roland, and after Rebecca had awakened, Roland returned to her house to see how the Ghost Hunter had fared. He hated to leave Rebecca's side, but Roland had to know if Henry died. He had expected the worst. Alvin had shot Henry in the gut, and Roland had seen too many men die from that type of wound and only a scant few survive. His own healing at the hands of Running Brook had given him some cause for hope, but Roland had entered the house with great doubts.

Much to his surprise, Singing Rock sat quietly beside Henry with his eyes closed. He had expected to find the Navajo still chanting over Henry's body and immediately feared the worst. *Doc's dead,* Roland thought numbly. The notorious gunslinger had cheated death for so many years, but Roland had found a way to end Henry's charmed life. Singing Rock, however, opened his eyes when Roland entered. "It took you long enough," he said calmly.

Only then did Roland notice the faint rising and falling of Henry's chest. Roland had rushed to the Ghost Hunter's side and looked down at him in amazement. His shirt had been ripped open, and he could see where the bullet had entered Henry's flesh. To Roland's amazement, it looked like a month-old wound, not a fatal one that had been received only a few hours ago. "Is he going to live?" He demanded from Singing Rock.

The Navajo nodded. "He has survived the most difficult part. He is too stubborn to die," he commented, and the corners of his mouth turned upwards in a tiny grin.

Roland had laughed with joy. Henry's wound had been the only thing making that night's victory incomplete. Roland always would have felt guilty if Rebecca's freedom had been bought with Henry's death. *Yes!* He exulted. His luck had turned around. But after his initial bout of jubilation, Roland remembered that Henry wasn't the only one wounded. Singing Rock had taken a bullet in the shoulder, but the Navajo cradled it against his chest, making it inconspicuous.

Singing Rock claimed that he couldn't heal his own wounds, and Roland only knew one other person who could attempt a healing. Roland looked the wound over briefly and was relieved when it didn't appear serious. Singing Rock had lost some blood, but the wound had already stopped bleeding. He breathed a sigh of relief that it wasn't as serious as Henry's injury. It would take quite some time to summon help, and he didn't want Singing Rock dying while he was away.

After listening to Singing Rock's brief words and making his cursory examination, Roland looked out the window exhaustedly. "I'll get help," he told the Navajo then tiredly went back outside. Roland stared at his horse for nearly a minute as he gathered his energy. With a sigh, he pulled himself into the saddle and began the long ride. The last time he had made the journey to the Cheyenne village, Roland passed out before he made it halfway. The only other times he had visited had been during the day. It was a long ride to make in the dark, but Roland stayed awake and alert through pure force of will. He needed to summon help for both of the Ghost Hunters, and Roland wouldn't stop until he had done just that.

Falling Thunder and Running Brook had been surprised to see Roland that night, but once he explained what had happened, the Chief's son quickly formed a party to gather the wounded pair. Running Brook had inquired about Rebecca then congratulated him when Roland told him that she had awakened. The Cheyenne Chief appeared almost as relieved as Roland. His dream with the raven and wolf had been quite vivid Falling Thunder didn't take long to gather a dozen men, and then the party began their lengthy ride.

The Cheyenne brave and his men knew the forest like the backs of their hands, and they did all the leading. Roland only had to keep his eyes open and follow them as they quickly navigated their way to the wounded Ghost Hunters. Singing Rock had fallen asleep while Roland summoned help, but he opened his eyes as Roland and a few of the braves entered the house. But Henry remained asleep and never twitched a muscle as Falling Thunder gently draped him over one of their horses. Singing Rock thanked him for his help, and Falling Thunder promised to send word on the status of the two Ghost Hunters as soon as there was news to tell. After watching them disappear into the forest, Roland had ridden back to The Last Frontier and collapsed in his bed for some much-needed rest.

All of Roland's time was spent with Rebecca during the next few days as she began eating and regaining her strength. He did think of the Ghost Hunters often as he hovered over Rebecca. By Wednesday, Roland had grown increasingly worried after no word came from the Cheyenne village, and by Thursday, Roland was ready to make the journey himself to see firsthand how they were doing. Luckily on Friday afternoon as Roland prepared to ride to the Cheyenne camp, Falling Thunder had arrived on the outskirts of town. Roland quickly met him before somebody could cause any trouble. Paul Henderson and his near riot were only three weeks in the past, and Roland didn't want to risk any trouble.

He instinctively thought the worst as he rode to meet Falling Thunder. His luck had run too poorly for too long to change overnight. Even with Rebecca awake, Roland's stomach tightened nervously as he talked to the Cheyenne brave. Falling Thunder, however, quickly put his fears to rest as he told Roland that not only were the Ghost Hunters doing well, they were planning to leave the village on Sunday evening. Roland was stunned. He had expected Henry to need weeks to recover, but then Roland remembered his own healing at the hands of Running Brook. After a few days of rest, he had jumped out of bed with no lingering effects.

Roland was anxious to see Henry and kept cursing himself as he raced towards the Cheyenne village. He hadn't thanked the Ghost Hunter for helping Rebecca and would be quite upset if he missed him. Even more so, Roland was anxious to see the notorious gunfighter one last time for his own personal satisfaction. He didn't know if he'd ever see Henry again, and Roland had always thought his adventure with Doc Holliday had been one of the greatest of his career. Roland knew that he shouldn't have spent so much time with Rebecca that morning, but he simply hadn't been able to help himself. *Hurry,* he tried to urge his horse, but there was no sense in pushing him yet. There was still a ways to go. At least the weather stayed pleasant as he raced under the summer sky. It felt more like a spring morning than a summer afternoon.

As the afternoon sky began to darken, Roland finally caught sight of the Cheyenne camp. *At last,* he thought in relief and slowed his mount to a walk. His horse snorted and breathed heavily as they approached the last segment at a slow pace. Roland had ridden his horse hard. He wouldn't have done so any other time, but he had no other choice. It was the only way that he'd get to see the Ghost Hunters before they left.

The camp was busy that afternoon. Roland saw children playing and running from one side of camp to the other, while women were busy talking amongst themselves. There were many braves milling about a newly returned hunting party, and they helped haul the carcasses of several deer into the village. Almost all of that activity stopped as Roland rode into sight. A few of the children ran for their mother's protection, and several braves picked up their bows. *Great,* Roland thought to himself, and his body tensed nervously. It would be just his luck to get shot when trying to visit Henry and Singing Rock.

A figure with long white hair quickly raised an arm, and the braves all put their bows down. *Running Brook,* Roland thought in relief. The Cheyenne Chief pointed at Roland, and a brave standing at his side jumped onto a horse and approached the Sheriff. Roland recognized him immediately. "Falling Thunder," Roland called out in greeting as soon as he was within earshot.

"Sheriff," the brave answered in his deep, quiet voice. "You are late. My father was beginning to doubt you would come." He pulled his horse alongside Roland's and escorted him into the village. His long hair rippled in the cool summer breeze.

"I was busy. Sorry," Roland apologized. He just hoped that he had made it in time.

Falling Thunder shrugged his shoulders. "You are here now. Your friends are here. That is all that matters," he observed and rode on silently. Roland nodded in satisfaction. Falling Thunder was right. Henry and Singing Rock were still at the village, and that was all that mattered. He had made it and, judging by the sun, only by the skin of his teeth. Sunset was no more than twenty minutes away.

Roland received a number of curious stares as he rode into the Cheyenne camp. Even though he had come to the village several times before, he was obviously a stranger and commanded attention. The brave led him directly to Running Brook. They had to weave between several teepees, and children scampered away then peered at the two men from behind the safety of one those teepees. Roland wanted to laugh. Children were the same anywhere. The children of New Haven always flocked curiously to Dennis's smithy.

Roland blinked in surprise when they reached Running Brook. Singing Rock stood by the Chief's side. All effects of his wounded shoulder were gone. He wore a shirt that covered the area, but Roland saw the Navajo move his arm freely. Roland just hoped that Henry's healing had been as successful. "Singing Rock, it's good to see you. How are you feeling?"

Singing Rock nodded. "I am fine, Sheriff," he answered and folded his arms across his chest.

Once again Roland was amazed. Singing Rock should have had his arm in a sling for over a month, but the Navajo had fully recovered in only a week. "Good. I'm glad to hear it. I wanted to thank you again for helping Rebecca. She sends her thanks as well." Roland waited for Singing Rock to respond, but the Navajo only nodded to indicate he had heard the Sheriff's words. "Where's Henry?" Roland asked finally. He had mainly come to see Henry, but Roland also wanted to thank Singing Rock. Roland hadn't planned on a long conversation with him, though. The Navajo had never seemed much of one for talking.

"I will take you to him, Sheriff," Running Brook told Roland and motioned for him to follow. Singing Rock walked with them although he continued his silence. Running Brook guided him to a teepee in the middle of the village and stepped aside. "He is inside," he told Roland.

"Thank you," Roland replied and scratched on the door. "Come in," a voice called out, and Roland pulled back the flap. Henry laid on his back in the middle of the teepee. Roland had expected the Ghost Hunter to be thin and weak like Rebecca, but Henry appeared as healthy as he had been the day he entered New Haven. His face was still pale, but Henry appeared completely recovered. "Damn, Henry," Roland whispered. The Ghost Hunter should have died from his wounds. "I don't believe it."

"He healed me up pretty good," Henry remarked dryly and sat up. He covered his mouth as he yawned loudly. "I'm still tired, but Singing Rock says we have to go to New Mexico." He shook his head ruefully. "I could use another week of rest, but I don't have much say."

Roland shook his own head. He still couldn't believe how much Henry had recovered. "New Mexico? What's there?" He asked curiously. If Henry was so tired, Roland didn't know why he didn't keep resting.

"Another spirit is causing trouble." Henry sighed. "There's always another spirit, Roland."

"Why don't you stay here then? New Haven could use another deputy, and you'd be perfect for it." New Haven's atmosphere would be even better with Doc Holliday as a deputy.

Henry looked tempted for a moment. His eyes looked off to the side as if he was considering the offer, but then he shook his head. "I can't, Roland. I still owe Singing Rock for saving my life." Then his lips curled into a wry grin. "Besides, everyone thinks I'm dead. Remember?" The Ghost Hunter pointed out.

Damn! Roland had completely forgotten about that. It seemed as if Henry's ruse had taken place months ago. He chuckled at his own forgetfulness and felt a bit foolish. "I forgot about that. Well, I just wanted to come here and thank you, Henry. Rebecca sends her thanks as well. We both appreciate your help. And Singing Rock's too."

"I was glad to have helped, Roland. I wish both of you the best of luck. When's the wedding going to be?"

"Tomorrow," Roland answered, and his face stretched into another one of his foolish grins.

"Not wasting any time, are you?" Henry commented dryly and chuckled a few times. "I'm glad you could make it, Roland. It was good to see you. But I need to get up. I'm sure Singing Rock is ready to leave by now. He's always impatient about these things." The Ghost Hunter started moving towards the exit.

Roland crawled ahead of him and waited outside. He had hoped for a longer visit with Henry. He didn't know what he wanted to say, but Roland felt like an old friend was leaving for good. Roland felt that there should have been something else to tell the Ghost Hunter. He hadn't mentioned what a thrill it had been to see the gunslinger again or how much he had enjoyed the trap that they had sprung on the Dark Riders. If nothing else, Roland should have told Henry how seeing him alive again had reminded Roland of the good old days when he had ridden in the West with a gun in each hand and eyes in the back of his head. But the words wouldn't come to his tongue.

Quietly he watched as Henry and Singing Rock spoke for a few moments. Then the Navajo said something to Running Brook, and the Cheyenne

Chief called out an order to his son. Shortly afterwards Falling Thunder walked two horses towards the party. Running Brook and Singing Rock exchanged a few words then the Navajo climbed into the saddle. Henry didn't waste any time and swung a leg over his horse without saying a word. Once he was in the saddle, he turned towards Roland. "You take care of that town. It's special."

"I will," Roland answered. "You take care of yourself."

Henry smiled a mischievous grin. "I always do, Roland. I always do." Then he turned towards Singing Rock and spoke to him in Navajo. Singing Rock nodded. "So long, Roland," Henry said, and the two men began riding out of the village.

Roland was tempted to follow them, but he stayed by Running Brook's side. As they left, Roland felt a bit sad. He knew that it was the last time he would ever see Doc Holliday again. Maybe it was the fact that he had lost so many friends recently and could have used an old gunslinger like Henry around, or maybe Roland just yearned for the old days. Whatever the case, Roland hated watching him leave.

"Farewells are never pleasant," Running Brook commented softly. Roland nodded but didn't say a word. The Ghost Hunters rode out of the village and onto a hill on the western border. The sun was just beginning to set, and when they reached the top, they stood directly in its path. For a moment they were silhouetted against a lush violet backdrop, then they slowly disappeared to the other side of the hill.

Roland exhaled as they vanished from sight. Then he shook his head. "Thanks, Running Brook. I appreciate everything. Can Falling Thunder guide me back to town?"

Running Brook nodded. "I will speak to him."

"Good," Roland answered. He turned his back on the hill and walked towards his horse. It was strange thinking that Doc Holliday was only a short distance away, but Roland pushed those thoughts from his mind. That was in the past. He had promised himself to move on from all the events that had taken place over the last four weeks and build a new life with Rebecca. She was all that mattered to him. Maybe Doc had left, but Roland had a wedding to attend and the most beautiful woman in the world waiting for him.

Falling Brook fell in beside Roland, and the two men mounted their horses. Then Roland began the ride back home.

Afterword

I tried to be accurate with my depictions of Native American culture, myths, and lifestyle, but I did take a few liberties along the way. No offense was intended to anyone of Native American descent. A few of the characters have names borrowed from other sources, but each of them is an original character of my own imagination except for their name. Matthew Brady was a famous civil war photographer. Roland's name was taken from the main character in Stephen King's Dark Tower series, which in turn was taken from Robert Browning's poem "Childe Roland to the Dark Tower Came." Singing Rock's name came from Graham Masterton's Mantiou series. Lastly, as far as my research shows, Doc Holliday died of tuberculosis in 1887. I visited his grave in the fall of 1997 and saw his tombstone, but I didn't actually see the body so anything is possible.

Bart Thompson
May 26, 1998

About the Author

Born in 1972 in St. Louis, Missouri, Bart Thompson has been a writer since his early teens. Although he has a large collection of manuscripts, The Ghost Hunters is his first published novel. He graduated from Trinity University in 1995 with degrees in Computer Science and Mathematics. He is hard at work on his next novel, Two Princes in Avalon, and hopes to publish it in 2003. In addition to writing, the author enjoys cooking, sports, and is a die-hard Houston Rockets fan. He currently lives in Texas with his wife and his two dogs.

The author would appreciate any comments or opinions you have about this novel. Please send them to Feedback@TheGhostHunters.com.

Coming in 2003

Two Princes in Avalon

The epic fairy tale by Bart Thompson

Once upon a time there was a fair kingdom named Avalon. It was a small kingdom filled with lush forests of fruit-bearing trees and crystal lakes. The Silver Mountains towered above the highest of clouds to the North of Avalon, while the Great Sea lay on the West, stretching all the way to the Far Lands. The kingdom of Scholari with its great universities of learning and its eternal quest for knowledge was to the East. Splendora bordered Avalon to the South with its luxurious mansions, countless treasures, and masses of jewels. But they all envied Avalon for the peace and tranquility that had ruled over the kingdom for as long as the bards could remember.

The people of Avalon were a happy people. Except for those who had come from other kingdoms, Avalonites were all dark of hair and pale of skin. They stood out when they traveled abroad, but then people seldom left Avalon. It wasn't that they were forbidden; they just didn't want to. Life in Avalon was easy and enjoyable. They spent half the year ensuring that the great fruit-bearing trees that grew only in Avalon produced their bounty. Then the people of Avalon plucked that fruit and sold it throughout the world. The fruits of Avalon were praised from the Marne Empire, where even the Lord Emperor loved to sink his teeth into an Avalon pear, to Skylar, where the rich Dukes and nobles treasured it for their opulent banquets. Ships would flock to Gi'mair to buy or barter for Avalon's harvest the very moment the fruit had been plucked from the trees. Gi'mair was Avalon's lone port, but it rivaled even Sylvanna's port during the Harvest Season, and everyone knows Sylvanna's port was the busiest in the world.

Tending the trees brought plenty of gold crowns into Avalon, but Avalonites had a great deal of free time for much of the year. For tending the trees never took all day, and harvest season only lasted a few months.

And so the commoners found ways to fill those voids. They loved to sing and dance, and some of the best musicians in the world could be found within Avalon's borders. The men of Avalon looked forward to the Harvest Season even though it was the hardest work of the year. When the fruit grew ripe and was ready to be plucked from the trees, the women of Avalon would take up lutes and pipes and serenade the men as they gathered the fall harvest. It is said that the harvest serenade is the most beautiful music in the world and could make the hardest man's heart weep. Better even than the Maestro Nealinor in Sylvanna, but perhaps you should judge for yourself. Everyone should hear the music of Avalon at some point in their life, and the palaces of Sylvanna are one of the most beautiful things in the world. I could tell you stories of Sylvanna…but I'll save those for another day.

They did more than just sing, dance, and play music. The people of Avalon were also fond of stories, and the bards made sure to travel through the fair kingdom. Wandering bards frequently stopped at a village and entertained not just a few families but an entire town with their stories. When they left the village with a full belly and a fat purse for their tales, the bards would journey to another Avalon village before leaving the kingdom with enough money to live luxuriously for several months. Games were also immensely popular in the kingdom. Avalonites ran races, threw wooden rings around a peg, and played an exciting game where people tried to kick a ball in another team's goal. Even those too old to run with the youngsters continued to compete at indoor games. On any given day in any given village, you could find at least a dozen games of Flip Chip being played. Sometimes they played Conquest, but that was mostly a noble game. With all their games, music, and harvesting, the people of Avalon never had time to be unhappy. They enjoyed their way of life and never even gave thought to moving somewhere else.

Ruling over the commoners was the King's responsibility, and that honor fell upon the Karvillian family, which had ruled Avalon for three hundred years. For eleven generations, a Karvillian King had marched through the halls of the Royal Castle Pai'shan with his Ki'tian dragging on the floor behind him and always remembering the golden rule: keep the people happy, and you shall keep the throne. There were taxes for the people of Avalon, but the Karvillians always kept them small. There was no need for a large army, and there was more than enough trade to keep the royal treasury filled. The people were happy, and no Karvillian would dream of changing that.

And that's how Avalon existed. The kingdom was surrounded by rich neighbors who lived in royal houses and hoarded magnificent treasures, but Avalon never strove to be the richest kingdom in the world. Avalon stayed within her means, and her people were always happy. And they all, from the lowest peasant to the King himself, thought it would last forever. Now, I know you must be asking yourself: what type of story is this then if everyone was so happy? Well, as it turns out, they were wrong. Dark times laid in wait for Avalon.